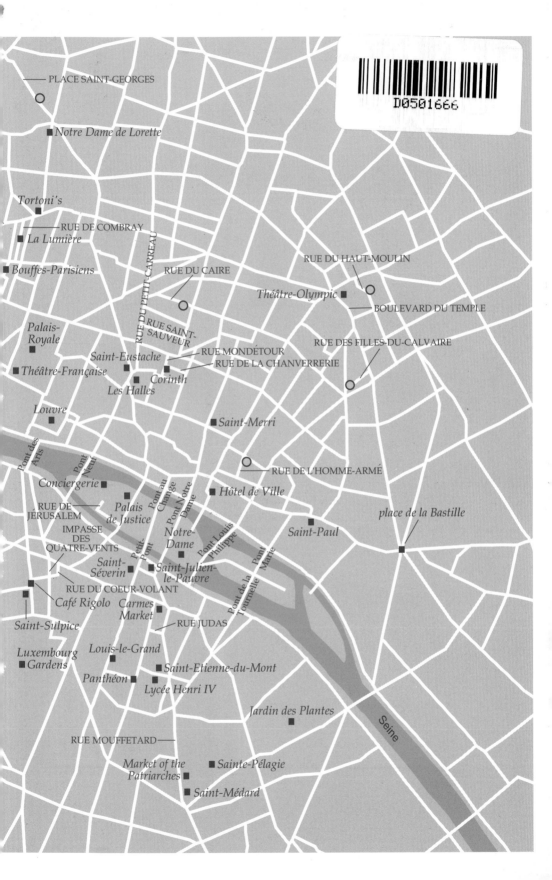

Cosette

ALSO BY LAURA KALPAKIAN

Cosette

The Sequel to *Les Misérables*

LAURA KALPAKIAN

HarperCollins*Publishers*

HarperCollins books may be purchased for educational, business, or sales promotional use. For information please write: Special Markets Department, HarperCollins Publishers, Inc., 10 East 53rd Street, New York, NY 10022.

FIRST EDITION

Designed by Laura Lindgren

Maps by Paul Pugliese

Library of Congress Cataloging-in-Publication Data

Kalpakian, Laura.
    Cosette : the sequel to Les misérables / by Laura Kalpakian. — 1st ed.
      p.   cm.
    ISBN 0-06-017222-3
    I. Hugo, Victor, 1802-1885. Misérables. II. Title.
  PS3561.A4168 6   1995
  813´.54—dc20   95-15841

95 96 97 98 99 ❖/RRD 10 9 8 7 6 5 4 3 2 1

This book is for my sister Helen,
la lumière de la famille

ACKNOWLEDGMENTS

Cosette has been fortunate in having many friends from the beginning. In Washington, Mary Alice Kier and Anna Cottle; in California, Michael Campus and Rowland Perkins; in Paris and New York, Phyllis Demarecaux Joseph and Robert L. Joseph. Additionally, the book and the author have had the good fortune to work with Larry Ashmead at HarperCollins. I also wish to thank Jason Kaufman at HarperCollins.

Unfailingly generous, cordial, and helpful, Dr. W. Scott Haine took time with the manuscript, answered my questions, and shared his own unique insights on nineteenth-century Paris. The librarians and staff at the University of Washington libraries extended courtesies on many occasions, especially Ms. Janice Thomas of Suzzallo Allen. I thank too Professor Mark Traugott of the University of California, Santa Cruz.

My sons, Bear and Brendan, lived around *Cosette* as much as with her, and did so with tact and affection. Thank you. My father, William J. Johnson, kept the home fires burning and, without complaint, ferried children to school and music lessons, and I thank him too.

Cosette follows my other books in being indebted to two people who have selflessly supported my work with their time, care, and unstinting affection. Meredith Cary, *merci mille fois*. And for my mother, Peggy Kalpakian Johnson, *merci toujours*.

So long as there shall exist, by reason of law and custom, a social con-demnation, which, in the face of civilization, artificially creates hells on earth . . . so long as the three problems of the age—the degradation of man by poverty, the ruin of woman by starvation, the dwarfing of child-hood by physical and spiritual night—are not solved . . . so long as igno-rance and misery remain on earth, books like this cannot be useless.

—Victor Hugo
Preface to *Les Misérables*
1862

CONTENTS

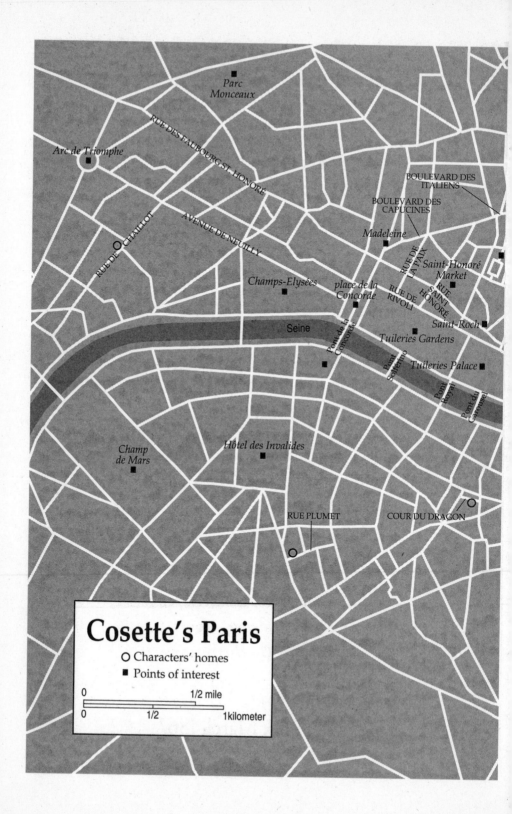

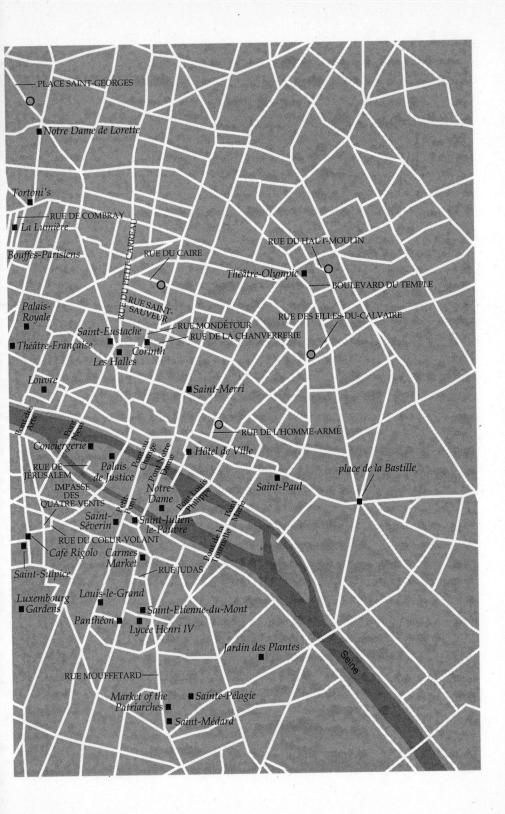

BOOK I

CHILDREN OF WATERLOO

Part I

The Fifth Man
1832

At this moment, a fifth uniform dropped as if from heaven, upon the four others. The fifth man was saved.

—Victor Hugo
Les Misérables

Chapter 1

*T*hey say that time and memory are shackled, forever fettered and forever out of step. With every passing year, time accelerates while memory slows, accumulating weight and girth, protesting time's velocity. The struggle between time and memory is unceasing, even in the quietest life. Cosette's was not a quiet life. But even the turmoil of her childhood did not prepare her for the tumult ahead.

She might have missed all that tumult and spent her life in celibate exile. The carriage had been called. Her bags had all been packed. The servant knocked to say the driver had arrived. Cosette ignored her, remained at the small writing desk in her room, her pen spluttering in haste as she scribbled.

My love my love my love

My father is moving us to Number 7 rue de l'Homme-Armé. We leave for England from there. We leave in a few days. You said there was one chance you could save me from England. You said you'd be back in two nights, but three nights have passed and I have waited in the garden for you and you have not come. I know that some terrible thing has happened, and now something even more terrible is about to happen. We are about to leave France. You must get this note. You must find me, Marius, my love, Marius. I don't care what else happens. I must see you. I must hold you. I must love you before I die or go to England. I have lived now three nights without you and I cannot bear the thought of a whole life without you. What if I live to be very old? Marius, come to me. Find me. Hold me. Love me.

Your adoring
Cosette
5 June 1832

She blotted the note and wrote the address of the apartment Marius shared with student friends before sealing it with blue wax. Hiding it in the folds of her skirt, she darted down the stairs. At the foot she nearly bumped into the driver, who was lifting their valises.

Cosette ran around to the back, to the walled garden, the wild, untended garden where Marius had come to her secretly, night after spring night. Now late-afternoon shadows slanted and the butterflies played amongst the weeds, bees nestled in the bosom of the wildflowers, but there was no one to take this note to Marius. Surely he would come here tonight, to the rue Plumet. He would think she had left for England and he would despair as she despaired. She wrapped her hands around the spars of the broken gate as if this gate alone remained of the wreck of her young life and clung there, crying softly, till a movement caught her eye. A young workingman, a boy really, clad in patched and tattered clothes, a cap pulled down over his face, crouched in a niche just outside. Cosette thrust the note through the bars to him. "Please take this note to Marius Pontmercy. See, there's the address. Please, I don't have any money, but he'll give you money."

"I don't want your money," said the young man angrily. "I'm not here for the money."

"Then, please," Cosette implored, "in the name of love, take this to Marius Pontmercy."

He took the note and sprinted away just as Cosette heard her father call her name and urge her to hurry. Gracelessly she wiped her eyes with her skirt and called back, yes, she would hurry, but under her breath she murmured over and over, *In the name of love, in the name of love, in the name of my love, Marius.*

Properly hatted and gloved, Cosette stepped into the carriage to take her seat beside Toussaint, their sole servant, while the driver, grunting audibly, swearing occasionally, continued to hoist their trunks and valises. Toussaint stuck her head out and told him, in no uncertain terms, to stop swearing; she gave one of those snorts perfected by the righteous when he finally complied and she remarked to Cosette, "Such language will upset your sainted father." Toussaint was tough, creased, pious as a prayer book, and next to Cosette she looked like an antique frame beside a picture of youth.

"I envy him his swearing."

"Young ladies never swear, *ma petite.* Young ladies respect always their elders, their religion," Toussaint crossed herself, "and those who know best."

"And who knows best?" inquired Cosette tartly.

"Did they teach you nothing at the convent?"

They taught me forever, love is forever, Marius, forever, even if we are to be forever parted. Cosette swallowed hard, gulping down tears and that peculiar metallic taste she recognized as rising anxiety. Ordinarily her coloring was too healthy for conventional prettiness, but today she was pale, and she sat now in this hired carriage, the very picture of maidenhood, though her hair curled in an unruly manner unlike the uniform ringlets decreed by fashion, and her mouth did not purse in the manner of contemporary beauties. Though she did not know it, Cosette had her mother's engaging smile, fine teeth, and dark-lashed blue eyes. She was trim and small-boned, and for the past year she had secretly suspected she was a pretty girl. Marius convinced her she was a beautiful woman. Girl or woman, pretty or plain, it little mattered now; she was powerless.

Her father got in the carriage at last and put the key to the house into his waistcoat pocket, where it clanged against the key to the apartment in the rue de l'Homme-Armé and also a key to yet another apartment. Cosette and her father moved frequently. That was just the way they had lived and she had never before questioned or contested any of it. Without Marius she would not have questioned this move, even going to England. But she could not imagine a life without Marius, and yet it lay before her, a cold certainty.

"It's a dismal place, England," Cosette observed.

"We're not going to England," her father replied. "I told you, we're going to the apartment in the rue de l'Homme-Armé."

"Yes, but later, in a few days, we are leaving France and going to England."

"And so we are," he declared emphatically.

"My friend at the convent, Helen Talbot, she is English and even she says it is a dismal place," Cosette continued argumentatively. "She has lived there and she says it's unendurable."

"Mademoiselle Talbot is entitled to her opinion, of course. We are not going to England to enjoy the climate. We are going on business and there's an end to it."

"You needn't euphemize to me, Papa, I mean about our going on business. We're fleeing France, just as we are fleeing the rue Plumet, as we have fled for years."

"You are a girl, Cosette, and there are many things you can't understand."

"And when I am a woman, Papa, what shall I understand then? Will you tell me then why we have lived this enigmatic life?"

Even Toussaint was abashed at Cosette's effrontery, but her father merely remarked that rebellion ill became her. He was a man of medium height, though his enormously broad shoulders, his powerful chest and arms, his visible strength contrasted oddly with his white hair and clipped beard. He had the thoughtful, considered speech of a philosopher and the physical presence of a stonemason, and this seemed to doubly fortify his pronouncements, giving them sinew of mind and, for that matter, the soul. "It is closed, this discussion."

"Papa, please—"

"Closed."

The valises secured, some thrust under their feet, the driver informed them that it might be a lengthy journey, that is to say, a hefty fare. "I'm taking the long route, monsieur, not across the river and through Paris. Going out to the *barrière*, beyond the city gates. I'm taking no chances. There's rioting in the streets. This nag and carriage, they're all I have in the world to earn a living, and these rioters take what they like, they'll build their barricades with anything at hand. They say, monsieur, that over in the rue de la Chanverrerie, they've overturned a whole omnibus and built it into the barricade, God's truth. They've freed the horses, but you know what that means—" the driver gave a swift Parisian gesture of derision. "Those horses will be warming plates and bellies by the week's end. Skewered, roasted," he continued distractedly, as though savoring the horsemeat, "maybe with a bit of onion and—"

"That's enough. Just take us to the rue de l'Homme-Armé."

"As you say, monsieur," said the driver, "but that's what I'm telling you, it's not safe. The city is not safe. Not the direct route—

of course there are no direct routes in Paris, eh? But we can't go by the Arsenal. They raided that this afternoon, looted weapons, and now they're armed, these hooligans. They say a man on horseback, a black horse, carries a red flag and leads the people on. Me, I'm an honest workingman, no politics at all, monsieur, but it's times like these, terrible times, make me glad I haven't any property either. You have property, you must sign up for the National Guard. You get a uniform, you get shot. They've called them out, you know, they're gathering the National Guard and the army at the Palais-Royal, so that route's out. They've arrested eight hundred people, so we'll want to avoid the prisons, won't we? And we have to stay clear of the hospitals too. It's not the weapons I fear, monsieur, not the crowd, not even the armed and angry crowd. It's the hospital. The cholera is everywhere." He crossed himself quickly. "The cholera is carried on the air and you have to breathe, don't you? They say you shit yourself blue with the cholera, and die in a few hours."

"No doubt this very long ride and very high fare will require something extra for service, which, the sooner we are on our way . . ." He regarded the driver expectantly.

Tipping his hat, the driver closed their door, climbed up, and the carriage lurched slowly forward. Cosette kept her eyes on her gloved hands, knotted into fists in her lap. Why could she not tell her father, simply say, *I am in love and I cannot leave Paris.* No, she should say, *I must not leave Paris. I am in love with Marius Pontmercy.* Pontmercy was an honorable name. Marius had inherited a title as well. He was a baron, really, if you recognized titles bestowed by Bonaparte. Marius had explained to her that not everyone did. Cosette had no idea if her father did or not. She and her father lived such a retiring life that politics had never crossed their threshold. In any event, Marius's father was certainly a colonel. Everyone would recognize that. Moreover, he had distinguished himself at Waterloo and had lived to tell about it, though not to tell Marius, who had grown up with his grandfather and then quarreled with him bitterly and left home five years ago. As a result Marius was poor. Very poor if the truth were known, completing his law studies while living in abject want. But certainly her father could not object to his being an impecunious student. Her father had brought her up with respect for the poor. The poor were to be helped whenever possible and pitied above all. Her father had taken her with him on missions of mercy amongst conditions of misery so shocking . . . well, her whole young life had been founded on her father's precepts of faith, hope, and charity. But Cosette knew that her inability—put bluntly, her refusal—to tell about Marius had nothing to do with his name or his politics or his poverty. It was simply this: once confessed, their love would be channeled into convention. She and Marius would shrivel, turn to human stumps, if they were forced into drawing rooms and the dreadful stilted forms required of young ladies and courting gentlemen, to address one another as monsieur and mademoiselle and in the cool, distant *vous*. Nights in the garden of the rue Plumet had left them free as lions in the jungle, and even now Cosette closed her eyes and remembered the heat of the garden wall baking into her back. The wall still held the afternoon sun, even after dark, and the warmth had radiated across her shoulders as the warmth of Marius's body radiated over her breasts and the warmth of his hands penetrated the silk of her dress.

As the carriage trundled toward the old city gates, the *barrière*, Cosette did not even hear the cries of distant violence. She ran her tongue over her lips as though the taste of Marius might yet linger there, as though she might find some crumb from the communion of their love. She hastily tried to cobble together prayers that would reunite her with her lover. Was there a saint for lovers? If so, nothing in her convent education had suggested that saint's name. A saint for profane love. It's not profane, she told herself; Marius and I, our love is sacred, central, as central as the sun. It is as Marius once said, *If we did not love, the sun would go out.*

But the sun was about to go out anyway, to go down in any event. Evening shadows were lengthening, and Cosette knew that later Marius would come to the garden at rue Plumet, that he would lift the broken gate and step through into the shelter of the garden walls, and she would not be there to press her lips against his lips, her heart against his heart, that only the tall, unkempt grasses would whisper in reply when he called out her name.

Chapter 2

*C*osette!"

He doubled his fist and pounded on the locked door, but the house and garden at the rue Plumet seemed to have been deserted for years rather than hours. Cosette had gone to England. And with her went the sum and substance, the meaning and the possibilities of Marius's life. At twenty-two years old, he had endured the loss of his mother, his father, his family, his patrimony, and through all this had clung yet to some shred of hope, conviction that life had meaning and grandeur. In Cosette he had met that conviction in the flesh. And now he had lost her—and gained the bitter knowledge that a man may endure every loss save that of love. Without love the sun will go out.

These thoughts pounding through his head, he ran, at breakneck speed, to put the river between himself and the empty rue Plumet. He crossed the Seine at the Pont des Invalides and found himself out of breath, heart pumping, on the rue de Rivoli. Marius leaned forward, hands resting on his knees, sweat dripping from the ends of his dark hair, breathing heavily, wondering if he'd been suddenly thrust into a theatre, a wholly artificial gaslit world.

There beneath the arches of the rue de Rivoli, frock-coated men escorted women in vanilla-colored silks and foamy laces through the gas-green flickering glare, sea-green shadows blending beneath their feet. These people moved in a slow pavane. The café tables were sprinkled with patrons indolently spooning ice cream in the evening heat or toying with the last of their confections. How can this be? "How can this be?" Marius shouted, hoping someone would answer and thus assure him all this was a dream. But no one did and he ran past and through these people, and they regarded him with the indifference one might bestow upon a passing fool. Perhaps he looked a fool. Distraught. Disheveled. The tramp of soldiers led by cavalry officers in brilliant uniforms sounded behind him and he bolted into the rue Saint-Honoré, leaving these rue de Rivoli actors resolutely oblivious of any world beyond the wings.

On the rue Saint-Honoré a palpable air of menace radiated from people running from a building where a huge carpet wagon stood hunkered in the street. Marius crossed to the other side. These wagons had been pressed into service as ambulances during the cholera epidemic, but people believed that to go to the hospital was itself a death warrant. More often the carpet wagons acted as hearses, whether the sick were dead or not, and with the cholera you sometimes could not tell; dead, the victims looked more alive. Rattling with empty coffins, the wagons made their rounds through the streets, picking up the dead and the near-dead indiscriminately. Eighteen thousand people had died of cholera that spring. Cries and lamentations echoed from the building, and a woman tore out of the concierge's lodge, wailing that her husband wasn't yet dead, that they were going to bury the living. But people ignored her, and on either side merchants and matrons alike were slamming their shutters, closing their shops, and locking themselves inside.

Marius collided with one of these matrons, a café owner hastily flinging her chairs inside the shop. She shouted at him, her fist doubled, "Lout!"

"Long live the French Republic!" cried Marius as he ripped past, nearly overturning a street vendor's stall.

"Long live King Louis-Philippe," she yelled, "and death to all—"

But he had long since passed her, sprinting along the rue Saint-Honoré, which echoed with the slamming of bolts and the creak of closing shutters and dogs whining piteously at doors already shut against them. Streetlamps strung overhead, suspended from ropes, cast shadows like enormous spiders dancing in the street.

The city seemed to close in on Marius, the streets tightening like the fingers of a fist as he plunged toward the medieval labyrinth of Les Halles, the old market district, where, at the Corinth bistro at the corner of the rue Mondétour and the rue de la Chanverrerie, he knew his friends had made their stand. The army knew as well. A sentry stepped before him and cried out, "Halt! No one permitted—"

Unheeding, Marius ran on, turned a corner just as the sentry fired on him. He darted along one ill-lit alley and then another and another, streets so narrow they were but cobbled threads. The old buildings sagged sadly toward one another, as though distressed to have come to such narrow ends, and often shored up by the same beam, reaching across from one house to the other, streets so insular, closed and narrow, they were their own prisons. At the corner of the rue des Bourdonnais, the street lamps ended altogether. Insurgents and army alike were obliged to go forth in total darkness.

As he made his way through coiling streets little wider than gutters, this inky blackness was to Marius a welcome palliative, obscuring the wreck of his life: there had been that one chance he might save Cosette from going to England. One chance: he could marry her. It seemed simple. Even possible. And so Marius had plunged every morsel of pride he possessed back into his pocket and gone to his grandfather, whom he'd not seen or spoken to in five years. He had asked the old man's permission to marry, but the interview ended much as he might have guessed. Now, as he groped blindly along wet walls and past garbage heaps, Marius consoled himself that if love were lost to him, if life had no more meaning or substance or possibility, at least death would. Without Cosette he would die. What did it matter when or how? The pain of losing her was so profound, physical pain paled beside it. He could hear patrols and the volley of gunfire in neighboring streets, but could see nothing, scarcely his own hands; not a single candle burned in the windows and the people who crouched behind these shutters did so soundlessly. He was not too far from the Corinth, but the way was twisted and desperate and dark.

Marius tripped on paving stones that had been ripped up, tore his trousers, and fell against an overturned cart. Apparently some insurgents had made a stand here and then abandoned it. His hands out before him, he felt his way along coarse wooden doors and shutters, along plaster so long damp it felt spongy to the touch. Somewhere overhead a woman's cry rang, a shriek of loss. Her wails counterpointed the nearby tramp of soldiers, random gunfire, and the deep bass, the low warning bell of Saint-Merri. The tocsin. Calling the people to arms.

He wondered if in answer to that summons these doors would open and the people pour out to support the rebels. But there was nothing. A cat in heat squealed. Marius hurtled through the darkling shadows, startled to turn a sudden corner, where he found two National Guardsmen. The sentries fired and the bullet ricocheted off a copper pot suspended above a barber's shop as Marius crouched in the first low doorway he could find, his heart pumping, determined to get to the Corinth and the rue de la Chanverrerie: if he were going to die, he would do it at the barricade, side by side with his friends, and not shot here, falling in the street like a thieving dog. He held his breath until the sound of soldiers' feet moved away and he could hear them firing at someone else nearby. At least he heard shots, shouts, and cries.

Collecting himself, he stepped out again, his pace reduced to a mere prowl as he stumbled over the rubble left by the day's riots and through the shadows. All he could do was lead with his hands, as though blindly trying to sweep the blackness from his path. Perhaps he'd actually done so, because the darkness split wide open, white, suddenly bleached and terrible as two runaway white horses bore down on him. Their eyes rolling, their fierce cries echoing, they careened along, their harnesses clanking, clattering desperately through the courts and stones, the narrow alleys. Marius flattened himself against a door and the huge horses plunged before him and then they too vanished, their white haunches swallowed up in the night.

He came at last to the barricade at the rue de la Chanverrerie, fourteen feet high. He saw the omnibus splayed and mortared there, with beams and paving stones and empty wine casks and a shattered billiard table. A single torch at the top cast an eerie light below. Four National Guard corpses lay stretched out before the barricade, their limbs twisted into positions unthinkable in life. A slow drip caught Marius's attention, and high up in a fourth-story window he saw a man regarding the corpses, his cap askew, his mouth open in amazement, and a seam of blood dripping from his chin. Marius could hear the voice of Enjolras telling Combeferre and the others to build up the back barricade at the rue Mondétour and ordering men to take paving stones up to the upper floors of the Corinth and block the windows there. Marius was about to call out to his friends and scramble over when he heard military feet approach. He cut and ran, ducked through the tiny streets and came at last to the back of the Corinth, the rue Mondétour, where torchlight flickered over the faces of Combeferre, Verdier, and a half-dozen others working to bolster this back barricade.

Verdier put down the empty cask he was about to jam into place. "So, you've come at last."

"Yes."

"And the girl?"

Marius could not reply. Combeferre and Verdier nodded sagely, even sadly. At last Marius said, "My grandfather told me it was ludicrous to marry a girl with no money, no name, no family. He said marriage should never be confused with lust."

"And love?" asked Combeferre. "Should it be confused with love?"

Marius slumped. "My grandfather does not believe in love. He told me to bed the wench and be done with it."

A furtive smile crossed Combeferre's face. He was a solid man, a bit older than Marius, perhaps twenty-six, but with the look of middle age and a receding hairline already upon him. Of all Marius's friends Combeferre seemed to have the broadest sensibilities and the most humanity, fittingly since he was studying to be a doctor. "What did you expect him to say?"

"Not that."

"My friend, your grandfather is a royalist goat. You are a man committed to honor and absolutes. He may have brought you up from a baby, but he knows nothing about you at all."

"He stole me from my father. My mother died, my father didn't. He told my father to give me up or I'd be cut from his will. My father thought he was acting in my interest."

"Well, you're going to be cut from your grandfather's will anyway, aren't you?" Verdier said grimly. "You won't outlive him." A printer with enormous hands, Eugène Verdier also had enormous political passions and barricade experience. He took an iron bedstead apart like a toy and thrust it into the barricade as supports.

"My grandfather always called my father the Brigand. My father, a colonel! Five years ago, when I left my grandfather's house, I said, *You will never insult my father again.* Today he insulted both my father and my wife."

"You have no wife."

"She is my wife in my heart."

"Till death do us part, yes?" Combeferre picked up the empty cask and put it in Marius's arms.

"Yes," replied Marius with a nod to his comrades, students and workers alike.

The students mostly wore threadbare coats, trousers shiny at the knee, and frayed cravats, clothes that nonetheless suggested bourgeois beginnings to their lives and perhaps bourgeois ends in ordinary circumstances. These circumstances, 5 June 1832, could not be called ordinary. For years workingmen had come together with students in political clubs all over the city, ready for this moment, eager for it. Clad in the loose blue smock and cap, as much the uniform of the workingman as the general's brass denotes a soldier, these men wore coarse, durable caps and clothes, bearing very often the signs and stains of their trades—plaster, ink, dust, dye. Their hands as well bore stains and scars. These men had skills. Perhaps they did not own property, but they had addresses, unlike that vast Parisian social sludge—the diggers and pickers and beggars and sweepers, people desperate, hungry, and nomadic, who lived amidst decay and slept in squalor, and whose bodies provided the main course at the cholera's banquet. The workingmen here had political passions, hopes, and grievances they could articulate with muscle. The students could articulate with pens. Together they saw themselves as the heirs of both the French Revolution and the American Revolution. Like the men of 1789, they wanted an end to the monarchy: no more kings for France. Like the men of 1776, they wanted a free republic, universal male suffrage, an unfettered press, and education free of the church. These same passions, hopes, and grievances would later fire the Revolution of 1848. But of the men gathered here at the Corinth, perhaps Marius alone knew how doomed they were in 1832.

A stranger to Marius had pulled a lumpy mattress from the third floor of the Corinth and dragged it back to the rue Mondétour, where Marius helped him secure it to the barricade. "It will break someone's fall," he offered. He was a big man with a well-fed solidity to him, young as the students, dressed like them, but lacking somehow their *esprit*. He sprinkled some bits of tobacco into small papers, rolled and smoked them. The tobacco seemed to color more than just his fingertips and teeth; his hair was the same gingery color, as was the beard sprouting on his unshaven cheeks. He had a jaw strong as a coal scuttle and close-set blue eyes, astute and intelligent. His wild eyebrows rested on his forehead like dragonflies, giving him an air of perpetual surprise.

"You're new to us, aren't you?" asked Marius.

"New to Paris. Not new to the fight. I'm from Lyon. I'm Achille Clerons."

Marius nodded, then frowned to see Eugène Verdier falter under a light load. "You don't look well, Verdier," Marius observed, knowing full well that Eugène Verdier never looked well. He was a lank, sallow man of perhaps thirty-five, with straight black hair and a mouth perpetually set in an unsmiling seam. His devotion to his trade was well known and a frequent subject of café humor amongst his friends. Sometimes they called him the Priest, mocking his sense of vocation to the press, and in his dour way Verdier tolerated their raillery at his expense. Perhaps he even enjoyed it.

"Verdier's skin is that color because of all the ink in his veins," chided his apprentice, a sixteen-year-old named Pajol, nicknamed the Monkey not only because he was a nimble compositor, but also because he was fast enough to elude the heavy hand of Verdier when his incessant teasing taxed the older man's patience. Pajol took off the paper cap of his trade and made a deep, low bow before the master printer—and just as quickly scooted away. "Verdier has ink in his prick and begets printers' devils upon his poor wife."

"And when he kisses her," another printer scoffed, "she spits out ink."

"No," protested Pajol from a safe distance, "she just spits."

When Verdier could not be roused to retaliate, Pajol mocked him further, but Marius sensed that more than the ink in his veins had made Verdier gray as newsprint, and he told Pajol to cease and asked the master printer what had happened.

Verdier's gaze went from one man to the next. "My wife will never taste ink on my lips again. She died of the cholera three days ago."

"Why didn't you tell us?"

"What is there to tell? How she went blue? How fast the cholera took her? How the cholera works, like poison, so swift and terrible?"

Pajol's jauntiness evaporated and he reached toward Verdier, who pulled away.

"*Merci,* but no, I can't bear your pity. Any of you. I prefer rage. The king, the government, they are behind this epidemic. They do not give a damn shit that we die of the cholera. They want us to die. Kill off the frail workers, the women, the children, the old folks. There are too many workers. Too many people to feed. Not enough work. Not enough bread. Invite the cholera in and let it do the bourgeois's dirty work. Kill off the excess. The doctors are government agents. You don't see the bourgeois dropping like flies, do you?"

"Casimir Périer died of it," said Combeferre, "the financier they buried the other day."

"Casimir Périer got it from fucking his chambermaid, who is ill fed and overworked and goes home at night to the rue Mouffetard, where twelve people sleep in one room, or to the place Maubert, where women and children sleep in the street, most of them drunk, or to those streets near the Bièvre River where no one can breathe for the fumes," Verdier replied bitterly. "No, when I see the bourgeois and the fatted pigs stoop to this, I know the only answers are armed answers. I have always hated the bourgeois, the bankers and bosses, the kings, the princes, the emperors, sorry, Monsieur Pontmercy," he nodded to Marius, "I know how you feel about Napoléon, that you are a committed Bonapartist, but they have to be stopped, all of them. And if the people do not rise with us this time, there will come another."

"We will not live to see it," said a tanner, who still smelled of his trade.

"Yes, we will." The voice was that of Enjolras, the student leader and *de facto* commander of this barricade. At twenty-four, Enjolras was a cold, committed young man, whose vision of the future had guided his life as a saint's life is guided by a vision of God, that is to say, to the exclusion of all else. Thin, sinewy, and fair, Enjolras had the pallor of a man who works too long by lamplight. "They're rousing all over Paris. They say a third of the populace has taken up arms. You can hear that tocsin from Saint-Merri. We're not alone. Of course, they've arrested a lot of men, but there are more joining every minute. The kings of France are finished. The time for the French Republic is now."

The rue Mondétour barricade fortified, Enjolras left sentries there, and with Combeferre and Marius walked back into the Corinth bistro, where a bleached sign overhead testified to the late owner's culinary abilities with carp. He had made a superb stuffed carp, advertised it as *carpe au gras,* but time and some waggish student's hand had altered the sign to make a pun in Latin, *Carpe ho ras,* echoing Horace's injunction to seize the hours.

"Fitting for us, yes?" said Marius. "We have only a few hours to seize."

Enjolras regarded the sign as though seeing it for the first time. "I don't believe in irony." He ordered the sign taken down and used to block a window in one of the upper stories. The barricade at the rue de la Chanverrerie had been built swiftly but cleverly and rose in jagged fourteen-foot-high splendor. Some of these builders were master craftsmen, joiners, carpenters, masons, and the strange materials yielded an edifice whose angles belied its navigability. It could be quickly mounted and maneuvered and defended from any number of positions. Enjolras ordered the sentries to look sharp and guard four others, whom he directed into the street below to take the National Guard uniforms off the dead. "Those uniforms may be useful before the night is over."

"More muskets, more carbines, more ammunition would be useful before the night is over too," said Combeferre.

"New men will bring weapons. They raided the Arsenal today and our men have real weapons, not just your father's old Waterloo sword. Sorry," Enjolras nodded to Marius, "I didn't mean that as it sounded. I know how you feel about your father's Waterloo sword."

"My grandfather pawned my father's Waterloo sword, so I hope they raided the pawnshops too and it's in the hands of some angry worker, but I have to tell you, my friends, I don't think we can count—"

"Listen to that tocsin from Saint-Merri." Enjolras, never given to affection, patted Marius fraternally on the shoulder. "Smell the smoke of gunpowder carried on the wind. They're fighting all over the city. This is it. Revolution!"

"My friends," Marius insisted, "I must tell you what I have seen in the city. The people are not rousing. The doors are all shut. On the rue de Rivoli, people are strolling beneath arcades and eating ice cream."

"I don't believe it."

"It's true. As long as we don't dirty their windows and gutters with our blood, the rich don't care. And the people are not rising with us. I'm afraid it will not be revolution, only insurrection."

"I would not have chosen this moment. This moment chose me, chose us," Enjolras admitted tersely. He seemed physically a rather frail vessel for so much intensity, as though a lighthouse beacon had been thrust into a votive candle. Enjolras met his friends' eyes with candor. "Now the cholera is killing us just as surely as the army. The epidemic has reduced all human feeling to brute fear. What *fraternité* can there be in these circumstances?"

"As a medical man, I tell you the cholera's ravaging the most wretched," Combeferre added, "the people who would have supported us."

"There's still the question of the army," suggested Enjolras. "If the army refuses to fire on us, if they side with the people, then we have revolution. That's how insurrection becomes revolution and how revolution becomes resurrection."

Marius followed him and Combeferre into the Corinth kitchen, which had been turned into a hospital and an arsenal, and the fire into a forge. Bullets and bandages were equally laid out, cartridges counted down to the last one, carbines, muskets stacked separately, even a couple of old muzzle loaders, and a single powder keg. Three metal workers were melting nails into shot, and the fierce heat and smell and smoke wafted all over the Corinth.

"Where we have cartridges," said Enjolras, "the army has caissons. Our every bullet has to count."

"Yes, but where they have officers, we have comrades. Besides, we know now the army is frightened." Combeferre pulled a cork from a bottle with his teeth, nodding toward a huge man clad in black, his hands and feet bound, who was tied to a post. He had iron-gray hair, gray eyes, and a gray beard that crawled along his jaw like lichen over granite. "If they weren't frightened, they would never have sent their police spy, would they?" Combeferre poured some wine into a cup, sipped, and passed it to Enjolras, who declined.

Marius took the cup and sipped reflectively. "Who denounced him?"

"Gavroche. You know that kid. The dauphin of the gutter."

"Everyone knows Gavroche, don't they?"

"When Gavroche denounced him, he hadn't even the wit to deny it. It wouldn't have mattered anyway, this *mouchard* is so stupid—" Combeferre turned to the prisoner. "Do you carry your brains in your bladder, Javert? What kind of spy carries his police identification?"

"A man of duty. A man of honor. Things you know nothing of."

With a shrug, Combeferre conceded that perhaps honor was not his personal strong point, but his friends, Pontmercy and Enjolras, they were men of absolutes and men of honor. "They could talk honor and absolutes to you all night, Javert."

"I do not speak of honor. I live it."

"Not for long," Enjolras added.

"Republican scum like you can't overthrow the king of France. One day more and you'll piss blood. I'll meet you in hell."

"I'm not going to hell, Javert. I'm going to be a free citizen in the new French Republic. The Second French Republic, you understand? No more kings living fat while children starve, no dogs like Guizot, licking sweat and blood and money off the backs of workers." Enjolras went on vehemently, "From now on the people will decide their own political fate. In the Republic, the press will be free, and education will be free of the blight of the church, and we will be free to assemble, free to speak, and every man will vote whether he owns property or not."

"*Liberté*," added Clerons, joining them. "*Egalité! Fraternité!*" Clerons picked up a wine bottle, took a sip, swished it around in his mouth, held it there briefly, then spat into Javert's face. "All police spies should be shot."

"All police spies will be shot," Javert replied laconically, unmoved by the insult.

Gunfire exploded from the back, and cries from the barricade brought them running to the rue Mondétour, where lay a young workingman, blood seeping from his outstretched left hand and black powder in an aureole across the back of his blue smock. Combeferre knelt and turned him over, while the sentry, Pajol, trembling, explained how quickly it had all happened. "The National Guard were right behind him. I thought they were going to jump the barricade too. They—he—well," Pajol took a steep, sad breath, "you can see for yourselves, they shot him in the back."

But the young man wasn't dead, and his lips moved as Combeferre tore open his blue smock to find the wound below. Combeferre looked up to Marius. "He wants you." His mouth tightened and he closed the smock. "She wants you."

"She? She?" Marius knelt, bracing her shoulders in his arms and pulling her cap off so red hair tumbled to the stones. "Eponine? Oh, God, Eponine—" he brushed the dirt from her face. "What are you doing here? Why have you—?"

"I came here to die with you, Monsieur Marius."

"You're not going to die. Combeferre, can't you—"

Combeferre shook his head, and Marius's friends melted into the darkness, leaving him with Eponine Thénardier, who was tall enough to have passed for a man and young enough to have passed for a boy.

"Monsieur Marius, you're all going to die here. You know that, don't you? Everyone else does." Eponine spoke slowly, softly, and with great effort, and though her face was creased, twisted with pain, a wisp of smile hovered near her lips. "I think I am a little in love with you, Monsieur Marius."

"You're bleeding to death. Oh, Eponine, don't—"

"I have been a little in love with you since you lived next to us in that filthy hovel near the *barrière* and you paid our rent that one quarter, you remember?"

"Yes, no, what does that matter now? I paid it because you were a family in misery." He stroked the hair from her forehead.

"You lived in misery too, Monsieur Marius."

"I was one man, a student."

"Because you are a man, my father thought you paid in advance for me. He sent me to your bed." The effort of laughing cost Eponine blood, which burbled from her lips, and Marius gently wiped it away. "I told my father, You misjudge Monsieur Marius, you old wolf. Monsieur Marius does not want that from me."

"I didn't want anything, Eponine. I only want you to live." He tore off his coat and pressed it protectively to her breast.

"It won't be long. It won't even be bad, Monsieur Marius, if you will stay with me."

"I'm here. I'll stay."

"If you'll kiss me."

Marius tenderly brushed her lips with his; she smiled as he pressed her cheek and kissed her closed eyes. "Why are you here, Eponine?" he whispered. "What in God's name brought you—?"

"In the name of love, Monsieur Marius. In the name of love." Her breath became shallow and labored, and each breath pulsated blood through Marius's coat. Her left hand lay useless with a hole through it, and in the other she clutched a piece of paper. "But not her love. My love, Monsieur Marius, my love for you. You'll keep me safe, won't you, close?"

"Yes. Yes, Eponine. I promise."

"Keep me warm?"

"I swear."

"We waited for you, both of us. In the name of love, Monsieur Marius. She waited in the garden and I waited in the street, but you didn't come to the rue Plumet."

"Cosette? *Cosette?*" The name was too much to bear and Marius began to cry. "Don't die, don't die, Eponine, we shouldn't any of us be dying."

"In the name of love, she said, and I said, Well, fine, fine, in the name of my love I will go to the barricade, but—" Eponine shivered, and her eyes widened in surprise. "Your coat is warm, but I am cold. I am very cold, Monsieur Marius."

"I will keep you warm." Weeping, he pulled her closer against him, his cheek to hers, his arms around her, his shoulders hunched protectively.

"You've kissed me. You don't have to love me. Take this in the name of—" She tried to raise her right arm but hadn't the strength, and with a raucous gurgle that sounded as if the life were being brutally sucked, not merely drained, from her body, her lips moved again, but wordlessly. She died while Marius wept against her pale throat.

Combeferre touched Marius's shoulder and took Cosette's note from Eponine's hand. Giving the note to Marius, he and Pajol lifted the body, wrapping Eponine gently in Marius's coat and taking her corpse to join their other losses in the makeshift morgue in the Corinth cellar.

Still kneeling, Marius regarded his bloodstained shirt and trousers, the note, in his hand, Cosette's handwriting and his own name, blood-smudged, and the tears he'd wept against Eponine's cheek fell again: tears for love, for loss, for the certainty that life without love was not worth living, that the only escape from the pain he felt now was to end all pain forever. With difficulty Marius rose, pulled himself up to his full height, flung his arms out and his head back to the enormous sky, the very stars picketed by the crazy roofs and chimney pots of Paris. With Eponine's blood in a sash across his chest, he walked slowly, Cosette's note in his hand, to a table where a single candle sputtered against the darkness, and the shadows it created leapt and flitted, fluttered like anxious birds nesting in the barricade.

Chapter 3

*T*wo tasks were vital to Jean Valjean's life: he must look after Cosette, and he must be true to the vow imposed upon him by the bishop. The bishop had bought his soul for God, bought it with two heavy silver candlesticks, which now stood on the mantel, here in the rue de l'Homme-Armé, though the rest of their valises remained unopened, in disarray. Jean Valjean stood before the candlesticks, struggling with his need for freedom, his vow to the bishop, his cherished integrity, and his love for Cosette, all these warring within him. For the first time in many years they had competing rather than complementary claims. He had always believed he loved Cosette selflessly, and now he knew he did not. Perhaps there is no such thing as selfless love, oh, maybe for humanity, or the poor, the meek, the orphans, perhaps in those sorts of aggregates and multitudes, but the love lavished on a single human being can never be selfless. The crisis before him tonight—and he knew it was a crisis—came as the result of a mere piece of paper, which lay between the silver candlesticks on the mantel: a passionate note of farewell from Marius, written to Cosette, delivered by Gavroche, and intercepted by Jean Valjean.

This boy Marius (Jean Valjean could not think of him otherwise, could not consider the name without the implicit sneer the wise reserve for the foolish) had written that he was throwing himself on the barricade because he was losing Cosette forever, because his grandfather would not allow him to marry her and save her from England.

"As if I'd let *her* marry *him!*" Jean Valjean crushed the note in his huge hand and cast it into the fireplace, dry and unlit this June night. "Who is he, this Marius? This no one!" And why had Cosette never mentioned him? Why had Cosette kept such a thing secret? She had never kept secrets before. These questions burrowed uncomfortably in the wainscoting of his mind. Well, this Marius, he was right about one thing. "Cosette is going to England. There's safety in England and no more fear."

Very soon Jean Valjean and Cosette would disappear again, this time across La Manche, what the English, in their insufferable condescension, were pleased to call the English Channel. Just as eight years before they had disappeared, scaled a wall and dropped into the garden of the Convent of the Perpetual Adoration. With the help of the old gardener there, Father Fauchelevent, they had passed themselves off as his relatives and made a life within the convent walls, Cosette Fauchelevent as a student, Jean Valjean (now Fauchelevent) as a second gardener. In deference to the nuns of the Perpetual Adoration, who were humble, reticent, and abstemious in the extreme, both Jean Valjean and the equally inoffensive Father Fauchelevent were obliged to wear leather knee patches with bells attached, so that when they moved about the grounds the nuns could hear these men and scurry away. It made Jean Valjean smile to think of those nuns. But he had struck an accord with the mother superior and repaid the convent for its kindness to him and his beloved daughter. Thanks to the nuns of the Perpetual Adoration, Cosette Fauchelevent was an educated young lady now, which meant that she could read, write, and speak elegant French, play the piano, and do fancy needlework. She could recite the kings of France and all important saints. She knew such history as pleased the nuns: in 1789 the Bourbon kings, given, alas, to excess, had fallen prey to irreligious mobs, and both Louis XVI and his queen had been executed, their heads cut off by the guillotine, as were many others during the Reign of Terror. However, they all died good Catholics. The nuns' obligation to history ended there.

Cosette grew up to be lovely, surprising everyone. Who would have believed that the scraped and ragged child of eight would emerge a few years later beautiful? And in those convent years Jean Valjean had almost achieved his own small worldly dream: to breed a blue rose. In his youth Jean Valjean had been a peasant, one of that rural tribe as stoic and dependent on the land as oxen. But in the convent garden, the rhythm of the seasons, the refuge of the thick walls, watching Cosette grow and prosper had all contributed to a sense of well-being Jean Valjean had never known—and indeed had never expected to know. And in this quiet interlude in his tumultuous life, Jean Valjean's hands had returned to the soil with pleasure; he had made the convent's garden bloom, and he had tried to graft, to create a rose so blue it would match the color of Cosette's eyes.

But she grew up before he could accomplish that. Father and daughter left the convent, Jean Valjean bestowing five thousand francs upon them, and the mother superior very wisely never inquiring how a gardener had come by so much money. The gardener, of course, had not. Jean Valjean had had many lives and identities, and in one of these he was Monsieur Madeleine, the wealthy manufacturer. As Monsieur Madeleine he had earned that money by dint of hard work and a few good ideas. But the past caught up with him and Monsieur Madeleine was forced to vanish forever as Jean Valjean took flight.

Now it merely remained for Jean Valjean to dig up the money (literally, for he had buried it in a forest), to book passage out of France, to arrange false papers, which would allow them to travel as Monsieur and Mademoiselle Fauchelevent, and then, neither Javert nor Thénardier would ever find them in England. Javert sought them at the behest of an obsessive belief in the letter of the law. Thénardier's motives were simpler, mere blackmail. Thénardier, that low, avaricious dog, he would sniff for his blackmail, all the way to La Manche, and there the trail would stop. In England lay perfect safety. Exile, perhaps, but safety. No more Thénardier. No more Javert. And no more of this Marius. Jean Valjean knelt and took the letter from the fireplace. It was scrawled on a bit of cheap student's notebook paper with a pencil and in a blurred and hasty hand, but there was no mistaking the passion, the ardor. And no mistaking that this Marius believed irrevocably that Cosette returned his ardor. How else would he dare to write to her in such a fashion? Cosette was in love. "Bah!" Jean Valjean crushed the note again, flung it back into the fireplace, and this time he brought the silver candlestick down, laid flame to it and watched it burn with great satisfaction. "She is seventeen, too young to be in love. She is a child. This Marius, he is nothing to her. She wanted a puppy once and I said no and she got over it."

However, the puppy was the only thing Jean Valjean had ever denied Cosette. And he had denied the puppy for good reason. A dog, after all, well, you never knew what it might do, how it might involve you unwillingly with the neighbors, or make it difficult to flee swiftly and without making a sound, to vanish if need be.

Indeed, Jean Valjean's fugitive past, in abeyance in the years they had lived in the convent, caught up with him almost immediately upon their leaving it. And so he had rented three residences, this apartment and one other, and the house in the rue Plumet, all in different districts of the city. He could thus move often and easily, protect his identity and maintain his integrity—which for Jean Valjean meant that he must exemplify the bishop's faith that the divine spark flickered in every human soul, however benighted. Why else would the bishop have taken Jean Valjean into his home all those years ago? Jean Valjean: a ragged convict so low, so reviled and repudiated, dogs would not share their kennels with him. The bishop fed this surly convict at his table, gave him a bed to sleep in—his first bed in nineteen years—and never asked why he had gone to prison. For stealing a loaf of bread. Nonetheless, that night Jean Valjean had stolen the bishop's silver. Nabbed by the police the next morning, he was dragged back to the bishop's home, facing certain death or perpetual imprisonment as a repeat offender. The bishop, carrying the two silver candlesticks, which he placed in Jean Valjean's hands, had merely, mildly inquired: *Why have you forgotten these, the best of all the silver I gave you? Why have you forgotten this gift?*

And with that gift of freedom—Jean Valjean prodded the ashes of Marius's letter—came the recognition that he too must demonstrate faith, hope, charity. Charity, alas, had unfortunately connected him once again with that thief, blackguard, and blackmailer, Thénardier. An act of charity had brought him (and, God forbid, Cosette!) to the hovel near the *barrière* d'Italie where Thénardier lived with his wife and their brats. Thénardier was one of those men who are cunning, careless, brutal, hungry forever, and drunk when he could be. Once the proprietor of The Sergeant of Waterloo Inn in Montfermeil (and the inn bought with money snatched off corpses at Waterloo), Thénardier had drunk himself into bankruptcy. Now he lived in Paris, which is to say he subsisted, a common thief, thug, forger, and the artful author of begging letters. Jean Valjean in his role as the well-to-do, benevolent Monsieur Fauchelevent had succumbed to one of these begging letters and very nearly lost his life when Thénardier and his band had set upon him to rob him and, worse, to kidnap Cosette and exact ransom. Jean Valjean had escaped them: one more successful flight. Cosette, thank God, was never even alarmed. But Thénardier was onto him.

At the bishop's whispered, ghostly behest, Jean Valjean could have forgiven Thénardier all that, could have forgiven Thénardier everything, save for what he had done to Cosette and to her mother, Fantine. Fantine had left her little daughter with them, to care for her till she could return. The Thénardiers had robbed Fantine of her every sou, driven her to desperation, to poverty, to prostitution, and death in short order. And at the same time they were unspeakably cruel to the child. They had beaten and bruised, kicked, starved, enslaved, and abused Cosette from the time she was three till Jean Valjean rescued her at the age of eight. No, Jean Valjean could not forgive the Thénardier family that. He'd tried. Truly, he had tried. Only by putting La Manche between Cosette and the corpse-robbing blackmailer Thénardier could Jean Valjean protect her. Nothing must ever harm Cosette. He and Cosette would go to England.

Jean Valjean was roused from his thoughts by the toll of a church bell. The mournful tocsin from the nearby church at Saint-Merri, where they had built barricades and where they were fighting. But this boy, Marius, he was not at Saint-Merri. What had the kid said? Jean Valjean had intercepted Marius's note from Gavroche, who said he was from the barricade at the rue de la Chanverrerie and in a hurry to get back to the fight. That's why Gavroche had consented to give Marius's letter to Jean Valjean rather than the young lady it was addressed to.

Jean Valjean regarded the bishop's silver candlesticks. They were two pillars of his life. Freedom and integrity. What if he lost one of them? Impossible. They were inseparable. They must be. If, in gaining his freedom, he lost his integrity . . . With his boot heel Jean Valjean ground Marius's charred letter into ash. The bishop had enjoined him to faith, hope, and charity. Charity was simple.

My God, charity was nothing! Giving away mere goods? Simple money? But faith and hope, they were allied to love. Jean Valjean loved Cosette. He had faith she loved him. She loved this Marius. That much was clear. The boy who wrote that letter was absolutely certain his passion was returned. Could Jean Valjean betray faith and hope, in effect lie to Cosette, take her to England and exile and never mention the boy she loved? The man she loved. Never mention that he knew she had loved a man? This Marius. Jean Valjean made himself say it, cleanly, shorn of derision, "Marius."

Once before he had been faced with a similar choice: an aged beggar had been caught stealing fruit and conclusively identified as Jean Valjean. Repeat offender. Death or perpetual imprisonment mandated. If this old, illiterate man were convicted in his stead, Jean Valjean—then Monsieur Madeleine and the mayor of his town—could continue to live in comfort and plenty, enjoying the fruits of his industry and ingenuity, Javert forever appeased. Then, with a mere beggar's life at stake, Jean Valjean had parted with his freedom in order to preserve his integrity. Could he do less now? Perhaps the life at stake was Cosette's. What had she said to him this afternoon, *And when I am a woman, Papa . . .*

"Are you a woman, Cosette? Has the child vanished without my even seeing her go? Has the woman appeared before me and I—no, I could not have been that blind." How could she be in love with this Marius? A penniless student. Who was this boy on the barricade? He paused: the bell from Saint-Merri had ceased to toll. Saint-Merri had fallen. It was near dawn now. By daylight troops would be massed all through the market district. By noon those barricaded in the rue de la Chanverrerie would be finished, dead, dying, arrested, imprisoned.

Jean Valjean put his huge powerful hands around the base of each of the silver candlesticks and drew them up close together, side by side. Then he took them and by their light went into his room, found his National Guard uniform, changed into it. Still carrying the bishop's gift, he went to Cosette's room, opened the door, and stood by her bed. The candlelight played over her young face and her hair tousled on the pillow. Hers was the dearest face in the world, and he was sorry to see her frowning in her sleep, tossing as though in dreams she sought something. Someone. He kissed her forehead. "I love you more than life itself, Cosette," he murmured, placing the candlesticks on the floor. "You are my child, and loving you has given me life, given me joy, given me heart. You will always be my daughter, even when you are no longer my child." He bent, blew out the flames, left the room, closing the door softly.

In the front hall there was a small bureau, and expertly Jean Valjean rummaged in its drawer and found the dagger he always kept there. He thrust it into its sheath, strapped it on, and went down three flights of stairs and into the street. An armed man in the rue de l'Homme-Armé.

Chapter 4

*T*hrough the night they readied the barricade for the morning assault as feverishly as one might have prepared for a wedding celebration, but the bouquets expected here were those of firepower and the ribbons those of smoke and the silver that of swords, and there was no food at all. Sporadic fighting throughout the night had left the insurgents with several wounded, and two more corpses joined Eponine Thénardier in the makeshift morgue.

From one of these men, dead of a bullet that pierced his brain, Combeferre took an unstained blue workshirt and gave it to Marius in exchange for the shirt with the banner of Eponine's blood. Marius drew his arms through the workshirt, which still smelled of the sweat of the man who had worn it, a mason's assistant. It was like putting on the other man's life: like wearing the hod that man had carried, the clay pipe he had smoked, the women he had loved, the garlic sausages and coarse bread he had eaten, the adulterated wine he had drunk in *goguettes,* cafés where he'd sung with his comrades, singing societies masking their political activities, their republican clubs, their ardor, their hopes for freedom beneath the veneer of drunken conviviality. Well, that mason's assistant was free now, wasn't he?

Clad in this man's unfamiliar workshirt, scented with his unfamiliar life, Marius had written his hasty farewell to Cosette and sent Gavroche off with it, telling the boy not to return. Marius helped his friends gather up spent cartridges emptied in the night's skirmishes, refilling them with powder, strengthening the redoubts, readying the upper floors of the Corinth for the fight they knew would come with the morning light. Marius also helped with the wounded. Combeferre's medical training allowed him to stanch the bleeding, but he had no medicine, no instruments, and nothing for pain, except the landlord's brandy. Through what was left of the night these insurgents stayed close to one another, drank the good wine the Corinth landlord would have never allowed them. They spoke in low voices. They relished their hunger, knowing that dead men don't get hungry, relished their fatigue, knowing that dead men don't get tired, and those wounded relished even their pain, knowing that dead men feel nothing. Perhaps dead men get nothing, not even remembrance. To that end, Feuilly, the fan maker, used his knife to scrape along the Corinth wall, *Vive le peuple!*

Sentries atop the barricade kept a fruitless lookout. The streets were so close and narrow, the darkness so devouring, they could see nothing. They relied, they all relied, on their hearing, on the toll of the Saint-Merri bell and its increasingly mournful call, *To arms, to arms, to arms* . . . As the night wore on, the tocsin seemed less alarming and more imploring. And when Gavroche, having delivered Marius's note of farewell to Number 7 rue de l'Homme-Armé, returned to the barricade (contrary to Marius's express orders), he had only the grimmest news: it was as Marius had said earlier, the hearts of the people of Paris were closed against them. The fists of the people would not be raised—5 June 1832 was not to be 14 July 1789, when riot became revolution. This was to be mere civil unrest, insurrection swiftly squashed. For days afterward the army would comb the narrow-veined streets, shooting anyone they found hiding in the heart of the city, and the police would fan through the sewers shooting anyone they found in its bowels. Labeled riot, the barricades at the rue de la Chanverrerie, the Corinth, the rue Mondétour and their defenders would be tossed into the dustbin of history.

"You're doomed, we're doomed," said Clerons. "All men who work for the Republic are doomed."

"Not forever," said Enjolras, a queer half-smile twisting his lips. "Tyrants will not forever triumph. The Republic will come. The Republic of France is a historical imperative and it will come, because the French demand freedom. They have since 1789. They will forever. The men who love freedom can be killed but they cannot be stopped. Close the back barricade. Sentries, take your places. The rest of you, get such sleep as you can."

In the feeble light of candles stuck along the tables, Marius studied the faces of each of his friends. We are all so young, he thought, there is so much we will never know. There is still so much to do. To say. So much to tell Cosette. Love, true love, requires a long life in which to prove itself true. Marius knew that now, fathomed it as a sort of last rite and too late. He took out his cheap notebook and pencil and wrote:

My beloved—

Time only matters to the living, and soon I will join those whom time can't touch. But I must tell you, even as that moment draws closer, that nothing will erode my love for you. I embrace you with my last breath. My love for you will live outside of time, will live beyond me and with you. I love you and shall go on loving you, as much outside of time as ever a man could within its confines.

Love is its own country, but not its own world. The world invades the country of love, but cannot destroy it. I shall live with you always in the country of love.

Marius
6 June 1832

To the finder of this note, please deliver to Mlle. Cosette Fauchelevent, Number 7, rue de l'Homme-Armé.

He borrowed Feuilly's knife and quickly dug a tiny tunnel in the wall beneath *Vive le peuple!* He wadded the note as if it were to be stuffed into a cartridge, and indeed made a sort of bullet of it, crammed the note at knifepoint into the hole, sealing it with a pared-down cork and the wax from a near-spent candle. Then he went to find Enjolras, who was sitting on an overturned crate, carbine in hand, staring at the barricade. Marius studied it too, the mass of stone and iron and wood, thinking something must be amiss. "What are you looking at?"

"The future."

"The Republic?"

"The Second Republic. We had the first, short-lived, in 1792."

"Do you really see it in the future?"

"Of course. You do too or you wouldn't be here."

"Perhaps I am here for less noble reasons than you."

"There are no noble reasons to die, my friend. There are only noble reasons to live." Suddenly Enjolras's pallid face blanched. The Saint-Merri bell had ceased to toll. The surrounding city was silent, and the two young men regarded one another knowingly.

Enjolras gathered up the men, including the sentinels. They stood before the Corinth, where the loss of the Saint-Merri bell seemed like the death of a friend, which, in the largest sense, it was. "Anyone who wishes to leave now," Enjolras addressed them simply, "do so. It's fine. It's understandable." His commander's air deserted him briefly.

"What do you think we are?" Courfeyrac, one of the students, called out jovially. "Rioters? Looters who smash and pillage and then cut and run back to their kennels? We're revolutionaries, not rioters! *Vive la république!* We'll fight like free Frenchmen, citizens of the Republic we won't live to see!"

"We'll die for the Republic!" shouted Pajol.

Enjolras was momentarily pensive. He scraped his feet through the dust where they had torn up paving stones for the barricade. "Our blood will run in the streets of Paris, my friends."

Marius stepped forward, "Better the sword than the scaffold. Better the scaffold than the gutter. This barricade is not a haphazard construction—an omnibus, a few wine casks, iron bedsteads, and billiard tables. Look at it again, men. This barricade is a mound of sorrow mortared with two ideas: freedom and the Republic!"

"Free press, free education!" shouted Pajol.

"One man, one vote!" cried Colville, the tanner.

"He who votes reigns!" Feuilly, the fan maker, cheered.

"The man who wields the shovel can wield the vote!"

"And the man whose hand is on the machine," said the printer, Verdier, "is the master of the nineteenth century."

"And the future," Marius cried.

"The Second Republic or death!" Their voices sounded in a single chorus.

"Very well," Enjolras paced nervously, "but not everyone stays. We know we have no chance. All married men must leave. I order it," he added when no one moved. "The family man who falls here does not merely die, he commits murder. He murders his wife and children. He condemns his sons to poverty and starvation. He condemns his wife and daughters to prostitution. There may be men amongst you—" and his gaze went out over the group of about forty, perhaps thirty of whom wore workingmen's clothes—"who have already seen this happen to your sisters and your mothers. Will you send your wives and daughters to the same fate? We all know that a man is paid twice a woman's wages. A workingman in Paris can barely live on his wages, but a working woman dies on hers, dies or sells her body. Or both."

"At the hospital," said Combeferre grimly, "I have seen women skulk away, leaving infants, whether dead or alive, on the steps. I have seen outright infanticide. I have seen abandoned children vomit straw and mud because that's all there is to eat. I have seen honest women, sewing for a living, their fingers stabbed blue with needles, and starving just the same. They turn to prostitution. They must. Prostitutes—the registered and the unregistered," Combeferre gave a Parisian's shrug, "the difference only matters to the police, not to the doctor—they come to the hospital beaten by the men they service. The diseases that ravage these women are not venereal but social." Combeferre took a deep breath and looked around him. The glare of the single torch on the barricade paled with the paling sky. Someone leaned over and blew out a candle. "Slow starvation, prostitution, if you leave your women and children, that's the fate awaiting them."

"I order the married men to leave," Enjolras repeated with finality, but still no one moved.

Marius stepped forward. "Leave your weapons here for the rest of us, and go. Keep our memory alive with your sons and daughters. Raise your sons and daughters to believe in the Republic. There are no noble reasons to die. There are only noble reasons to live." He shot Enjolras a conspiratorial nod. "I wish before God I had such a reason, a wife, a family of my own. Verdier, go on, put down your gun, my friend, my brother, go back to your press and your family."

"My wife died of the cholera. I told you that."

"But you have children."

"Four."

"They'll starve on the streets." The gamin Gavroche jumped out before Verdier. "They'll look for bread and bite into stones."

"You don't starve."

"Me? Of course not! But look at me—I am the baron of the Bastille! I am the comte de Paris! I am the dauphin of the gutter! I am bred from the streets and the stones. Go on, feel my arm—" Gavroche held up a bony arm. "There, you feel the stone there? See? Me, I made my choice. I prefer my new parents, the street and the gutter. My old man, he calls himself Jondrette one day and one day Fabantou and one day the pope and king together. What do I care what his name is? He and the old lady, they beat me around, kicked me, saved the best scraps for themselves, till I said, Enough of this *merde*. I have a new mother and she is the street. I have a new father and he is the gutter, and I am made from their clay, but others, runts who just get left, they get lost, they starve, they freeze." Gavroche didactically poked his finger at Verdier's chest. "It's what happens, old man."

Finally Eugène Verdier held his gun out to Marius and said he would leave because he had another weapon. He held up his enormous hands, still rimmed with ink. "These are my weapons. I'll find someone who can write and I will set the type and I will live to bring down the king and see the Republic."

Four other men stepped forward, Blanchard, a journeyman joiner who had lost three children to the cholera, but still had two sons, a wife, and an aged mother dependent on him. Colville, whose woman had just given birth a few days before. Latour, a dyer who lived along the Gobelins River, whose skin was bright yellow and clothes streaked with colors like mold. And Clerons, whose wife and children were in Lyon. Enjolras scrutinized the rest of them. He nodded at a man who was sitting on the ground, clinging to his musket. "You have sons, Aulard, you have brought them to our meetings."

"I am not leaving," replied Aulard in an iron voice and without looking up.

Combeferre stepped over and, taking Aulard's jaw in his hands with a professional air, turned his head this way and that. "Open your mouth."

"No."

"You have it, don't you? The cholera."

Aulard used his musket as a crutch as he rose. "Yes. I have it, and I hope to God my corpse gives it to those bourgeois pigs who wallow in troughs while we die in hovels. I have the cholera, but I will die fighting instead of shitting my guts out. My sons know I am not coming back, so choose someone else to be saved." He lingered corrosively on the last word.

They all stepped back. Even those about to die salute the plague.

"What's the good of leaving?" protested Colville. "Look, it's light. The city is swarming with soldiers, with police, with spies like Javert in there. Once over that barricade, we'll be shot anyway."

"No, you won't." At a word from Enjolras, Courfeyrac brought out the uniforms of the National Guardsmen who had died in the skirmish the night before. The uniforms were damp, the bloodstains on them turned to the color of muddy rust. The wearer would certainly have been mistaken for a wounded soldier, not an escaping insurgent. "Put them on," said Enjolras.

But there were only four uniforms and there were five men.

"I'll stay," Clerons volunteered. "I'm new to Paris, and if any of us have a chance after this, I do. I'm not known. I'll stay and shoot the spy, Javert. It's my duty."

"Very well," Enjolras ordered the rest of them to change clothes. "Quickly. You must leave now."

As the four were pulling off their own shirts and donning the uniforms, a cry went up from the back of the Corinth, where Courfeyrac had been wrestled to the ground, hobbled by a National Guardsman who had bounded over the back barricade and leapt into their midst. He was spry, solid, and bearded, and he pushed the fleshy Courfeyrac forward, a knife at his throat, with a strength and agility shocking in a white-haired old man. "I'm one of you," he said, lowering his knife and releasing Courfeyrac. "How else could I get through the streets except in this uniform? " Jean Valjean regarded the half-clad uniformed men before him. "I see I am not the only one with this idea."

"And who are you?" demanded Courfeyrac, rubbing his throat.

"I am a man who saves others," replied Jean Valjean, stripping off the National Guard uniform.

Clerons handed Jean Valjean his frayed student's coat and pulled on the National Guard uniform. Gravely he clapped his hands on the shoulders of Verdier, of Blanchard, Latour, Colville, all of whom were about to vanish over the back barricade, and asked to be reminded of their names to remember them in the future. "And yours?" he turned to Marius. "But for your words about the scaffold and the gutter, I would never have consented to save my own skin."

But Marius did not hear him. Dumbfounded, his eyes never left the face of the newcomer. Surely that was Cosette's father. Impossible. No, not impossible. Unlikely. After all, he had seen Monsieur Fauchelevent often, walking in the Luxembourg Gardens with Cosette. Seen him from a distance and some time ago, true, and never in a uniform. Still, this man, could he be anyone else?

"And you, father?" Clerons asked, a comradely hand on Jean Valjean's shoulder. "I should know the name of my savior."

"I am not your father," replied Jean Valjean. "And your savior is Jesus. Now get out of here." Years chained to others' bodies made Jean Valjean shrink from human touch, and physically he shook Clerons off while mentally he took the measure of the man before him. This Marius beloved of Cosette. Beloved of and by Cosette. This Marius radiated an inborn dignity at odds with an equally evident intensity, something rash and passionate discernible in his eyes, even in the way he held his body. Jean Valjean longed to ask, *Are you worthy of my beautiful daughter?* But full dawn lit the sky and there was no time. Perhaps there never would be. Someone put a gun in his hand; Jean Valjean declined. "I have no wish to fight, but I will help as best I can. Where are the wounded?"

Enjolras called Marius to the barricade. Though it was light they could see nothing. Still they heard the army on the march. "They're moving everywhere through this whole district," said Enjolras, "like vermin on the back of a rat."

And so they were. The tramp of military feet became more audible, the tattoo of drums. Because the filament-thin streets did not permit maneuvers, the troops had broken up into single files, but they all knew where to reconvene, and a bird flying over the district at that moment would have seen soldiers marching through stone capillaries, swelling in the larger arteries, their bayonets glinting in the first rays of the sun as it rose over the crooked chimney pots, patched roofs, the sagging façades of this ancient district. If ever the people were going to rise and fight, this was their chance. But the only missile to fire against the army was a chamberpot full of shit hurled by an old woman.

At the rue de la Chanverrerie, everyone fell silent. Pajol, the Monkey, scrambled up to the top and took down the useless torch. "What's that sound? It's not troops. It's something else."

Combeferre and Marius and Enjolras, already atop the barricade, strained to see, but it was not possible to make wood and mortar, however rotted, dissolve with their eyes. They listened. As the sound drew closer, the ancient houses around the Corinth shuddered as though their very decrepitude could not bear the groan, the growl rumbling underground, echoing: the rattle of brass, the beat of iron on stone, the wheels of war. Cannon. And right behind it caissons, heavily freighted with ball and canisters of grapeshot, and behind, further caissons bearing muskets, boxes of cartridges lined up perfect as molars, and bringing up the rear (some infantry ahead, a larger contingent behind) a dozen gunners carrying torches, useless to light the dawn, but essential to light the cannon.

"To your places!" shouted Enjolras.

"We can thank God for these tiny streets," said Combeferre to Marius. "That little eight-pounder is all they can fit through. If we were on a field of war—"

"The eight-pounder will suffice," said Marius.

"Yes, but not just now." Combeferre leveled his musket and shot one of the gunners.

A wave of infantry fired; the men on the barricade returned fire and, despite the smoke, the infantry replied with a charge and a murderous barrage, though the insurgents did not retaliate. Their every bullet had to count. As gunners tried to fix the cannon's trajectory, the men on the barricade shot at them, killing them off one by one. The army did not count their losses in men, only in regiments, so when soldiers fell, the infantry still advanced through the smoke, till at last the order came, "Fall back!"

In the acrid fog of battle the men on the barricade hastily reloaded, carried the wounded to the Corinth kitchen, but they grew wary when no further assault ensued. Enjolras peered over into the street. He could hear the groan of the wounded soldiers below, and beyond he could just make out through the gray fumes that the army had taken a leaf from the insurgents' book: they were tearing up paving stones to make a breastwork for themselves, while their gunners still maneuvered with the cannon. Enjolras shot one of the gunners. Pajol shot another. They braced for another attack.

Just then an officer, resplendent in his blue-and-white brass-laden uniform, his sabre raised, stepped forward and cried out as the smoke lifted in the morning light. "Surrender! Save yourselves. No one is coming to help you to fight! Your revolution is dead! Surrender or die!"

From his post at the far end of the barricade, Marius called out to his comrades, "You remember our history, men? You remember the battle of Waterloo? You remember General Cambronne? The English called on him to surrender and he said—"

Enjolras scampered to the top of the barricade, stood atop, and yelled to the army, "*Merde!*"

Chapter 5

*T*he first blast of the cannon at dawn in the rue de la Chanverrerie killed three insurgents. In the rue de l'Homme-Armé,
some distance away, that same blast woke Cosette from a difficult
slumber. She flung open the window, sending a nest of starlings
spiraling into the sky. No one had lived in this apartment for a long
while, and no doubt the birds considered themselves secure. They
soared above the rooftops, their squawks echoing to the court
below. Cosette peered out, as though she could will Marius to
materialize there. Surely that young workingman had delivered her
note. Surely Marius now knew where to find her. That metallic
taste of anxiety settled on her tongue, not merely the grim
prospects of England. Something else. Something more. Something worse. She could feel it to her very fingertips, a dreadful certainty that knelled throughout her body with every heartbeat. She
lay back, already exhausted at dawn, and tensed to hear loud crackling to the west, which seemed to speckle the sky overhead with
menace.

"I can bear it no longer," she whispered. "I'll have to tell Papa.
I'll have to ask his help in finding Marius." Papa would be unset-
tled, of course, even unbelieving that she was in love, and he would
tell her she was too young. He might be upset. Very upset. She had
kept Marius a secret for so long. And doubtless he would think her
conduct in the garden at the rue Plumet (any unchaperoned conduct in the garden) unbecoming of a young lady, but she would risk
his ire, even his outright anger. The stakes were too high to flinch.

She rose and reached for her wrapper, but stopped short when
she saw her father's silver candlesticks on the floor beside her bed.
"Papa? Why. . . ?" She picked one up. They were solid silver, as
long as her arm, very heavy, ecclesiastical in their weight and substance, in their implied moral weight and substance; they served as

torches, not mere candles. But unlit and inexplicably on her bedroom floor, the sight of them filled her with dread.

Flinging on her wrapper, Cosette ran toward her father's room, nearly colliding with Toussaint, who was already up and, in her stolid way, going about the business of unpacking.

Cosette knocked, rapped sharply at his door. "Papa? Papa—how can he sleep through that racket, Toussaint?"

"Because your father is a saint."

"Oh, you can be so foolish. Papa!" Cosette stopped when the sound of the cannon again burst over the city. "What is that?"

Toussaint crossed herself. "You heard the driver yesterday. Thugs. An armed mob. Without the National Guard, the army to protect us, we'd be murdered in our beds."

Cosette opened the door: her father's iron bed had not been slept in; the blankets remained drawn up with their usual military rigor. Jean Valjean's quarters always had this air of an officer's encampment, spartan and unembellished. That was how he lived. How he had always lived. He gave Cosette every comfort and some luxuries, but he never indulged himself. She was most alarmed to see the valises opened, clothes strewn about the floor. For a man so methodical, the disorder here would have been intolerable.

"Papa? Papa?" Her voice strangled slightly. "He's not here. He hasn't been here all night. Something terrible has happened. Where has he gone?"

"Perhaps on a visit to heaven. Perhaps your sainted father will tell us what the angels say about us on his return."

"Well, I'm going to find him."

Toussaint followed in Cosette's wake, picking up the clothes she discarded, protesting continually: girls did not go into the streets unescorted. Monsieur Fauchelevent could be anywhere. His habits were irregular. He would be angry if she went out alone. Cosette must wait.

Cosette gathered her hair up and with one swift motion secured it atop her head. "I can't bear to sit—stupidly—and wait, not when I have such a terrible feeling here," she touched her solar plexus. "Some sense of loss, a fear—"

"It is the lot of woman, *ma petite*, to wait and pray, to suffer."

"Then wait and pray, Toussaint, suffer. I refuse to." She pulled on her stockings and silk boots, lacing them badly, fastened her skirt, and asked Toussaint to help her hook the bodice, but the old woman was already on her knees praying before a small shrine to the Virgin, begging the Holy Mother to give this girl humility and patience. "I'm going, no matter what you say, Toussaint. I cannot lose Papa and Marius in the same night. Or the same day."

"Marius?" Toussaint quit praying, and her face wizened with suspicion. "Who is this Marius?"

"Hook me up."

Toussaint folded her arms over her ancient breasts.

"I'll tell you if you'll hook me up."

"Your father will be very angry to know there is a Marius."

"Saints don't get angry," Cosette rejoined, knowing full well Toussaint was absolutely right. She struggled with the hooks of her own bodice as best she could, inwardly berating fashion that assumed all women had four arms. Inadequately dressed, she flung a voluminous shawl around her shoulders, took a gauze scarf in lieu of a bonnet, and ran out of the apartment, down three flights, while the old woman wailed after her about the Four Horsemen, pestilence, and death in the streets of Paris.

Cosette pounded at the door of the concierge's lodge. "Have you seen my father?" she asked when at last the door opened. "Did he leave last night? Maybe earlier this morning?"

"It's only just dawn now," replied the concierge, his breath redolent of last night's fish, his nose hairs visibly quivering. "And who is your father, anyway? You arrive here yesterday and you expect me to know your whole family?"

"Monsieur Fauchelevent is my father."

"Monsieur Fauchele—who? Believe me, in times like these, it's best not to know your own brother." And he shut the door in her face.

The rue de l'Homme-Armé was empty at an hour when Cosette would have expected to see water carriers hoisting their barrels off dripping wagons and ragpickers with their staffs and baskets going through the garbage accumulated at their accustomed corners, street sweepers pushing yesterday's dung and refuse into piles, cesspool carts collecting their horrible sludge. But

Cosette saw no one, save for a cat across the street licking its paw in the doorway of the shop that had given the rue de l'Homme-Armé its name, a plaster relief carved above a doorway. The armed man was naked, sitting on a cannon, pike in hand. Blasted vines bore fruit on either side of him.

As she started toward the rue des Blancs-Manteaux, she heard the rattle of wagon wheels behind her and was surprised to see a carpet van out so early. When it passed her, she noticed the stacked coffins and she crossed herself and quickly turned the corner. In this street, too, shuttered windows seemed to frown down upon her, keeping their tight-lipped silence. Cosette knew that when she found her father (and she must find him) he would indeed be angry and she would deserve his anger. She had never before walked about Paris without his arm. On their long strolls she never paid any attention to direction. That was Papa's task. Hers was to be the ornament of his life. She was not an ornament now. She might have thought herself lost, save that she had no known destination, save that she could hear gunfire and knew she must follow it. Pulling the shawl more closely around her, she started to run, and now more than anxiety made her heart hammer and her mouth dry.

Her silk boots splashed through the muck sludging down long central gutters, which were cut like spines through the old streets. She ran beside the walls of ancient convents, long decayed along with their tombs of the illustrious dead, the whole district seemingly still housing the dead, as no human life stirred. Tradesmen's baskets lay broken, bricks spilled in the street. A cart with three wheels lay crippled, unmoving, while cats crawled over its contents. She ran on, stumbled into one impasse after another, courtyards with no outlets, and in trying to retrace her steps got hopelessly confused, passing streets again and again, plunging under a dark arch where two dogs copulated in the shadows. She screamed, the dogs broke apart and scampered away, but Cosette screamed again as she ran headlong into a soldier in a bloodstained uniform.

"Where are you going?" he demanded. Despite the splash of gore across his breast, he was upright and not staggering. He was lanky, with black hair and wild-looking eyes, and he towered over her. "What can bring a girl out today?"

"Nothing that concerns you," Cosette retorted with more confidence than she felt, brushing his terrible blood from her shawl.

He flung her up against the wall, held her pinned there in the shadows of the arch and asked her again, this time grimly, his lips peeling back from his teeth: where was she going? When, from fear, she could not reply, he rattled her shoulders fiercely. "Are you deaf? Don't you know what that sound is? What it means?"

She shook her head, nauseated by the smell of death wafting off his uniform. The cannon sounded again and his hold on her faltered. She twisted out of his grip and darted away.

Not fast enough, though. Grabbing her roughly above the elbow, he pulled her close to his face. Tears came to her eyes as his fingers tightened over her flesh. "You can't go that way. You mustn't." His tone softened, though his hold did not. "It's finished. It's over. Whoever you have there, you can't help him now."

"Where?" Cosette spoke over the stone in her throat. "Where?"

"In the rue de la Chanverrerie, the rue Mondétour."

"I don't know what you're talking about. Leave me alone! Let me go! I'll scream."

"Your own mother wouldn't come out for you today." Another blast of the cannon shook the street, and the wounded man blanched.

"What is that sound?"

"It's an abortion, mademoiselle."

"A what?"

"It's the Second French Republic aborted before it can be born. Do you have men there?"

"No. Of course not."

"Then you must be a bourgeois fool."

"And you are a thug. Let me go."

"Where do you live?"

"I won't tell you anything, you—"

He twisted her arm up behind her back till she did tell, and without releasing her, Eugène Verdier dragged her back through the streets of Paris, while she screamed and fought and kicked. But it was as he said: no one so much as opened a shutter or a door to come to her aid, and she vowed loudly he would regret treating her like this when she told her father.

"And who is your father, mademoiselle?" Verdier halted, yanked her up close to his bloodstained uniform. He was panting, looking furtively about, angry with himself for the risks he was running—he could be shot for wearing a stolen uniform—to take this chattering goose of a girl home. "Tell me, who is your father? Some fat banker? Some peer of this stinking realm? One of the king's ministers? Perhaps you are Mademoiselle Thiers, eh? Mademoiselle Guizot? Perhaps your father is a member of the Chamber of Deputies, where they squat over the rights of man and shit on the working people."

"No, it's not like that." Cosette started to cry. "My father is a saint."

"Ah, and this saint, he's waiting for you in the rue de l'Homme-Armé?

"No," she said, weeping, "he left in the night, or at least before dawn. I got up and my father was gone."

Verdier's grip on her arm loosened slightly, but he did not relinquish his hold and he remained brusque. "What does he look like, your sainted father?"

Cosette used her free hand to wipe her face. "He's big."

"He's only big, mademoiselle, because you are little."

"I'm seventeen! I'm looking for someone else too. I'm frightened for him—for Marius."

"Marius Pontmercy? Are you the girl?"

"Have you seen him?" Cosette grabbed his arm. "Please, tell me. I love him. I love—"

"I know him," growled Verdier. "I haven't seen him."

"Is he—there—where the gunfire—"

"I haven't seen him," Verdier repeated.

"I'm so frightened for him."

"Everyone is frightened today." He pulled her after him swiftly down the rue Blancs-Manteaux, Cosette no longer resisting, till they arrived at Number 7 rue de l'Homme-Armé, and Verdier beat on the door of the concierge's lodge.

"Why, you're not even armed." Cosette noticed this for the first time.

"I'm armed." Verdier doubled his huge ink-rimmed fingers into a fist and slammed that fist against the door. "Don't doubt it." Finally the concierge, still only half clad, opened the door, and

Verdier roughly thrust Cosette inside. "If you stay here, your men will find you, mademoiselle. If you leave, you'll just endanger them further."

"How do you know they're in danger?"

"Everyone is in danger today. Everyone and everything—the past, the present, the future."

The concierge, on seeing a female tenant brought back roughly by someone in uniform, immediately protested that he would never have rented to her if he'd known she was a prostitute.

Cosette gasped with outrage, but Verdier stepped up close to the concierge, close enough to endure the full bouquet of his breath. "I command you, in the name of His Majesty the king of France, to keep this girl off the streets, under lock and key. Fail in this and His Majesty's fusiliers will relieve you of your balls."

The concierge yanked Cosette behind the door and bolted it. Twice.

Defeated, Cosette slowly ascended the stairs, her shawl dragging after her, while the concierge repeatedly patted his balls, assuring them that he and they would not part company.

Chapter 6

*F*our balls and two canisters of grapeshot had breached a great hole through the belly of the barricade. Portions of it burned, and in the smoke and debris, infantry massed just behind the cannoneers and moved in divergent lines toward the barricade, where the insurgents picked them off, and were, in turn, slaughtered. Enjolras gave the signal to fall back into the Corinth, whose façade had crumbled under incessant fire.

"I'll hold here!" Marius cried through the acrid smoke swirling everywhere. A slashing wound across his head dripped into his eyes and over his ears, and blood ran down his neck and over the shirt of the mason's assistant.

In the momentary lull, Enjolras guarded the door of the Corinth while his men retreated hastily inside. Jean Valjean stepped out. "The police spy, Javert," he demanded.

"What about him? Hurry, hurry, men, up to the first floor."

"I ask permission to kill him."

"Well, monsieur—" Enjolras swiftly reloaded and urged the others on up. Infantry sabres gleamed in the smoky sunlight, and a bullet stopped Aulard before he could reach the door. "Since you saved the life of the fifth man today and since he was to have killed Javert, you are certainly welcome to the life of the spy, but we need every bullet, so slit his throat like the swine that he is. To the second floor, men! Hold the first floor before you go on up!"

Marius fired and reloaded. His high perch on the barricade was protected from the outside, but the infantry had begun to swarm in. Beside him Feuilly fell. As the infantry was about to rush their redoubt, Marius turned to see Monsieur Fauchelevent leading the roped and bound Javert out of the Corinth and around to the rue Mondétour. Enjolras and Marius exchanged a last salute, a farewell, as the flood of soldiers and bayonets engulfed them, swept their poor protest into oblivion. Enjolras vanished into the Corinth, bolted the door, and secured it behind him.

The door slowly splintered under repeated assaults of gun butts, and in the street soldiers took aim at the upper stories, where the insurgents fired down on them. Marius used his last bit of ammunition, his gun no more sophisticated now than a tribal club, when a bullet shattered his collarbone and his shoulder, and he fell backward into Jean Valjean, who had just come back around and who grabbed him and dragged him into the ephemeral safety of the smoke.

The infantry had broken through the Corinth door. Some soldiers fired up from the street, and once inside other soldiers chased the insurgents up to the next floor, and then to the top and onto the roof. Pajol leapt successfully to a neighboring roof, clinging there, about to scramble out of sight, when a shot shattered his right leg and he tumbled slowly to the street. Soldiers scurried after the others, the combat now hand to hand as the insurgents' ammunition was exhausted and their fight was swiftly ended. From his hiding place behind a pile of debris, Jean Valjean held Marius and watched as Combeferre took three bayonet thrusts in the chest and Enjolras's brains splattered from his broken head and dripped down the walls of the Corinth, where his body lay draped across a bullet-riddled window, incongruously holding in place the sign that said *carpe ho ras.*

Seize the hours. But their hours had passed.

Jean Valjean did not stay to see any more. The army was being called back, off the roof, out of the empty Corinth, and ordered to search the district, to shoot anyone who had powder on his hands or clothes, anyone wounded, anyone suspicious. His arms still around the unconscious Marius, Jean Valjean pulled him through the thick curtain of smoke and the fires burning where the barricade had once stood. The only way out of the rue de la Chanverrerie was into the pitiless mouth of the cannon. Bent double, draping Marius's body over his back, Jean Valjean ran for the back of the Corinth and the rue Mondétour. Though he could feel Marius's blood soaking his clothes, Jean Valjean was not hit, but he was not saved either. There was no safety unless God Himself should intervene.

They did not ascend into heaven. They descended into the underworld. There at the back barricade, Jean Valjean saw a huge iron grating, perhaps three feet wide, buried under some fallen stones. Bent under Marius's dead weight, he scattered the stones and wrapped his powerful hands through the transverse iron bars. Jean Valjean had many times proven himself to be the master of escape. What was needed now was the combustion of sinew and conviction, and with a deep, visceral, animal groan, he lifted the grate enough to move it off to one side, and the great maw opened. With the bleeding Marius still on his shoulders, he climbed down into the sewer. Depositing Marius on the wet stones ten feet below, he went back up the iron ladder and with both hands pulled the grate into place, just before the tramping feet of soldiers ran over it and their boots broke up the light of day, shattered it into tiny flecks of sunlight mixed with flakes of rust that fell upon Jean Valjean. He quickly shouldered Marius and ran, seeking the indissoluble darkness of the sewers, the only true democracy this side of the grave.

Part II

The Opera of Love
1833

In this opera which is called love, the libretto is almost nothing.

—VICTOR HUGO
Les Misérables

Chapter 7

*T*he Changer did a gaudy bit of business on Mardi Gras, his
trade very brisk, far better than the usual costumes in
demand, a suit for every swindle, liars' luxurious raiment. On
Mardi Gras all Paris took to the streets, reenacting the ancient rites
and privileges of carnival. Comedy and infamy met, rubbed shoulders, rubbed elbows, rubbed more than that. Hidden behind their
masks, the duchess and the dairy maid might fairly compete for the
affection of the potboy or the duke. All along the avenues, from the
Bastille to the Madeleine, the nobility mixed with mobility. It was
this latter, the mob, who frequented the Changer's warehouse and
on Mardi Gras emptied his cavernous emporium, left there clad in
plumes and satins and laces freighted with forty years of time and
grime, clothes last legitimately worn in 1793 by aristocrats shaved
by the revolutionary barber during the Reign of Terror.

On Mardi Gras a rabble in ribbons poured out of the Changer's
shop, sporting curled wigs, some so light and fine and well preserved that uniformed, the wearer might have passed for Lafayette
himself. And some wigs so old, full-bottomed, and ponderous they
were snatched off heads and thrown over the backs of horses and
ridden about the city, where vehicles of every description thronged
the thoroughfares in an erratic, erotic uproar of paint and tumult.
Every spring cart, hackney coach, cabriolet, and fiacre, every water
wagon, milk wagon, and market wagon had been pressed into carnival service. Light vehicles meant to bear the weight of six people
groaned under the weight of twenty. Revelers clung to the shafts
and blew their horns while hanging from the carriage lamps. Even
the infamous carpet vans, which had rattled with coffins last spring,
now supported bouncing jesters and costumed Turks, who turned
their backsides to men clad in bishops' robes and crowned with
chamber pots. False noses hung from the faces of false nobles, and

codpieces bulged over rosy tights, which showed young men's muscular thighs to advantage and old men's skinny haunches for what they were. A painted savage cavorted with a squealing mock marquise and hundreds of particolored Harlequins sang out ribald songs and shouted lewd invitations to costumed Columbines. Men in the garb of Bacchus dropped hothouse grapes down the dresses of women whose high skirts matched their high spirits, whose masks concealed their features, though their frocks scarcely concealed their breasts. All this bawdy spectacle, this makeup daubed over mud, was undimmed by the February cold. Thick flannel-gray clouds growled overhead, grumbling like pump-sucking parsons outraged by these intemperate goings-on.

In the middle of the congestion on the rue Saint-Antoine, one carriage was festooned simply with a white ribbon on the door, and inside, the bride, an aureole of orange blossoms on her honey-brown high-piled hair, waved to the painted brigade all around her. Cosette's blue eyes and fresh young face sparkled, and she glowed in her wedding dress of Binche lace over a skirt of thick white taffeta, a long rope of pearls against her throat, a lacy veil melting over her shoulders. She smiled and waved to the masked revelers as a princess might to her milling subjects, and so they seemed, the rabble shouting good wishes for the wedding day—and others for the wedding night.

The groom, as custom dictated, rode in a separate carriage. Marius had only his old spinster Aunt Adelaide for a companion, and she, not the best of company even in the best of times, was appalled that they seemed to be awash in a sea of vulgarity. Oblivious of the crowd, Marius cared nothing that a whistling Spanish-clad urchin jumped on the roof of their carriage. Marius heard no song except the one inside his head, *Cosette, Cosette, Cosette.* Breathing deep, Marius closed his eyes, prayed only that the crowds would thin, the horses hasten, that rites enough to satisfy the church and the civil authorities could all be completed quickly so he could hold the dream of Cosette, hold the woman Cosette, hold his wife Cosette. He had reason to believe God would answer his prayers. Surely any God who had spared him the death sentence meted out to everyone else at the Corinth barricade, any God who had provided an anonymous angel to float him through the sewers of Paris, who had brought him slowly back to life when even the doctors believed him dead, surely any God that almighty could clear the path through the rue Saint-Antoine, couldn't He? Marius wanted to jump out, damn the dictates of custom, and fly back to Cosette's stalled carriage to carry her to Saint-Paul's.

In her carriage, Cosette was equally dismayed by the noisy quarrel that locked their wheels and their driver in argument with the driver of a cart whose fourth wheel had fallen off. She too might have got out and run to Saint-Paul's, but her father said gently that he thought the Church of Saint-Paul would not dissolve before they could arrive.

Sitting beside Cosette, gravely dressed in his modest black broadcloth, Jean Valjean's arm was immobilized in a white sling. The injury was a useful fiction, like many he had told. To fulfill the forms and documents necessary for marriage, Jean Valjean well knew how to arrange a family of dead people for Mademoiselle Fauchelevent. After all, he had once been Monsieur Madeleine, the mayor, and his knowledge of civil forms was thoroughgoing. On these documents he was identified only as the guardian of Cosette Fauchelevent, an orphan. His injured hand kept him from signing anything and from walking her down the church aisle, so her civil and religious transition from mademoiselle to madame was safely made with nothing to impede or imperil it. Her identity as Madame Pontmercy would be unquestioned, and he could rest knowing Cosette was loved and safe and protected. He kept his other hand in hers and basked in her luminous happiness.

The carnival lewdness everywhere around their carriage was so broad, so raucous, so profligate that Cosette worried for her father's spartan sensibilities. Riding with them was Marius's grandfather, and she was worried for him too—though for very different reasons. Ninety-two years old, in high good health, unrepentantly lascivious, Monsieur Luc-Esprit Gillenormand, dressed in his *ancien régime* best (mauve satin knee breeches, a flowing blue coat, a waistcoat worked in gold, and lace cascading from his knobby chin), clearly reveled in carnival. If Cosette's father was a saint, Monsieur Gillenormand was a sybarite. When a passing Columbine clung to the door of their carriage, begging a flower from the bride, Monsieur Gillenormand toggled her chin with his bony claw. "Bend over and I promise I'll kiss you."

"Promise you won't," jeered the girl as she jumped off, though once down, she promptly bent over, her skirts flying for just a flash of white bottom. The old man, skinny as pike, laughed out loud.

When Cosette had first met Marius's grandfather, she had found him rather shocking. Well, very shocking. He talked so much. More than talking, he declaimed, he orated, he declared theatrically. He was so very different from her own quiet father. And even more different from Marius. She wondered how Marius—passionate, intense, careful of his honor and his conscience—could even be related to Monsieur Gillenormand, who did everything in such a shallow and uproarious manner.

Monsieur Gillenormand was enormously proud of his original thirty-two teeth, and he would laugh often to show them off. Vain and stubborn, he was an easy mark for the servant girls he routinely "seduced." Shown a squalling brat and being told it was his, he never doubted it. As an old royalist (he'd found it expedient to leave France during the Reign of Terror), his sense of *noblesse oblige* at least made him maintain his bastards: forty francs a month till they were thirteen—a fortune for their mothers. Monsieur Gillenormand's suggestion to Marius, *Bed the wench and be done with it*, was (as Combeferre had suggested that night on the barricade) absolutely in keeping with his own character, and absolutely ignorant of Marius's. However, during Marius's long convalescence, when Monsieur Gillenormand met Cosette, he was instantly smitten. The old man positively fell at her feet, and far from forbidding their marriage, he insisted: nothing would do but that his darling boy should marry this girl. He declared (truthfully, for he never wanted to lose Marius again) that he cared nothing that Cosette had no family, no fortune, and a name no one had ever heard of. (Fauchele—who?) Marius loved this girl and they must marry. In his bullheaded way, Monsieur Gillenormand adored Marius as well.

Imagine then Monsieur Gillenormand's happiness when it was revealed that Cosette, though she still had no name and no family, nonetheless had a fortune. One of her dead family (who still preferred to remain anonymous, according to her guardian, Monsieur Fauchelevent) had endowed Cosette with a dowry of nearly six hundred thousand francs. Told this, the spinster Aunt Adelaide had an immediate seizure of the vapors and had to be brought round with vinegar. But the grandfather, with a confirmed royalist's disdain for mere money, had remarked, "But of course, Marius and Cosette are truly Fortunatus and Fortunata," and then he declaimed for an hour about true love. Enraptured with each other, Marius and Cosette heard none of it. Jean Valjean cared little, as long as he was certain of his daughter's welcome into this family and into the house in the rue des Filles-du-Calvaire.

Cosette knew that Marius's grandfather adored her, which made it easier for her to excuse his frequent lapses of taste, such as the one just now with the bare-bottomed Columbine. However, she scolded him just the same, while he laughed.

"You must excuse an old man," he wiped his eyes with a lace handkerchief and gestured floridly over his heart. "But for the infirmities of age, I would leap into that girl's dirty arms and dance in the streets myself."

"You wouldn't want to miss the wedding, would you, Grandfather?"

"Miss the wedding! My dear young lady, God Himself could not make me miss this wedding. Truly, if He ordered me to die this minute, I would decline. I am happier this day than I have been for half a century." He took out a five-franc piece and tossed it to a fiddler dressed as Nero and another to an urchin boy playing kitchen utensils. "This blessed day. A fine day to marry. An excellent day to marry, a marvelous day to marry. You know the old saying, 'Marry on Mardi Gras, beget no ingrate brats.'"

"Marius is an angel, Grandfather, so we couldn't possibly have ingrate brats."

"Very well, Cosette, if you say Marius is an angel, I'll believe you. I'd believe anything you said. I'd do anything you asked, Cosette. I'd embrace Napoléon! Robespierre! Marius's brigand father! I'd embrace Liberty leading the people!"

"You would probably do that anyway," said Jean Valjean in a droll voice, it being understood between the men that Liberty went about bare-breasted.

"Nonetheless, Cosette, you're wrong about Marius. He is an

ingrate. He left me for five years. I could have died in those five years!" Monsieur Gillenormand looked suddenly alarmed. "He never told me where he went. All those years I never knew where my dear boy was living." This was a patent lie. Monsieur Gillenormand had known where Marius lived, had tried to send him money, which Marius returned, preferring to support his law studies doing translations for paltry fees from publishers who were loath to pay anyway. "He broke my heart," the old man concluded, whipping out his handkerchief again.

Cosette and her father exchanged indulgent looks. "The time for heartbreak is past, Grandfather." She patted his dry hand with her white glove, and he looked relieved, indeed, restored beyond all measure. "Today is our wedding day, and beginning tomorrow we will all live together, happy as larks, you and Aunt Adelaide and Papa and I and Marius, unless this is a glorious dream."

Cosette was startled by the impromptu appearance of another masked girl hugging the carriage door, begging flowers from the bride, her coarse hands wagging before Cosette. She was big-boned and red-headed, wearing a plain black mask, and her costume consisted only of red and purple ribbons pinned to her threadbare dress, the colors streaking in the chill, thin rain. She clung to the carriage door, studying the three people in it as if sizing them up for shrouds. The carriage lurched forward and Cosette's face lit: they were moving toward Saint-Paul's. In gratitude she put the whole bouquet of yellow freesias into the girl's hands just before she jumped off.

"You've given them all away," said her father, dismayed.

Cosette put her hand over his. "Oh, Papa, it's from you I've learned to give."

"Then I have done you only half a service, Cosette. I hope I have also taught you to receive."

"In marriage," pontificated Monsieur Gillenormand—who had been married twice, first for money and then for love, reversing the old adage—"you must do both. Give and receive. Can you love each other too much? Can there be too many nightingales? Too many roses? Too many blossoms on the chestnut trees? Can there be too many lilies? Too many young girls to lie in the green grass? Can there be . . ."

The carriage with its single white ribbon made its way down the ribald rue Saint-Antoine.

Once they were inside the church of Saint-Paul, the carnival cries, the profane shouts receded, vanished like the rain. Cosette looked down the long aisle to see Marius waiting there. Six feet tall, he held himself with his father's military bearing, an attitude of immense physical dignity he must have inherited, his shoulders squarely back. His broad chest and lithe build were suggested beneath his fine clothes. Beneath those clothes, too, Marius bore the scars of last June's battles; the wounds that had nearly killed him had forever altered his face. Where the bullet had grazed his temple there was a deep scar, cutting through one eyebrow, dangerously close to the eye itself. The effect of this downward path across his face had left him with an expression of ineffable sadness, although at this moment the joy of seeing Cosette eclipsed everything else. He beamed at her as if she were the medal of the Légion d'honneur, the great gift given him for his valor, the girl he had lived for, the woman he could not live without.

The smile on Cosette's lips was one in which gravity mixed with triumph as buoyantly she took the grandfather's arm, offered at a courtly angle, and they walked down the long aisle. Her father, his right arm in a sling, followed behind. In the high-vaulted church, cold drafts eddied, flickering candles in the banks of votives before which knelt worshipers so pious they spent Mardi Gras in the church. These were mostly middle-aged women with little to repent and much to mourn, but the click of their beads ceased and the incantation of their prayers died away as they turned and saw the bride. Hoping to catch a bit of bride's luck (surely as efficacious as prayer), the sound of their feet echoing as they shuffled and convened at the front, they joined those emerging from little side chapels. The pews behind the bride and groom filled up with matronly faces gone suddenly roseate and lively. At the back of the church, shaking off the rain and shivering, stood the girl with the bouquet of yellow freesias. She remained in the shadows, watching the ceremony, stroking the flowers under her nose, breathing in their fragrance.

The young couple stood in the pool of light cast by the tapers, the pews of penitents at its shore, all of them surrounded by the whiff of incense, honey-smelling smoke pouring from the censers. The priest's vestments glittered over Cosette and Marius, who both knelt before him. The wedding ring too gleamed in the candle-light, and as Marius slipped off her glove and put that ring on, Cosette knew that no human touch could ever move her as his did this moment. Marius's eyes, more eloquent than spoken vows, met hers and his hand returned her pressure. This was one of those moments you carried to the death, one of those moments in which you realized the central possibility of life. The low drone of the priest's voice rolled heavy as a morning fog, through which Cosette's and Marius's bright, clear replies pierced like shafts of light.

Chapter 8

*B*y the time the bridal carriages pulled through the gates at No. 6 rue des Filles-du-Calvaire, the rain had turned to snow falling softly in the last light of the waning afternoon. Snow slowly framed the high, bright windows and softened the stones of the drive. The big-boned girl, still clutching her handful of freesias, jumped off the back of the carriage just as it turned into the gate; she noted the number and hurried away in the cold.

Guests crowded into the drawing room, and despite the cold, they pushed the windows open and their handkerchiefs waved and fluttered. Cheers went up as Marius and Cosette, their faces radiant, peered from the carriage. As he stepped out, Marius offered his hand to Cosette, who instead responded with her arms. He bent over her, their lips brushed, and she whispered, "So it's true at last. My name is Marius too. I am Madame You and my every dream fulfilled."

The servants (some of them borrowed for the event) stood outside, their breath fogging before them, and each offered a curtsy and a flower to Cosette as she walked up the steps of her new home. The carriage bearing Jean Valjean, Aunt Adelaide, and the grandfather rattled in next. Seeing the open windows crowded with an audience and the servants before him like a chorus, Monsieur Gillenormand hobbled out and announced to one and all, "May I present to you the Baron and Baroness Pontmercy!"

To give the guests their due, they cheered. Ordinarily they would never have recognized a title bestowed by Bonaparte. Nearly all these wedding guests were octogenarian friends of Monsieur Gillenormand, royalist ultraconservatives, an exclusive mummified elite practicing invented and remembered affectations and with a taste for undercooked heretics. They felt consummate disdain for the century they had been thrust into and kept up with the world only insofar as the near blind read to the near deaf. But they were all there for this wedding, doddering, tottering, or pushed in chairs.

Monsieur Gillenormand escorted the newlyweds, one on each arm, into the house, transformed for the wedding. "Adore one another! Idolize each other!" he cried. "Make the rest of us rage with envy that we cannot do as much. Love unto excess! Give your joy free rein! Don't you know that in making this love match you have already snatched the great prize of living? None of your nine-teenth-century frock-coat prudence this day! I've spared no expense so you may jubilate, my angels!"

The house defied the winter day outside. Garlands festooned every chandelier, every wall sconce; every candlestick had a ribbon and a flower. Beribboned bouquets of forced freesias, narcissuses, and gold mimosa exhaled their fragrance in the warmth of the company. For five years this house had sheltered only the lonely grandfather and the querulous old aunt, but now the shrouds were off forever, all the plate polished, the crystal gleaming, the servants whisking about filling gilt-rimmed goblets with champagne chilled in the ice house. Everything had been brought out of cold storage (truly, including the guests) to honor the bride and groom. From an antechamber just off the drawing room, three violins and a flute played Haydn quartets, eighteenth-century music spilling every-where through the rooms, completing for these octogenarians the sensation that they had been invited here for this last gavotte of the *ancien régime*. They had no need to powder their white heads, and the men all wore satin knee breeches and the women wore frothy lace fichus fifty years out of fashion. As they each were introduced to the bride, the whiff of pomander and moth repellent teased Cosette's nose.

On the arm of her handsome dark-eyed husband, Baroness Pontmercy greeted her guests with a graciousness one would not have expected of someone so young. Jean Valjean glowed to watch her take the first steps in her new world, the way in which she instinctively assured each of these people she recognized their best selves, though that best self might have been buried, especially for these bitter old royalists, as Pompeii had been buried. Without guile or artifice, Cosette shared her intrinsic warmth and light with her guests, in the way a candle provides light and warmth, because it cannot do otherwise. Hers was not a learned charm. Even Jean Valjean's reclusive life had taught him charm could be slathered on a young lady like shellac and then, just as surely, it cracked with age. Cosette's gifts would be enhanced with age. Jean Valjean knew he would not live to see it, but that's the way it would happen. Declining champagne from a passing servant, Jean Valjean pensively watched his daughter and her husband. Already their steps had picked up a kind of unison, not constricting as in a march, but as in a dance, complementary, expressive, intuitive. Reserving a father's right to believe no man is good enough for his daughter, Jean Valjean equally believed Marius loved Cosette. That much was certain. And perhaps that's all that needed to be certain.

Marius was as cordial to his grandfather's royalist friends as if they had all been his comrades in arms. He remembered fleetingly that his true comrades all lay in narrow graves, but even that memory could not dim this day's joy, especially when he and Cosette caught sight of the only other young people present, Marius's cousin Théo, a dashing officer in the army, and two of Cosette's friends from the convent, the blushing, dark-haired Mademoiselle de Bélessin and her English friend, the prim, clever Miss Helen Talbot.

Cousin Théo flirted outrageously, spread his charms equally between Mademoiselle de Bélessin and Mademoiselle Talbot, who protested his imputations of wit. "This is a wedding," Mademoiselle Talbot rebuked Cousin Théo smartly, "and you would do me no favor to sentence me to spinsterhood. Please don't tell anyone I'm smart or witty again. If a girl once gets the reputation as a bluestocking, she'll never find a husband in France."

"And a married woman who is a bluestocking will never get a child. Wit in women is like a frock coat on a cart horse," quipped Cousin Théo, causing Mademoiselle de Bélessin to flush and flutter.

Amongst themselves the old royalists, still critical of Marius's political views, nonetheless extolled his good fortune: just imagine, they purred, all that money for her dowry and no one has ever heard of the Fauchelevents.

"No one in our circle, certainly," conceded a duchess who had spent the Reign of Terror paying exorbitant rent to her former groom. "But who knows where their money might have come from?"

"Money, like smallpox, ought to be quarantined," advised a superannuated marquis, taking snuff. "Three generations at least. It's quite appalling, the number of people with money nowadays. Where are they all coming from?"

"Of course, young Marius is fortunate to be married to such a rich girl, but he's fortunate to be alive at all," confided one of the near blind. "They say he was brought here last June half dead and reeking of—" her eyebrows raised expressively.

"They say he came from the sewer dripping shit," one of the near deaf declared, "carried on the back of a man who has disappeared and cannot be found. They thought young Marius was dead."

"It serves him right for fighting with that republican rabble."

"He could have been arrested anyway, you know," the duchess's fan rattled with palsy and conviction, "after that June fracas. All doctors were ordered to report any wounded to the authorities."

"I'm sure Monsieur Gillenormand paid the doctor well for his services—and his silence."

"The girl, though," the count said, smiling, watching Cosette and Marius kissing beneath a candelabra dripping with ribbons and hothouse flowers, "the girl is absolutely ravishing, isn't she?"

"That old man over there is supposed to be her father." The marquis pointed to Jean Valjean, and sneezed. "But it's impossible. White hair? White beard? He can't be her father."

"And why not?" demanded the wheezy count didactically. "An old man may beget a child. Besides, see the way he looks at her."

"He has no one else to look at. Not a single person here from the bride's family," sniffed the duchess. "They are nobodies."

"The Baron and Baroness Pontmercy are quite somebodies," Monsieur Gillenormand pontificated, coming upon his friends. "You mark my words. Now come, this may be our last chance. Warm yourself at the fires of youth," he added, offering his arm to the duchess to go in to dinner.

The cook (hired especially for this occasion) had convinced Monsieur Gillenormand that, although she was a woman, nonetheless she had trained with the late, great Carême himself. The master's recent death, she claimed, had obliged her to take catch-as-catch-can employment. And perhaps she was telling the truth. Certainly for the wedding of Cosette and Marius she had created spun-sugar confections that reflected the light, cupids in puff pastry, and platters of quail glittering and shivering in aspic. Rare conceits and strange delights, culinary sculptures adorned the long table, some of them gleaming in dishes made of sugar plate so artfully constructed it looked like silver plate. Marmalade molded as oak leaves melted languidly, decorating platters of perfectly matched medallions of beef, and on silver trays poached fish shimmered, their scales slivered from silvery scallions.

At the far end of the table Cousin Théo sat flanked by the alternately flushing and paling Mademoiselle de Bélessin and the sprightly Miss Talbot, whose tidy ringlets shook with pleasure when she laughed at one of Théo's gallantries. Lining either side of the long table, all the white heads turned toward the bride and groom: side by side, hand in hand, Marius and Cosette. Grandfather Gillenormand (never known to pass up an audience) extolled at length the joys of love, the holy injunction to live together, to love, to produce no ingrate brats, and finally, winded rather than finished, he called on his grandson, Baron Pontmercy, to offer a toast.

Marius rose, glass in hand, and offered a simple toast, thanking his grandfather and their guests, and then with his old passion and conviction, the flash and fire that had always so thrilled Cosette, he lifted his glass higher. "Many people may marry, but this celebration today, this is more than a wedding. This is a triumph for love." He offered his other hand to Cosette and she rose, faced him, held tightly in the circle of his arm, her breasts pressing against him, her chin tilted back. To Marius this great golden happiness seemed almost impossible, the opposite end of a scale of events that would have brought him to the prison or the grave. "Love is its own country," he said, gulping with emotion, "but not its own world. Sometimes the world invades the country of love, but cannot destroy it."

Cosette rose on tiptoe to meet his lips, to whisper to Marius alone, "Take me with you to that country of love and we will live there always."

Chapter 9

*T*he snow had thickened and deepened in the night, and laced their bedroom windows while the crackle of flames played pizzicato to the sizzling wax, running cream-colored down the candles by the bed. Their bed. Cosette rolled onto her side and stroked the scar that zigzagged from Marius's temple through the eyebrow, cutting down toward his ear, where his dark hair had grown back over, obscuring it. Marius lay very still, exhaling finally, so deeply he seemed to have relinquished every anguish he had ever known.

"Are you frightened?" he asked at last.

"No. I've never been frightened."

"I have," Marius confessed. "There, in the garden at the rue Plumet, sometimes I was frightened of what I felt for you, how I wanted you. I've never known anything so powerful as that hunger. Sometimes I wanted you more than I loved you. If we hadn't been able to marry—"

"Nothing but death or England would have kept us from this, Marius, from loving each other with our bodies as well as our souls. I would have been yours, Marius, no matter what," she added with a long kiss and a sweet smile. "Marriage or not."

He rolled over her and she lay back, her hair spilling across the pillows. "It might hurt," he murmured, his lips at her cheek.

"I don't care. I know there's some great mystery here, some secret the world keeps from well-bred girls. Whatever it is, this secret they all keep, I want it," she stroked his hair. "I've wanted it since I met you. I'm not afraid. I want to learn to love you with my body, that's all I—" her voice thickened as he untied the ribbon of her wrapper and his fingers slid across the rims of her breasts— "want to be, your love, your lover."

His hand moved down the length of her body, lifting the frothy nightdress up, following the incline of her knee and down, along the smooth white inner thigh till he touched some coil, some spring that made her wince with pleasure, groan audibly, and give herself to the sheer beauty of his hands, the thrill of his weight, the loss of all time.

A candle sputtered and died and Marius moved to blow the other candles out, but Cosette restrained him. "One day I will know your body so well I won't need the light, but tonight I want to see everything, my love, tonight . . ."

Marius stood, undid the buttons of his stiff pleated shirt and those on his long trousers. His beauty took Cosette's breath away. His lean flanks, long legs, and broad chest were pale, and across his chest the black hair grew in a thicket, dwindling into a perfect seam down his belly and luxuriating out again. A tortured scar sliced over his left shoulder, and she winced to see the knob where the shattered collarbone had not healed properly. Marius would carry the scars of 1832 all his life.

Rising from the bed, Cosette embraced him, inhaled his scent, kissed even the scar and the imperfectly healed bones, stroked the fine long lines of his body. Then she raised her arms up; Marius pulled the silky nightdress over her head, and candlelight flickered over both their bodies. Unclothed, Cosette's body lost its suggestion of fragility and gained in suppleness, her breasts small, but high and well defined, and she exulted in the adoration in Marius's face. At his behest Cosette turned slowly, while he followed her curves and contours with his hands, kneeling before her, his lips tracing a path on the plain between her hip bones. She held his head in her hands, pressed him, and in a husky and uncertain voice said he would have to tell her the names, what everything was called.

"You don't know?"

"In a convent the word *love* is never mentioned with a man in mind. The girls know nothing. The nuns know less. Please give me these words, Marius. I want you," she lay back on the bed and held her arms out, "to give me everything, my love. Even the words."

"This is a nipple." Marius lay beside her, naming with his hands and lips and words, naming much as an old explorer might name some new land, some heretofore unseen country so beautiful it both demanded words and diminished them in the same moment. Cosette's breath came faster and sweeter with his every touch, when he rose over and braced his weight on his strong arms and lowered himself on her. Their lips met and that was the end of words. Cosette followed the suggestion, the direction given her by his body, and she was rewarded with a thrill so deep it seemed to pull her very being taut and knotted, and she wrapped her arms around his back and closed her eyes and plunged somewhere with Marius she had never been before, over some glorious precipice, down some wonderful palisade, and into a pool of the most profound contentment she had ever known.

Chapter 10

*T*he knock that roused Marius the following morning was quiet, apologetic, but insistent. He threw on a dressing gown and cracked the door. In a low voice a servant explained that a man awaited him in the drawing room who insisted on seeing him. Even today. "Tell him I'll be down directly," Marius said with a shiver, for the fire had gone out in the night and the room was chilled.

But Marius did not go down directly. He got back into bed, naked beside his new wife, parted the hair from the back of her neck and brought his lips over her smooth shoulders and down her shapely back till she woke with a shiver that had nothing to do with the February morning. The shivers gave way to giggles, the giggles to visceral groans, and they rolled over and over in bed, their thighs slick and shiny and wet. Marius's hands wrapped round Cosette's arms and she bent over him, her hair creating a honey-colored curtain, her erect nipples tracing a path all over his chest, and she lowered her body to engulf him, till he seemed to vanish altogether into the woman he loved, into love itself.

It was past noon when Marius roused again, Cosette's head on his chest, her hand across his scarred shoulder. He lay there for a bit, savoring the moment, the heady, novel combustion of lust and protectiveness he felt, the satisfactions he had never even dreamed of before, the energies he had gained in a single night, and the prospects—just think of all the nights that lay before them. Then he remembered someone awaited him. It must be urgent for this individual to appear the day after a wedding. Urgent or tactless. Reluctantly, he slipped out of bed and dressed quickly, but before he left the room he made certain the covers were up over Cosette's shoulders and the bed curtains closed to keep her warm. He paused one last time to look at her again, her light brown hair tumbled out across the pillow, her young body drawn up into the space vacated by his warmth, her mouth slightly open, the sleep of a woman much beloved.

All down the sweeping staircase and into the foyer yesterday's finery now drooped and draggled, and a small corps of servants, their foreheads uniformly marked with ashes, were replacing candles burnt to their sockets the night before. They nodded obsequiously to Marius, smirked if he was not mistaken (and he wasn't). He walked down the stairwell with a too-leisurely pace, relieved to come to the drawing room and altogether surprised to see his father-in-law there.

Monsieur Fauchelevent stood before one of the tall windows, looking out to the fog-wreathed drive. He turned to Marius without smiling. He was pale, and rings encircled his eyes. Clearly, the old man had not slept all night. The pang of concern Marius felt was tinged with chagrin; after all, Marius had not slept all night either. And no doubt all the world knew why. He thought perhaps Monsieur Fauchelevent was concerned for Cosette, but how could you assure a girl's father that the wedding night, well, that . . . To cover his discomfort, Marius blustered about, calling out in the foyer for someone to bring coffee, vowing that the servants should have had their ears boxed for not telling him the visitor was Monsieur Fauchelevent. "Father, I mean," Marius tasted the word. His own father had died before Marius could get to his bedside; he'd never even said farewell. "If I'd known it was you, I would have come down immediately."

"Would you indeed?" queried Jean Valjean. "Probably just as well you didn't. My reason for being here is not a happy one."

"How can it not be happy? Today of all days? Today—well, look, you can see what a beautiful day it is." Marius went to the window as though he expected the weather to cooperate choreographically and the chestnut trees to sprout instant white spires. "Cosette has your room all ready for you. It's next to ours and looks over the garden. She insists, we both do, you must leave that grim apartment and . . ." Marius faltered. His father-in-law stood behind a whist table like a witness in the box.

"I am not who you think I am," he said without further pleasantries. "I am a former convict. I served nineteen years in prison for stealing a loaf of bread. My name is Jean Valjean. Jean Valjean," he repeated it, claiming the name, clinging to it much as a monk pulls the comfort of the cowl over his bare, unsheltered head, as he gave Marius that part of the story that was his to give, the story of the prisoner's chain and branded flesh, the iron collar, nineteen years of degradation, his name stripped from him, identity sundered and hammered into a number he wore. Even more fantastical, he told Marius how, years later, he had come not merely to a beggar's rescue, but to his salvation when the man had been wrongly identified as Jean Valjean. Again condemned to the galleys, Jean Valjean had effected an impossible escape, plunging into the sea from the yardarm of the prison ship, plunging, as the authorities believed, to his death. For Jean Valjean it was a fortunate fall into salty obscurity, into years of evasion and fear and feigned identities.

Marius could hardly breathe. But neither could he seem to move toward the window and its promise of cold, untainted air. He was grateful when, with a light knock, a servant entered bearing a tray with coffee, interrupting them. The servant moved to mend the fire, but Marius at last found his feet, rose with difficulty, and ordered him out harshly. When the door had closed and they were again alone, Marius demanded of Jean Valjean, "And who is Fauchelevent?"

"A friend. A fiction. A way of life. A way to live." He shrugged. "Nothing more than that."

Suddenly parched, Marius poured himself some coffee. The china rattled in his hand. "Why are you telling me this today—of all days?"

"I could not come into your home an imposter, to live in lying silence." A look of scholarly perplexity crossed the old man's face. "Would it have made a difference to you yesterday? Would you not have married Cosette knowing this?"

"I love Cosette and nothing will ever change or touch that," Marius declared, the old fierce protectiveness making him the more passionate. "I ask because you have raised the point, Monsieur Fauchele—Monsieur Val . . ."

"Perhaps you prefer Number 24601."

Marius bit down on his anger and confusion. "You have said you are not who I think you are. My love for Cosette has nothing to do with this bizarre and terrible story of yours."

"It is not a story. It is the truth."

"Then it is a confession," snapped Marius, "and you should have taken it to the priest."

"The priest has not married Cosette. You have married Cosette."

Marius brought his hands down sharply on the table, and the china bounced in alarm. "What do you want from me, old man? Why have you brought this rat from your past and released it into—" he gestured about the room with its wilted flowers and drooping wedding finery—"into my marriage? You tell me no one pursues you now, that the police believe Jean Valjean dead. Fine. But why make this wanton revelation now?"

"From honor. For nineteen years I was number 24601. My honor and my identity, who I *am*, Monsieur Pontmercy. Don't you know what that means? You must. Why else would you have left your grandfather's house when you discovered he had maligned your father, kept your father from you, kept you from your father's deathbed? Monsieur Pontmercy, *you* did not know who *you* were until that day."

"I was too late," Marius dryly replied, accosted by old emotions, still fresh as wounds. "My father had already died when I got there. I will never forgive my grandfather for that."

"You are a young man and too hard. All young men are hard. You have no idea the kind of charity and tolerance, forgiveness, that will be obliged of you in this world."

"Is that why you've brought me this sordid tale? To receive my charity? My tolerance? I am not the judge to pardon you, Monsieur Valjean, nor the priest to forgive you, nor the holy spirit to beatify you. I am only a man and—"

"You are the husband of Cosette. I could not come into your home, into her new life, unless my honor and my identity, my integrity, were intact, united, no longer separated. I have buried myself, don't you see, under a rubble of names and identities, and I must, now—"

"I see your arm is out of the sling," Marius commented. "That injury, I take it, was also a fiction, a story?"

"You have studied the law. I should not need to tell you why I did it."

"You should not need to tell me any of this!" cried Marius, fighting his rising rage, even as he unwillingly adjudicated through the evidence: clearly, the false injury to the arm relieved Jean Valjean from the necessity of signing civil or ecclesiastical documents. His lies about the Fauchelevents were all attested to by righteous nuns and seconded by Marius's own grandfather, who, because of the injury, had signed the necessary papers in his stead. But if Monsieur Fauchelevent were Jean Valjean, who was Mademoiselle Fauchelevent? The former Mademoiselle Fauchelevent. "Who is Cosette?"

"An orphan."

"You are not her father or her grandfather or in any way related to her?"

"I am related to her. Oh yes, I am tied by the bonds of love and time and duty, of affection and even a kind of grace. That's what she brought to my—"

"But legally you are not her guardian."

"Legally, monsieur, I am dead."

"The birthdate you gave Cosette on those documents, 18 June, 1815, that was—"

"A larger truth rather than a smaller one. I used the one date known to everyone in France, to everyone in Europe."

"Waterloo."

"You are all the children of Waterloo."

Despite the cold Marius went to the window and flung it open, drank in deep drafts of air. He thought about the young woman in his bed upstairs. He thought about the night before and the nights to come. He thought of the way his body had sunk into her body, his life into her life, his spirit into her spirit, about the miracle that had somehow united and bedazzled them. Perhaps, he told himself in an effort to be calm, he was merely disappointed, having believed their adversities were over, having believed that the wedding, that marriage, had provided them with a fabled happy ending. Perhaps it was merely the end of youth to recognize there are no endings: there are only beginnings that feel like endings. Marius spoke clearly, but into the wafting fog at the window. "As you are so eager to confess today, Ash Wednesday, perhaps you will tell me, at last, what you were doing at the barricade last June in the rue Mondétour. I have asked you before and you have denied even being there."

"I deny it again. You are mistaken. That day, that street, they mean nothing to me."

"That's what you've told me in the past, but I'm certain it was you," Marius contended, though he was certain of almost nothing connected with that day. His memories were incomplete and confused, a jumble of smoke and shot and shell, of pain and loss, shattered bones and splattered blood, so scattered, all of it, that memory itself seemed to have dissipated during his long convalescence, drained out of him with the blood he'd lost, burnt up in the fever. Marius closed the window, turned back into the room from which all festivity had fled, the wedding splendor now merely tawdry, limp, and withered. "What do you want from me?"

"I want to go on seeing Cosette. I had planned, that is, I thought, after your wedding, I would leave Paris, knowing she was loved and cared for. But I can't. I can't bear to be parted from her. I can't tell you what . . ." Jean Valjean swallowed hard. "For ten years she has been my life."

"Ten years!" cried Marius. "You mean, that's all—"

"She came to me by chance. Ten years ago, Christmas Eve, 1823, Cosette came to me by a holy chance. God gave her to me and God gave me the opportunity to love."

"But how did you find her?"

"She was an orphan, alone in the world. Together we are a family. She is all the family I have. She is all I have. I cannot leave Paris and give up my daughter. But neither could I come to your home as an imposter. I am here to ask your permission to continue to see Cosette."

"But she is not your daughter?"

"No. She is my life."

"She is my life now, Monsieur Valjean," Marius corrected him, "but I would never deny you the right to see her. Cosette loves you."

"One other thing. You must never tell her any of what I've told you."

"With all this talk of honor, you would tell me the truth, but not her?" Marius scoffed. "You want too much."

Jean Valjean seemed to weave slightly on his feet. "Once, a few years ago perhaps, maybe more, we were at one of the city gates, walking there, outside the *barrière*, when a wagonload of convicts bound for Toulon went by, chained by their necks, their collars clanking like harnesses, filthy, covered with running sores, their hair matted, their feet unshod. Cosette was so frightened of them, so appalled. She could not even believe they were human. They are human, I assure you, but I could not bear for my daughter—"

"She is not your daughter," Marius protested.

"If you like, I will not allow her to call me father in the future, only Monsieur Jean, but I beg of you, let me see her and promise you won't tell her I was once one of those filthy and inhuman wretches, one of *les misérables*. The humiliation would kill me. To be a thief, a convict is nothing, but to have my daughter know—"

"Cosette is not your daughter. Cosette is my wife. Your integrity, your identity are your own affair. Please don't expect me to hand them back to you wreathed in glory, because I can't, and, by God, I won't!"

"I want only to do my duty."

"Damn your duty!"

"Duty!" cried Cosette, opening the doors, the whoosh of her embroidered organdy wrapper whispering across the parquet floor. Her hair was loosely tied with a random ribbon and she billowed in under a full sail of joy toward her husband, kissing him, reaching her arms around his neck. Marius rose to hold her, keep her close, pressed her with more fervency than he had meant to display. "I won't hear of duty today," she added, humming a little wisp of yesterday's Haydn melodies and frowning to see the fire had gone out and the coffee was untouched and cold. Though a twilit fog pressed against the windows, she declared it a gorgeous day, and neither man contradicted her. "Are you well, both of you? You don't look it. Marius, the scar on your eyebrow has gone all white, and Papa—"

"We're fine, Cosette." Marius reached for her hand and pulled her again into a swift embrace.

"Papa! Your arm is out of the sling," she said brightly, insisting now that he must move out of the rue de l'Homme-Armé. "Away from that loathsome concierge. Come live with us. I am madame now, Papa, no longer mademoiselle. Madame can insist. A made-moiselle can only entreat. I quite like being madame. But baroness—that will take some getting used to. I don't think I can be the baroness until I am at least nineteen." She plucked a handful of mimosa off a wall sconce and it made her sneeze.

"Cosette," Marius said gently. "We must be left alone to talk."

"Not of duty. I loathe duty. I forbid it in this house. No duty, no politics, no business. At least for today, no, not till the spring. Maybe in the spring I'll let you talk of those boring things. Men's tolerance for boredom astounds me. Too much politics and duty and business will cross your eyes forever. It's true. I read about a man in Lyon and this happened to—"

"Cosette," Marius declared decisively. "We have to talk."

"So talk, my love. I'll listen."

"Alone."

Cosette glanced over the rim of her own happiness at these two best-loved men. Marius's eyes were filled with adoration, but his lips were taut, tight-set in a brooding expression. Papa, of course, Papa always looked contemplative, though not so penitent. But of course it was Ash Wednesday. Fleetingly she considered what she might give up for Lent. Not Marius. Certainly not Marius. She flashed him a conspirator's smile.

Jean Valjean took her smooth hand in both of his rough ones. "Just this once, excuse us, Cosette—Madame Pontmercy. And then I shall leave you to your married life."

"I don't want to be left to my married life. None of us do. We all want you to come live here, Papa. Marius's grandfather will teach you to play whist. I'll never learn. I loathe card games, so it will fall to you. And when Marius is in court, working with all that boring law, you and I will walk in the Luxembourg Gardens, just as we used to."

"To see you so radiant is all the happiness I'll ever need, Cosette. You are the light of life itself to me, and to know—"

"We're discussing business," said Marius abruptly.

Cosette with an imperial gesture lumped the boring law with business in the vault of her disdain, but it was clear they both opposed her. At the tall French doors, she vowed she'd return in one half hour. "By the clock, gentlemen. No more long faces." She closed the door and left them, trailing her wistful Haydn melody like a last bit of wedding whimsy. The tune fell from her lips, tumbled, and bounced, echoing all the way down the long staircase into the drawing room, where two silent men faced each other grimly: the past, like a cadaver, stretched out stiff before them, Jean Valjean the resurrectionist having brought it here, and Marius the reluctant physician.

Chapter 11

*H*e's dead," said the doctor to the turnkey, putting his taper on the rickety table and taking out a small leatherbound register. "Sign here and I'll have someone come take away the body."

Finishing his sausage hastily, the turnkey took up the pen and signed with a careful hand, adding as well, Cell XII, 28 February 1833, leaving a greasy smudge for an official seal. The turnkey's uniform had been embellished with a silk waistcoat, a few filthy laces, a bit of gold chain that might once have held a watch. He could not fleece his prisoners of very much because by the time they got to him they'd already been pretty well denuded of any valuables. He presided over that section of the prison where those tried and condemned awaited transport to grimmer destinations yet. "And the other one?" he asked. "Number 23974?"

"Oh, he'll live for a while. They'll bury him at Mont-Saint-Michel. One splash into the sea and burial's over. At high tide," the doctor added with what passed for humor. "Here in Paris, I have to write and sign a thousand forms, registrations, death certificates, burial certificates. Is there any end to it?"

"You won't bury the dead man anyway," sneered the turnkey, "you'll sell him to the medical school, a little cadaver for the students to slice?"

"That's enough out of you."

"What did he die of?" The turnkey nodded toward Cell XII.

"The usual. Scurvy, jail fever, something like that."

"I don't want the cholera back in here." The turnkey spat out a bit of bone he found unground in the sausage.

"The cholera was last year."

"And a very bad year it was."

"Certainly for that poor dead bastard in there. And that other one," the doctor snapped his book shut, "the bones in his leg must have been set by a horse doctor."

The turnkey pondered this and then observed that horses with broken legs get shot. The doctor pronounced him brilliant and took his leave.

Lifting the taper high, the turnkey went down the narrow passage, lit by flares on either side, though the cells themselves had no light beyond that afforded by small barred windows. Prisoners could not be trusted with fire. As he walked, there sounded intermittent groans and whimpers, a man crying out a woman's name, stifled weeping, the gibber of fever, the bray of pain, the dissonant oboes and cellos of the music of misery. These men were to be moved out of La Force tomorrow and sent to Mont-Saint-Michel, the prison for political crimes, though this sorry bunch, to the turnkey's practiced eye, scarcely qualified as political. Rioters. That's all they were. Rioters, although throughout their trials they'd been called revolutionaries, so that all the implicit perils in the word could be invoked—the specter of destruction, the threats to property, the streets running with blood, and so on. All that had been trotted into the courtroom and into the pages of those newspapers friendly to the government. Thus, the stiff sentences given these men would seem merited, and the methods used to apprehend them could be excused in the public interest. Last June, despite the raging cholera epidemic, the government had ordered doctors to give to the police the names of anyone treated for gunshot wounds. Some doctors had not bothered. Some thought it beneath their professional ethics. Some sold their silence. But wounded men with no luck and no money found themselves arrested.

At Cell XII his keys jangled percussively, iron against iron, and the door swung open. The cell was tall enough to stand in and long enough to lie in, but then so is the grave. Chill February winds blew in, carrying up the fetid air from the courtyard below. Against either wall there were beds stacked like wooden shelving, stuffed with straw, room for as many as half a dozen prisoners (and certainly more had been and could be accommodated), but at the moment there were only two. One, discounting the dead. The turnkey put his candle on the floor and had a quick, practiced feel over the corpse. Then he struggled with the dead man's jaw, which resisted opening.

"You're too late," said a flat voice across the cell. "The doctor already fleeced him."

The turnkey cursed the doctor. The prisoner cursed them both.

"The doctor says you'll live, Number 23974. Jail fever won't get you out of here. You'll be thrown into the sea."

"Why do I care what they do with my body, since I don't even care what they've done with my life?"

"Well, you'll have a private apartment here, as soon as they get your friend out. Phew! They'd better come soon. He's starting to get ripe."

"Of course he's ripe. He died yesterday. He's not my friend."

The turnkey picked his candle off the floor with evident disgust. "Don't you pigs ever shit in the pot?" He kicked the chamberpot over and it clanged dismally, but only rolled as far as its chain would allow. "You are all animals. You live in shit."

"Maybe I live in shit, but you lick it up the asses of—" Number 23974 received, as he'd expected, a couple of blows, and he turned so that his back would absorb the worst of them. He groaned, but did not resist or fight back. The turnkey, on his way out, kicked over the water bucket and told 23974 he would have to beg to get another. And then he left him to the merciful darkness.

Even had there been light, no one would have recognized in Number 23974 the cheeky apprentice Pajol, the compositor so sprightly they'd called him the Monkey. Pajol was so emaciated, wasted from scurvy, his body could not fight the jail fever and vermin eating him up. On 6 June, he'd fallen from the roof and smashed to the stones below, breaking his leg, but in the smoke and confusion he'd still managed to crawl away. But the doctor who treated his wounds turned him in. If he lived, Pajol would always walk with a limp anyway and the doctor, in Pajol's case, had done him a double disservice. He'd spent the summer, fall, and winter rotting in prison, so sick and weak and wounded the trial itself passed in a fog. Only the verdict and the sentence seemed to strike through his consciousness: fourteen years penal servitude at Mont-Saint-Michel, that rock off the northwest coast of France where men had hung in cages since the fifteenth century. That was the night Pajol cried his last tear. All his capacity for human hope or sorrow passed with those tears. He was seventeen years old.

Now Pajol lay in his straw, providing the usual banquet for vermin, mildly surprised to hear feet in the stone passageway and light again bobbing in front of his barred door. The doctor must have wanted the corpse badly to send men for it so soon. "They'll have your bowels open before midnight," Pajol remarked to the corpse. "Stink in their nostrils, *compagnon*. Give them all the jail fever."

But these men had not come for the corpse. The turnkey escorted into the cell a frock-coated individual, who brought with him the odor of tobacco. The smell made Pajol's mouth water, though from nausea or desire even he could not tell.

"The stench here is enough to kill an ox."

"I'm sorry, monsieur," the turnkey said, bowing, "but the man is dead through no fault of mine."

"Which one is he?"

"Number 23974 is the other one, monsieur."

The turnkey left and the man brought the candle closer to Pajol's face. Pajol remained, eyes closed, undifferentiated for all intents and purposes, from the corpse. "Number 23974? Victor Pajol? Answer." He brought out a small well-shaped cudgel much favored by the police and used it unceremoniously to prod the prisoner, but not until he gave a sharp rap on the broken leg did Pajol comply with the order. He answered, but he remained supine and unmoving. "Your republican friends have cost you your life, haven't they, Pajol? You'll end up like your friend here." He nodded brusquely toward the corpse.

"He's not my friend."

"You deserve jail fever and scurvy. All of you republican rabble. You're ulcers in the side of society. Carbuncles on the social order. Order is necessary in this world, Pajol, don't you know that? *Liberté, égalité, fraternité* are impossible. The rights of man are not important, but the rights of property are. You don't understand power and property. Power and property do not pass into the hands of men like you and your friends. Property consolidates with power, reinventing itself. You radical republicans are powerless and always will be." He stopped abruptly. "Do you know me?"

"Why should I?" Pajol sat up slowly, fascinated by the man's bushy eyebrows.

The man took out some small papers and ground bits of tobacco between his fingers and rolled them up. He brought into this cell a fleshy insistence on breathing. With the candle, he lit the thing he had rolled and smoke filled the cell. Pajol coughed and gasped. "I'm here finishing up the last bit of my work, Number 23974. Accounting work."

"Go shit yourself, bourgeois pig," was Pajol's interested reply.

"We got them all, you know, except those two. The students died and those few workers who lived, we got them. We got you."

"You've got the pox."

"We even got those who left in the National Guard uniforms. Blanchard, Latour, Colville. Ignorant artisans, not even smart enough to burn the uniforms they escaped in. You'll probably see them there at Mont-Saint-Michel. Ah, I see I've got your interest at last. You're not as stupid or near dead as you look. The other one, Verdier, your old master, he was the only one sufficiently intelligent to burn the uniform. We'd have got him too, but it seems that the whole of the rue du Caire was ready to testify that Verdier, the priest of the press, was safely tucked up at home on the fifth and sixth of June, playing Papa to his motherless brats."

Pajol roused from his torpor, peering into such light as the candle offered, straining against darkness and memory and the void into which his life and spirit had fallen.

"You didn't see Blanchard, Latour, and Colville, any of your other vermin friends at the trials?"

"I remember nothing of the trial."

"What do you remember of the barricade at the rue Mondétour?"

Pajol's lips drew back from his blackened teeth. "You're the fifth man. The man from Lyon."

"Monsieur Clerons to you."

"You filthy police spy. *Mouchard!*" With what strength he had, Pajol drew a great wad of phlegm up and spewed it at Clerons's feet. It gleamed there on his polished boots.

"Spit another oyster at me and I'll have your tongue torn out.

No one will care and no one will stop me. Or you can use your tongue to help yourself."

"By sucking your short cock? *Merci*, no."

Clerons smacked Pajol hard across the face. "I want some names. We are mopping up the books on this one. They've all been accounted for except two, and perhaps they died of their wounds. You lived. And for what?"

"To see *mouchards* like you strangle on their own vomit one day."

"At least I won't be hung in a cage at Mont-Saint-Michel."

"You will hang by your cock in hell."

"But I will live first. You don't look too healthy, Number 23974."

"I'll live long enough to come back to Paris, to kill you myself."

"I need some names, Pajol. Two names. Two men from that barricade have not yet been accounted for. One was the old man, the one whose uniform I took, the one who came in at dawn."

"To save your worthless ass."

"The other was a young man, the dark-haired one, the one who spoke of the sword and the scaffold. These are the two we can't account for. What are their names? What was that young man's name? You knew him."

"Chiffonnier," replied Pajol, invoking the ragpicking trade.

"I could help get a few years taken off your sentence in return for your cooperation."

"I know nothing. I care nothing. I have nothing. Nothing matters."

"You're young. These people misled you. There's no reason for you to die on a rock like Mont-Saint-Michel."

"My life is over. I have squandered it for nothing. That will not change. Nothing changes. There is no Republic, the same pigs are in power, and all my friends are dead."

"Not Verdier. He's not dead. He's free while you rot here."

"Verdier was not at the barricade. It was as he said. He was home at the rue du Caire." Pajol closed his eyes, picturing his old master at home with his children. Verdier was not an affectionate father, and everyone used to tread carefully around him, everyone except the Monkey. "I have nothing more to say." Pajol lay back down. Let this *mouchard* beat him to death if he wished. That would not matter either. The ravages of scurvy and jail fever and dehydration, the infestation of vermin rendered Pajol helpless against a fatigue that felt like death, that could be differentiated from death only because he dreamed. He heard Clerons finally leave the cell, and he could feel the warmth of the candle left on the floor, but Pajol did not open his eyes. Instead, he followed the dream that beckoned him, the Monkey, down the twisting, turning streets of old Paris, all the way out to the *barrière*, where the countryside rolled and the taverns abounded, where the wine was cheap and the girls flirtatious, and where he saw his friends, the living and the dead.

Chapter 12

*I*n Cosette's schooldays at the Convent of the Perpetual Adoration, the students had passed Lent with spartan rigor, but this winter of 1833 the days of Lent passed in a dream of delight, the winter everywhere belied by the warmth Cosette and Marius created. To marry for love was, as Monsieur Gillenormand had said, the great prize that they had captured. Cosette's joy that winter was dimmed only by her father's eccentric insistence: he would not come to live with them, or even dine with them. True, he came to see her every afternoon, but he insisted that these visits should take place in a little basement room behind the kitchen. Of course Cosette knew her father was the most self-effacing of men, but she protested nonetheless, acquiescing only when he agreed that yes, it was only for Lent.

The little basement room, the morgue of flies and spiders and empty bottles, its street-level window barred, was down a short corridor from the kitchen. Another door opened to the outside under the sweeping staircase at the back of the house, but it was rusted shut, so Cosette's father went in through the kitchen like a servant. The basement room—cleaned up now, two comfortable chairs installed and a carpet and table placed before the small fire—represented a compromise between Marius and Jean Valjean. In this room the older man could see Cosette daily and avoid her husband. Actually Jean Valjean much preferred it to the grand drawing room; the simplicity and quiet were soothing, reminiscent of their old life with Toussaint (since sent to live with her daughter).

But one day in March, bringing a small vase of crocuses for the table, Cosette found that the fire had not been lit and the room was dank and chill. "Really, Papa," she said as she took the worn cloak from his shoulders and hung it on a peg, "perhaps you don't need a fire, but think of me. Toussaint always said you were a saint, but I'm a mere mortal, Papa, and if you insist on meeting here, fine, but must we freeze? You mustn't tell the servants not to light the fire."

"I told them nothing."

Cosette went back into the kitchen and asked the cook (known as Madame Carême) to make some coffee and bring some cake to the little basement room. "And I want that fire lit every day before my father comes." She used her best baroness voice. Over her father's protests, Cosette herself built up the fire while she scolded him. "You don't look well. You were always so robust. It's a crime the way you take care of yourself. You were better to yourself when I lived with you. At least then you didn't give all your money to the poor and all your warm clothes." The fire crackled obligingly and she stepped back, regarding it with some satisfaction. "I am going to have Marius's own tailor make you a proper coat, Papa, and I will be very cross with you if you don't wear it. You don't want me to be cross with you, do you?"

"No, Cosette," he replied obediently.

The fire snapped smartly and the dank implicit in the room seemed to retreat before the flames. Cosette took the tray from Madame Carême and poured her father a steaming cup of coffee. "Our roles are reversed now. All those years you took care of me. Now it's my turn to take care of you. That's how it should be, and I will be glad when Easter comes and all this Lenten dreariness of yours can pass and you'll come live here."

"The idea of its being a Lenten vow was your own, Cosette. Not mine. I will not move into this house. I will come to this room every day as long as you permit it—"

"Permit it! How can you say that, Papa?"

"And you know I have asked you not to call me Papa, not to call me Father. You should call me Monsieur Jean if you want to make me happy."

"Well, I don't. If that's all that will make you happy, then I refuse," Cosette declared grandly. "You are my father and I am your daughter."

"Truly, Cosette, you are my child, my daughter, the joy of my life."

"I am the joy of Marius's life, too. Why can't I be the joy of both of your lives? What's happened between you?"

"Nothing has happened, dear girl. I am a simple man. I lead a simple life. Allow me to go on visiting you here and continue my simple life in the rue de l'Homme-Armé. Now let us have our favorite topic of conversation. Tell me all about Marius. Yes, I will have another cake. Your cook is quite a treasure."

"She is a miracle. Such stories she has, of working with Carême."

"Odd that he would teach a woman, don't you think?"

"Of course it's odd. I told you she was a miracle."

Jean Valjean gave a quiet laugh and settled down to hear all about Marius. How he was continuing his search for the man who had brought him—broken, wounded, unconscious, and near death—through the sewers of Paris, back to his grandfather's house, and then vanished. The man was so covered in fecal filth he could hardly be called a man, but Marius would not give up. Marius must find him. It was a debt of honor, and Marius's sense of honor was one of his sterling characteristics—one of the many. Oh yes, and Marius was hating the law (speaking of honor). He'd been educated for it, but now he chafed under it. The law itself seemed so often wrong; how could Marius honorably continue to believe he was doing right in supporting something wrong?

"Why doesn't Marius do something else then?" Jean Valjean inquired idly. "He has plenty of money. You brought a substantial dowry, six hundred thousand francs, to this marriage. There's no reason for him to stay in the law."

"Marius says we can't touch the money."

Jean Valjean's face darkened. "Why not?"

"I don't know why not. He says it's just so. At least for the time being."

"But you should have the good things money can buy, Cosette. You should have a carriage, a box at the theatre, and fine clothes, and give lovely dinners for your many friends."

Speaking of her friends launched Cosette into the courtship of Mademoiselle de Bélessin and Marius's Cousin Théo. Théo was the grandfather's brother's only grandson. The grandfather's brother had died very young. Eighty-three. Théo was giving up the military. The glory of France was all in the grave with Napoléon.

Even Napoléon's son, Napoléon II, was dead. War was over for Théo, but love—well! Théo was truly smitten with Mademoiselle de Bélessin, but her family . . . Jean Valjean smiled happily, responding when obliged to, content to let the sound of Cosette's voice wash over him and the smell of coffee perfume the room. He shook his head sadly and said "What a pity" when told that Mademoiselle Talbot was going back to England. Mademoiselle Talbot had vowed to write Cosette daily just to keep up her French.

Cosette declared, "I told her, well, Helen, you should just refuse to go. Refuse! England's a grim, dismal place, especially for Catholics. They say London is filthy. Not at all like Paris." Cosette nattered on, then stopped and shivered. "Oh, Papa—do you ever think how terrible it would have been if *we* had gone to England?"

"Yes, Cosette. I often think what might have been."

That year the spring pirouetted in uncertainly. One day in April a chill rain sluiced down, and by the time Jean Valjean had walked from the rue de l'Homme-Armé to the rue des Filles-du-Calvaire, he was soaked clear through. He came in through the kitchen, and Madame Carême dusted flour from her hands and advised him to dry at the kitchen fire. He thanked her and declined, but when he went into the basement room, he saw why she had offered. The fire was unlit. Cosette was not there. Marius was.

"I wish only a word with you. I have some questions." Marius closed the door.

"I have already told you the truth."

"But not the whole truth. My question is about Cosette's dowry. To whom does that money truly belong?"

"Enjoy the money. You don't know how poverty can—"

"I have tasted poverty. I lived for five years in the most abject poverty, in a hovel at the *barrière* d'Italie—"

"You lived there by choice, Baron Pontmercy. You chose to leave the comforts of your grandfather's house on a point of honor, as I recall. There is poverty one does not choose, poverty that kills your soul and spirit before it kills your body. The honor of people who live in that poverty is much less tender than yours."

Marius demanded, again, to know to whom that money rightfully belonged.

"The six hundred thousand francs are in no way tainted, Monsieur Pontmercy. I will say no more about it. You may believe me or not as you wish."

"I do not believe you. I have investigated all this carefully, and my inquiries so far have linked that money to a Monsieur Madeleine, a wealthy manufacturer, who vanished ten years ago, vanished in 1823 and no trace of him was ever found, but they think he was murdered."

Jean Valjean was not appreciably moved by the fate of Monsieur Madeleine.

"I would rather throw those six hundred thousand francs into the Seine than to accept money tainted by blood. I think you stole that money and I intend to see it returned to its rightful owner, if he is still alive."

In a small, obscure way, Jean Valjean chuckled.

"I have another question. Ever since last June I have been looking, ceaselessly trying to find the man who saved my life, who carried me through the sewer and brought me here and vanished that day, the sixth of June."

"What has that to do with me?"

"I have discovered certain things. That *mouchard* we had bound there at the Corinth, the police spy, Javert, he was known to you, wasn't he?"

Jean Valjean drew a deep breath. "He was as known to me as my own shadow."

"You came to the barricade—and it was you, you gave your uniform to that fifth man, don't deny it—but you came for the express purpose of killing Javert, of ending his pursuit of you. You came to kill him and you did. I saw you lead him to the back of the Corinth. It was the last thing I saw."

Jean Valjean slumped and availed himself of the chair. "If I had not gone to the rue Mondétour, my whole life would have been different."

"If you had not put a bullet in the brain of Javert, you would be a convict again. You shot him and then you escaped."

Marius went on, a barrage of accusation that Jean Valjean endured stoically. He had long ago decided to keep his secrets in the sewers; to do otherwise might drag that sewer into his daughter's life. He wanted Cosette free of the sewer, the prison, the bloody barricade, free of reprisals by the law and the heavy hand of the state. She had the man she wanted, the man she loved, the man who loved her. What did the rest of it matter? He did not begrudge Marius his conjectures; the evidence put together in a certain fashion could well have led Marius to these conclusions. It was the young man's vehemence he found chilling. He'd always heard that passion made men burn, but Marius's passions seemed as pointed as icicles. Any charity he might have felt for Marius ebbed, succumbed to the cold, not in the room but in the man before him. "Are you happy with Cosette?" he interrupted.

"What kind of question is that? And what right have you to ask it?"

"I have a father's right."

"You're not her father," Marius insisted. "You said she fell to you by chance."

"She fell to you by chance as well."

"She fell to me by destiny. There is a difference."

"Ah." Jean Valjean collected his dignity about him as a convict gathers his chain. "You think me a monster, don't you? And you think Cosette an angel."

Marius assented and demurred at the same moment.

"And do you sometimes look at her sleeping beside you and wonder how such an angel could have been loved, protected, and raised by a monster?"

"You are not her father. You said she was an orphan."

"Do you look at Cosette, sleeping there, and wonder if something of the monster does not lurk invisibly within her, like the worm in the rose, perhaps? Like the butterfly who can't quite rid herself of the ugly cocoon?"

"Cosette has nothing of you."

"Sometimes do you look at her and wonder if, having married the angel, you have also married the monster? Has it happened in the past three months, perhaps, that in your wife's eau de cologne you sometimes catch a whiff of the prison? That in the tinkling of her bracelets you hear the clank of leg irons?"

"She is not your daughter!"

"Oh yes, she is. Before God she is my daughter! By every standard of love we are given to live by, she is my daughter. I told her not to call me father so as to soften what for you must be a painful association, but I repent of that now. I am her father." Jean Valjean rose from the chair and stepped toward Marius. "Does she know you feel this way?"

"She knows nothing of this. I do not feel that way," Marius stammered.

"That day, Ash Wednesday, in your drawing room, I told you the truth of my past and I asked only one thing of you. I could not bear for Cosette to know I had once been one of those miserable wretches. I begged you not to tell her."

"I never have. On my honor, I never have."

Jean Valjean's brow furrowed, and it was a while before he spoke. "Listen to me carefully, Monsieur Pontmercy. Cosette's dowry is as clean, as free from wickedness or taint, as if it had been earned by a peasant by the sweat of his brow—which it was. As you know, I was born a peasant, we were starving, and I stole a loaf of bread. I spent nineteen years a convict. But that money, I earned that money with these hands—" Jean Valjean held up his still-powerful hands. "My daughter's dowry is clean."

"Cosette is not your daughter."

"Just listen. Second, you will never again have cause to regard your beautiful young wife with anything but devotion and affection. I will not be coming back here. I will never see Cosette again, even if it kills me. Had I known your thoughts would take this morbid turn, Monsieur Pontmercy, I would have gone to the grave with my hideous secret."

"If this is morbid, it is not my doing. In these two things—the question of the money, the questions of the sixth of June—quite separately, my investigations keep coming back to you, to deeds you've done. Possibly to murders you've committed. You brought the whiff of prison. You brought the clank of leg irons. It suited your honor to bring them to my attention. It suits my honor to tell you—"

"My honor is nothing compared to Cosette's happiness."

"My happiness, Papa?" Cosette opened the door. "Marius! What are you doing here? Why is the fire out? Papa, you're dripping wet—what's wrong?"

Marius excused himself quickly and left, closing the door behind him. Cosette might have gone after him except her father announced he was going away, leaving Paris altogether.

"What? Where are you going? Where is there for you to go?"

"I will call on you when I return."

"Call on me? Am I the minister of finance that you should call on me on your return? What has happened, Papa? What is so final and tragic, please—" Cosette flung her arms around him, soaking cloak and all, and held him. "Don't leave me. You saved my life, don't leave—"

"Don't speak of that. It's a time that is past."

"But it's not gone. I dream of them, the Thénardiers. In my dreams, that horrible sign, the Sergeant of Waterloo, I hear it creaking in the wind, and the chains on the gun carriage rattle, Madame Thénardier beats me with her broom, or old Thénardier, he comes after me, the girls laugh, scream at me, sing, sing, Lark—" She wept against the rough wool of his cloak.

"Cosette, my angel, my sweet, hush, have you ever told this to your husband?" He patted her back. "No? Good. Shh."

Cosette raised her face to his. "That night, that Christmas Eve, Papa, you took that heavy bucket from me, you put your hand in mine, you gave me your strength. Don't take it away from me now. I have prayed always since then, lit candles and prayed, thanked Saint-Joseph, the father-who-was-not-the-father, who worked with his hands as a carpenter as you worked with your hands in the convent garden."

"You were a child then. You are a woman now." He brushed the tears from her cheeks and held her face in his hands. "Listen and heed me. That brutal past is finished. Over. Dead. Madame Thénardier truly is dead, she died in prison, but if she ever comes after you in your dreams, then snatch the broom from her, sweep them both from your dreams, and if you can't, then wake, yes, pray to Saint-Joseph, but never, never speak of all that misery. You are Madame Pontmercy now, not a little girl all alone on Christmas Eve. You are the baroness, not a hapless waif. Revel in your present, Cosette, the past is only a shadow. Our life—yours and mine—was lived in shadow, but your life has come into the light."

"All the good I know, Papa, I learned from you."

"Perhaps. But your strength comes from your mother. Your mother, Fantine, lost everything except her love for you, and so, no matter what happened to her, she remained beautiful. You have a beauty beyond your lovely face, Cosette, a beauty that comes from strength and grace. There will be those who will try to pilfer that strength, erode that grace, ridicule it and tell you these things are unbecoming on a woman. Don't believe them, dear girl. While you grew up, I was only the nettle protecting the rose. Remember that, Cosette. You are the rose and not the lily. Roses have thorns. Keep your thorns, my blue-eyed rose, my beautiful daughter. I'm going away because I love you. I'll be back. I'll write. Often. Daily. Let me go now. Please—" He kissed her forehead and pulled her hands from his shoulders. He turned, and with what was left of his great strength he pulled open the door that had been rusted shut as long as anyone could remember, and left Cosette alone, weeping, her skirt still damp from his cloak, the rain blowing in and around her, disturbing the ashes in the grate.

Chapter 13

*P*aris is endlessly intolerant of the dying, of the feeble young and the feeble old, Malthusian remnants, all of them, too weak to live, too strong to die, the butt of jokes, the prey of thieves. Along a certain route between the rue de l'Homme-Armé and the rue des Filles-du-Calvaire, urchins in the spring of 1833 came to recognize a certain old man, no matter what his disguise, because he could be teased into tossing coins, and it was more fun to irritate him than to pick his pocket. His route was constant and daily, until finally Jean Valjean lacked the stamina for the streets. He could not walk all the way to the rue des Filles-du-Calvaire to hazard a glimpse of Cosette. His route dwindled and by June he scarcely stirred from the rue de l'Homme-Armé. Indeed, the concierge there with his repugnant rheumy eyes began to wonder idly to whom he'd next rent, and he wondered too why he had been paid to tell the old man's daughter, on her every visit, that he had left Paris and there were no messages for her.

Cosette kept up her daily prayers to Saint-Joseph, and waited for word from her father, but it was spring after all. May rolled in, so magnificent she wondered if the world was always this beautiful and she had simply failed to notice. On trees all over the city the tiny fists of buds broke into applause and a colorful pageant of tulips followed the daffodils; lilac curtains lifted on peony theatricals, and in the garden of the Convent of the Perpetual Adoration the old nuns marveled over the appearance of a blue rose, counting it as a miracle given their dwindling order.

The nuns might have concurred with Cosette and Marius that there never was a spring like this, though for very different reasons. Marius neglected the law and Cosette neglected the rest of the world, and they moved to that country of love; they made love in the afternoon and afterward they played whist, idly naked, Cosette discovering she could abide the game after all if she could also watch Marius stretch out sinuously across their bed. They discovered that neither of them had ever seen the sea, and so they took the poste chaise to Boulogne-sur-Mer and spent a week at an especially hospitable inn, Gérard's Inn, where the food was simple and appetizing, the catch fresh daily, the wine good, the beds warm and clean. They walked along the beaches and tried to see who could shout to England, while the sea rolled in like long gray muscles, breaking white upon the rocks, the wind tugging at Cosette's hair and chafing their cheeks. They talked together, huddled in the long grasses. To Marius's surprise and delight, Cosette showed him the cartwheels she'd been famous for in the convent, infamous for actually. There, by La Manche, they made voyages of discovery on the great galleon of their bed. They felt like the very first man and the very first woman, Adam and Eve. So of course they had their serpent too.

This serpent—able, evil, and ubiquitous in their lives—had been outfitted by the Changer for his appearance at their door in Paris. As the devil appeared to be a snake, so this snake appeared to be an aging statesman. The costume was fine overall, wanting only in the particulars, the missing buttons, the fraying waistcoat, the coat shiny at the elbows, but there were ambassadorial accoutrements, little green spectacles and a wig that Talleyrand might have admired. The man who wore these clothes was sixty or so, gaunt, his skin coarsened by age and smallpox scars, his hair the color of dried and powdered snuff, and his knees creaked, the result of rheumatism, which had been exacerbated by a recent stay in those apartments of state, Conciergerie prison. With some outside help he'd managed to escape those apartments without paying his full rent, which is to say, without serving his full sentence. Accompanying him as he walked toward No. 6 rue des Filles-du-Calvaire was his sole surviving daughter, a girl of about eighteen. This was the same girl who had clutched Cosette's yellow freesias on her wedding day, who had accosted the bridal coach in the first place because Thénardier had recognized Jean Valjean riding in it when they were stalled in the rue Saint-Antoine. One individual of ambivalent identity always recognizes another.

Zelma Thénardier was large, angular, and strong, the image of her late mother, a dragon if ever there was one. Even old Thénardier knew better than to cross his wife, and fear of her wrath had kept him a faithful husband (for the most part), so there was at least one of the Ten Commandments he had not abused time and again. Zelma had strong teeth, fine, full lips, and a tigerish expression even when she smiled, which wasn't often. She too had been outfitted by the Changer. She wore a respectable gown too narrow through her broad shoulders and straining across her scrawny bosom. Her reddish hair had been jammed into a matronly bonnet, and she carried soiled gloves and cursed and swore at her pinching shoes.

"Shut your gob," Thénardier ordered as they walked through the gates. "You deal gently with the bastard baroness. We may need her later. There's no reason to pluck the cock and the hen at the same time. You understand?" They ascended the high steps. "I'll deal with Baron Pontmercy, the son of my old colonel from Waterloo. Can he bear to see an old soldier like me—his father's savior—go forth naked into the New World?"

"Save it for the pinchprick baron."

Thénardier gave the door a sharp rap and he asked to be shown to the Baron Pontmercy, with all the proper diplomatic flourishes, save, of course, for a calling card. No matter, he had a letter for the baron and would the servant be so good as to show mademoiselle to the baroness?

Cosette was in the garden, at the back, digging in the strawberry beds that lay before the garden wall, baking in the June afternoon. A climbing rose spread across the wall, and a splintery gate led to the outbuildings, the stable and carriage house. Marius's grandfather sat on a marble bench, his hands resting on his cane, appropriating strawberries from Cosette's basket, which she had entrusted to him (knowing very well he would eat them). Trowel and scissors in hand, she stepped gingerly amongst the plants, sampling the season's first offerings. She turned to see a tall woman coming toward them, past the fountain in the courtyard and up the narrow graveled walks, past the statue of Diana, past the scarlet peonies alternating with blue delphiniums that stood like protective sentinels.

The grandfather, nibbling thoughtfully on a strawberry, also watched the woman's stride and gait. He rose and leaned upon his cane as though a buyer at a cattle market. "Good haunches," he remarked to Cosette, who hushed him quickly, though to no avail: as soon as the woman had come up to them, he asked her if she'd like a quick one behind the garden gate.

"Grandfather!" cried Cosette. "Please! This woman is—who are you?"

"No stranger to—" the grandfather made an indecent suggestion with his hand.

Cosette blushed and banished him instantly, but the woman before her seemed to take no notice of any of this. Struck dumb, she looked up and down the garden, following the grandfather's bandy-legged progress toward the house, with its fine, high windows, its green shutters, its clean, vanilla-colored stucco. Her eyes bulged, and she seemed apoplectic and about to swallow her tongue.

"I ask you to forgive him," Cosette stammered. "He is an old royalist, and really, what can you expect? You know how incorrigible they are when it comes to women. You—"

"I have to go to America."

"Ah. Well, I—"

"America. With its savages and slaves and filthy forests. I am a Parisian and I have to go to America, shipped over there like a cheese. God! This is all wrong!"

Cosette stepped out of the strawberry bed and peered down toward the house to see if some explanation came with this woman, whose breast was heaving and eyes flashing as she began to laugh, hoarse, coarse, horrible laughter.

The woman stepped closer and her bony forefinger waved in Cosette's face. "You ask who I am? Who are *you*? You are scum. You're filth. Your father was a convict, and your mother was a whore who sold her hair, her teeth, and her body, and you are a bastard. Yes, the baroness is the rut-spawn of a prostitute and a convict! The baroness was a slave. Oh, Cosette—" she spat the name out like something rotten—"you fought the dog for scraps!"

As though struck, Cosette winced and wavered, while overhead, in memory, the sign The Sergeant of Waterloo squealed on its hinges like the coarse, hoarse laughter of Madame Thénardier, the ghost of whose flailing broom roused the dust of dreams and chains clanging in nightmares.

"I've watched you and the dog chewing the same bone. You were a slave to us, Cosette. We kicked you for the fun of it, just to hear you cry, you bitch. You went barefoot in the snow while my mother dressed us, my sister and me . . . we always, oh Eponine," she choked and heaved and sobbed, "we had the warmest, sweetest little clothes—"

"*Eponine?*" Cosette backed against a tree for its protection. "*Zelma?*"

"Yes, me, Zelma." She quit blubbering and snarled, "Me, I had a bed. You slept with the dog—till he died, and left you his ticks and fleas. Why should you be married and safe and happy and rich and have all this—" Zelma gulped and gazed around her—"while I go to America? My father is in there now, screwing money from your pig's prick of a husband because we have to leave. In France, if my father's caught again, he has a death sentence over him, so it's America for us, and it's all your fault, the fault of your mewling husband and your jailbird father, Jean Valjean."

"Jean Valjean? Who is Jean Valjean? I don't know—"

"You don't know that name? Maybe you know the number branded on him." Zelma jabbed Cosette's chest with every digit. "Number 24601. Maybe when Jean Valjean put a leg over your mother he still wore his lovely iron collar and his lovely green convict's cap. Don't you believe me? It's true! Your mother was a whore! She'd fuck anything that walked for money. She fucked convicts for free. It's all true, and if you think I am calling you baroness, you don't know your cunt from a cauliflower! Don't turn your head from me, you bitch." Zelma moved in, toe to toe, pressing Cosette against the tree. "Your father, Jean Valjean, the convict, one of those handsome men who wear square cravats with iron bolts, who are chained like beasts to wagons, those gallant green-caps with their running noses and their running sores. You once had sores. Sores and frostbite. My mother once beat you senseless because you were too weak to pick up the broom, because you couldn't push Eponine and me on our swing."

"*Marius!*" Cosette cried, her arms held over head, her back scraping against the tree. "*Marius!*" She wept, sinking to the ground. "*Marius!*"

"Cosette, the Lark, that's what they used to call you. Up and singing at dawn. Such a sad little song. I should have stoned you then and you wouldn't have such fine tail feathers now, would you, Lark? I told Eponine, Kill the Lark, kill the bitch, take the man, but no, my sister"— great sobs raked up through Zelma's chest and spewed from her lips—"my sister famishes away from love, dies with that bunch of drunken rabble rioters last year, and for what? For love," Zelma spat on Cosette's head. "For the love of your husband. Didn't you know? Your husband was bedding my sister the whole time he lived next to us in the filthy chamberpot of a room at the *barrière* d'Italie. My sister was in love with him, and he loved her. He told my sister, Eponine, You are so beautiful, because she was so much more beautiful than you. How could he love some twirping bastard of a virgin lark? He couldn't. He never did. He loved Eponine because she gave it to him whenever he wanted it. Free, she gave it to him—"

Zelma's tirade was cut suddenly short by a shove that knocked her off her feet and into the strawberries, where she landed, winded and with a splat.

"If you were a man," Marius said, "I'd beat you senseless."

"If you were a man, I'd show you a good time."

Marius knelt over Cosette, his arms around her. Her shoulders shook with sobs, and he called her name again and again, pulled her to her feet as though pulling her back from the abyss. He held her tightly, chafed her hands and cheeks. "Cosette, darling Cosette, listen to me. Listen. We have to fly. Now. No matter what's happened here, we have to go to the rue de l'Homme-Armé, immediately. We must find your father, your father, your father." Marius pushed the hair from her face and kissed her, repeated, *Your father* till her eyes opened. Marius's voice was low and urgent. "We have to go, my love. Quickly. I've been such a fool. Oh, God, I've been—" He put his arm across her back and held her as they hurried down the garden path toward the house, Marius calling out for a servant to call them a carriage, to hurry, to forget it, it would take too long and at the front steps they bumped into the aging statesman, who gave an elaborate bow.

"The baroness? Have I the pleasure? Or is it the Lark?"

Marius and Cosette flew past him toward the street as though pursued by demons.

Thénardier chuckled and sauntered down the garden path with an air of immense satisfaction. His pockets bulged with bank notes and were further filled out with a few little items he'd nicked after Marius left the library in such a tearing hurry. He found Zelma recovered, inasmuch as she was no longer sprawled on the ground, but sitting on the marble bench, trembling and hyperventilating, fists clenched. He dusted off a few strawberries and chewed them reflectively. "I hope you haven't let fly with something you shouldn't, Zelma. I told you I wanted to save the baroness for later."

Zelma's eyes seemed to focus slowly on the money protruding from his pockets, and like smelling salts to the faint, the sight brought her around. Her big teeth gleamed. "You filed him, didn't you?"

"Neither picked his pocket nor ruffled his trousers." Thénardier pulled out a couple of bank notes. "He gave it all to me."

"And I'm a wood grub in ermine."

"In all my long and honorable life as a poor child of cruel necessity, such good fortune has never smiled on me. I wish I knew what I'd done right. We're twenty thousand francs the richer."

"Twenty? Get off it, there's not twenty thousand francs there."

Thénardier patted his crinkling pockets. "There? No. This was quite separate. There will be twenty thousand francs waiting for us in the bank in New York when we arrive."

"No!"

"Courtesy of the baron, so you can see, my little peach pit, can't you, why I'm puzzled. What did I do right? I'd figured to file a couple of hundred francs off him, just to buy my silence, a bargain really, a little blackmail. So I told him his father-in-law was Jean Valjean, the convict, and to my surprise, he said, Very well, I know that. I went on. I told him Jean Valjean was twice a convict. Very well, said the baron, I know that. I brought out those two bits we got from the newspapers, the one about the mysterious manufacturer, the benevolent Monsieur Madeleine, turning out to be the convict Jean Valjean, and the other bit of print, the one from last year about that poor police inspector drowning himself in the Seine. Poor Javert." Thénardier drew out a silken scarf he'd filched from a table in the foyer, wiped his eyes, assessing its worth at the same moment. "To see the young baron's face at the moment I showed him those, Zelma, his face would have broken your heart as he broke Eponine's—"

"Don't talk about my sister. Just get on with it."

"I've seen corpses with more color than the baron had after he'd read those two. Naturally I upped the price I was asking for my silence. I thought, Well, I've got his mouth stuffed with grass, I might as well lead him to slaughter, so I said Jean Valjean was not merely a convict in the past—which might have been forgiven, time healing all wounds and—"

Zelma rose. She was taller than her father and she outweighed him. Perhaps it was the memory of her mother that made Thénardier trot along with his story.

"I said Jean Valjean was not merely a convict from the past, but just last year he was up to his rotten old tricks. I knew it for a fact. I'd seen him, hadn't I? The assassin. The thief. I told the baron how I had found Jean Valjean with a dead man on his back, there where the sewer opens into the Seine. You'd have thought I put a pike through the baron's heart, Zelma. He stands. He staggers. I think he's going to put his hands round my neck and throttle me. But he comes right up on me, breathes down my cravat, grabs me, and shouts—*When?* When did Jean Valjean commit murder and robbery?" Thénardier popped sweat at the memory. "Let me think. The time of the great rioting and the cholera. June. Jean Valjean had the corpse of a young gentleman over his shoulder—it must have been a gentleman, there'd be no point in robbing a ragpicker, would there? I had the key to the sewer grating, the key to freedom and the river. I traded him a turn of the key for cash. Fair enough. An honorable exchange. But all the time I was discussing with him the fare, the toll you might say, I'm thinking, I know that voice. You couldn't see anything of the man, either man, for that matter, the dead or the living, they were covered in shit. To here." Thénardier sliced along his chin and gagged. "They had been through that lake of shit where better men have died. Later it came to me, *Jean Valjean.* And then, Zelma, you'd have thought I'd told the baron Jean Valjean was Christ and I had a piece of the True Cross to prove it. Baron Pontmercy opens every drawer in his desk, showers money on me, cries and shouts and showers more money. Well, you can see for yourself."

He patted the notes bulging from his pockets and Zelma snatched several and thrust them down her bosom before he slapped her hand away and warned against greed in girls.

"He tells me *he* is the man Jean Valjean had on his back. *He* is the man Jean Valjean carried through the sewers, through the lake of shit. He is that man! He wasn't dead—and so I quickly reminded him, Well, your eminence, then you also have me to thank for your life, don't you? I did turn the key, after all. Let's not forget that. Let's not forget that the same service—the gift of life, you might actually say—I gave your father on the field at Waterloo. It was I recalled him to life, pulled him from a mound of corpses. Of course I pulled Colonel Pontmercy out of the bloody heap at Waterloo to take his watch and money, so how was I to know I'd saved his life? I'd got his everlasting debt of honor," Thénardier sucked on the last word, "and his son's."

"Who are you talking about?"

"Colonel Pontmercy, my little unlicked cub."

"Don't call me that."

"The first Baron Pontmercy, who swore his son, Marius, to everlasting gratitude to me, the Sergeant of Waterloo. It was a good harvest, Waterloo." Thénardier sighed sentimentally. "Of course, young Marius called me a thief and a corpse robber and said if he ever saw me in France again he'd see to it I was shaved by the guillotine. I assured him I preferred America. Ah, America!"

Zelma spat. "We have to go to New York to get our twenty thousand francs?"

"America is the land of opportunity. Truly, Zelma, our fortunes have changed. Fate and twenty thousand francs smile on us." A look positively beatific crossed Thénardier's gaunt face. "I am one of those holy men. I can walk in shit, sit in shit, sleep in shit, eat shit, drink shit, and still my turds come out in perfect golden bricks."

Chapter 14

*T*he concierge, his keys clanking, his banner of bad breath waving behind him, led them upstairs at the rue de l'Homme-Armé, protesting all the while, he had called the doctor, he had looked after Monsieur Fauchelevent, was it his fault the man was dying?

"Dying?" exclaimed Cosette. "He's dying?"

Marius seemed to crumble in the stairwell, and when they got to Jean Valjean's apartment, Cosette was appalled to find it stripped so bare. The concierge slavered, scraped, swore he had touched nothing, stolen nothing, as Cosette ran through the apartment toward her father's room, calling his name.

Flinging open the door to his room, she saw the afternoon sun eking in behind the shutters, laying a sort of grill across the floor, her father's narrow bed, the crucifix above, the silver candlesticks on the mantel. "Papa!" she tore to his bedside, and took his hand as Marius fell, bowed down on the other side.

Jean Valjean roused only slowly, erratically, as though doubting his senses or his whereabouts. Not until his eyes flickered open and rested on Cosette did he seem to fathom that he had not died. Turning his head with difficulty, he saw Marius bent on the other side of the bed, weeping. He raised his hand and gently stroked Marius's dark hair. "So you know then?" he said, only mildly interested. "You know the truth of it."

"I beg your forgiveness. Please don't die without forgiving me. I can't forgive myself, but I beg you—"

"Of course I forgive. I am an old man. How can I not?"

"Papa, you're not going to die. I won't let you. I'm going for the doctor, I'm going to get you some medicine, I'm going—"

"Shh, Cosette. Calm. All this furious energy, Cosette, don't waste it on what can't be changed or altered. I'm so happy to see you, to rest my eyes on your sweet face, my child, my daughter, my daughter and my son—" he patted Marius's hand—"my family."

"How could you save my life and never tell me?" Marius wept.

"Salvation comes to us in strange ways. I was a thief and salvation came from the bishop, a man I stole from. There, Cosette—" he pointed vaguely toward the mantel. "Do not leave without the silver candlesticks. They are my freedom, my integrity, my identity, all I have to give you—"

"You've given us life, Papa, a life together, you've given us—" But she broke down, wept, could not say what he had given her, could not say he had rescued her, saved her from death at the brutal hands of Thénardier; instead, she whispered, her lips at his ear, "That night, Papa, that Christmas Eve you put your hand in mine, you gave me your strength. Now see, Papa, I have your hand. Feel my hand in yours, Papa. I give you my strength. I will be the one to save you, to pull you back and give you everything you need to live."

"You have already done that, my child, Cosette," he lingered over the sweetness in her name, "my dear, dear girl. You've given me everything I need to live, with your love, your trust, you've given me everything I need to die in peace. You're here, you love me, you both love me, you love each other—"

"Always, Papa—"

"The candlesticks," he murmured confidentially, "take them, please. Don't leave without them." He seemed satisfied, fell back when they both vowed they would take them, keep them, cherish them forever. "The concierge will steal them otherwise. It would be a pity to have them stolen," he mused, "after so much."

"Come home with us," Marius implored, "allow us, allow me to—"

"You are allowed," said Jean Valjean. "You are forgiven. You may one day be required to forgive someone else. Perhaps it will be easier for you, now that I have forgiven you."

"Papa," Cosette clasped both his hands in hers, smoothed the white hair back from his much-loved face, "Papa, don't leave me."

He smiled. "I'm not leaving you, dear girl. The grave is for the body. Love is from the soul. Oh, Cosette, Cosette, bless you. Please—" he motioned to Marius—"open the shutters, will you? The bars across the bed, I can't bear to see the bars across the bed."

And when the shutters were opened and the shadows fled, the bars removed from his body, Jean Valjean's life was freed and Cosette held him while he breathed his last.

As the priest's words fluttered with his lacy surplice, June sunlight dappled through the branches of a yew tree in an unkempt section of Père-Lachaise, where wild oats and grasses gossiped with the wind. Jean Valjean was buried as he had wished, in an unobtrusive corner in the simplest manner possible, the place not even to be marked with a stone. The man who had worn many names would not leave one behind.

The priest finished, closed his book, and with a nod to Marius and Cosette he turned and left, followed by the grandfather and Aunt Adelaide. The young couple—pain, strain, tears, grief, and confusion evident all over their faces—stood in the restless shade of the yew. Nearby two gravediggers waited, smoking, chatting low and leaning on their shovels while lizards scurried over an ancient gate. Cosette cleared her throat. "You need to tell me the truth of it, Marius. Of everything that happened between you and my father, Jean Valjean." She said it as though the name were foreign and could only be pronounced with difficulty.

"The truth is I treated him like vermin."

"I mean the other truth. The larger truth."

"You've read the newspaper pieces Thénardier left before I burned them," Marius said after a while. "Jean Valjean did not murder Monsieur Madeleine, he was Monsieur Madeleine. He did not murder Javert, Javert killed himself. Your father let me believe he was a criminal, and I treated him like vermin. He could have told me the whole truth, and I would have honored him all my life."

"That possibility isn't closed to you, Marius."

"I could have honored him all his life. That possibility is closed to me."

Indeed it was. The gravediggers moved out of the shadows expectantly. Cosette took her husband's arm, and the two walked the paths where stone urns and angels monumentally testified to mortality, Marius stooped by grief and shattered with guilt. "He said he couldn't bear for you to know he'd been a convict. He wanted to protect you. I promised. I wanted to protect you."

"I'm not a child to be coddled. I'm a grown woman."

"You were his child."

"I am your wife."

Marius stopped, turned, lifted the black veil from her face, and met her blue eyes candidly. "You're a woman to me, not a child, and I swear I will never again keep secrets from you. I promise you. We have to promise that to each other."

Cosette promised. And lied. Not a very big lie, she told herself, more a sin of omission, and so not a proper sin at all, so minuscule it would not even require confession. There was one secret Cosette would keep, the secret she prayed he would never discover. Please keep Zelma in America forever. Please, Saint-Joseph, let Marius remain forever ignorant of the enslaved Lark of the Sergeant of Waterloo, the child with fleas and lice and running sores, who fought the dog for scraps, a child beaten with the strap and the broom, the bastard baroness, daughter of the whore and the convict. Clearly and for reasons known best to himself, Thénardier had not given Marius that information. The nameless whore had appeared in one of the newspaper articles he'd left, something about how Monsieur Madeleine had kept as his mistress a prostitute who died of shock at the moment of his rearrest, but nothing to connect this prostitute to Cosette's mother.

Were they lovers, Fantine and Jean Valjean? Could Jean Valjean (in yet one more bit of truth unsaid) have been the man who had fathered her, as well as the man who had been her father? Whatever they had done with their bodies, Fantine and Jean Valjean were united in their devotion to Cosette. Would Marius have understood such devotion? He had spurned the convict. Imagine how he might respond to the prostitute. Over the past few days Cosette had fathomed, unwillingly but fathomed nonetheless, that her beloved Marius—for all his passion, his intensity, his care for conscience and his sense of honor—harbored a streak of cold correctness, unfeeling as marble, unmoved as granite, that impelled him to sacrifice affection to a notion of uncomplicated rectitude.

As they left the cemetery Cosette felt the cold clutch of the unknown. The past? The future? She put her father's death behind her, but not the enigmas of his life. As a child Cosette had never questioned those enigmas. Why should she? Why should any child who knows herself protected and adored? Perhaps for the first time now Cosette perceived how mysterious was her childhood, with its elliptical changes of address and identity, its underlying assumption that identity was fluid, but integrity was not. As an education, that had to be at least as useful as the names of the kings of France.

Chapter 15

*O*n a brilliant day in early October, Cosette went to the library to find Marius as she had expected to find him, as he had been all summer: drapes drawn, room dim, candles burning in Jean Valjean's silver candlesticks, Marius at his desk awash with unopened books, blank papers, his pen dry. The death of Jean Valjean had struck in him the chord of all those other deaths he regretted—his father, the men on the barricade, the best of his generation. Fatherless, friendless, Marius came to the library every day and closed the drapes that Cosette had resolutely opened in the morning. He had wrecked on the shoals of grief and guilt, but there were no bottles, no empty glasses, no stain or stink of drink or dissipation in this room; Marius's despair was in keeping with the rest of his life, pure and formal as a sonnet.

As the summer progressed Cosette's grief for her father had submerged in her fears for her husband. His suffering sank into a profound torpor before which she was powerless. Neither Aunt Adelaide nor the grandfather had the capacity for such suffering, and so they could not touch Marius, nor guide Cosette. Desperate for resources, she had even gone to the Convent of the Perpetual Adoration, and no sooner walked behind its walls than she knew that these nuns, shut away forever from the world, could not possibly help her with a grief-stricken man. Ironically, though, they had helped her, given her the resolve she brought with her this October afternoon in 1833.

She sat down primly on the sofa and looked about the library (a wholly masculine preserve) as though she were about to put it up for auction. Two walls were lined floor to ceiling with books, two fireplaces faced each other, two sofas. Marius brought his head up off the desk. Ordinarily she would have gone to him, wrapped her arms around his shoulders as she had all summer, tried to infuse him physically with the tonic of her love, but today she sat quite still and told him he slept too much.

"I sleep so I can dream. In my dreams I right all my errors of judgment. In my dreams my friends are still alive. We laugh. We talk. In my dreams I call your father *Father*, and I take his hand as I should have done on Ash Wednesday, and he embraces me. In my dreams I reach my father's bedside before he dies, and I am able to tell him how much I love him and admire him. How I think I am like him."

"He was a brave man and a soldier."

"I don't mean that I am brave. I meant that I would do the wrong thing for the right reason. Or vice versa. Perhaps I don't know what I mean." Marius put his head in his hands. "Why did your father tell me the convict's past and not the hero's? Why not tell me he saved my life when all my friends died? Would it have been so terrible for me to know he was the man I'd been searching for?" He looked up beseechingly. "Sometimes, Cosette, my anger turns on him and I'm enraged. He could have clarified every mystery, and he did not do it."

"Perhaps he was testing your faith in him. Perhaps he was testing your faith in me. Testing your faith at all."

"And I failed that test of faith." Marius slumped again and his chair creaked like an old complaint.

"We're young, Marius. There are bound to be other tests," she replied, hoping there wouldn't be.

"That day, Ash Wednesday, he told me he had to keep his integrity and his identity intact and together or he would have felt dishonored. Why couldn't I understand that? Accept it? It seems simple enough now."

"It seems simple now because he is dead. It is not simple. It never was. For my father honor was not all neat and simple and cut from a single bolt of moral cloth, the warp and woof equal, the color uniform, the whole coat worn in the sunshine of everyone's approval. Sometimes to have honor you have to embrace uncertainty, the roughness and stubble of life. Sometimes you have to maintain your honor in the dark."

"In the sewer?" he taunted her. "In the prison?"

"Very well, then, Marius. Yes. In the sewer. In the prison." She endured the lengthy, empty silence, then announced, "I went to the

Convent of the Perpetual Adoration. The nuns told me my father's blue rose had bloomed this summer. At last."

"I don't care about the nuns or roses."

"He worked so hard to breed that blue rose, but he never saw it. Still, it bloomed without him. So all his work and effort and time—I mean, it might have pleased him more to know the blue rose bloomed this summer than if he had seen it, I mean," she faltered, "to know that the things you work for, the things you believe in, do not die with you, that the time he'd lavished on that blue rose had been rewarded."

"It was luck."

"It was not." Cosette rose, and with a decisive step she went to the green velvet drapes and gave them each a snap, and thick autumn sunshine spilled into the library. Dust motes swam and flew and tumbled crazily about. She stood, her small figure silhouetted in the flood of light, her honey-brown hair illuminated. Marius squinted against the dazzle till his eyes adjusted to the light and to the sight of his eighteen-year-old bride in an act of audacity. "I forbid you to close those drapes again." *Forbid* was not a word wives used on their husbands. Even the nuns knew that much. "My father forgave you, Marius. You have to forgive him."

"I cannot forgive myself."

"Sometimes death gives a kind of clarity to life, a clarity so bright and so terrible that you can't bear to see it, you want to keep everything closed up, as you have kept this room closed up. But you can't go on like this."

Cosette crossed to the desk and pushed the unopened law books, which fell, thudding, one after the other, to the floor. She pulled out some fresh, clean paper and set it before him. Marius turned to her, buried his face against her while she stroked his hair. "Marius, my love, my sweet, you can't live like this any longer. We are about to test your grandfather's old adage, 'Marry on Mardi Gras, produce no ingrate brats.'"

She enjoyed the shock on his face, enjoyed it the more when it turned to pleasure, to outright joy. "Oh, Cosette! Really?"

"Really."

"Well, when? How do you—? How long? How soon?"

"Not long, my love. And not soon. But certain. You see, everything is changing. Our lives, our futures—we can change the past too, Marius. You can. It's not set in stone. Only epitaphs and statues are set in stone. The past is fluid in the present." She took the pen and dipped it in the inkwell, held it till the fluid past dripped in a present splash, blue ink upon the white paper. She put the pen in his hand. "You've been hating the law for a long time, so leave the law. We have money. We have six hundred thousand francs, money my father earned. Let's take that money and put it to use. That money and this pen. There are newspapers all over Paris. Why not one more? It takes a lot of money to start a paper, but we can afford it. We could be using that money to fight the laws that would condemn a man to prison for stealing a loaf of bread. We could be using that money to fight the grief you feel for your friends."

"There are no words for the grief I feel."

"Yes, there are," she insisted. "You lived and they died. Then you should be their voice. There are words. Your friends believed in the Second Republic and the Rights of Man. My father believed in the goodness of man. You can do the work, write the words these dead cannot. My father's blue rose bloomed after his death. Why shouldn't your friends' ideas bloom after their deaths?" Cosette turned to the mantel and took down one of Jean Valjean's heavy silver candlesticks and used it to soften a bit of red sealing wax. She dripped it on the paper beside the blue ink, and setting the candlestick on the page before him, she said, "You see, there is your tricolor—paper, ink, and a seal, all in this light."

"*La lumière,*" remarked Marius.

Chapter 16

Jean-Luc Gillenormand Pontmercy, the eldest child of Marius and Cosette Pontmercy, was born 2 May 1834. Named in part for Marius's grandfather, the boy clearly seemed to have inherited Monsieur Gillenormand's insouciant charm and high-handed ways, and the old man recognized this instantly, although he died the following year, passed one night quietly—and completely out of character—without a single theatrical remark.

Jean-Luc Pontmercy grew up believing himself the center of the universe. Why shouldn't he? He had his mother's blue eyes and his father's black hair; he was lovable and loving, adorable and adoring, delightful especially when he got his own way. On those occasions when he did not, he was given to fearful tantrums, wheedling, even outright lying. He could do this with perfect confidence, knowing his Aunt Adelaide would back up any story he chose to tell. She doted on him as if he were her own son, indeed, more lavishly than if he were her own, since in that event she would have been responsible for him. As Aunt Adelaide saw it, her only responsibility was to indulge Jean-Luc and she did so with relish, going so far as to draw up legal documents settling her whole fortune on him upon her death. This was a considerable sum inherited from her mother, Monsieur Gillenormand's first wife, the one he had married for money. Marius's grandmother was the one he had married for love. Aunt Adelaide had never married at all, and loving Jean-Luc provided her with the passion she'd been denied all her life.

From the time he drew breath, Jean-Luc was so beloved by his parents that his mother refused to send him out to a wet nurse, despite the prevailing customs and beliefs. She nursed her daughter Fantine too. Cosette told Marius she had got the unusual name from a best friend at the convent, who had died, alas, of the cholera. Born in 1836, Fantine Marie Louise Pontmercy was equally adored by her parents, but her character was altogether different from her brother's. She seemed content to walk in Jean-Luc's shadow, joining happily in the general will of the world to give him his way. Fantine was a watcher. Her small mouth pursed pensively, and her great brown eyes watched the world with an astute, amused expression. She seemed always to be in the process of forming some unstated conclusion, while Jean-Luc was always in the process of conquering.

As these beautiful children grew and played and prospered, put their small hands unquestioningly, uncritically in Cosette's, she sometimes thought her heart would burst with joy, with pity for her own mother's terrible sufferings and gratitude to Jean Valjean.

He had endowed her life with love. When Cosette was a child he had protected and sheltered and taught her; he saved her from the stony grimness of the nuns with his smiles and ever-present affection. He had saved Marius's life so that in marriage Cosette could bloom as a woman. And with the six hundred thousand francs Jean Valjean left them, they took up the work that would both fulfill and imperil their lives. They took on, though they did not know it at the time, the work that would unite them and divide them, carry them to the highest reaches of French society and plunge them into the hovel and the prison. They too would have to find their way through thickets of identity, to balance, even choose, between integrity and freedom.

But as young parents, their lives seemed a sort of opera of love, not without its low notes, but full of happy arias as well. They had a carriage to convey them around Paris, to balls, concerts, salons; they had a box at the Théâtre-Française, and in Madame Carême a superb cook, whose dinners were legendary amongst their many friends—writers and poets, painters and printers, critics and editors. Cosette developed a reputation as a *lionne*, one of those witty women so frightening to Cousin Théo, and contrary to his warning, Cosette did have two beautiful children, though she lost a third in a miscarriage. She had beautiful clothes and a beautiful husband, believed in those years that time and memory balanced. In this she was wrong. Time and memory could no more be kept in step than Cosette could have sewn the waves to the shore at

Boulogne, where together she and Marius escaped Paris, winter and summer, so often in fact that the innkeeper, Monsieur Gérard, did not believe they were married.

Monsieur Gérard, an expansive romantic, concocted a fanciful notion of two lovers, snatching a bit of time from madame's husband, whom he pictured as a gouty provincial aristocrat, unworthy of his beautiful young wife. Now the dark-eyed lover, Baron Pontmercy, clearly he was worthy of her. Gérard was a man of about thirty whose father had died in Napoléon's débâcle in Russia. Monsieur Gérard himself had no need or wish ever to leave Boulogne. The world came to his inn. When Monsieur Gérard discovered that Marius's father had been a colonel in Napoléon's army, he was certain their fathers had been brothers-in-arms, and as an ardent Bonapartist, his infatuation with the young couple was complete, and he declared himself at their service for the rest of their lives.

At the time, it was enough for Marius and Cosette to walk the Boulogne beaches as the buoys clanged in the harbor and the boats groaned against the pilings, and in that time, the sea freed them. Cosette teased Marius that he loved the sea because it was gothic and unpredictable just like he was. But Marius knew the truth: he was altogether predictable and it was Cosette whose spirit was free and reckless as the waves. The strength of their union was that he was the beach she returned to again and again, faithful and forever as the tide.

But other than to Boulogne, they did not travel, save for back and forth between their home and the rue de Combray, the offices of *La Lumière,* the newspaper they founded with Jean Valjean's six hundred thousand francs. Before they could begin to print, they had to pay the government twenty-five thousand francs in caution money and endless obligatory stamp fees. Like all the other Opposition newspapers, they had to fight the government at every turn, in ongoing litigation, lawsuits the government instigated, capriciously invoking stringent press laws against Opposition editors.

The politics of *La Lumière* were simple and radical: free press, free rights of assembly, education free of the church, and the conviction that all men should have the vote and no man's labor should be exploited, the belief that no woman should be degraded into prostitution, and no childhood should be atrophied. Their masthead was a torch.

Marius hired talented writers and journalists, critics, an artist for caricatures, but only one man could print *La Lumière*: Verdier. Marius and he were, as far as they knew, the sole survivors of the barricade, though they kept the anniversary in June yearly in hopes someone else might yet appear. They went to the new nondescript café where the Corinth had once stood; undistinguished cuisine (certainly no *carpe ho ras*) and undistinguished clientele had replaced the roistering camaraderie, the high spirits and high hopes of the students and workers, but those spirits and hopes lived on in the pages of *La Lumière*. It was—as Verdier had vowed—words as weapons. In *La Lumière*'s spacious quarters on the rue de Combray, near the Boulevard des Italiens, Verdier took charge of the pressroom on the ground floor. And as Marius worked in the editorial offices above, the constant creak and rhythmic thump of the presses pleased him, reminded him always of the groaning of a great ship on a voyage of discovery.

Entr'acte

*B*efore dawn on the sixth of August 1840, Madame Gérard, always the first to rise, visited the ample henhouse she kept out back of the inn, gathered up the eggs, and selected six fat pullets to make their début on her table later in the day. She'd wrung their necks with her own fair hands and laid them out, along with an axe for the ministrations of the servant girl, a pale young person, already complaining the day's heat had given her a rash. Madame Gérard threatened her with a rash of a different sort if she didn't immediately pluck the chickens and cut off their heads. Then, grumbling, Madame Gérard climbed upstairs to wake her husband, who was no doubt deep in a vinous dream. He had been up late drinking, exchanging war stories with several of their guests, British and French. The Gérards' inn, the whole town of Boulogne in fact, had enjoyed a nice flush of tourist trade with the British the past few years, and Madame Gérard had altered her prejudices against them. They had money to spend, after all. The inn, which had prospered (no thanks to her husband), had begun as a cheap hostelry and now served such fine people as the Baron and Baroness Pontmercy, who came at least three or four times a year. Her husband thought they were runaway lovers. The fool. Love affairs don't last for seven years. No, they were married, Madame Gérard concluded, and besides, she didn't care if they were Napoléon and Josephine, they had money to spend. In fact Baron Pontmercy—and the young baroness too, if you can believe it— stayed up late last night, with her husband and the rest of the old soldiers, listening raptly to these fools, French fools, English fools, warbling on about their adventures, about Wellington and Waterloo and Cambronne and Marengo. What a lot of rot.

With little tolerance and no sympathy, Madame Gérard woke

her husband roughly and ordered him down to the fish market. Never mind his aching head, his furry mouth. She wanted the freshest fish. None of that stinking catbait the other places served. When you were the best, you could charge the most. Monsieur Gérard, cursing his wife genially, pulled on his clothes and set off toward the harbor.

To his shock a prattling Italian in an ancient French uniform ran into him in the street. Armed with a paste pot and a sheaf of papers, he was slathering proclamations on the walls and strewing them everywhere. Monsieur Gérard grabbed one of these and read: *Frenchmen! I see ahead a brilliant future for the country. I feel behind me the shadow of the Emperor, which pushes me on.* "Can it be?" Monsieur Gérard consulted the heavens gratefully. "Bonaparte!"

He bumped into another soldier, who thrust a handful of these proclamations at him along with a five-franc piece and told him to shout, *"Vive l'empereur!"* *"Vive l'empereur!"* cried Monsieur Gérard, leaping, throttling the pages, reading quickly: *To the French people: It is essential that glory and liberté should stand by the coffin of Napoléon, who always chose his lieutenants, his marshals, his princes, and his friends from amongst you.* "Vive l'empereur!" cried Monsieur Gérard repeatedly. *Voilà,* a glorious new era! Napoléon! That was the signature on the documents: *Napoléon.*

The name worked its magic on Monsieur Gérard, though the conqueror had been dead for years. This Napoléon, Louis-Napoléon, was the conqueror's nephew, son of his brother. To people like Monsieur Gérard, it was clear that Louis-Napoléon Bonaparte had landed his military might here at Boulogne and was about to snatch France back from their stuffy, stinking bourgeois kings and return her to the glories of empire. Crying the fabled, the sacred name repeatedly, Monsieur Gérard turned, tore back up the street toward his inn. He would call the fighting guard from last night! They would show those English swine with their talk of Wellington! This would be young Pontmercy's chance to do his father proud! The new Napoléon! Louis-Napoléon!

"Long live the king!" cried a neighbor, pulling on his National Guard uniform and running headlong into Monsieur Gérard, who decked him. (He would be fined for this altercation.) Monsieur Gérard was so beside himself with joy he was very nearly incoherent; he clutched the proclamation, gave his wife the five-franc piece, and raced up the stairs to the room of Marius and Cosette, banging on their door. "Louis-Napoléon! Prince Napoléon, the nephew of the Emperor, has invaded France! He's come from English exile to claim his rightful place in France!" He hammered on every door, all along the upper reaches of the inn, and all the old soldiers, French and British, and Marius and Cosette along with everyone else in Boulogne, tumbled into the street.

The whole crowd rippled down toward the column of the Grande-Armée, where the invaders were apparently heading. The night before, their force had been rowed ashore, landing in a nearby fishing village, crossing the fields in stealth and coming to Boulogne, where the city's garrison, the 42nd, had already engaged them, at least that was the rumor. One of many.

The August sun had already begun to broil down, and in the heat and tumult some of Monsieur Gérard's English guests were roughly handled when word ripped around that it was not Napoléon, but a British invasion. There was a British warship in the harbor with cannons leveled at their shores. No, cried a prostitute, it's Louis-Napoléon's ship! Our whole 42nd Regiment, the garrison of the town, has gone over to Louis-Napoléon! *Vive l'empereur,* she shouted as Monsieur Gérard embraced her. Nonsense! cried a baker, his floury hand grabbing Marius's sleeve, Prince Louis-Napoléon, you say? The men he brought with him, most don't even speak French. They are London waiters outfitted in old uniforms. Before waiters all France is supposed to cower? The king's army should capitulate to waiters? Ha! Confronted by Louis-Napoléon, the brave captain of the 42nd declared himself for the king and drew a sword on the invader and his foreign rabble. Some poor bastard of a soldier got shot right through the jaw. Shot in cold blood. Never mind the 42nd, cried a hobbling veteran of Marengo, the National Guard has gone over to Bonaparte! Maggot turd! cried out a National Guardsman, buttoning his uniform as he too joined the throng: the National Guard is loyal to the king. All the world is loyal to the king.

Perhaps, but amongst the swell of men and women and children running toward the column of the Grande-Armée, it was declared that those with penises were for Bonaparte. Scuffling, fighting broke out, fisticuffs. A mason called out *Vive la république,* and he and half a dozen republicans fought off four legitimists, two orleanists, and a priest, nearly getting left behind as everyone else surged downhill, the crowd thrilled to meet the subprefect, who showed off a rip in his waistcoat, where he'd been stabbed by an invader's pike. It wasn't a pike, it was a sword. It wasn't a sword, it was a broom. Listen, men!—cried out a carpenter, leading them on down the column de Grande-Armée—revolution has broken out all over France! Stand up and see Louis-Napoléon go by. Tell your children you've seen this day! Hurrah, cried a pickpocket cavorting through the crowd, making off with a week's work, pinching Cosette's embroidered cambric shawl right off her shoulders. She saw its lace fringe vanish before her eyes, but she and Marius ran on toward the docks, the beach, where they found the milling populace who had already had the invaders on the run, who had fired cabbages at them and flung oaths and now an old woman pitched a dead cat carcass which hit one of the soldiers who gibbered out something in "Polish?" Marius asked of Cosette, who shook her head. How would she know?

They saw him at last: Louis-Napoléon, nephew and scion of the late Emperor, the hope of the house of Bonaparte, a mustachioed man in a military uniform with a crop of thick hair, short legs, and a long torso, retreating comically with his gang of London waiters toward the harbor. The townspeople ran after them, the whole farcical troupe tumbling downhill, jeering to see Louis-Napoléon commandeering boats, jumping in with too many men, and beginning to row toward, yes—see, there it is, an English boat at the mouth of the harbor. No warship this: a wheezy steamer, the *Edinburgh Castle,* laden with food, wine, nine horses, two carriages, and a tame vulture tied by one claw to the mainmast, playing molting opéra-bouffe to the Imperial Eagle.

A naked bather just emerging from his morning dip found uniformed London waiters about to seize his small boat. He told them to cease, and all eleven men surrendered to him and dropped their weapons. His clothes held modestly before him the bather marched them back toward the dock, where the National Guard knelt in formation and opened fire at the other waiters and the fleeing prince, all of whom were futilely, stupidly splashing about the harbor, since no one knew how to row. The National Guard fired, killing one man instantly, and in the ensuing fracas, the boat overturned and another man drowned, but both the prince and his colonel swam to a buoy and clung there while it clanged mournfully, a tocsin calling to the fishes. Finally the *Edinburgh Castle* (boarded and overtaken by French customs officers) steamed in and plucked the two off the buoy. The steamer huffed toward the customs dock, and under heavy guard Prince Louis-Napoléon and his colonel were marched, dripping and draggled, into the Customs House.

By one o'clock the pullets Madame Gérard had selected at dawn lay crackling, golden, running juices and hissing steam, on plates along with roasted onions and sausages, so thick they burst under the fork. The diners at Gérard's Inn ate heartily, talked of nothing but the morning's antics. They laughed until they cried. Monsieur Gérard did not laugh. Monsieur Gérard wept. Marius sat on one side of him and Cosette on the other, comforting the crestfallen Bonapartist. Monsieur Gérard was about to wipe his eyes with one of the proclamations, but Marius traded him for a handkerchief. Marius read the proclamation, folded it neatly, and put it in his pocket to take back to Paris.

The invasion of Boulogne was opéra-comique, but the trial in Paris was pure Racine. Looking subdued, dignified, exemplary, tragic, the prisoner, Louis-Napoléon, declared that in his person he embodied a cause and defeat, "the cause that of empire, the defeat, Waterloo."

Marius avidly followed the trial, surprised to hear the nephew of Napoléon echoing the convict Jean Valjean: "All true Frenchmen know in their hearts we are the children of Waterloo, and before we die, we must fulfill the burdens imposed upon us by Waterloo." The press, including *La Lumière*, printed his every word. Speaking with a martyr's conviction and military aplomb throughout his trial for treason, Louis-Napoléon Bonaparte indicted not merely the current king, but all the kings of France. "There is but one victor and one vanquished," he declared before his judges, the Chamber of Peers. "If you are the victor's men, I cannot expect justice from you. And I will not have your generosity."

This was probably just as well since he did not get it.

"Unless," Cosette observed, "you count it generous that they did not execute him."

"They can't execute a Bonaparte," Marius insisted. "They'll probably invoke the law that says no Bonaparte may step foot in France and banish him."

"Again?" asked Cosette. "They banished him the last time, and clearly that didn't work."

Indeed it had not. Four years before, in 1836, Louis-Napoléon had invaded France at Strasbourg—an invasion equally inept, though not so comic. He had been quickly captured and just as quickly banished. The French government shipped Louis-Napoléon to America, where he lived for several months in New York, welcomed into a coterie of New York's literary and social élite and meeting, naturally, other well-heeled French exiles like Zelma Thénardier, who, like many women, found him absolutely irresistible.

But in 1840, after the Boulogne fiasco, the king's justice came down much more severely: perpetual imprisonment in the grim northern fortress of Ham. "Is anything in France perpetual?" inquired Louis-Napoléon laconically.

Six years might have seemed perpetual at Ham, a gaunt medieval castle near the village of Saint-Simon. Here Louis-Napoléon Bonaparte studied and wrote, called these his university years, and, if not treated quite royally, neither were his toes nibbled by rats. Comfortably housed in a three-room apartment, he had good food, good wine; he had papers, books, writing materials, newspapers (one of which was *La Lumière*), a dog, and the services of a valet, a physician, and a mistress, the laundress who washed his clothes and bore him two sons.

The collusion of the valet, the physician, and the mistress, and the fact that the castle was undergoing repairs, allowed the future president of the Second Republic, the future Napoléon III, Emperor of France, to shave his beard and mustache, don wooden clogs, a workingman's smock, a clay pipe jammed in his mouth, his face rouged (it would not be the last time he wore rouge), with a wig atop his head and a plank over his shoulder, and walk out of the fortress of Ham. A prearranged carriage took him to Valenciennes, a train to Brussels, and on the evening of 27 May 1846 he stood, hatless, at the rail of a steamer crossing La Manche bound for England, watching a storm obscure the coast of France.

The evening of 27 May 1846 Cosette and Marius were returning to the Boulogne harbor in a small borrowed sailboat after a day's picnic when the storm struck La Manche. Marius gave Cosette the tiller while he furled the sail and tightened the halyards, fastened them to a spar, and secured the boom so that rising winds would not capsize them. Then he took the oars. Cosette remained at the tiller, using all her strength against it. They could see the town, but it never seemed to come any closer. Night came on and before them the lights of Boulogne lit, but the wind swept them willy-nilly back and forth, or merely in circles, despite their best efforts and their failing strength. In the dark, waves troughed and billowed, bellied up and plunged down; the rain drowned their voices and they were certain the sea would drown their bodies. Knowing they were going to die, they clung all the harder to the tiller, to the oars, to life.

They thought perhaps they had already died when they saw the feeble light of a lantern tossing incongruously on the stormy waves, coming closer. Their shouts and screams caught the attention of this fishing boat, also making its way against the odds and toward the port. It dared not come too close, but the fisherman cast them a line and a grappling iron; three times he cast it before it caught. He tied that line to his own boat and pulled with both hands, bringing their sailboat close enough so he could throw them a stout rope, which Marius caught, then tied securely around Cosette's waist, and told her to hold tight and jump.

They burbled to her lips, all the reasons she would not leave him, but the rain, the wind, the seawater washed the words away, and so she did his bidding, took the line with both hands, gripped that thick rope, closed her eyes and leapt. The sea clawed at her skirts, dragging her down into its embrace, until she felt two strong hands wrapped round her wrists, and she was pulled up and on board, flung on deck as if she'd been a fish herself. Cosette scrambled to her feet, raced to the side, crying over the gunwales to see that the little sailboat had smashed itself against the larger vessel and the sea was gulping its hull, while Marius clung weakly and with one arm to another line held tight by the fisherman, who heaved and hoisted, wrapping his arms at last around Marius's chest while Cosette grabbed his legs, and they dragged him on deck, where he fell in a heap, moaning in pain, his left arm broken when their little boat broke up against the fishing vessel. Cosette held him in the pelting rain, wept with joy that he was alive, wept in fear that they would all die. The fisherman cut the grappling-iron line, and all trace of the sailboat vanished.

Scudding before the storm, they lurched toward port, where, avoiding the other moored boats, which were all tossing and flinging, slapping the waves, he slowly, expertly brought them up alongside pilings which themselves seemed to heave. He secured his lines to the pier, and shouted at Cosette she'd have to get Marius off as quickly as possible; he dared not tie up very close to the pier for long. He would stay on board; in this foul weather he would not abandon his boat, the *Saint-Joseph*, but slacken his lines and wait out the storm. The *Saint-Joseph* touched in close enough to the dock for Cosette to clamber out and help Marius, whose broken arm was swollen, the bone at an unthinkable angle. Marius leaned on Cosette and, buffeted by the storm, they made their way unsteadily through town, toward the shelter of Gérard's Inn, grateful for the firm street, if not dry land.

The next day, though his arm was set, Marius was in too much pain to leave their bed. Cosette asked Monsieur Gérard to stay with him while she walked back down to the harbor to find the *Saint-Joseph*, to thank the man who had saved their lives, to reward him. Her hands were swathed in thick bandages and she still felt shaky, though it was a fine day in May and the storm had passed in the night. Fishermen stood on the piers smoking their clay pipes, mending their sails, repairing their vessels, comparing this storm to others in the past (all of which were worse). She wandered over all the docks, searching, but with no luck. The *Saint-Joseph* was nowhere to be seen. The fishermen could not answer Cosette's questions, no, they had not seen a *Saint-Joseph*, not last night and not this morning, and word around the port was that no one had even ever heard of the *Saint-Joseph* and that there was no such boat.

BOOK II

THE REVOLUTIONARY WIND

Part I

The Lark and the Starling
JANUARY 1848

Do you not feel by some intuitive instinct . . .
that the earth is quaking once again in Europe?
Do you not feel . . . as it were, a gale of revolution in the air?
This gale, no one knows whence it springs, whence it blows,
nor, believe me, whom it will carry with it.

ALEXIS DE TOCQUEVILLE
Speech in the Chamber of Deputies
27 January 1848

Chapter 1

*H*ulking before the old Sergeant of Waterloo Inn, abandoned in the wake of some defeat—perhaps that of time over memory—there was a monstrous gun carriage, left there no one knew how or why, its iron and wood smothered in rust and mud. Across the axletree, riveted at either end, a huge chain looped from side to side. Madame Thénardier had put these wheels of war to more prosaic use and rigged up a swing for her little daughters, Eponine and Zelma, rocking them when they were too little to swing the heavy chain themselves. Its every link was as big as a man's fist and, to a child, each was heavy as an anchor. Maternally gratified to see her darling daughters gracing the chain, Madame Thénardier would rock them and sing "Partant pour la Syrie," a forgettable ditty written by Louis-Napoléon's mother, Hortense, who had the dual pleasure (if that's the correct word) of being the great Napoléon's stepdaughter as well as his sister-in-law, married off in 1802 to the emperor's syphilitic brother.

When Eponine and Zelma were old enough to swing the grotesque chain themselves, they would resolve their childish quarrels by having Cosette push them. So Cosette pushed and pushed, the muscles in her little arms twisting around her bones as she pushed Eponine and Zelma, who, when they tired of their own voices, insisted Cosette should sing "Partant pour la Syrie" and amuse them: sing, Cosette, you're the Lark, sing and push, the groan, the rusty moan of the chain for accompaniment, sing till your voice breaks and your heart breaks and your loveless life breaks and the chain breaks and Eponine and Zelma tumble, plunge beyond the reach of clock or compass, while Cosette fights her way to wakefulness.

Instinctively, she moved to wrap her aching arms around Marius's chest, to breathe in his spicy scent, his warmth, to put her head on his shoulder. But the place beside her in bed was cold, and Cosette pulled his pillow close and lay there, eyes wide, relieved to hear the silence, not Madame Thénardier's horrible laugh. It was 5 A.M. and the empty bed seemed full of fear and longing. She pushed open the bed curtains, lit a candle, pulled on a cashmere dressing gown with Venetian sleeves, and slid her feet into heelless *nonchalantes*. Shivering, she went to the fire and rekindled it, kneeling there, her feet tucked up. She watched the flames.

There were times when Cosette would have parted with her every principle just to have her love in her arms again. Marius would never have said the same; he seemed sometimes like those old explorers, certain of that better country that lay in the future, certain too the route could be navigated by the stars alone. Marius steered *La Lumière* toward some destination he could all but see. In the beginning of this great voyage, Marius had scooted *La Lumière* around the government's gagging press laws like a skiff outwitting a frigate, though in recent years it seemed to Cosette that he had become less the captain of this ship and more its figurehead, and it was, moreover, an expensive and uncertain voyage.

Since 1843 the government had arrested Marius sixty-seven times for seditious libel, and he had endured the drain and strain, the cost and anguish of the trials, though he'd suffered only thirteen convictions. Cosette went to court every day that Marius did, and like him she was pleased when juries refused to convict. It was refusal, not failure, to convict. The mood across France, across all Europe, was changing. With one bad harvest after another for the past few years, people grew hungry, restless, hungrier yet, angry, and Cosette wondered how the well-to-do, those in power, could fail to see that the people's anger was viscerally connected to their hunger.

Those sixty-seven trials exacted a terrible toll on Marius, on *La Lumière* as well, a newspaper powerful without being popular; subscriptions never numbered more than about four thousand, but its influence was felt all over France, and its insignia, the torch, became a sort of symbol amongst radicals of every stripe. Marius believed the sedition trials served some higher purpose. The trials certainly provided a fine public forum. All France—people denied the right of political assembly—could gather after work, a few at a time, in their cafés, over a glass of wine, a leisurely smoke perhaps, a rousing gathering of the *goguettes*, where in between songs they could talk about the government's vendetta against *La Lumière*, discuss sedition—without engaging in it. The trial provided a field day for the other republican papers; from constitutional republicans to radical socialists, they could all report on sedition—without engaging in it. Everyone discussed the sedition trials; even in the Chamber of Deputies they waxed eloquent; café pundits, people in salons and on street corners, in boudoirs and bistros waxed eloquent—while Marius Pontmercy continued to pay the fines and enter Sainte-Pélagie prison with a kind of gallantry no one else could have equaled.

Sometimes Cosette longed to tell Marius that the sacrifices he made were not wholly his own. The suffering he endured he also inflicted. Little Fantine had started keeping a scrapbook of all her father's trials for sedition, carefully cutting accounts from the other papers, and with a great pot of glue slathering them inside a book she called *Papa*. When Jean-Luc had school holidays he resisted spending them in the courtroom or visiting his father in prison. In his thirteen convictions, Marius served sentences of six weeks to six months, and Jean-Luc resented it when his mother declined to allow him to join wealthy friends and their families, citing his obligations to his father. For Cosette, Marius's long hours in the courtroom, the long weeks in Sainte-Pélagie prison meant that she took up the pen on his behalf more and more often. She wrote under his name and sometimes Marius was indicted for articles Cosette had written, but she could not embrace his conviction that fighting these sedition laws would ever bring about a free press. Sometimes, she pointed out, the arrests were so swift it seemed as though the government knew what they were going to print before they went to press. Cosette admired Marius's courage, but she did not want to share it with all France. She wanted his courage, his body, his warmth here, in their home, in their bed, with her. Still she could never quite bring herself to say these things; they might have seemed disloyal, perhaps even cowardly. She glanced from the fire to the bed and rested her head on her hands. Well, if she could not sleep, perhaps she could work.

She took a candle to light her way through the dark house and went to the library, where she opened the drapes, lit the lamp, the fire, and her father's silver candlesticks. The work lay before her as it had for years: when Marius was in prison, they would smuggle out his notes, and Cosette took them home and fashioned them into eloquent articles for *La Lumière*. To the readers of *La Lumière*, it looked as though its editor were absolutely unstoppable and the torch undimmed even in the prison. But in the small, acrimonious world of Parisian journalists, it was well known that Madame Pontmercy did much of the work, and it was rumored as well that the sedition trials were draining *La Lumière* of funds and of much of the talent Marius had originally assembled. As *La Lumière* became more and more radical, committed to the broader notions of social justice, more men left. It was all very well to whisper about rights of workers among like-minded men, but not many had the courage to go to jail for them.

Each time Cosette brought the finished pieces into the rue de Combray, the managing editor, Achille Clerons, with a cloying excess of courtesy, always told her not to bother her pretty head with the workers in the white-lead factories who died such grue-some deaths, or the number of suicides fished out of the Seine, or the effects of the potato famine on France. Women were not meant to take up the pen. Women unsexed themselves in print. His atti-tude, he always hastened to explain, did not extend to gossipy columns or frothy novels serialized in the major papers. Even Del-phine Gay, wife of Emile de Girardin, of France's biggest paper, *La Presse*, wrote such a column and no one thought the less of her. However, Clerons quipped, some thought the less of Girardin.

Such a remark passed for humor with Clerons. Cosette had tried to like him, and couldn't. But Marius relied on him. And of course the more time Marius spent in the courtroom and the jail, the more the day-to-day running of *La Lumière* fell to Clerons. Marius admired Clerons and felt for him a fraternal bond forged in memory, the reflexive loyalty of battle and shared losses and values.

Where the old Corinth had once stood, there was a new café, modern and gleaming, but with none of the old character or cama-raderie of the place that had been completely destroyed by the cannon. On the very back wall, though, where Feuilly had scratched *Vive le peuple!*, the inscription remained, and faithfully, every year on 6 June, Marius and Verdier sat at that table and ordered a bottle of wine and drank to the friends they had lost. In 1842, ten years after these deaths, the two men began with the youngest name, *Gavroche*, and drank to him, and then *Pajol*, and drank to him. A solitary man sitting nearby had approached them. Gingery beard, a strong jaw, wild eyebrows, his fingers stained with tobacco, he wore good clothing, though frayed and untended, and he carried a satchel. He said, *Better the sword than the scaffold, better the scaffold than the gutter.* He opened the satchel and drew out the National Guard uniform that had changed Marius's life—indeed saved Marius's life—Jean Valjean's uniform. The uniform given to the fifth man, Achille Clerons.

Clerons explained to Verdier and Marius that he had come to the site of the battle to have one last drink, then he intended to put on the uniform and jump into the Seine, so sad and fruitless had been his life these past ten years. The wife and children he had lived for had died. Marius clutched the uniform that had saved his life as well, said he could not offer Clerons family, but he could offer him friends; he could offer him work. And so Clerons came to *La Lumière*. Over the years he seemed to Cosette quick to take offense, long to remember that offense, methodical, occasionally malicious, and efficient in a way she found chilling. Most radical journalists might quarrel into the night, denounce one another as idiots, and argue about the relative merits of a Republic no one truly expected to see, but they had for the most part a messy vivacity Cosette always found appealing. Clerons remained enigmatic, a man with no private life, no mistresses, no wife, and no mention ever of the family he'd lost.

Ah, well, she told herself, little as I like him, he's loyal to Marius. She drew the silver candlesticks across the desk so their light fell more evenly over Marius's notes, notes she had smuggled out of Sainte-Pélagie prison. They lay here now in disarray, creased and wrinkled, some words blurred with dampness, the ink swollen with her perspiration, the notes inflammatory in more ways than one.

When she went to visit him in Sainte-Pélagie, a few francs slipped to the turnkey would buy them undisturbed time, and they made love on the narrow bed in his cell. Afterward Marius helped her dress, and page by page he tucked these notes in her bodice and every time she moved her arms, she felt them crinkle. He tucked them in her stockings and she felt them every time she moved her legs, and sometimes the act of smuggling was so aphrodisiac that half-clad couplings lengthened her visits, and the pain of walking away from him was all the more intense for the pleasure he had given her. But when she left Sainte-Pélagie, her gloved hands were free, her pockets and basket empty. These pieces of paper, secreted amongst her clothes, still reeked of love, of the smell of Marius's hands and body, of the fragrance she and Marius made together, which wafted up from the desk like a renegade hyacinth and made her smile. For Cosette to take his notes and ideas and fashion them into cogent arguments was another act of love. A different kind of act, the same love.

Cosette dipped her pen in the ink and set to work on his notes as the January dawn skulked into the library like a great gray cat, settled on the carpets, then crept up the lined walls.

Later a servant came in, surprised to find the fire already lit and Madame Pontmercy up. She asked if Cosette wanted coffee and a brioche. "The schoolroom is ready, madame, and Mademoiselle Fantine is having her breakfast in the kitchen."

"Merci." Cosette rose, stretched and walked to the window. She well knew that Marius did not like Fantine to eat breakfast in the kitchen, chatting with the cook. Well, if Marius went to prison for the French Republic, he could not expect to rule in the domestic Republic, could he? The fact that Fantine was being educated at home was a victory for Cosette. She'd given in to his wish that Jean-Luc should board at the famous Lycée Henri IV, but she did not want to send her daughter to a convent school. Cosette could not bear to think of little Fantine sleeping in cold stone dormitories, her childish laughter stifled by long hours of prayer, her bright imagination channeled by nuns. Cosette's own convent education had not been repressive because her father was there in the gardener's cottage, a daily source of affection and support, his warm embrace redolent of the garden, not the cloister. In truth, Cosette could not bear to be parted from Fantine. But these were not the arguments Cosette used. In order to win her point she'd simply

said she did not want to see their daughter preserved in religion like a bonbon in sugar. This convinced Marius because like most Opposition editors and confirmed radicals, his biases were wholly anticlerical. Indeed, the piece Cosette was writing today was resolutely anticlerical.

She stared out over the garden, clad in the rag ends of winter, and smiled to think how Pascal Beaujard would take her words and make them vivid. Beaujard was the best caricaturist in Paris, and no doubt he would sketch some sepulchral bishop throttling a steamboat in one hand and locomotive in the other. Perhaps he'd have church prelates, ugly as starlings on roof tiles, squatting over Knowledge, Science, Progress, treading the nineteenth century underfoot.

The servant returned with a tray of coffee, and Cosette set back to work while the life of the house went on around her. Faintly she could hear Fantine's two cousins, Théo's children, arrive to share her lessons, and the little girls' bright voices echoed down from their schoolroom on the floor above. The tutor arrived, his jaunty tread unmistakable. Aunt Adelaide returned from early mass at Saint-Denis. The servants padded up and down, but suddenly all that was shattered by a crash in the front entry, and a great altercation ensuing.

Cosette rushed downstairs to find her son standing framed in the doorway, yelling, "Damned thief!" at a coachman who had scrambled off his carriage and followed Jean-Luc to the door, calling him a baby-pricked bastard, while the servants stood gaping or snickering. Upstairs the little girls hung over the banister eagerly, the tutor right behind them, while Aunt Adelaide hyperventilated, a letter in her hand.

"Jean-Luc!" Cosette quickly closed the door, without the slightest effect on the cabdriver, who pounded against it, calling down more curses. "What's wrong? Why are you here? What's—"

"He's stealing me blind for a ride across Paris, the thieving—"

"Jean-Luc," Cosette cried in dismay, "not the cab! Why aren't you in school?"

At thirteen Jean-Luc Pontmercy was more solidly built than his father, and he had his mother's blue eyes and smile, but his features were still caught in the crosscurrents connecting the province of the child to the country of the man. He wore the student's school uniform—black coat, high collar, white necktie, and blue woolen stockings—but on his face was a thoroughly adult amalgam of chagrin, defiance, and contrition. He said he needed money to pay the cabman—still pounding on the door—and he took the letter from Aunt Adelaide and gave it to his mother. It was written on heavy cream-colored stationery, with the seal of the Lycée Henri IV, the signature of the headmaster.

Chapter 2

$\mathcal{A}$ balding man, blue-eyed and dazed, stumbled through the red umbrellas dappling the old market district amidst the cacophony and stench of Les Halles, wandering, seemingly lost amidst the cold splash of coins, bouquets of scent, bunches of rosemary and thyme hanging in the herb market, and the odors of straw and animals. Horses brayed and whinnied, steamed in the midmorning cold. The smell of earth, of raw vegetation, rose from wagons carting winter vegetables, and the smell of blood rose from wagons carting whole quarters of beef and game. Across the top of one of these, strung like an amber necklace, a dozen iridescent pheasants hung, lurching rhythmically with every roll of the wheels over the paving stones. This man's feet were shoved into wooden *sabots* that country people wear for shoes, and his ankles were ringed with sores, many festering; his wrists too were chafed and angry, his clothing frayed, inadequate to the season. His thin chest was blue, the hair as sparse as that on his head. Ample farm women, their hands as tough as hooves, bright scarves over their heads, stared at him, assessing him knowingly. For his part, he stared at their breasts and their cabbages with equal hunger.

He made inquiries where he could, where people did not spurn him on sight, but amongst this tribe of vendors, auctioneers, inspectors, hawkers, people whose color and corpulence and good spirits testified to steady employment, to plenty if not surfeit, this man looked like a wraith. Shivering before the church of Saint-Eustache, he was scorned by people who scurried away from the dark church and the pale man before it. Even those few who listened to his question, who heard him out, shrugged, shook their heads, and moved on, no, they had never heard of a Corinth bistro anywhere around here. He was in the wrong street. The rue Mondétour? It was over there, yes, over there somewhere. They pointed vaguely to the east and moved on when they noticed the sores on his ankles, the great bruised knobs of his wrists, the squint in his blue eyes. The eyes of a man dazzled by daylight.

Finally he accosted an old man, smock-clad and stinking of fish, hoisting heavy baskets of silvery herring, one after the other. No, the Corinth was long gone, destroyed in 1832 when a band of gallant men held out there for the Republic and were slaughtered by the National Guard.

"Vive la république," said Victor Pajol, the phrase rusty on his tongue.

"Number 102 rue Mondétour," said the fishmonger. "There's a café there, yes, but it's not the old Corinth. The Corinth—" His shoulders lifted expressively, his palms opened to the sky, his mouth contorted around the unsaid: all that, long vanished, mortar dissolved with memory, hope ground under the heel of time.

Chapter 3

*T*he Pontmercy carriage was well oiled, polished, and the horse a sleek animal, but the driver, Abel, reeked of sweat and smoke and alcohol so pungent it seemed to circumvent his liver altogether and pop out of his pores. Muffled in a huge greatcoat, he guided the horse through Paris, where the traffic stalled and tangled, as omnibuses, cabriolets, fiacres, lumbering wagons and vending carts, huge old diligences leaving the city for provincial destinations, and every other form of modern motion struggled in the medieval streets, as pedestrians cursed and darted amongst the wheels. Abel crossed the Seine at the Pont au Change, passing in the shadow of the Palais de Justice, and on the left, the Ile-de-la-cité, disfigured by sheds and hovels, low cabarets, rotting and clinging together there since Saint-Louis left for the Crusades. People who lived here had a well-deserved reputation as thieves, thugs, and assassins; their romantic adventures were chronicled in the pages of Eugène Sue's *Mysteries of Paris,* enjoyed by all France when it appeared serially in *La Presse.* The reality was not so picturesque and Abel hastened the horse across the Ile-de-la-cité. He had no wish to have his courage tested by these low, lurking creatures; he had been without a drink now for hours. The carriage wheels churned up a spray compounded of slushy snow, animal dung and urine, effluvia, ground garbage, and the contents of a hundred chamberpots. As they crossed the Pont Saint-Michel, drove along the quai Saint-Michel, and thence down the rue Saint-Jacques, the massive Panthéon loomed over the whole quarter, dominating the sky, its dome dusted with snow, sparkling in the afternoon light. Fair and foul hunkered cheek by jowl in old Paris.

He turned the horse into the rue Clovis, stopped before the Lycée Henri IV, and opened the door for Madame Pontmercy, who bid him wait for her. Abel shivered noisily. "If you please, madame, if it gets too cold, you won't mind me waiting in the church, would you?" He nodded toward the church of Saint-Etienne-du-Mont.

"Not if I truly believed that was the church you worshiped in," Cosette commented crisply, holding her breath against Abel's vinous presence.

The porter at the Lycée Henri IV gasped to see a lone woman passing through the school's ancient gates. His breath fogging and puffing on the January air, he sputtered and naturally denied Cosette's request to see the headmaster. She debated the wisdom of an outright bribe, but decided to hold that possibility in abeyance. "I'm here on behalf of my son, Jean-Luc Pontmercy." His wizened face wrinkled into a grin, and he twisted his mittened hands, kicked the snoozing servant boy curled up behind the door, ordering him to go to the headmaster's office and ask if monsieur le directeur would deign to grant an audience (that's how he phrased it) to Madame Pontmercy. "Baroness Pontmercy," she corrected him, having learned over the years that the title could be effectively used like a lever, smoothed as an emollient, brandished like a weapon. But it had no effect whatever on the porter, who slammed his door against her, muttering imprecations against women coming to the school and women in general.

Left alone, looking to an enclosed courtyard where the gray stones were powdered by snow that itself seemed gray, she pulled her velvet cloak closely about her shoulders and chafed her gloved hands. At thirty-two Cosette's youthful beauty had mellowed into something more dramatic and expressive. Her thick hair was worn simply, knotted high on her head, stray curls escaping from under her bonnet, and her blue eyes were brilliant and direct. She exuded a sort of complex bouquet bred of paradox—a woman at once fulfilled and spirited, content but not complacent, energetic but not frenetic, at ease in the world because she had some great secret from it: vintage love in a cask of loyalty. Marius took no mistresses and Cosette took no lovers, and in the circles in which they traveled their unique domestic arrangements were the occasion of mirth amongst the men and envy amongst the women.

The young servant returned to say no, the headmaster would not see her. This was hardly surprising since his letter had been addressed to Baron Pontmercy, as though Jean-Luc had no mother at all. Resorting to a bribe, she produced two francs, which had the immediate and desired effect. Her boots snapped smartly as she followed the servant down passageways that were low, dank, and medieval. Lycée Henri IV, like other schools for young gentlemen, prided itself on the punishment it could inflict on their bodies while enhancing their minds. The regime, the order of silence, the buildings themselves reeked of the cloister and indeed, Cosette reflected, the jail.

The boy knocked at the headmaster's door, swung it open, and bolted; Cosette stood face-to-face with Monsieur Liancourt, who had been a teacher here when Marius was a student. A dozen candles burned on his desk so he could read a newspaper spread there, and the little spectacles perched on his nose could not conceal the surprise on his face. He wore academic robes and over them a shaggy, thick sort of shawl and matching shaggy cap, which seemed to curl atop his head. He had yellowish eyes and coarse skin, which was scrubbed around painfully close-shaven cheeks. All in all he looked like a sheep in sheep's clothing, but he announced in no uncertain terms that he could not discuss this matter with anyone but Jean-Luc's father.

"My husband cannot be here, so it falls on me to—"

"These are not matters I can discuss with a woman."

Cosette glanced at the newspaper lying across his desk, the *Gazette de France*. "Since you read the royalist press, you must know that my husband is serving a sentence for seditious libel in Sainte-Pélagie."

"It is against the laws of France to criticize the king or his government. As the king's minister, Monsieur Guizot is above reproach. Just or unjust, it is the law." Like his chamber—unplastered stone walls hung with fading tapestries and heavy funereal furniture built to accommodate ogres—his certitude was gothic. "I am not an admirer of your husband or his politics. He certainly did not learn the history lessons I taught here. History is a cart, an old cart best pulled in grooves, in ruts even. Sometimes the cart breaks down, loses a wheel. It sits there in the path of progress. One repairs it so it may go on revolving. Your husband's notion of revolution destroys the cart."

"And the rut," she observed.

He folded his newspaper carefully. "I shall discuss this with you, madame, so that when your husband is released from prison there will be no need to repeat this regrettable interview."

He paused, clearly waiting for her to say *merci,* and she obliged him. With one yellowed hand he gestured toward the stiff chair opposite his desk; she sat down, as though perched on the lower mandible of a great beast. She wondered how often Jean-Luc had sat here.

Monsieur Liancourt asked if she had his letter with her. "Did Jean-Luc tell you his offense? Did he elaborate?"

Cosette rather tiptoed around this because Jean-Luc would say only it was a stupid misunderstanding, and then immediately Aunt Adelaide had swooped into the conversation, heaping abuse on the Lycée Henri IV and on the headmaster, berating the teachers, the ushers, the other students, attacking anyone who could be so benighted as to misunderstand when a boy—Jean-Luc, for example—when asked to hand over a note a friend had written him, had refused. Naturally he'd refused. Who could fail to understand why the boy—Jean-Luc, say—had torn that note up, chewed it, and swallowed it in the headmaster's presence. Aunt Adelaide declared Jean-Luc ought to be rewarded for such bravery, taken to Tortoni's for ice cream. Cosette had sent him to his room.

Sitting here now in those same chambers, Cosette offered in her son's defense, "The punishment—expulsion—seems unsuited to the minor offense."

His vellum-colored eyes rested on her. "Minor offense? Jean-Luc declared himself ready to suffer the torments of Inquisition, indeed the pain of the Reign of Terror, rather than divulge this note. Moreover, he recited all this as though the pits and galleries of the Théâtre-Française hung upon his every word, rather than—as you can see—a more modest and disapproving audience. Me." He folded one great paper-dry paw over another. "Jean-Luc then tore the note to tiny shreds, thrust them into his mouth, and swallowed them. I assume they will shortly pass through the usual portals."

"Who wrote the note?"

"My question precisely."

Cosette unbuttoned her cloak, removed her gray leather gloves, and loosened the ribbons of her bonnet; though the day was cold and the fire inadequate, she could feel herself pinking and perspiring under the headmaster's obdurate gaze.

"The letter of itself is of little consequence. Rather it was an expression, how shall I say, of levity, of irreverence, a spirit of frivolity"—Monsieur Liancourt drew the latter word out as though strangling on a piece of tripe—"inconsistent with Lycée Henri IV. I do not approve of your husband, but at least he was a serious boy. Your son continually undermines discipline. He smuggles in forbidden books—Hugo, Balzac, de Musset, the dreadful George Sand, Eugène Sue. He shows no remorse when apprehended. One outrage follows another. This business of the letter was but the straw that broke the proverbial camel's back." He harumphed phlegmatically and in keeping with his allusion. "Lycée Henri IV cannot tolerate such behavior. We are raising up a new generation of statesmen here. Doctors! Diplomats!"

"Journalists," Cosette countered. "My husband was a student here. So was Emile de Girardin of *La Presse*."

"*La Presse* is scarcely any better than *La Lumière*."

"Indeed, *La Lumière* quite outshines it."

"Wit in women is like a frock coat on a cart horse." Monsieur Liancourt turned to study a few freezing pigeons fluttering along the roof slates, before continuing, "If you have followed your son's academic progress at Lycée Henri IV, then you know that in Latin, Greek, philosophy, rhetoric, mathematics, and religion, his progress has been less than sterling—put bluntly, fruitless. He is weak, mediocre, shallow—in and of themselves not bad traits—but he is irreverent, madame, and such a combination is intolerable. Jean-Luc pays not the slightest heed to the rules and has struck up a dangerous friendship with a day student, Arsène Huvet. Do you know this name?"

"Yes, of course. My son often speaks of him, but I've never met him. He returns to the provinces during holidays."

Monsieur Liancourt's fleshy lips curled in distaste. "His father is a grocer in Clermont-Ferrand. Arsène lives in Paris with an aunt or some decrepit female relative in the Chaussée-d'Antin. He entered this academy under false pretenses, under the patronage of a great lady of Clermont-Ferrand who—" he paused, sucking uncomfortably on his teeth.

"Repaid her debts by sponsoring the grocer's talented young son into one of France's premier academies?"

"Arsène Huvet has the instincts of a man committed to totting up the cost of sugar."

"What has that to do with Jean-Luc?"

"Your son is a young man of considerable charm. Personally, I disapprove of charm, save in the aristocracy, where, unfortunately it is very much wanting, but you keep your son on a rather tight tether for an allowance, if I'm not mistaken."

"An adequate allowance."

"Not for the pleasures he seeks. Arsène Huvet, on the other hand, has a good deal of money, but he lacks charm. He lacks, well, everything that makes a gentleman, and he needs Jean-Luc for an entrée, shall we say, into the world of pleasure, I speak of the theatre, madame," he bleated vehemently, "days at the Chaumière, nights at the Bobinot, frequenting cafés and cheap student eateries like Flicoteaux, where they eat potatoes like the Irish, who, of course, are not eating at all these days. I speak of money spent to buy wine, madame, used to bribe the porter, the ushers, the servants, and other students of Lycée Henri IV, so that your son might trump up his bedclothes so as to look like a boy sleeping safe in his dormitory bed, while actually he and Arsène Huvet are out cavorting in the Latin Quarter with women twice their age."

"That isn't possible. He's not yet fourteen!"

"Nonetheless, it has come to our attention"—he spoke as though he and the ghost of King Henri IV had been together apprised—"that many's the night Arsène Huvet escapes from his elderly relative and your son takes the measures I've described, and with Huvet's money, off they go to the *grisettes*. Yes, madame, *grisettes*. I know many people believe *grisettes* are harmless shop-girls looking for a bit of good time, a few trinkets from student lovers while their looks hold out and the boys are away from familial supervision, but I assure you none of that is true. They are prostitutes. Apprentice prostitutes."

"Surely you're being too harsh."

He raised his bleary eyes and tied the strings on his strange cap as though fearful Cosette might snatch him bald, staring out the window to the thin snow, wondering aloud how a woman of

Madame Pontmercy's station in life could condone sexual union outside marriage.

Cosette believed Monsieur Liancourt had never known sexual union in any state, or province for that matter, but she waited till he had quite finished before she asked when her son would be allowed to return to Lycée Henri IV.

"When he has learned religion, respect, humility. When he takes less interest in the girl who sings at the café-cabaret and more in the Holy Fathers of the church. When he reads less Balzac and more Pascal, a writer who reminds us of man's eternal misery."

Pompous old pedagogue, miserable philistine, Cosette thought, as she rose, defeated. "I will send a servant for Jean-Luc's things tomorrow."

"The books—Hugo, de Musset, Balzac, the poems and plays— they will all be gone," he reflected gloomily. "The other boys will steal them."

Chapter 4

*T*he gates of Lycée Henri IV slammed soundly behind her, and once in the rue Clovis, Cosette was dismayed to find not only the coachman gone but the horse and carriage too. She cursed Abel's drinking, and while prudence dictated she should walk to the Panthéon, find a cab, return to her home, and wait for Abel to come groveling back, she was too angry to wait idly. Besides, how far away could Abel be and how could one misplace a horse and carriage?

She turned into the rue Descartes and went down the rue Mouffetard, a street whose path was first beaten out by Roman legions and whose reputation for lawlessness in the Middle Ages was succeeded by a reputation for stench. For hundreds of years tanners and skinners and horse knackers set themselves up here beside the river Bièvre. Even now the first shop she passed was a *charcuterie,* where greasy sausages gleamed on hooks, pale blood ran in the snow, and dogs fought audibly over the offal. The rue Mouffetard was one of those energetic arteries, crass, commercial, some shops solidly and clearly there forever, presided over by families who had taken three generations to come down from the garrets and up from the cellars, to have the shop on the ground floor and a comfortable apartment above, the petit bourgeois. But most of the commerce in the rue Mouffetard was on foot. From makeshift stalls vendors offered mussels with the seaweed still clinging to them, or hoisted baskets of corrugated cauliflowers, cabbages of indifferent color. In the rue Mouffetard peddlers crying out the splendors of their fried potatoes stood before tobacconists' shops and grocers where the smell of grinding coffee tinged the air. Now, at the end of the day, one set of commercial transactions was coming to a close and another just beginning, as the women moved in on the vendors—whose wares were well past their first freshness—and began to harangue them, waiting till the late afternoon to drive their bargains home. A turnip seller grasped two of her wares high overhead and waved them about, crying out lyrical comparisons between the size of her turnips and the balls of the men who ate them. A juggler's balls spun high in the air, and given the thin, flappy garment he wore, no doubt his other balls contracted with the cold.

In the early winter evening Cosette pulled her blue velvet cloak closer just to look at ill-clad street musicians squeezing wheezy concertinas and rattling battered tambourines, playing to the mostly empty hats that lay before them on the pavement. She stopped to watch a family of street musicians provide accompaniment for a little blue-lipped girl who sang and danced. Cosette reached in her pocket and threw a five-franc piece at her feet; the girl's face—and the faces of all her family—lit up. The music stopped instantly and all of them repaired to the nearest café. Cosette followed, glancing inside for the inebriate coachman, but through the smoke and noise she could not see him. She could not see the horse and carriage in the street, for that matter.

Sidestepping brewers' wagons and laundry vans (and grateful she was wearing high-heeled boots for all the horse dung and urine stinking up the street, some so fresh it steamed), she made her way through the clamor of the rue Mouffetard, where vendors' pipes and horns and cries chimed in a crazy crescendo, a concerto of commerce at the end of the day when tinkers and crockery menders, porters, and knife grinders tried for a last few sous before the lamplighters took up their tasks. Cosette's cloak and fashionably ruched bonnet contrasted vividly amongst the brown and black, rusty-clad matrons hawking their wares. One of these women, standing guard before her secondhand clothing stall, reached out for a feel of the blue velvet cloak.

"When you're ready to sell, dearie—" she cried after her—"I'll give you good weight for that cloak."

Men ogled Cosette and women assessed her as she made her way through the calls of hawkers; sweat streamed down windows of the laundries and steam billowed out the transoms as half-clad girls, their faces rosy with heat and exertion, lifted great groaning baskets. Outside a butcher shop a rag-and-bone man quarreled with the owner, and it ended with the butcher telling the rag-and-bone man to take his own ugly carcass off the step and the latter retorting that the butcher was the son of a whore and the husband of a slut. As he hoisted his pack and walked away, Cosette saw thick, still-bloody thigh bones hideously protruding.

All along the rue Mouffetard, evenly spaced as the Stations of the Cross, were beggars, beggars as various as the vendors. There were veteran beggars wearing the last bits of their ragged Grande-Armée uniforms, legless beggars, disaster beggars, crippled beggars, bandaged beggars, beggars clad in respectable clothing worn to its final fray, who chalked out on stones or walls, "I am starving," and smiled with black and broken teeth. There were beggars with sores and beggars without. And amongst all these there were bouncers and besters and skinny waiters scurrying to evening shifts, there were fences and bawds and bullies and cadgers and cloak twitchers (of whom Cosette was especially wary), short-heeled wenches, and light-fingered boys.

Straw in the street before one building suggested someone mortally ill in an apartment above; the unsoftened wails of babies and domestic discord rang out despite windows closed against the cold. A scrawny girl with a toddler clinging to her skirts kept up her pathetic cry selling bootlaces. A man carrying a high rack of toys—including dolls hanging in hideous postures suggestive of the gallows—sang childish songs in a lugubrious voice. Most of the children loitering on the rue Mouffetard reflected Cosette's own childhood—big eyes, dirty faces, insubstantial clothes, mouths cinched from want, wary expressions looking out for the next blow, wearing the bruises of those they'd not been able to dodge, working, toting loads too big, or looking after babies too small to look after themselves. The smoke from a chestnut roaster's charcoal burner blew in her eyes, and she screamed when, pirouetting in front of her, a ragged, pale young man, hands clasped to his bosom, eyes cast to heaven, cried out, "Bread! Bread! I'm dying of hunger in the streets!" With a wretched rattle in his throat, he fell at her feet, face down in the muck, unmoving.

Cosette stared at him, horrified to hear laughter behind her, a cackling chorus coming from two street vendors, one with a tray full of apples and one with a basket of onions. "Don't give him anything, madame," cautioned the apple seller, "he'll die in the rue Saint-Denis tomorrow."

"And he'll die in front of the Odéon tonight." The onion seller gave him a swift kick in the backside.

He roused, doubled his fist, and brushed the straw and horse dung off his rags as he cursed the women for not minding their own business.

"We have to rid ourselves of beggars like you," the onion vendor spat, "get you off the streets and make room for honest working women."

"You're only honest because you're too old to whore," replied the recently near dead.

"Have you seen a horse and carriage?" Cosette asked the two vendors. "My coachman—"

"Drunken bastards, coachmen. Yours has left you, has he? Sack his drunken ass."

"There—" the apple vendor pointed down the street. "That looks like a lady's carriage. You'd better get to it, madame, before the knackers get your nag. A good horse, why that's worth a lot of money in the rue Mouffetard." She patted her own hungry dog, who sniffed at Cosette's hem.

"There, see, opposite the church, try that café for your coachman, madame."

It was a corner café of unsurpassed ugliness, plastered with handbills long since tattered unto scraps and blowing in the cold wind. Its mangy façade glowed mustardy in the gaslight and encroaching darkness. Cosette would have marched in to apprehend the erring Abel, but her attention was arrested by a figure darting, like a moth to light, a boy perhaps, a child certainly. The child wore a cap and a coat many times too big for him; its lining hung down in shreds, matching the shredded ends of his trousers, and his feet were thrust into mismatched shoes. She watched as he ducked swiftly between carts and wagons, upsetting a thick-armed milk merchant lifting the last of her empties onto a wagon. He paid no attention to the curses she rained down on him, but moved swiftly toward some objective invisible to Cosette.

Right next to the tattered café, a baker's window cast squares of buttery light on the pavement, and framed inside the window were golden breads and brioches. The child tucked himself behind a stack of baskets underneath the window, and in his hand the blade of a knife gleamed. With amazing swiftness born of genius or practice, he inserted the point of the knife into the corner of the windowpane, and as he flicked his wrist quickly, the pane cracked upward in an almost perfect arc. He ran the knife up to the highest point on the crack, inserted its tip again, gave a slight twist, and the pane, in a half-circle, popped out. Immediately the boy reached in, wrapped his hand around a loaf of bread, and pulled it through the hole, jumped up, ran, and might have escaped altogether. But the glass clattered, shattered in the street, attracting the attention of two men just emerging from the café. They blocked Cosette's view of the boy and nabbed him, crying out, "Thief! Thief!" till the baker came running out of the *boulangerie* just as the boy squirmed out of their grasp and tore up the street, running headlong into Cosette, almost knocking her over. When she caught her breath she heard the whole of the rue Mouffetard shouting, "Thief! Thief!"

"Oh, no you don't!" The onion vendor caught the boy, dragged him back to face the baker. She gave his neck a vicious twist. Her onions had fallen into the street, but her colleagues collected them, stealing only just a few as they congregated and congratulated her for having caught Le Sansonnet, the Starling, "The filthy little Starling," she snorted.

The baker thrust his way through the group, drew his arm back, and smacked the boy's face. "You and your knife, that's how you did it, isn't it? You star glazer, I'll take that knife and rip it across the roof of your mouth!"

"He's mine first!" shouted the secondhand clothes dealer, joining them breathlessly, having run the length of the rue Mouffetard. "That's my coat!" She brushed past Cosette and rattled the boy till his teeth chattered. "The little bastard filched it yesterday from in front of my shop. Snatched it off the hook! I saw him with my own—"

"Lying cow!" cried the boy before she punched him.

The onion vendor held his neck while the other woman stripped him of the heavy coat, and the bread fell into the street, gleaming golden on the stones. The baker cursed him again. And when the coat was turned upside down, out fell the knife, an onion, an apple, three centimes, and a clean white handkerchief, which the secondhand dealer snatched. The baker reached for the knife, the onion vendor gave his neck another snap, and the boy bit her inner arm viciously, leapt when she screamed and involuntarily released him. He seemed to sprint, to fly, but a butcher just emerging from the café snatched his arm in a thick-fisted embrace and dragged him back. At least Cosette hoped he was a butcher to account for the blood-stained apron. Between him and the white-floured baker, they seemed to be ready to tear the boy to pieces.

The girl who sold shoelaces sauntered up to the thief and picked the three centimes off the street. "Why don't you go to work for your old grandmother? You'd be a natural going through the clothes of the dead."

"You're a spavined slut, Germaine—"

The butcher lifted him off the street by his neck. Without the heavy coat the boy looked pathetic, like a hooked fish or a kitten about to be drowned.

"Go for the police! Get the Municipal Guard," cried the baker. "You're going to get it now, Starling. Someone get the police."

No one seemed much inclined to include the police in this fracas until the baker offered money, and then the young man who had so nearly died at Cosette's feet said he'd call the army and march Le Sansonnet to Algeria for five sous.

As he tried to wriggle from their grip, Le Sansonnet's cap fell off, and there were a few more stolen goods up there, including a roll of ribbon, the worse for wear and the gutter.

"A present for your whoring mother?" asked the butcher.

"At least she doesn't have the pox like you!"

"You'll piss when you can't whistle, boy," the baker vowed, referring to the action of the guillotine on the larynx. He drew his hand back to strike again.

"How much for the bread?" Cosette called out. The little crowd silenced, stared at her as she pushed through in her sumptuous velvet cloak. "I'll buy it. How much for the bread?"

"You don't know the price of bread!" crowed the incredulous turnip vendor. "What are you doing in this street, madame, if you don't know the price of bread? Come to see how the people of the rue Mouffetard suck the stones?"

"I asked a simple question." Cosette was not a tall woman, but she had been married to Marius for fifteen years, and she could at least imitate his innate physical dignity. "I expect a simple answer."

"Seven sous," said the baker.

"Seven sous this year and six last year," grumbled the onion vendor, "four the year before, and if it goes above eight, these people, look around you, madame, these people will starve."

"Me, I'll starve before that," said the military beggar, "my empty guts curse my vacant lips."

Cosette addressed the baker. "I'll buy the bread. It's been in the street. It's dirty. It's wet. No one will eat it." In the sudden silence she regretted her words, knowing that each rise in the price of bread consigned more of these people to slow starvation, knowing that any of them would eat that bread, that she would have eaten it as a child and counted herself fortunate. "I'll give you eight sous for the bread if you'll give me the boy. Let him go."

"Don't be reckless with this brat," counseled the onion vendor. "He's a sneak, a thief, a filcher, a filer, a journeyman pickpocket, and a liar. Just look there." The apple seller pointed to the things in the street.

"Whore!" cried the boy before he was silenced summarily.

"He's a little shit-of-a-thief," cried the secondhand-clothes woman, folding the coat over her arm, petting it like a lost puppy.

"That's how he got his name, Le Sansonnet, the starling, a curse, a thief—"

"Me, I'm an altar boy at Saint-Julien-le-Pauvre," cried the culprit.

"An acolyte at Saint-Monday," croaked the butcher. He turned to the baker. "Well, what will you do?"

"Give me the boy and I'll buy the bread," Cosette repeated. "Quickly, before the police come."

Reminded of the police, many of the little crowd began to melt toward the tattered café.

"Ten years old," muttered the turnip vendor, "and a curse to the name of France."

"Thirteen, you filthy sow!"

"Fatherless scum," said the apple seller as she drifted away.

"Motherless whore!" he cried after her.

He might have said more but the baker smacked him another good one, and at that moment Abel came tearing out of the café, wringing alternately his hands and his cap, running toward the horse and carriage, crying all the while and begging forgiveness of Cosette, of God, of Saint-Fiacre, whoever would heed him first, promising reform, rehabilitation, sobriety, truly and on the soul of his dead mother. The few people left in the street watched the exchange between the coachman and Cosette with mercenary interest, and surely it crossed more than one mind that the baker could get more than eight sous from a woman dressed as Cosette was and rich enough to have her own horse and carriage. It crossed Cosette's mind too. "Five francs for the boy and the bread," she said flatly. "My last offer."

Abel bobbed and apologized all around her, his walk uncertain, his words unclear, his breath unbearable.

"There will be plenty of time for you to tell your story to my husband when he gets out of prison," Cosette said sharply. Mention of prison brought a look of collective curiosity to the faces around her. "It's a political offense," she felt obliged to explain, "Sainte-Pélagie, just a few streets away," before a series of signals, clearly timed hoots and whistles, sounded, and everyone vanished save for the butcher and the baker, who still had hold of the boy.

The *sergent de ville* was indeed on his way; the young man had earned his five sous. The baker took Cosette's five francs with one final threat against the Starling, and the butcher released him. Abel brought the carriage around, and with police coming down the street, the boy jumped in, swooping up the dirty bread first.

The carriage clattered through the twisting streets, back toward the rue Saint-Jacques, and in the dusky light, Cosette scrutinized the child across from her. Without the coat he looked altogether pitiful, his trousers held up by one brace, his frail shirt held together with string tied through hooks, and his mismatched shoes both too big for him, the soles stuffed with newspapers whose matted gray print fell out in clumps to the carriage floor. Dirt and grime streaked his face and arms, and his legs were black and scabby. His nose went oddly to one side, giving the impression of a congenital squint, and his dark hair had been cropped very short and stuck out queerly all over his head.

"How old are you?"

"Old enough to know piss from holy water," he said, tearing off a chunk of bread with his teeth. "He'd have done it, you know, that filthy gutwad baker. He'd have had me in the leg bracelets for sure. Playing the iron tune." He gulped down his bread and whistled some street ditty before biting off another chunk and adding thoughtfully, "Back to La Petite Roquette for me, or maybe not. Second offense, they might have transported me. So I guess I have to thank you, eh?"

"I guess you do."

"Well, *merci*." He stuffed the uneaten bread into his meager shirt and leaned out the carriage window, watching the lamplight flicker on the Seine as they crossed the river. He turned after a while, studied Cosette. "Why did you do it? What do you care what happens to my sorry ass? What do you want from me? Eh? Tell me, what do you want?"

"I knew a man once who stole a loaf of bread." Cosette spoke more to the gathering darkness than to the boy. "He went to prison for it and he carried the shadow of the prison with him always. He dragged the shadow of the prison through a life that was blameless. It was a sad story, and I could not bear that it should happen again, that history should repeat itself."

Chapter 5

*T*he kitchen at Number 6 rue des Filles-du-Calvaire resembled a medieval castle with battlements of cookware and turrets of iron. The cook, Jeanne-Louise Poillard, who had adopted the prestigious sobriquet Madame Carême, commanded this kitchen with the panache of Napoléon in the field. Though the Pontmercys' home was not by any means palatial (the old grandfather had moved here in 1818 to retire from the world), the reputation of their table was unsurpassed, and many of their guests had tried to tempt their cook away. Madame Carême was flattered, but why settle for the possibility of being a field-marshal when here she was indisputably commander-in-chief? She had built in the rue des Filles-du-Calvaire not a mere reputation but a palace to her art. The huge fireplace had cranes and roasting spits and grills and country ovens, where coals could be thrust down the center of a hollow iron pot. Hanging all alongside the fireplace were an array of pokers and tongs, hooks and ladles, forks and strainers, and a variety of *pelles-rouges,* heavy iron devices that could be heated red-hot, passed over the top of a dish to brown it to perfection. Suspended from the ceiling on a rack that could be raised or lowered to the cook's direction were her artillery—saucepans, frypans, casseroles, *bain-maries,* and *braisières*; great *marmites* hunkered on the sideboard, some with spigots, and lined up, gleaming, on the shelves were whips and funnels, mortars, pestles, knives, and an arsenal of devices for cutting fruits into fantastical shapes, molds for perfect figures of meringues. A shelf sagged slightly under the weight of tomes like *La Physiologie du Goût,* by Brillat-Savarin, and all the works of Carême, the maestro. Once she had been a scullery maid in his kitchen, an exceptionally astute and observant scrubber. She'd taken more than Carême's name; she'd absorbed his culinary techniques. An ample, yeasty woman, Jeanne-Louise had hands as strong as a mason's and a touch as light as a nun's. She was about to stuff forcemeat into a half-dozen young partridges when she heard the carriage come around the back, and she quickly sent the scullery girl upstairs to fetch a servant with a lantern to light madame's way into the house. "You'd best tell the boy his mother is home too," she called out. Everyone at Number 6 knew where the baroness had gone—and why.

From her low kitchen window Madame Carême watched Abel trying to decide if he should get down or fall down from the carriage. "Drunken sod," she muttered, returning to her partridges with a practiced hand. "He'll kill them all one day, drive them into the Seine."

"Madame Carême! They say Mama's home!" Fantine tumbled into the kitchen. At eleven she was still coltish, all eyes and legs, a doll and book pressed against her narrow chest. She had her mother's watchful expression and her father's stubbornness, but she had quarreled severely with her parents only once, over her education. Fantine maintained that girls don't need rhetoric, mathematics, Greek, or Latin, everyone knew girls only needed a bit of this and that. But she had lost this battle and pliantly succumbed to a regime of education better suited to a boy. She flung the book down now with a great smile: with Mama home, the two of them would take this late-afternoon hour together—as they always did—to read, or sometimes Cosette simply brushed and plaited Fantine's long, fair hair. "Is it true, Mama's here?"

"Yes, little peach, but don't go outside. Go upstairs and wait for her. It's too cold for you, *ma petite,* and you have only those little silk shoes. Go on, wait in the library where—"

"They're not going upstairs. Look. They're coming into the kitchen."

Madame Carême left the partridges and returned to the window, shocked to see the baroness herding a filthy urchin toward the house. In a great gust of January cold, Cosette blew into the kitchen, pulled off her cloak and gloves, and flung her arms around Fantine, showering endearments on her.

"Mama, you act as though we've been separated for years!"

"Oh, Fantine! If you only knew!" Cosette brushed her daughter's thick straight hair back from her fresh face and kissed her cheek, then she ordered a fire built in the basement room and a tray of food—soup, bread, tea, and meat—brought in.

"Who is that awful boy, Mama? He stinks and he's filthy."

"Mind your manners, Fantine."

"Why is his hair sticking out all over his head?"

"Lice. Want some?" The boy ran a dirty hand over his stubbled head and then he blew toward Fantine, who jumped back in alarm. "I got more. My grandmother did it, held me down and cut my hair. Next year I'll be too big and she can't get me. I like my lice, but she likes to tear down their little hovels and leave them homeless."

"Revolting little beggar!"

"I'm not a beggar. I'm a thief."

Cosette ordered him into the basement room, to wait there, then she reprimanded her daughter again and Fantine sulked, picking imaginary lice off her doll.

"Is this food for that boy, madame?" inquired Madame Carême. "Don't do it. Feed a brat like that and you'll just make him sick. He'll vomit on your floor," she vowed darkly. Without replying, Cosette poured water into a basin, washed her hands and face, and dried them.

"Is Jean-Luc still expelled?"

Cosette put her arm around her daughter's shoulders, and together they went into the basement room, where a small fire crackled in the grate and candles had all been lit, but the January cold still pressed against the barred windows. The boy warmed his brown hands before the fire, and in the light Cosette could better assess him. His thin legs stuck out of the oversized shoes, and once warm, his clothes gave off a pungent odor. Scrawny, savage, and fearless—certainly he'd proved that in the rue Mouffetard; all in all it had taken four or five adults to hold him—his lip was cut and swollen and his eye was beginning to swell, turning a livid purple, visible even under the dirt. Blood from his nose had dried on his upper lip and sprayed across his shirt. "Do you want to wash those cuts?" Cosette asked. He shrugged and shook his head.

"What is that sticking out of his shirt?" asked Fantine. "Why, it's bread! It's dirty bread. He isn't going to eat that, is he, Mama?"

"Hush, Fantine. Don't be rude."

"He's not a guest," she protested.

"Nonetheless," replied Cosette with all the maternal weight she could muster behind the word. She asked Le Sansonnet to sit down and he obliged her. "Where are your parents?"

"In heaven with the angels," he replied with wry, sly modesty.

"They're both dead?"

Shrugging in a wholly Parisian fashion, he retorted, "My father—well, who knows. My mother, she's licensed."

"What does that mean, licensed?" Fantine asked Cosette.

"A *fille publique*," explained Le Sansonnet, clearly delighted to expand the girl's education. "Prostitute, registered with the Morals Brigade, they give her a certificate and everything, and she can walk the streets anytime she likes, as long as she's inspected regularly—like the sewers, yes? No pox in my family. She's best found at the Café Rigolo behind Saint-Sulpice every day at five, six in the summers."

"That'll be enough," snapped Cosette. "Where do you live?"

"Why, me, I live with a countess sometimes. When she doesn't come after me with the Jondrettes and the scissors." He pulled again at his queerly cut hair, and it stood out even more weirdly. "It's the truth. Countess Crasseux is my grandmother, once shackled to the staff and basket, now slaps only, no slops, no credit, no pox, that's her motto."

"What is he saying?"

Le Sansonnet's lip curled up over brown teeth. "She's a great lady now, my grandmother, but she used to scrape through shit your chambermaid threw in the street!"

"Mama! Did you hear—"

"A ragpicker," he added with pride. "The lowest of the low."

"A convict is the lowest of the low," Cosette reminded him tartly, "and unless you'd like to achieve that status, then you'd best confine yourself to my questions. Can you read?"

"And write. Me, I'm a graduate—really—of La Petite Roquette."

"Whoever heard of such a school?" Fantine said to her mother. "It's not in Paris."

"It is in Paris," Cosette replied. "It's a prison for children."

"A fine school, La Petite Roquette. They'd give us bread toasted all over with sugar, meat twice a week, feather mattresses, and oranges when we learn our lessons. I remember my lessons, 'Other people's property is sacred and we must respect it,'" he parroted. "See? I'm as learned as Saint-Antoine's pig and better looking. But me, I'd rather boil a book in water and drink the soup. The glue in the bindings, it can be tasty."

At that moment Aunt Adelaide burst into the basement room. She had all the vanities of the aged virgin, lace caps with fluttered ribbons, milk baths to rid her hands of liver spots, her white hair crimped and unmercifully curled, but at the same time her pieties were equally well preserved; a rosary hung from her waist, a heavy gold crucifix dangled across her breast. Certainly it was with religious zeal that she demanded to know if that wretched headmaster had conceded he'd been altogether wrong, or at the very least, that he'd made some tactless error, that the dear, sweet boy (Jean-Luc, who came in right behind her) was naturally innocent. Before Cosette could frame an answer, Aunt Adelaide spied the Starling and screeched. "So it's true, what the servants say! You've brought the mob to murder us in our beds! He'll steal everything! And Marius not here to protect us! Oh, Jean-Luc, protect your sister's virtue! Stand between her and this—"

"Stay away from him," Fantine cautioned her brother. "He's got lice."

"I will steal everything," Le Sansonnet snarled. "I'll steal your ass and you'll have to shit through your ribs."

"Oh! Oh! Oh, Cosette—look what you've done!" cried the old lady breathlessly as she bustled out, calling for the servants to lock up the silver.

"You're taxing my patience," Cosette advised the Starling, who gave a shriveled grin in reply.

Carrying the tray, Madame Carême came in and placed it on a little table before the boy, and with a last muttered warning to Cosette about the inadvisability of feeding people who were not accustomed to eating, she left the room.

Dazzled at the feast before him, eyes wide, the Starling stroked his pointed hair as though comforting those lice still making their home there, and when Cosette asked why he was called the Starling, he seemed not to hear. She asked again.

"The starling is the most hated of birds," he said at last, tearing off some bread and slathering it with ham and stuffing it in his jaws, swallowing quickly and in a single audible gulp. "It raids, it shits, it steals. It shows no mercy and plays no favorites, and it doesn't give a damn shit what people think."

"Are you a thief by choice or a thief at heart?" When he did not reply, his mouth being too full, she turned to her son and asked him to have a servant go upstairs and bring down some clothes Jean-Luc had outgrown.

"He can't wear my clothes!"

"He'll grow into them."

"It's not size! You can't dress a guttersnipe like a gentleman, Mama!"

Stepping quite close to Jean-Luc, Cosette said very clearly, "As a gentleman, Jean-Luc, you will be obliged to defend your conduct at the Lycée Henri IV."

"The headmaster's lying."

"The headmaster is a great prig, but I do not think he is a liar. I'm very angry with you, not merely that you have behaved impudently and disrespectfully, but because this will break your father's heart. Papa will return home and find that you've been expelled. When I think what it will do to him, I—" Her anger at Jean-Luc was interrupted by the sound of Le Sansonnet, who, having picked up the bowl of soup, drained it noisily and in a single slurp. He took the uneaten bread and pressed it too into his shirt, where, with the other loaf, it gave him almost the appearance of paunch. Fantine laughed, Jean-Luc left angrily, and Cosette returned her attention to the Starling. "Are you a thief by choice or a thief by nature?"

He poured some tea, bolted it in a gulp that widened his brown eyes and burned his mouth. He wiped his lips with the back of his hand, rubbing the blood under his nose into a gelatinous mess with the snot. "I ask nothing of no one. That's how it is. See? Me, I don't beg and I don't whore. I may squat, but I'll never kneel."

"Then I take it you are a thief by choice."

"Take it however you like, I've said *merci* for your salvation in the rue Mouffetard. If you want something else, then you have to wash it in clear water, eh? This is all dark beer to me."

Jean-Luc returned and lounged in the doorway, studying the Starling with a look at once interested and insolent. Caught between them, Cosette endured one of those moments when time leaps over memory, the whole moon visible in the pale shadow of the crescent. Coals in the grate tumbled, a shower of sparks flew up, and the pang passed. "I have work for you," she addressed the Starling. "Real work. Not squatting or kneeling, but running. The kind of work you would be good at. My husband, my husband's paper, *La Lumière,* has need of a dispatcher, a courier."

"A courier who looks like me?" He laughed rudely and, noticing the sugar bowl, heaped sugar into his cup and dissolved it with the tea.

"A courier who knows Paris. Who can run through Paris, who can fly over Paris like the starling."

"Or scurry through the sewers like the rat?"

"I saw what you did this afternoon, how fleet and fast and accomplished you are."

"Yes, and I'd have been balls-up if you hadn't seen it."

Jean-Luc protested, "Papa can't have people at *La Lumière* like him, with lice and blood, with black eyes, foul mouths, and the police after them! What can you be thinking of, Mama!"

"I'm thinking of *La Lumière.* I'm thinking of the old veterans who totter out on errands and come back winded or drunk. A starling can go where a man cannot, he can know and hear and see things that would be hidden from a man. These are terrible times. No one takes a child seriously, but a serious child could be of great help to *La Lumière.*"

"He's a filthy little beast," Jean-Luc corrected her. "A thief by his own admission—and you want him to go to *La Lumière*? He'll steal the pens and presses."

"He ought to be kicked," Fantine maintained.

"He has been," retorted Jean-Luc. "Look at his eye swelling."

Cosette returned her attention to Le Sansonnet. "If you want to work, you can work for *La Lumière.* If you want to thieve, well— the choice is yours."

"They're all rags, newspapers are. Some people blow their noses with newspapers, some wipe their asses. Royalist, radical—I put them in my shoes." He lifted up one foot, where the sole flapped sadly from the rest of the shoe and gaped gray with newsprint.

"*La Lumière* is a republican newspaper. It is committed to the notion of a republic for France."

"Mama!" Jean-Luc cried. "Be careful what you say to someone like him. You could get Papa arrested!"

"Papa is already arrested. Well?" she demanded of the Starling.

"I don't give a damn shit for any of that. I ask only to eat regular and sleep warm."

"You sound very bourgeois."

The boy sulked and asked what they would pay.

"You can settle that with Monsieur Clerons tomorrow. He is in charge of *La Lumière* at the moment."

The maid brought in a bundle of clothing and gave it to Le Sansonnet, who picked through it as if checking for vermin. "There better not be a uniform in here. I won't wear no uniforms, no man's uniform and no man's livery. No monkey-garters and no wigs, none of that." He rose.

"There's none of that."

"Do I have to tell people I'm working for a rag?"

"You have to promise not to steal while you're working for this rag."

He looked dubious, disgusted, and judicious in the same moment.

"Meet me tomorrow at ten at the offices of *La Lumière* in the rue de Combray. Look presentable and don't mention La Petite Roquette. If they ask you where you learned to read, tell them your grandmother taught you."

"She did. She's the one taught me. That's why I was the prize student at La Petite Roquette—I could already read and write." Having caught the grain of Jean-Luc's current dilemma, he turned to him and added impudently, "My headmaster loved me, wept to see me go, he did. Said with my education, my abilities, I'd do great things one day. Governor of Algeria, maybe. Head priest of Mont-Saint-Michel. Guillotined before I grow a beard—or have a woman. It was all honey or turds with him," he added adroitly, hopping toward the door. "Maybe I'll be in the rue de Combray tomorrow," he called on his way to the kitchen, "and maybe I won't."

He gave a deep bow to the cook, who stood poised with a cleaver hidden in the folds of her skirt just in case he should try to nick the spoons, and then he sprinted through the kitchen door and out into the night.

Chapter 6

*I*n the short, dirty winter dusk, Pajol lingered. Here at the intersection of time and memory, the past had been everywhere effaced, mulched into obscurity, the stones not merely mute, but dumb. In the street where Enjolras had vowed their blood would run, new paving stones refigured the pattern of the barricade, and the walls all around, once pocked with shot and shell, had been replastered, repainted, the shutters and doors replaced. The façade of the Corinth shattered by the cannon—all that had come down and a new café had taken its place, with higher ceilings, new stairs, new floors, and a broad-faced, beef-handed landlord behind the zinc counter, who eyed Pajol as though he visibly brought with him the pox.

"I have money," protested Pajol.

"Get out! I can tell just to look at you, you're a convict—or you ought to be."

"Answer me, this used to be the old Corinth, didn't it? Somewhere here there's scraped on the wall *Vive le peuple,* yes?"

"Are you a *mouchard* as well as a murderer?"

The man's lips twisted. "You dog, call me anything but that."

"They're everywhere, *mouchards.* There are more spies than socialists in Paris nowadays. Gag it, and get your red republican rags out of here! I'm for the king, you hear!"

"I'm looking for a printer," he went on desperately, "a man named Verdier who used to—"

A shiny pistol, muzzle up, made its appearance on the zinc, and the other drinkers—sausage makers, fish inspectors, a street sweeper, and a man cuddling a bag full of goose feathers—watched with interest as the landlord threatened again to call the *sergent de ville.* "At best you're a vagrant. At worst you're a thief."

So Victor Pajol left, pulled his cap down low, closed up his shirt, and walked along the rue Mondétour in the rain, pausing there briefly when from the upper stories laughter fell on him; bright, coarse, feminine laughter splashed down upon him like counterfeit coins of a country in which he would be forever foreign.

Chapter 7

*A*s the prison door of Sainte-Pélagie opened on the third of February, Marius was dazzled by the brilliant winter sunshine and by the sight of Cosette awaiting him in their carriage, her face alight, her arms open. He held his hat and gloves and walked out a free man, tipping the turnkey.

"It's been a pleasure to serve yourself, monsieur," said the turnkey truthfully. His was a lucrative post. The Opposition editors—kept happy, allowed books, pens, paper, letters (sent in, not sent out), visits of wives and children, mistresses, good cigars, good wine, meals brought in from the outside—were always generous when they left. Monsieur Pontmercy was no exception. "Your things will be packed and sent to your home. I hope to see you again, monsieur." He meant it. Freedom of the press would have left him destitute; the other prisoners in Sainte-Pélagie were debtors.

"Forgive me if I do not return the compliment," Marius said, laughing. He was pale from his prison stay, but his spirits did not seem affected. The sad scar still streaked down his temple where his dark hair was just beginning to gray. At thirty-seven only incipient creases fanned out from his eyes, and in the passing years his mouth had softened, though he still left the impression of a man whose humor could be taxed before his intelligence.

Once the carriage clattered through the gates in the rue des Filles-du-Calvaire, Fantine ran out of the house, down the steps, never minding her flimsy silk shoes, to throw her arms around her father, who embraced her, beamed, held her at arm's length, embraced her again, declaring she'd grown up and grown more beautiful in a mere month. Behind Fantine, Marius was surprised to see Jean-Luc. "Has the old royalist Liancourt had a change of heart," asked Marius, delighted, "to let you come home to celebrate my return?"

"Not exactly," replied Jean-Luc.

"Perhaps we'd better discuss it in the library," said Cosette. "Perhaps you'd prefer to wait," she added, knowing full well Marius would not.

Marius paced back and forth before the fireplace, and Jean-Luc sat dejectedly on the sofa while Cosette explained why the headmaster had expelled him. Watching all this was the portrait of the old grandfather, which hung above the library mantel, and to Cosette's eye the old man's lascivious grin seemed enhanced, as if he were enjoying the sight of the brash, headstrong Marius confronted by someone equally brash and headstrong. Cosette offered, on Jean-Luc's behalf, that Monsieur Liancourt was an insufferable prig, and anyone would have felt obliged to defy him.

"I well remember Monsieur Liancourt," Marius snapped. "The character of Monsieur Liancourt is not in question here. Jean-Luc's is. I am appalled at your conduct. I return from prison to find you have been expelled from one of the finest schools in France for frivolity! For swallowing a note! For sneaking out at night!"

"You were in prison for sedition," Jean-Luc retorted. "I was following your example."

"Jean-Luc!" Cosette exclaimed. "Your father has suffered public sedition trials, months in prison, and certainly not for frivolity. How can you say such a thing?"

Jean-Luc shrugged. "He rebelled, I rebelled. He fights the authority of the king. I fought the authority of the school."

"I am not a student," Marius informed him. "You are a student. A student must—"

"You rebelled even when you were a student, Aunt Adelaide told me. She said you left home when you were seventeen, left this home, moved into a filthy tenement, and broke your grandfather's heart."

"It was not for frivolity, I assure you."

"Jean-Luc," Cosette reminded her son tartly, "your papa does not have to defend his conduct to you."

"I left on a matter of principle," said Marius.

"Isn't it just always principle?" sulked the boy. "The principle of the right to work, the principle of the free press, the principle of free political assembly, the principle of free education, it's always some principle or another, isn't it, Papa? You care more for the rights of workers and wages paid to women who huddle in garrets than you do for us. You love the Republic better than you love us, and there isn't going to be a Republic. France needs a king!" Perhaps Jean-Luc could make such a speech because he knew his father (unlike his teachers at Lycée Henri IV) would never strike him, would never strike anyone. His parents were stunned speechless, and in the void he ventured on, "You'd go to prison to protest an unjust law and think yourself and the world better for it, but when I have a little fun—"

"A little fun?" Marius inquired, as though Jean-Luc had spoken a foreign language. "The world is not here to amuse you! The world is here to instruct. The school is there to instruct, to educate—"

"Monsieur Liancourt says he failed to educate you. He says that just because we live in the nineteenth century does not mean history is a locomotive. He says that you believe in the locomotive and not the cart. He says you're dangerous and France needs a king."

"Monsieur Liancourt said that to you?" Cosette asked, incredulous. She turned to Marius. "It's unthinkable that he should tell a boy his father is dangerous."

Marius himself looked up to the picture of the grandfather, and he too seemed to see an unwonted twinkle in the old man's eyes. Perhaps Marius might be fated to endure as a parent the pain he had inflicted as a young man. Perhaps he and Cosette were raising the grandfather in the guise of their son. Certainly Marius recognized in Jean-Luc his grandfather's high spirits and love of frivolity, his stubborn refusal to see the world as a serious place where men make serious choices. Still, in the years since Jean Valjean's death, Marius had made an effort to learn tolerance; it was not his native element and he achieved it often only with a struggle. He struggled now, keeping his voice even, as though he were addressing the Chamber of Deputies and not this recalcitrant boy. "My grandfather was an avowed royalist, and so it was in keeping with his beliefs that I should attend Lycée Henri IV. We are not royalists, and so perhaps you would be better served by a different school, perhaps Louis-le-Grand."

"He would be spared the company of Arsène Huvet," offered Cosette.

"You are forbidden the company of Arsène Huvet." Jean-Luc nodded sourly as Marius went on. "You are forbidden cafés and theatres and *grisettes*." He lingered meaningfully over the last word. "You will study for the law as I did. In school you will do your duty and you will learn. You will demonstrate honor. You will not board at school any longer, but be a day student and return here nightly, so that we may watch over your evenings and improve your habits. There will be no more frivolity. You will give me your word."

Jean-Luc gave his word, thinking there would be no more frivolity ever, that he would live and die a prisoner here, serving a sentence for sedition of another sort.

Chapter 8

*A*s was the unstated custom amongst the Opposition, when an editor was released from Sainte-Pélagie, the other editors, writers, and critics poured in to welcome him, to apprise him of the mood, to share news of the changes, the chances, the strategies—and all this accomplished in a sort of informal gathering that sidestepped the ban on political assembly. All that afternoon and throughout the evening, the Pontmercy servants raced about, taking hats and gloves, showing people into the drawing room, where a dozen tables had been scattered to hold the plates, the trays of food, the empty glasses, as one after another, bottles of champagne were popped and corks drawn on old Bordeaux. The men of *La Lumière* arrived first, since the daily fare of artists and writers does not usually include champagne and oysters. They ate, drank, and shared with Marius what he'd missed in the month he'd been in Sainte-Pélagie and their enthusiasm for the new hire, Le Sansonnet, the courier Cosette had brought to *La Lumière*.

"The courier," said Coligny, the theatrical critic, "the Starling lives up to his name."

"Yes," said Clerons, "he's filthy."

"No, I meant he can fly. The old soldiers we used to use for messages, it's best they should stay there at the subscription desk. It takes them days just to cross the river and this boy does it, well, like a bird. He must know every impasse and courtyard in the city."

"And every gutter," added Clerons, holding his glass to be refilled.

"Perhaps that's what we need," said Marius, "someone who can report from the gutter because he comes from the gutter. These are the people *La Lumière* is committed to serving, workingmen and working women and this boy—"

"His mother is a whore," said Clerons, "a *fille publique*."

"How do you know that?" asked Coligny.

"I've inquired. The boy is the bastard son of a *fille publique* and the grandson of that notorious old bawd, the Changer. I don't think he should be on our premises and I told Madame Pontmercy as much, but she insisted on hiring him. I said I would abide by your judgment," he turned to Marius, "when you were released."

"We'll keep him. This boy can do more than take messages around Paris, he can bring messages to *La Lumière*. My wife tells me he's smart, literate, fast—"

"Foulmouthed," Clerons offered, "a little savage."

Marius smiled. "I would like to think that *La Lumière* is not so puffed up with itself that it can't tolerate a little savage, as long as he stays honest. His parentage is nothing to me, as long as he's not a *mouchard* or a thief."

"The boy is honest," Beaujard spoke up. "I sent him around to my tailor with enough money to keep me out of debtors' prison and it got there without him nicking any."

"Why couldn't you take the money yourself?" asked Marius.

"If I had, the tailor would have snatched the coat off my back!" Beaujard's cultivated congeniality masked the one true passion of his life: his painting. Destined by his military father for a career in the army, Beaujard had rebelled, run away to Paris, and after a while his father gave up on him, paid for his artistic education— and cut him off without a cent. Perennially short of money, Beaujard was never short of friends, many of whom he painted when he wasn't working for *La Lumière*. He had set himself an impossible task—to garner the world's recognition for his painting while refusing to paint in the way the world praised. His work had been consistently declined for the Salon because it was not thought academic or high-minded; his work collected ridicule because he clearly believed that contemporary lives had heroism worth painting. He was bearded, brown-eyed, and dapper; he had a studious air, as though constantly framing what he saw, compounding color with vision.

They were joined by Paul Gallet, a bitter man who wrote art criticism and poetry and reviewed books for *La Lumière* and in general found everything wanting and hopeless. Gallet grumbled that there were more poets in Paris than cats.

"There are more playwrights than rats," declared Coligny, spearing another oyster. In the warmth of the gathering, his round face had gone quite flushed and his hair curled around his face, giving him the look of an outsized cherub.

"Ah, Coligny," said a critic from a rival paper, "I've heard the rumor that your wife is married to the dullest man in France."

"That isn't true," said Cosette, joining them. "The king is the dullest man in France. The competition is for the second dullest." She caught Marius's eye and smile and the old flash ignited between them, the more understated for the years of practice; they'd developed so close a bond their thoughts chimed like the twin prongs on a tuning fork.

Her attention was caught by Cousin Théo, just arrived and looking rumpled; he bolted one glass of champagne, and Cosette saw that he'd taken note of his wife deep in conversation with Flocon from *La Réforme*. Théo's wife had no radical sympathies whatever, but she enjoyed her husband's affiliation with *La Lumière* (he wrote for the paper, but his great talent was being related to Marius) because it gave her access to Cosette's salon, to the drawing rooms of important people. Sophie Gillenormand, the former Mademoiselle de Bélessin, no longer blushed and paled at Théo's every word; in thirteen years of marriage, her mouth had settled into a pinch thought by some men to be quite kissable. Indeed, the marriage of Sophie and Théo proved the old adage that in order to get into society a woman must first marry and pass through the bedroom, and for a man to get into a married woman's bedroom, he must first pass through society.

The room began to fill; editors, writers from *La Presse, Le National, Le Siècle, La Réforme, L'Atelier,* all argued and congregated and broke up and congregated again. The talk was unanimously of the reform banquets scheduled to take place in the Champs-Elysées on 22 February. The emphasis was more on reform; the "banquets" allowed people to convene without being arrested for political assembly. People paid to eat, drink, and harangue the government, to argue vocally for reform, to consolidate opposition. While Marius was in prison the government issued a decree forbidding these banquets, and now the question here among these Opposition leaders was that of tactic and strategy. Would they defy, or would they acquiesce? The more moderate counseled obeying the crown; the banquets were a small thing, not worth a fight, especially when the government had the troops. The radicals argued that if the king won this small battle, the Opposition would have lost more than mere banquets: they would lose all possibility of bringing people together to protest, to oppose the king and his ministers. Tempers in the Pontmercy drawing room grew heated and contentious; bickering disintegrated into argument, those who foresaw trouble versus those who relished it, but no one here could have guessed that this seemingly minor question—would the reform banquets scheduled for Tuesday 22 February proceed or not—would ignite a revolution in France. No one could have guessed that on 24 February many of the men in this room, Flocon of *La Réforme,* Marrast of *Le National,* the poet Lamartine among others, would stand on the balcony of the Hôtel de Ville and proclaim the Second French Republic, would become leaders of the provisional government. No one here could have guessed that before the month of February was out revolution would explode: the king would abdicate and flee to England, the monarchy in France finished forever.

Some of these men Marius admired. Some he respected. Some he liked. Some he trusted. But they were not all the same, and in truth, looking amongst the frock coats, the pleated white shirts, the well-knotted cravats, and silk waistcoats, Marius saw men he thought no better than adventurers. They believed in *liberté,* yes, but *égalité, fraternité?* Those might be more difficult. To grant *égalité* and *fraternité* to men of substance, like themselves, would be an easy proposition, but too many equated the laboring classes with the dangerous classes, as though every workingman were but a criminal in embryo. There were men here who believed that it was the natural order of things that some should starve, that blunted lives and stunted hopes, empty guts and filthy hands entitled people to *égalité* only in heaven.

As the swift February dusk descended, the servants lit the lamps and all the candles in the drawing room, and fueled perhaps by the champagne and the old Bordeaux, the quarrels within the Opposition grew more vehement. The poet Lamartine caught their collective attention and raised a gold-rimmed glass for a toast. Marius smiled; he found Lamartine vain, insincere, and posturing, but there were moments when the poet's poses could be effective. Lamartine offered a toast to celebrate Marius's release from prison, offered it at length, till men's arms grew weary of holding their glasses aloft.

"We're here to drink your wine," said Emile de Girardin, editor of *La Presse*, "to enjoy the company of your pretty wife and thank you for bringing the government's shortcomings to the attention of the people, though it cost you a prison sentence. To say," Girardin turned toward Marius, "prison cannot extinguish *La Lumière*. The light will never go out."

Armand Marrast of *Le National* stepped forward and proposed, "A toast to seditious libel!"

"Seditious libel," they echoed.

"To the king," someone offered, "the crowned pear."

"To the government, a fraternity of ne'er-do-wells!"

"To the day when the press will be free and the church shackled!"

"*Liberté!*"

"*Egalité!*"

"*Fraternité!*"

And on that note they all returned to their various squabbles.

Marius smiled to watch Cosette weave through the crowded room toward him. She wore a dress of claret-colored silk, the skirt flounced in white lace matching the lace at her wrists. The deep wine color of her bodice set off her skin, and her eyes glowed like blue opals. She was the most beautiful sight he'd ever seen, and he longed to part this crowd as Moses had parted the Red Sea, tumble them up and over and clear an open avenue for him to embrace her. "It won't be much longer now," she whispered. "They'll soon go. Come with me and rescue Jean-Luc. Emile de Girardin's got hold of him, recounting *his* schooldays at Lycée Henri IV in grim detail." She took his arm and drew him into the world he had chosen, indeed, the world he had helped to invent.

"Yes, Monsieur de Girardin, I agree Lycée Henri IV is loathsome." Jean-Luc's enthusiasm was tempered by the approach of his parents; the scene in the library was all too fresh in everyone's mind.

"I always wonder when I meet Englishmen how they can be so stupidly sentimental over their schooldays," de Girardin mused. "I'd sooner join the convicts in the galleys at Toulon. Lock me up in the cages of Mont-Saint-Michel rather than spend another moment at school. Here's your father. He was a student there—ask him."

Salvation for Jean-Luc appeared in Lamartine, who drew Marius away, wanting to know what *La Lumière*'s stance would be if Thiers and others decided to go ahead with the reform banquets, no matter the king's ban.

Pascal Beaujard interrupted de Girardin's return to his schooldays by asking Cosette if she liked his caricature of the church strangling France's progress in the nineteenth century.

"It was exactly as I'd expected, Monsieur Beaujard, oh, perhaps with more zest than I'd imagined. You have a most energetic pen."

Strolling by with Sophie Gillenormand on his arm, Achille Clerons remarked idly that the energy of a man's pen could be used as index to another sort of energy. "Everyone knows the pen is truly, well, the 'male member.'"

"That explains why it grows in women's hands," Cosette replied with a suppressed smile. "Don't you agree that George Sand and Daniel Stern are fine writers?"

"Amazons!" scoffed Clerons, escorting Madame Gillenormand over toward the knot of constitutional republicans.

"Frenchwomen are more intelligent than their men," de Girardin observed as he swooped a glass of champagne off the tray of a passing servant.

"Then why are we denied the vote?" inquired Cosette. "Why does universal suffrage apply only to men?"

"Women can't vote!" Jean-Luc advised his mother.

Maternally indulgent, Cosette explained she was well aware of that.

"Men are afraid to let them vote." The champagne had loosed de Girardin's expansive nature. "How could we possibly keep women in the boudoir if they once proved they could do things better than we can? I ask you—" he pointed to the men around them, who had fragmented into suspicious cliques and whose bickering over tactics was audibly disintegrating. "Can you imagine women doing that? Frenchwomen, I mean. Frenchwomen know how to make a profit from their men, and they are criticized all over Europe for it. Profit, perhaps, but where else do women profit by giving so much pleasure? The Parisian woman is like a man distilled down to his essences—then a dollop of shrewdness thrown in, denied to men, alas, at conception. Our women collect more visitors to their salons than do ministers of state."

"For the simple reason," Cosette interrupted, "that ministers of state are hopelessly tedious and famously dull."

"No sooner said than tested," Beaujard nodded toward the door. "You have your own minister of state now, madame."

"Monsieur Thiers is no longer a minister of state," de Girardin reminded them over the gold rim of his glass. "He's been expelled from the government, and I understand the king quite hates him."

"Everyone hates him," added Beaujard.

Adolphe Thiers in the company of the editor of *Le Constitutionnel* made his way across the drawing room toward Marius. A tiny man with an enormous head set atop narrow shoulders, Thiers had a close-lipped smile suggestive of the sphinx. His hair, heavily streaked with gray, had receded from his forehead as if to leave more room for his immense brain, and he was caricatured often (perhaps best by Pascal Beaujard) as a naked, big-headed baby with a patriotic sash across his belly and ever-present tiny spectacles on his nose. Ruthless and unlovely, he was nonetheless one of the most powerful men in France and had been since 1830. He was much sought after in Parisian society, even though he was now out of the government, having quarreled with the king. He voiced his opinions through *Le Constitutionnel,* his paper in the truest sense, shackled to his policies and the editor wholly dependent on Thiers's goodwill.

"I shall have to rescue Marius presently," Cosette said. "He can't abide Monsieur Thiers."

"No one can," said de Girardin. "I have twenty thousand readers. Ask them."

"Marius loathes his prudence."

"Prudence, property, and order," said Beaujard, "that's all that's inside Adolphe Thiers."

"And is he 'nasty, brutish, and short'?" quipped de Girardin, quoting from a recent article in *La Lumière.*

"He's more complicated than that." Cosette watched the little man, no taller than she was, brewing a quarrel with Marius. "Excuse me." Cosette crossed through the servants and journalists and took her husband's arm, greeting Thiers cordially and asking him if he had returned to the writing of history now that he was out of power.

"Madame, I may be out of office, but I am never out of power. I only write history when I am not engaged in making it." Thiers still spoke with the thick rind of his Marseille accent and in a thin, reedy voice. "But you are a feast for the eyes and your husband the most fortunate man in Paris, married to a woman of beauty, charm, intelligence, and wit."

"*Merci,* Monsieur Thiers, but I do hope you will spare me the quip about the cart horse and the frock coat."

"On the contrary, madame, wit in women appeals to me. Yours is the only salon in Paris where a man need not dredge through his trunk of *ancien régime* compliments, century-old affectations, in order to talk to a woman. Everywhere else, before a man can have a conversation with a woman, he has to decide first if he wants to bed her or not."

Coming from Thiers, sexually nondescript (though he lived with a wife and her behemoth mother, the joke in Paris being that the latter was the one he'd wanted), his remark about bedding women seemed comical. Rather than laugh, however, Marius gallantly placed his hand over Cosette's and said, "At least we have in common that we both admire Cosette."

"We have more than that, Monsieur Pontmercy. We both trained for the law and forsook it for journalism."

"But you forsook journalism for politics."

"Perhaps you will too."

"I could only serve the Republic."

"You already do—and there isn't one. As you know, I've no misguided faith in the mob, or their ability to rule themselves. I believe France needs a king, but I would agree with *La Lumière* that the whole gang in current government are neither honest nor sensible. You should run for the Chamber of Deputies, Monsieur Pontmercy, since you are honest, even when you are not sensible."

"Surely it's sensible to be honest."

"Not in France today. A sensible man would follow Monsieur Guizot's advice when he told us all to enrich ourselves. I see no admonition to honesty there. And truly, Monsieur Pontmercy, would a sensible man allow himself to be tried time and again for seditious libel as you do? No, you are a rare individual. Even dangerous."

Cosette thought it odd that Thiers would echo Monsieur Liancourt in his assessment of Marius, and she disputed the notion that honest men were dangerous.

"It's not the honesty that makes your husband dangerous, madame. There are honest men, then there are honest men who are also scrupulous."

"The distinction seems academic," contested Marius.

"But it's not. Lastly, on the top of humanity there are men both scrupulous and honest who are willing to sacrifice themselves for their country, and that's what makes them dangerous."

"Are you such a man, Monsieur Thiers?"

"Not at all. In my defense I could say my contempt for mankind is mixed with pity rather than hatred, and that is enough to distinguish me from the rest of the government, but I will never be dangerous like Monsieur Pontmercy." He patted his heart. "Constitutional infirmity."

"Are you ill?"

"Constitutionally, madame, I am incapable of trusting to anything. Certainly not in France. I trust to nothing in France. Look at the last century, the old regime had every right to believe itself secure—money, power, that vast weight of tradition—and yet they fell. And with them fell a whole structure we have not replaced, not in fifty years. The current government is certainly inadequate. No one contests that, save perhaps Guizot and the king."

"They are unworthy of their power," Marius said. "Their power and property rest on a cruel foundation, unnecessary in a century when we have seen such dazzling progress. There's no reason we can't enjoy social justice as well. Perhaps people could endure these terrible inequities in the Middle Ages, when all they had were lives, as Hobbes said, nasty, brutish, and short."

"People have said the same of me." Thiers did not smile.

Marius colored, took a glass of Bordeaux from a servant with a tray, and coughed. "Each French revolution is an attempt to amend the one before, 1789, 1830, 1832—"

"That riot in 1832?" Thiers demurred. "That doesn't qualify as a revolution."

"Lives were lost."

"Lives are lost in fights at *barrière* bistros. Lives are lost in duels on the Champ-de-Mars at dawn. That doesn't make it a revolution."

"In 1832, it was not a duel, Monsieur Thiers. It was not a brawl. It was an insurrection. Insurrection is the bud. Revolution is the flower. Insurrection is immature revolution."

"Very, very immature and precipitate. The men who died in 1832, they died of gesture, Monsieur Pontmercy. Gestures killed them, futile gestures that better belonged on the stage, gaslight before, chorus behind."

"That's not so!"

"I remember eating in the restaurant Rocher de Cancale, not far from the fighting in the rue Mondétour, and the sound of gunfire ruining my dinner, the troops thundering past." The room had grown quiet, but Thiers was not unaccustomed to controversy; indeed, he courted it, but not for its own sake. Adolphe Thiers did nothing for its own sake. Despite the palpable tension, he went on, "If those men in 1832 wanted to die, why didn't they simply walk down the rue Mouffetard, along the old rue Perdue, sit in the place Maubert, and wait for the cholera? No, that June a handful of students and workers got drunk, looted the Arsenal and the pawnshops, built a lot of barricades, and got themselves stupidly killed. The world rolled on, none the worse for it. None the better, either."

"Spontaneous uprising is the way history happens!"

"On the contrary, Monsieur Pontmercy, it is the way legend happens. History, I'm happy to report, is a much more orderly sort of business. Have things truly changed since 1789? Are we not still howling outside the Bastille, trying to bring it down without knowing what's inside?"

"You think Napoléon made no difference to France?" cried Marius incredulously.

"To France and to a whole generation of Europeans, but Napoléon is dead and his era is dead, and to look back at the glory is short-sighted and as silly as Louis-Napoléon, his great booby of a nephew, who imagines himself the emperor's heir."

"Marius and I were in Boulogne when Louis-Napoléon—" Cosette paused, looking for a word to incorporate the comic and the pathetic—"arrived."

"'Arrived' is the very word, madame. He is the *arriviste* par excellence. Escaped from the fortress at Ham, he arrived in London, where he makes love to British ladies, and their money," Thiers had a particularly unpleasant snicker, "and he dreams of arriving in France and putting a laurel wreath on his own pointed head."

In Thiers's slur against Louis-Napoléon, Cousin Théo saw a slur against the great Bonaparte dynasty, and he swaggered over. Since Théo had left the military, he'd developed an exaggerated and nostalgic view of the glories of the empire, and the sacred duty of the French to lead a united states of Europe, of happily conquered Europeans. Moreover, he was quite drunk by now and would have challenged Adolphe Thiers to a duel—did, some later said—but in the mêlée turned his anger on Armand Marrast, who had been absorbing the attentions of his wife, and some said he challenged Marrast to a duel. Some said he challenged his wife to a duel, but all agreed that at the end of the evening Sophie had hauled him unceremoniously from the Pontmercys' drawing room, and the other guests broke into their respective cliques and claques to continue their arguments about the reform banquets as they collected their coats and went home.

At last Cosette and Marius closed the bedroom door. Their arms around each other, they fell on the bed, rolling over and over till Cosette's hair tumbled down and she lay finally breathless beside him, arms outflung, eyes closed. She turned on her side and smoothed his hair, whispering at his temple, right where the scar had sliced through his eyebrow, "Keep your eyes closed and let me do everything."

She undressed him, starting at his feet and working up, and then she led him to the great tin tub the servants had placed in front of the fireplace, the water hot and two more kettles warming. The smell of woodsmoke and honey-scented candles wafted over them as Marius, with a sigh of pleasure, eased himself into the water and Cosette, barefoot and clad only in her simple chemise and a single petticoat, handed him a fluted glass of champagne. Taking the bar of lavender-scented soap, she began with his chest, where she rested her hand on his heart.

"Do you think he was right, Thiers?" Marius asked, his eyes closed and head back. "Do you think he was right about them dying of gesture?"

"Of course not. He was being spiteful to get you back for the nasty, brutish, and short."

"It would be a poor thing to die of gesture."

"Oh, don't, Marius. Don't believe Thiers. Why should you start to doubt now?"

"Maybe doubt is something you grow into, like the way Le Sansonnet will have to grow into Jean-Luc's coat."

"My love, don't worry about Thiers."

"Before this, I simply loathed Thiers. Now I despise him. Imagine, all that gunfire interrupting his dinner . . ." When her hand came up over the knob of his once-shattered collarbone, he caught it and drew her up close to kiss. "I thought I would die for missing you when I was in prison, the hunger for you, I'd lie there and see the snow falling outside the barred window and picture you in our room, here as you are now—" He kissed her fingers and leaned back. "Without you I would have no life at all. My grandfather was right, it's the great prize of life we've snatched. Love. The oldest gift of all." Marius relaxed at last. "You can't buy it. You can't win it. You can't force it. You can't even earn it."

"You can find it. Or lose it," Cosette added, drawing her hands along his thigh, lifting each foot from the tub and pressing it against her breasts as she soaped his legs one at a time. "Can you share it?" she asked lightly, but the question had troubled her for years. Was Jean-Luc's accusation just? Did Marius love the free press, the memory of his dead friends, the conviction of *égalité*, some notion of humanity's final intrinsic worth more than he loved his family? More than he loved her? Cosette did not love these things. She honored them, but she did not love them. She would never love them. She loved the man before her, who stepped from the tub and rubbed down roughly with a bath sheet. She watched his beautiful body in the firelight, and he reached out for her, pulled her up against him, unhooked her chemise hastily, and pulled the ribbon on her petticoat, which fell like a pile of magnolia petals at her feet. She closed her eyes and wrapped her arms round his shoulders and gave herself up gratefully to his hands and lips. "Never leave me," she murmured, "never, never leave me."

Chapter 9

*T*he Café Rigolo lay in the shadow of Saint-Sulpice in a cluster of streets with bad sanitation, bad ventilation, and bad reputations. The café itself was clean, the zinc scrubbed, the steps swept once a day, the floor less often (on the theory that if you swept the steps the floor would not get so dirty). The windows, heavily streaked with smoke, nonetheless admitted enough light so that customers could play cards or read the newspapers without lamps till afternoon. Like all cafés, this one had its own social code and habitués, who would tolerate newcomers if they bought a round of drinks and made no trouble. The proprietor, Madame Fagennes, claimed she could smell trouble as fast as a fart. Once there was a Monsieur Fagennes, but the story was he'd run off to America with a serving wench half his age in 1843. Madame Fagennes referred to them simply as *les disparus*. Then she'd smile. Madame Fagennes cultivated good relationships not simply with her customers but with the police, with the local *mouchards*—every workingman's café had its resident police spy and every urchin knew who it was—and with the few prostitutes she suffered to use her premises as a rendezvous. Madame Fagennes tolerated only registered prostitutes; if she caught an unregistered one lurking about, picking up men, she hustled the woman out immediately. Unregistered prostitutes were unreliable, amateurs who brought with them always the possibility of a *razzia*, a raid from the Morals Brigade. Bad for business. The registered ones were docile for the most part, reliable, like Mimi Lascaux. Madame Fagennes ran Mimi Lascaux a tab and Mimi's regulars knew where to find her, and it was agreed between them that Mimi's customers paid cash for their drinks. It worked out. Besides, Mimi always wore good-quality clothes, much mended, but they brought up the tone of the place.

Mimi's clothes and accoutrements came from her mother, the

Changer, also known as the Countess Crasseux, a former ragpicker who by dint of extremely good luck and hard work (and no doubt some well-placed blackmail) had inherited the old Changer's business. Now she played wardrobe mistress to the mobility—the mob—with clothes snatched from the deathbeds of the nobility by servants undistracted with grief. They sold everything, from stockings to spectacles, to the Countess Crasseux, a name befitting a woman of such power and substance. Mimi accepted these clothes from her mother, though they had quarreled bitterly some years before when Mimi declared her contempt for the countess and said she'd rather whore than work for her; the countess warned Mimi would end up a ragpicker, that a ragpicker was only a whore who'd lost her looks. Mimi retorted, "The day I find myself with the staff and basket is the day I throw myself into the Seine." They could agree on nothing save that they both doted on Mimi's son (her only living child, as she was her mother's only living child). Neither, however, was quite certain what the Starling did with himself all day, where he slept at night, where or how he lived. He was resourceful and independent.

He was a thieving brat, Madame Fagennes thought, and she had been glad to see him sent to La Petite Roquette, hoping he'd stay there till he could be transported to Algeria. So she was surprised one afternoon in mid-February, doing a perfunctory washup in a basin of greasy water, to see him enter the Café Rigolo. She almost didn't recognize him with his hair cut in that alarming way and Jean-Luc's old coat, far too big for him, and far too fine, trousers not torn or ragged. "You're looking quite prosperous," Madame Fagennes observed. "Quite the young gentleman."

Le Sansonnet made a florid bow and said he was working for *La Lumière,* the best newspaper in all Paris. An itinerant cobbler sitting nearby, drinking adulterated wine and reading *La Lumière,* burped enthusiastically.

"You men and your Republic," snorted Madame Fagennes. "I piss in the chimney of your Republic. Will the Republic allow women to vote any more than the king allows us to vote?"

"No one allows women to vote," said Le Sansonnet, shocked.

"Very well, then. My point is made." She rinsed out a few more glasses. "She's had a bit of bad luck, your mother. No, don't look so tragic, she's all right, but it's one of her regulars, Léon. His landlady came in here and she tells me he broke his arm in three places, fell off the scaffolding and had to be taken to the hospital."

"The poor bastard's dead for sure then, isn't he?"

"He won't die. But he won't be working for a good long time either. He was your mother's regular. Saturday night, just like clockwork. Sunday too, then Saint-Monday. She could count on him for that."

At that moment Mimi entered the Café Rigolo in a dress of mustard-colored wool, the hem spattered brown, her bonnet at a jaunty angle. When she saw her son, her whole face lit and she exclaimed how well he was looking.

"He looks to be eating regular and sleeping dry," said Madame Fagennes, pouring Mimi a glass of wine, adulterated with some mysterious substance that gave it a blue cast; in the Café Rigolo one might ask for *vin rouge* or *vin blanc,* but one inevitably got *vin bleu.*

"Except for your hair." Mimi took her glass and sat across from him, took off her bonnet and placed it carefully on the bench beside her. "Did you get arrested again?"

"The countess," he shrugged. "The Jondrettes wrestled me down and she cut it. Lice."

"That woman would find lice in the hair of the Virgin." Mimi Lascaux pulled her gloves off with a flourish, and fidgeted with the tattered lace at her wrist. Her coat was held together with frayed velvet frogs, and the smart bonnet belied her tired eyes and mouth, the way her expression seemed to sag from her temples. Her prize possessions were two sets of false ringlets pinned to her own hair, which was thin like her son's, and dark, and a pair of black jet earbobs. Mimi's meek, abstracted air (Madame Fagennes was quite right about the docility of registered prostitutes) allowed her to be bullied by everyone—the police, her customers, even Madame Fagennes—and remain numbed and pliant. *Vin bleu* helped. When *vin bleu* was not strong enough to help, Mimi had recourse to a near-lethal brew of beer, brandy, and absinthe, which produced on the breath and the brain of the drinker a kind of combustible fog, comforting when it did not kill.

"I'm working now," the Starling volunteered brightly. "Why don't you let me buy you a meal?"

"Léon will buy me a meal later. Léon or someone like him. You don't need to use your money. Unless—" She sipped audibly.

He bought a second *vin bleu* and set it before her. "Did you know I have work?"

"Yes. Someone told me. I can't remember who."

"Aren't you going to ask me what I'm doing?"

"Didn't I?" She toyed with her earbobs and false curls.

"I'm a courier, an errand runner for *La Lumière*. They used to have a bunch of old gaffers, veterans from Napoléon's time, for runners, men who could not get around Paris on a beggar's sled. Me, I go all over the city. They trust me with everything, even money. I'm fast. No one's fast as me. That's what they say."

"*La Lumière*, what's that?"

"The newspaper!"

"The one with the candle?"

"The torch. It's a torch on either side of the masthead."

"The what?"

"Never mind. Yes, a newspaper. We have advertising. On our back page like *La Presse*," he added proudly when she failed to respond. She finished her wine as if it were a solo and delicately began another. The boy began again, "*La Lumière*, they have their own theatre critic, Monsieur Coligny. He gets tickets for everything. He said he'd get me tickets, too. Would you like to go to the theatre, Mimi? Me, I could take you."

"I go sometimes."

"I don't mean a cabaret, or a café where they sing, I don't mean some *guignol* in the park, I mean really, the theatre! To see the great actress Rachel! To go to the opera even!"

"You go, Gabriel. You go and then come home and tell me all about it, and that will be better than if I go. I'll like it better, to hear it from you. It will be—well, like having your eyes. You can come home," she said pointedly, "and tell me all about it."

"I can't," he said at last. "You know I can't."

"There's been nothing like that. Nothing at all. You can come back and live with me now. You know I have two rooms. Only one is for business. The other—well, you're a big boy now, you could have the other room. All to yourself. Really, it would be so nice to—"

He put his hands over hers. "*Merci*, Mimi, but no." At thirteen his hand was as big as hers and their skin was equally pale, but Mimi's was blue-veined and the little vanities she'd once taken with her fingernails had come to an end. "At *La Lumière* there's a pallet at the back of the print shop, by the stove, so it's warm, and Monsieur Verdier, he says I can sleep there. He gave me a blanket and a pair of shoes. I have my own place to live." She tried to pull her hand away, but he held it tightly. "They pay me three francs a day, Mimi."

Her eyes grew round and rapt. "Three francs! For larking about Paris! Three francs!"

"They trust me. I pick up money. I pick up information. I'm good. The best."

"You are the Starling after all," she said with some pride.

"I have a place to sleep and I don't need much to eat, besides, Madame Pontmercy, sometimes she brings whole meals to the rue de Combray, feeds all the men who work there. People like us, we could live for a month on what the Pontmercys eat in a day, but you see what I'm saying, don't you? Me, I don't need the three francs. I can live."

"I need another wine. Léon will be here soon."

The Starling fetched her a third *vin bleu,* and when he did, Madame Fagennes informed him in an undertone that Mimi didn't yet know of Léon's accident. "You tell her. It will hurt less."

"It won't hurt at all," he snarled. "She's not in love with him. He's a—"

"He's a regular, boy. That's better than love."

Taking the wine to the table, Le Sansonnet explained, patiently as if he were giving a lesson in arithmetic, "Three francs a day, Mimi. I can give you those three francs. When you were a seamstress you used to make two francs a day. With my three, that will be five. You can live on five. Live well. Nicely. Not nicely like Madame Pontmercy lives nicely, but you can live without—without a lot of men and a police certificate."

"The police aren't bad. There's a ruffian now and then, but mostly they're just bullies. It's a joke they call them the Morals Brigade, Gabriel. Really. They're not very moral. I can tell you that. A brigade yes, moral no, eh?"

"You take my three francs," he went on, speaking in a schoolmaster's tone. "You earn two sewing. You have five francs a day. Bread. Shelter. A bit of ribbon now and then. No police. No Léon. Oh, don't you even hear me?"

Mimi sipped her *vin bleu* vacantly. "Do you remember that stupid story she used to tell? She used that story for everything. I hated that story."

"Listen to me—Mimi, please—I have three francs—"

"You know the one I mean, don't you?" Her eyes had bleared and her mouth had gone slightly slack. "'The Costly Omelette?'"

"I don't want to hear that now. I want you to listen—"

"It's true. I choke to say it, Gabriel, but it's true, that story."

Gabriel's grandmother had heard "The Costly Omelette" from the original Changer, and she retold the story to anyone who would listen, and many who wouldn't. She used it continually as one might a biblical warning. The story went like this: In 1793, with his friends' heads falling daily, an aristocrat had made a daring escape from La Force prison in Paris. Dressed as a peasant, he fled across France to Calais, where he could catch a boat that would take him to safety in England. He'd made good his disguise, got all the way to Calais, and at the inn there he ordered an omelette. When the innkeeper asked how many eggs, the so-called peasant said twelve. Everyone knew—instantly—not who he was, but what he was, an aristocrat in disguise. Arrested, sent back to Paris, he was guillotined within the week.

Mimi's droopy eyes fastened on the floor where the house cat toyed with a hapless cockroach. "The Countess always said it's not enough to change your clothes, to change the outside. You must change the inside. The outside of me is the inside. I can't change that."

"I don't need three francs. You need the money. Let me give you three francs."

"Once," she held her little hands up and told herself a singsong story, "my fingers were blue with pricks from the needle. I was not very good with the needle, ever. I could sew—who can't?—but not fast, you see, Gabriel. Not fast and not accurate. And anyway, I couldn't undersell those sluts in convents. None of us could. The nuns, they don't have to buy bread, shelter, your bit of ribbon, do they? They undersell us and we starve. Not all the girls maybe, not the clever ones, not the ones with men who'll stay by them, marry them even, but the rest of us . . ." She dropped her hands down on the table, and took a drink. "Me, I'm not clever. I used to sew velvet flowers, but I wasn't good with the needle and I'd prick my fingers and the blood got on the velvet and it was no good. My work was wasted. No lady would wear a bloodstained velvet flower, would she? Show me the lady with a bloodstain on her flower. I dare you. I couldn't—"

"Léon isn't coming anymore," he said coldly. "His landlady told Madame Fagennes he'd had an accident. His arm is broken in three places. He's finished, Mimi. He'll have to live on his savings and buy his bread by the notch and hope the landlady doesn't throw him out of the boardinghouse where he and the other workers sleep twenty to a room and shit eighty to a latrine. So there's no more Café Rigolo for old Léon. No more Sunday nights, payday at the *barrière bal,* no more Saint-Monday in your bed. You understand? You see? He can't pay anymore. You need to live. I can help."

Mimi began to blubber and cry, and in dismay Le Sansonnet ran his hands roughly over his still-spiky head. When he was almost ten the Starling had intervened in a quarrel between Mimi and one of her customers, a man who was beating her savagely; in the fracas both Mimi and the boy had gotten broken ribs. The boy's nose was broken, which accounted for its still crooked appearance. Worse, they'd been evicted. Mimi had found new rooms in the impasse des Quatre-Vents, one room tarted up for business and one, considerably plainer, for living in. But the boy could not bear it anymore, to be in the next room, to hear, even when they were not beating her, he could not bear it. He left. He was resourceful, resilient, and adept at thievery, able, nimble, a good student, but he was a novice pickpocket and this was what had got him sent to La Petite Roquette. Mostly he stole from those nearly as poor as he. Sometimes he merely mudlarked along the river, fishing out rope, wire, wood, coal, iron, or canvas, selling to marine dealers, to anyone who would buy without asking questions.

He developed a wide acquaintance with boys like himself and with men like the kind of man he would grow up to be. He'd learned to "star-glaze," to take out a pane of glass with a flick of the knife, from a boy, an accomplished thief known only as the Pincher, who declared the Starling a natural talent. His reputation spread, and once a gang of thieves had approached him to star-glaze a window of a jewelry shop and split the take with them, but Le Sansonnet declared he worked independently. It was his trade-mark, if not his trade. He'd felt the fists of men, the boots of police, the pinch of empty guts, the fingers of winter wrapped round his thin shanks. He was fleet and foul and foulmouthed, ugly, and stubborn, but not stupid. He slept where he found it convenient to sleep, easy in the summer when an overturned boat on the bank of the Seine or dry arches under a bridge could be very accommodating. Harder in the winter. In winter he'd show up at the Changer's more often. His grandmother chafed and rattled at him for being bruised, filthy, and hungry, but he'd got a taste for the independence, and like the starling he was named for, he could not be caged.

He was dubious about working for *La Lumière*, but the freedoms were many and the money a novelty. He was still occasionally tempted when darting through Paris and seeing an old man whose watch or pocket handkerchief cried out, *Steal me.* But in taking on the work of courier, he discovered he was a thief by choice and not by nature. This surprised him. At *La Lumière* he liked the work, he liked the people, printers, proofers, apprentices, and old veterans alike. He liked being paid on Saturday night. Three francs a day! Unthinkable riches. He could fulfill all his dreams, fulfill the grand stories he had told himself over and over while he had listened to men boffing his mother, while he had walked the exercise yard of La Petite Roquette, as he had huddled under overturned boats in July or warmed his hands at street fires in November, as he had hunkered in alleys listening to police run by, or crouched under the blows of men stealing his bread, endured the blows of drunks. Through all this ugliness, he told himself the kind of stories that gild bitter lives, promises brandished against brutality, sugar-on-shit: how he would come for Mimi, in a carriage, yes, that's how it would happen, an open landau, and he'd have fine clothes and he would tear the police certificate up before her eyes and waltz her out of the Café Rigolo and into the Café Anglais. No more *fille publique.* No more Morals Brigade. No more men to beat her and strip her and make her cry. And now here he sat across from her. He had three francs a day. Three francs. And still his childhood dreams were about to be defeated and he did not know why.

"Poor Léon," she sniffed and wiped her nose. "It's a real pity."

"You didn't love him. You couldn't have loved him."

Laughter rasped and bubbled to her lips. "No one in Paris loves. Didn't you know that? Thirteen years old, graduate of La Petite Roquette, the terror of the rue Mouffetard, dauphin of the place Maubert, and you didn't know that? This is what they do in Paris." She made a slow, obscene gesture. "Sometimes they pay. Sometimes they don't. Me, I insist on being paid. I didn't always. It used to be—your father, I lived with him. It was a free union, I did not ask to be paid. I asked to be loved. He didn't pay, but he didn't love either. No one does." She rose and stroked the Starling's spiky head, his cheek, and said she would still take the three francs. She had some clothes at the pawnshop, a pair of boots that would be nice in this wet, cold weather, especially now, without Léon, she could not wait in the dry café.

Le Sansonnet gave her the money and watched her leave. He cast an angry look to Madame Fagennes, who shrugged. On his way out, he kicked the cat and the wounded cockroach escaped.

Chapter 10

*T*he stones ran black with ink, mottling gray in a fine evening rain, as the Starling sprinted into *La Lumière*'s courtyard. A young apprentice, given the thankless job of washing down the inking brushes, told him to be quiet in the pressroom because Moses was snoozing by the stove. That's what the young men called Verdier now, no longer the Priest, but Moses, his long hair having gone entirely gray, his temper Old Testament–short, and his way of making pronouncements having something of the Ten Commandments; he was a perfectionist, determined that *La Lumière* should be the finest and the best-printed newspaper in all France, and anyone not subscribing to that view was brought sharply around to share it. Le Sansonnet tiptoed into the press-room, where the gas was turned down, and in the half-light, the huge presses stood black and silent like so many idling guillotines.

His feet stretched out to the stove, Verdier slouched in one of the chairs, hands crossed over his leather apron. "You're late, Starling. Monsieur Pontmercy wants you upstairs and don't leave again without stopping here." Verdier said all this without opening his eyes.

"Yes, your holiness," muttered the Starling, making his way to the front and the large windows on the rue de Combray, where the last of the old soldiers were closing up the stamp and subscription books for the night, quarreling about Austerlitz and the day's receipts at the same time. Their medals clinked and clanked on their bosoms as they bid the Starling good night.

He mounted the stairs to the editorial offices, where a few cubicles were partitioned off from a large, airy central room. Here half a dozen baize-covered tables were pushed together in the center and surrounded by chairs with cheap straw bottoms. Over-head all the lamps burned and two stoves kept the room comfortable. The windows, one fronting the street and one overlooking the courtyard, were stippled with rain. Of all the men usually at work here—the runners and the writers and the proofers—only Marius and Clerons remained, but even near empty the editorial chambers still had the air of dash and battle, haphazard energy, as masculine as the pervasive smell of tobacco. Papers and proof sheets and messages and caricature drafts were pinned along the dull green wallpaper above cracked wainscoting; stacked on the floor were other Parisian papers of every stripe and variety of opinion; on the table whole regiments of ink bottles and blotters, flotillas of pens, the wax and seal imprint of the torch, stood ready for action.

Marius looked up from his desk, beckoned to the Starling, and asked him to go to the rue des Filles-du-Calvaire and tell Madame Pontmercy he would not be home for quite a while. "And tell her not to come here and work. She mustn't. She's done enough."

"I'll tell her, monsieur, but as you know—" the Starling shrugged. "She does as she pleases."

"I have been married to her for sixteen years this month," Marius's serious face took on a pleasant glow, "so you needn't inform me about my wife."

"I only meant, monsieur, that I'm doing my job. I take the message. I can't oblige your wife to obey."

"Are you being flip with me, Starling?"

"No, monsieur."

"Very well." Marius picked up the pen and returned to his work.

"Excusing your pardon, monsieur, but I'm late for a reason."

"That is?" Marius did not look up.

"I've been around and about, as you'd asked me to, monsieur. I know a lot of people along the river, those poor neighborhoods on the other side of the river, Saint-Julien-le-Pauvre, the place Maubert, the rue Mouffetard, places like that. I know the people there and I must tell you, monsieur, it's not going to happen like you think."

"What's not going to happen?"

"The reform banquets."

"They aren't going to happen at all," Marius explained patiently. "Last month the government forbade these reform banquets to go on, and the Opposition toyed with defiance, but now, at the very last minute, the organizers, Thiers and the like, decided they will not defy the government. The reform banquets are canceled, Starling, not by the government, by the organizers. So much for *Vive la réforme.*"

"Excusing me, monsieur, but the people, the men who work and starve anyway, I don't think they much care for your organizers."

Marius beckoned for Clerons to join them. Then he said to the Starling, "I don't see."

"The organizers, Thiers, Marrast, Lamartine, and them, they call out *Vive la réforme,* but they are bourgeois without balls or spine, if you will forgive me, monsieur. When the government says, tells them, Please do not cry *Vive la réforme,* it disturbs the king's sleep, do not hold your reform banquets, they upset the digestion of Monsieur Guizot, then the spineless bourgeois, they rattle their sabres for a bit, they splutter, they flash their hash of words, but when it comes down to it, what happens? They get down and lick the rust off Guizot's balls."

"Your mouth is going to get you into a lot of trouble, boy," Clerons warned him.

"Maybe so, monsieur, but it won't be for sucking the dimples off the king's ass."

"Take your hat off inside, Starling," Marius ordered him, "and sit down."

"Is that what a gentleman does? Take his hat off inside?"

"It's one of the things a gentleman does. Now, go on."

"You think when the bourgeois agree with the king, then nothing will happen? The men who work—and the men who don't—" he added significantly—"they don't care what Thiers says. The bourgeois have kept workingmen out from the beginning. Why should they obey? Why? See? When word first goes around about these reform banquets, the price is three francs. Very well, three francs, that's steep, but possible. Then the men you call Opposition, suddenly they raise it to six, knowing very well no workingman can pay six francs. And what about those poor country sods who come to Paris from all over France, carrying their tools on their backs, come to find work, but no one is building in Paris. So they live and starve like cattle. They couldn't cough up six francs if their own mothers were to be shipped to the Montfaucon boneyard."

"Get to it," Clerons muttered.

"That's how the bourgeois treat the workingman. But that's not enough. No, the reform banquets were to be held on Sunday when working people have off and could have gone—"

"They're all drunk on Sunday," Clerons interrupted. "They get paid on Saturday night, they get drunk on Sunday, they celebrate Saint-Monday in bed with whores and hangovers."

The Starling paused, but he finished up quickly, saying that changing the date of the banquets to Tuesday meant that working people couldn't possibly come. "Now—after we have been kept out, and kicked out—they want us to obey them and forget everything?"

"Us?" inquired Clerons, pointedly.

"I should not have included you amongst those with balls, your excellency." Quickly the Starling ducked the blow he knew was coming.

"They'll fetch you up on the scaffold one day," Clerons said, breathing heavily, "they'll guillotine that tongue right out of your head."

Marius rose and came around the other side of his desk, as if to put himself between his colleague and this troublesome boy. He admonished the Starling to keep a civil tongue and show some respect. "You said it would not happen as we thought. So tell me, how will it happen?"

"I don't know," Le Sansonnet confessed at last, abashed at having made such a fuss.

"Tell me, Starling—" Clerons lit one of his ever-present cigarettes. "Look at me when I'm talking to you. Do you see riot in the street?"

"No."

"Do you hear people singing revolutionary songs, chanting slogans, demanding bread and equality?"

"No."

"Do you see them raising the workers' red flag?"

"At the bordellos, the whores are hanging red drawers out of their windows," snapped Le Sansonnet, "and when the Morals Brigade comes along, they say they're airing their linen."

"What do you know of bordellos?" asked Clerons, with an arch smile.

The boy sulked and shrugged.

Clerons smoked. "In your travels do you see anywhere evidence of blind and hostile passions against the government?"

"No."

"Against the king?"

"No."

"Then what makes you think—"

"Because I do not see them doesn't mean they don't exist! Because you don't see them means nothing! Because I don't see the *merde* in the street doesn't stop me from stepping in it!" The Starling returned to Marius. "These are the wrong questions, Monsieur Pontmercy! You should be asking yourselves, Why don't we see these things? Everyone knows they are there! People are starving and freezing and there's no work for the honest. Men come from all over France, find no work here, and have no money to go home. Women in the rue Mouffetard try to live, to support children by selling bootlaces for ten centimes. How can they buy bread that costs seven sous? Eight in some places, double what it used to be. How can she pay rent by the week? If she's thrown out, how can she keep warm? She can't. They find these women, children, beggars, they are frozen in the doorways, monsieur, they die. Some slow, some fast. They die because they have no work, because those with work are not paid enough to live, to buy bread, to pay rent—"

"You don't die," observed Clerons mildly.

"I am fast and young and the Pincher's taught me well. The gutters run in my blood. I am not a woman with three brats and no man, sewing twelve hours a day for two francs. These people are angry, monsieur. Hungry. They care nothing for what Thiers says, or the rest of them, your bourgeois Opposition. They care for the full belly. Why should workers care what the bourgeois say? At six francs and on Tuesday they could not go to the banquets anyway, so who cares? Frock coats put them on. Frock coats called them off, eh? But you wait, monsieur, on Tuesday," the Starling faltered. "Well, because you don't see these people starve in front of you doesn't mean they're fed."

"Why don't we see them?" asked Marius.

"I'm just—well, you asked—fine. I answered."

But Marius had not been talking to the boy; he was talking to himself. "Why don't we see them?" Marius crumpled the page he had been writing, staring at it thoughtfully. At last he said, "*La Lumière* will advise its readers to gather in the place de la Madeleine the 22nd of February, regardless of the king's ban and the Opposition acquiescence."

"That's sedition!" cried Clerons. "The government's forbidden these reform banquets! Even the Opposition has declared they won't go on! And they won't."

"Something will go on," said Marius, picking up his pen. "Count on it."

"It's incendiary! It defies the ban on political assembly. You will have men collected there with no better aim than riot. You will insult Thiers, the other moderates, by defying them."

"Have you seen our masthead? The torch? Better the torch than the trough." Marius paused. "Go on, Starling. Take the message to my wife."

Le Sansonnet whisked out of Marius's cubicle and through the editorial rooms and downstairs while the men's quarrel proceeded—Clerons arguing that Marius would be instantly back in Sainte-Pélagie prison, this time for treason.

No longer snoozing by the stove, Verdier emerged from the shadows in the pressroom, and to Le Sansonnet's surprise he was smiling.

"On your way to the rue des Filles-du-Calvaire," said the master printer, "take a message to my apartment in the rue du Caire. Tell Thérèse I won't be home, probably not all night. I've got something to fix before we can run again tomorrow."

"Yes. Fine. I'll do that." Jamming his hat on his head, the Starling paused. "Why are you smiling? What's so funny?"

Verdier raised his eyes overhead, where they could hear the quarrel ongoing. He took a long clay pipe off the shelf, tamped some tobacco in it, and brought a candle up to illuminate his cadaverous face. "Does it not seem strange to you, Starling, that something so silly, so inconsequential as all this—whether or not a reform banquet should be held—should be the pivot on which turns the revolution?"

"All they want is reform. Do you think it'll come to revolution?"

"Revolution has come before, Starling. The question is, Will it stay? That's the question."

Chapter 11

*L*e Sansonnet took a different route tonight, turning, twisting through the streets of old Paris, a city divided vertically for the most part, where the squalid garrets and the lowest courtyards, dank dwellings, were reserved for the poor, who sandwiched in between them the comfortable flats of people of prosperity. The rue du Caire was populated by printers, lithographers, and hatters, and Verdier's flat was near the top, but mercifully far enough from the latrine to have a bit of fresh air. He gave the message to Thérèse, with whom Verdier lived in a *union libre*. A worker in the ribbon trade, Thérèse had buried two husbands before she took up with Verdier; she had four children of her own and raised his three as well. (His youngest son had followed Verdier's wife into the grave, dead of the cholera in 1832.) Thérèse was unflappable, and the Starling wondered how someone so good-natured could live with Moses.

From there he ran zigzagging through the theatrical district, the broad boulevard du Temple, and from there, quickly to the rue des Filles-du-Calvaire, Number 6. The cook answered his knock and his heart rather sank. Madame Carême did not like him.

"I hate to see your face," she announced, marching back to the marble chopping block.

"I might say the same," he retorted, scooting inside, adding as she came after him with her cleaver, "if I was a great brute and a liar! I love your face, madame! I do, really!"

"Is it the same thing tonight, then?"

"My message is for Madame Pontmercy," he announced grandly.

"Yes, but the burden is on me. Look at this—" she pointed to her elaborate preparations for dinner, her face falling dejectedly when she regarded a baking dish of pears of perfect shape, peeled, set upright in custard and baked with meringue collars. "The pear crowned," she lamented, "wasted."

"I'll eat it."

"Never, you brat! Food like that would be sacrilege in your foul mouth! Now get out. Go on up and give your message. Madame is in the library."

Madame Carême had never before bade him go up, always sending some lesser servant with the message and making him wait. Either she had thawed, or she had given up, and he wasn't about to tax her by asking directions, so he moved quickly through the kitchen doors and up the steps. Le Sansonnet might have been able to navigate all Paris, both sides of the Seine, and the *barrières* with winged ease, but the Pontmercy home unraveled him. In looking for the library, he felt like a starling caught in a cage. He'd never seen such empty rooms, such vaunted space, so high-ceilinged, such long windows and heavy drapes to keep out the cold. He opened doors into the drawing room, to the dining room, both so cavernous he feared the void inside, certain it would swallow him up; worse than being lost, he felt giddy, as though gravity itself had failed him.

Startled by a servant whom he had likewise startled, he said he had a message for Madame Pontmercy, and he was subsequently led upstairs to the library, where Cosette sat on the sofa before one of the fireplaces, Fantine on the floor at her feet, Cosette drawing a brush through Fantine's long, fair hair. The servant announced him and showed him in.

Quickly removing his hat, he said, "Message from Monsieur Pontmercy, madame."

Cosette sighed. "I hate to see your face."

"I guess everyone does."

"I mean, in the evening, it can only mean one thing. Am I correct?"

"Yes, madame."

"My husband will be very late and I should wait here."

"Yes, madame."

Swiftly Cosette plaited Fantine's hair while the little girl stared at the Starling; clearly, she too hated to see his face.

Le Sansonnet could scarcely look at either of them; his eyes followed the shelves from the floor to the ceiling and the books in them, the bindings of multifarious colors, green and yellow leather, dark inky blue, maroon, every shade of brown from snuff-colored to amber to deepest chocolate, some books so old and well thumbed the titles had been rubbed off the spines. He caught Cosette watching him. He said stupidly, "Leather."

"Paper too," she observed.

"Yes, lots of paper. Lots of paper in books."

"Do you read, Starling?"

"I can. Not to say I do."

"I'd lend you a book, but you might throw it in the pot, boil it for its binding, and drink the soup."

"Depends on how hungry I was."

"How hungry are you?"

"Not as hungry as I used to be."

"There, Fantine!" Cosette finished off her braids and tied two ribbons at each end, making her daughter look quite festive despite her frown.

"Don't go, Mama."

"I must, angel. Your papa needs me."

"He did tell you not to come," offered the Starling, unasked.

"See, Mama?" Fantine's sweet face brightened.

"The fact that Papa told me not to come makes it very plain how much he needs me." Smiling, Cosette stroked the girl's head. "One day, when you're older, you'll understand how messages go back and forth between people who love each other. They understand what they cannot say. Now I'm going to change."

"Why?" implored Fantine. "You look fine. You look lovely."

"But I'm going to put on something truly dazzling, my new gown with the tea-colored lace, I think, and when we're done I shall insist that your papa take me to the Café Anglais for supper. The food is grand there, though not as grand as Madame Carême's if the truth were told, but your Papa needs the lights and the gaiety of the Boulevard des Italiens as much as anything. Now, Fantine, you can have your supper in the kitchen with Madame Carême. She'll be delighted. I'll go down and tell her. And Le Sansonnet can go rouse Abel and he'll drive us to the rue de Combray."

The Starling made a face. "Abel drinks the brew of all nations to the death of the horse."

"What?"

"I'll tell Abel you ordered him not to breathe on the horse, madame."

"Yes. That's a fine idea." Cosette rose, kissed Fantine's cheek. At the door, she turned to the Starling. "You may choose a book if you'd like, and take it with you. Only you may not return it to me in soup."

"Yes, madame. I mean, no, madame."

"Can you really read," Fantine inquired, after Cosette had left them, "or were you lying?" When he did not reply, she pestered him further, interrogating him until finally he nodded, agreeing with he knew not quite what. "And was it really your grandmother, a ragpicker, who taught you?"

He thought he had swallowed his larynx, but perhaps not, as he could reply in his grandmother's behalf that she was no longer a ragpicker. "She was once. She's the Changer, the Countess Crasseux."

"She changes countesses?"

"She changes people."

"That's ridiculous! What does she change them into? Little toads?"

"Whatever they want to be. If they want to be little toads—"

"What do you want to be, Starling?"

He regarded her queerly and she asked again, slowly, as though saying each word for the benefit of the blind, deaf, and dumb, till he replied at last, "I guess I want to be what I am. I don't know. No one's ever asked me that before."

"What were you before you were the Starling?"

"I've always been the Starling."

Fantine walked along the bookshelves, stopping here and there, pulling a book off, glancing through it, and moving on and perusing another. "You really are ignorant. I meant—what did your mother call you? You have a mother, don't you? Everyone does."

"You and your brother have a beautiful mother. If she was my mother, I wouldn't make her go to the headmaster to find out what I'd done, I'd tell her myself. I'd tell her the truth."

"You'd lie."

"So did he."

"How dare you call my brother a liar! A thief calling my brother a liar! That's rich! You have no right to say that."

"I'm sorry. I beg your pardon."

"My brother's going to a different school now. Louis-le-Grand. He's a day student. Do you know Louis-le-Grand?"

"Me, I call no man *le grand,*" he declared, "citizen, that's the highest honor."

"That's what my father thinks too. My brother thinks it's clap-trap."

"What's that?"

"Garbage. I'm sure you know what garbage is."

She paused at the shelves, pulled a book off, turned a few pages, and pressed it against her. "What is your real name? You must tell me if you want the book. No name. No book."

"Maybe I don't want the book."

"You want it."

"Gabriel," he mumbled at last, "Gabriel Lascaux."

She repeated his name once or twice as though it were a stale biscuit. "Come and get the book, Gabriel Lascaux."

His feet mutinied and would not move. "My feet—my feet are dirty. Your carpet is clean."

"Do you still have lice? Your hair still looks terrible. Not as ter-rible, but very queer."

Picking dubiously at the warp and woof of Jean-Luc's coat, he said there were no more vermin. "This is too fine a house for vermin. Vermin only go where they're wanted."

"Who'd want them?" She crossed the room and held the book out to him, arm's length, as if she were a small queen with a scepter to pass. "La Fontaine's *Fables*. You'll like them. They're about ani-mals. Put it in your shirt. Beside the bread."

He snatched the book from her hand, and pivoting toward the door he rattled down the staircase, the shoes Verdier had given him making an awful racket on the marble since they had soles. He fell and got lost at the foot of the stairs till a perplexed servant pointed him toward the door that led into the kitchen, where he went flying past Cosette and Madame Carême, who were packing up a hamper of wine, biscuits, olives, and cheeses to take to the rue de Combray. He dashed out the door and into the garden, running along the gravel path toward the carriage shed, stopping for breath only at the statue of Diana under the chestnut tree, whose heavy boughs groaned overhead and whose branches rasped and whispered terrible things about him in the winter wind.

Chapter 12

Gilt gleamed on the spine of La Fontaine's *Fables*, and a tiny gold line rimmed the perimeter of the book. The leather, mottled with age, had softened, gone shiny under a hundred years of hands, and the pages were thick, lusciously so. It smelled of, well, of Book, the Starling supposed, since he had never held a book before. No doubt they all smelled this ambrosial. Certainly they smelled different from newspapers. He tucked himself up beside the stove, while Verdier worked on one of the presses, and upstairs the Pontmercys and Clerons worked on. After a few hours, true to her promise, Cosette insisted her husband should take her to the Café Anglais.

"I've put on this beautiful new dress," she smoothed her lacy overlay on rose-colored satin, "and I can't possibly go home till everyone on the Boulevard des Italiens has admired me."

"I admire you," said Marius, smiling.

"Then you'll take me to the Café Anglais?"

"I'd be honored."

And as they descended the stairs, it was clear that Clerons would be also honored. Hats, cloaks, gloves on, the three left *La Lumière* to walk toward the brilliant beckoning lights of the Boulevard des Italiens.

Verdier and the Starling finished up the light supper Cosette had brought for all of them, but Verdier still had the better part of the last bottle of wine. He took the chair beside the Starling at the pressroom stove, poured himself a glass, and sat there, taciturn and inscrutable as ever. He'd finished that glass and poured another before he asked where the Starling had stolen the book.

"Madame Pontmercy lent it. Honest. It's hers. It's from her library."

"She is a saint as well as a beauty. Who else would lend a book to a beggar and a thief, eh?"

"I'm not a beggar," he snapped, but he did not conclude as he had in the past because he was no longer a thief either. He wasn't sure what he was.

"You're a scamp and you'll end on the scaffold." Verdier burped in an un-Moses-like way and then toasted Madame Pontmercy, "A saint and the daughter of a saint. Her father was a saint."

"What did he do? Change ink into wine and type into bread?"

"He saved lives, you little savage. Let's have some respect for the dead."

"When did he die?"

"After."

"After what?"

"After he saved the lives." Verdier sipped his wine. "If not for him, Monsieur Clerons, even Monsieur Pontmercy, they would be eating the grass banquet, dead and rotted like the rest of them."

"The rest of who?"

"Don't ask so many questions."

Verdier finished the bottle of wine slowly and told him the story of the rue Mondétour, the barricade at the Corinth, coming finally to the five married men and the four National Guard uniforms they'd stripped from corpses, uniforms that would allow these men to escape, and how Cosette's father had appeared in a fifth uniform, how he took it off and saved Clerons's life. "He saved Pontmercy's life as well. Monsieur Pontmercy fought outside the Corinth, and he was wounded—you've seen the scar down his temple?—it would have been fatal, but this man, this stranger, lifted him, carried him on his back through the sewers of Paris, and left Monsieur Pontmercy at his grandfather's. Asked no reward. Told no one. Not even Pontmercy. Not even his daughter. He saved the life of the man his daughter loved." Verdier frowned. "Don't know that I would have done the same. My daughter's husband . . . ah well, women have a hell of a time of it, Starling. That's why they give us such hell." He held the empty bottle up to the feeble light of the stove. "Another cadaver. Goodnight, Starling. Think I'll stretch out on your pallet if you don't mind."

"Be my guest, Moses."

"What did you say?"

"I'm honored, monsieur."

Verdier must have fallen asleep immediately; his snores, deep and even, put the Starling to sleep, curled up in the chair, Jean-Luc's coat pulled over him and the book pressed close. He dreamed of animals. A mule, like one of those in the *Fables* of La Fontaine, pulled a cart with only three wheels, and with each revolution, the cart fell and thumped. Thumped. Thumped. He woke and the thumping did not dissolve with the dream. He thought perhaps they had returned from the Café Anglais, but looking toward the door at the rue de Combray, he saw nothing and no one. The thumping was coming from the door at the back of the pressroom. It was not at all urgent, only steady, slow and steady as a three-legged cart and a mule. The Starling wondered how long he'd been sleeping.

Taking no candle, he went back to the pressroom door, unbolted it, cracking it slightly, so as not to let in the cold—or the caller. They might have been one and the same: two blue eyes, pale as the winter moon, stared at the Starling from a white face framed by stringy hair that had deserted the top of the man's head and tangled with his sparse, matted beard.

"Priest?" he croaked. "I'm looking for the Priest."

The Starling cursed him, told him to go to the church, tried to slam the door shut, but the man's wooden shoe jutted in and blocked it. All the Starling's might was not enough to keep out the phantom, whose bony fingers curled around the door.

"Priest," he insisted.

"Go to hell and find your priest."

"He's here. I know he's here." The voice had a raw, breathy edge.

"There's no Priest here! Damned fool! Why would there be a priest in a printshop?"

"Priest! Priest, are you there?" he called through the crack in the door.

"Priest?" The voice was Verdier's behind the Starling. "Who wants the Priest?"

The vagrant seemed to sag against the door, and the boy would have kicked his foot away and closed it, but Verdier clapped a hand on his shoulder.

"I need the Priest." The voice seemed to have come from a sepulcher. "I am the Monkey."

Verdier flung the Starling aside and opened the door wide to admit the night, the cold, the phantom. He cried unto God, something the Starling had never heard from old Moses, nor had he ever seen him weep, tears coursing down his face unashamedly. Verdier and the pale man strained to see one another, as though they must look not the distance of an arm's length, but down long avenues of the past, dwindling into some finite obscurity, as though each must take not the measure of a man, but a memory. Memory's shroud fell from their eyes, time's crust and dust and mortar and mold crumbled between these two. "My God!" Verdier wept over and over. "You lived! You lived!"

"No, *maître,* you lived. I died. I am Lazarus." Laughter scrabbled up through his lungs like a dull blade sawing wood. "I am Lazarus now, but you are still the Priest."

"He's Moses!" declared the Starling, ready to defend the old man if need be from this terrible wraith.

But Verdier wanted no protection; he drew the vagrant into the pressroom, and the Starling closed the door and watched the stranger's queer lopsided walk. Taking the blanket from the Starling's pallet, Verdier threw it over Victor Pajol's shoulders and brought him over to the stove. Pajol looked anxiously around the dark pressroom, and then he began to nod, slowly at first, then picking up his pace and losing rhythm, bobbing spasmodically, whether from the cold or some internal, involuntary command the Starling couldn't tell.

"Pajol!" Verdier embraced him. "You see, Starling? You see this man? He lived! My friend, my brother, you lived!" Verdier's eyes shone with something close to beatitude, crying out joyfully, "This is the Monkey! My apprentice."

This man could not be an apprentice, so Le Sansonnet thought. Apprentices were boys who washed off the ink rolls; apprentices were blackened-up little imps who rolled the paper in, tied and stacked the newspapers, got kicked by the master, and helped distribute *La Lumière* to the hawkers, who would take the papers into the street. Apprentices were sullen or cheeky or sly, as suited them, but they were boys. To a man, they were boys. This man had never been a boy.

"Bread?" His head still bobbed up and down and his teeth chattered too. "Bread."

Verdier cursed himself for eating everything Madame Pontmercy had brought and drinking all the wine.

"I have bread," said the Starling. "In my stash at the back of the pallet I have a notch of bread." He brought it out, tore off a chunk, and gave it to the stranger, whom Verdier had seated before the fire, the blanket over his shoulders. Le Sansonnet watched rapt, as the stranger tore the chunk into tiny little pieces and put it, one bit at a time, into his jaws. The rest of the bread the vagrant clutched close to him, pressed against his breast like a holy relic. His gums bled profusely over the bread.

"My God," whispered Verdier, "my holy God."

The Starling took some water from a copper basin nearby, poured it into a saucepan, and set it on the stove. He tore off more bread, and to Verdier he explained, "I can soften it in the hot water. It will be easier for him to eat if it's soft. My grandmother has to do this."

Verdier scarcely heard him. "Pajol, oh Pajol, what did they do to you?"

"Fourteen years hard labor. Mont-Saint-Michel. You know Mont-Saint-Michel, Priest? Are you still the Priest? Tell me."

"No one has called me Priest since you died—I thought you died."

"Political prisoners, we didn't have it too bad at Mont-Saint-Michel. Not like the criminals. We didn't kill ourselves. Some died, but we didn't kill ourselves. We didn't kill each other." His head bobbed more furiously. "Finally, these frock coats, they come to inspect the prison, to see how men are treated at Mont-Saint-Michel."

"De Tocqueville," cried Verdier. "I remember the prison inquiries. We published all that in *La Lumière*."

"That's this paper, *La Lumière?* Nice. Nice, Priest. Good."

Le Sansonnet handed Pajol a warm cup with bread softened in warm water. He put his few other crusts in it, and as his fingers, sinewy and white as worms, folded around the cup, his shivering and involuntary nodding slowed.

"I can't take my eyes off you, Priest. I kept your face before me always so I should know you when I saw you again. Me, I kept your face, but I don't know it. It's your voice, I know your voice. But your face . . ."

"I am gray."

"Yes. You are changed."

"You are changed too."

Pajol slurped down a chunk of soft bread and, to the Starling's horror, he said he was thirty-one. He looked as old as Verdier. Older. For the first time the Starling considered what prison might do to a man. La Petite Roquette was certainly not the Academy of Amusement, but it had seemed to the Starling only grim and occasionally grisly, not an experience to destroy the spirit. Only the worst boys there were chained up. The Starling had never been chained. He had been beaten, but not broken, and he recognized that his resilience had never been truly tested.

Pajol finished off the bread and warm water, but held on to the cup. "Five years ago, after the frock coats come through, they moved us, the political prisoners. We were down to twenty-three men. They put the iron collars on and chained us to the transport wagon and took us to another prison, in the north—somewhere. I spent the last years there. When my fourteen years were over and they gave me my ticket of leave, I said to them, Point me to Paris, just shove me toward Paris and I will find it. That was—the autumn? Sometime. Now, it is what? January?"

"February."

"Ah. February," he replied as if softening that thought before he could chew it as well. He put the cup on the floor and pulled the blanket closer, squinting at the Starling. "This is your son?"

"No." Verdier regarded Le Sansonnet, seeming to see him for the first time.

"But your children lived?"

"Some of them." Verdier sank into the chair beside his old comrade. "Oh, Pajol, Pajol, why didn't you send some word, some message, some—"

"The only messages off Mont-Saint-Michel are those carried in the shit of seagulls. Don't fret, Priest. There's nothing you could have done. It was the doctor who turned me in, mangled my leg, too." He frowned and shrugged. "My hands are still good, though. Ugly, but useful. I can still set type. The doctor turned me in, but—"

he eked out what might have been laughter. "I saved you, Priest. I helped to save you."

"I escaped, Monkey. I wore the National Guard uniform and left the barricade before it fell."

"You alone, Priest. All the others, even those who escaped, they're dead, all dead, no, my friend, listen—" Pajol reached out and grasped the master printer's hand—"I kept your face before me and I swore I would find you, but I didn't live to find you. I lived to kill someone. Why not? It's a good reason to live, eh? Keeps you going. I will kill him and then I will die. It won't matter. But, Priest, I had to see you. We're orphans, yes? But we're two orphans. At least we're two." He began to shiver and nod again.

"No, Pajol, we're more than two. Others lived. Two others lived."

"Who?" He clung to the older man's arm. "Who?"

"Pontmercy. This is his newspaper. You remember Pontmercy, the student. *Better the sword than the—*"

At that moment the key to the door fronting the rue de Combray rattled, and sparkling feminine laughter flew into the pressroom, like glittering moths fluttering toward the light of the stove, and behind Cosette's laughter, Marius's voice. They stepped inside. It was perhaps two in the morning and all else deserted. Verdier ran to the front—Le Sansonnet had never seen any grown man move that fast—"Come!" Verdier cried, "Look!" He pulled Marius toward the pressroom, Cosette and Clerons behind. They brought with them the sharp odor of tobacco and the lilt of Cosette's cologne as they walked into the pressroom, the dark and silent presses surrounding them all like a forest.

Slowly Pajol turned around. Slowly he recognized Pontmercy. Slowly his eyes adjusted to the vision of Cosette, radiant in her blue velvet cloak. And the other man? Pajol's face twitched, his jaws working as if he were trying to spit out something disagreeable. He stood, slid the blanket off, and ignoring the Pontmercys, ignoring even the Priest, he paced slowly, purposefully around Clerons, looking him up and down.

"Who is this filthy beggar?" Clerons demanded. "Isn't it bad enough you bring beggar boys into the pressroom—"

"It's *you*. It is *you*. You don't know me? I know you! For years I have reached down into your throat and pulled your filthy tongue out by its dirty roots, I have—"

"Verdier," Marius implored, "what—"

But Verdier stood speechless as Pajol circled Clerons, who outweighed him by a hundred pounds, Pajol growling, "Filthy, filthy . . ." like a rosary. "You are the fifth man, but I am the last man." He sprang at Clerons, neither strong enough nor heavy enough to knock him over, but clinging to his throat with scrawny hands tightening. Clerons choked and sputtered and backed against the presses, while Marius and Verdier tried to pull Pajol off, Cosette watching in horror as they all four fell against the composition boxes, which were knocked over; and the men tumbled amongst the spilled alphabet, Marius and Verdier unhooking Pajol's hands from Clerons's throat long enough for the big man to scramble away.

Pajol shrieked like an animal, "*Mouchard! Mouchard!* Murderer! You killed them. You killed them all. Oh, Priest, how can you know this man? This swine? This—"

Clerons stepped up smartly, slapped Pajol hard, the crack of flesh against flesh like a rifle report. The others gasped, and Cosette lit a candle and handed it to the Starling, lit another, which Clerons snatched from her hand. He held it before Pajol's gaunt face.

Haltingly, Verdier said, "This is the other survivor, Monkey." He moistened dry lips. "This is the only other man who lived—" He turned to Marius. "Pajol lived, Monsieur Pontmercy. My apprentice, the Monkey. He lived."

Marius took Pajol's face in his hands, searching the cold blue eyes for some remnant of the lively Monkey.

But Pajol loosed himself from Marius, from Verdier, pointed his long, worm-white finger at the solid figure of Clerons. "You know this man? This lying dog?"

Marius felt as though some terrible tide had begun to ebb and pull, to reveal the wrecks heretofore shrouded. He looked from Pajol to Verdier to Clerons. "He is the fifth man."

"He's the king's man! He's a police spy! *Mouchard!* Everyone who escaped with you, Priest, he hunted them down. You got away because your wife's family, your whole building, vouched for you, but he, this *mouchard,* he came to me in La Force and that's how I knew you lived, Priest, and he told me two others had escaped, Pontmercy and someone else, the old man who came over the barricade in uniform—"

"Jean Valjean," said Marius, paling, his eyes meeting Verdier's horrible gaze. "Jean Valjean is dead."

"He was looking for those two men," Pajol repeated, "one young, one old."

Verdier's lips twisted as though he'd been shot. "I guess he found you, Monsieur Pontmercy."

"He knew when to look." In the wavering candlelight Marius studied Clerons's face: the gingery whiskers, strong jaw, unflinching blue eyes. "You knew where too, didn't you? Fifth of June. Old Corinth. It took you ten years, but you found me."

Clerons dusted off his clothing. "Fourteen years at Mont-Saint-Michel have played tricks on this man's mind."

Cosette brought her candle forward to Marius, the scar gone livid down his face, his dark eyes filled with pain. To Marius alone she said, "No one said fourteen years. No one said Mont-Saint-Michel."

"Have you betrayed us at every turn, Clerons?" Marius spoke in a hush. "Have you been the *mouchard* all along? Is this why I have been singled out for sedition time after time? The government has come down on us, as though they knew what we were going to print . . ." Marius swallowed hard and looked wildly from Cosette to Verdier. "Every meeting of the Opposition, every time the editors and Opposition deputies have met, you've been there. The government has followed our step, haven't they? The king has known everything."

"I thought you had died," Clerons said to Pajol with no particular animosity.

"I told you I'd live to kill you, and I will."

Marius gasped as if strangling, "You never had a wife and children in Lyon. My father-in-law gave you the uniform that saved your miserable life!"

"He didn't save my life," Clerons snapped, lighting up one of his ever-present cigarettes. "The officer taking the barricade knew Javert and me, knew we were spies. We would have escaped. So you see, I have no particular reason to be grateful to Jean Valjean. But you do, Monsieur Pontmercy. Jean Valjean, the convict, saved your life, and then you married the convict's daughter."

Marius bolted, brought the full force of his hand sharply across Clerons's face; the cigarette flew out of his lips and Cosette screamed to see his fist double up to hit Marius, but not before the Starling flew at him, buried his teeth in Clerons's cheek. Screaming, Clerons fought him, flung him off, but the Starling's teeth tore a chunk of the cheek and Clerons wailed in pain, pressing his hand to his face.

"I say kill him," cried Verdier, "don't let him out on the street again. I say kill him right here."

"Kill him," Pajol agreed. "There's three of us, kill him."

"Get out," Marius spoke to Clerons through clenched teeth. "Get out of Paris, Clerons. The next time I see you I will kill you. What have you cost us?" he whispered harshly.

His hand still gripped over his bleeding cheek, Clerons reached down and picked up his cigarette, where it lay near Cosette's feet. "The beautiful baroness, up from the gutter," he murmured. "The daughter of a convict, the daughter of a thief."

"He stole a loaf of bread!" Cosette cried out, and she too might have flown at him with her fists, but Marius pulled her into an embrace, his arm across her shoulders.

"You've done enough damage, *mouchard*. Leave."

Le Sansonnet mopped his lips again and again and spat out the taste of Clerons's blood, stunned to hear that the man Verdier had called a saint and the man who stole the loaf of bread were one and the same, the father of the Baroness Pontmercy.

"Prison awaits you all," Clerons growled, putting the cigarette between his lips, where it trembled.

"Leave before we kill you, you lying swine," cried Verdier.

"Leave before it ends in blood," said Cosette, weeping.

"It will all end in blood. It began there. It will end there." He left the pressroom door open, and the dank February night blew in, spluttering the candles, chilling the five of them through to their marrow.

Part II

The Sword, the Scaffold, and the Gutter
FEBRUARY 1848

The conflict of the right and the fact endures from the origins of society. To bring the duel to an end, to amalgamate the pure ideal with the human reality . . . this is the work of the wise. But the work of the wise is one thing, the work of the able another . . . As soon as the revolution strikes the shore, the able carve up the wreck.

—VICTOR HUGO
Les Misérables

Chapter 13

*B*y Tuesday, 22 February 1848, everyone in Paris knew something would happen, but no one knew what. With the expectant air of a crowd of playgoers—as yet uncertain if the curtain will rise at all—perhaps five hundred people gathered that morning before the church of the Madeleine, which rose like a vast Grecian dream uprooted from the Aegean sunshine and settled, all massive fifty-two Corinthian columns, in the pearly, cold light of Paris. Even before it was finished—eighty years in the building—the Madeleine was already a great relic, a monument of the eighteenth century, which valued static, classic symmetry, and completely at odds with the nineteenth century, which valued above all movement, momentum, and energy. Movement, momentum, and energy were everywhere evident early that morning, as people of all sorts and varieties walked and lounged, jostled, ogled one another. In the crisscross of carts and carriages, beneath bare trees, vendors called out their wares, newspaper hawkers did a brilliant bit of business, and in the chill rain, umbrella menders, working swiftly, did a rousing trade. The Pontmercys' carriage pulled up behind half a dozen others in front of Durand's restaurant fronting the huge square, and Cosette stuck her head out for a glimpse of the crowd, which she described to her husband and son as neither actors nor audience.

"Not yet," replied Marius.

A vendor's pipe played nearby, echoing the cry of a cornet as an umbrella mender advertised his availability. "Hardly the overture for rebellion," Cosette remarked.

"The overture was a long time ago. Whatever this is, it is no longer the overture." Marius turned to Jean-Luc seriously. "You will remember your duty at Louis-le-Grand? You will study and be a credit to your family? You have given your word, you know."

"Yes, Papa."

"Above all, Jean-Luc," Cosette took Marius's hand and stepped out, "you must stay out of the streets today. There could be trouble."

"Really, Mama, this crowd looks like they're waiting for a fair, not a riot." But Jean-Luc agreed to all her instructions. All sons agree to their mothers' instructions. The carriage pulled into the wheeled mêlée and took Jean-Luc to Louis-le-Grand across the Seine.

Walking toward Durand's Marius saw a flower stall, which in winter had but few pickings. The fragile flowers, upright in tins, stood shivering under tarps. Marius paid the vendor and put in Cosette's hands a nosegay of yellow freesias. "You remember?"

"That was the happiest day of my life, our wedding." She gave him their old secret smile, encoded after all these years of marriage to suggest the kiss they could not publicly share. Holding the yellow flowers up against her blue velvet cloak, she crossed the vast square on his arm.

Durand's restaurant was the best-known hub of Opposition opinion in all Paris, so much so that spies outnumbered the waiters—and very often the spies were waiters. A festive air pervaded here too; the place was crowded, every man with a newspaper under his arm, more than one, and the splash of brandy enlivened both coffee and conversation. From the back, Coligny and Beaujard gestured to them.

"The Comédie-Française will close its doors tonight," Coligny informed them, his cherubic face creased with a frown. "That confirms the emergency, doesn't it?"

"Only if the actors aren't paid," Cosette remarked.

Armand Marrast deigned to stop at their table, to ask if it was true, what he'd heard, "That the very able Monsieur Clerons has left *La Lumière,* on short notice."

"He was more able than we knew," Marius said bitterly, while under their table Cosette put her hand in his.

"Ah, well," Marrast replied brightly, "very soon perhaps all police spies will be out of work." And he glared pointedly at the waiter who brought their coffee.

Through the crowds—the men mixing, talking, gesticulating, arguing, planning for different contingencies—they saw Thiers enter Durand's, his wife, engulfed by her bonnet and cloak, invisible on one arm, his massive mother-in-law on the other. Between these women Thiers looked like a bright-eyed spider about to be ground up by a pebble and a boulder. He deposited his ladies at a table and made his way through the Opposition thicket, men who might fear him or flatter him, but very few who liked him, and no one who trusted him. He came to the Pontmercy table. "Well, Monsieur Pontmercy," he beamed with satisfaction, "I defy you to show me the resistance you were so certain would happen this day. As I recall, the pages of *La Lumière* predicted rebellion."

"The day is early, Monsieur Thiers."

"Barricades? Looting? Riot? Bloodshed? The usual Parisian bill of fare?"

"We have seen it before."

"I find it rather unthinkable, Monsieur Pontmercy, that *La Lumière* would urge its readers to defy, not the king, but the Opposition. You knew we had decided not to press the issue."

"Yes, but that was after you had decided to charge six francs and move the reform banquet to Tuesday, effectively cutting all workingmen from the event. If you truly want to be the Opposition, Monsieur Thiers, then you must represent all the French, not merely those with property."

"They are the only ones who count."

"When there is universal suffrage, you'll see that change."

"Ah, Monsieur Pontmercy, I don't share your enthusiasm for the French worker, for his intrinsic worth or his intrinsic rights. Property creates order, order creates stability, stability creates profits, profits create property—and so on. That is how it works." Thiers spoke with pedagogical exactitude.

"Such a notion leaves too many people without either property, profit, or order. It leaves their lives unstable, uncertain. Men have rights to their own labor, the labor itself confers rights."

"That sounds suspiciously like revolution. All we've asked for is reform, for the king to dismiss Guizot, primarily. But, ah, freedom of the press, that would be something worth having."

"It would be one thing worth having. There are others."

"There will be no revolution, Monsieur Pontmercy. Only when God is down to dubious means does He give a revolution. In the same way that a merchant whose credit is low gives a ball. He keeps up appearances, but beneath the gilded ceilings the dancers all tread on cracked floors and threadbare carpets. One wonders who is the more duped, the guests or the host."

"Only a cynic would say such a thing."

Thiers sighed, glanced in the mirror, and smoothed a stray hair from his enormous forehead. "You see my virtues as vices, I'm afraid."

"And no doubt you see mine the same way."

"Not at all, Monsieur Pontmercy. Both your qualities and your defects allow you to see the truth, but impede your taking action. I may choose to follow either my virtues or my vices, but it's not a choice for you. You are unbendingly upright and can be no other way. I might admire you, Monsieur Pontmercy, but I do not envy you. Save, naturally," he gave Cosette his lemony smile, "in your choice of a wife. Madame, if you will permit me to say, you look lovely in forest green. It complements your blue eyes."

"*Merci*, Monsieur Thiers," replied Cosette, amazed really that Thiers had sufficient imagination to distinguish between forest and any other kind of green. A man from *Le Siècle* came up and asked the diminutive Thiers whether, if the king invited him back into the government, he would serve. Monsieur Thiers declared, *Never*, and they walked away, while Beaujard, Coligny, even Marius teased Cosette that Thiers was half in love with her. "Don't be ridiculous!" she chastened them all. In truth she found Thiers physically repulsive and his intelligence abrasive. Worse, he had the habit of offering up as casual conversation things one could not say even to oneself. His observations on Marius touched her own worst fears for the man she loved: Marius's unbendingly upright quality, the very thing that made him a powerful figure, made him predictable, and for less scrupulous men—men like Clerons, men like Thiers, for that matter—easy to defeat.

Outside in the great place de la Madeleine, still more people had gathered, Verdier, Pajol, Thérèse amongst them. Pajol had shaved, and burned his prison rags; he was warmly dressed and no longer had the look of wizened innocence. The whole huge square around the columned church filled with palpable expectation; everyone around them wore a festive face, as if half of Paris had taken a half-holiday to collect here. Even in the grip of winter, goodwill was everywhere abundant, *fraternité* amongst all manner of men: frock coat and shopkeep alike, smock-clad men carrying their tools, velvet weavers who had deserted their looms, hatters from the Sainte-Avoye *quartier*, carpenters, joiners, and cabinet-makers from Saint-Antoine, metalworkers from the *quartier* Popincourt, mechanics from the *quartier* Poissonniers, men with no trades, only their sheer brute strength, who had made the tour of France, migrating seasonally to Paris, though there was no work for them now. By midmorning, following an invisible telegraphic excitement communicated all over the city, sudden infusions of workingmen streamed into the square, as workshops shut and stores closed up and stalls closed down, and even though it was a Tuesday, women who sewed by candlelight in tiny rooms blew out their candles and walked toward, gathered at the place de la Madeleine, dazzled by the metallic glare of winter sun on the church's cold marble. Stockbrokers from the Bourse, police and postal workers, porters milled with market women, merchants, the fat with the lean, the warmly dressed with the flap-shoed, and from their accustomed crevices at the corners, ragpickers appeared, looking biblical with their long, tattered clothes, their beards, their packs and baskets, their staffs reminiscent of shepherds watching over an unruly, unlikely flock.

Across the Seine, in the shadow of the Panthéon, another great monument to classical repose, a different crowd gathered that same morning. Here, in the *quartier* Latin—where there is more learning per square inch than any other place in Europe, perhaps the world—most students were still cloistered in their schools, toiling under the merciless gaze of their masters. Jean-Luc Pontmercy ought to have been one of those boys, but when he arrived at Louis-le-Grand, he grinned to see his old partner in crime, Arsène Huvet, lounging before the austere portals of learning.

Arms crossed, his cap at a rakish angle, Arsène slouched with the practiced, worldly air of a boy of thirteen. Sly, wistful, cavalier of money and hungry for approval, Arsène put himself, whenever possible, in the company of clever, charming people, the better to take on their coloration. Jean-Luc was perfectly willing to lend his coloration, since it cost him nothing.

"You can't be thinking of school today, Pontmercy," Arsène called out cheerfully. "Don't you know there's a rebellion in the king's honor? The fun's brewing over by the Panthéon."

"I'm sick to death of people waxing themselves over reform banquets. Who cares if they go on or not? Not me. I wouldn't care if every worker in Paris chewed stones for bread."

"You should have parents like mine, Pontmercy! Figure in francs, in weight, in volume, tell my father how much it will cost him to cart it to market and sell it at profit, and he is a font of wisdom. But he hasn't read a book since the last revolution."

"Which one?" Jean-Luc asked glumly. "Politics are lethal."

"Look at it this way, if there's a revolution, they'll close the schools!"

Brightened by this thought, they raced toward the Panthéon, and in the great square there the boys found a crowd of about three hundred, some clad in school uniforms, but many were servants, ushers, or porters for the great schools, some mere loafers and loungers, some, judging from their ink-stained hands, were earnest young journalists from the *Avant-Garde*, a rag with a minuscule readership and passionate views whose offices were nearby. Unlike the crowd before the Madeleine, the gathering here was mostly young and male and less like a holiday outing. A serious young journalist harangued the crowd. His arms waved windmill-like and he was as thin as the rails around the Panthéon, which gloomed over him, its classical symmetry implicitly disparaging all his intensity.

"Thinks he's Camille Desmoulins," observed Arsène with a snicker, "going to lead us all to the Bastille."

"He couldn't lead a bag of kittens to the river," said Jean-Luc rather too loudly. A man behind him gave him a shove and told him to shut his gob.

The boys bought hot fried potatoes off a vendor who scooped them into newspapers (*La Lumière*, Jean-Luc was happy to see), and with their hands thus wholly occupied in holding and eating the potatoes, they were in the perfect posture for Le Sansonnet's old friend, the Pincher, to inspect the lining of their pockets with his long, nimble fingers. Jean-Luc's pockets were a disappointment, but Arsène's proved fruitful. Sensing someone too close behind them, Jean-Luc turned around.

"Vive la réforme!" cried the Pincher ecstatically. "Down with Guizot! An end to tyrants!" he added as the crowd picked up his cries and his mood, and these chants ricocheted off the august stones around them. If the Pincher had had a sense of irony, he might have realized this was an inauspicious square for plying his trade, surrounded as he was by the Panthéon, the mayor's office, and the faculty of law, which is to say, the state, the city, and the notion of justice (and nearby, just down the rue Clovis, the church, Saint-Etienne-du-Mont). But the Pincher did not deal in symbols, only in stolen goods, and he was happy to have shaved ten francs off Arsène. He made his way through the throng, shouting the occasional slogan. Pincher was perhaps seventeen, lithe and wiry, and he walked with a curious crablike step that was a product of his profession.

Here in the precincts of the great schools of France, the Pincher was happy to see his own student, the Starling, milling about. "I heard you went legit." The Pincher spat the last word from the corner of his mouth and inspected the Starling's new coat, rubbing the threads together with the sagacity of a wool merchant.

"I'm a courier now. They sent me here today, to see what's brewing on this side of the river."

"They've got you up so fine and fancy I'd have taken you for a mark, boy, if I hadn't seen your scrawny self beneath this fine coat and scarf."

"You'd take the king for a mark, Pincher."

"That soggy old pear? He'd beat me to death with his umbrella. Now, in a fair fight—" The Pincher turned a quick twirl, thrusting his foot out with alarming—and potentially deadly—grace, a *savate* kick, a Parisian form of street boxing much practiced by young men and much admired by boys. The Starling was in awe, begged to be shown how to do that; he flattered the Pincher's sterling record as a teacher in all the other arts, and at last the Pincher consented. They moved to the edge of the crowd, and the older boy demonstrated, the Starling imitated, as quick to learn the *savate* kick as he'd been to learn star-glazing.

The Pincher ruffled the Starling's coarse hair, which had grown back over the past month. "You're doing all right, Starling, but you'd better watch out for that fine coat. It'll get in your way every time."

The Pincher's thin jacket barely met over his chest. In exchange for the lesson, the Starling gallantly took off the wool scarf Cosette had given him and presented it to his teacher. "Well, this is fine, Starling." Pincher wrapped it around his pale neck. "Just fine. I'm off to glean the fields, pluck the sheep of dinner's ransom. But you be careful. Some of these sheep have lead in their wool."

"This lot? They're not armed."

"A few. I went to filch a few sous of one and put my paws round cold, hard metal."

"Pistols?"

"Not saucepans. They're flashing a lot of hash here, but it could get hot. I'm off now, but if you ever get tired of flying for *La Lumière,* come back to me. You're a natural. With a little practice, you could file the gold off Guizot's teeth. Down with Guizot!" shouted the Pincher as he winked and moved away. "Down with the king and all his ministers! *Vive la réforme!*" he shouted directly behind a man whose arms were raised in protest and his pockets thus ripe for picking.

Flushed with the Pincher's praise, and practicing his newly learned *savate* kick, the Starling strolled through the crowd, whistling "La Marseillaise," his hands tucked in his pockets, where in one he fondled some bread he'd stowed, and in the other a handkerchief in which he tied up meat scraps bought cheap off a pork butcher.

"Link arms, men!" cried the would-be Camille Desmoulins, the journalist from *Avant-Garde.* "By threes! Link arms by threes! To the Madeleine! We'll join our brothers at the Madeleine!" The crowd roared its approval and, gathering themselves, they followed toward the rue Saint-Jacques.

Jauntily and full of republican goodwill, the Starling offered his arm to the person on his left, who happened to be Arsène Huvet, and beside him, "Jean-Luc!"

With the cool disdain of a patrician bred to the manor, Arsène demanded, "How dare you be so familiar with my friend?"

"He knows me, don't you?"

Jean-Luc regarded the Starling indifferently. "You're wearing my clothes. I guess I know my own clothes. Huvet, meet the Starling, filthy, foul, and ugly."

"That's true," Arsène concurred.

"It was my mother's fancy to pluck him from the gutter and put him into the pressroom. He's a self-confessed thief so beware your money."

Arsène checked his pockets and his face went quite white. "Ten francs! Gone! You little—"

Arsène lunged toward the Starling, but using the maneuver just learned from the Pincher, he slammed his foot into Arsène's chubby hand, and the rest of his money went flying. In the confusion, the Starling flew away, to the head of the column marching toward the rue Saint-Jacques, calling out behind him that he didn't steal anymore.

Some streets in the *quartier* Latin were so narrow that marching three abreast the crowd constituted a virtual phalanx, and on their way to rendezvous with destiny, the marchers made a detour to the place de l'Ecole-de-Médecine, where the medical students threw down their books and their scalpels, hastily covered their indecent cadavers, and spilled into the streets three abreast, marching down the rue Dauphine singing one of Paris's most popular tunes, "Song of the Girondins," whose lyrics declared all France's children were ready to spill their blood for her, to lift their voices to the roar of the cannon, to vanquish or die!

They crossed the river at the Pont-Neuf, Le Sansonnet still at the front, having a look back for pursuit by Jean-Luc and Arsène, but they seemed to have vanished, or perhaps they'd merely been swallowed up in the crowd, whose numbers had doubled.

Their voices grew stronger as they entered the broad rue Saint-Honoré, and they reclasped each other's arms and, five and six across, they spread out, "La Marseillaise" echoing between the buildings, reverberating as they collected new marchers. Shutters came down, chairs and tables, baskets of goods, children were stashed inside, doors slammed. Men and women joined the procession, some shopkeepers whose aprons had only just come off, some mechanics, clerks, and carriers, waiters, navvies, and potboys. Men of property and substance too were hastily donning their National Guard uniforms, and these men draped their arms around the smock-clad shoulders of the workers. Clerks traded caps with masons, and students loosed the red neckties of their uniforms and tied them around their heads like banners.

It was about eleven o'clock when they surged to the place de la Madeleine, where the holiday atmosphere still prevailed, and before the colossal church there still swarmed the mélange of merchants and mechanics. The Starling flew up the high steps of the church and looked over the great expanse before him, thronged now with perhaps two thousand people, and there, near where the flower vendors were closing down their stalls, he saw Verdier, Thérèse, Pajol, and the Pontmercys, and he swooped through the crowd to join them.

"Well, Monsieur Pontmercy," he said with pride, "you sent me to the other side of the river to watch, to see, and I thought, Well, why should I just watch? I'll bring them all back with me!" He stretched out his arms as the marchers from the Panthéon milled about with the Madeleine crowd, the very air bubbling with excitement, possibility.

"With all this *fraternité*," said Marius, smiling and drawing Cosette's arm through his, "can *liberté* and *égalité* be far behind?"

As if to confirm Marius's brightest hopes, the proprietor of a confectionery shop locked up and gallantly offered his hand to a beggar with two wooden legs; she rose unsteadily, he held her crutches, and the beggar and the bourgeois joined the throng, as a great cheer went up as all of Paris joined in common cause. "To the Chamber of Deputies!" shouted the young journalists. "*Vive la réforme! Vive le peuple!*" as the people surged forward.

"Look," cried Verdier as someone from the Panthéon crowd pulled from a pack on his back an enormous red flag, the flag of the workers of Paris, long outlawed and first seen as a symbol of resistance in 1832, when, legend had it, a man in black, riding a black horse, had unfurled a red flag and ridden at the front of the marchers. Verdier, Pajol, and Marius slapped each other on the back and cheered as a mason offered his quarterstaff, and the flag was attached. The quarterstaff—the Parisian weapon of choice—was a huge stick, six to eight feet long, hewed for defense, weighted for attack, could be wielded only by men of tremendous strength, and the mason not only lifted it, he hoisted it high in the air to a great chorus of cheers as he marched to the front to join the journalists. Three days before it would have been impossible to imagine that frock coats would follow the red flag, impossible that it would have been carried in the streets at all. The flag and all political clubs who espoused it were unlawful, but now men from these underground clubs swarmed out, raised their fists and voices, and with this jubilant parade, Marius, Cosette, Verdier, Pajol, Thérèse, and the Starling plunged into the rue Royale, marching toward the place de la Concorde and the Seine.

Arms linked, the crowd fanned out through the vast square, where their cheers and voices, their singing of "La Marseillaise" swirled. The holiday atmosphere evaporated, and some greater expectancy took its place, as though in passing through the place de la Concorde, beneath the gaze of the stone-eyed statues ringing the square, these Parisians had passed through a great forge and emerged a single, shining instrument in the hands of—whom? That was the great question. Marius thought they were in the hands of history; Cosette believed they were in the hands of God. Perhaps they were in the hands of mere Chance. As they came to the pont de la Concorde, the bridge separating them from the Chamber of Deputies, seventeen armed Municipal Guardsmen barred their way. On either side of the bridge colossal sculptures, massive stone figures, regarded them pensively, as if they had, all along, been contemplating revolution. And perhaps they had: the pont de la Concorde had been built with the stones of the Bastille.

"Fix bayonets!" shouted the officer, sweat pouring down his narrow goatee.

"Join us!" cried the young journalist.

"Join us or die!" crowed someone else.

"Throw them into the river and let's get on with it!"

"Down the royalist bastards! Cross the river!"

The officer's eyes darted from this unruly throng to his men, and all seventeen men dropped their weapons and bolted. With a great cheer the people scooped up the fallen guns and bayonets and swarmed over the pont de la Concorde. At two thousand strong they were certainly a crowd. Were they a mob? A riot? An insurrection? A rebellion? No shot had been fired. The laws had been broken, but as yet no bones, not so much as a window. But the bridge had been crossed.

Once across the river, they found to their dismay that the Chamber was certainly there, but the deputies were not. It was only just past noon and the session had not yet started. The rain had stopped and the clouds thinned, and since there was no one to harangue except one another, the crowd climbed fences, milled in the huge stone courtyard, shouted slogans, verses from "Song of the Girondins" and "La Marseillaise," and cheered all orators and all would-be orators. Someone in the crowd recognized Marius and shouted, *"La Lumière! La Lumière!,"* the cry taken up as Marius was disengaged from his wife and his friends and pushed to the front, up the steps of the Chamber of Deputies, where he protested he was not a speaker but a writer, an editor, a shaper of other men's thoughts. But as he looked out across the crowd, Marius was moved to words, moved very nearly to tears, saw in this *fraternité* the old coalition of workers and students, all men of conscience. Anything was possible.

"Why have we come here? To demand the vote for all men! To free the press! To have the right to assemble! To free education from the church! To assert that all men have the right to work! No woman should starve! No childhood should be atrophied!" Rousing from the crowd cheers for each of these demands, Marius went on, "We are brothers, the same nation, the same God, we are joined, united. As long as men are hungry, and women are degraded, and children grow up in the dark, as long as these things persist in France, we must fight them. And we must fight those who put their feet on our necks and call it God's will!"

The cold wind that came up off the river snapped skirts and tugged scarves and pulled caps and hats from heads and rippled in the red flag, still tied to its quarterstaff, waving now before the Chamber of Deputies, an affront to the men who were not even there to see the insult. That same wind took Marius's words and spewed them upward, over the city, a city whose enduring vivacity was paradoxically set in stone, in its stone monuments and squares, its vast cathedrals and threadline alleys, its columns and obelisks and arches all testifying to France's significant moments. This was one of those moments. Perhaps even one of those dates, like 14 July 1789. From his perch it seemed to Marius as if he might fly, as if spread before him, nearly three thousand strong, all of these men and women might fly, that the power of their numbers and the strength of their convictions could fuel them, release them from gravity, liberate all Paris, all France, unchain the world.

Marius was up so high he was amongst the first to see the cavalry. Others heard it: hooves clattering as they approached, not at a full gallop, but with an air of menacing decision and with metronomic intensity. Behind them marched a battalion of foot soldiers, bayonets gleaming in the winter sun. The infantry massed behind the cavalry. Sabre upraised, the officer ordered the crowd to disperse. Soldiers and civilians stared bleakly at each other while no one moved. The sun spun out from behind a cloud, sheeting the river with a metallic glow as the officer's sabre came down and cavalry charged into the courtyard.

Marius's eyes met Cosette's, and he tore down the steps, plunging into the crowd, flailing his way through cries and screams and horses trampling, sabres slashing as marchers caught in the courtyard pressed against the walls in their effort to flee, to reach the quay and the bridge, were beaten back by the incoming flood of infantry, their bayonets primed. Cosette, bolting from Verdier and Thérèse, was perhaps alone in running toward the steps, where at the top the Starling darted behind a pillar, pulling Pajol after him and then leaping down; their fall broken by other bodies, they cut their way through the crowd toward the quay. The red flag fell, torn apart by hooves and then bayoneted, but the quarterstaff was still in the hands of the burly mason, who knocked a horseman from his mount, and a clerk nearby grabbed the soldier's fallen sword and used it on him ineffectively.

A horseman rode up the steps, his sabre catching the light as Marius jumped aside, seeing in the churning mass of bodies Cosette's blue cloak before him. Horses' hooves rang on stone and screams echoed, splashes of silver blinded Marius, and he felt the thud of one blow after another, as he pushed and shoved a horse's enormous haunches that stood between him and Cosette. And when he reached her, he pulled her swiftly against him, pressed her against the wall, his body sheltering hers as they made their way, staggering with the others, toward the gate and the freedom of the quay. The beggar with the wooden legs rode on the back of the bourgeois, flailing at the soldiers with her crutches as Marius and Cosette scrambled out through the gate, reached the quay, and joined the mob—and now they were a mob—retreating.

Sticks and stones pelted the soldiers. These were the weapons the mob had at hand; those with pistols either hadn't the wit to use them or hadn't time as they fled, stumbling over the wounded, running across the bridge with its stone-eyed statues, back toward the place de la Concorde, and once there they fled that vast unprotected space, the crowd dissolving, pursued by soldiers till they vanished into side streets.

Marius and Cosette ran east and north toward the rue de Combray, reaching the rue Saint-Honoré, where, at the church of the Assumption, men and women were already tearing up the pavements, building barricades. They ran on, to Saint-Roch, and there, melted into the dim, votive-lit church, fell into pews, breathless, Cosette weeping, Marius calming her, smoothing her hair, whispering that they were fine, they were fortunate. "Fortunatus and Fortunata," he murmured. Marius himself was breathless, badly bruised, even beaten, but ebullient. He put his head back on the pew, looking at the ceiling of Saint-Roch and thinking that truly the Starling had been right: it did not happen as they had thought. Blood had been spilled in front of the Chamber of Deputies, on the pont de la Concorde, and in the place de la Concorde, where more than half a century before the guillotine had done its grisly work, where severed heads had dangled free of bodies, even the head of a king. The festival was over. The February Revolution had begun.

Chapter 14

"ainte-Marguerite refused the advances of the proconsul Olibius, and so he ordered her cast into the darkest dungeon of the most terrible prison in all of Antioch,'" Cosette read.

"She couldn't have been a saint then. She must have been plain Marguerite. To be a saint she'd have to be dead," observed Fantine with perfect clarity.

She sat close beside her mother on a settle by the enormous kitchen fire, their attention not so much on the page but on the door. They expected Le Sansonnet at any minute. They had expected him at any minute for hours. It was the night of the 23rd of February, and sporadic fighting had broken out all over the city; they could hear it even here at the rue des Filles-du-Calvaire, where Cosette had promised Marius she would stay with their children. Marius had left well before dawn, vowing to send word by the Starling by nightfall. But the short February twilight contracted into darkness, and no Starling appeared. Each time wind rapped naked branches against the kitchen window she looked expectantly up.

"It's only the wind, madame," Madame Carême counseled. She too was keeping the vigil.

"Yes," Cosette replied, not unconvinced but disappointed. "Send someone up for my cloak and bonnet, will you please? If the Starling doesn't come soon, I'm going to the rue de Combray by myself. I've told Abel to ready the carriage."

"You promised Papa you wouldn't go," Fantine reminded her. "I heard you."

"I'm not breaking that promise," Cosette explained. "I'm keeping the one I made when I promised to love him."

Fantine frowned. "Don't you have to promise to obey too when you get married?"

"Let us return to the perils of Sainte-Marguerite."

"What does it mean she refused his advances?"

Cosette pondered this and Madame Carême made a very noisy show chopping up bones for bouillon. "It means Olibius wanted her to do something and she refused to do it."

"To do what?"

"They don't say exactly. To marry a man of the Roman Empire, to do something inconsistent with her faith. That's why she's a saint."

"No, she's a saint for what comes next." Fantine loved fantastical stories, tales of geese turned into princes, witches and crones, and younger daughters from whose lips jewels fell. As saints go, she was bored by those like Saint-Martin, who merely cut his cloak and gave half to a beggar. Perhaps not everyone would do that, but anyone certainly could. Fantine preferred her saints with peril and terror. "Go on."

"'In this terrible dungeon, lit only by a little rag floating in oil, there flickered and lapped the red tongue of a terrible dragon, whose breath was foul and hot and whose hot tongue flickered up and down Sainte-Marguerite.'"

Fantine took the book away. "'And then he swallowed her whole. But once inside the body of this fearsome beast, Sainte-Marguerite made the sign of the cross, and the dragon rose up, crashed through the stone and mortar of the prison where he had been chained, his pain so terrible and his strength so towering that stone walls could not contain him. His wings created a gale that sent soldiers cowering, and he spewed Sainte-Marguerite back up, whole, alive, unharmed, unchanged, enshrined in glory and all the pagan—'"

A sharp knock sounded at the door, and Cosette jumped up as Madame Carême unlocked it and the Starling bolted in, bringing with him the gale of revolution. "Guizot's gone!" he announced, "It's happened! He's finished!"

"Thank God," cried Cosette, hugging Fantine. "Oh, Marius must be ecstatic."

"The whole city, madame! All Paris is wild with joy! There are rumors everywhere. They say the king's asked Thiers to form a government and—"

"He vowed he'd never serve the king again!"

"People are leaving the barricades, abandoning them, workers from Saint-Antoine, from the boulevard du Temple and Popincourt, even from the other side of the river, from the place Maubert and Saint-Julien-le-Pauvre," he added with evident pride, "workers from as far away as Saint-Marcel and *barrière* d'Italie. They're all marching toward the Madeleine to celebrate. The fighting's over!"

"Jean-Luc will be furious," Fantine announced, folding up her book. "He will have missed everything. He says all his friends, all the students, are in the streets leading the revolution, and he has to stay home and watch over a lot of women. Aunt Adelaide's barred herself in her bedroom, she's so afraid."

"Well, it was a swift revolution," said Cosette, pleased, "and Jean-Luc can be angry as he likes that he missed it, he's staying out of danger. Ah, *merci.*" Cosette took her cloak and gloves and bonnet from a servant.

"Madame—" the Starling looked perplexed. "I promised Monsieur Pontmercy I would deliver the message and return alone. I promised you would not come."

"Then it was a foolish promise, Starling. Perhaps you'll think better of it next time." Cosette took off her shoes and pulled on sturdier boots.

Fantine regarded Le Sansonnet archly. "Have you finished the book? La Fontaine's *Fables?*"

"Not entirely, mademoiselle." The Starling removed his hat.

"You can't have another till you return it."

"Yes, mademoiselle."

"My brother says you are still a thief. He says you stole ten francs from his friend Arsène Huvet."

"No, mademoiselle! It wasn't me!"

Cosette looked up, disappointment, chagrin, and anger in her eyes.

"Madame," he protested, "I swear it wasn't me. Your son and his friend—"

"Jean-Luc's been forbidden to see Arsène Huvet. Where did all this happen?"

"It wasn't me, madame! It was the Pincher. He was in the crowd too, there in front of the Panthéon. It must have been the Pincher. It wasn't me."

"I believe you, Starling." Cosette rested her gaze on this ugly urchin, whose face would always bear the marks of a brutal childhood, comparing him to her beautiful son, her only and beloved son. Why could she believe the Starling and not Jean-Luc? Jean-Luc had again defied his parents, lied, regardless of having given his word to them. She turned to her daughter. "Jean-Luc told you the Starling stole ten francs from Arsène Huvet?" Fantine's silence answered. "Did he swear you to secrecy?"

"Yes, Mama." Fantine shot the Starling a hateful glare.

"I am going to your papa now, but you will be so good as to ask Jean-Luc if he can forgo his own pleasures long enough to look after the people in this house." Cosette flung her cloak over her shoulder, tied her bonnet, and pulled on her gloves. As her back retreated toward the door, the Starling looked helplessly from Fantine to Madame Carême.

"What could I do, mademoiselle? He accused me wrongly. It wasn't me."

"Thief," Fantine whispered harshly.

"Beggar," Madame Carême echoed.

Chapter 15

*W*ith every crack and snap of the whip, Cosette vowed to put Abel in the Republic of the unemployed, as he drunkenly urged their horses forward. Barricades sprang up as soon as the carriage turned into the boulevard du Temple, and though these barricades were abandoned, they still impeded traffic. All their defenders marched by torchlight, eastward, toward the Madeleine, the crowds gathering pace and momentum, especially as they wended through the narrow streets of the market district, which were clogged with overturned carts and tumbrils splayed at intersections. Still Abel flogged their horses on toward Saint-Eustache, where the crowds were swollen by whole contingents of secret political clubs long outlawed (and, no doubt, long infiltrated), who hoisted banners and the equally outlawed red flag of the workers, openly declaring themselves, as though *Vive la réforme* had also done away with the death penalty for political offenses. They shouted *"Vive le peuple!"* and swirled around Cosette's carriage, raining curses on the departed Guizot. As the carriage approached the rue Montmartre, increasingly Cosette heard *"Vive la république!"* ring out, gaining conviction and crescendo over *"Vive la réforme!"* echoing all along the buildings as though the essence of Parisian *esprit* and love of liberty had been uncorked and could never again be contained in the bottle of *Vive la réforme.*

At the entrance to the rue Montmartre, the crowd surged and thickened, arms locked, but Abel whipped his horses on and very nearly ran over people, who split in two streams around the carriage, cursing the driver, who cursed them back. "Move on! Move out!" shouted the drunken Abel, snapping the whip over the horses' backs, unseeing, urging them toward a three-wheeled cart that was helplessly stalled, its driver shouting over the horses' fearful whinnies. Abel cursed again, and this time the whip came down over the heads and backs of the knot of people to his right, while the horses pawed ahead.

"I must stop this!" Cosette's hand was on the door, but the coach rocked and jostled as a man clambered up to relieve Abel of his whip, snatched it, and began beating him.

While Abel brayed in inebriated anguish, the Starling, kicking open the opposite door, reached for Cosette's hand and quickly pulled her out behind him, drawing her into the crowd, which began swarming over the carriage. He kept her hand, dodged toward the rue Saint-Marc, and turned up the rue de Richelieu, which finally spilled out on the broad boulevard des Italiens, where, breathless, they joined celebrants gathered in front of all the brilliant gaslit cafés and restaurants, people dancing down the tree-lined boulevard, cheering the fall of Guizot, frock coats and workers cheering together, milling with students, recognizable by their youth and their school uniforms, especially the great élite military school, Ecole Polytechnique, whose students had distinguished themselves in the short-lived fighting.

Cosette caught her breath, braced against a wall. "*Merci,* Starling—that was quick thinking."

"Ah, madame," the Starling said, grinning through the gaslight, "I must get you to the rue de Combray or never show my face at *La Lumière* again."

They pressed and wended through crowds of revelers, whose liberation was as infectious as their cries, their songs, and their slogans, the smoke from torches lying heavy on the air. Everyone stepped back, cheering, when a unit of the National Guard carrying a banner *Vive la réforme!* marched through, their pace kept even by a single drumbeat. The National Guard had gone over to the people, refusing to fire on their neighbors, and now they were cheered through the streets. Suddenly a single crack of gunfire sounded. The drum stopped, the National Guard seemed to halt, and as if by some invisible order, everyone on the boulevard des Italiens, stranger and comrade alike, froze, stared at one another with dazed and scholarly intensity.

A volley of gunfire rang out from the west, explosions reverberating deep in the belly of the central city, rippling along the walls, the old buildings, from garrets, through arches, and echoing percussively along the windows and balconies, shattering the winter night: gunfire roared, burst in a barrage followed by screams, shouts, and the thunder of running feet.

Revelers on the boulevard des Italiens dropped their cigarettes and glasses, the National Guard broke ranks, and everyone streamed westward toward the boulevard des Capucines, only to be overwhelmed, crushed beneath a tide of humanity, a mob, panicked, shouting, bleeding, fleeing eastward, screaming, *Save yourselves! Save yourselves!*, running with bloody hands out before them, *Massacre! Massacre!* parting the crowd, parting Le Sansonnet from Cosette, colliding with Cosette, who was pushed to the ground and scrambled up only to see, pummeling toward her, the anguished face of a woman holding her right eye in its socket, blood gushing between her fingers.

"Massacre! Massacre!"

"The army! They're killing us!"

"Run! They're riding us down!" cried men and women jostling Cosette, who hurried against the tide, against the warnings, toward the rue de Combray, fearing that every bloodied hand or face she saw might belong to Marius, caught in a rubble of human debris, flying against the panic and the current toward a figure she saw ahead, saw from the back, Marius too running toward the battle, not away from it.

"Marius!" she cried out, again and again, till at last he turned around. "Marius!" She ran to him, riot erupting all around them, but he did not take her in his arms; he took her shoulders and shook her violently, asking why she'd come. They were both horrified to see the wounded still streaming from the boulevard des Capucines, though the gunfire had ceased and only human voices shook the night, people who cried and wept and warned that the army was coming to kill them. But it was not the army Cosette feared, not the mob, not the avalanche of blood and bodies. She locked her fingers into Marius's coat as if he were the branch and she the autumn leaf that this revolutionary gale was about to blow apart forever. Yesterday it seemed they'd seen the future, tonight Cosette feared the past: the cries and groans, the fury of 1832, which had come to claim Marius, to take him back, to finish the work begun there. His features were bathed in a kind of wild joy, not fear, but joy, release, a release so physical, so deep, she recognized it from wild couplings, from times when he had held her arms, his body high above her, his eyes closed, the moment of release so profound it seemed to flood her as well, to drown her as this crowd was about to drown her, as they had once very nearly drowned in the sea at Boulogne. As she had held him then, she held him now, but this time he fought her, fought to leave her. "Don't go! I won't let you go!" she cried as he pried her fingers off his arms. "Don't go back! They'll kill you if you go back!"

"Back! Go back where?"

But there was no need to go back, because the past, 1832—that rough draft of revolution—was about to be revised, revisited, its latent energy unleashed, set in motion, as an officer from the Fourteenth clattered up, riding toward them, people screaming and scattering in his wake. Marius pulled Cosette from the path of his horse as the soldier roared up the boulevard des Italiens, crying out, "There was no order to shoot! The army gave no order to shoot! We were defending ourselves!"

He pulled up before Tortoni's at the corner of the rue Laffitte and got off his horse, waved and shouted to the anxious throng, congregating as the word *massacre* rattled telegraphically along the boulevard and through the city. There before Tortoni's, the most venerable and splendid of the boulevard cafés, the officer approached, his arms raised in a gesture of surrender, even imploring, crying out the whole while, there was no order to shoot. "The army did not fire the first shot! The army was defending itself. It was an accident!"

"It was a crime." A man stepped from the knot of people, his blue smock stained with blood, "The blood of my brother! The blood of my brother who is lying dead in the boulevard des Capucines!" He pulled an ancient pistol from under his shirt, and as the officer's gaping mouth made wordless gurgles of protest, he shot him in the face, and his blood and bones and brains flew everywhere about, into the face and hair, spraying the clothing of everyone standing nearby.

They all looked westward, expecting a torrent of horsemen to ride down on them, and when that did not happen, they ran toward the boulevard des Capucines, Cosette's hand fiercely holding Marius's. Once there, they stopped, looked upon forty or fifty already dead, many who had crawled out of the street toward the gutters and against the walls of the fine old buildings to die. Many more lay groaning and gasping, others silent, their skins and skulls split open, their torches extinguished, still smoking in pools of blood.

Marius immediately took off his coat and draped it over a woman who lay moaning until a man cried out her name and took the fallen figure in his arms. People everywhere rushed to the aid of the wounded, to wail at the unhearing dead. Cosette wanted to be brave, to be heroic, to be of service in the face of all this terrible suffering, but she could not move. She gulped, looked this way and that, at the frantic activity to aid the wounded, at the dead who lay sprawled, eyes open, jaws slack, surprise still slathered over their contorted features. Cosette brought her hand slowly to her throat and unfastened her cloak. Marius snatched it from her, and two men made a litter to carry a wounded woman away.

A cabdriver brought his rig up and offered to convey the wounded, another offered to convey the dead, but a group of workers from Saint-Antoine gathered, several pulling carts behind them, small, one-horse vendors' carts hastily emptied of whatever they had once carried. "You take the wounded," said the worker to the cabdriver. "The wounded need the closed carriages. To the dead it doesn't matter. The cart will do."

Cosette stood and watched while they began to load, Marius gently lifting the wounded into the cabs while the dead were stacked like bleeding wood on open carts and two-wheeled tumbrils.

"Where will you take them?" Marius asked the workingman.

"If you are asking me where they will be buried, monsieur," he added the term of respect out of cool recognition of Marius's fine clothes and uncalloused hands, "I can't say. Where their people will come to claim them I can't say." He nodded to his comrade, and the two took hold of the bridle and turned the cart horse around in the street. They were joined by others carrying torches. "All I know is that the task of these dead is not yet finished."

Lifted unceremoniously, the rest of these dead were loaded on carts like the one that had just left. Bodies not yet cold were heaped on top of one another, blood running over the wheels, their anguished limbs hanging off the sides while Cosette—hatless, coatless, tearless, and speechless—stood rooted and unmoving in the winter night, altogether aware that the torchlight, passing by, gleamed and winked in the blood running along the stones under her feet.

Chapter 16

*B*y the morning of the 24th the dead had done their work. All night long the living walked, a city-wide cortège, accompanying these dead on carts and calling out, calling all Paris to arms, waking those who squatted under garret roofs and hunkered in dank cellars, rousing those who curled up in warm beds. The living lifted these dead from the carts, held them aloft as their limbs stiffened, and the cry went out that the king's troops had done this to the people.

That night those barricades that had been abandoned in the wake of Guizot's dismissal were strengthened, defended by armed men, often men of the National Guard, who this time aimed their guns from behind the barricades, siding with the insurgents against the army. Between the Panthéon and Ecole-de-Médecine, all across the south side of the river, whole streets were torn up under the leadership of students from the élite military schools; students and workers manned these redoubts, and from high apartment windows women sniped at the army. In the face of all this opposition, the army seemed to wither; its *esprit de corps* vanished and its will to fight, to defend the king, crumbled. By noon on Thursday the king had abdicated the throne of France, fled Paris, limping across France disguised as Mr. Smith, bound for England and obscurity.

That afternoon, the poet Lamartine stepped out on the balcony of the Hôtel de Ville and declared the Second French Republic to a crowd gone mad with jubilation, a throng that included Le Sansonnet, Pajol, Verdier, Coligny, Beaujard, Gallet, cousin Théo and his newest mistress, indeed everyone connected with *La Lumière* was there to sing "La Marseillaise," "Song of the Girondins," shout *"Vive la république!"* They were all there save for Marius. The omission was the more odd because the provisional government was comprised primarily of literary men, newspaper editors, Lamartine,

Marrast, Flocon, and a handful of others. The upheavals wrought in France in February 1848 were fueled by ink, the revolution itself the work of newspapers with less than four thousand circulation. Has the pen ever been more powerful? Before or since?

From where he sat, at Number 102 rue Mondétour, the rebuilt café, Marius could hear the rejoicing, could hear the whole city of Paris tremble, shaken to its very geological core, triumph seeping down to all the bones there buried and the blood spilled on behalf of those ideas whose moment had at last come: *liberté, égalité, fraternité.* Marius could hear that triumph. He sat there with his bottle of claret and he drank to it. That is where Cosette found him.

All through the night Cosette had followed Marius through the streets like a dinghy pulled in the wake of a revolutionary clipper ship as they followed the carts of the dead, and roused sleepers; people tumbled into the streets to build barricades (she recognized their carriage in one of them). People knew Marius, shouted, *"Vive La Lumière!,"* embraced him, and gave him a red cap for his head, and Marius, joy, certitude, passion all reflected in his face with the torchlight, embraced them back, the old *fraternité* of 1832 born at last and again.

At about four in the morning, chilled through and wet, they turned in to the gate at Number 6 rue des Filles-du-Calvaire to find, tucked in the shadow of the wall, Le Sansonnet, who jumped up, making Cosette scream.

He pulled his coat more closely around him and explained that when he'd lost sight of Cosette in the crowd he'd gone to *La Lumière,* and then he'd come here to wait. What else could he do? "Honestly, Monsieur Pontmercy, I told her not to come, I—"

"You've waited out here all this time?" asked Marius.

"She was my responsibility and I feared—"

"Come inside."

The three went around to the back, where lights blazed in the kitchen window and Madame Carême and Fantine slept fitfully by the fire. At the first sound of their approach the cook woke and unbolted the door, gasped at the sight of them, bloodstained, shivering, filthy, and wet. "Oh, madame! Monsieur! Where have you—"

"Mama!" cried Fantine, rubbing her eyes. "Papa! What happened? Starling, what—"

Madame Carême led them to the fire, bustled about, heated up some water, and bade Cosette sit down, to take off her shoes, but Cosette did not comply. Or reply.

Marius sat her down on the settle, knelt, and began to unlace her boots.

There in the dancing firelight, the warmth of her own home, Cosette beheld her husband. His waistcoat and trousers, his shirt, his cravat, his hands, his sleeves, his face were splattered with the blood of strangers. She looked at her own feet; they too were covered with mud and blood, and the hem of her blue skirt had turned a mauvey brown, mud- and bloodstained. Cosette began to cry.

"Oh, Mama—" Fantine rushed toward her.

Madame Carême held her back. "Don't. Your father has to do this."

As Marius whispered her name, Cosette continued to shiver, tears dripping off the end of her chin, and she bit her lip white against the torrents that threatened. "You never told me," she said, gulping, "you never told me what it was like. You never said it was like that. You never said, you never, you said they fought and they died, and it was terrible you said, but you never said it was like—" her whole body trembled—"like that. Like those people lying there with their brains gone, like—"

"Cosette." Marius dipped a cloth in hot water and daubed her face. "How could I? My love, how could I?"

Her hand swooped up and caught his. "Promise me you'll never leave me."

"I will never leave you."

But when Cosette woke late the next morning, the place beside her in bed was cold and he was gone.

She threw on her dressing gown and went downstairs to find that Le Sansonnet, who'd spent the remainder of the night in the kitchen, had likewise flown and Madame Carême did not know when or where. Madame Carême handed Cosette a cup of coffee. "No milk has come into the city in days."

Wrapping her hands around the cup, Cosette stared out to the wintery garden. The sound of fighting, probably from the rue

Saint-Antoine, echoed overhead, echoed for Cosette from the past. "I know where Marius is," she said at last. "He needs me. I have to be with him."

Cosette washed and dressed, and pulling on an old cloak, less sumptuous than the one she'd lost the night before, she set out to recreate her journey of sixteen years before, walking westerly toward the rue Mondétour, but this time the city was not deserted—save by the king. This time the city was filled with excitement. This time she was not seventeen, her bravery born of ignorance. At thirty-two her bravery was born of conviction, per- haps necessity, she wasn't certain which, but she knew that for six- teen years Marius had labored to give the deaths of his friends dignity and meaning, and now, as the cries rang out around her in the cold winter morning—*Vive la république! The king has abdicated!*—she knew that history was making revolution of Marius's 1832 insurrection and that this was the moment he had longed to see, not simply for himself, but for those who had not lived to see it.

She'd no sooner turned from the rue des Filles-du-Calvaire into the boulevard du Temple when cries of joy rang out, metallic as bells in the cold, "The king has fled," celebratory as bells, "The king has abdicated!," pealing as bells. She took a deep breath and picked up her pace as freedom, palpable as frost, settled over the city, and crowds—from cheeky urchins to the grimmest old concierge—cavorted on the boulevard du Temple, the great enter- tainment avenue of old Paris, where the out-of-work could still earn a living performing in the street: acrobats, tightrope walkers, street singers, dancing dogs and dancing girls, savages from far away and savages from nearby. It was also known as the boulevard du Crime for these latter savages, who often acrobated their way through the pockets of the unsuspecting. This morning it rang with cries and calls and rough music, as though the theatres along the boulevard du Temple had been turned upside down and their entertainers all shaken into the street. There, before the Théâtre Olympic, Cosette saw people in thin clothes with blue lips and black-toothed smiles, scrawny urchins, drunken beggars, and joyous crones, who liberated a nag from a cart, cheering as upon the gaunt beast they hoisted a general. Really, was it? Cosette paused and stared at the strange procession. He looked like Lafayette, waving and accepting the adulation, applause, the cheers of his adoring audience, the ragged troupe augmented by the jugglers and stilt walkers and girls in silly shepherdess costumes, all of whom crowed with delight, shouting, "On to the Hôtel de Ville! Make way for the governor general of the Hôtel de Ville!"

Cosette laughed, but made her way steadily toward Les Halles, walking around or climbing over barricades, abandoned now by everyone except the dead, who lay there, eyes open, seeing only the Republic of heaven. She averted her gaze from the corpses and blessed God the stones were not spongy with blood. In truth, the fighting had been swift, decisive; the army had abdicated as much as the king and the casualties were painful to see, but truthfully, not many to count. The smell of gunpowder still lingered, acrid here and there, but the National Guardsmen who accosted her had wine bottles in their hands rather than rifles.

Avoiding them all, Cosette walked with purpose toward the past and completed, at Number 102 rue Mondétour, the journey she had set out to make sixteen years earlier when Eugène Verdier had intervened.

Chapter 17

*T*heatre might wait upon revolutions, but it does not wait for
them. The Théâtre Olympic, a minor theatre in the boulevard
du Temple, was no exception. In keeping with the revolutionary
fervor of February, the Théâtre Olympic was putting into hasty
production—hasty resurrection might be the better term—the
Parisian hit musical from 1793, *Au Retour*, a rousingly patriotic story
of a young man, Justin, who will not wait for conscription, but
insists on joining the army of the First Republic to the tearful
sorrow of his fianceé, the shepherdess Lucette. Despite her sorrow
at losing him, Lucette and the whole company send young Justin
off to fight for the First Republic with a stand-up chorus of *Au
Retour*, everyone confident he will return replete with honors, all
his limbs, and both his eyes.

In the role of Justin's general (with, alas, no lines) was an actor of
modest talents, Alexis Châteaurenaud. In his cold, nasty cell of a
dressing room, which he shared with a dozen others—mere soldiers,
he was the only officer—he'd just finished putting on his costume
for rehearsal. The play was to go on that very night, never mind that
all true theatre had moved into the streets. Châteaurenaud stood
before the cracked mirror regarding himself carefully. He was about
thirty, with a thick mustache, thick nose, thick paunch, which he
had corseted in so that his chest swelled out. He practiced
breathing. He had a round face and long, lovely chestnut hair, his
great vanity. He could, as they say, strike the pose. He could not act
it, but he could certainly strike it. He did this before the mirror,
checking the brass buttons and epaulets of his costume, adjusting his
tricolor sash and the gold tassels, and sheathing his stage sword in a
real scabbard. He held his gloves at the appropriate military angle.
To powder or not to powder: that was the question. He was justly
proud of his chestnut locks. Nonetheless, character is all in the the-

atre, and so he dusted white powder over them and tied his hair at the nape of his neck with a tricolor ribbon, and with his plumed, beribboned hat, he declared that Lafayette could not have done it any better.

Another extra, a girl with tumbled, coarse blond hair, great gray eyes, and an impudent manner, wandered past as he was in his Lafayette mode, and made an insolent remark regarding not merely his performance, but his pretensions. Ordinarily, since she too was a lineless extra, a shepherdess in Lucette's entourage, he might have said something foul, but as Châteaurenaud was in the uniform of a great general, he withered her (he hoped) with his gaze.

The girl, undaunted, followed him. "Oh, Lafayette," she implored, pretending to swoon, "thou stirrest in me such thumpings of patriotism. How might I serve your greatness?"

"Nicolette," Châteaurenaud observed haughtily, rolling a cigarette, "it is well for the French stage that you have no lines."

"I won't always be lineless," she retorted.

"But you will never play a general." He regarded himself with great satisfaction in the mirror and left to smoke in peace via the stage door.

Châteaurenaud had no sooner turned the corner into the boulevard du Temple than a commotion in the street, a mob, mad or drunk with revolutionary fervor, surged past, crying out, "Vive la république! The King has fled!" caught his attention, as indeed he had caught theirs.

"A general!" cried a woman with only two teeth.

"A general of the First Republic!" cried a ragpicker bereft of his staff and basket.

"Lafayette!" cried a woman who scavenged low tide on the Seine, and who with some chimney sweeps, ragpickers, and a nomadic tribe of urchins with scrawny chests streaked with mud made up this procession.

Châteaurenaud was not perhaps a great actor, but he was enough of an actor to know a cue when he met one. He saluted this populace of about fifty persons. The mutual recognition was instantaneous and infectious, and at the bidding of this appreciative rabble, General Châteaurenaud took up a new command. *Au*

Retour went on without him that night. He never returned to the theatre, at least not to the stage.

The crowd swelled with passersby and entertainers and they freed a nag from a vendor's cart. With help from the mob, the general mounted this steed, and on horseback they led him through the streets of Paris, people joining at every street, everyone falling in behind, saluting and chanting, *"Vive la république,"* and on to the Hôtel de Ville. In their path there were some corpses lying splayed, some, eyes still open, unmoving since the night before, but the crowd parted around them, swift and uncaring as a river separates to accommodate a boulder.

Le Sansonnet and Pajol caught up with this parade quite by accident in the rue des Lombards in front of the church of Saint-Merri. They joined the throng, including the sassy blonde extra who came along to watch her comrade. Escorting the new general to the Hôtel de Ville, they cheered and cried through streets where people hung out their windows and off their balconies and men stepped out of cafés, glasses raised high, to salute the new general and the new Republic. Châteaurenaud was the man of the moment, drawn by the irresistible magnet of revolution, a corps of urchin officers, scavenging sergeants, and an army of filthy foot soldiers, arriving finally before the Hôtel de Ville, where Châteaurenaud was drawn, led, escorted up the stairs by a regiment of ragpickers up to the first floor. They burst into the salons of state and presented him to the provincial government. The poet Lamartine greeted him as "Citizen."

"As a general," Châteaurenaud corrected him, "I salute you, Poet-President."

Visibly moved, Lamartine stated, "The address of *citizen* is the highest appreciation the Second Republic can bestow."

"Except for general," Châteaurenaud insisted.

"What business do you bring before the provisional government . . . General?" inquired the poet.

The recently lineless actor walked to the balcony and extended his arm so that the poet could see whence and why he'd come. There, below, his entourage, his army, his horse—well, his nag—awaited him; certainly Le Sansonnet and Pajol were amongst those who lent their voices to these shouts and cheers that greeted his appearance on the balcony with Lamartine. *"Vive le gouverneur de l'Hôtel de Ville!"* In a chorus of approval, the cheer was taken up, the title chanted and repeated, the blonde extra in her shepherdess costume cheering as loudly as any of them.

"Voilà," said the new Lafayette to Lamartine. "That is who I am. The governor general of the Hôtel de Ville."

"You will be obliged to be sworn in, General."

"I am ready to die for the Second Republic."

General Châteaurenaud and the poet-president embraced in an excess of *fraternité,* but sadly for the spectators, the drama there ended, the general disappearing with the poet, to guide the new Republic forward.

Pajol, the Starling, the ruck and rabble of Paris flowed westward toward the Tuileries Palace in an alluvial mass, spread out on the quays, crowding the narrow streets, stepping over corpses. Now and then gunfire sounded, but never a volley, only an excess of celebration.

The fighting had finished so quickly the people of Paris were dazed. Military (saving for the National Guard, who having gone over to the rebels no longer counted as military) had vanished from the streets. No one could remember a time when the streets of Paris weren't thick with soldiers of one sort or another. Every *quartier* had its barracks, sometimes two, but all uniformed authority had vanished, even at the Palace of the Tuileries, where not so much as a guard remained. Taking advantage of their new *liberté,* people of all sorts indulged in *égalité* and uproarious *fraternité,* streaming in and out of the Tuileries, where late the king had lived. The doors were all open and the heavy velvet drapes twitched involuntarily in the winter wind. Pajol followed the tide inside, but the Starling's attention was caught by a body that lay on the stones of the courtyard, shot cleanly through the heart. Le Sansonnet recognized him; it was the young man who died twice a day, "starving to death" in the rue Mouffetard, getting a pittance for his performance.

An old man, bald and with a boot-shaped liver spot across his pate, knelt by the body till a screaming woman fell over it, pulled the corpse up close to her, rocking back and forth. Tied to the young man's back was a sign, SHOT FOR STEALING.

"What did he steal?" the Starling asked the old man.

"Six francs and a roll of ribbon."

"From the palace? The soldiers killed him for six francs and a roll of ribbon!"

The old man began to blubber and cry that it was not the soldiers who had shot him, if the soldiers had done it, he could have understood. "After all, that's what soldiers do, kill people, but they executed him," the old man pointed to the palace where dirty faces grinned from the windows and shrieks and shouts of abandon resounded. "They did it."

"They wouldn't execute him. Those are people just like him."

"Just like him," the old man wept. "Starved and cheated and broken and beaten by the fat ones all their lives. They walked into the palace, the first wave of them, and they were dumbstruck, they stood like cardinals dropped into a tomb of holy relics. I tell you, they breathed the air the king had breathed and they took off their caps and genuflected!"

"No! It couldn't have—"

"I saw it, I tell you! They walked through the palace without touching a thing! And what this boy did—lifting a roll of ribbon and six francs—it was childish, but not criminal. They caught him and they took the king's justice upon themselves. Is that justice? Why the revolution if that is justice?" he implored. "The people, the mob, they tied the sign to his back. I begged them not to, I tried to reason, and there was another worker, a boy like you, we pleaded with them, begged them to see what they were doing, killing one of their own, but they said, if we didn't shut up, we would get the same." He wiped his nose ineffectually with his blue smock. "They stood him up against the palace wall and they executed him in the name of the Republic."

"But look, these same people, they're looting themselves sick!" cried the Starling as if the old man didn't have eyes of his own to see them, crazed and jubilant, shirtless in the cold, their blue smocks serving as packs and bags to cart silver down the broad stairs.

"I swear to you, that's how it happened." The old man watched the wild crowd. "All my life I have longed for the Republic, and the first thing I see it do is to devour its own."

"He died twice a day for years," said the Starling sadly. "On 24th of February he only died once."

Clearly the rabble had recovered from their early awe and care for the king's possessions. They streamed out of the Tuileries now, onion sellers wearing the gowns of the princess royal, ragpickers carting blankets that only the night before had warmed royal bodies. Women sashayed out, their old rags torn off, the royal rags but half on, and men wrapped themselves in velvet drapes and enough gold braid for regiments of generals. A troop of people shrieked to hear a huge grand piano bounce down the palace stairs, its thick legs finally giving way, and the piano's protest was deep and abiding. A horde of men carried the throne aloft, crying that they would burn it at the place de la Bastille. The Starling did not join them: without the king on the throne, what was the point?

He walked up the broad steps and into the Tuileries Palace, where parquet floors squeaked under his feet. Overhead, around sparkling crystal chandeliers, cherubs floated, their little pink bottoms picking up the hues of dawn painted over the high ceilings, each vault meeting in great ribs of gilt and brilliant rosettes painted scarlet at their centers. The Starling walked from gilded room to gilded room, each opening onto the next, like never-ending flowers, making him rather dizzy, as he came to the royal family's personal apartments, judging from the number of wardrobes and mirrors and cabinets and the high-curtained beds. On one of these a half-dozen mud-daubed men and women rolled about, and at the king's desk, chair tipped back, sat a prostitute, her legs gloriously apart, blue silk boots with silver tassels on her feet. River ravagers pawed through cabinets, and a line of books hit the floor with reports like gunfire. Each room was painted blue and gold, all walls plastered with huge pictures of well-fed nudes looking coy or desperate, as well they might, the Starling figured, surrounded as they were by goat-men or naked fops.

He found Pajol admiring a young woman who smirked and flirted with him as she fastened a brooch on her tattered bodice. A great swath of lace was wound around her waist, and on her feet, where she usually wore wooden *sabots*, little silken shoes twinkled. She grinned at the Starling in the mirror. It was Germaine Fleury, the girl who sold bootlaces in the rue Mouffetard. Pajol was enchanted.

"How do I look, Starling?" she asked, mincing, flinging lace over her shoulder.

"You know her, Starling?" asked Pajol, clearly smitten.

"Well—I—"

"The Starling and I are great friends, aren't we? How do I look? You'd better do it right or I'll cripple you where you stand. I haven't forgotten you called me a spavined slut."

"Starling!" cried Pajol.

"You look glorious."

She smiled appreciatively at Pajol and told the Starling he'd find his grandmother upstairs in the Galerie de Diane.

"What's she doing?"

"Business. What else?" She turned back to the mirror and Pajol.

Le Sansonnet made his way through these apartments to the great central stairs of the Tuileries Palace and ascended, like a child in a dream, dizzy with the height and dazzle. Had he seen turtles and crabs upright, waltzing in each other's arms, he could not have been more amazed than to watch his own dirty brown hand move up the marble balustrade, then to be nearly knocked over by a handful of tumbledown drunks, a ragpicker in ermine, a potboy in satin, the military beggar in a dressing gown and lacy cap. But they were not all ruffians, navvies, and beggars cavorting here. There were men in frock coats looting, and bloodthirsty-looking young matrons in smart bonnets tearing clothes from the claws of seamstresses; men in National Guard uniforms, some even officers, sauntered downstairs with bottles of wine in one arm and pretty prostitutes on the other. A dozen women who seemed to have fled the madhouse, loose caps covering shaved heads, screamed and cackled. Ham-handed masons, whose enormous muscles rippled along their backs and biceps, bent double, some of them, under gilded chairs and inlaid tables, looting, to the squealing delight of their women. There were shopkeepers still wearing their white aprons, metalworkers still in their leather aprons. He knew some of the ragged boys climbing up, snatching swords off the walls, and using them to stab the royal portraits. There were students in the uniform of the élite schools, Louis-le-Grand, Lycée Henri IV, Ecole Polytechnique. There was even

Arsène Huvet lounging at the top of the grand staircase, smoking a cigarette.

"Hello, thieving brat," he said by way of greeting. "I see you've joined your brothers for the looting."

"Shove your ankle up your ass and talk with your toes," replied the Starling, walking on.

"I want my ten francs back! I want it back! You hear me?"

"The more you cry, the less you'll piss."

"Thief!" Arsène shouted. But the assembled—though uninvited—guests of the palace gave him queer looks, and the fact that men in broadcloth were the minority was not lost on Arsène. He sauntered downstairs and found some school friends from Lycée Henri IV.

In the huge Galerie de Diane the king's table had been laid, a long elegant affair for perhaps three dozen people, where now more than a hundred clambered, boggled, ogled, flirted, took their ease, smoked the king's cigars, drank his wine (the wine cellars, some four thousand bottles, were quickly emptied), and perplexed themselves over what you were supposed to do with the lobsters. They choked on date pits and chewed the bones of ortolans, which one man remarked "was like eating blackbirds, only drier." He was a dwarfish, portly man, wearing a greasy hat and tattered trousers. His gray beard appeared to have been scraped off with a knife, and recently at that, and he wore a long silk scarf, which once had graced the rather cleaner neck of a duke. "Why, if it isn't the Starling!" he cried, pulling the prostitute next to him into his lap so as to make an empty chair for the boy.

"Hello, Captain." Starling sat down and put his feet up on the table.

"Eat up!" The Captain gestured expansively over the table and himself spat out another bone.

"This stuff'll give you the bloody flux. Not for me."

The Captain guffawed and gestured to the prostitute on his lap, who was falling out of a purple satin dress far too big for her. "Have you met the Ark, Starling?"

"Why are you called the Ark?"

The woman howled. "I'm like Noah, dearie! I've been known to take on two of everything at one time or another!"

The boy flushed with chagrin and quickly changed the subject.

"The last I heard, Captain, you were caught stealing, and you were living off the fat of the Conciergerie."

"And so I was, boy. I was number 4361421, Conciergerie Prison, and happy as a maggot at Montfaucon to be there, too. In Paris, at least, a poor convict has his chance. If they'd transported me to Algeria, why, my bones would be banquets for dumb animals, and as it is, here I am at the great Tuileries Palace, guest of the king of France!"

All around them cries rang out—*Vive la révolution! Vive la république! Vive Lamartine!*—as the Captain bounced the Ark on his knee and nuzzled her bosom, making her squeal with delight and affection. "Now we're all free men of the Second Republic!" he shouted. "Going to have the vote just like any other man, the right to assemble where we likes, freedom of the press for them who can read. Oh, it's grand, Starling. Your own father would have loved it, he would. This boy's my godson, in a manner of speaking, given we're godless," he explained to the appreciative Ark. "His father died in my arms, perished as I held him, when we was prisoners together long ago."

"Take care, Captain," said the Starling, moving off, as a shot rang out and everyone screamed, but it was just a man, virile with wine, who had climbed onto the table and fired a pistol into the belly of one of the portraits that lined the wall. A handful of the Starling's old urchin friends looked about for knives to fling, but the silverware had long since departed this table, and everyone laughed to watch a beggar pissing into the royal stove.

Sunlight had broken through the heavy matting of February clouds outside and spun across the brilliant parquet floor as the Starling walked down the Galerie de Diane, wondering why he felt so angry when everyone else was so happy. Heretofore his rages had all been directed against things or people he knew, anger against the police, against his mother's men, against other thieves and mudlarks who'd stolen from him, anger against men who'd beaten him or tricked him, stolen his food, cruel jailers at La Petite Roquette. But he had never once thought to be angry with the cold, the hunger, the dirt and disorder he'd lived in or lived with. Before he'd become the courier for *La Lumière,* he'd quite taken these things for granted, assumed he would die as he'd lived, as everyone he knew lived and died—perishing with cold in winter, perishing hot in summer, lousy, hungry, dirty, diseased more often than not, fighting over the same scraps everyone else fought for, filthy water, straw beds, no light, little shelter, and food to be hunkered over, hoarded. It had never occurred to him to live like that—in that despair—degraded men and women, ravaged children. That it was despair had never occurred to him. As he walked down the gallery along satin-covered walls, gilt-framed portraits of corpulent men and proud women, Le Sansonnet felt toward them, toward everything in this palace, a growing loathing, a rage the more intense for its novelty: rage against an idea—the assumption that most of humanity should live as he had lived, in pinch and misery, despised and diseased.

A high, sharp whistle followed by two quick, short blasts brought him up short. At the end of the gallery, sitting in a regal chair, he saw his grandmother, the Changer, the Countess Crasseux, doing a great business in royal goods, flanked on either side by the Jondrettes, men perhaps best described as her serfs, though they acted like her knights. They were in their twenties, but looked older. The Jondrettes were always spoken of in the plural. They were indistinguishable; they wore huge butternut-colored smocks and neatly hemmed trousers, identical blue caps, and wooden shoes. They were fanatically loyal to the Countess since that day in December of 1832 when she had found two boys freezing in a doorway. Their parents had sold them to a woman who had inadvertently abandoned them when she went to prison. They were starving, hacking and coughing, bruised and bleeding and freezing to death, until she came upon them. She was not the Countess then. She was Dahlia Drion, a ragpicker, shrewd, energetic, restless, but a ragpicker just the same, and could ill afford two more mouths to feed, but she took them home and raised them as sons. They'd never left her. They'd never left each other either, but they had given up the habit of speech, which is to say, perhaps they could talk, but they preferred to communicate in a wordless parlance known only to urban birds like the Starling.

Seeing her only grandchild, the Countess's face brightened, and Le Sansonnet wandered around the periphery of her circle, waiting till she finished. He climbed up on a gilded chair to see himself in a gilt-framed mirror, wishing that he hadn't. His hair had grown back, but his nose would never straighten out, and he was ugly, brown with dirt and gray with fatigue. His eyes looked like two mud puddles and felt just as gritty. He had slept only fitfully for a couple of hours in the Pontmercys' kitchen, knowing he had to be out of the house before that cook rose. He lived in mortal fear of her cleaver.

The Countess dismissed all protest from a woman whose gown she had declined to buy. "I can't use it, I tell you. It's shredded."

"But I had to get it off the back of that slut, the Ark, it was mine and—"

The Jondrettes escorted the woman away, and approaching the Countess was a frail, tubercular prostitute affectionately known as Les Genoux for the services she perfected on her knees. From Les Genoux the Countess bought a gown of black lace over white satin, with green velvet bows, and a pair of soft yellow leather gloves, a glory to behold. Les Genoux flushed with pleasure and profit.

The Countess graced a chair where bottoms more royal than hers might have sat, but none could have been more regal. A great, gorgeous wreck of a woman, the Countess had fine, high cheekbones, but her mouth had collapsed, entirely toothless, and she worked her gums incessantly. Her eyes were bright, unclouded by age or misfortune, and her hands were wrinkled and hard, but clean. Her white hair was piled atop her head severely: no false ringlets for the Countess Crasseux. She rose from the chair and took her grandson's arm, asked him if he'd like to have the yellow leather gloves.

"No, *merci*, you have them, Countess. They suit you."

She hugged him against her enormous bosom and ruffled his head. "No more lice?"

"Only the strong survive."

Taking his arm, they made a stroll round the Galerie de Diane, the Countess as though she'd been born to it. She was one of the few people in the world absolutely clear about what she valued. Le Sansonnet was one of the things she valued. "I've brought cash," she said proudly.

"To the sacking of a palace?"

"Cash is the first law. And the first love. No one really loves this—" she kicked a courtier's chair out of the way. "Give the mob the thing they really love, that's what I say. Hard money. Cash money. Why should I fight for these rags? They'll fight to sell to me. They are. Look for yourself. Me, I'll turn some fine threads here, but I have to get them now, while they're whole. These clothes won't be worth a damn shit after they go out of here on the backs of Saint-Lazare whores like that Ark."

"The Captain's out of prison too. Did you see him—"

"He'll be back in prison before the summer. He's a choir bird, Starling. Sung in all the great choirs of Paris—La Force, Mazas, Conciergerie, Sainte-Pélagie."

"People aren't going to live like that anymore, Countess. Every man will get a vote in the Republic. There's a poet now in the Hôtel de Ville. This is the revolution!"

"Republic, empire, king—phhtt!" The Countess spat an invisible seed at the parqueted floor. "I've lived long enough to know. Don't tie your nutmegs in a knot over this Republic."

"I believe in it. Something truly new has happened here! Look, the frock coats and workingmen are friends, united. It's finally come, we have *fraternité* between the workers and the white-hands, we'll have *égalité* with the vote. We'll have *liberté*, Countess!"

"And after the revolution, my boy, do the dogs still do it in the streets? The cats still squeal at night? Do the poor still squat in squalor? And do the rich always—somehow—scramble back to their pedestals?"

"Not this time! Can't you feel it? It's like—"

She kissed his cheek. "Why do you think they call it revolution, Starling? Because it turns and turns and comes back round to where it always was."

Chapter 18

A brilliant splash of winter sunshine fell across the floor when Cosette opened the door of the new café at Number 102 rue Mondétour, its illumination stretching all the way back where Marius sat alone.

"Vive la république!" cried the landlord (who had so recently declared himself in favor of the king to Pajol). Gratified to find it was only a woman, the landlord had no need to flog his new loyalties, and he busied himself with his washing up, watching from the corner of his eye as this beautiful woman in plain clothes walked over to his sole customer and took the man's hands in hers.

"Marius?" He looked up; his eyes were darkly ringed with fatigue, and the scar at his temple looked gray against his pallor. She took off her gloves and ran her fingers through his crisply curling hair. "I knew you would come here."

"It was the dream of my youth, the Second Republic, and I have lived to see it come true." He poured a little wine. "The dreams of youth died here for all but three of us, Pajol, Verdier, and me. And Clerons, of course. We mustn't forget the fifth man."

"Ironic, isn't it? He was working for the king, now the king is gone. What would he have done, do you think? Who would he report to now?"

"He'll find some other master to serve." The landlord brought another glass, and Marius poured them each a splash; it was bad wine, but not *vin bleu*. "There are men like that. They have the souls of dogs, who must always have masters. They're necessary to their masters, they're good dogs, but they are not men."

"With the Republic," Cosette declared, "we'll be free of *mouchards* altogether."

Marius gave her a sad smile. "You see this, here, scratched on the wall?"

"*Vive le peuple!*" She ran her fingers over the words.

"Feuilly carved that with his knife. He was a fan maker. And you see this—" he pointed to a spot below it and to the left, at the edge of the table. "You see this bit of candle wax? It's been painted over but you can see it."

"Yes, I can."

"I wrote you a note that night. I wrote you that love is its own country, but not its own world. If I could not live with you in the country of love, if the world would not let me, then I would go to that other country, the one from which no one returns."

"We have lived in the country of love," she assured him, fearing the sadness that seemed to have engulfed him. "We are our own country, Marius."

"Yes." His white face lit and he smiled expansively. "We always will be. Do you want the letter? I can get it out for you. It wouldn't be hard."

"No, I have the man. Leave the letter in the wall. The paper is not important to me." Cosette wrapped her hands around his. "In the streets they say a mob is looting the Tuileries."

"Good. Loot it. Pull out all the old royalist gilt and silver. The royal family's fled and the beggars are in their beds, but the wine here is no better than it was in 1832. Worse. *Carpe ho ras,*" Marius said wistfully. "Lamartine seized the hour when he proclaimed the Second Republic, Cosette. He showed real courage for a man so vain and posturing. It makes me proud to have a Republic led by a poet, led by writers and editors, my peers, if not my friends. They even asked me to be part of the provisional government, but I declined."

"Oh, Marius, I would have thought to serve the Republic—"

"Perhaps I've already served it. And I haven't the mettle for the task before these men. My virtues, as well as my flaws, make me unsuited to it. I'm not preening and strutting and insincere like Lamartine. I'm not cynical like Marrast. I'm not a reed in the wind like Flocon. I'm not able and efficient like they are, and the structure of the government interests me less than the effect it has on men's lives. I'm a brooder, I guess, a writer, certainly, not an actor, and that's what's needed right now."

"An actor?" she asked, thinking of the costumed general she'd seen carried off by the mob.

"At the Hôtel de Ville, in the Chamber of Deputies, all over Paris the actors in the Second Republic are rummaging through the revolutionary trunk, pulling out the swords and plumes and periwigs, the brocaded waistcoats of 1789, the red caps of 1793, the great military plumes of 1800. The men of that great revolution are alive in everyone's mind, their deeds, their words, we can all recite them from our schooldays. We can sing their songs and strike their poses and slash our way passionately using their rhetoric, imitating their gestures, their flourishes."

"I hope we don't look to the Reign of Terror for their actions."

"We are but poor provincial actors, Cosette, in a noble under-taking." Marius sighed. "But I fear a tragic ending."

"Marius, how can you? This is the event you longed and hoped for. This is the moment your friends died to see. You are here. You are part of it."

"So are you. Together, you know, Cosette, all those things we wrote for *La Lumière*, we lit the way into this revolution, into the Republic. With *fraternité*, God has granted us *liberté* from the king. But the test is yet to come. How far will *égalité* go? I came here to celebrate with ghosts, with men who died of gesture, as Monsieur Thiers said."

"Oh, don't even think about him. On my way over here, I heard in the streets that Thiers is half mad, worrying what will happen to him, cowering in his house."

"I wish him no ill will personally, but I fear people like him, who hear only the great machinery of history and care nothing for the lives it grinds up. The mechanics of power and profit, that's all he understands."

"He's not part of the provisional government."

"No, but we've only unleashed the actors with our revolution. The play's not fully written, the play of 1848, and the question is, who will invent the ending?"

Chapter 19

*M*arius Pontmercy was not the only man who saw, or at least saw the possibility, that the February Revolution would end in a civil war, but few would have been so unflinchingly honest [Cosette wrote many years later to her granddaughter].

You say you have read his Recollections of 1848 *and that the pages are rambling and not chronological. Your grandfather did not see the world in simple linear time; his was a larger vision, broader, and for him time warred always with memory. So naturally you will not find his* Recollections *neat as a railway timetable. But as for your suggestion that I take them and fashion them into order, I must say* merci, *no, my dear. For years I took his notes and wrote from them, and we were in that regard a sort of duet, he the deep cello and I the violin. But I am old now, afflicted with memory and infirmity. The task is best done by you. For me the past is overwhelming. I know too much.*

Perhaps my best contribution would be to give you some notion of that spring of 1848, of what it was like to be alive and living in Paris during the February Revolution, to have had that indelible moment before the June Days steeped us all in blood and left France an enduring legacy of resentment, distrust, and indifference.

As the winter of 1848 closed, we felt we had created a country that would in turn create its own aristocracy of talent and courage. The word went out from Paris, Vive la république, *and all over Europe, kings and tyrants trembled, even the dour matron who yet occupies the throne of England. She trembled too. It was as though we French had invented a dance new in the history of human feet, a dance to trample all the old forms and assumptions, the old oppressions, and bring forth vintage revolutionary wine.*

After the king's abdication, we witnessed the most progressive twenty-four hours in the history of mankind. In the course of the next month, the shackles unsnapped all over France. The provisional govern-

ment granted universal male suffrage, total liberty of assembly, abolished the death penalty for political offenses, abolished imprisonment for debt, limited the working day to ten hours, and granted complete freedom of the press.

All France floated in paper, nearly two hundred new journals in Paris alone, some admittedly for a very few issues, but what of it? Anyone who could read could write, and anyone who could write could print. No caution money, no fines inflicted, no trials for sedition. The day they declared freedom of the press, there was not a dry eye at La Lumière. We sent the Starling and the apprentices out for wine and bread, for cake and champagne, and celebrated one of the most glorious afternoons I can ever remember.

I wish you could read the old issues of La Lumière, dear girl. Perhaps someone, somewhere still has them. I don't. When they tore down the rue de Combray, I've no idea what happened to such records as we kept. But if you could find La Lumière for 1848, you would know, far better than my poor words here can convey, the euphoria of that early spring. In March, for instance, I remember your grandfather was so confident of the revolution and the Republic that he wrote a long article about changing the prisons of Paris into schools. Swords into plowshares, prisons into schools. He believed we would have no more need of prisons, that with new institutions we could abolish base servitude, starvation, the degradation of women and children, abolish even the impulse, and certainly the necessity, for crime. And these institutions seemed to be in place. To absorb the tide of young men, hungry, eager, unattached to any trade or profession, Lamartine and the provisional government created the Mobile Guard, inviting free men of the Republic between the ages of sixteen and thirty to join. They would protect the revolution, and in turn the Republic would clothe, shelter, feed, and arm them, pay them one franc fifty centimes a day.

On 25 February the Republic proclaimed its belief in the right to work. But as the spring progressed, it became clear that we had swept the monarchy off the throne, but whose hand was on the broom? What did it mean, this right to work? To Marius it meant that an honest man should not starve. There were literally thousands of these men in Paris, men with skills and trades and experience, connected to neighborhoods and quartiers, men with families, who were reduced to beggary, who were evicted and watched their children freeze and starve because at *that time there was no work to be had in Paris. The rich weren't buying, the richer yet weren't selling, and so the poor weren't working and went hungry.*

For these honest, impoverished men the Republic established national workshops, a nightmare's web of madness to organize, but affirming the principle that an honest man could sign up, and the national workshops would help him find work, would create work if need be so these men and their families would not starve. A married man with four children received less than twenty francs a week, so you can see neither did they grow fat.

In short, my dear girl, in February, the revolution turned to the workingmen of France and answered the cries of their children with a resounding yes! *And in June the Republic slaughtered these men. In June, the Republic—which began its days with a poet at the head of the provisional government—granted dictatorial powers, vested all powers, military and civil, in the hands of a general. General Cavaignac was ruthless and savage with the people of Paris as he had been savage subduing the people in Algeria. The dead are always subdued.*

I cannot convey to you the horror and betrayal. Truly, it was as the novelist Flaubert once said of the June Days, "Intelligent men lost their sanity for the rest of their lives." Just before they closed down the national workshops and the violence erupted, we wrote in the pages of La Lumière, *"In 1789 Marie Antoinette paid with her head for saying if the people of France have no bread, let them eat cake. Now the government says, If the people of France have no bread, let them eat lead." Bread or lead! That was the cry of June 1848. The response was not bread.*

Do you see now, dear, why I cannot take the task of forging Marius's Recollections of 1848 *into a coherent whole? Hindsight is always so garish.*

Throughout that spring, as March gave way to April and April to May, Marius saw, more clearly than anyone else, how the Assembly was retreating from the freedoms of February, how, you might say, the Republic was withdrawing from the revolution.

On 15 May the Starling *came to the rue de Combray with the news that massive demonstrations—two thousand workingmen—had invaded the Assembly. Marius and I quickly crossed the Seine, where we found them haranguing the representatives. These workers had not invaded, but* they did indeed occupy the Assembly. They were not a mob, but they were not a regiment either. They were not, that we could see, violent, or even armed. They were a single voice imploring the Republic to honor the revolution. And what did the Assembly do? They sat there, patient as donkeys in that stifling hall, and waited for soldiers to rescue them. The workers' leaders were all arrested and imprisoned without trials, taken far from Paris.

To foresee is one thing. To see quite another. Marius went on working, long, terrible hours, the more so after it was clear we were the only newspaper who supported the rebels (as the workers were called once they took up arms against the men who betrayed them). I watched the sorrow and the pity of it undermine your grandfather's health, and it broke my heart, not just that his hopes for social justice in France were dashed, but the dreams of his generation, the men who had died in 1832.

Still, he labored on heroically until the day they arrested him. Before that day, I only saw him falter, truly, once. It was at the Fête de la Concorde, a bit of empty self-congratulatory pageantry staged by the government and held on 21 May—exactly a month before they closed down the national workshops and the carnage of the June Days began.

In the Champ-de-Mars they had set up huge stands for a thousand dignitaries, all the members of the Assembly, and as well, Paris was filled with porcine provincial officials, each more verbose than the last. Ah, my dear, you should have heard the stands groaning under the weight of all that governmental majesty!

All of us from La Lumière, and all the rest of Paris, we milled about in the merciless heat, breathing in the dust raised by endless armies of the line, parades and parades of soldiers, and following them, every straggling suburban militia marched. There were three hundred girls clad in white, supposed to be virgins, walking past the stands, flinging flowers at the governmental luminaries (bouquets like bricks, I commented to Marius). They were followed by three hundred sullen young men, supposed to be ploughmen, and many of these young people rode in carts pulled by oxen supposed to represent Agriculture and Industry. Poor affairs, these carts, crude wooden wheels, wooden axles, they moved only because the drivers used whips on the dull oxen, and they churned up dust and dug ruts before the stands. Then one of them, quite late in the procession, broke down. Its wheel cracked, really just cracked in half, fell off, and the white-clad virgins (not to put too fine a point on it) all *tumbled in the dust, and the driver and his whip fell out and the poor ox just kept dragging the crippled cart through the ruts and the dust, using its dumb brute strength, until it stopped. I knew what Marius was thinking, but I was not prepared for the look on his face. He was speechless with horror, and there are times, dear girl, when I wonder if indeed he ever quite recovered from that horror. He whispered to me—Monsieur Liancourt was right and I was wrong. History is a three-wheeled cart, broken and sitting in the path of progress.*

No doubt in the pages of the Recollections of 1848 *your grandfather explained all about Monsieur Liancourt, so I shall not. Also, I tire easily these days, but I wanted you to know that at that moment perhaps Marius Pontmercy alone knew that we would watch the Republic devour the revolution, that we would see the triumph of men who had power without conscience, men of sense without honor, of pride without valor, shriveled spirits, withered shanks, small minds, and large pockets. Such men are their own dynasty, their power passed down like a scepter, and their roads paved with the spines, the bones, the muscles of working people, and once that road is paved with their backs, history rolls over them.*

Part III

Bread or Lead
June 1848

Intelligent men lost their sanity for the rest of their lives.

—Gustave Flaubert
The Sentimental Education

Chapter 20

From his perch here in the tower of the church of Saint-Séverin, the Starling could see across the river where the towers of Notre-Dame imposed themselves upon the summer sky. To his right, the narrow streets in and around Saint-Julien-le-Pauvre twisted, streets like the rue Galande, he knew like the veins in his own hand, and behind him rose the dome of the Panthéon, glowing in the late-afternoon light.

Well below, encircling the church tower, were the chimney pots and crazy roofs of old Paris. If he had truly been a starling and able to fly, Le Sansonnet could have seen the whole eastern half of Paris sliced, severed, carved apart by barricades, fourteen hundred of them, built since yesterday afternoon. Perhaps, too, he could have seen that one hundred thousand people were about to fight in three days of civil war, in which hundreds would die in the fighting, three thousand summarily executed after they laid down their arms, eleven thousand arrested, six thousand of those later imprisoned or transported. The Starling, fiercely loyal to the stones that had nurtured him, would have come in any event to fight at this first barricade between rue Saint-Jacques and the river, but he was here as well at the behest of Monsieur Pontmercy and on behalf of *La Lumière.* He was to report back to the rue de Combray on the other side of the Seine. "If I live," he muttered, adding an oath, because from his lookout point here over the Saint-Séverin gargoyles he also saw cannon on the Petit-Pont.

It was a Friday in June, near the summer solstice, the shortest night of the year. Maybe my shortest night ever, the Starling thought. The cannon was mounted, ready to creak over the old wooden bridge and down the long rue Saint-Jacques, the gunners alert and soldiers massed in even formations. Worse, metal flashed from the windows of the hospital right next to the bridge. Soldiers had lined up, two by every sickbed, their guns aimed into the street below, and from that high vantage point, the men and women behind the barricade could be picked off like trapped birds. The barricade would offer no protection from above. It would be better to move the fight into the buildings there, at the draper's shop and warehouse on the corner, at the sign of the Deux Pierrots, where two painted harlequins eyed each other maliciously.

He stared more intensely at the soldiers massed behind the cannon. They were not regular army at all. These were Mobile Guard, that ragtag bunch created by the February Revolution, which promised any able-bodied tradeless young man a wage, a weapon, bread, shelter, and a fine new uniform. In the Starling's old impoverished precincts, the young men swaggered insufferably, bragging how the girls fell all over themselves at the sight of the Mobile Guard uniform.

He left the tower, padding swiftly down the stairs to the door that led to the roof, and gingerly made his way to the back to have a better look down the rue Saint-Jacques. The masonry up here was all in patterns that were themselves dizzying, and occasionally his foot slipped, dislodging a tile, and he winced to hear how long it took to crash to the pavement below. All around him, as far as the eye could see, in every building, unshuttered windows framed armed, red-capped men and women, snipers, who saluted him. Since Thursday afternoon, the Starling had served as courier, a runner amongst the barricades from the Seine to the *barrière* d'Italie, so most knew his face, if not his name.

From the church roof he could see thin seams of smoke, which laced the underside of clouds, bivouac fires from armies camped in the Champ-de-Mars and across the river as well. No other burning as yet was visible and no shooting sounded, only the weird discordant call of drum and trumpet, the call to arms all over the city. The insurgents—the army of the poor—their call to arms was sounded on the tin trumpets and cornets of vendors and menders, those and the low tocsin tolling from church towers, like Saint-Merri. All these melancholy tones wafted over the river, down the streets, across market squares, and through trees all leafy with June.

Scampering off the roof and out through the church, Le Sansonnet ran back to the rue Saint-Jacques, where he took the news to

Pajol and the others. The cannon, of course, they could see for themselves, but the barrage of fire that would come from the hospital, that would have been a surprise. Pajol ordered half a dozen of them to go into the Deux Pierrots and tie up bales, bundles of cloth, attach long ropes to them, soak them with whatever they could find, oil from lamps, anything that would burn. Since February, Pajol's strength and health had returned, though his hair would not, and his walk remained impaired, but his eyes were clear, and what had given him impudence as a youth gave him spirit as a man. He lived with Germaine Fleury now in a low, stagnant street near the river Bièvre, and in protecting this first barricade, he felt he was protecting her. Pajol was a veteran of revolution but an unlikely leader; he was the leader here only because the men who might truly have led the workers were already imprisoned far from Paris for their part in the foolhardy "invasion" of the Assembly in May. This ragtag bunch behind the barricade, what had they left—what had they left to lose, for that matter? The lyrics of a popular song called them "soldiers of despair," and their true weapon was the willingness to die in defense of their families, who were starving anyway. Bread or lead.

A sentry alerted them to an approaching parlay party, and Pajol and a few others climbed up on the barricade, peered over to see three men, regular army, one carrying a white flag, one a drum, and the other, an officer, armed only with a sabre, sheathed.

"In thirty minutes, at six o'clock," the officer called out, "we will commence firing. Lay down your arms."

"*Bread or lead!*" shouted Pajol.

"Bread or lead!" echoed voices behind him and all down the rue Saint-Jacques.

Pulling himself up on the barricade, an unemployed mason whose foot had been crushed in an accident grabbed the quarterstaff where the red flag was nailed and waved it. "It's death or liberty for us! Either we die in the democratic Republic, or we die fighting for it!"

"You have taken up unlawful arms against the Assembly and against the Republic."

"The revolution has taken back its promises of February! The Republic has turned its back on the workers! We want social justice!" Pajol shouted.

"General Cavaignac has called in all troops and National Guard from the provinces. They will be descending on Paris. We have men, supplies, officers, ammunition. You have nothing!"

"We have the right to work!" cried a grizzled dyer, whose skin had been mottled and eroded by chemicals.

"We have the right to bread!" shouted a ragged tool grinder.

"We have the right not to watch our children starve, to die of want and cold and disease," cried a tanner whose hands and wrists were a terrible ocher color.

"It's time for the meek to inherit the city!" cried his shoeless wife.

"Lay down your arms or die!"

"Join us!" cried Pajol. "Cross this line and join your brothers. You are men, not suckling pigs crowding up to the belly of that great sow, the Assembly!"

"You have taken up arms against the revolution!"

"We are the revolution!"

Everyone at the barricade took up this cry, and it resounded back as well, to and from the snipers in the unshuttered windows, and down the rue Saint-Jacques and the barricades behind them, *We are the revolution!*

"Very well, then," said the officer, "we are the Republic."

And he turned and marched back across the wooden bridge.

Still perched on the barricade, Pajol looked down on the ravaged faces in the street below, men and women, young and old, those with skills and those without, who had built this barricade, appropriated their environment to build it, constructed it from the simple facts of their lives: timber and scrap and rubble, paving stones piled up, carts, barrels and staves, axletrees, anvils, café countertops, shelves from businesses, bales, beds from homes, all splayed across the street. Pajol implored these soldiers of despair, using Enjolras's old argument that married men—and women too—should leave. But these were not the passions of 1832, content to wait for the revolution. The revolution had come, and in a mere four months the Republic had betrayed it. No one departed.

Across the ancient *quartier Latin*, the great clocks in towers and courtyards tolled, and on the first stroke Pajol told his men to light torches.

"But it's not dark yet," protested the tanner.

"Light them anyway. Take them with you into the warehouse."

On the final toll of six o'clock, the cannon's blast rumbled under the streets of Paris, shaking the earthly rug on which they all stood. The noise knocked the Starling over; at thirteen he had never heard a cannon, and the shock he felt was painted on all the dirty faces around him: the path they'd chosen was in the path of the cannon, and the Republic they had all greeted so rapturously four months before was going to wipe them out like vermin.

After every barrage, the cannon moved slowly forward across the Petit-Pont, like a mill on wheels grinding up the barricade at the entrance to the rue Saint-Jacques. From the windows of the warehouse of the Deux Pierrots, Pajol and the others fired on the gunners, on the soldiers taking aim from the hospital windows. For every gunner the insurgents felled, five more took his place as ball after ball breached the barricade, and behind the great gun marched the Mobile Guard who, at a sign from the officer, swarmed into the warehouse, bayonets fixed.

Pajol gave a signal and they all moved up the stairs, where the tanner was pulling the great bound bales of cloth in their wake; at the top, the tanner ignited one of them with his torch, kicking it downstairs. Cries and screams from the Mobile Guard flared at its rolling approach.

"You! Starling!" Pajol shouted. "Go! Warn the other barricades before you go back to *La Lumière*."

"I can fight, Pajol. Let me fight!"

"You can run too. Go, Starling. Along the roofs."

"I want to fight here—"

"Fly. Fly down the line and tell them all the way out to the *barrière*, we're holding the best we can. You tell them that. The cannon is coming. Tell them—over here, men—fire into the street!" Pajol himself fired and brought down a Mobile Guard. He pulled the red cap off his head and put it on the Starling's. "There, that's so you won't be mistaken by our own!"

"I'll come back."

"Not here. Go to *La Lumière*. If you don't, no one will ever know we fought here."

Or died, thought the Starling as he left, ran up to the top of the draper's warehouse, which was already filling with smoke from the guns, from the bales of burning rags, from the cannon. Being careful not to look down, he scampered out along the roofs and jaunty chimney pots, hearing a few bullets whine overhead. Someone at the hospital must have got a bead on him because bullets followed him across the roof till at last he could dangle himself over a top-floor balcony and jump down, kick the shutters in, and run through the abandoned apartment, down the stairs, and into the street, darting to the next barricade in the rue Saint-Jacques, and the one after that and the one after that. Thirty-eight of them. He brought the news as the cannon rumbled under his feet and shots ricocheted inside his skull. He looked back now and then to see a great pillar of smoke rising like dragon's breath from near the river, and he guessed it to be the warehouse of the Deux Pierrots. The cannon would push past that and blast down the rue Saint-Jacques, which was long and fairly straight, so the cannon could establish its trajectory. As he sprinted, carrying his warnings, Starling advised the people defending these barricades to abandon them when they saw the cannon approach, to defend the smaller barricades in the side streets, those twisted lanes that turned at queer, oblique angles where cannon could not fire and artillery would be useless to the attackers.

He was breathless when he reached the Panthéon, and here, by contrast with the rest of the *quartier Latin,* the barricades were paltry, defended only by a handful of veteran redcaps, mostly with white hair. The Panthéon—huge, glowering, solemn in the summer twilight—did not need defense. Government troops would not fire on the Panthéon, nor, he realized, would they fire on Louis-le-Grand, or the Sorbonne, or the Lycée Henri IV. Filthy streets around the place Maubert, the rue Galande, they would be rubble when this finished, but the great schools of France would not be bombarded. In June the students, of course, were gone, and all the schools' courtyards and hearts closed against the insurgents.

One of the old veterans told the Starling he'd send someone else down the length of the rue Saint-Jacques. Would the Starling turn west, see if more troops approached from that direction?

"It would make sense," said the Starling. "They're bivouacked at the Champ-de-Mars. I'll be back," he promised, barreling off, running till his lungs burst, coming on barricades at the rue des Grès and the rue de la Harpe. At the place Saint-Michel, rebels held the police station, and they too believed an army approached from the west and the Champ-de-Mars.

Black smoke lay in palpable banners all through the streets, the June heat intensified by wind-borne embers from burning buildings, gunfire, gunpowder that blacked the Starling's hands, his face, and his clothes as he raced toward the Odéon, where rebels blocked a whole quartet of streets. The defenders there too said they knew why the government had waited so long to begin their attack. "We started building the barricades Thursday afternoon," said a scrawny woman, whose eyes were ringed with muddy shadows, "they knew it. Why wait till Friday night?" In the distance the cannon coming down the rue Saint-Jacques sounded. "Unless they wanted us in place for—"

"I'll be back," promised the Starling.

Between the Odéon and Saint-Sulpice his mother lived in two tiny rooms in the grimy impasse of the Four Winds, so called no doubt because of the drafts. He ran to her building, to find it deserted, even the concierge had fled, and in the smelly, forlorn courtyard some kittens played with the body of a rat. Mimi did not answer her door, and indeed, it was even unlocked; the disorder here, the clothes and bottles overturned testified to a hasty departure, though the room still smelled of her scorched hair and alcohol.

Coming on the back of Saint-Sulpice, he saw the Café Rigolo was dark, looted, its window smashed, empty casks and barrels, its very zinc counter no doubt forged into a barricade somewhere. He ran toward the Croix-Rouge, only to be met by its defenders, falling back, retreating into the smaller streets. The army was marching from the west.

"They're marching for the Panthéon," a slaughterhouse worker told the Starling.

"There's an army coming down the rue Saint-Jacques too."

"Well, from there they'll have us, won't they?" the worker said, his clothes already matted with dried blood.

The Starling was off, sprinting, speeding, crying out to the rebels he passed on his way back to the Panthéon. Once there, clearly, the armies would branch, one going down the rue Saint-Jacques and out to the *barrière*. The other would destroy the rue Mouffetard all the way to the *barrière* d'Italie. The *barrières,* the wild edges of the old city, were the insurgents' only hope for supplies. Or escape. There were no reinforcements—they knew that.

Despite his red cap, Le Sansonnet kept to the side streets, running along threadlike lanes. He breathlessly called out, as he darted from one barricade to another, warning the defenders of the approaching armies: the one from the west, the one from the north. Other young runners fanned out toward the *barrières*. The Starling was determined to warn the rue Mouffetard.

Coming to the Panthéon once again—his flying feet tapping against a tempo of percussive, incessant gunfire—he warned the red-capped graybeards and then ran along the rue Clovis. From a window high in the walled enclave of Lycée Henri IV someone took a potshot at him. The Starling took off his red cap, waved it, cried out, "Bread or lead!" so he could be identified, and clearly he was, for they fired again and this bullet whizzed so close to his ear the Starling was certain he heard it whisper his name. He paused then at the corner of the rue Clovis and the rue Descartes; this last street alone stood between him and the rue Mouffetard. He took a deep breath, peered around. Save for a sniffing cur, the way looked clear. The dog looked up and whined.

The barricade crossing the rue Mouffetard at the rue de l'Epée-de-Bois was buttressed not merely by the carts and axles he'd seen elsewhere, but huge iron pots from the sausage maker at the corner, and even a dead horse had been jammed in with the paving stones. On either side of the rue Mouffetard, the windows were shattered, the shops were all looted, the cafés were open, and the mood here oddly jubilant. Even the grim news the Starling brought did little to dampen the enthusiasm of people whose stomachs were suddenly well filled, some of whom reeled out of the tattered café, a bottle in one dirty hand, bread in the other. These soldiers of despair, the ragpickers, beggars, street vendors, launderers, skinners, tanners, dyers, greeted each other joyfully, as if a holiday loomed, and in his heart the Starling cursed the stupid "invasion" of the Assembly last month. Now we are the ones being invaded, and where are the leaders to forge these people into an army? The army of the poor, he thought bitterly, their holidays would be in heaven.

The onion vendor who had so nearly snapped the Starling's neck that day in January called his name gleefully, embraced him with gusto, as though this time she would snap his neck from affection. Her breath was thick and vinous and she was armed with a great gutting knife and an ancient sword; her hair was down and wild, and she clutched a wine bottle against her like her firstborn child.

"Bad news," said the Starling. "Two armies are meeting at the Panthéon and—"

"Here, Starling," the onion vendor handed him her bottle. "Drink and go on. Go out to the *barrière* d'Italie. Don't worry about us, the poor beggars of the rue Mouffetard. We'll hold them. Anyway, listen, it sounds like the fighting's letting up."

"That doesn't have to be good news. It could mean all the barricades have fallen to the enemy."

"Whatever it means, it gives us time." She took her bottle back. "It gives you time to get to the *barrière*."

Time enough. Without fighting in the streets or soldiers to be wary of, the Starling's way down the rue Mouffetard out to the *barrière* d'Italie was unimpeded, and so fleet was he, he had got all the way out there and back up and still the rue Mouffetard had not fallen to the army. It had not even been fired upon yet. It was nearly dark now, well past nine, and though gunfire still crackled persistently, the rumble of full-pitched battles no longer sounded in the Latin Quarter. Smoke blowing from the river lay thick upon the air and the short summer night. Other runners had brought word that everything between the river and the Panthéon belonged to the government troops and the Mobile Guard. The Starling was advised to stay behind the rue Mouffetard barricade and make his stand with them, but he declined. "I'm going back to the Petit-Pont. I have to cross the river tonight. They're counting on me at *La Lumière*. I have to get back with word."

"Don't cross at the Petit-Pont!" advised the military beggar. "Go farther east, over by the wine market. Between here and the

Petit-Pont they say the Mobile Guard are shooting everything that moves."

The Starling took his red cap off and jauntily placed it on the onion vendor's old head. "*Merci,* but I can't face Moses without word of Pajol. I have to see if Pajol's still there."

"If he is," snorted the onion vendor, "his soul isn't with him."

Le Sansonnet climbed over the barricade, left the rue Mouffe-tard, cautiously made his way up toward the rue Descartes, where the first casualty he saw was the cur who had whined at him earlier. His feet crunched on broken glass and splintered doors that had been torn off hinges as the army had invaded buildings. His heart pounded and his breath came in short, painful stabs. But he did not run, did not dare; he moved stealthily, stayed close to the build-ings as screams and oaths and cries echoed all round him. Bodies of insurgent snipers hung, doubled over their unshuttered win-dows, like so much bedding hung out to air, and the barricades he encountered in these dank streets were deserted, certainly by the living. Soldier and insurgent alike sometimes lay together in what was clearly a last lethal dance.

Barricades down the straight rue Saint-Jacques had no doubt been demolished altogether by cannon, but these, built in narrow streets, still stood, their defenders dead or piteously, hideously wounded, and the Starling was horrified to step over and around bodies and overcome with a terrible, impotent pity to hear whim-pering cries for Jesus or Holy Mary, inchoate grunts of pain, which he was powerless to aid or comfort. He took a kitchen knife from the hand of a woman, the look of outrage on her face familiar: the secondhand clothes dealer whose coat he had once stolen. She lay frozen, in mid-gesture, her clothes black where her ribs used to be. "*Merci,* madame," he gulped and moved on, not running, not trusting his feet, or his luck for that matter, but treading carefully in and out of doorways (those opened, those closed, those smashed) along the rue des Carmes, listening to the running feet of soldiers, their barking voices, the shattering of doors and windows and the screams of men and women pulled from their apartments.

He was nearly at the Carmes Market Square when, at the corner of the rue Judas, the tramp of marching feet broke on him suddenly, and he humped himself into a nearby doorway, tapping at the door, begging to be let in. A man's voice told him to shut up and go away. He didn't go away, but he certainly shut up; he held his very breath for the noise it might make and stayed hunkered down, clutching his knees, his back pressed flat against the wall, when not ten steps from him the tramp of feet stopped and a voice ordered, "Faces to the wall."

"You pinchprick," cried a woman's voice. "Your mother should have strangled you at birth! Traitor! Coward! Can you kill a woman to her face, you swine—"

A shot rang out.

"Now, the rest of you, faces to the wall."

"Time to pray," a man beseeched. "In Christian charity, give us a moment to pray!"

"Face the wall and I'll give you five minutes to pray."

Almost instantly a barrage of shots rang out. Then, amidst thumps and groans, the occasional cry (followed by another shot), the feet marched back off toward the market square.

Peering out into the empty street, the Starling edged furtively toward the rue Judas and found there a pile of corpses, making their own barricade of sorts. Though he had had nothing to eat since the morning, nonetheless the Starling threw up what he could, and swallowed, ingested viscerally what he knew would be a lifelong lump of hatred.

He managed to flatten himself against the building, scoot past the pile of bodies, and then avoiding the Carmes Market Square at all cost, he zigzagged through the alleys and hovels, stinking passages that coiled around the back walls of the Ecole Polytechnique and the rue Saint-Victor, coming at last to the place Maubert, the streets in and around Saint-Julien-le-Pauvre. He felt oddly protected here, certain these streets somehow cared for him; surely these stones, witness to his earliest life, would warn him of danger, would open up and swallow him before they would allow their own son to die. The stones, however, had clearly shown no such loyalty to others. *Bread or lead.* Denied bread, they'd taken lead, these soldiers of despair, in the guts, the head, the torso. A quarterstaff still lay clutched in the strong hands of a tanner who would never again touch leather, and a woman who had crawled out of the public pawnshop, her loot still in her hand, lay bleeding to death in its doorway. It was Les Genoux, the prostitute with the practiced knees. The Starling watched, horrified, as a white butterfly fluttered around her, rested momentarily in the blood across her breast, a butterfly, unchanging token of summer, drawn to a sticky substance not at all sweet. The Starling moved toward Les Genoux, but she cautioned him away, raising one finger in benediction and farewell.

Stealthily he prowled the rue Galande, stepping over the dead, pushing debris from his path and keeping close to buildings, where from the shattered windows he heard weeping, screams, or some low half-human groans. He could see the tower of Saint-Séverin, but kept looking over his shoulder, feeling all the while that someone was at his back. Soldiers surely would have fired. Finally he turned and saw them: phantom figures tiptoeing around the dead like goblins, plucking from them such trinkets as they would clearly have no further use for.

Fearing these pickers of dead pockets more than the soldiers, the Starling ran, made at last the corner of the rue Saint-Jacques. The cannon crossing the Petit-Pont had done its work and moved on, and sprawled in the street lay men and women who had fallen from the roofs when they'd tried to flee, their heads cracked, their blood pooling and turning purple, some directly under the gargoyles of Saint-Séverin. He did not see Pajol, but the sign of the Deux Pierrots lay face up amongst the blood and bits of blasted barricade, the two harlequins grinning maliciously skyward. Slowly the Starling followed their gaze, where bodies bent double in the windows; the tanner's yellow hands hung uselessly and the knife grinder's gray eyes were open, peering, unseeing. Smoke billowed from the upper stories, and a section of the roof gave way, a rush of red and gold, thickly curtained in black smoke, cascaded from the windows, and flames flew up against the milky summer sky, and the Starling felt a swift, sharp bayonet jab between his shoulder blades.

The Mobile Guardsman who disarmed him of his kitchen knife had a beard sprouting amongst a thicket of pimples on his chin. He marched Le Sansonnet back along the streets of Saint-Julien-le-Pauvre. The stones Le Sansonnet had known all his life did not open to swallow and save him. When they passed the pawnshop, Les Genoux still lay there, still alive, groaning, and the Guardsman took aim, shot her in the head.

They brought the Starling into the Carmes Market Square as another four insurgents were being marched toward the rue Judas. A crude trestle table, barrels serving as chairs, had been set up before the fountain. In the center of the fountain stood a narrow obelisk topped with the face of a woman, whose stone eyes gazed out impassively to watch torchlight dance a devilish caper in her watery reflections. They flung the Starling amongst a dozen others, "incarcerated" behind a few market carts, and guarded by heavily armed skinny men. No one spoke, some wept. Like the Starling, their hands, faces, and clothes were black with gunpowder, one woman trying feverishly to wipe it off, as if she could erase all evidence of ever having participated in the rebellion. Among this ragged band, the Starling recognized (from the boot-shaped liver spot on his bald head) the old man from the Tuileries, the man who had tried to save the beggar shot by the mob for stealing six francs and a roll of ribbon. The old man did not see him, saw nothing; he was the next pulled out and made to stand upright before the trestle table where three Mobile Guardsmen sat on barrels.

The Starling peered out between carts. The old man shook off the rough hands of his captors and stood with dignity, his gaze on the stone-eyed woman above the fountain. The men questioning him, despite their hats and uniforms, had young faces, their youth more odd for their swaggering certainty, their coarse voices. One asked the old man his name, which he gave, and his occupation.

"*Merde!*" cried the Mobile Guardsman in the center. He was thin-chested, and his lanky form sprawled uncomfortably on the barrel. He held a gun in his right hand and a near-empty bottle in his left, which was horribly deformed, the fingers rigidly curved inward, the nails long and yellow like claws. "Don't ask his occupation. Who gives a rat's ass what he did yesterday? Today he took up arms against the Assembly, the government, eh? From now on just write *rebel* under occupation."

"Very well, Griffon." The guardsman on the left complied. He asked the old man his age.

"He's old!" cried the Griffon, the name clearly resulting from the claw. "Can't you see he's old! Do you really give a damn shit *how* old?"

"He's not getting any older," said the guardsman on the right, picking his teeth with a knife.

"Old man," said the one on the left, "what were you doing this evening in the place Maubert?"

The old man brought his gaze down from the woman in the fountain and rested his eyes levelly on the three young men before him. "Shooting dogs like you, bastard curs. You'd kill your own father. You've turned on your own kind. Yes, you, you the Mobile Guard. They give you a uniform and a weapon, and you turn on your own people, people like us. You're killing your own! I know you boys! I know who you are, and in your fathers' names, I spit on you!"

The center guardsman, the lanky one with the deformed hand, took the old man's spit full in the face. Rising slowly off his barrel he walked around the table. The look on his young face, made more ferocious by torchlight, was the most terrible thing the Starling had ever seen, his features twisted in rage and glee. He walked over to the old man and with his right hand struck him hard in the face.

"Cripple," said the old man, eying the claw.

"A crippled hand is better than none." He ordered one of the guardsmen to hold the old man's left arm out. With a slow, indolent motion, he picked up his gun, rested the barrel on his deformed fingers, and pulled the trigger with his right hand, but not before the old man, seeing what was to happen, cried out and loosed his bowels.

The hand blasted to a thousand bits sprayed everywhere, and the man fell into his own blood and body fluids, screaming till the Griffon shot him again. First in the groin. Then he shot him in the head. "I'm going for a drink," he announced. "I'll be back."

Two others carried what was left of the old man toward the rue Judas. Le Sansonnet felt his own bowels weaken as he was nudged out at the point of a bayonet, and to his horror, ordered to stand where the old man had stood.

They asked his name, repeated the question, but the Starling could not reply, did not, his voice was somehow still tangled round his bowels, holding them tightly.

"Name," the guardsman insisted. "Tell me or I'll—"

"Gabriel Lascaux," he strangled out.

"Age—well, never mind."

The one picking his teeth with the knife took up the interrogation. "So, Gabriel Lascaux, what were you doing in the *quartier Latin* tonight? You're just a suckling babe, aren't you, Lascaux. I'll bet you go to school here, don't you—Louis-le-Grand?" He chuckled and his friend guffawed. "You're a student, eh?"

Student racketed in the Starling's head as his whole short life shimmered before him, resisting, defying the void of death. *Student?* "Yes! Yes, I'm a student, Pincher! Pincher! Is that you? Under that cap?"

The one who had been picking his teeth rose, reached into the fountain, slathered water over the Starling's face. "Starling! Who in hell is Gabriel Lascaux?"

"It's my real name, Pincher—"

"My name's not Pincher. I'm Sergeant Lorin. What are you doing with this rabble? I thought you were a smart boy."

"I thought you were a free man, Pincher."

"What do I want with freedom? Freedom to starve like the rest of them? Look at me, the Mobile Guard gives me one franc fifty centimes a day!"

"For one franc fifty centimes a day, you'd kill your own, Pincher? You'd kill the men and women you've known all your life? You'd kill people who've been hungry like you?"

"Not anymore. I'm not hungry. They give me bread, shelter, a uniform. Women love this uniform. You should have joined."

"I'll never wear a uniform."

"You're too young anyway."

"I didn't think the Mobile Guard took thieves."

"I'm a fan maker." The Pincher grinned. "Can't you tell from my hands?" He held out his long, spidery fingers. "I bless the Second Republic. I'm loyal to the Assembly."

"I looked up to you, Pincher! You were a great thief and now you're a traitor, I hate you!" The Starling wept for the first time in years; after the man's work he'd done, he succumbed to the tears of the boy he was. "I regret everything you ever taught me, you scum, you pig—"

Pincher smacked him and his nose started to bleed. "You have a big mouth, Starling. First I'm going to stuff your mouth with turds, and then I'm going to close it forever," he announced as the first guardsman returned to the table, carrying an open bottle of wine in his clawed hand and settling his lanky bones on the center barrel. Pincher kicked the Starling's feet out from under him, kicking him again, face down on the purple-brown stones. "I'm going to kill this one myself."

The Griffon shrugged and ordered the next prisoner out from behind the carts.

Bayonet at the Starling's back, the Pincher marched him around to the rue Judas, where the mound of corpses and still twitching bodies had grown. He pushed the Starling's cheek to the cold wall, his hand splayed against the boy's back. He stepped away, the bayonet still between the Starling's shoulders, pointed the musket suddenly skyward, and fired. "Fly, Starling," he whispered hoarsely, moving in close behind the boy. "Get to the river and don't come back!"

Le Sansonnet ran, flew as he had never flown before; he sprinted through streets where soldiers combed the buildings; he jumped over bodies, over the living and the dead, ignoring cries and shots that shrilled past his ears, till at last he came to the river, and plunged into the Seine. The slow, cold water closed over his head, and he went under gratefully until he could bear no more, and then he burst to the surface, breathed deep, and plunged back, giving himself to the current, washing the soot and smoke from his face and hands, the blood and shit from his shoes and clothes, diving down, paddling back up, till at last, he crawled out of the river and lay weeping and breathless on the embankment in the brooding shadow of Notre-Dame. Thick clouds rolled over the twin towers of the cathedral, and its ancient flying buttresses were bannered with battle smoke. Rain clouds and smoke clouds blew, shredded noiselessly, torn by gargoyles who had crouched there for a thousand years. Thunder unfurled, so deep and rumbling the Starling thought it was the cannon bearing down again. But it was only a summer thundershower, unleashing itself upon the towers of Notre-Dame, sluicing its roof slates and stained-glass windows, pelting the gargoyles, falling on the streets of old Paris, on rebel and soldier alike, on the dead and the living, on the Starling, crying and shivering, hugging his knees, knowing that neither rain nor river would ever wash him wholly clean again.

Chapter 21

When at last Le Sansonnet came to the rue de Combray, it was very close to dawn, but all the lights blazed at the newspaper and theirs were the only unshuttered windows in the street. In any street, for that matter, although in these *arrondisse-ments*—between the smart boulevards and the rue de Rivoli, those deserted avenues of wealth, commerce, and amusement—there were soldiers, but not barricades and no fighting.

He went around to the back, opened the door, and leaned there, absorbing the welcome sounds, the clank and groan of the presses, the voices, the ceaseless activity as the pressroom worked through the night. "It's the Starling," cried an apprentice, and Verdier dropped his work and pulled the shivering Starling into an embrace.

Gabriel thought he might cry against Verdier's smock, sweet with the smell of ink and sweat and metal. He lingered in the warmth of the embrace. "Pajol?" he asked at last. "Did he come back, Moses?" Verdier's face fell and the Starling wept, "They're wiping us out like vermin."

Cosette clattered downstairs from the editorial offices, Marius right behind her, and they joined Verdier and the other printers and apprentices near the cold stove, where they had wrapped the Starling in a blanket.

Cosette pushed his wet hair away from his face; his lip was cut open and his eyes were fierce and horrible. She stroked his hair. "What's happened to you? What have they done to you?" She chafed his hands. "Do they make war on children?"

"They make war on everyone in their path."

To Marius, Verdier announced he was leaving for the barri-cades. "Pajol did not come back. Thérèse is on the barricades. They're fighting all along Saint-Denis, right near my house. I can't stay here."

Marius put his hand on the older man's shoulder. "You are the only one who can do this work. We are the only paper supporting the rebels. This is your barricade."

"I only just got Pajol back." Verdier swallowed a great lump of emotion. "When he came back, he brought with him, I mean, he reminded me of the man I was, the man who—"

"You're still that man," said Marius. "You've kept your vow. We have kept our vows, Verdier. We worked for the Republic. How could we know it would betray us? Now we have to work for the revolution. The revolution and the Republic have split. The Republic belongs to Thiers and men like him. Property, profit, and order, that's what they're setting in place of the king. Nothing's changed. We have a new government and the same old enemies— want, poverty, ignorance, and disease."

"I want to kill the Assembly, those pious frauds." Moses's mouth set in a grim seam.

"Kill them with ink," advised Marius. "We need this edition out by noon and then get ready to print again. Starling, will you come upstairs please and tell us everything you've seen?"

"Could I have my bread first, monsieur, my notch of bread?" he nodded, trembling, toward the pallet where he habitually slept.

"What does that mean?" asked Cosette.

The Starling shrugged eloquently. "You buy your bread and the baker makes a notch on a wooden stick that has your name, and at the end of the month, he tells you what you owe, and if you don't pay, he keeps your stick and gives you no more bread till you do." One of the apprentices handed him the bread, and he tore into it gratefully.

It was full dawn now, and in the editorial offices Cosette turned out the lamps. The air hung heavy with tobacco smoke, though the place was deserted. The three of them sat at the green baize tables in the center, and the Starling, still clutching his blanket, told his tale, while Marius and Cosette, both of them gray from lack of sleep, listened grimly, Marius playing with a pencil, making notes, asking questions. When the Starling told of the Mobile Guard's summary executions, Marius swore under his breath.

"Where were their officers?" he asked. "Who authorized these executions?"

"They had no officers. They had uniforms. They had guns. That was enough. The army just set them loose on the people. Like dogs, like a pack of wild dogs. The men and women they shot should have been prisoners. By noon the Mobile Guard will be down the rue Mouffetard, out to the *barrière* d'Italie." Starling's lip shook and he rubbed the grit from his eyes. "And the rest of the city, monsieur?"

But Marius could not speak. He rose and walked to the window, still playing with his pencil.

"They're still holding out on this side of the river, as best we know," Cosette explained. "The rebels are running from one barricade to the next, defending when they can, sniping. At the rue Saint-Antoine they've got a huge barricade guarding the whole place de la Bastille and everything around it. They say there are a hundred barricades between there and the place du Trone."

"If they could just capture the Hôtel de Ville," said Marius from the window, "perhaps . . ."

The guns started up again, not nearby, but insistent.

"It's General Cavaignac who has unleashed the carnage." Marius turned back to Cosette and the Starling. "They brought him back from Algeria, where he was celebrated for his ruthlessness in putting down the natives. Now he once again is ruthlessly putting down the natives, isn't he? The native French. The native Parisians. He'll pull his troops off the south side by the end of the day and bring everything against the rue Saint-Antoine, Saint-Denis, all along the eastern half of the city."

The Starling flung off his blanket and jumped up. "Listen to the guns, monsieur! The rue des Filles-du-Calvaire, it's an island in the midst of the fighting. Saint-Antoine to the east, place de la Bastille to the south, Saint-Martin, Saint-Denis, all to the north and west, monsieur. Mademoiselle Fantine is not safe there!" He gulped and added, "And neither is your son, your servants, your sister."

"My sister?" inquired Marius.

"The old lady—I mean the other mademoiselle."

"Aunt Adelaide," Cosette suggested. She bit her lip, listened to the sounds of the fighting escalate as the dawn rose over the city. "I wish now we had taken Jean-Luc and Fantine to Cousin Théo's, Marius."

"They're protected at home. There are gates, thick walls all around the back. Jean-Luc is responsible." Marius frowned. "If the Starling can be trusted to go from the *barrière* d'Italie to the rue de Combray and bring back word of a battle, surely Jean-Luc can be trusted to keep the house locked up and stay vigilant."

"Can he?" asked Cosette fearfully. "When we left the fighting was farther away, up by the canal, but now—"

"Please, monsieur, madame, let me go to your house and bring your children back. It's better here. They aren't fighting here near the boulevards. The soldiers aren't—"

As if to belie him instantly, the sound of a drum and the tramp of military feet sounded in the rue de Combray, stopping before the door of *La Lumière*. Marius looked down into the street. "Regular army," he said, putting on his coat as the knock sounded below.

Cosette ran to the window to see an officer and perhaps half a dozen men in the street. "What do they want, Marius?"

He took her shoulders firmly in his hands. "Whatever happens here, you go home with the Starling, get the children, and all of you go to Théo's. Starling," he turned to the boy, "you'll see she gets safely home and—"

"Count on me, monsieur."

"I have counted on you, more than you know." He pulled Cosette close and kissed her cheek, held her, and by that time Verdier was up the stairs, the look on his face pure hatred.

Cosette and the Starling followed Marius and Verdier into the pressroom, where everyone crowded forward as the officer saluted.

"Citizen Pontmercy, editor and proprietor of *La Lumière*?" At Marius's nod, he handed him a piece of paper. "My orders. I am commanded by General Cavaignac to seal the presses of *La Lumière*—"

"Cavaignac has no authority here."

"Citizen, the Assembly has declared Paris in a state of siege. The Assembly has granted, with a single dissenting vote, to vest all powers, dictatorial power, in the hands of General Cavaignac. The general alone can save the Republic from the rebels!"

"But the general can't close down newspapers."

"The general can do whatever he likes in a state of siege." The officer nodded to his troops, who brought in with them huge, rattling chains and heavy locks. "I am under orders. Your presses are sealed and you are under arrest."

"Swine!" Verdier lunged at him, but the officer drew his sword.

"Everyone is ordered to leave the premises or be arrested."

"How long?" asked Marius. "How long must my presses stay silent?"

"Till General Cavaignac decrees otherwise."

The terrible rattle, clank, and thump of chains wrapped around the upright presses sounded. But the horrible groan those presses would have made had they been animate came from Verdier.

"I alone am arrested?" asked Marius, his calm more horrible than Verdier's passion. The officer nodded and Marius told his staff to leave.

"Where are you taking him?" cried Cosette. "Where—"

"To the Conciergerie prison."

"And a trial?" she implored the officer. "A trial?"

"There will be no trial for arrested editors."

"Doesn't the Republic require a trial?"

"Madame, until the Assembly decrees otherwise, General Cavaignac is the Republic."

"We begin with a poet and we end with a general?" she said incredulously.

"We have not ended," the officer informed her coolly.

Somehow the chill of that thought, the fear of worse yet to come, permeated the whole pressroom, and Marius told everyone to leave immediately. Verdier said he was on his way to the Saint-Denis barricade and Marius nodded sadly.

The soldiers finished chaining the presses, and the room was eerily silent. Printers and apprentices filed out into the street, Cosette and the Starling following Marius and the soldiers. The officer asked Marius for the key to the premises of *La Lumière*.

He gave it to him, but his lips were taut and his unshaved cheeks ashen. "I have fought for the Second Republic all my life. Now the Republic—not the king, but the Assembly, they cower like sheep, give away their responsibilities to a butcher. The butcher tells his soldiers to execute whomever they wish, men, women—" he looked at the Starling—"children. The Assembly allows the butcher to take lives, to take rights. The press is chained and I am imprisoned without a trial." Marius looked to Cosette, no shock or outrage on his face, only the impenetrable sadness, the look of a man who attends the funeral of his best friend, or his youthful dreams. "Cavaignac does well to silence me. I am indeed the enemy of the Republic. But I am the friend of the revolution."

"That's enough. Will you go quietly, or shall I manacle you?"

"By all means," Marius thrust out his wrists, "never let it be said I went quietly."

Cosette wept to hear the fetters snap. Not since the day of Jean Valjean's funeral had she seen Marius so despairing. "I'm going to get you out," she vowed. "I will. I will move heaven and earth, Marius, but you will not stay in the Conciergerie. I will find a way! I'll go there right now!"

"No," he said. "Let the Starling take you home. It's not safe. I can endure anything if I know that you are safe."

"I'll take her home, monsieur. Your family will be safe with me, but after that, I'm going to the barricades at Saint-Denis and fight with Moses."

"You can't!" cried Cosette. "You're just a boy."

"Not after last night," he replied in a voice that truly was not that of a boy.

The soldiers formed a phalanx around Marius; the officer put the key in the lock, and it turned with metallic finality.

Chapter 22

*T*here were days in June after the June Days. There were days in July. Days in August. There were evidences everywhere that the city was finding, or would slowly find, its equilibrium. Doctors, lawyers, and judges were frantic with activity. Gravediggers too. Slowly the deposits of the dead were cleared; nearly every body was claimed by someone, and the rest were dumped into common graves. Goods and supplies found their way back into the city as the markets tentatively reopened, although the Carmes Market Square did not pick up its old pace till the following year, and there were those who said the stone-eyed woman in the fountain still sometimes wept and that her waters ran pink.

The whole eastern half of the city was torn up, much of it destroyed, reduced to rubble. There was the work of rebuilding, but fewer workers to put their hands to it: many of the dead, the wounded, the arrested, the imprisoned, and the soon-to-be transported were joiners, carpenters, glaziers, masons, hod carriers, the men who erected scaffolding, the boys who scampered over it, builders of one sort or another. Well, perhaps they would build in Algeria. Even the ranks of the ragpickers had thinned considerably. Someone had to sweep and sift and process the waste, the litter and rubbish, into bundles and cart it away, and inevitably, there were nasty surprises amongst the debris; only ragpickers could be expected to delve into, to rummage and touch, such disorder.

Perhaps the most encouraging sign of recovery was the number of carriages. Slowly the wheeled traffic of the city picked up; omnibuses, carts, carriages, cabriolets, fiacres, and wagons rattled percussively on the paving stones, thumped where the paving stones had been torn up, trotted past the empty shells of burned-out buildings and over the bridges.

On Friday, one week after the fight at the Petit-Pont, a cab pulled up in front of the Café Rigolo, where Madame Fagennes had got her window fixed. And as for the zinc counter, well, she'd made do with a plank flung across a couple of chairs stacked, and though her stocks were depleted, she adulterated the wine still further and opened for business. A woman got out of the cab and came into the Café Rigolo, inciting Madame Fagennes's interest, which is to say her immediate distrust. This woman was blue-eyed, her honey-brown hair fixed smoothly, plainly under a gray bonnet of good quality, tied with scarlet ribbons, white satin ruching framing the striking face. Madame Fagennes had a weakness for bonnets. Well-dressed, expensively dressed, the woman wore a frock of lavender gray, and to Madame Fagennes's eternal surprise, she asked after Madame Lascaux.

"She's back to work," declared the café landlady, "but you're too early. She's not here yet. It's six in the summer."

"I see," said Cosette, clearly disappointed. "Actually it's her son I'm looking for."

"Little beggar."

"You've seen him then?"

"Little beggar's gone off and got himself killed."

Cosette paled and Madame Fagennes poured her a glass of adulterated cognac, charged her double, and said she did not know that for a fact. She did not know anything for a fact. He hadn't been seen, that's all. The fighting finished on Monday and it was Friday, and nothing had been seen or heard of him, save for a rumor he had fought at Saint-Denis. "Here's Mimi now. Be careful what you say. It's tough on her. He was a little shit and a thief, of course, but—"

Cosette took a chair opposite Mimi Lascaux, who ignored her; she wasn't a customer, after all. As though speaking across a great chasm, Cosette introduced herself, but Mimi only squinted. Her eyesight was bad, which accounts for her poor performance in the seamstress trade. She toyed nervously with her ringlets and earbobs. Not until Cosette mentioned *La Lumière* did Mimi's expression brighten, though perhaps it was the approach of Madame Fagennes with a glass of *vin bleu*.

"I'm looking for your son, Madame Lascaux. I've been looking since Monday. I've looked at the morgue and the hospitals and I haven't found him. The prisons—well, there's such confusion there. They won't tell me anything at the prisons and I—"

"He was a good boy. I don't care what he done to others, he was a good boy to me."

"Is he dead? Did you claim the body?"

Mimi burst into tears. "I couldn't do it, claim his body. I thought, I can't be walking through those aisles and aisles of dead people, can I? What if there's people I know? There's sure to be people, men I know lying there, all dead and horrid. I couldn't do it. What if one was Gabriel? Shot by those dogs of soldiers. I don't care if he made war on them! He was a boy!" Shoe blacking ran off her eyelashes, and powder and rouge ran down her face in pink rivulets.

"Maybe he's not dead, Madame Lascaux. If you didn't claim him and he wasn't at the morgues or the hospitals, he's alive. But if he's a prisoner, they'll start trying the rebels soon and I'm afraid for him, for what they'll do to him. There won't be real trials," Cosette added bitterly. "They'll transport anyone whose clothes were stained with gunpowder."

"Gabriel would not want me to go to the morgue. I can hear him. *Don't you go walking through that morgue and upset yourself, Mimi.* That's what he'd say. He looked after me." Mimi drank her wine and wept softly. "I'll tell you who would have claimed him," she said at last. "I'll tell you who wouldn't let no one stop her. Cavaignac himself could not stop the Changer, my mother, the famous Countess Crasseux. I didn't go to the morgue. I didn't have to. I knew she would go. I know what she would do. She is her own June Days, that woman."

"Where can I find her?"

"Walk to the river where the scum washes up. That boy was all I had. Now I don't have him."

"If he's alive—"

"He's a prisoner. They'll transport him to some stinking prison, some hulk of a prison ship, some desert hole in Algeria. Whose fault is this, madame? Whose fault? Is it yours? Maybe it's yours. If he hadn't gone to work for your husband's wretched radical rag, maybe this wouldn't have happened." Mimi wept, wiping her nose with her arm.

"I will find him. I'll help him, Madame. I—we—cared for him, care for him. He is a fine boy. You can be proud of him." But Mimi continued to sob, and so Cosette asked if she could buy the drink. "Five francs. I'm sure it must be five francs."

"Yes," Mimi gulped. "It is. Five francs."

Before she left the Café Rigolo Cosette asked Madame Fagennes where near the river she could find the Changer.

"The Changer isn't the sort of shop to hang out a sign," Madame Fagennes explained with lethal condescension. "You either know it, or you don't."

"Would five francs help me to know it?"

Five francs found it. It had once been a tobacco warehouse and stood at the end of a long, ugly courtyard, where centuries of dirt and bird droppings stained its walls, where the sun could not penetrate, and even on these days of high summer, such light as fell was slivered and splintered and thin. Mold furred the stones in the narrow impasse, and the frame of a wooden shed gaped over empty baskets and a forlorn three-wheeled cart. Rags lay heaped in piles at random intervals, rotting dully. Despite the bright summer day, all the windows were shuttered and all the four doors flanking this impasse equally forbidding, but she heard dogs barking behind one and so she knocked there.

Dogs' snouts and bared teeth protruded through the slightly opened door, and a pair of eyes peered at her. In a faltering voice Cosette asked for the Changer. The eyes appraised her, tallying up her means and the extent of her desperation. "I need to see the Countess on a matter of some importance," she said, adding regally, "Tell the Countess Baroness Pontmercy wishes to see her."

In a single movement, he pulled the dogs back, and when Cosette stepped in, the door slammed shut behind her. He drew the dogs toward another man, who sat at a table fingering a deck of cards in the light of a single tallow candle. The man whistled queerly and the dogs lay down. The two men looked exactly alike, in butternut-colored smocks, with bony faces and waxy coloring. The first man returned to her, making succinct, silent gestures, moving his fingers in an oblong pattern.

She reached into her pocket and drew out a visiting card with its ornate script, *Baroness Pontmercy*. The man turned, left—vanished really—into a door Cosette had not even guessed was there. She smiled ineffectively at the other man, who made no noise whatever.

Slowly Cosette looked above to the enormously high ceilings, which were spanned by thick rafters, beams stretching from end to end, and in the musty shuttered light, she saw suspended, high above her, clothes: ball gowns looped around their middles and seemingly bent double, most in huge sacks like the cocoons of monstrous butterflies, thousands of them, so it seemed, hideously suspended, and the smell of tobacco still pungent with the damp and dried perspiration of the bodies long since turned to dust. The clothes seemed to hang there as if they expected at any moment to be warmed by human flesh, reanimated by human laughter, released from their melancholy gallows.

When the man returned, he bade her follow him through a maze of corridors, stacked, packed with wardrobes and trunks, shelves of footless shoes. At last he brought her to a set of double doors, which turned into a parlor of sorts, at least a room with pretensions to formality, windows with shelving holding broken bric-a-brac and lit by candelabra. On a ragged Napoleonic couch there reclined the Countess Crasseux, scraping Cosette's calling card across her lips. The Countess seemed to dwarf the couch, clad, as she was, in a crazy garment without fashion, but not altogether lacking in style. Many styles. The bodice was Empire, the fichu snatched from Marie Antoinette, the skirt was many skirts, and the sleeves fell in cascades of lace gone amber with age, as indeed had the Countess's amber-spotted hands.

"I'm looking for the Starling," said Cosette without preliminaries, which, she guessed, would be inadequate here in any event. "I've been looking for him since the last barricade fell on Monday. I will not rest till I've found him."

To Cosette's surprise, the Countess snarled, remarked that it was Cosette's fault he was lost at all. "There he was, leading a perfectly fine life, picking up the odd bit of business when necessary, watching his tail, skylarking about Paris. Oh, he'd get his wings clipped now and then, but at least when he was in La Petite Roquette, I knew where he was. Didn't I, eh? Then you come along, take him to the other side of the river, put him in fine clothes, pay his way, fill him with a lot of swinish ideas about liberty and equality, and send him off to fight!"

"I never sent him off to fight! I begged him not to go!"

"And to fight for what? For your husband's newspaper? I wipe my ass with *La Lumière.*"

"But I saved him from being arrested, from prison, the baker would have—"

"Yes, and look what you brought him to." The Countess glared at her. "Keep your white fingers where they belong, Madame Pontmercy, keep them out of the river and out of the place Maubert and out of Saint-Julien-le-Pauvre and out of the ragpickers' baskets and away from the children of the ragpickers' families."

"If it pleases you to blame me, Countess, then blame me—"

"I do! He never listened to me. Do you know the story of the Costly Omelette?"

Cosette shook her head.

"I thought not." She spat out the invisible seed that always plagued her.

"I want to help him."

"Can anyone help him now?"

"Is he alive? Answer me that."

But the Changer answered nothing, remained grimly indignant.

"Please, tell me he's alive. Tell me he didn't die with the rest of them." Tears welled in her eyes, and she tilted her chin so they would not fall. "I can help him. If you care for him, tell me where he is, which prison. He's a prisoner, isn't he? One of the arrested? I will get him freed." Cosette licked her lips, continued more carefully, "I will do everything in my power to get him freed, everything in the power of the people I know."

"Who do you know?"

"Many people." Cosette drew a deep breath. "I know Monsieur Thiers."

"A pig. You know him well?"

"Well enough."

"He is odious."

"He is powerful. Please let me help the Starling, Countess, whatever you think of *La Lumière,* or my part in changing his life—"

"It didn't need changing!" The Countess rose, pulling her impossible gown after and around her, and stalked up and down. "His life was fine! Look around, madame! He did not need to pick up your leavings. If he wanted to pick through the shit of the rich, he could have lived here! People like you and your husband, you live your overheated lives, you know nothing of freedom. You are slaves. You think your money buys you freedom? It fetters you, madame! Gabriel, now, he was one of us. He was fine, he was free till he met you! He was the Starling. Now he wants to be a nightingale. He envies you," she added sourly.

"I protected him from arrest," Cosette declared in her own defense.

"And sent him to the barricade. Tell me, madame, your son, his name is Jean-Luc, yes? Oh, yes, I have heard of your fine son. Was he following in his father's political principles? Was he fighting on the barricade, thirteen years old?"

"Fourteen." Cosette's mouth was dry, her palms moist. She would have chained Jean-Luc to the wall before she would have let him near the fighting. She understood the depth of the Countess's passion, knew too that passion is unarguable; she would not offend that passion by asserting that she and Marius too loved Gabriel, loved him, admired him, were indebted to him; Starling had got her back home through all the fighting around rue des Filles-du-Calvaire that awful Saturday, and then, against all her protestations, he had left for the Saint-Denis barricades to fight with Verdier. "Is the Starling alive?" she asked again. "I don't want to see him transported with all the others."

The Countess's eyes flickered over Cosette, who pulled herself up, trying for the dignity to conceal from this appalling woman that she had not even known the Starling's true name when she went to search for him. Fantine had told her. Madame Carême had reminded her of the boy's remarks about the Café Rigolo and his prostitute mother. Cosette hoped she possessed sufficient physical bravado to conceal from the Changer that Jean-Luc had said the Starling was a liar, a thief, and a coward, that someone brave would have tried to stop the arrest of Marius. Cosette hoped she could conceal that she had been speechless with shame, not merely that Jean-Luc had committed offenses against a set of rules deemed good behavior, but at some fundamental rip in the fabric of her son's character. She had wished more than ever she had Marius with her. Marius would know what to do with Jean-Luc. But her immediate task was to get Marius freed from the Conciergerie prison, where he had languished since last Saturday, when they'd closed the press and arrested him. Each time Cosette went to the prison, even from outside, the stench was overpowering.

The Countess frowned and spit out the invisible seed. "Do I know you, madame, eh? I look at you, I wonder if we've met."

"How could we have met?"

The Countess brooded.

"Please tell me if Gabriel's alive."

"I have friends. A friend in the prison, not there for getting his ass shot off in the rue Mouffetard for republican fun, *merci*, but for a good reason, a solid reason, an honest reason. Thievery. The Captain has sent word to me that Gabriel's there."

"Which prison?"

"The Conciergerie," grunted the Countess. "Why do you look so pleased, madame?"

"My husband, that's where they're holding my husband!"

"Do you think for one minute your husband and my grandson are sharing a jolly little cell with a view of the river and meals brought in from Tortoni's?"

In fact Marius shared his cramped and fetid quarters with eleven other editors and two dozen National Guard officers who had gone over to the rebels. The Starling lay on filthy straw with thousands of others in a deep vault under whose medieval arches nineteenth-century men pissed and wept and groaned and relieved their guts and anguish in the dark. And if, seven hundred years before, Saint-Louis once graced these stones dispensing alms, he'd left nothing behind, nothing to soothe or comfort, no alms for the certain oblivion awaiting the men of 1848.

Chapter 23

*W*hen Cosette arrived at Thiers's home, an opalescent summer dusk dripped down over the place Saint-Georges, reflected in the sparkling fountain in the middle of the square and the shining windows of fashionable homes all around it. Thiers's home had five high windows on each floor fronting the street, and a curling walkway led guests to the front door. Imposing without being palatial, the house met the place Saint-Georges with an air of satisfaction, the mood maintained by an iron railing, though whether its purpose was to keep the satisfaction in or the trespassers out wasn't entirely clear. At least that's what Cosette thought as she approached, uninvited, exhausted, the hem of her lavender-gray dress dim with dust, her hair coming undone under her bonnet, and perspiration beading along her bodice, a layer of city grit over all. These were not the clothes in which one ordinarily went to visit a former minister of state, but then this was not an ordinary visit, and she cared less for manicured effects than for results.

This was perhaps a mistake on her part. She sensed as much the minute the servant regarded her with obvious dismay, and probably he would not have let her in had she not brandished her calling card, *Baroness Pontmercy.* Perhaps she ought to have groomed herself for coquetry, she thought, as from the drawing room voices lilted into the hall, different accents, different languages even. However, the card seemed to have the same effect on Thiers's servant as it had on the Countess Crasseux some hours before. In those intervening hours Cosette had, with great difficulty and a good deal of money, extracted from the keepers of the Conciergerie prison information that, indeed, one Gabriel Lascaux was there imprisoned, and no, she could not speak to him; neither could she speak to her husband. No one could speak to Citizen

Pontmercy, who, they reminded her tartly, had been jailed at the express orders of General Cavaignac, and the general remained in absolute power, even though the rebels were completely defeated. Cosette had left and gone directly to Thiers.

Who better? Thiers was one of those who had brought the king to power in 1830—and who had seen him out in 1848; Thiers had ushered in the Second Republic in February and applauded the state of siege in June. He'd aggravated everyone in the government, in the press, in the diplomatic corps, in business and politics for twenty years, but in or out of office, he had deep pockets of power. If, as Marius had teased her, Thiers was half in love with her, so much the better, thought Cosette in his front hall. Jean Valjean had gone through the sewers to save Marius; what did Cosette care if she had to beg Adolphe Thiers?

The servant returned, followed by Thiers's mother-in-law, the enormous Madame Dosne, dressed for an evening party. She regarded Cosette as if she'd just crawled off the rue Mouffetard and stated emphatically, "All business must go through Monsieur Thiers's secretary, and for an appointment—"

"This will not wait, madame. Lives are at stake."

"Then, tomorr—"

"I will not leave till I have spoken with Monsieur Thiers."

"About?"

"I shall only talk with him."

Madame Dosne pulled her pince-nez up, peered down at Cosette, who stood at a cadet's unflagging attention. Trailing a servant behind her, Madame Dosne disappeared into the drawing room.

When the servant returned, he led Cosette to Thiers's study, a long room set about with innumerable bric-a-brac and huge paintings in heavy gilt frames and low shelves filled with endless uniform volumes all bound in chocolate-brown leather. High windows faced west, and thick slabs of summer dusk fell across the intricately worked carpet. She walked to the fireplace at the end of the room, dismayed to see her untidy, dirt-streaked reflection in the mirror over the mantel. She lifted up her skirts and, raising her petticoat, rubbed the dirt from her face, or at least rubbed it around her face. Taking off her bonnet, she began hastily repiling her hair, and it was in this attitude, her hair caught in her hands, a gesture at once intimate and self-indulgent, that Thiers found her when at last he bustled in. He smiled. Cosette hurriedly, ineffectively, put hairpins in while he invited her to have some wine.

"I did not come for wine."

"I must say you look unusually distraught and not at all your impeccable self."

"I am here on a mission of mercy."

"It sounds expensive."

"My husband—"

"Of course. All Paris knows. How delicious that Emile de Girardin is locked up with eleven others, editors of newspapers with less than four thousand readers."

"It's absolutely illegal what they did to my husband, unconstitutional, against the laws of the Republic—"

"The Republic is rather too young to have a constitution. We won't until the autumn."

"Against the principles of the Republic," Cosette maintained.

"The principles had to be suspended, owing to a military emergency, madame, now mercifully behind us, as our gallant forces have won the day." He laid some stress on the word *our*.

"They were not gallant. And they were certainly not mine, Monsieur Thiers. They slaughtered their own countrymen."

He continued in his schoolmarmish fashion, "Surely you are astute enough to realize that if this Republic succeeds at all, it will not be because of the efforts of men like your husband, men who have worked for it. It will be because of the acquiescence, the acceptance, of men who have opposed it."

"Like you?"

"Absolutely like me. Men who believe in power and order and profit and property."

The thought of one of his paeans to property and order was unendurable. She came straight to the point. "I need—I must have—your help in securing my husband's release, Monsieur Thiers."

"Your husband will be released when Cavaignac decides to release him."

"Surely Cavaignac can be persuaded," she implored.

"Why come to me?"

"You can do anything."

A smile curved Thiers's prim little mouth, and he gestured to a chair for her. He pointed to his *History of the French Revolution,* volumes and volumes of it. "Have you read it?"

"I'm sorry to say I haven't, but my husband has. I'm well aware of your reputation as a historian, Monsieur Thiers. Everyone is. They say you have no equal on paper." She felt some sticky-sweet wafer dissolving on her tongue, and she tried to swallow it quickly.

"Have you talked to Cavaignac, or his staff, madame?"

"I can't get near them. I can't imagine they'd be very sympathetic, since Cavaignac ordered the arrest."

"Do you imagine that I am sympathetic?"

"You are a man of some principle, Monsieur Thiers," she said sweetly. "The same cannot be said of the general."

"He threatened to have me shot. Did you know that? The rebels were taking over the whole city, they held the place de la Bastille, they were about to attack the Hôtel de Ville, and I told him, Withdraw your troops from the city, coalesce outside, at Versailles, say, and move in from there, crush them from the outside so they have no place to go. It was perfectly good advice. I gave it to the king in February—and you see how he suffered from not following my suggestion. Cavaignac declared if I said anything more he would have me shot. Can you believe his pique?"

"In any event, the government prevailed," she said dryly.

"Yes, but many of the rebels escaped through the *barrières.* If the troops had entered the city from the *barrières,* the rebels would have been trapped."

In fact Verdier and Thérèse had escaped through the *barrière* Saint-Denis; word had reached her just that morning through a chimney sweep crying through the rue des Filles-du-Calvaire; he had come to the back, offered to clean their chimneys, and given word that Moses was safe, Thérèse too.

"There is another matter," she went on hastily, "another prisoner. A boy. The courier for *La Lumière,* a boy known as the Starling. He's a prisoner in Conciergerie as well."

"Sharing a cell with Emile de Girardin?"

"No."

"A pity." Thiers gave his grimacing little smile. "With a name like the Starling, I take it he's unwashed, unlettered, underfed, and ill-mannered."

"He can read."

"It's unbecoming that a lady of your stature should beg for the life of a guttersnipe."

"I'm not begging for his life. His life has been spared. I'm begging for his freedom. He's just a boy. He'll be tried as one of the mob and transported."

"He is one of the mob," Thiers observed.

"But he's so young, surely—"

"These people," Thiers bristled with assurance, his mouth pinched into a seam, "constantly running around declaring revolution. It's civil war that they get. Victory always goes to those who have order, power, and property on their side. Why is it that every generation feels they must tear up the streets of Paris and pretend *liberté, égalité,* and *fraternité* might yet be possible? Revolution!" he sputtered. "How much *liberté* and *fraternité* did you people find during the Terror, madame? Everyone was equal before the guillotine. How much *liberté* under Bonaparte? The *liberté* to die in Russia! The *fraternité* of the dead. You and your husband are misguided. Why should there be universal suffrage for every ragtail drunken man slumped over a gutter? Why shouldn't Property have rights? Why shouldn't Order prevail over liberty? No, madame. You will find the June Days to be very costly indeed. People of sense are appalled. Reaction is inevitable. But—" he took a breath—"in the matter of this boy, I advise you to let the law take its course."

Was that not exactly what the baker in the rue Mouffetard had said? *Let the law take its course.* And if she had, would the Starling be imprisoned now? Would he be in La Petite Roquette with the juvenile offenders instead of packed into the Conciergerie with six thousand rebels? Was the Countess right? Had Cosette ruined his life? She had certainly intervened to alter it. To rescue Le Sansonnet from the baker in 1848 seemed the chance to reach back in time and rescue Jean Valjean in 1796, to repay Jean Valjean's intervention in her own life, rescuing her from the Thénardiers. Yes, she had intervened in the Starling's life, and perhaps the change she'd wrought was irremediable, but Cosette's faith in the notion of rescue remained. "I'm begging you, Monsieur Thiers, to intervene on behalf of this boy's life, to intervene on behalf of my husband's release. I implore you to rescue them from prison. I know my husband. I know what prison will do to his health and his spirits."

"It might sober him, madame. Perhaps a dose of prison without the comforts of Sainte-Pélagie will make Monsieur Pontmercy think better of property and order. Just because he flung himself against the barricades when he was a young man—"

"Why should he let go of his youthful dreams? Have you?" In truth she could not imagine what youthful dreams Adolphe Thiers might have, but anyone with his colossal vanity would require dreams to feed it. "My husband should not be sacrificed to the whim of Cavaignac."

"It was not a whim. Your husband sided with the rebels. I'd have done the same in Cavaignac's place. *La Lumière* is a very influential paper."

"The rebels have been defeated. My husband is languishing in prison. Is the Second Republic the better for it? And the life of a boy, the freedom of a boy—how will the Second Republic be better for sending him to Algeria?"

"Ordinarily I'd say he won't make trouble next time. But I don't think there will be a next time. As I say, madame, reaction will set in. The rebels will be the worse for their insurrection. They've lost and they've badly frightened the rest of France."

"I care nothing for politics. I care for my husband and this boy."

"I admire your spirit, madame, your gallantry, if that's not too strong a word to apply to a woman. It must be a terrible affliction to be a woman with spirit and wit and brains and no avenue for ambition," he mused. "I can't imagine anything worse."

"I beg of you, Monsieur Thiers, use your influence, please, see this boy released—my husband—his health—prison will shatter Marius. He's fragile in some ways."

"In ways that you are not?" Thiers drummed his fingers on the mantel, waiting for a reply that was not forthcoming. He adjusted the bric-a-brac there and turned, resting his eyes not on Cosette but on the globe dominating his desk. "If I fail, you will hate me."

"I won't hate you."

"If I succeed, you will owe me."

"Owe you what?" she asked with an inward gulp. She tried to picture Thiers naked, but kept seeing Beaujard's caricatures of him as a big-headed unclothed baby.

"*La Lumière* will owe me. Perhaps I shall need to collect on this debt when this floundering Republic finally gets around to electing a president for France. Oh, not this time, not this fall. In December we'll elect some fig leaf from the past, if you'll forgive the expression. Lamartine thinks he can win, which shows you the extent of his self-delusion. There's been the odd talk of Bonaparte, Louis-Napoléon. Imagine—electing a man who still, by law, cannot set foot in France. He's in England now awaiting the repeal of that law. That silly fool." Thiers's laughter came out in tight little pellets. "Oh, it's really too amusing. No, my guess is it will be Cavaignac. People are slavishly grateful to him for quelling the rebellion. But whoever it is, the constitution will forbid him to succeed himself. That much has been decided. We need only just endure Cavaignac for four years. A figurehead for now. In the next election, in four years, 1852, that we shall need a real president for France—and then *La Lumière* will owe me."

In her musing about Adolphe Thiers's youthful dreams, Cosette would never have guessed that he fancied himself president of the Republic. Thiers? The man whose distrust of the people was legendary? That he should be president was unthinkable. There was something truly repulsive about this tadpole of a man with overwhelming ambitions, but with the ability nonetheless to make himself indispensable to any regime. Absolutely indispensable. Why else was she here? She replied with something flattering and reassuring, adding, "You have your own paper, the *Constitutionnel.*"

"Yes, but if I do this for you, I won't have to buy the good opinion of *La Lumière* in the future. Four years from now."

"Is the Parisian press so routinely bought, Monsieur Thiers?"

"All of them except *La Lumière*. Didn't you know? Your husband thinks he can fill his coffers with subscriptions and advertising." At this Thiers again laughed his nasal laugh. "Has Monsieur Pontmercy never suggested to you that *La Lumière* might fatten itself at the usual troughs? Selling influence? Peddling loyalty? What is the name of this boy?"

"Gabriel Lascaux. He's about thirteen or fourteen. My husband has never suggested any such thing."

"They say *La Lumière* is running out of money."

"That's not true."

"A silly rumor then." He wrote the boy's name on a scrap of paper and tucked it into his waistcoat pocket.

"The buying and selling of opinion," Cosette inquired, "of the press, is it always that simple and corrupt?"

"It is never simple." A servant knocked on the study door and beckoned him. "But it is always corrupt. You'll excuse me now, madame, I have guests."

Four days later two men in butternut-colored smocks had the effrontery to knock at the front door of the Pontmercy home. It was odd that the Countess should have sent men who had forsworn language to deliver a message, but she did. The servant refused to admit them and they refused to leave; they clicked and clucked and whistled and made such a racket that at last the servant went for Madame Pontmercy, who, when told two gibbering idiots were at the front, lifted her skirts and ran to the door. "You have word?"

They did not have word. They had a picture, a swiftly sketched starling in flight, soaring over the twin towers of Notre-Dame. Cosette clutched the picture to her and laughed out loud, and the Jondrettes made equally jubilant noises as they took their leave. At that moment a hired cab turned in to the carriage gate, its wheels crunching on the gravel, and Marius Pontmercy alighted. He had ten days' growth of beard and he had aged visibly, and Cosette, the Lark, flew into his arms.

Entr'acte

*I*n the Louvre there hangs a portrait by Pascal Beaujard called *Garden Study*, odd because it is neither a garden nor a study, but a portrait of a man of middle years sitting by a window. Below the window are collected a pen, an inkwell, creamy paper, a blotter, an unlit candle, and a pale, half-peeled lemon. The light from the uncurtained window is amber and green and takes up perhaps a third of the painting, but it does not touch the man, who is surrounded entirely in black. Black seems to seep from the background, absorb the man's frock coat, his hair and beard as well. His cuffs and cravat are matte white, but his skin tones stand out with luminous clarity against the black. His hands, though they hold no object, look as though they ought to. They're poised, but tense, the more emphatic for their being empty.

It is a mature face, a thoughtful face, pale; a scar stitches visibly through the right eyebrow, the nose is straight, but the mouth is hidden by the beard. (Beaujard took artistic license with the gray in Marius's hair; it would have interfered with the unremitting black.) But the man's gaze is what has always held and troubled viewers— from the painting's earliest detractors, one of whom scoffed in print at its "impossible realism, suggesting we should believe in it while it conforms to nothing else we believe in," to students who yet today stand in the Louvre and wonder how Beaujard could have portrayed those eyes, fixed on some faraway point, something dreamy and distant, and yet have made the man's gaze so penetrating. Contrastingly invitational is the window beside him. If you could have dissolved yourself in the amber-green light of that window, which is large and deep-set, you would have stepped out into the garden of the ramshackle farmhouse Cosette rented that summer of 1848 near Boulogne, its shutters all open, worn steps leading in, floors sanded by time and the wooden shoes of two hundred years. Monsieur Gérard had secured it for Cosette when she wrote him saying that Marius's health and spirits had been severely impaired, though she did not say how, or why.

This old farmhouse had room for all of them, including Madame Carême, a few servants, guests, and the imagination as well. Cosette tried to fill it with laughter and diversion to heal Marius's spirit. Coligny came briefly, paced by the pond, smoked, reciting lines from the play he was eternally writing. (Theatre critics are always writing plays.) Beaujard came, set up a studio of sorts in a dilapidated greenhouse and garden shed, where the glass was so thick and old it whorled the light. For Marius there was a desk, but Cosette moved it from the back room to the window painted in *Garden Study*. Marius claimed that here the desk was no good for writing, since the window served (as it does in the painting) as an avenue to imagined possibility, in short, day-dreaming. (This is why Cosette had moved the desk.) But it was here, perhaps daydreaming, that Marius began to toy with the idea of writing his classic *Recollections of 1848*. The actual writing he did later and under sadder circumstances, but the notion came to him here, at the desk that figures in Beaujard's painting. It seemed to Marius, then, in the summer of 1848, that if history were always written by the victors perhaps the voice of the vanquished should also be heard. The book was not published till 1901.

As Marius sat at the desk, ruminating on these questions, looking through that window he might have seen black-clad Aunt Adelaide, sewing on a bench set on flagstones and surrounded by crazy lilies and renegade poppies amongst the weeds. He might have seen birds quarreling in splintery arbors and wisteria groping the roof. Beyond the garden there was a sunny orchard of apple trees, ancient, wormy, and gnarled, good only for cider, and here in the afternoons he might well have found Fantine, reading beneath the trees or playing at dragon fighting up in the branches. Not far from the orchard was the pond, the water murky, mucky, and here, Jean-Luc threw stones into a rowboat till he sank it at last, and then there was nothing to amuse him.

Cosette might be found in any of these places, or in Beaujard's studio, where she patiently submitted to a portrait. Here too Beaujard used the black background; light from some unseen source illuminated her face. The eyes are clearly the center of the picture, their gaze direct, and the mouth curved, though not coy, but not pensive either. The whole bespeaks vitality, modernity. "Appalling modernity," said an early critic, one of many who heaped ridicule upon *Portrait of Madame P.* "Here is a modern woman, her hair simply pulled back, a narrow black ribbon at her throat, an open summer dress, simply in the act of being?" The eyes in *Portrait of Madame P.* (Metropolitan Museum of Art) still arrest audiences, and she still looks modern.

The Boulogne farmhouse was close enough to the sea that frequently the lot of them packed up for all-day beach picnics, where sometimes the clouds piled high about the bottle-green sea and rock-stubbled beaches. Another of Beaujard's paintings, *The Walker* (Los Angeles County Museum of Art), shows a slender male figure in the distance, a figure seemingly taking its sustenance from the play of light and water, the bare feet of Jean-Luc emerging from the sand but his body caught in the fog. Another, *The Steamer* (private collection), shows Cosette holding Fantine's hand, wind whipping their skirts back, hats sheltering their faces, and a rippling strand of smoke from a distant steamer carving up the horizon.

The days Beaujard captured in these paintings proceeded at the usual mere-mortal pace, but to everyone who lived them they seemed elongated, even to Marius, who by mid-August—that fine, high moment that fulfills spring's promise and harbors its killer— had slowly begun to emerge from the dark cowl of June.

Cosette was rewarded. As she passed his window one August afternoon with a basket of windfall apples, he looked up and smiled. For no reason. Just a smile. The sort of instant-complicity smile they'd exchanged in the Luxembourg Gardens nearly twenty years before, when she, a young girl on the arm of her father, had unabashedly returned his gaze and Marius had fallen passionately in love, not truly with the girl in the Luxembourg Gardens, but with the woman here, framed by the window, dressed in white sprigged muslin lit with blue flowers, hatless, gloveless, her blue eyes expectant and hopeful, a basket in her arms. That night Marius and Cosette left the house, made love under the trees in the orchard, and Cosette thought her heart would break for the joy of it, the intensity, the satisfaction, the conviction that his health, his spirits, his old unquenched energy had all returned.

The pleasures of the summer of 1848 proliferated, compounded logarithmically, evident in one of Beaujard's best-known paintings, *The Conversation* (Musée d'Orsay, Paris). A rough table covered partially by a white cloth is set up beneath the gnarled branches of an apple tree in the orchard, and there—under its black limbs and black shadows, its glowing rubescent fruit—are the ends of a meal: the wine in a glass decanter, to show off its color, a half loaf of bread, remnants of poached trout careless on a bed of shallots, everything evoked as if ordinary life could actually be endowed with significance beyond its temporal content. In the picture an old woman in black (all his long life Beaujard remained fond of black and all its nuances) sits at one end of the table, intent upon peeling an apple in her hand. Beside the woman is a girl with great dark eyes playing with spindles of peel. At the other end of the table, across a gulf of light, a woman whose face you cannot see has her arms draped over the shoulders of the same man from *Garden Study*. She is whispering something to him. The expression on his face is altogether different from that in *Garden Study*, and his hands, though empty, are no longer tensed over something he has lost, but poised to catch something he has yet quite to find.

Conversation of a less conventional sort took place that September at the Changer's warehouse, when a young woman, visibly pregnant, with stringy hair and a small child tugging at her skirt, knocked at one of the four doors in the dirty impasse and was greeted—as were all comers—by the snouts of the dogs and one of the Jondrettes. The child burst into tears, and the young woman picked it up but offered it no comfort, other than "Hush." To the Jondrettes she announced, "I've a message for the Changer. It's the Republic now, boys, and I don't have to call her the Countess or Your Holiness, even though I know she thinks she's the queen. No, I don't want a change either" (which is why Germaine could afford to be so flip). "My message isn't even for her. It's for the Starling. Is he here?"

The Jondrettes' eyes glazed over with ignorance.

"Is he here, or is he dead with the rest of them? If he's here, he's hiding out till the trials are over, yes? That's smart. At least he can breathe here," she added, swaggering in. The child tugged at her hair and she pushed its hands away. She balanced him oddly on one thin hip. He had been begotten on her by the master in the house where she had been a servant; his wife threw her out when she "turned up pregnant." That's how Germaine Fleury came to be selling bootlaces in the rue Mouffetard and living in a single room near the Bièvre River, the foulest place in all Paris, save perhaps for the Montfaucon boneyards. So Germaine had reason to appreciate the air in the Changer's warehouse, tobacco tainted though it might be.

Germaine had come to Paris from the provinces, from a family so poor they could hardly feed their own, a life Germaine found numbing. With a great show of spirit, she'd come to Paris at fifteen. The city had betrayed her hopes. The master betrayed her trust, but she could hardly go home with a brat and nothing else to show for her bravado. She loathed the confines of the needle trade, which employed most women. Not averse to thievery, she just wasn't very good at it. She confined her crimes to robbing the occasional drunk. Not very lucrative. She was afraid to take up informal prostitution, for fear of being caught in a Morals Brigade raid, a *razzia*. What would happen to the boy? When he was a baby she could scarcely abide him, but as he grew, she gradually forgot how he had come to be conceived, and she rather liked him. He was hers in any event, and she was fiercely possessive. Her friends assured her that to be licensed by the Morals Brigade and practice prostitution as a *fille publique* was not so very bad; at least you had a few laughs while you were starving and freezing and fucking anything with six francs. They advised Germaine to take it up while her looks still held. She was getting on.

In February, however, Germaine's prospects brightened. From the looting of the Tuileries she took the princess's brooch and assorted other bits of finery. (It was amazing how much of the Tuileries ended in the rue Mouffetard and places like it.) Along with the brooch that day, Germaine also took Pajol home with her. That glorious spring he left the rue de Combray every night, crossed the river, and came home to her. He slept in her bed. He brought his wages from *La Lumière*. He loved her. Germaine had had a child, assorted men for pay, a couple of lovers, but no one had ever loved her. Germaine and Pajol, to whom life had been so brutal, found a measure of love, of those joys that can imbue the grimmest life with hope and pleasure. By June, Germaine was pregnant, and Pajol forbade her to go with him to the barricade. She forbade him to go too, but he went just the same.

"My message is for the Starling," she said again, louder, as if the Jondrettes were deaf as well as mute. "Is he here?"

They shrugged and rolled their eyes in an orgy of ignorance.

"You can't write, can you?"

They shook their heads.

"Me, I can't write either." She put the toddler down and walked into the vast gloomy expanse of the warehouse, like a theatre with the audience all hanging upside down. She planted her feet apart, cupped her hands around her mouth, and called out, "Starling! It's me, Starling! Germaine Fleury! You remember me, don't you? The spavined slut?" She waited but no reply came; dust motes spiraled overhead, illuminated by chinks in the high shutters. "If you're alive I have a message for you! It's from the Deux Pierrots, Starling! The man from Deux Pierrots, he says he wants his red cap back. When you decide to fly again, Starling, fly down to the rue des Mar-mousets-Saint-Marcel and give him back his red cap!"

That same September of 1848, Zelma Thénardier was having several "conversations" of her own. Some were in French with her husband, Emile-Charles Touchard, a handsome, indolent man she'd acquired in New Orleans, who had polish and pretensions, but no backbone; the combination suited her. The conversation of the moment, however, in English, was with the sheriff of Helena, Arkansas. Under his direction, a few black men and women were moving all Zelma's furniture and other goods into the front yard of her home (the house was rented) and putting price tags on them, preparatory to this forced sale of her property to settle a debt long owed.

Zelma's path from New York City—twenty thousand francs awaiting them in the bank, wining, dining, and sleeping with Louis-Napoléon Bonaparte, to Helena, Arkansas, and the forced sale of her household goods—was a tortuous one. Along the way she had acquired and lost many things. She had lost her father, who had lost their money, and acquired the above-mentioned husband (in a manner of speaking), a slave, Polly, and two daughters, the eldest, Eponine, a dark-eyed, ill-tempered vixen, and the younger girl, Corinne, sulky and indolent like her father. (Touchard was not Eponine's father.) Zelma loathed America and the Americans, but she had lived amongst them, lived off of them, and learned a good deal from them in the last fifteen years and, as she tried to explain to the sheriff, it was an oversight, a tiny misunderstanding resulting in this unforeseen debt, and if the sheriff would just prevail upon the major to discuss it with her—

"Miz Touchard," (the sheriff pronounced it Touch-urd), "The major's give me orders if you was to come near his home again I'm to shoot you."

"Then you and the major are goddamned skunks, and every man in this town is nothing but a fungus-livered coward to watch a lady treated so!" (Language was one of the things Zelma had learned from the Americans.)

"Still, them's my orders." And the sheriff went back into the house.

Zelma felt like crying. She would have cried if she hadn't already tried it to no avail. In the merciless September sun she strolled through her household goods, stooping now and then to scratch a chigger bite on her leg. She sat down, one last time, at her beloved pump organ and worked the pedals to get its steam up and thumped out "Shall We Gather at the River," singing in heavily French-inflected English and with melancholy finality. The family was unwillingly packed up to go north, to Cincinnati, which meant she'd have to sell the slave. She'd heard people in Cincinnati were even more uncouth and in need of refinement than Helena, Arkansas. If that were possible. Where else was there? She couldn't make a living in New Orleans; in New Orleans people already had the graces, the language, the refinements Zelma traded in. It's true: Zelma Thénardier, daughter of a thug, thief, and forger, indeed a *fille* of the streets of Paris, "finished" young ladies in America. She had made a living out of her French accent, her exaggerated manners, her ardently expressed and self-taught music. At thirty-three Zelma was still a fine-looking woman, though life had told somewhat on her red hair, which had gone a dull, brickish color, and motherhood had done nothing positive for her bosom or her temperament.

She quit playing and looked up, incensed to see Polly helping to carry things out of the house. She marched over, slapped her, and snatched it from her arms. Zelma unwrapped newspaper from around a little china dog, late of her mantel, whose noble, sweet smile made her really want to cry. Instead she flung it, smashed the china dog against the side of the house. She wadded the newspaper and was about to fling that after the china dog when her glance caught something. It was a New Orleans paper and it said there had been another revolution in France in June, but the rebels, "mostly low class," had been put down, and the Republic was firmly in place. Zelma read on:

> *In December France will elect her first president. Vying for this honor are Mr. Lamartine, General Cavaignac, and Mr. Louis-Napoléon Bonaparte, nephew of the great Emperor. Mr. Bonaparte has only just returned to France from England. Though Mr. Bonaparte has spent most of his life outside of France (including several months on our fair shores), he carries with him a tide of good feelings among new voters, peasants, and workingmen. This is the first election these people can vote in. Many believe a strong hand is needed to keep the Republic on course. Who better to give a strong hand than the nephew of the man who terrorized all Europe? Our friends in Paris write that men admire Mr. Bonaparte, but no one knows him.*

"I know him," Zelma said to no one in particular, reading the article again. "I know him. I know him!" She whirled about, arms open, head back, "I know him! I know him!," spinning and shouting amongst all her household goods gathered there at the river in Helena, Arkansas.

Cosette and Marius did not know him, so they were astonished one night in October 1848 to have their servant bring his calling card into their home in the rue des Filles-du-Calvaire. They were drinking their after-dinner coffee and told the servant to show him up. Short, ill proportioned, and with ungainly but vaguely military bearing, Louis-Napoléon Bonaparte entered their lives and their drawing room.

He had cultivated manners, but he spoke French with an unappealing accent, German perhaps, and his fingertips were stained with tobacco, which Cosette regarded as impossibly vulgar. (Clerons was the one person she'd known who smoked that much.) Louis-Napoléon wore a plain republican frock coat, fresh linen, white cravat, smartly blacked shoes, but his glorious name, *Napoléon,* he wore that like a mantle, its evocations whispering round him almost audibly. With that name he carried his star, his sense of destiny. Nonetheless, he presented himself democratically, the soul of republican courtesy. He listened raptly while Fantine stumbled through something Mozartian on the piano. He treated Jean-Luc with the grave regard young men take for recognition of their gifts. He told Baron Pontmercy (naturally he recognized the title) he knew of Marius's father's bravery serving his uncle, especially on the battlefield of Waterloo. Indeed, the last time he'd seen his uncle, Napoléon, was just before he had left Paris to fight in June 1815. "I was only seven, but vowed then," Louis-Napoléon said, his simplicity contrasting with the weight of the words, "if my uncle should fall, I would carry on his work, his name, his mission, which was the glory of France. But I do not return to France now to become another Napoléon. I want to be France's George Washington. I want to serve the Republic, to see it triumph over its enemies."

"And who, in your opinion, are its enemies, Monsieur Bonaparte?" asked Marius.

"The ancient enemies of all mankind: poverty, disease, starvation, ignorance, and superstition. The latter two go hand in hand when the church has power over education. Free education from the church and you have freed men's minds. Free men's minds and you have freed France. Free France and you have liberated Europe. France must be delivered from the church, and the Republic must be delivered from the military. We do not need a General Cavaignac. We need a statesman."

"We need a man," said Marius crisply, "who will guarantee the freedoms of the press and assembly. We need someone who will guarantee men the right to work and the right not to be exploited for their labor. We need a Republic that will not exploit women's ruination because they're starving, or exploit the bodies, minds, and spirits of children, sir. That is what we need."

"That's why I've come to ask your help, Baron Pontmercy. *La Lumière* stands for all that. I have admired *La Lumière* for years.

I've read it since 1840 when I was imprisoned at Ham. I'm asking for your support. The election is in December, and Cavaignac, after all, has the gratitude of many."

"We despise Cavaignac," said Marius.

"As do I."

"As do the working people of Paris," interjected Cosette. "Lamartine betrayed them, and Cavaignac slaughtered them."

"I will vote for you!" chirped Jean-Luc. "I'll soon be old enough!"

Louis-Napoléon thanked Jean-Luc and sipped his coffee.

"There is a great groundswell of Bonapartism in your favor," acknowledged Marius, "amongst all sorts of people, people who wouldn't ordinarily agree. They love you for your name, but they don't know you."

"If you know me, Baron Pontmercy, I am satisfied. If you support me, others will come to support me. I offer much more to France. Have you read my pamphlet, 'On the Extinction of Pauperism?'"

Marius had and he'd been impressed.

"I wrote it during my 'university years,'" he gave a diffident smile, "the six years I was imprisoned in the fortress at Ham, a terrible medieval pile of stones. I am also a firm believer in prison reform." Louis-Napoléon had a sallow face, tapering at the chin, which accentuated his taciturnity. "I shall be the only president to know firsthand the prisons he seeks to reform."

As he spoke Cosette tried to align the manners and evident humanity of the man before them with the queer duck they'd seen fished from the buoy at Boulogne and marched ignominiously dripping into the Customs House, who had tied a vulture to his mainmast and invaded with an army of London waiters. Such a scene could only be declared a swaggering parody, not of military glory but of the empty notion of it. She tried too to reconcile his sincerity and ugliness with rumors she'd heard of his debauches and endless women. People said that he was penniless, save for money lavished on him by his wealthy English mistress, Miss Howard, who had come to France with him. He spoke with modesty, but his expression was veiled. And yet, she considered, might it not be as likely that his odd accent, his unappealing physical characteristics could be ascribed to years of exile and imprisonment? Except for prison, he had not lived in France since 1815. Perhaps these very contradictions finally made him very appealing, while his illustrious name only dazzled. Perhaps he was not the booby Thiers made him out to be.

Marius believed in him, that much was clear. *La Lumière* would support Louis-Napoléon in the coming election. Perhaps Marius had always believed in him, Cosette thought. Marius's veneration for his dead father had somehow fueled his imagination with respect, even a reverence, for the first Napoléon, as though the two dead soldiers were one.

And though he could not have known it, Louis-Napoléon's talk of prison reform touched Cosette's heart, reminded her of her father, Jean Valjean, his sainted life tainted always by the stink of prison. They're all mortared-and-pestled together, she thought— pleased to see Marius's expression reflect new hope and focus and purpose—the personal and the political, the public and the private, the causes that light our imagination, the dreams that fuel our days.

Part IV

The Rat in Satin
MAY 1851

*What were the Thénardiers? . . . They belonged to that
bastard class formed of low people who have risen and
intelligent people who have fallen. . . . They were of those
dwarfish natures which, if perchance heated by some sullen fire,
easily become monstrous.*

—VICTOR HUGO
Les Misérables

Chapter 24

Cosette added a last touch to the high cascade of her curls in the drawing-room mirror, and Marius came up behind her, laid his lips at the back of her neck. "At least if I must go to this damnable ball, I shall have the pleasure of escorting the most beautiful woman in Paris."

"Will it be worth it?"

He frowned, regarding the invitation on the mantel before them. The prince-president's invitation. The very notion was ridiculous, impossible, a contradiction, but Louis-Napoléon had insisted on the unconventional title immediately on having been elected. However vigorously *La Lumière* had endorsed his candidacy, they could not support a prince-president. "We haven't used our theatre box in months," Marius complained to his wife. "We always have to attend these awful official balls and dinners and receptions, and I don't understand why we're even invited. Surely I've offended everyone. I haven't played any favorites. *La Lumière* has attacked the president and the Assembly, the military and the clergy as much as we dare without getting three warnings and being closed down."

"My love, I'm sure you have offended everyone, but I have a beautiful new ball gown, and it's a fine spring night, and I won't hear anything that's not amusing or flattering. Preferably both." Cosette turned in his arms and brought her lips up to be kissed.

"Mama!" Fantine breezed in. *"Elegantissima!"* She drew the word out to show off her Italian, which was better than her English, which was better than her German. No longer coltish and awkward, at fifteen Fantine gave every evidence that as a woman she would have her mother's radiant high spirits and her father's intensity. "Oh, how I wish I could go to the prince-president's ball."

"Don't call him that," Marius scolded her. "The very phrase annoys me beyond description." He was, though, more gentle with Fantine than with anyone else. He adored his daughter and had always been her willing slave. When she was little, he had sat through endless doll parties. This spring her new fancy was carriage rides about Paris, with stops at Tortoni's to show off her new clothes, indeed, her new figure, and her papa was happy to oblige her. His relationship with Jean-Luc was more complicated, but with Fantine, simple adoration sufficed.

"I'd like to go to any sort of ball." Fantine dipped and glided about in the manner prescribed by her dancing master. "Everyone is doing something exciting but me. Even the Starling is going to a ball."

"What sort of ball would he go to?" Cosette asked.

"When he came to deliver those proofs, he said he was escorting a great lady to a ball. I told him he couldn't borrow the Balzac novel if he didn't tell me who, and still it took twenty minutes before he admitted that the lady was his grandmother, and it was a ragpickers' ball. Wouldn't it be too funny? Going to the dressmaker's and saying, I want the perfect gown—lace from the gutters of the rue de Richelieu and I won't touch a morsel of ribbon not plucked from garbage heaps around the Palais Royal."

Marius took up his top hat and offered his arm to Cosette. "Soon, Fantine, you'll be going out dancing every night, costing me a fortune in dancing slippers. Young men will line up for the mere pleasure of your smile."

Cosette kissed her daughter's cheek, picked up her coat of green silk; it matched the mint color of the dress, with its tiered skirt and acres of lace wreathing her shoulders; the long rope of pearls from her wedding rested on her collarbones, and a pair of emerald earrings gleamed beside her face.

Fantine waved to them from the drawing-room window as the coachman opened the door and helped them into the carriage, a new carriage and a new coachman (the inebriate Abel having disappeared altogether three years before). Then she turned and started upstairs, noting the time on the somber hall clock. Sitting on a stair, obscured in the half shadow of candles in a wall sconce, she waited. Eighteen minutes later she heard her brother bid Aunt

Adelaide an unctuous good night and come down the stairs. She jumped up and frightened him.

"You're so predictable, Jean-Luc," she said, laughing. "Mama and Papa go out, and—twenty minutes! You're ready for the boulevards."

He refused to reply, immensely pleased, however, to be recognized as a man of the boulevards. At almost seventeen, he, Arsène Huvet, and their set cultivated an air at once spirited and world-weary. Jean-Luc was taller than his father, but whereas Marius carried himself with something of the old military bearing, the son affected a lounging walk.

Fantine followed him downstairs. "Three francs for my silence."

"Thief. It takes all my allowance to buy you off. You know what Papa would think if he knew your silence could be bought?"

"He wouldn't believe it. But he would believe it if I said that you and Arsène Huvet—"

"That's enough." He fished the money from his pocket.

"Besides, you don't need the money. Arsène's father is rolling in it. Didn't you tell me his father's just bought some sugar beet farm and factory? Sounds dreadfully boring, sugar beets, but at least it lets Arsène bathe in gilded lilies."

"Never you mind what Huvet bathes in."

She ran down the stairs before him, her head held in an arch and actressy fashion. "Does she act like that? The beautiful palm-frond waver at the Théâtre-Française? Are you going to swoon at her feet? I intend to have men swooning at my feet. One day very soon."

"Nobody would swoon for you." Jean-Luc pulled on his gloves.

"To get back into the house must cost you something," she observed. "The servants' silence probably comes more dearly than mine."

"One expects to buy the servants' silence. One does not expect to buy a lady's."

"When I am a great lady, I shall have my silence bought routinely." But her brother did not stay to hear the rest of her grown-up plans and left her there to sulk, cursing the fate that had made her a girl, while boys like Jean-Luc got to stroll the boulevards, and boys like the Starling got to run the streets.

*　　*　　*

The chandelier had not yet dimmed and the orchestra was playing some lively *divertissement* when Arsène and Jean-Luc opened the door to the Pontmercy box at the Théâtre-Française, which was draped in red velvet, the gilded uncomfortable chairs sociably arranged—and with people already in them, to Jean-Luc's considerable surprise. Introductions were hastily made: Cousin Théo of his latest conquest, Madame Something, and Beaujard of his newest model. Jean-Luc introduced Arsène Huvet. Then they all stared at one another uncomfortably. Jean-Luc knew the silence of Beaujard and Cousin Théo could not be bought for three francs, but he needed their complicity in his duplicity—knowing, as they all did, that no one loathed a lie like Marius. "I'm here because I'm in love," he announced. As he expected, this aroused the adults' interest, even their sympathy. "It's true, there's a girl in this theatre I'm going to marry."

The orchestra *vivaced* on and the adults looked out over the opulent house, expecting Jean-Luc to point out one of the brilliant young women below or across from them.

"You can't see her. She hasn't come on."

Beaujard inquired, "She's an actress?"

"She's a goddess."

The music softened, the curtain rose, the play ensued, the actors casting the orchestra leader visibly ugly looks when he forgot himself and ebullient music rose over their voices. The orchestra leader seemed careful only of the star's lines. Mademoiselle Rachel came on stage and wreaked her tragic magic on the audience. Jean-Luc was not as enchanted as the rest of them, his attention only truly arrested in the middle of the second act when a quartet of young women came out in togas waving palm fronds to cool the tragedienne's brow. Jean-Luc leaned forward between Cousin Théo and Beaujard and whispered, "There she is. Second from left."

Unfashionably tall when taste called for dainty women, she had thick blond hair escaping from its classical moorings and beautiful gray eyes. Slender, stately, sumptuous, though not, perhaps, a goddess, she had no lines. "Me," murmured Jean-Luc, "look at me." Last week she had; he was certain. This time, however, her gaze seemed oddly to rest on the music director, a man of unsurpassed angularity. Tall, with a huge beaked nose, he tilted his head back as though the music were printed on the ceiling or he had to keep his pince-nez from falling. "She can't be interested in him," Jean-Luc muttered. "He's ugly as a gargoyle."

Leaning back, Beaujard whispered, "That girl? The blonde with the way about her? Nicolette Lauriot?"

Jean-Luc's voice plunged into his stomach, his whole chest seemed to fill with rose petals, and a flurry of violins in the orchestra obscured the pounding of his heart. "You know her?" Beaujard's reply was lost in the thud of drums, but it seemed he'd said yes. He knew her. She modeled for him. A lineless actress has to support herself somehow. She modeled for Beaujard twice a week. Tuesdays and Thursdays at four.

"Clothed or—" Jean-Luc cleared his throat—"not?"

The girl's long white arms extended the palm frond; she stepped an inch too far forward, so the divine Rachel also took an extra step, flung her arm out so as to cast a shadow across Nicolette's face, but in that moment Jean-Luc was certain her gray eyes rose to his box, that she singled him out to share that single ravishing moment that might last forever.

"Come see for yourself," added Beaujard. "I'll expect you."

Chapter 25

S ome distance from the Théâtre-Française the Starling was about to be entertained with very different music: squealing fiddles, pealing one-key flutes, coronet, bugle, and barrel organ, the musicians flap-shoed and thick-bearded, culled from the ranks of the ragpickers and performing at a *barrière* bistro called the Three-Colored Pot. A wooden sign to that effect hung over the door, the three colors entirely effaced by rain and time. The food was bad, the wine was bad, the brandy bad, and the air all too close to the boneyards of Montfaucon. (There were those who said the food was too close to the Montfaucon boneyards.) But the pot room was quickly filling with the fraternity of the staff and basket, and for the occasion one of them had chalked up on the pot room door ASSEMBLY OF THE TRUE PROLÉTAIRES. Since nearly everyone here was illiterate, this had to be read out and repeated at length. The landlord had to be assured it had no political content whatever; he had no wish to antagonize the authorities, and perhaps even ragpickers had their *mouchards*. The rights of political assembly had been revoked, and one had to be careful. Indeed, the free press and universal male suffrage had been revoked as well; in three years, the Revolution of 1848 had become merely revolution, one more turn of history's ungreased wheels, nothing more. Assured that a *prolétaire* was only a man who had no property and no civil rights, the landlord calmed. That he understood. He personally greeted all guests, demanding a deposit against the disappearance of the spoons. (The cups were chained to the tables.) He even insisted on a deposit from the Countess Crasseux and her party.

The Jondrettes made outraged noises. Dressed for the ragpickers' ball, they were in threadbare military garb of Napoleonic vintage. The Countess, in keeping with her station, her sheer physical opulence, wore a gown she had adapted from the resplendent robes of a bishop of the *ancien régime*. By contrast, the Starling looked fairly plain in a white ruffled shirt, fine black cravat, silk-embroidered waistcoat, coat and trousers his grandmother rented to people in banking swindles. As he'd grown up, and he was now nearly seventeen, his broken nose had come to have a sort of winsome symmetry with his impudent smile. His dark hair was thin, smooth, and well combed, and he was clean-shaven, though no beauty. Still, he had a sort of errant charm that brought him friends on both sides of the Seine, and his experience in 1848 had left no permanent scars on him, save for a long, invisible streak of radical fervor.

The Starling paid the deposit on their spoons, and with the great lady on his arm, they made their entrance into the Three-Colored Pot, thronged with ragpickers in plumed finery; even those with the most miserable clothing had tucked flowers here and there for festivity. Daisies sprouted in unlikely beards and bosoms. Most faces were washed. The first to greet them with a deep bow was none other than the Captain.

"No thieves here, Captain. Ragpickers only."

"Ah, Dahlia dear, what's a thief but a ragpicker of the night?"

"We're honest."

"I'm honest, Dahlia! I've left crime behind me forever. Now I've an honorable profession." He scraped his three days' growth; he seemed to maintain his beard at three days' growth. "The Ark and I are honest as you now, maybe more honest. We're ragpickers new to the profession, but not to the streets. And here's the young Starling, taller than you, Dahlia, and the image of his late father."

"His late father," the Countess corrected him imperiously, "was not the sort of man we want to see recreated. He was a scamp and a liar."

"You've fallen for the occasional scamp, as I recall."

To the Starling's surprise, a blush crept up the old woman's puffy cheek, but the Captain was snatched away by the Ark with a proprietary air.

The music picked up and the pot room filled with noise and smoke and laughter, gossip and argument as the landlord's shrewish wife made the rounds collecting for dinner in advance. A rumor floated in the smoke that the government had yet another plan for refuse to be collected by city dust carts. "They're snatching our rights," cried a delegate from the rue Saint-Antoine, her cap askew.

"They snatched those a long time ago. They give us all the vote, ragpickers too, and two years later snatch it back!" snarled a tattered crone. "Property!" She spat out the word. "They want you to have property before they let you vote on which fat ass is sitting on your neck."

"No one sits on my neck," shouted a young man, scion of a family who had been ragpickers for generations, "no one's ass and no one's boot."

A man doubled over with years hobbled through the throng, muttering about 1832. "They tried it then, taking away our livelihoods and putting in those damnation dust carts."

"We had a great time burning them," remembered the Countess.

"So we did," he said nostalgically. "I can smell the burning ash now."

But it was the embers from a clay pipe having fallen on his coat. Controversy over the threatened dust carts, over the snatched right to vote, over the revoked rights of assembly made the ragpickers collect themselves (as the title on the door to the pot room suggested) into a mock Assembly. Fueled with spirits, they hilariously harangued one another with toadying speeches, fatuous toasts, and false promises, till the younger people began to flirt boldly, and gradually they pushed tables back to dance. The old folks collected along the walls to smoke and argue. The first to dance by the Starling and the Countess were the Captain and the Ark. The Captain winked at the Countess.

A black-toothed compatriot came up to them and the Countess greeted her warmly as Toutes-Nations. The Starling, no longer a boy of thirteen, did not ask how she had come by the name.

"And this wine, Countess, the piss of many horses, yes, for flavor?" Toutes-Nations picked up a nearby cup to see if it held anything.

"They put wine in for flavor. The rest is horse piss. How have you been?"

"The pox is carrying me off," Toutes-Nations sighed, waxing on briefly about her ailments, while her eye, cold as that of a trout laid out in the marketplace, looked the Starling up and down. "This is your handsome grandson, eh, Countess? Quite the heir apparent, isn't he? Runner for *La Lumière*?" Toutes-Nations reached out and drew through the gray ribbons of smoke a young lady, perhaps fifteen, with a sassy smile and knowing eyes. "This is my granddaughter, Marie-Josephine."

The Starling mumbled some sort of greeting while Marie-Josephine, who regarded him with a plainly assessive smile, quite liked what she saw. Toutes-Nations pushed the girl into his arms, and he obeyed, not the old lady, but the old laws inherent to pretty girls and music, and the two reeled energetically around the floor. Toutes-Nations, beside herself with black-toothed joy, didn't even take offense when the Countess inquired if Marie-Josephine had inherited the pox. "I swear on my daughter's grave," Toutes-Nations vowed, "it stopped with me."

At last, amidst the gabble and gamboling, the ragpickers were called to dinner, the tables moved back over the dance floor, and the Countess (as was her due) took her place at the head table with the other notables. The priest on the Starling's right, a flush-faced lower priest from the parish of Saint-Julien-le-Pauvre, blessed the gathering. On the Countess's left there rose the new president of the ragpicking fraternity, the prince-president as he liked to be addressed. (If it worked for Louis-Napoléon, why should it not work for him?) He said a few heartfelt words about the new fraternal association, not political in any sense (said loudly for the landlord), but so that the sick and the lame amongst them should have some succor from their friends and fellows, instead of dying like dogs in the streets they had served. The ragpickers must care for their own, protect one another, see that the old were cared for and the dead decently buried. There wasn't a dry eye in the house by the time dinner came, each guest served a steaming, stewish dish called *olla podrida*. Heavy on the onions.

The Countess leaned over and sniffed hers. "This is from the same horse as the wine."

Nonetheless, there followed a cacophony of slurping, sloshing, gulping, and lip smacking, clearly occupying everyone who didn't also have a hand on someone else's knee, which, judging from the yelps and squeals of pleasure and surprise, must have been a good many. The food couldn't have been a source of pleasure. Surprise, perhaps.

Across the room the Starling caught Marie-Josephine's smile. Her eyes were big with promise.

The Countess gave a low, coarse laugh, "Oh, you're in for a good time tonight, boy."

"Her grandmother has the pox."

"She swore on her daughter's grave it stopped with her."

"That's good news for whoever sleeps with Marie-Josephine."

"What? Don't you think she's pretty?" Before he could reply, a couple of ragpickers from the rue Saint-Denis approached the Countess, explaining that their son, a commercial swindler, had not returned the suit he'd rented because he'd been arrested in it, and as soon as he—and it—were out of jail, it would be back. "You've lost the forfeit money then," said the Countess. "Once something's been in prison, the vermin are of an entirely different class, and I can't possibly take it back."

"We could wash it."

"You should. But I can't take it back." The Countess turned her attention to the Starling. "What's the matter with Marie-Josephine? Look. She's pretty. She's eager."

"Nothing is the matter with her."

"What is the matter with you?"

"Nothing."

A man in mourning came up to thank the Countess for some kindness she'd shown his late wife, but she waved him away and returned to her grandson. "Then why not? Why not take advantage of what's given you?"

"I don't want Marie-Josephine. Given or not. She's not the one I want."

"Who is?" The Countess looked out over the broad and crowded Three-Colored Pot. The ragpicking profession, though generally a more mature one, had brought to the ball daughters and granddaughters: some, pale girls sewing for a living, some tarted up and well embarked on livelier careers, some already with brats of their own. "Which one?"

The Starling protested, but she rattled and nattered and insisted he tell her which one of these local beauties. Even if the woman was married, that was fine, in fact that might be best.

"I don't want any of these girls," he finally declared. "I'm not in love with these girls."

"Love?" She spat out her invisible seed and turned to the prince-president on her left. "The boy wants love. Can you believe it? Love?"

His red-rimmed eyes glistened tearily. It was the wine, but the prince-president looked out over the room as if some one person shimmered there, instead of a rowdy band of *olla podrida* eaters. "I used to believe in love."

"Old fool." Peeved, she turned back to Gabriel, who passed his *olla podrida* on to the priest. "Don't you be a fool, Gabriel. You don't have to be in love with Marie-Josephine. You don't have to be in love with any of them. Love is claptrap. You know the story of the Costly Omelette."

The Starling laughed out loud. "Does everything have to be tied to that story?"

"Love is just a costume over nasty old urges. Love is wax, sops, slops—"

"Have you ever been in love?"

"Never. You listen to me. You take this girl, this Marie-Josephine, you take her and have a good time together. Look at her. She's dying for you."

"She's not dying for me." He nonetheless acknowledged Marie-Josephine's little wave, while his grandmother extolled the virtues of Marie-Josephine over any of these belles. "I'm in love with someone else," he said finally. "If I can't have her, then—"

"Who?"

He paused, debated; he'd never admitted this to anyone and it seemed too coarse and profane to say it at the ragpickers' ball. He had carried his impossible love like a secret. But here, somehow, amongst this garish gathering, the clank of chains on cups, the rattle of the paid-for spoons, its impossibility overwhelmed him with sadness. He said her name like a tonic chord.

"Fantine?" It lost its musicality in the Countess's mouth; she chewed on it, coming as well on a shard of bone in the *olla podrida*.

"I knew a girl named Fantine. Who is she? Some *grisette* with a heart of gold and an old procuress for a mother?"

"Fantine Pontmercy."

The Countess's fine-planed face darkened, her jovial mood evaporated, and she shooed off a gaggle of well-wishers who had swooped down upon their table. "This can't be true. Oh, Gabriel, you have the pox of the heart! What Toutes-Nations has is nothing compared to what you have! Does the hound mate with the hare? Oh, they have got to you, haven't they? Nasty yipping little high-class dogs. I despise them. Felons in frock coats. That goat of a baron," she waxed on while the Starling played with his spoon, not meeting her eyes, not even looking up. "First they nearly get you killed—"

"No one got me killed. Madame Pontmercy got me out of the Conciergerie—"

"And into it! That woman! That woman—Pontmercy? That woman has a daughter named Fantine? Who names her daughter Fantine? It's not a name. Not a proper name." The Countess rubbed the creases in her brow as if ploughing thought furrows. She finished her wine in a gulp. "Forget Fantine Pontmercy. She is the baron's daughter."

"How can I forget her? I see her, sometimes every day. I'm always running back and forth between rue de Combray and the house, picking up pieces Madame Pontmercy has written or taking proofs for her to correct."

"Why doesn't she work in the rue de Combray if she's going to write for the paper?"

"She did. But—well, the men, Monsieur Pontmercy's Cousin Théo, Gallet, some of the others, they didn't like having a woman around the office. They don't like having a woman write for them at all, but—"

"And they're right! Madame Pontmercy should be doing what those rich, silly women do—those stupid, flatulent beauties. She should take lovers. Buy bonnets. Sit in front of the mirror while some foppish hairdresser curls her up and whispers nasty gossip. Her daughter should be in a convent."

"*Merci,* no." He gave her his lopsided grin. "Then I would never see Mademoiselle Pontmercy. I live for those moments when I see her, when she hands me a book."

"Do you know the disaster you're courting?"

"Heartbreak, maybe. She'll marry someone else. Not disaster. How can it be disaster? It's impossible. I love her and it's impossible. I know that. I've always known it, but when I see her, the sun comes up. All over again."

The Countess spat again, and she rolled her eyes to heaven. "Forgive me, God, for teaching this boy to read. If he couldn't read, *La Lumière* would have never hired him." She finished her conversation with the Almighty and turned to the Starling. "You stay away from this baron's daughter, this girl with the *grisette*'s name—"

"And the angel's face."

"She is no angel. She doesn't want you. Enjoy the girls who do."

As if she'd heard the conversation, Marie-Josephine rose with the music; the tables were pushed back again and she danced a dainty jig with a man old enough to be her grandfather, whose toothless smile suggested he too remembered love, and slowly the plumed and painted ragpickers crowded onto the floor, clapping, keeping no real time but their own.

Marie-Josephine's view of the Starling was blocked by a courtly ragpicker of mature years and a particularly ripe smell, who came to pay tribute to the Countess. "Tell me, Countess, what's the fashion in swindles these days?"

"The rage is all for foreigners," stated the Countess with papal authority, her pronouncement collecting an interested group around them, the knot of people thickening as the Countess explained how every swindler in France now presented himself at the prince-president's door, or desk, or stateroom, to remind Louis-Napoléon of a past act of kindness when he was in exile, a pretender to power, or a prisoner.

"Or a pauper," snorted a ragpicker from the rue de la Paix. "I saw him every day when he lived in the place Vendôme, and I tell you he didn't have a sou. He lived off his English mistress."

"It's true," the Countess declared, "they're truly a ragtag bunch, these people in power. No names—of course—but you wouldn't believe the numbers and sorts who come to me and want to be outfitted, got up like the Swiss, like Germans or Italians, English. Even Americans." This last caused a ripple of noisy disbelief till they were reminded that Louis-Napoléon had been exiled to America after his invasion of Strasbourg.

"Oh, that's why they call him Boustrapa—" cried the overripe ragpicker—"for his escapades in Boulogne, Strasbourg, and Paris."

"They call him Rantipole," said Toutes-Nations, chuckling, "half-fool, half madman."

"Rantipole suits him," contended the Countess. "Any day now I expect someone to come to me to rent Chinese robes to swindle him in."

"You can't do that." The sloshed priest from Saint-Julien-le-Pauvre raised his head off the table. "The Chinese are heathens."

"I can do anything," replied the Countess proudly, though with a quick glance at her grandson she added under her breath, "Almost. Landlord!" she shouted, to diminish the pain of her implied failure. "Another bottle here! And another for my friends as well."

As everyone knows, this last phrase is guaranteed to ignite an infusion of warmth and goodwill in all manner of men, and the ragpickers of Paris, who might have been excepted from everything else in society, were not excepted from this. Suddenly the Countess had as many friends as she had admirers, and when the plate passed to collect for the new fraternal organization, the Countess made a great show of donating twenty francs and became quite the heroine of the hour.

"Business is good," she said modestly to her well-wishers. "With Louis-Napoléon in office, business is very good. With Louis-Napoléon, the knaves and sharpers all have their day."

Chapter 26

"The Baron and Baroness Pontmercy!" Marius and Cosette moved into a vast gilded room, where ball gowns floated like bejeweled water lilies on a pond of money and influence: five hundred people, five thousand candles, an orchestra of fifty. A hundred servants bobbed amongst the guests, and the windows and balconies were open to the warm night. Light and music seemingly beaded in the heat, rolled down crystal glasses filled with cold champagne, with ices, lemonade, and punch. Waltzing in Marius's arms, Cosette whispered she didn't care how awful these people were, to have the pleasure of dancing with him was worth enduring every one of them.

However, when Louis-Napoléon asked her to dance, Cosette wondered if she hadn't overstated this. Louis-Napoléon liked to bestow his dancing presence on the wives of men he'd singled out for one reason or another; his whims were unfathomable and his tastes were catholic. Cosette continued to wonder how such an ugly man could have such a debauched reputation. He was awkward on the dance floor, with no feeling for music; moreover, the "Radetzky March" was an awkward piece, better suited for a review of the troops. Louis-Napoléon's breath grew short and he begged off. Punctiliously, Cosette inquired after his health, though she could hear his breath scraping up and down his lungs. He thanked Cosette in a courtly fashion, thanked Marius for the pleasure of allowing him to dance with his beautiful wife, and left them to have a smoke, trailing behind him a line of well-upholstered flatterers.

To Cosette these presidential gatherings always had the air of upscale market day, the guests—with varying stripes of subtlety— here to buy or sell or bleed one another, to root out a bargain, to peddle influence or information that could be turned to money, as in the old story in which straw could be turned to gold in knowing hands. There were men here whose hands were thick and dry from rustling insubstantial bonds and notes and credit, and men whose hands were thick and calloused from being immersed in solid goods, coal and sugar beets, wheat and iron. Their women were a gorgeous array of female possibility, from puff-breasted, pinch-lipped matrons to gaudy demimondaines, whose hands were slender and soft and skilled, women like Miss Howard, Louis-Napoléon's English mistress, whose oddly accented French mixed with that of numerous other foreigners. Assorted English, Americans, Romans, Neapolitans, Piedmontese, Spanish, Swiss, Mexicans, and a few Russians gathered under this gilded roof and painted ceiling, along with thick-set individuals from German principalities with equally thick-set names. There were impoverished young men with glittering Bonapartist titles, trading on their grandfathers' exploits of fifty years before. In short, a collection of knaves and sharpers, a few even outfitted by the Changer. She would not have been out of place here herself; after all, she had a worthless title, a military escort, and bishops' robes.

The clerics at the prince-president's ball were not priests from Saint-Julien-le-Pauvre with a fondness for the bottle, however, but splendidly robed prelates with satisfied faces, accepting congratulations all around, since the Assembly had recently put primary education for all French children back into the hands of the church. Compliments seemed to be passed with the champagne, the ices, and the lemonade for and amongst the military. The many uniformed chests here blazed with medals, men whose parade-ground strut betrayed them on the ballroom floor, whose foreign exploits were much touted, befitting a nation led by a Bonaparte. Deep in conversation with General Cavaignac was the former actor Châteaurenaud, who, after the glory days of '48, never went back to the theatre. Both of them greeted their old comrade-in-arms Lamartine coldly, coolly, dismissively. In three years Lamartine had been reduced to a relic, an artifact of the passions of 1848, spurned by the parvenus of 1851.

Not so, Cosette noted, Thiers. If anything, his prestige in the Assembly, as the manipulator of all things, had grown. He flitted over this gathering like a water spider with prestige to bestow, to prevaricate and pontificate in equal measure. Sipping her champagne, Cosette watched as he made short work of a group of vulgar *arrivistes* attempting to ensnare his attention and goodwill. Their attempt failed, the group returned to their own amusements as a big woman in a florid purple satin gown regaled them with terrible stories of the uncouth Americans, how they spat on the floor; she paused for a moment, as though debating if she should demonstrate. She had broad shoulders, reddish hair, a long nose, and when she smiled, big teeth. She looks like a rat in satin, thought Cosette; she looks like *Zelma*—the name rose up, not a question, but a statement of devastating clarity. Cosette held tight to Marius's arm as the ballroom spun around her, and Marius took her glass with a wordless inquiry, introducing her at the same moment to a Monsieur Haussmann, a civil servant who had been a student with Marius at the Lycée Henri IV. Perhaps Cosette responded with pleasantries. Perhaps she did not. She remained rooted, recognizing Zelma not merely across a ballroom but across a chasm of time, the battlefield of memory, the squealing chain, the abandoned gun carriage in front of The Sergeant of Waterloo Inn.

"Cosette?" Marius's voice brought her back. "Cosette?"

Zelma turned back to her rapt audience, went on to amuse them, and Cosette's blue eyes met Marius's. Protectively he pulled her arm through his, and she was surprised to find the overbearing Monsieur Haussmann gone, and in his place before her was the diminutive Monsieur Thiers.

Thiers mentioned how happy he was to see *La Lumière* still operating, since freedom of the press was a thing of the past. "Three warnings and it's off to prison with the editor. Why are you here, Monsieur Pontmercy?"

"Perhaps my title makes Monsieur Bonaparte sentimental."

"Nothing makes him sentimental, except for talk of his mother, that tart Hortense. You see comte de Morny over there, Louis-Napoléon's illegitimate half-brother? They are both worthless sons of a worthless mother, probably Louis-Napoléon no more legitimate than Morny. And probably they've fathered between them a tribe of bastard brats. But Morny at least understands power and money, and doesn't believe himself fated for empire. Next year we can get rid of Louis-Napoléon, that fool and booby, and elect a true president for France."

"I find it odd, Monsieur Thiers, that you so welcome an election, since it was you and your people in the Assembly who rescinded universal suffrage," Marius observed tartly.

"A necessary measure. You don't want France to look like America, do you?" Involuntarily Thiers shuddered and, with Cosette, glanced over to the redheaded woman in the purple satin dress with the big teeth and the broad shoulders.

"My point is," Marius went on, "if the Assembly is willing to change the constitution to rescind universal suffrage, then why shouldn't the constitution be changed so that Louis-Napoléon may succeed himself as president? That he may run again in 1852?"

"Do my ears deceive me? Is *La Lumière* now *supporting* the prince-president?"

"I loathe that term as much as you do, though for different reasons. *La Lumière* withdrew its support from Monsieur Bonaparte a long time ago, but we remain committed to the Republic."

"I'm glad to hear that. Then you'll be eager to support the man best suited to lead France, the man best able to protect property, instill order, and keep power in hands that can wield it."

Marius had gone rather pale. "Who might that be?"

"Why, me, of course."

"Monsieur Thiers, while I esteem you as a historian, I oppose you in every other way. I always have."

"Which is not to say you always will," Thiers replied, strolling off.

Their carriage rattled eastward along the rue Saint-Honoré, and moonlight fell in an oblong patch through the window as Cosette told Marius of her conversation with Thiers, what he had wanted in exchange for his help getting Marius and the Starling released from prison after the June Days.

"He wants to be the next president of the French Republic?" asked Marius, incredulous.

"I'm afraid he does. He sees Louis-Napoléon as a temporary, a fig leaf, I think was the word he used."

"Unfortunate choice of metaphor, considering Monsieur Bonaparte's reputation. But Thiers as president! Impossible!" Marius rumbled around the possibilities and then asked, "And did you promise? Did you say that *La Lumière* would support him?"

Cosette bit down on something that tasted of metallic anxiety. "I would have promised him the fish in the sea and the stars in the sky if he'd asked for them. But I didn't commit us. Either way."

"For the Starling's sake, you would have been right to. I got out of prison sooner than the rest of the editors, and even they were all released by mid-July. But the Starling . . ." He pulled her arm through his and shook his head. "We could hear them, the others, held, crammed in what amounted to a common pit. We could hear the cries, the shots."

"Shots?"

"Jailers shot men who begged for bread. People disappeared. Bodies lay where they fell. They arrested eleven thousand and sent six thousand to prisons or transported them. They would have gone very hard on a boy who was a known thief. The Starling took a man's part in the June Days. He should not have had to pay a man's price."

"Thiers was the only one with enough power to cut through martial law, but I should have told you earlier what he demanded. He said now he wouldn't have to pay for *La Lumière*'s goodwill. He called it the usual trough."

"And so it is."

"He said you were alone in not allowing yourself to be bought."

"Perhaps I should have been bought."

"How can you say that?"

"I have to say it. I have to tell you the truth. I haven't wanted to. I don't want to now, but I must." He listened to the horse clip-clop, and said finally, sadly, "I'm afraid *La Lumière* is going under."

"Going under what?"

"Do you remember when we were nearly drowned in that storm at sea in Boulogne, when the *Saint-Joseph* came to our rescue? How the weather changed drastically? We'd set off on a fine day, a fine sea, and found suddenly it had all turned against us?"

"Yes." She searched his face in the half-light.

"The same thing has happened to the times we live in. When all the Opposition papers and editors were working toward a Republic, there was a kind of, well, *fraternité* amongst the Opposition. Now they are the government and we are still the Opposition. People seem content without social justice. They seem content to roost on their power, to hunker over their property, to consolidate all that without regard to anyone else's welfare. From the time we supported the workers in the June Days, we've become more and more isolated."

"Oh, Marius, *La Lumière* can go on, even if they don't like what we say—"

"Our subscriptions are down by half, Cosette. And you know we never exactly rivaled *La Presse.*"

"But in influence!"

"We have readers. We have influence. We just don't have readers with influence. Or money."

"I have noticed," Cosette said with a sigh, "that the advertising on the back pages, well, there hasn't been as much of it. I couldn't bring myself to say it."

"There will be less. Less and less. I think next year, 1852," he mused on the date, said with a bitter finality, "*La Lumière* will go out."

"How long can you go on publishing?"

"Till spring. Perhaps summer."

"We don't need this carriage, the box at the theatre. Look, Marius, these pearls are a fortune and the emerald earrings—"

"All that might matter to us, personally, but it's not enough to float the newspaper. *La Lumière* is badly in debt. I have squandered your dowry, Cosette. For richer or poorer, I have squandered your father's hard work in a cause completely lost."

"You have squandered nothing."

"I'm sure Verdier can find work, Pajol, no doubt. Of the writers left to us, only my cousin is truly talentless. He will find a hard time of it. And as for the Starling—where will he go? What will happen to him when *La Lumière* closes? I can't bear the thought of him cast into the streets without a home, without money or skills."

"You have squandered nothing," she insisted, pressing his hand in both of hers.

"I worked my whole life for a free press—and saw it for four months, only February to June of 1848. I worked so that education should be free of the Church, and now the Church has more of a stranglehold than they did under the king. I championed the rights of workingmen and working women, and still, even after the revolution, even under the Republic, their backs and hands continue to be exploited, while people like those we saw tonight at the palace, knaves and frauds, most of them, they grow fat. I supported Louis-Napoléon because I thought he truly believed in the 'Extinction of Pauperism,'" Marius shook his head sadly, "and in social justice, but he wanted to be the prince-president. He said he wanted to be George Washington, but that was a lie. He wants to be Napoléon III. I'll go on fighting him as long as I can, fighting all of them, Thiers too, but I have lost everything I have ever believed in. Except for you."

"You have me and you have your family and you have your honor. You have not lost your convictions. Even if they have been betrayed, they are not lost, Marius. They are not even changed, my love. Perhaps we cannot call ourselves victors, but it doesn't change what we believe in."

"All the same, if we are to be swamped by the tide of events as we were in Boulogne, I wish the *Saint-Joseph* would appear. I guess the only difference is this time we see the storm coming."

Do we? Cosette wondered wordlessly. *Do we?*

Chapter 27

S he was not naked. She held the pose Beaujard required of her, held the blue hat, which became the painting's title, though the model was bare-headed in the harsh light of a high window, wearing a dress of cascading white. Beaujard introduced them, but demanded silence while he worked, so Jean-Luc could only look at Mademoiselle Nicolette Lauriot. At least the view of her here was not over footlights in a darkened theatre. Compared to that, this studio on an unfashionable street going toward the *barrière* Clichy seemed almost intimate, the very air scented, tender, and extravagant. Mademoiselle Lauriot, however, ignored him. She held the pose. When the afternoon light altered and the session was over, she asked Beaujard for her money, put on her bonnet, her gloves, and hurried off.

"Where does she go?"

"Don't begin with that question." Beaujard cleaned his brushes. "It's only fair to tell you you'll have a very rough time with women if you begin with that question."

"Have you had a rough time with women?"

"Very."

Jean-Luc, however, had already a fatal sense of his belonging to Nicolette Lauriot—and vice versa, that the right to know where she'd gone did not have to be earned or granted, but merely discovered. In that regard, he was very like his father; the same absolute conviction had drawn Marius to Cosette. Jean-Luc and Marius were men who loved once. Denied that love, everything else would be forever wanting, and for Marius—the romantic idealist—unthinkable. Jean-Luc was not a romantic idealist. Denied Nicolette, he would not have thrown himself on the barricades in an excess of gesture. He would have sulked and hungered in turn, resorted to subterfuge.

He'd certainly had practice in subterfuge; he continued to sneak out of the house, to use his parents' theatre box, even after he'd been caught (they left a reception early one night and came to the theatre). After this unpleasant incident he had been forbidden the theatre, theatrical girls, forbidden (again) the company of Arsène Huvet, punished with a particularly harsh course of study, which would serve the dual purpose of keeping him perpetually occupied and preparing him to attend the Faculty of Law, as Marius had. His parents and tutors supposed him to be studying while he sat in Beaujard's studio, staring at this tall young woman who regarded him with less interest than he gave his law studies. Nonetheless, every Tuesday and Thursday, with a kind of religious zeal, Jean-Luc came to the studio, the time bought with lies.

Jean-Luc would have lied to the pope for the pleasure of Nicolette's smile—which, finally, she gave to him one Tuesday, altering the pose slightly so she could see him from the corner of her eye. One Thursday she altered the angle of her head so she could regard him more directly. Beaujard must have been working on the white of her skirt, the black of the background, the blue of the hat, instead of her luminous gray eyes. He seemed not to notice. The following week she allowed Jean-Luc to escort her when she left the studio. As far as the rue Saint-Lazare. No farther. But the pleasure of that first touch of her gloved hand on his arm, of keeping step with her on an afternoon in early summer, remained etched in his memory forever. He was Parisian, born and bred, but he had never before noticed his city's enchantments, the splash of water in the public fountains, the narrow, dirty streets, the humid alleys, the dank impasses, high overhead windows, each its own little theatre as everyone watched and participated in everyone else's lives beneath Watteau skies.

He walked her to that corner every Tuesday and Thursday for two weeks and waited, watched her walk away, stood still, hoping she would remember him, hoping she would turn and wave. But she didn't. Then one day she asked how old he was and naturally he lied.

"You're not nineteen. I know you're not older than I am."

"I'm taller."

"Yes, that's nice. Not many men are."

"What difference does it make, my age? Nothing."

"I am a grown woman. I have a living to make. You're still a student living at home."

"I won't always be."

"But I shall always need to make my living. I've run away, you know. My family are dreadful provincials. Stuffy, boring, bourgeois, and ugly. Their lives, the same."

"No one related to you could be ugly. They must all be beautiful."

Nicolette rewarded him for this with an intimate smile. He was learning to distinguish amongst her smiles, to know the artful gestures from more natural ones. She had the knack of a born actress, moving to an inward, unfailing tempo, adjusting it to achieve effect. At eighteen, instinct stood in for practice, but she had long since learned to take off a bonnet so it seemed a wonderfully indecent act.

"My family tried to make me marry a doctor. They said it was a great match. What? A widower twice my age with three brats and a mother still living? They locked me up till I said yes."

"Brutes."

"The very day of the wedding, me, I ran away and came to Paris. To be a singer."

Jean-Luc had no wish to be equally brutish, to remark that she was not singing; she wasn't even speaking on stage; she was waving palm fronds. So he nodded.

"Would you like to take me to one of the boulevard cafés, Monsieur Pontmercy? I only go to cafés where it's worthwhile being seen."

The cafés where it was worthwhile being seen were all perilously close to the premises of *La Lumière,* but Jean-Luc took the risk and took the girl to Tortoni's. The looks Nicolette collected from other people there made the risks seem trivial. Over their ice creams, she told him that the Théâtre-Française musical director, Monsieur Offenbach, had heard her singing in the wings. "He said I had the perfect voice. Monsieur Offenbach is a composer, and when he has his own productions, I shall be the singer. He says he'll have no one else. Monsieur Offenbach thinks I can be more famous than Mademoiselle Rachel, who is a great cow. If only you knew. Everyone hates her."

"Monsieur Offenbach is that gargoyle of a—"

"Please," she touched his arm slightly, warningly, and withdrew her hand. "I will hear nothing against Monsieur Offenbach. His taste is exquisite and his music is wonderful, don't you think?"

"I never notice the music when you are on stage." Jean-Luc envied the ice cream on her spoon; he envied the spoon. "And in the meantime, till you sing for Monsieur Offenbach and are the toast of all Paris, do you model for painters for a living?"

Nicolette's gray eyes met his candidly. She licked the spoon and set it down. "I don't sleep with critics, if that's what you mean. I despise the girls who do, and I don't sleep with the men who organize theatrical claques, buy up rows of seats, and have their men hiss or applaud as they've been paid to. When I get applause and good notices, it will be because I'm really splendid."

Jean-Luc agreed she was really splendid, but he wanted to ask who she did sleep with and then kill the man.

"I have a protector, of course. I must, to live."

"Do you love him?"

"Don't be silly. Besides, I want more than a rich protector. I want an audience. I want to be applauded and adored. Do you understand?"

"Perfectly," he lied. "Is he rich, your protector?"

"Not rich enough, but he'll do for the moment. I call him Monsieur Needlemaker. He has a little factory that makes needles."

"If he were rich, would you love him?"

"Are you rich?" she asked bluntly.

"I will be. I'm sole heir to my old aunt. She has lots of money, and my father owns *La Lumière.*"

"The newspaper? That radical newspaper? I would never have believed it of you."

"That's good, because I think it's all rubbish. My father fought his whole life for the Republic, and look what it's got him. The Second Republic. I ask you," Jean-Luc snorted, "is that worth fighting for? He spent twenty years slinging ink and going to prison on principle for the freedom of the press. I'd call that a wasted life."

"You're very harsh with him."

"I know what I don't want." Boldly he picked up her hand, brought her fingers to his lips. "You know what you don't want."

She withdrew her hand, patted her lips with her napkin. "I must be going."

She let him accompany her all the way to the corner of the boulevard de Bonne-Nouvelle and the rue Saint-Denis. She said *au revoir*, turned, and left him. She had a distinct walk, chin up and insouciant, and as her white dress receded before him, he remained rooted. Would she? Would she turn and wave before Paris engulfed her, before the walkers and hawkers and menders and vendors, before the drays and cabs and crowds all swallowed her up? Would she turn? Nicolette continued away from him, lifted her skirts smartly to avoid something in the street, paused and turned, waved to him. An omnibus crossed her path, and when it passed, she had vanished.

The following day Beaujard must have been painting her head because he grew exasperated with her and said if Nicolette couldn't concentrate, he wouldn't allow Jean-Luc to come anymore. "Perhaps you'd better not come anymore in any event." Beaujard put down his brush and frowned. "I don't want to contribute to your parents' unhappiness. Things are going very badly for *La Lumière*. You know Gallet is gone, don't you?"

"Left Paris?" Jean-Luc didn't care if Gallet had died.

"Your father worries so much and your mother is working too hard. When I last saw her, she looked so pale and worn. You haven't noticed?"

"No, I've had other things on my mind. Perhaps—" Jean-Luc gave Nicolette an imploring look—"perhaps there are other places I can see Mademoiselle Lauriot."

"Where do you want me?" Nicolette ostensibly asked the painter, who posed her in the light.

After the session she accepted her modeling money from Beaujard, took Jean-Luc's arm, and together they ran down the four flights, stopping only at the gate before the concierge's lodge, uncaring at the stares as Jean-Luc brought Nicolette close against him, kissed her, and she raised her arms as gracefully as she did the palm frond, only this time they wrapped around his neck.

"Take me home with you," he whispered hoarsely against her lips, her cheeks, her hair.

"I don't dare. Monsieur Needlemaker might—"

"Risk it."

In time Jean-Luc discovered that Monsieur Needlemaker, who paid for Nicolette's apartment, was also boring, stuffy, and ugly. Like the doctor she'd nearly married, he had three brats and a living mother. He also had a wife. But twice a week he had Nicolette Lauriot in this apartment in the rue du Haut-Moulin: two tiny rooms fronting a street in the labyrinth of the old theatrical district, just off the boulevard du Temple (and not so very far from the rue des Filles-du-Calvaire). This tidy arrangement helped Nicolette to meet expenses while—like every palm-frond waver since the beginning of time—she awaited opportunity. Nicolette kept, at any given moment, three or four cats; any stray animal elicited her instant affection.

But Monsieur Needlemaker was not there that first afternoon (nor indeed subsequent afternoons) when, as the cats watched stoically, Nicolette fell into bed with Jean-Luc Pontmercy with a splash of white from her dress and a great groan of pleasure from the bedsprings. They both laughed out loud, couldn't stop kissing to get their clothes off, boots to be unlaced, stays, braces, buttons, snaps and tabs, stockings all tumbled to the floor, spilled in the afternoon light, which lay sliced in neat golden rectangles by the open window, and below, on the rue du Haut-Moulin, passersby grinned, giggled, winked to hear the laughter and excitement pealing out of that open window.

"Go close the window," Nicolette whispered.

Naked—not posing nude, but truly, gloriously naked—Jean-Luc stepped to the window, looking out over the chimney pots, cracked plaster, patchwork roofs, and laundry festooning balconies (acrobats lived across the way). He searched for the high mill that had once lent its name to this glorious, this beautiful street, the rue du Haut-Moulin, this hallowed garden of a street, whose salutes to summer bloomed bravely, white geraniums in a nearby window, and urchins splashed noisily in the cobbled gutters below. He stood there believing, even fearing, that he might fly, feeling so strong, so free, so fine that a single wish might lift him out of the window and over the rue du Haut-Moulin, to the high buttes of Montmartre, that he might soar over the huddle and jumble, the roofs of old Paris.

He closed the window and returned to the bed where Nicolette, her hair loosened over her shoulders, lay amongst the tousled pillows. "I have loved you since the day, the night I first saw you at the Théâtre-Française, Nicolette. I knew I'd always love you. I knew it then."

"Oh, Jean-Luc." She ran her hand through his crisp curling hair. "This has to be just for fun. It can't be anything else."

"That's not true. You know what this is. You know as well as I. This is for love."

"And what if Monsieur Needlemaker comes in?"

"What does it matter? You love me, not him."

"I want a man with money," she said good-naturedly. "I don't think there's any romance in shivering next to your beloved in a garret. I won't live sewing for eleven hours in a sooty room, or going to some workshop at a quarter to five, weaving till nine at night, eating two bowls of broth a day. I don't want the brightest moments in my life to be going out to the *barrière bal* on Sunday, getting drunk, in bed with a hangover on Saint-Monday, and believing yourself deliciously fortunate just to be in love. I won't live like that. I want jewels on my garters and diamond earrings. I want the adoration and men and audiences and—"

"I can give you all that. I will. And I will love you in the bargain."

She kissed him as if tasting the nectar at the heart of the honeysuckle. "Then it's a bargain. And I will love you too."

"This is forever."

"Oh, you're hopeless." She laughed. "Nothing is forever."

Chapter 28

Geographically speaking, the rue des Filles-du-Calvaire was but a short jaunt from the rue du Haut-Moulin, but Nicolette's magical street was worlds away from the Pontmercy home, with its carriage gate, high windows, garden, its fine eighteenth-century façade, which met the world with enviable certainty but no élan whatever. That's what Jean-Luc thought as he left the dishevelment and medley of Nicolette's street in the old theatrical quarter and flew home. For truly it did seem to him that he flew, perhaps only moving in time with the revolutions of the earth, certainly enjoying a sense of harmony he'd never dreamed possible, and so he especially resented entering the house and hearing the lugubrious thump of some awful piano piece undermining the music in his heart.

Opening the drawing-room door, he saw a big-boned, red-headed woman at the piano, two brightly dressed girls sitting on either side of the fireplace, looking bored. In her accustomed chair sat Aunt Adelaide, looking bewildered without her ear trumpet, and standing behind her, Fantine, looking miserable.

"That," said the woman, plunking down the final chord, "is 'Camptown Races,' one of the prince-president's favorite American songs. He absolutely adores to have me play it for him."

"Jean-Luc," Fantine said tentatively, nodding toward the woman, who wore a satin day dress, too heavy for the weather, too yellow for words, "this is Madame Touchard. She came to see Mama. Mama is not here. She insisted on waiting and meeting us, Jean-Luc. Madame Touchard, this is my brother, Jean-Luc."

"*Enchanté,*" said Zelma, rising from the piano and offering her hand to Jean-Luc, who behaved with the elaborate courtesy instilled in him. "I was just telling your adorable sister and your lovely aunt how I sometimes go to the prince-president's just to play his favorite Stephen Foster songs. The prince-president adores all things American."

"Are you American, madame?" asked Jean-Luc.

"We are," piped up one of the girls, a snippy black-haired, black-eyed young lady, younger than Fantine. "Ma isn't, but we are."

"*Mama*," Madame Touchard corrected her. "My daughters, Monsieur Pontmercy, schooled in French, English, music, dancing, all the arts. This is my eldest, Hortense."

"My name is Eponine and well you know it, Ma."

"*Mama.*" This time Zelma bit down on the word with steely finality. The girl sulked visibly. "Eponine-Hortense is her real name. Her family name. Sometimes we merely shorten it for convenience. My younger daughter," she pointed to a little girl of about ten, "Corinne, named after the great novel, of course—"

"Excuse me, madame, but what is the purpose of your visit?"

"I came to pay a call on the Baroness Pontmercy, but alas, she wasn't here, so I waited, and *voilà!* I am rewarded for my patience. I get to meet the son. The handsome son."

"Have you business with my mother?"

"Business?" Zelma seemed to step around *business* as one might avoid something a horse left in the road. "Not at all. Friendship. Friendship brings me. You see, we've only just returned to our native land from America, where we have vast estates—slaves, cotton fields, three plantations. Have you ever heard of Arkansas, Monsieur Pontmercy?"

"I don't believe so."

"All our money is tied up in Arkansas. And, naturally, in railways in New York, where we had most rewarding and intimate acquaintance with the prince-president."

"I didn't," Eponine-Hortense commented. "I never met him before we came here. He lives in a pretty grand place now."

"We are returned to France for good, Monsieur Pontmercy, and I thought to call on your dear mother and father. I was a friend of their youth. Indeed, I knew them before they knew each other. I grew up with Cosette—you'll pardon the familiarity, but she was like, well, like my sister. Dear little Cosette. I can see her now as a child. How you resemble her, Fantine."

Fantine shot a desperate look to her brother.

"I haven't seen Cosette for eighteen years. We called on her just after her marriage, my father and I. My late father. In fact, my family has been connected with the Pontmercys for generations. Did you know my late father fought right alongside your grandfather at Waterloo? Your grandfather, the first baron, he was a colonel. My father was the Sergeant of Waterloo. We—"

"If you have a card, Madame Touchard, I will be happy to leave it with my mother," said Jean-Luc, as he helped his addled aunt up from her chair. Adelaide had gone mercifully deaf since the June Days, but she could see he meant to rescue her, and her eyes were rapt with gratitude. "You will excuse us, I hope, Madame Touchard."

"Of course."

"The servants will show you and your daughters out," he said, glancing at Corinne, who despite her romantic name was chewing on a fingernail, and Eponine-Hortense, who regarded him with idle contempt mulched with curiosity.

"I shall call another day." Madame Touchard stood up and flung an embroidered shawl around her great shoulders. "Please do give your dear mother and father my regards. And, do you mind, might we, before we leave, take a turn around your garden, Monsieur Pontmercy? I have such vivid memories of that lovely summer day, that last visit here in your garden before we left for America, the last time I saw Cosette."

Chapter 29

One by one she gathered them up, the pages she'd written all morning. They crackled in the fire. Like laughter, Cosette thought, watching the ink burn. She looked at the silver candlesticks on the mantel, lit them, just to see them lit. How much longer would they have such *lumière?*

A knock sounded and Le Sansonnet came in, still shaking rain from the ends of his hair, and bringing with him a whiff of November and the bad news that Cousin Théo had left a note for Marius, that as of tomorrow, 1 December, he had joined a Bonapartist rag.

"Perhaps he's right to," said Cosette with a sigh. "Théo is not exactly—well, he'll need his options."

"That's what Monsieur Pontmercy said. I thought he'd be crushed. I mean, if it was my cousin who deserted me for Bonaparte, I'd be crushed."

Cosette smiled wanly. "I don't have anything for you to take back to the newspaper. Not yet. It's been very difficult lately. I used to just dip the pen in the inkwell and the words would cling to it, as if they lived there and only needed me to ferry them to the paper. Now they seem to fight against me."

"You're tired, madame. If you'll pardon me for saying so, you look very tired."

"That evident, is it?"

The Starling frowned, wrung his cap in his hands. "Is it true, what we've heard? About *La Lumière,* that it might be going under?"

"We are the Opposition, Starling," said Cosette with forced cheerfulness, "we have always been the Opposition. We always will be the Opposition."

Fantine walked in with her schoolbooks and papers and put them on the floor in front of the fire. "Hello, Starling. Did you finish *The Hunchback of Notre-Dame?*"

"Yes, mademoiselle. Here it is." He drew a thick volume from under his coat. "I kept it dry."

"Did you like it?"

"I thought it was very sad, the hunchback so crippled up and ugly to the world, but he loved Esmeralda so much."

"That's the way it is in novels, Starling," said Fantine didactically. "If you are going to be my student, you must learn not to take things so personally."

"Is he a good student, Fantine?" asked Cosette.

Fantine regarded the Starling judiciously, "Yes, he is. Quite good. The best," she added as a servant entered and handed Cosette a card: *Madame Touchard*.

"I don't know a Madame Touchard."

"Oh yes, you do." Fantine began prowling the bookshelves for the Starling's next assignment. "She's known you since you were a child. Papa too. How could you have been friends with someone so vulgar? She wore the most horrible dress and sang awful American songs. And her daughters—one chewed her hair and one chewed her fingernails. They revolted me. Didn't Jean-Luc tell you they'd come?"

"When did this happen?" Cosette sank into a chair.

"Months ago. In the summer. Jean-Luc took Madame Touchard's card. He didn't tell you? He's so impossible. Have you noticed?"

"The rat in satin," Cosette murmured. "The rat in satin approaches."

Cosette sent Fantine and the Starling downstairs to the kitchen and the servant to fetch Zelma Thénardier, and then she drew herself up, smoothed the lace at her bodice, and when Zelma entered, she said, "I've been expecting you."

"For eighteen years?"

The two women appraised each other warily. Cosette saw the nightmares of her childhood; Zelma saw the nightmares of her youth. Maturity had shaped both the lineaments in their faces and the lineaments of their characters. Cosette's strengths had been forged, hammered, refined from love, durable as the silver candlesticks on the mantel, but she recognized that in some fundamental way her life was changing, the balance irrevocably shifting, and that Zelma was the fulcrum of that change.

The strengths Zelma had achieved in eighteen years were cobbled of necessity, desperation, impulse, and instinct, but her life too had reached a crucial juncture and she was in the ascendant. In that vein, she chattered at length about her long and close friendship with the prince-president, the corridors of power in which she now walked, the fact that the prince-president had all but acknowledged her daughter, Eponine-Hortense, born in 1837, the fruit of a bittersweet liaison with Louis-Napoléon, which, Zelma suggested, would have doubtless ended in marriage had the original Hortense not died and Louis-Napoléon been obliged to return to Europe for his mother's funeral.

"If you have business with me," said Cosette, after listening to her natter, "please get on with it."

"Business?" Zelma's big teeth gleamed; she was dressed in ostentatious grape-colored satin and a heavily beribboned bonnet. "How crass. But I should expect crass of you, Lark, the pitiful lark chirping at dawn, the broom bigger than she was, licking bones the dog didn't want. Luck alone kept you from your mother's fate, Cosette. How pleased would your daughter be to know she was named for a prostitute? Would your handsome son be proud to know that clanking in his own family tree he has the convict's chain and a prostitute who lifted her skirts under the bridge?"

"I trust you speak from experience in that regard, Zelma."

Zelma flushed, but collected herself quickly. "How good of you to be so familiar with me. We were like sisters, yes? Like my sister Eponine, who slept with your husband. He loved her. He thought she was beautiful. She told me how he loved her, what he did for her and to her and with her." Zelma lingered over the implied possibilities, then continued headlong. "He only married you because she died. She went to her death on that barricade for him! Your lout of a husband cost me the life of my sister! My sister slept with him all the while he lived next door. He paid our rent, he was so grateful for her body. But then, your family is no stranger to the selling of bodies. Jean Valjean did the same for your mother, the prostitute." Zelma made an obscene gesture and walked around the library, fingering the furniture as if putting it up for auction. "Jean Valjean must have been desperate, to sleep with Fantine. She'd sold her hair and teeth by then. They'd pulled the teeth right out of her head. Truly. My father found out. Cut off her hair and pulled out her teeth; there wasn't any part of her body she wouldn't sell."

"Is there no part of your soul you won't sell?"

"Spare me the soul. Anyone who retreats to the soul is defeated. Meet my price. Five hundred francs."

Cosette walked to the windows, watched the rain pulley down the glass, mottling the late November garden into a pool of gray, making everything so indistinct that the whole could only be imagined, not constructed. She thought about that day in the garden eighteen years before when Zelma had so shocked her she'd slid down the tree weeping. She was not that eighteen-year-old bride any longer. She turned to face Zelma. "It's a pity no one rescued you as Jean Valjean rescued me. Your father brutalized both of us, Zelma, but I escaped before you did. We can still be free, though, both of us, free of the squalor and the past and the pain, free of The Sergeant of Waterloo. Why shouldn't we be? Let go of all that, Zelma. You have possibilities now your parents could not have dreamed of. You have an entrée into the highest society. You have—"

"I don't have money."

"Let's both escape the past. If we don't," Cosette persisted, "we'll stay trapped at The Sergeant of Waterloo forever."

"Five hundred francs. Little enough for the death of my sister."

"So it's revenge and not the money?"

"It's the money. The revenge, well—I'll settle for the money. I want my five hundred francs, but payments are fine. Tomorrow is the first of December: one hundred francs tomorrow. One hundred on the first of January. And so on." Zelma gloated.

"Do you remember the chain, the swing on the abandoned gun carriage, Zelma? Do you remember the hideous squeal? I sometimes hear that in my dreams. Do you?"

"I hear my sister telling me how she loved Monsieur Marius. That's what she used to call him. In bed," Zelma added for spite.

"All those years you were in America I had nightmares about The Sergeant of Waterloo, your terrible mother, your horrible father, but perhaps the nightmares weren't so much the fears of the past but fears for the future. I prayed God would keep you in

America, but yes, I have expected you, and yes, perhaps for eighteen years. I'm glad you're here so I can banish you at last."

"You can't banish me!"

"I can banish you from my sleep, from my family, from my prayers. I no longer have to hope you'll stay in America. I don't care where you go, or to whom you tell your nasty story. Perhaps Jean Valjean was a convict, but he had more integrity in his little finger than you have in your whole body. In your whole family, for that matter. Perhaps my mother was a prostitute. Now that I am a mother, I pray she never knew what your family did to me, because whatever degradation she endured, she did so to earn money to pay your mother and father for caring for me. Caring? Caring! I pray she never knew what they did to me, and I tell you, Zelma, whatever she did with her body, my mother's soul was clean—and you cannot say the same of your parents. My mother loved me, died loving me, my father died loving me. What of your father, Zelma? How did he die?"

Zelma blanched, but repeated again she would go to Marius with the story, and after Marius she would spread it like manure, dirty gossip all over Paris.

"Spread it however you like, Zelma. I will not pay your blackmail."

"I'm sure your children will love to hear it."

"No doubt it will pain them. Life is full of pain. Sometimes we invite it, sometimes we don't. If the money is the revenge, then you'll just have to find something else, won't you?"

The next morning in the Luxembourg Gardens, the trees all stood like skeletal sentinels, a few scattered tiny leaves clinging to their topmost branches. The fountains were silent, the little vendors' stalls for toys and newspapers, confections and other pleasures of summer all closed and forlorn. Only the statues, naked, impervious to the season, stared out across the foggy paths, their stone-eyed gaze unchanging, regarding the few strollers whose feet left faint imprints in the snow-dust. Dressed warmly in a cloak of burgundy velvet, Cosette kept her arm in Marius's, and their feet crunched in unison on the gravel paths this first day of December. She had waited to tell him, wanted to come here, to the place where twenty years before, chance—fortune, in their case—had brought them together: Cosette a young lady on the arm of her adoring father, Marius an impecunious student estranged from his family. She watched in the distance a young couple, their voices indistinct, ringing on the winter air, their laughter rippling. The girl wore a gray cloak trimmed with white, the hood obscuring her face, until the well-dressed young man wrapped his arm around her, bent her back slightly, and the hood fell away from her fair hair, and they stood, thus poised momentarily, like statues themselves. Then he kissed her, a long, sweet kiss, public and uncaring as the statues embracing all around them. In one fluid motion he brought her upright and she put her arms round his neck.

"Could we have done that, Cosette?" Marius asked wistfully, "been so free that we kissed in the Luxembourg Gardens?"

"We kissed in the garden of the rue Plumet."

"Yes, we had to keep our love a secret from your father, and then your father kept his love for us a secret. It seems so tortured, so unnecessary."

Perhaps this talk of secrets was the best place to start and Cosette was about to, but she watched the young couple more closely, listened to the ripple of their voices as she and Marius drew nearer. The girl had a brash, too-quick laugh and a teasing, insinuating manner. The young man—"Jean-Luc?" she said incredulously.

"Where? There? Those two?"

Stunned, Cosette and Marius stopped, stared ahead. The girl kept talking and laughing, but when Jean-Luc saw who shared the Luxembourg Gardens with them that wintry morning, his face went as gray as the sky overhead. Nicolette, sensing some alarm, looked from him to the people opposite. Jean-Luc stood immobile, stammered out, "This is a surprise." To which his parents speechlessly agreed, as did Nicolette when he added, "Mama, Papa—"

"Mama? Papa?" Nicolette gulped.

"I would like you to make the acquaintance of Mademoiselle Nicolette Lauriot. Mademoiselle Lauriot, my parents, the Baron and Baroness Pontmercy."

"Charmed," said Nicolette weakly.

A hundred horrified questions came to Cosette's lips, but Marius put his hand on hers. "All further discussion will be held at home. You understand, Jean-Luc? We will see you there directly."

"Yes," he said miserably.

"Immediately," snapped his father. "You will return home. You have gravely disappointed us, betrayed our trust. You have broken your own word time and again." He spoke from some deep well of pain and then retreated into anger. "Perhaps you should be sent to school outside Paris, where your infirm mettle will not be so severely tested. Perhaps you will be better educated in Switzerland." Marius nodded curtly and with sterile good manners, "Mademoiselle Lauriot, I hope you will excuse us."

Marius and Cosette walked away, not daring to look back or speak, since it was clear from Jean-Luc's familiarity with the blond, brash girl that his defiance was of long duration. When at last they could hear no footsteps but their own, Cosette wept. "Oh, Marius, Marius, I'd brought you here to walk where we had met, so I could tell you about the past, and instead—"

"Don't cry, my love, I will punish Jean-Luc. I would never have believed our son could be capable of such deception! Where is his sense of honor?"

"No, no, it's nothing to do with Jean-Luc. It's to do with . . ." She brought her gloved hands together, twisting them before her. "Do you know a Madame Touchard?"

"You mean Zelma Thénardier," he said to Cosette's surprise. He spoke abstractedly, clearly still undone by Jean-Luc's betrayal of trust. Finally, he added, "She is a harridan. No better than her father, Thénardier, Jondrette, whatever name may be carved on his tombstone in America. I hope they left him to the wolves in the forest. A vicious, unredeemed villain. His wife was a brute and he was a blackguard and Zelma is both. Madame Touchard is her father's devilish daughter. As you are your father's angelic daughter."

"Oh, Marius, I'm not at all angelic. Please don't say that."

"She tried to blackmail me. Yes, it's true. Pitiful, don't you think? She demanded I pay five hundred francs or she would tell you I had bedded her sister Eponine all those years ago, back in my student days. I was so impoverished, I lived in the room next to theirs in a crumbling tenement near the *barrière* d'Italie."

"And what did you say when she threatened you?" Cosette looked up at him.

"What would anyone say? I told her blackmail was an indecent act committed against the memory of her sister. I would have none of it."

Cosette walked to an empty bench and sat down, shivering, pulling the burgundy cloak around her.

"So she did come to you?"

"Yes."

"It was all lies." Marius sat beside her. "I held Eponine Thénardier in my arms as she lay dying of her wounds that night at the barricade. I held her as the life left her body. I kissed her. I pitied Eponine, but I have never loved anyone but you."

She brushed the dark hair salted with gray from his face, touched the creases fanning out from his sad eyes. "She didn't come for that."

Marius paused, perplexed. "What did she come for, if not for that?"

And so Cosette told him. How Jean Valjean had rescued her from the Thénardiers, The Sergeant of Waterloo Inn. She told him she was the bastard daughter of a desperate woman, so desperate she eventually sank into prostitution. "So you see, Marius, all these years you and *La Lumière* have fought for the rights of women not to be starved into degradation, fought for decent wages for women, I have always thought that in some ways, ways you could not know, you were helping my mother, helping women like her. Her name was Fantine." Cosette bit her lip. "I lied about the girl in the convent with the name Fantine. I couldn't bear it, to tell you the truth of my mother."

"And why should you? Cosette, what was I then? Priggish at best, reflexive, and I committed a great wrong against your father, and all the while I went about feeling moral and upright. I nearly died of the remorse when your father died, but I don't blame you for not trusting me. You had watched me be stubborn and sanctimonious. Your father was testing my faith and I failed that test."

"You forgive me, then, for not telling you all this before?"

"I blame you only insofar as if I had known Thénardier had ever hurt you, ever laid a hand on you, I would have killed him, shot him where he stood. No, Cosette, Cosette, it is for you to forgive me."

She kissed him there amongst the cold statues and the black trees, kissed him as though they were lovers, not young lovers perhaps, so young, so free that they could kiss in a public park, but lovers free at last. "Love is its own country," she whispered against his lips, "but not its own world. Let's go to that country, Marius. Today. Let's go to Boulogne. Now."

"But Jean-Luc. I told him I'd be home, I'd deal with him."

"Let's go right to the railway station, Marius, now, and send the coachman home with the message we'll be back late tomorrow. And as for Jean-Luc, you can see that's already beyond our poor power to control. Nothing we do today will make any difference to him."

"We have somehow lost him, haven't we? He repudiates everything we've tried to instill in him."

"Let us leave Paris, Marius. Take me to the country of love. Let's sleep at the Gérards' inn and walk by the ocean, and let everything wait until tomorrow."

Part V

Free the Larks
DECEMBER 1851

*The act of December 2nd is an infamous, insolent,
unprecedented challenge to democracy, civilization, liberty . . .
I do not know that we shall conquer, but we ought to
protest. Protest first in parliament; parliament closed, protest in
the street; the street closed, protest in exile;
exile accomplished, protest in the tomb.*

—VICTOR HUGO
History of a Crime

Chapter 30

On the night of 1 December 1851, the conductor at the Théâtre-Française, arms raised high, commanded his musicians to new heights, his eyes closed, hearing only the dash and rapture of his own music. Even those actors supposed to be expiring stepped forward into the gaslit proscenium and delivered their lines with undisguised ire at Monsieur Offenbach. The palm-frond wavers, on the other hand, moving in tutored unison, smiled to hear the actors' lines drowned out, all the better for the audience to look at those without lines. Certainly there were several in the audience with eyes for Nicolette Lauriot alone. In his accustomed seat (he was too prudent for a box), Monsieur Needlemaker, sans wife and children, anticipated his regular Monday assignation with the beautiful Mademoiselle Lauriot. From her vantage point, stage right, Nicolette looked across the theatre, surprised to see, in the Pontmercys' box, Jean-Luc, a gorgeous grin on his face. After the incident in the Luxembourg Gardens this morning, Nicolette half expected to hear her lover had been exiled to Switzerland. And yet here he was, his eyes alight, his clothes impeccable, his friend Arsène Huvet at his side.

Side by side at the Gérards' inn, Marius and Cosette sat before the fire, a bottle of Bordeaux between them, the wind from the sea rattling the shutters. Surprised to see them in December and without notice, Monsieur Gérard had hastily lit the fire in their room and now refreshed their glasses, cleared away the plates of oyster shells, and left them in the empty taproom, where firelight played on Cosette's bright hair and Marius listened, frowning sometimes, often wincing. Cosette told him what little she knew of her mother, what she could remember of her childhood before Jean Valjean had rescued her, how she had come by the name the Lark. Up at dawn, broom in hand, water buckets to carry, assured only of the strap, the cold, the fear, fatigue and hunger at The Sergeant of Waterloo, where the abandoned gun carriage served as a swing for Eponine and Zelma. "I had to push the two of them, and sing their favorite song." Cosette drew her knees up under her warm skirt and rested her cheek there while Marius stroked her hair. "To this day I can sing it, that loathsome song, 'Partant pour la Syrie.'"

The military band struck up "Partant pour la Syrie," the song Louis-Napoléon's mother, Hortense, had written. Here, in the presidential Salon, he hosted the usual Monday-night reception, five or six hundred people, most of the men resplendent in military uniforms or prelates' robes, many decorated with the Légion d'honneur. Amongst the many pretty women, Madame Touchard looked especially fetching, her gown—black lace over white satin, decked all over with green velvet bows—sumptuous enough for a princess. (Indeed, it had once belonged to a princess, looted from the Tuileries in 1848. Zelma had rented it from the Changer and no one the wiser.)

On the arm of the obliging but undemanding Monsieur Touchard, Zelma approached the prince-president and curtsied. With a rather confused grimace, Louis-Napoléon reminded her this was a Republic. "I look back happily, then," Zelma replied sweetly, "to the days of empire, when a woman could acknowledge a prince among men."

Louis-Napoléon rewarded her with a wayward gesture of his index finger, half papal blessing, half waggish invitation.

The conversation was desultory, the band lackluster, the prince-president more than usually restless and taciturn. "It's said," one of the guests whispered, "he knows five languages and can be silent in all of them."

The reception lasted an hour only. Amongst the guests, however, were four men who would reconvene in the study with Louis-Napoléon at one in the morning, who would pull an envelope marked *Rubicon* from a drawer, open it, and cross not merely the metaphorical Rubicon but from history into infamy. These men were a courtier of long standing, a general, the head of the Parisian police, and Louis-Napoléon's illegitimate half-brother, comte de Morny, a well-known bon vivant, who left the reception and went directly to his box at the Théâtre-Française. He arrived at intermission.

*   *   *

In his haste to get backstage at intermission, Jean-Luc very nearly bumped into the comte de Morny, excused himself, and made his way to the stage door, tipping the porter handsomely and asking directions to the extras' dressing room. It was at the very back of a narrow labyrinth, and he made his way among scene-shifters and rope-and-pulley men to a damp room Nicolette shared with a dozen others. Lit by unadorned gas jets, a single grilled window, a single slop pail, and a single cracked mirror served all of them. Black and green mildew crept colorfully up the walls, and the other girls cursed him and told him to get out of the way.

Nicolette took his arm, led him into the dirty passage, where gas hissed close to his head and he was nudged by a prop man carrying an armful of spears. Still clad in her toga, Nicolette shivered and kissed him again and again, chastised him for coming backstage, inquired what had happened with his parents.

"They're gone! They've gone to Boulogne and won't be back for days!"

"You mean, without even—"

"I didn't even see them! They never said a word, or left word—or anything. You see what this means for us? We have all night. We have the whole night together."

"It's Monday night. Monsieur Needlemaker. His night."

"You don't love him."

"Of course I don't love him," she said, laughing. "I love you."

"Well—"

"Well, what? That doesn't matter."

"It matters to me." He caught her arm and pulled her up against him, whispered harshly. "I have all night, Nicolette. To sleep with you."

"And tonight is arranged. I can't change it."

"You could."

"But I won't. You know very well I won't. It's unfair of you to ask me. It's unfair. Now don't look like that. You know I love you. You know that's true." She kissed him again. "Monsieur Needlemaker pays the rent." In the green, gaslit glare her face had a peculiar metallic cast, and her full lips settled into an unflinching line.

"Tonight," he whispered.

Nicolette freed herself. "Tomorrow."

"Tonight," said the Duchesse de Galliéra to the esteemed dinner guest on her right, "they are taking bets on the boulevards: will Monsieur Bonaparte oust the Assembly before the Assembly ousts him? Where will you put your money, Monsieur Thiers?"

"Whatever the shortcomings of the Assembly, it is committed to order, madame. A coup d'état is illegal." The duchess's servant put a slice of duckling *Rouennaise* on his plate, and Thiers sipped his wine, a very good wine, and smiled his smug smile. "Next year, in 1852, we shall elect a true president for France."

The duchess toyed with her diamond earrings. "Isn't that disingenuous of you, Monsieur Thiers? All Paris knows Louis-Napoléon won't stand by idly while the Assembly denies his right to be reelected."

"Christmas and New Year are coming." Thiers picked up his heavy silver knife and fork to cut the duckling. "It is the season of celebration, of gifts, and little mechanical toys. Parisians aren't in the mood for politics, and the merchants are too fond of profit to allow a coup d'état."

"Do you really think Parisian merchants can dictate to Louis-Napoléon?"

"Merchants are like debutantes, madame. Any man who trifles with their affections will find himself in serious difficulties. Indeed," he chewed reflectively, "this duckling puts me in mind of Louis-Napoléon."

The duchess smiled mischievously and glanced down her table.

"The duck, after all, is a most ordinary barnyard creature, a mere fowl who can only be ennobled by a cook. Louis-Napoléon is a duck in search of a cook."

"'A king may look further for a cook than for a general,' that's what the maestro would say," Madame Carême stated decisively, making a requisite well in the center of her flour for the maestro's puff-pastry recipe. "Of the two, the cook is more important. A diplomat with a fine cook at his service can effect with a skewer what the general can only do with the sword."

Fantine wrapped her hands around her cup of chocolate and asked to be told again the story of Carême's diplomatic triumphs, watching as, under Madame Carême's expert touch, flour, a bit of butter, two egg yolks, a little salt, and a glass of water were transmitted into a paste as smooth and supple as yellow satin. "It is miraculous how you do that."

"Experience, *ma petite,* that's all."

Finishing her chocolate as Madame Carême finished the story, Fantine wandered to the window, looking out at the chill December night. "Why do you suppose Mama and Papa would just go off with so little warning?"

"Perhaps they want to remember, to imagine themselves young, impulsive lovers."

"It's hard to think of them that way."

"Why? Your parents are extraordinarily fortunate people. They married for love and the love never left them. Now that, my dear girl, is miraculous."

"In novels it happens all the time. It's either that or people are getting their hearts broken and dying for love."

"Piffle and nonsense."

"I won't have my heart broken." Fantine lifted a sugared slice of apple from a bowl. "I intend to marry for love. A very rich man," she added, licking the sugar, "for love."

"You'll marry the man your parents tell you to marry, like all the other girls."

"I think it's criminal what people do to girls, keeping us locked up, no fun at all, till your family decides to marry you off to someone you scarcely know. There you are, married and stuck forever kissing him. And why is it, once you are married, then you're free to do as you like? Why should married women be free? Unmarried girls can't even meet a man's eye, can't go out, can't—"

"Parents know best."

"That's why girls die of heartbreak. It's all very well to read about it," she plucked another slice of apple, "but I'm sure heartbreak is tedious in real life."

The street name had changed, but the brothel kept its old appellation, *Coeur-Volant,* the symbol of the flying heart above the door, run by a notorious old bawd known to all as Mother. In winters a legless fiddler played in the ground-floor public room, where Mother's half-wit son poured the drinks (and broke up fights) and Mother herself tended the greasy till. A couple of underclad, underemployed prostitutes sat performing intimate rituals, cutting their toenails and chatting, waiting for customers. Mimi Lascaux sat apart from them, nursing a brandy nervously: Mother didn't like to see people underemployed. Mimi shivered, but at least she wasn't shivering on the street in this wretched cold. Still, she thought with a sigh, there was something to be said for the independent Café Rigolo days. Now she went to the Café Rigolo every day, no longer for *vin bleu* but for absinthe, and she worked here. At the *Coeur-Volant* she had a place to live and didn't have to freeze on the street; however, she had to take on whomever Mother sent her—and the half-wit son now and then without complaint. All the girls did. She brightened to see a soldier enter, a nice-looking boy, Mimi noted, but truly a boy, not much older than Gabriel. Mother took his money and pointed him out to Mimi. He grinned and offered her a cigarette, which she was pleased to take. He had some class, she could tell because he wasn't smoking a clay pipe. She blew out a wreath of smoke and commented on the number of soldiers in Paris the last few days.

"*Vive Napoléon,*" said the soldier taking her upstairs.

"I am the image of Napoléon." Eponine stood before the mirror, hand on her bodice, raising her chin, and staring straight ahead as if regarding a predestined future.

Corinne reshuffled the deck and dealt another hand. "He has fish eyes, Louis-Napoléon does."

"He does not."

"Papa says he has eyes like a fish, legs like a toad, and a mustache like a third-rate musician."

"You're all just jealous," Eponine retorted.

"At least I'm not a bastard."

"Say what you want, catfish guts, the prince-president won't come to your wedding."

"He won't come to yours, either. Bring the candle back. You know Ma says no more than one."

Eponine brought a stool up near the mantel, the better to see the mirror over the pawn tickets and the ancient sign of The Sergeant of Waterloo nearby. She pulled her dark hair back from her face, which was sallow and round. She had black button eyes and an impudent mouth. "Ma says by the time I get married, they'll quit all this shilly-shallying around with a Republic and make my true father Emperor." Defiantly she reached into the coal box and put a few more on the fire. When this coal ran out, they'd have to find a new merchant. They'd spent the last week avoiding the wife of their last coal merchant, who had come to collect on a debt of long standing. "If only they'd make Louis-Napoléon Emperor. Think how rich we'd be." Eponine-Hortense held her hands out to the fire.

A street fire in the rue Mouffetard had attracted a crowd of rowdies, the remnants of the parish of Saint-Monday. Emerging from the cafés, where lights were blinking off, men and women in varying stages of drunken ebullience or pathos were drawn irresistibly toward the fire, the warmth, the flames leaping up. A cart of straw had been oddly abandoned here near the corner of the rue Pot-de-Fer across from the public fountain, and some enterprising soul had set it afire. Gradually people gathered in the street, some leaving heatless apartments in nearby buildings, some bringing crates and broken baskets to keep the blaze going, the welcome conflagration, which snapped skyward and lit the faces of Le Sansonnet, Pajol, Germaine Fleury, who was seven or eight months gone with child, and about two dozen others. They extended their hands for the warmth, clapping time to a couple of fiddlers, a flute player, and a drunken cornet player, who did the best he could with the old dance *La Poule*.

"Hello, Starling," said a man standing beside him, hands out to the blaze. "Got the pox yet?"

"Pincher!"

The Pincher's face was brown and swarthy, emaciated, and his wrist bones stood out in knobs. His clothes were no more ragged than anyone else's in this crowd, his shoes flapping inadequately, but his eyes were not like theirs. "I don't remember you being taller than me, Starling."

"I almost wasn't."

"That was the devil's own time, wasn't it?" The Pincher

chuckled. "The June Days. We nearly did the job for the fat ones, killing each other off. Too many mouths to feed anyway." He gave Germaine a passing glance.

"You saved my life, Pincher, and me, I never had a chance to thank you."

He shrugged. "It's a cheap thing after all."

"It's dear to them who have it."

"Maybe."

"Where've you been all these years, Pincher?"

"They let us go, the Mobile Guard, our enlistments were for a year and they let us go, and by that time, well, I'd got a taste for it."

"For what?"

"Blood." Someone passed a wine bottle around; the Pincher held it possessively, but only took his single swig and passed it to the Starling. "So I joined the army. Been to Algeria, Starling. Real savages in Algeria."

The Starling took his sip and passed the bottle to Pajol. Everyone laughed as the cornet player passed out; they dragged him to the public fountain, revived him, and he rejoined the crowd, ready to play, struck up his tune. Finally the Starling asked if perhaps the Pincher had found he had not the taste for blood after all.

"If I did, I don't anymore." He smiled; three of his teeth were gone. "Ah, France is in my debt, Starling. My country owes me. I fought for France, for, well—got any money?" He pulled his thin coat closer over his chest.

Le Sansonnet dug down in his pockets and pulled out one franc, fifty centimes. "I'm in your debt, Pincher. You saved my life."

"You're a good man. Are you still honest?" Pincher's hand closed over the money.

"I suppose."

"Not very smart, Starling. How long can you keep running for that radical rag? You're not a boy anymore. Runners don't live forever. You've wasted your youth. You should have got yourself a trade. You could have been a first-rate thief." He turned to the crowd, the musicians now warbling out the old revolutionary ditty "Ah ça ira, ça ira," and he called out that the Starling could have been a first-rate thief, then he wandered away into the darkness and the rain drizzled down on the fire and festivities.

The crowd cursed the weather and someone blamed the Assembly for ruining their fun. "They've sent the rain to break up our radical meeting!" cried a blue-lipped prostitute, looking for a last conquest for the evening. "Come get us, lardbellies! We're planning another revolution!"

The laughter swiftly silenced as a clatter of hooves sounded, and they turned to see two officers on horseback before a column of infantry marching up the rue Mouffetard from the *barrière* d'Italie. The horses were sweating and foaming, ridden hard and a long distance. The officer demanded to know who had set fire to his straw, forage for his animals. Without replying, the crowd fell back into the accommodating shadows, Pajol, Germaine, and Le Sansonnet all watching as the doors of the nearby barracks were thrown open, lamps lit, and the infantry marched in. Several men put the street fire out and led the officers' horses around to the back. Then the rue Mouffetard was quiet, save for the occasional note of domestic discord falling from an upper story, a croupy baby, a wheezy concertina, a woman's laughter.

He heard her laughter, recognized it, though her window was high and dark and closed. Perhaps the laughter was not hers at all, just the last of the theatrical crowd closing up with the cafés; they wandered homeward, the puppeteers and cabaret singers, ballet girls and impecunious musicians, leaning on one another, save for stilt walkers who drunkenly reveled through the streets, high on their stilts, avoiding the mud and the filth and presenting a hazard to everyone. Then the lamp in Nicolette's window lit and her figure silhouetted there, a man beside her. Jean-Luc pulled his hat down against the grim rain, the cold invading his bones, jostled by the acrobats returning home across the way in the rue Haut-Moulin, a street that once seemed so enchanted the very rats were gay and painted. To Arsène, Jean-Luc made vulgar remarks, equating Monsieur Needlemaker's penis with his trade. He called Nicolette a whore. He cursed the cold. He cursed the rue Haut-Moulin, the luck that had given him a whole night to spend with her and the money that made her spend it with another.

Arsène tugged at his sleeve. "Come on, Pontmercy, don't be a fool. Paris is full of women, brothels full of women. Why are we standing here in the cold? Look, here come the police. You want to get us arrested?"

"For being in love?"

"For being a fool." Arsène tipped his hat to the police, three of them, who ignored him, marching at a sharp pace to some other destination.

At the Prefecture de Police, the commissaire in charge was in the midst of his speech when the three truants entered. He glared at them and said they would suffer double the usual fine, as these were exceptional circumstances and the absolute fealty of every man required. "We have our orders from the head of the Parisian police, who has them from Bonaparte," Commissaire Clerons informed them. "Tonight Louis-Napoléon will see that the Republic is saved. Louis-Napoléon will give us order, stability, protect property. We will see that he is unopposed. We have the list of names. One commissaire and two guards for each house. Twenty minutes per arrest. Everyone opposed to Napoléon will be arrested and imprisoned tonight, from the most reactionary royalist to the most radical socialist, all important members of the Assembly, the military and Opposition editors. The arrests shouldn't be too difficult. They'll all be in bed asleep and unthinking." Achille Clerons, resplendent in a double-breasted brass-buttoned greatcoat that accentuated his bulk, paced gravely before his men. No longer a mere *mouchard,* three years after the king had fled, Clerons was prepared to serve a new master in a capacity befitting his talents. He had made certain that he would be the one to go to the Pontmercy home, relishing the irony of it, the opportunity at last to see Marius Pontmercy arrested, not for mere sedition, but this time arrested as a prelude to exile.

Beginning at two in the morning, Clerons's men marched, swept through the city, meeting, crossing with whole regiments of military and swarms of bill posters, who flew from the brilliantly illuminated government printing office all over Paris, all over France: the railroads commandeered, the telegraph entirely in government and military hands, the gasworks as well. The bill posters were armed with freshly printed decrees of 2 December and paste. The military were armed.

The coup d'état was orchestrated with operatic precision by the comte de Morny (who understood theatre). Food, forage, artillery, and ammunition materialized all over the city; the various barracks provided shelter and the parks became bivouacs for the one hundred thousand soldiers who descended on Paris that night. Trains running on military timetables disgorged troops into the city. Some troops fanned out to gag the press, and all but two papers were shut down, presses sealed, printers evicted, guards posted. They occupied the building where the Assembly met. They marched to the National Guard headquarters in each of the city's twelve *arrondissements*, where soldiers broke every drum in sight, silenced instruments that might have called neighborhood men to defend the Republic. The National Guard, after all, might not fire upon their neighbors; the regular army would fire on command. Other soldiers broke into churches in poor and working-class neighborhoods and cut the bell-tower ropes, so that no tocsins should ring to call the people to arms. The church bell at Saint-Merri was cut first and its clapper hung like a mute and rootless tongue. On every wall, bill stickers slathered the decree that went out all over France: *The Assembly is dissolved, martial law declared, new elections are to be held, universal suffrage is returned to all males.* The singing of "La Marseillaise" forbidden. *Liberté, égalité, fraternité* will be erased from all public buildings. The military will effect it. The church will bless it. The police will enforce it. The coup d'état complete. The Republic dead.

Reeling home from a brothel where he'd gone with Arsène, Jean-Luc stopped to pee against a building and saw a decree freshly plastered there. He read it with difficulty. There was a public fountain nearby, so he splashed his face and went back, reread the decree just as a uniformed messenger on horseback rounded the corner and nearly ran him over.

He cursed the man on horseback, cursed Nicolette and women in general, but as he walked on, troops took over the streets and every public building was lit, and in the place de la Bastille cannon were being set in place with a clear trajectory down the rue du Faubourg-Saint-Antoine, where during the June Days the last barricades had fought to the last man. All around the place de la Bastille, buildings that the rebels had held in June '48 were being evacuated, hastily dressed people filing out as the troops filed in, women wailing. Jean-Luc pushed through the crowds, some still in nightcaps; he ran, colliding at one point with a bill poster and his armful of decrees, arriving at the rue des Filles-du-Calvaire, panting, to find every light burning there as well, a police van in front of the steps. He dashed and beheld the servants assembled on the stairs in their nightclothes and the fifteen-year-old Fantine comforting their aged Aunt Adelaide, who wept and blubbered.

Before this group there paced a tall, dark-clad bearded man. Jean-Luc didn't recognize Clerons at first because of the beard, and he had grayed slightly in three years. The beard only partially concealed the circle scar on Clerons's right cheek, where the Starling had left him an indissoluble reminder of the passions of 1848. Perhaps that reminder inspired his vehemence now. He eyed Jean-Luc appraisingly and demanded to know where his parents were. Jean-Luc watched as soldiers trooped over the house, coming down from the library with armfuls of papers and dumping them at Clerons's feet, as his Aunt Adelaide shivered and wailed and Fantine glared. Jean-Luc asked, stupidly, still trying to clear the wine from his head, what had happened.

"Your parents are under arrest. Now tell me where they're hiding. I can get no answers from these pigeon-livered idiots."

"Why? How can they be under arrest?"

"They are known enemies of the state. The new state. The new regime. Louis-Napoléon has dissolved the Assembly, declared martial law, and given universal suffrage back to the men of France. Of course, he's the only one they can vote for."

"The Reign of Terror," bellowed the old lady.

"We don't know where our parents are," cried Fantine. "I've told you a hundred times, we don't know."

Clerons ignored her and stepped closer to Jean-Luc. "You stink of the bottle and the brothel, young Pontmercy. If you do not wish to add the stink of the prison to that, you'll answer me. Your parents will be safer in prison," he added, "they won't be shot in prison. They'll be exiled rather than transported."

"You mean they can't come back to Paris?" he stammered.

"Arrested, exiled, ordered to leave France. That's what will happen to them."

"And to us?" The specter of being educated in Switzerland hovered before Jean-Luc."

Clerons shrugged. "That's not my place to say."

"And if they're not arrested—"

"Jean-Luc!" Fantine exclaimed, "Clerons is a traitor! You know that. Papa forced him to leave *La Lumière* because he betrayed them!"

While Aunt Adelaide blubbered about Wellington and Madame Carême's fingers itched for the cleaver, Clerons stepped up to Fantine and fondled the long ribbon of her nightdress. "I never worked for *La Lumière*. I never worked for Marius Pontmercy. He is a blot on my professional honor. He got away from me in 1832, but I brought him to the attention of the authorities in 1842 so he could spend a lot of lovely time in jail, and now it is nearly 1852, and I intend to see him out of France. I intend to finish the work assigned to me twenty years ago."

"Cur," Fantine retorted, "louse—you are vermin on a dog's back."

While Aunt Adelaide broke into fresh squeals of terror and trembling, Clerons returned his attention to Jean-Luc and repeated again that his parents would be safer in prison and exile. "Otherwise, your father is very likely to be leading rebellions again. I am defending the Republic. I'm not the traitor here, boy."

"I'm not a boy."

"Then you understand these things. You understand your father's a rebel by nature, and it's up to you to protect him from himself."

"They've gone to Boulogne."

Fantine seemed to crumple. "Oh, Jean-Luc, Papa will never forgive you for this."

"Gérard's Inn. I should have remembered." Clerons turned to one of the police with him and told him to go to headquarters, telegraph Boulogne, and have the police arrest Madame and Monsieur Pontmercy at Gérard's Inn. Another policeman came out of the library and added an armful of papers to those already scattered about the floor. "No one is to leave this house until your parents have been arrested."

They woke languorously, curled up like spoons, Marius's cheek on Cosette's hair and her hands pressing his against her breast. The morning light that fell into their room was thin, cloud-clotted, and overhead they could hear gulls squealing, fighting raucously over the scraps and slops Madame Gérard threw out. The gulls' cries drowned out the sounds of Marius and Cosette making love, their tenderness refreshed, their ardor renewed, their love brightened, their time their own, their knowledge of one another deepened, Marius careful to bring Cosette to that high clear peak, that vanishing pinnacle, moments before he went there himself.

They ordered coffee, drank it slowly, and ate Madame Gérard's freshly baked bread. They dressed, bundled against the December day and the wind blowing from the sea, and walked to the harbor, Cosette holding her skirts off the streets, her color high, her laughter ringing, her arm in his. The town only slowly roused itself in weather like this, and thin seams of smoke etched upward, abandoning themselves to the clouds, as Cosette and Marius made their way to the docks.

The bay was full of whitecaps and only steamboats braved it, nothing under sail. Along the harbor sulking gulls roosted singly on the pilings, where the tides washed over long-established columns of barnacles and the bright, sharp stench of the sea wafted up through slats on the wooden docks. Against the brown dock, the leaden skies, and the gray and dun of the fishing boats, Cosette's burgundy-colored cloak stood out vividly.

Except for the sound of the waves, water sloshing against the docks, and the fishing boats tied there, it was quiet until a single halyard began to ring, to ping and clang, a small bell ringing like a tocsin, calling from the end of the dock. Cosette meandered out there and looked down into the moored boat. The *Saint-Joseph*. Worn, shabby-looking, paint peeling, the lines gray, frayed with age, the name *Saint-Joseph* itself faded. "Hello!" Cosette called down, but the only reply was the continued clang of the small ship's bell, ringing in a melancholy fashion, urged on by the choppy water. "Marius, look!" she cried, but at that moment, Monsieur Gérard's voice also rang out, and he ran toward them, his arms waving, his face contorted, and flapping in one hand a proclamation and in the other a yellow telegram.

As Monsieur Gérard, breathless and overwrought, talked, the

ship's bell on the *Saint-Joseph* clanged louder, the warning, wind-borne, seemed to overpower Monsieur Gérard's account, prepos-terous account, of the police coming to his inn to arrest them. Both of them. "There's been a coup d'état." Monsieur Gérard thrust at them the proclamation that had been posted all over Paris, now going up all over France. Cosette read the announcement, read the telegram, but heard only the warning bell from the *Saint-Joseph*.

"I've left the police there with an open bottle so I could warn you. You mustn't come back. You mustn't go to Paris."

"England," said Cosette, echoing the insistent bell of the *Saint-Joseph*. "England."

"Yes, madame. Yes! England. From here, Boulogne, you can almost see England. You'll be safe there. I can arrange passage for you now, this morning."

"Paris," said Marius.

"No!" Cosette cried, over the bell, over Marius's protest, over Gérard's pleading, and over another sound, distant and indistinct. "Please, Marius, we'll be safe in England. You go to England. I'll bring the children later. Oh, my love, Marius, listen to—"

Marius put his hand gently over Cosette's lips and moved his fingers up to brush away her tears. "My freedom has been given to me for a reason. If I don't use that freedom, I will have betrayed the last nineteen years, betrayed you, betrayed my friends, betrayed the sacrifice your father made in saving me. He could have taken you to England nineteen years ago. And he didn't."

"Please, Marius."

"Did you see the name on the telegram?" He took it from Monsieur Gérard and handed it to her. *Clerons*. Cosette paled and Marius remarked bitterly that the fifth man had indeed found a new uniform, a new master like the dog he was. "You go to Eng-land, Cosette."

"Without you?" She reached up and followed the line of the sad scar down his temple, the smooth beard, the best-loved lips. "What safety is there for me without you?" Without further protest, she took his arm and walked toward the town, her back to the *Saint-Joseph*, the sea, the coast of England. The world had invaded the country of love.

Chapter 31

*D*awn comes late in December, and in its gray and pearly light a young woman clad in a cloak and bonnet of matronly brown made her way through Paris toward the Seine. The night's rain had turned to snow, and working people roused that Tuesday morning to find they had no newspapers, only decrees slathered on the walls, that Paris—the most musical of cities—had been silenced, no church bells, no vendors' cries or cornets. People huddled and muttered before the proclamations posted everywhere. Fantine read the first one she saw, read it aloud for the benefit of the illiterate pressing near her: the Assembly was dissolved, universal suffrage restored, new elections and martial law declared. Martial law was certainly everywhere evident. Soldiers in tight formations guarded squares, their artillery already in place, their bayonets fixed, their officers on horseback, their breath steaming in the cold air. The omnibuses were running, but squads of police had commandeered cabs, and heavy traffic in the direction of Mazas prison proceeded in an orderly fashion. No one stopped or bothered Fantine till she came to the Petit-Pont, where soldiers had set up a checkpoint. A young soldier demanded to see her papers, to know her reason for crossing the river, remained unmoved when she said her mother was sick, until she added the magic word *cholera*, and then he stepped back and let her pass.

With the complicity of the cook (coffee and the apple tart made the night before, which Madame Carême used to lure the guard into the kitchen) and in Madame Carême's plain cloak and bonnet, Fantine had managed to leave the house. She made her way across the river to find the Café Rigolo and the Starling. If her parents were arrested in Boulogne, then they were arrested, but if they weren't, she knew they would return to Paris, and she knew the Starling could help hide them from Clerons. At Saint-

Séverin, she asked people clustered about the decree on the church wall the way to the Café Rigolo, and finally someone pointed her toward Saint-Sulpice. Like most Parisians, Fantine had limited experience outside her own district, and this side of the river, this slummy neighborhood, seemed to her a completely different country.

Ironically, in the rue des Aveugles, the street of the blind, the decree was plastered on the back of Saint-Sulpice, and there Fantine found the Café Rigolo. Even this early, it was smoky inside and so warm steam ran down the windows, so insular that the sight of a stranger dimmed conversation. She went to the zinc counter and asked for the Starling.

Madame Fagennes made a few deprecating remarks about the Starling, and then, with a dry snort, she directed Fantine to the Changer's. "If you get lost, just follow the good republicans. They'll all be looking for a new suit of clothes and a passport out. It's that or prison. Revolution is good for the Changer's business."

"This is not revolution," declared Fantine, her father's daughter, "this is a coup d'état by cowards."

But Madame Fagennes was correct about the good republicans. There in the dreary impasse, before the uninviting doors, harried by the barking dogs, Fantine was not alone in being ushered into the vast warehouse. Perhaps half a dozen others, all muffled against the cold and detection, waited here too.

"Wait your turn," snapped the Countess when Fantine came up to the table where the old woman sat with a pen and a huge, leatherbound ledger.

"I'm not here for—for changing. I'm looking for someone. That's all. The Starling."

"What for?"

"I need him."

The Countess put down her pen, regarded Fantine sourly. "You're in trouble then?"

"Yes, madame."

A look at once gratified and resigned crossed the Countess's face. She told a Jondrette to go get Gabriel and pointed Fantine to a chair. The Countess studied Fantine. "Do I know you?"

"I don't think so. I can't imagine that you would."

The Countess busied herself with a middle-aged man, a journalist, in fact, from a socialist newspaper, who desperately wanted changing—and a passport out of France.

When Jondrette returned with the Starling in tow, he was still rubbing sleep from his eyes and pulling a shirt over his head till he saw Fantine. He stood up straight, slicked down his hair, and said her name.

"Mademoiselle Pontmercy?" cried the Countess, looking up. "Fantine Pontmercy?"

"Pontmercy's been arrested," said the journalist. "His name is on the list."

Twenty minutes later the Starling, wearing a slouch hat, crossed the Pont-Neuf with Fantine, followed at a short distance by a Jondrette, armed with a ragpicker's staff and a basketful of garbage, including the stiff carcass of a cat, which he used to good effect when he was stopped by soldiers checking all parcels.

The snow continued to fall, but it did not stick to the ground as they made their way along the rue de Rivoli and the rue Saint-Honoré toward *La Lumière*. By now all Paris was up and about, all Paris had read, all Paris knew and talked of nothing else; there was muttering and mumbling, but the omnibuses ran, cabmen swore at their horses, most shops were open, and the cafés doing brisk business in coffee and brandy, but no newspaper hawkers crowed in the streets, indeed the whole noisy commercial life of Paris was subdued, silenced, but not resisting.

At the rue de Combray they walked past the military guard, bayonets fixed, who stood before the door at *La Lumière*. No one was permitted in, the soldier told them.

"And Monsieur Pontmercy?" asked Fantine.

"Arrested."

When Fantine, the Starling, and Jondrette arrived back at the rue des Filles-du-Calvaire, the police van still stood before the house and a police guard still stood by the carriage gate. They left the Jondrette, his staff and basket, to keep watch for the Pontmercys; should they try to return home, he would warn them. Then the Starling led Fantine around to the back, to the stable. The driver was nowhere in sight, but the horse and carriage were still there. The garden gate was locked.

"I don't want to go home," said Fantine. "I want to stay with you."

"No, you'll be safe here. Your parents will want to know you're safe. It's not safe on the streets of Paris."

"They seem quiet enough."

"It will take a while. Maybe a few days. The Opposition is scattered, arrested, silenced, but the people of Paris will not be herded without protest. No, mademoiselle, I thank you for coming to get me, and I will hide your parents if they come back to Paris, but I am responsible for your safety too."

"No, you're not."

"I am now." He found a barrel and used it to clamber up to the carriage-house roof, pulling Fantine after him, holding her hand across the slick, frosted roof tiles and leading her to the garden wall, easily reached from the roof. In a single bound, he jumped down into the garden and beckoned her to follow. The wall was thick and perhaps eight feet high, but his fall was broken by the remnants of herbs and strawberries, winter weeds and the ground not altogether frozen. "Jump."

"I can't. It's too far. I'm afraid."

"You won't get hurt."

"I can't. I'm afraid."

"Jump. Just close your eyes and jump. I'll catch you."

He did catch her, but fell back himself, and they rolled over into the broken mint and sage, the crushed leaves of strawberry plants exuding a winy smell, at once heady and dank. They lay there longer than they needed to perhaps, just a moment longer, then slowly sat up and brushed the leaves from their clothes, awkwardly, self-consciously.

The kitchen door was bolted, though once Madame Carême saw them she opened it quickly, cursed the Starling, fussed over Fantine, and told them Clerons was in the library with Jean-Luc. The servant who had taken up their coffee had good news: Monsieur and Madame Pontmercy had escaped arrest in Boulogne. Then she drew them back into the little basement room, where Verdier stood by the fire, looking more taciturn than usual. He greeted Fantine respectfully and remarked to the Starling there would be a lot of work for a runner over the next few days. "When you find Monsieur and Madame Pontmercy, you can take them to my apartment in the rue du Caire, Starling. They'll be safe there for a while and you can tell him that what's left of the Opposition will gather at the Café Roysin. The password is *What is Joseph doing?*"

"Who is at the Café Roysin?"

"Whoever escapes arrest. Not many. Anyway, I'm off to find a press. A printer needs a press."

"But they're all closed up."

"I'll find something, though I think we're doomed."

"Why are we doomed?" asked Fantine.

Verdier nodded toward Gabriel. "You remember the June Days?"

"The working people of Paris, the ones who fight, they don't care that the Assembly has been dissolved, mademoiselle," said Gabriel. "Why should they? Three years ago the Assembly sent the army out to kill us—and they did. The Assembly took away the right to vote for most of these men. The Assembly betrayed the revolution more than Bonaparte. Will the workers of Paris fight for the Assembly? No."

"They might fight for their freedom," mused Verdier, "if they once understand what this means. But—" he shrugged in the Parisian fashion. "There are a hundred thousand soldiers in the city now. Six thousand cannon in the forts, field pieces set up in every major square. They have ammunition, guns, food, fodder enough for the Russian campaign. And the Opposition are arrested, to a man. Everyone from Cavaignac to Thiers—"

The Starling laughed. "So Cavaignac will taste prison bread. Good. I hope he chokes on it."

"That's what people are saying," observed Verdier. "That's why it will be hard to rouse them to fight. You know the old saying 'The enemy of my enemy is my friend.' Monsieur Pontmercy will return to Paris. I know him. I have known him for twenty years. But, mademoiselle, please listen, if you see your parents, tell them to flee. If they stay in France, they'll be jailed. Exile is all they can hope for. I'm sorry to say this, but it's true." Verdier pulled open the little door to the basement room, and a rush of cold December hurled in. "Bonaparte has the army, the telegraph, the press, the railways; it's criminal what he's done, but brilliant. He's made the coup d'état look like the coup de grâce."

Chapter 32

*I*t was the wind Cosette remembered, the wind, the words, and the shot. She remembered the shot as if it were singular. Impossible, of course. There were many shots, many words, and the wind was ubiquitous, chilled, wrung from the stones of Paris, which upon their return was at once so familiar and so foreign, so dangerous and uncertain that they had to change their meeting places with other Opposition leaders seventeen times in forty-eight hours. Years later, when Cosette tried to remember, that same wind came up and sheared time off memory, tousled memory, jumbled memory to defy chronology, so that the single shot stood clean and unencumbered by causality.

Sometimes she thought she had heard the shot before it happened, that she had heard it on the dock in Boulogne, over the clang of the *Saint-Joseph*'s bell, on the desperate journey back to Paris, in the two days they spent on the run, having been warned away from their own home by a Jondrette. Sometimes she thought she had heard it in those few moments of sleep she could snatch, even in their furtive meetings with other Opposition leaders to frame, finally, a document. Verdier, the printer, found a press, though not without cost—two men lost their lives for this press— but it got out five hundred copies dated 3 December 1851. *To the people: Louis-Napoléon is outlawed, the state of siege is abolished, universal suffrage is reestablished, long live the Republic! To arms!* (signed) *The United Radicals.* They had five hundred copies, to the five hundred thousand copies of Bonaparte's declaration.

Then, on 4 December, as she and Marius hurried through the streets, they saw the wind pick up the United Radicals' declaration and blow it, high overhead, down into the street, dancing along in the wet gutters till it got too sodden to move any farther. Marius reached down, plucked the resolve of the United Radicals from the mud and the gutter, held it gingerly, remarking that it had cost two lives to get it printed, and yet it blew like ash, the flotsam, jetsam, the wreck of an idea.

She heard the shot then and it hadn't been fired yet. Perhaps she had it confused with all the other shots because, while the Declaration of the United Radicals blew about Paris, the announcement of 1 December stayed plastered firmly to the buildings, despite the rain, despite the snow, as did the edicts following, those of 3 December, they stayed on the walls. To pull them down was an offense punishable by death and anyone doing so WILL BE SHOT, anyone having political meetings, posting political documents, crying any seditious phrase WILL BE SHOT, people arrested in constructing or defending barricades WILL BE SHOT, people with weapons in their hands WILL BE SHOT, and, as it turned out, people with smoke or powder on their clothes WILL BE SHOT, anyone with three days' growth of beard, anyone who looks like he hasn't slept WILL BE SHOT, representative Baudin of the disbanded Assembly WILL BE SHOT three times in the neck and head, will die, a man singing "La Marseillaise" on the boulevard du Temple WILL BE SHOT, anyone robbing the gas men of keys or gaslight rods, trying to control the darkness in the fighting districts, WILL BE SHOT, anyone wounded and many arrested WILL BE SHOT—how better to empty the prisons, which are filling with men who are tearing up the streets of Paris, especially in the workingmen's *quartiers*, Bonne-Nouvelle, Saint-Denis, Saint-Martin, Saint-Antoine, Saint-Eustache, and the market districts, where the streets are twisted and defy the logic of an army, where barricades can be quickly built and defended, insurgents ducking in and out of passages, streets, alleys, knowing that the object is not to defend these barricades to the death but to buy time, to keep the fight going till Paris could be roused, till the people who had been betrayed in June 1848 could be made to understand they were being betrayed again.

Early in this struggle, the casualties inflicted on the army were more than those suffered by the insurgents, who knew the streets, the twists, the lanes, and impasses. The army was comprised of French peasants, who would follow orders, but the workers of Paris follow instincts. Perhaps that's why the army took the fight from the gutters, and put it on the broad and fashionable boulevards, where people can and WILL BE SHOT. To that end, there were gathered over sixteen thousand troops—lancers, grenadiers, gunners, infantry, cavalry—moving eastward from the boulevard des Italiens to the boulevard Montmartre, where holiday crowds gathered, while the military marched and the cavalry rode, their horses' hooves clanging on the cold paving stones. A single shot rang out. Who fired and from whence? No one knew. No one ever knew. Cosette did not hear this shot, though she heard ones subsequent; all Paris, all France heard the ones subsequent, the shots and screams, as the army swept the boulevards with fire, and the unarmed WILL BE SHOT, at Tortoni's they WILL BE SHOT, as it and the other fashionable boulevard cafés are raked with fire; the cannon follows the lance at the Maison d'Orée and the Café de Paris, and they, the rich, the well-fed, the fashionable, WILL BE SHOT, from the Madeleine to the boulevard Montmartre, they WILL BE SHOT: a seamstress, a bookseller, pharmacists, servants, a gaggle of nursemaids, people standing in front of theatres on 4 December WILL BE SHOT, children WILL BE SHOT, a boy running, taking refuge in a toy shop amongst the mechanical toys displayed for the season, WILL BE SHOT, all along the boulevards, the military run riot, unchecked, attacking the citizens of Paris, who WILL BE SHOT. Men, women, children, frock coat and smock, cloak and bonnet, they are, they become, the dead, phantom witnesses to the transformation of Louis-Napoléon. By the time the short winter dusk falls on 4 December 1851, the man who had invaded Boulogne with a vulture tied to the mainmast has the vulture tied to his reputation forever.

But the shot Cosette heard for the rest of her life was not in these volleys on the boulevards, but in the barricade on the rue du Petit-Carreau, the intersection there at Saint-Sauveur, there in that last knot of paving stones, that last labyrinth of fortified streets, which had not yet fallen to the army on 4 December. Not so very far from the rue Mondétour, not so very far from the past, which she knew had come to claim him: nineteen years later Marius was again behind a barricade with Verdier and Pajol. Only this time Cosette was there too, huddled in a doorway, and her father was not there to save him, and the *Saint-Joseph* was not there to pull him from these waters, and the long, clawed hand of death he had eluded nineteen years before would surely snare him now. She knew all this and still she stayed, refused Marius's entreaty, ignored his wishes, his express orders that she should leave and find safety without him. Finally she had said simply, "If you do not succumb to my beseeching, why should I succumb to yours? If your life is yours to command, why should my life not be at my own command? I will not leave you." So, in the dark, the cold, the hunger, the fatigue, and with Marius, Verdier, Pajol, the Starling, and perhaps two dozen others, Cosette hunkered behind the barricade at rue du Petit-Carreau and rue Saint-Sauveur, waiting for the attack they expected at dawn.

But by dawn it would be all over. Because at ten-thirty that night they heard cannonade, and following that, the volley of musket fire; the flash of firepower lit up the sky overhead and shook the ground beneath their feet. The army had set up a cannon in the small square behind Saint-Eustache, pointed it at the barricade at the rue Mauconseil—the only defended barricade between Saint-Eustache and the rue du Petit-Carreau. When Mauconseil fell . . .

The barrage from the rue Mauconseil rocked the whole area as it exploded. Its defenders stayed till their ammunition ran out, or until they died, and the soldiers scaled the barricades at the rue Mauconseil, bayoneting the already dead, the wounded, battering in the doors of houses lining the street, running upstairs, dragging men out and insisting the women light the candles in every window, ordering the people of Paris to light the army's way to the rue du Petit-Carreau, to illuminate their advance. In an hour's time the way to Petit-Carreau was freckled with light from every window, and the army fell back to get ready for the assault.

Behind this barricade Verdier handed Marius a gun, and said, "*Carpe ho ras,* my friend."

Marius embraced him, but declined the weapon. "In civil war I will only go halfway. I will die if need be, but I will not kill my countrymen."

Marius turned to Cosette, pulled her close against him, whispered to her. Unhearing, she nodded; she thought he smiled, but perhaps not. Perhaps he said something else. If he did those words were lost in the shock of his next words, after he had loosed her hands and stood, at the top of the barricade, unarmed and bare-headed, and Cosette screamed and Verdier caught at her.

"Citizens!" Marius cried out. "Citizens of the army! Hear me! Have we not bathed and waded and supped on the blood of our countrymen? Why do we fight? We are men of the same nationality, the same country, the same God. The people are the army and the army cannot fire on the people. Have we not—all of us—eaten the bitter bread of civil war? Citizens!" His voice echoed up and down the narrow street, between the buildings, and every man behind the barricades, every woman near a window, perhaps all the people of Paris listened to him, to his words, wafting out, blowing, as the appeal from the United Radicals had blown about in the wind, the revolutionary wind sweeping through Europe.

He told the army that the soldiers of France who had fought at Austerlitz could not, in conscience, take the lives of their own men. "We are your men as you are ours!" and then Marius climbed over the barricade and started walking toward the rue Mauconseil, where the soldiers were readying their attack. "You are the peasants of France," he called out to the army who awaited him at the end of the street. "We are the workingmen of France. We are brothers. I will not kill! Join us! Join your brothers!"

As he walked, one by one, the candles in the windows went out; perhaps the people in the buildings blew them out, wishing to protect the speaker in the mantle of darkness, perhaps the candles were blown out by that same revolutionary wind, but Marius vanished into the night, swallowed up by the darkness, and only his words and the sounds of his footsteps reached his friends, footfalls splashed through the central gutter, his words calling out to end civil war, blowing back toward 1848 and forward toward 1871, blowing back toward the rue du Petit-Carreau and forward to the rue Mauconseil, where there came another word, a singular word, a command, *Fire!* But the silence persisted. No one obeyed the command. *Fire!* again cried the officer into the darkness, the narrow street, and again there was silence, save for Marius's voice calling out to the army—his arms outspread—calling to them to ignore their officers and answer their hearts, to join their *fraternité*, the *égalité* of workingmen and women who cherished *liberté*, to oppose Louis-Napoléon, who had put his bootheel on the neck of France.

And behind the barricade at the rue du Petit-Carreau, Cosette, Verdier, Gabriel, Pajol, and the others stood up, looked over, peered into what they could not see, only believing that the man, the words, the unarmed appeal had defeated the enemy, the army who resisted yet another command to *Fire!*

Then there was the shot. That was the shot Cosette heard. The one she heard over and over for the rest of her life.

Chapter 33

*H*e was a runner, after all; he had a runner's body, a runner's instincts, a runner's luck dodging, darting, avoiding troops and sentries, armed squads mopping up the last of the resistance, and when he did not have a runner's luck, he had the *savate* kicks he'd learned from Pincher, which he could deliver with strength and, often, precision. He was the red specter, his clothes soaked through with blood, his hands and face and hair black with smoke and powder, running through the streets of Paris, which he knew better than he knew his own mother. Perhaps his own mother would not have known him.

Certainly Madame Carême did not know him. She opened the kitchen door at the rue des Filles-du-Calvaire, screamed, gasped when she recognized him. "Where are you wounded, Starling?"

"It isn't my blood."

"Then whose is it?" She drew him over to the fire and lit a couple of candles. It was about four in the morning.

"I can only talk to Jean-Luc, I mean Monsieur Pontmercy. Please."

She popped open a bottle of cognac, put more coals on the fire, and set some bread before him. One good swallow of the cognac made him instantly light-headed, and he sank into the chair before the fire, refused her questions, insisted on talking to Jean-Luc.

"Is it that bad then, Starling?"

"It's that bad."

Madame Carême was gone a long while, and he stared into the fire, seeing and not seeing, thinking and not thinking. Physically, all he could feel was the heat from the cognac pulsing in his very fingertips. It tasted of the powder that blackened his lips; the bread did too. He was afraid everything would taste of powder and smoke now as long as he lived. But he was alive. Or maybe he wasn't: looking up he saw Fantine, like an angel, clad in a long, white nightdress with ribbons at the high collar and the sleeves, a voluminous shawl wrapped round her shoulders, and her hair spread out across her shoulders. Surely she was in some unworldly dream, which could not possibly be concocted of the same terrible flesh, rampant blood as the rest of them, the flesh and blood he'd seen this night in the rue du Petit-Carreau. She reached out to touch him, but he recoiled, and insisted on talking to her brother.

"Jean-Luc isn't here."

"Where is he?"

She paused and then said, "There is a girl, Nicolette Lauriot, who lives in the rue du Haut-Moulin. That's where he is. Whose blood is this, Starling? Why have you come here dripping blood?"

"I can't say these things to you, mademoiselle. You're just a girl."

"Where are my parents, Starling? Where are they? Why aren't they with you? What message have you brought? What's happened to them? You must tell me."

He turned back to the fire and finished the glass of cognac; he rose, as though he faced the firing squad, and perhaps he did, because finally he had to tell her that her father was the bravest man he ever knew, that he had died in the bravest act, not fighting, but uniting.

"Oh Jesus—" cried Madame Carême, coming up behind Fantine and catching her in an embrace while Fantine wept. "And madame?"

Regarding his bloodstained rags as if seeing them for the first time, he replied, "I carried her, Pajol and I. She's wounded, but the bullet went through. Madame Pontmercy is fortunate, truly, that's what Thérèse says. It was the shoulder, not the heart or the head, but once she was hit—well, we had no ammunition anyway. Verdier said, leave me your guns and go, it's finished, it's over. And so Pajol and I, we left, carried Madame Pontmercy between us. We ran back to the rue Thévenot and cut up through the rue Danielle and over to the passage du Caire. Pajol tried to force the lock but couldn't, so we had to go the length of the rue du Caire, soldiers everywhere, till finally we got to Verdier's building. The concierge let us in only because she recognized Pajol. Thérèse, well, she knew. She guessed."

"Guessed what?" Fantine's eyes were wide, her face pale, her lip bitten white.

The Starling leaned against the mantelpiece, the heat from the fire cooking his clothes to a rust color, drying his hair in matted clumps. "Verdier is still at the barricade. He stayed there so your mother could live, mademoiselle. So I could live. And Pajol." He turned back to face the weeping Fantine. He longed to take her in his arms and comfort her, but even if he could have touched her, he wouldn't, not in these bloodstained clothes. The gulf between them yawned the wider for her white nightgown and his red rags. "Please don't cry, mademoiselle," he said ineffectually, "I mean, go ahead and cry. Cry all you want. What else is there to do?"

"We need a doctor," declared Madame Carême. "We'll take a doctor with us."

"No, it's too dangerous. A doctor will betray her."

"A doctor wouldn't!"

"Ask Pajol. She's safe there at Thérèse's, at least she's safe unless the army comes through. They're marching off all the wounded, taking them to prisons."

"They wouldn't take a woman!" cried Madame Carême.

"They would take the Holy Mother if she had powder stains and bloodstains."

"What can we do then?" asked Madame Carême, as Fantine seemed to sink in front of the fire.

The Starling ran his hand over his face, his dry lips. "The only possible safety is in exile. She will have to leave France. I don't know when. I don't know if she can travel, but when she can, she must leave. Somehow. We'll have to wait in any event," he thought aloud. "The army has stopped all civilian railway travel, and only troops are moving now in France. But when she can," he came back around to his thought, "she'll need plain clothes, some kind of disguise. My grandmother can help, probably, arrange some papers. She'll need money. Any jewelry that she has should be sewn into the clothes and—"

"What can we do *now?*" Madame Carême rephrased her question.

"Now? Wait. Stay here and I'll come back when—"

"No." Fantine looked up at him. "I won't wait. I won't wait and suffer. I'm going to my mother. If she can't have a doctor, fine. I will be there. I'm going to the rue du Caire with you."

"It's too dangerous, mademoiselle. Please. I came to tell you, not to take you."

"I'm going, Starling."

"We're going." Madame Carême pulled two baskets off hooks overhead and began filling them with bread and wine and cheese and brandy. "You will not go alone, *ma petite*, you—" She broke down and wept into her hands. "I will stay with you through these times, these terrible, terrible times."

"You see, Starling," Fantine regarded him levelly through her tears, "we are going."

"Not till dawn then. It's too dangerous to move about in darkness."

"You did it."

"Me, I have done it all my life, but you, you don't know how. Besides, I must find Jean-Luc. I must tell him . . ." The Starling swallowed with difficulty. "The truth. He should know. He must know."

"At dawn, then," said Fantine, "we'll get Jean-Luc and go on to Mama. Take those bloodstained clothes off, Starling. I'll fetch you something of Jean-Luc's to wear."

Slowly he pulled the bloodstained shirt over his head and, shivering, he dropped it into the fire. "The first time I came to this house, I walked out with Jean-Luc's clothing. This last time I shall do the same."

"This is the last time, isn't it?" Fantine stood beside him and watched the shirt burn.

"Everything is changed," he said, as though he'd bitten down on something sweet and found an iron core. "Everything we knew is over. Everything is gone."

At dawn, when the Pontmercy carriage rolled out, gray clouds groveled overhead, lit by flames from burning buildings near Saint-Denis, and the smell of smoke and powder laced the air. On the boulevard du Temple there were soldiers, and the driver, forewarned, turned quickly off that street and rattled through narrow lanes. Fantine and Madame Carême sat across from each other, the Starling, his face and hands washed clean, dressed in unstained clothing, peered out the window, looking for trouble. When the carriage halted in the rue du Haut-Moulin, the Starling jumped out and told the driver to wait, unless he saw soldiers, in which case he should return to the rue des Filles-du-Calvaire.

The concierge in Nicolette's building, an acrobat herself till rheumatism set in, barred his way with a broom. Despite his clean clothes, clean hands and face, she called him a red republican and radical thug.

"I'm for the Emperor," he declared, *"Vive Napoléon!"*

She stood in the courtyard and watched him go up to the top floor, evidently reassured when, on the third-floor landing, he met Arsène Huvet coming out of the latrine. Arsène looked shaky and gray and did not recognize the Starling. Not until Gabriel made some insolent remark did Arsène's eyes clear, and then he followed him to Nicolette's.

"Pontmercy won't be happy to see you," commented Arsène, opening the door.

"He never is."

Frost curtained the windows and the fire was out. On the mantel and the few tables there were candles burned down to the sockets, and empty wine bottles stood in crazy formations amongst plates where the remnants of a late supper lay congealed in grease and the cats stepped gingerly in and out of the plates, nibbling this and that. The air was thick with cigarette smoke and patchouli, and on the floor in a pile of finery there was a good-looking bare haunch. When Arsène sat down beside this haunch, the girl rolled over, burped, and groaned.

For a moment Gabriel thought perhaps he'd come to a foreign country. How could they not have heard the cannons, volleys of musket fire? How could they still lie here, eating, drinking, smoking? After everything he had seen this night, Gabriel found this room and the people in it inconceivable. He called Jean-Luc's name, and finally Jean-Luc came out of the bedroom, followed by a girl with tousled blond hair. They were both barefoot; she was pulling on a tawdry satin wrapper, and he was fastening his trousers.

"You're still wearing my clothes, I see," he said tartly.

"I have some sad news."

"You always have bad news," but Jean-Luc had paled significantly, and he walked to a table, tried two bottles before he found one that still had some wine. Hands trembling, he poured some into a glass. "Is it my father?"

"Yes."

Jean-Luc drained the wine. "Is he dead?" he asked in a flat voice.

"Yes."

"On a barricade?"

"Rue du Petit-Carreau."

"In a damp gutter? Behind paving stones and overturned carts? Fighting with people like you?"

"Yes."

"Fighting for people like you, Starling?" he added with a sneer. "Giving up his life as he gave up his freedom, so people like you and your vile ragpicking relatives can have the vote—" he took another swift and trembling swill—"can walk upright and not stooped over like beasts of burden?"

Nicolette, behind Jean-Luc, put her arms around his shoulders, murmured something consoling, and held him while the Starling stood silently tense.

Jean-Luc spoke with exaggerated control, swallowing swiftly. "You see now, Starling, how much better it would have been if Clerons had arrested him? He'd be alive."

"Maybe. There are rumors of executions of prisoners in the Champ-de-Mars, at the Prefecture of Police. They say they're shooting prisoners above the sewer grating in the rue Jérusalem."

"Those are common people, you fool!" Jean-Luc freed himself from Nicolette's embrace. "People like you, picked up for drunkenly singing 'La Marseillaise' in the street. Influential people would never be shot like that! Bonaparte just wants the influential people out of Paris, out of France. That's all. Bonaparte only wanted my father's voice stilled and his pen stilled."

"His voice and his pen are stilled now."

In the thick, ensuing silence, Arsène volunteered, "Perhaps it's not the time to say it, Pontmercy, but you are the baron now."

"It's not the time to say it," Nicolette snapped.

"I have other bad news." The Starling drew himself up, consciously imitating Marius's dignity. "Your mother went with him. She would not leave his side. She was at the barricade. She fought too. When he fell, she nearly went over the barricade herself."

"Over the barricade?" asked Nicolette incredulously, as Jean-Luc fell into a chair, doubled up his fists, and hit the table repeatedly. "Why would she go over the barricade?"

"Because he went over the barricade, because Monsieur Pontmercy walked toward the army without weapons, with only words. He was the bravest man I ever knew."

"And Jean-Luc's mother," Nicolette asked, "what of her?"

"She stood up to go after him, and Verdier pulled her back down, but in the fight, before we ran out of ammunition, she was hit."

Jean-Luc looked up from the table. "And?"

"She's wounded. I don't know how badly, I just—"

"Oh God, if only they'd let themselves be arrested. She'd be whole. My father would be alive. This is your fault, Starling. Where is she?"

Warring within Gabriel were all the duties of his class, the obligations incumbent on him simply for being born the bastard son of a *fille publique,* the grandson of a ragpicker, spawn of the street and gutter, and all those social roles and rules fought against his intelligence. Or was it intelligence? Might it not be simple, instinctive revulsion against the decadence here? Or the old reflexive enmity with Jean-Luc? Perhaps it was the losses the Starling had suffered this night, or the sense he had of having saved Madame Pontmercy, as she had once saved him. Perhaps no one had saved anyone at all. Perhaps Jean-Luc was altogether right, and if Monsieur Pontmercy had been arrested, at least he would have been alive.

"Well, where is she?"

"I can't tell you," he said at last, adding, "I won't tell you."

"She's my mother!"

"For the moment she's my responsibility."

"You dogmeat! You filthy jail louse!"

"I don't trust you. You might tell Clerons and that would endanger many others as well. Perhaps you're right and she should have been arrested, and if she wants to give herself up later, when she's well enough, that's her decision. For the moment, me, I'm committed to keeping her out of prison. I'll send you a message."

"You are a thief, a guttersnipe, and a bone licker. You haven't the right to touch her hem!"

"And where were you, Monsieur Pontmercy—Baron Pontmercy—" he snarled, "when I carried her through the fire and out of the battle? Where were you when your father, his words his only weapon, walked into the arms of the enemy?"

"I'll kill you one day."

"Jean-Luc! He's in shock," Nicolette protested to Gabriel. "He doesn't mean it."

"Next week," said the Starling, feeling the stale air here suck the last of his strength, "cross the river and go to the Café Rigolo, rue des Aveugles near Saint-Sulpice. There'll be a note for you. If not a note, a message."

"You have no right to do this," declared Jean-Luc, turning as though he might lunge at Gabriel. "You are not her son!"

Gabriel regarded the girl on the floor, the fallen wine bottles, the cats with their paws on the plates, and the blond, disheveled girl at Jean-Luc's side. "Are you her son?"

Jean-Luc did lunge, reached for a wine bottle, cracked its neck into a jagged weapon, and came at the Starling, who, with one swift *savate* kick, sent it flying from his hand. Then Gabriel backed toward the door, left the apartment, clattered down the stairs, and said, *"Vive Napoléon,"* again to the concierge.

The carriage was still waiting and he got in swiftly, curling up on the floor, where they piled blankets and baskets around him, and Fantine put her feet up on his back.

They were stopped twice by sentries. The first, seeing only two women in the carriage, waved them on. The next was not so obliging. He ordered them back, saying that no one was allowed into the Bonne-Nouvelle district because of the fighting. The sentry's bayonet had blood dried on it. Fantine pulled Madame Carême closer to her, the older woman's bonnet obscuring her face. "Cholera," she whispered. He waved them on quickly, and the carriage clattered over the stones; where the stones had been pulled up and fashioned into barricades, the wheels sank slightly into mud, churned into a bronze color, mixed with blood and suffering.

The Starling, knotted uncomfortably on the carriage floor, could feel the cold penetrate underneath him and the warmth from Fantine's feet on his back. He could feel her warmth through her shoes, through the blankets, through his clothes. That warmth radiated out through his whole body, and still he wept silently, knowing this would be his only opportunity to cry for a long, long while.

Chapter 34

On Christmas Day a bearded sergeant at the Gare du Nord sat at a makeshift desk checking the papers of everyone with tickets for the train to Brussels. On either side of him stood two young guards, armed. The train had not yet arrived at the station, but nearly everyone came early, knowing these checks were mandatory and time consuming. For the most part, the French submitted without protest, but then there was an American journalist who reacted very badly, railing against Louis-Napoléon, declared he had stolen the Republic, stolen liberty from the French people, "Snatched it in an infamous deed!"

"Have you not heard of the recent elections?" inquired the sergeant. "With universal suffrage, monsieur, five million Frenchmen have endorsed the coup d'état. We French, we love Louis-Napoléon."

"The army loves him. The church loves him," sputtered the American. "France does not love him."

The sergeant gave the American a garlicky grin. "Soon they say Louis-Napoléon will declare himself Emperor—and what might France not do with another Emperor? Perhaps this time we'll invade North America," he warned the American. Moving on, he took papers from a French family, bourgeois, with scampering brats, and then a Scots couple, and next a troupe of actors with trunks full of costumes and scenery, all of which had to be opened and inspected.

Behind the actors a nondescript group waited, two women, a young girl, and a young man who told the sergeant he was not going with them, only there to help his mother and aunt get their few things on the train. The sergeant rifled through their two parcels each, clothing tied up in shawls, checked their third-class tickets and their papers. *Jeanne-Louise Poillard, age 38, brown eyes, round face, heavy build. Distinguishing scars, burn on the left hand.* "Your left hand, please?" The sergeant turned it over, found the ancient burn. *Occupation, cook. Reason for travel: work.* "You can't cook in France?" inquired the sergeant.

"Everyone can cook in France. I must go where my talents stand out."

"Go to England," he said sourly. "Next."

"This is my daughter, monsieur le sergent. She's just a girl. Surely she doesn't need papers."

"She doesn't look like a girl. She looks like a woman."

"You are too kind," said Fantine with a curtsy.

"Next." *Madeleine Lascaux, age 36, eyes blue, light build, small features, distinguishing scars, none. Occupation, domestic servant.* "You don't look very strong for a servant."

Madame Carême put her bulk between the sergeant and Cosette. "She could throw you downstairs fast enough if she found you in the wrong bed!"

Behind them, the rest of the line laughed and the sergeant eyed Madame Carême. "Your bed? I like women with meat on their bones." Then he reminded them there would be another check before the train left, "So don't anyone think he can sneak on."

"No sir," replied the Starling.

The four found a bench along the wall, Cosette between Fantine and Gabriel. Fantine took her hand, whispered, "Just keep your strength up, Mama. Tomorrow night we'll be in London."

"He'll come, won't he? Jean-Luc?" The twill cloak was not heavy enough to keep Cosette altogether warm, but at least it was big enough to cover the bandages swathing her left shoulder and the sling in which rested her left arm. Pale, pinched, and hunched, Cosette kept hold of Fantine's hand as they both searched the station for Jean-Luc. "You gave him the message, didn't you, Starling?"

"I wrote down the day and the train and Madame Fagennes assured me he picked it up. It was him. He'll come."

Hawkers and vendors plied their wares along the tracks where family groups gathered; quarrelsome children were quickly hushed, often with a single swat, and lovers bade farewell. Old women huddled together, criticizing the young, and well-dressed men and women read the papers. There were only two papers in Paris to read: the official government organ and the unofficial government organ. The actors lounged and flirted, and it seemed to Cosette that the whole world had gone on in a way that was unthinkable. Marius was dead. How could the rest of the world continue without Marius? People traveling, quarreling, reading, eating, buying sweets and fruit and fried potatoes. Didn't they know Marius was dead? Didn't they know he could so easily have escaped to England from Boulogne—so swiftly, so certainly—and yet he chose to return to Paris, to unite the radicals, to embrace at last his enemies, the men who killed him. Men like that leering, good-natured sergeant. Didn't people here know all that? "I need to walk," she said, patting Fantine's hand and rising swiftly so her daughter would not see her tears. They came unbidden. Always. They could be fought, but they could not always be hidden.

Shivering, Cosette moved along the platform under the huge vaults of the station, looking for her son, whom she had not seen since that day in the Luxembourg Gardens. That last day. There was so much to say to him. So much to know. So much to tell. But it would all have to wait till they got to Brussels. Jean-Luc would ride first class, of course. From Brussels they could be together on the passage to England, to safety, to London, where her dear friend Helen Talbot lived.

"Free the larks, sir? Free the larks?"

Cosette's attention was caught by a bedraggled old woman nearby, pulling a sack and approaching the American journalist. She was squat, her shoes flapping, her face wizened as a spider's belly; her hands were black with dirt, very strong, and the sack she pulled was tied up and churning somehow. "Free the larks, sir?" Even from this distance Cosette could see the sack was alive, the churning caused by birds stuffed into it, and over the station noises Cosette could suddenly hear their squeals, their frantic chirping, their imprisoned cries. "Free the larks? Twenty centimes for a lark's freedom?" she wheedled the American, who, disgusted, brushed past her. She approached the well-dressed family with the scampering brats, and with one long, yellow nail, she beckoned the children toward her and her terrible sack. "Free the larks, pets? Twenty centimes each, thirty for two."

The children got the money from their parents and the old woman reached into the sack, wrist deep, and came out with a lark, which she gave to the girl, who screamed. The lark fell, and stunned by the blow, writhed on its back, squawking desperately till it flung itself over and flew away. The girl cried out she wanted another, but the old woman held out for more money while reaching in for one to give the boy. This lark was dead. She flung it down and got him out a live one.

"They're a great delicacy cooked," the old woman said, approaching the actors. "They say the peasants of France have been told that with Louis-Napoléon for emperor they need only walk into the fields, heads back, and cooked larks will fall into their open mouths. Would you like a lark? Fifteen centimes, ten for you, handsome," she teased an actor, who kicked the sack, and the birds squealed louder. The old woman moved away, coming toward the Scots couple, who waved her on with a look of revulsion. Cosette could not flee, stood rooted with horror as the old woman approached her.

"Free the larks?" She had a great wen on the side of her nose and her eyes were muddy, the whites yellow. "Free the larks?"

"Free them from . . ." Cosette licked her lips and tried again. "Free them from what?"

"Bondage," whispered the old woman confidentially, *"bondage."*

A gruff, masculine voice ordered the old woman to move on, and Cosette looked up to see her son standing before her. He gave the sack one final kick, and Cosette began to cry, whether for the sheer sight of Jean-Luc's face or for the larks, she did not know.

"Please, Mama, don't cry." He glanced suspiciously around. "Please, I can't bear it if you cry."

"Yes." She wiped her eyes. "I'll stop. I must. People will wonder what a fine gentleman like you is doing talking to me, but oh, my darling son, the sight of you!"

They did look odd, this well-dressed young man lavishing such courtesy on a small, plain, fragile-looking creature. He wore leather gloves, a high hat, a waistcoat, a frock coat, and a greatcoat over all. He lowered his head and his voice. "I would have come to you that night, that very night, but the filthy Starling wouldn't tell me where you were. Wouldn't tell me anything. I would have come before this."

"It's best, Jean-Luc, really. I don't want you implicated. When we're all in England, we'll be safe, but I must know now, your papa, did you find your father's body? Did you claim Marius's body and see he was decently buried? They say that all the dead were taken to Montmartre Cemetery, that people have to go there to claim their dead, and they make them bury them there so there will be no funeral cortèges in the streets. Did you find your father?" Tears spilled unheeded down her face.

"No. I didn't. Thérèse found Verdier, though. I saw her there. Did you know Verdier died?"

"I knew," Cosette said bitterly. "We held our hope till the very end, till Thérèse came back from the cemetery."

"Is that where you were? At Verdier's?"

"Has Marius gone into some common grave," she beseeched her son, "buried in an unmarked grave as though no one ever loved him?"

"No one seems to know," Jean-Luc admitted. "And now, well, they say there are no records of the dead."

"They don't know who they are?"

"They don't even know how many. Some say two hundred. Some say two thousand. No one knows for certain. I couldn't find Papa's body."

"Oh, Marius," Cosette wept. "Marius, Marius . . ."

Glancing about for soldiers, Jean-Luc nonetheless took her arm and steered her back to the little family group on the bench, where he nodded to his sister and exchanged uneasy glances with Gabriel. He took off his greatcoat, folded it, put it over his mother's knees, and knelt there before her. "Please, Mama, don't leave for England. Let me talk to Clerons."

"Clerons?" Cosette's tears dried instantly. "That Montfaucon *mouchard?*"

"Maybe they wanted to arrest Papa only, and perhaps you can be free."

"Please don't say anything more, Jean-Luc. I've endured everything else, but you are breaking my heart." She frowned. "Where is your valise?"

Jean-Luc took a deep breath. "I'm not coming with you. I'm not leaving Paris. I'm not going to go into squalid exile for nothing."

"For nothing?" exclaimed Fantine.

"I have no quarrel with Bonaparte—"

"Bonaparte killed your father," whispered the Starling harshly.

"You stay out of this. This is not your affair." Jean-Luc put his hands over Cosette's. "Mama, Bonaparte has no quarrel with me. He won't come after me. He won't come after Fantine."

"I am going with Mama," Fantine declared. "You astonish me."

The train heaved into the station, a great steaming, gasping, panting mechanical beast, and soldiers collected along the platform to check the tickets and papers of everyone getting on. "Free the larks!" shouted the old woman with her sack, emerging from the swirling steam and ash and smoke. "Free the larks!"

"Mama, I mourn my father and I would do anything to spare you more sorrow—"

"Then come with us, Jean-Luc," she implored, "I beg of you, don't desert me. We need you."

He rose. "I can't leave Paris. I won't go to London and I don't think you should. Let me talk to Clerons—"

"If you bargain with Clerons," said Cosette grimly, "you will end up as dirty as he is. If you bargain with Bonaparte, you will be a traitor to the Republic and your father."

"I'm not leaving France."

"You're deserting us?"

"You're leaving and I'm not coming with you." He pressed his coat into her arms and told her to keep it. "But you wear it. I'm sick of seeing the Starling in my clothes." He kissed both her cheeks, and then he rose and left them, his tall figure quickly swallowed up amongst the crowds on the platform in the chuffing vapor of the train, amidst the cries and calls of porters, passengers, soldiers.

"Free the larks!"

Cosette could not move at all. It required all three of them to get her ticket and papers verified, to get her into the third-class carriage, numb, struck dumb and vacant-eyed. They seated her beside Madame Carême

Across from her, Fantine stumbled over words, trying to thank the Starling, trying to say—something, she didn't even know quite what, and he, replying scattered, incoherent words, jumbled words, as he looked into her eyes, her beautiful young face framed by the plain bonnet. He hoisted their bags to the wooden rack over her head as the Scotswoman tripped on boarding, and fell against him. He caught himself, arched protectively over Fantine, his hands sliding down the walls to rest momentarily on her shoulders. Fantine's hand flew up to press his as she wept, tears unabashedly coursing down her face as she held his hand there.

The actors needed to board, and the Starling had to get out of the carriage so they could hoist their trunks in, one actor shooing his little dogs before him. The dogs yipped and yapped. Cosette closed her eyes over the shrill yammering, heard instead the cry and shriek of seagulls overhead in Boulogne, that morning, that last morning they had made love, that morning she had slept in Marius's arms, his body close to hers, his breath warm upon her neck, his hands . . . Now he lay in an unmarked grave, the body she had loved, buried amongst the people he had always believed in, amongst the anonymous dead, in the service of an idea he had always cherished. I have lost my husband, my son, and now my country, she thought, I am leaving France as I was supposed to have left nineteen years ago. Was this the journey she should have made then? If she had gone to England in 1832, would Marius have died then? Jean Valjean had saved Marius's life, and in saving Marius's life, he had saved Cosette's. That journey to England she was to have made nineteen years ago had been interrupted. Was this journey now a memory outside of time, and was she traveling toward possibilities discarded nineteen years ago? In France she risked prison. In England did she not face the prison of the past? In France she had no home she could return to, no son, no money, no safety, no husband. In England what would she have? Without Marius, what did it matter? With Marius dead, Cosette did not care where she lived. Perhaps, she thought, I am only truly native to the country of love. At least let me defend it.

"Free the larks!" The old woman hauled her roiling sack along the platform.

Cosette stood up, so hurriedly the blood drained from her head; she stepped over the dogs and parcels tucked underfoot and stashed overhead, over the shoes and knees of men, the smell of garlic sausages, stumbled, stopped before Fantine and kissed her.

From under her cloak she pulled out a small purse and pressed it into the girl's hands. "This is the money you brought from home. Five hundred francs. Keep it. Go to England. You must be safe from Clerons, but I cannot go."

"Mama! You must! It's for your safety—" Fantine cried, heedless of the other travelers, the soldiers strolling the platform.

"No, my sweet, sweet Fantine, I can't. Not now. My dearest, my sweet, beautiful daughter—" She turned to Madame Carême as the train heaved to life, panting, steaming, hissing. "Please, look after her."

Madame Carême wept as Cosette opened the door and stepped down to the platform, to the Starling's unabashed shock and protest. Cosette clung to the train window, to Fantine's hand, exclaiming endearments, trying to explain that memory had caught up with time; she wept and begged Fantine to understand, to wait for word in England. "You'll be safe there," she cried as conductors slammed compartment doors shut and the soldiers all stepped back.

"Free the larks! Last chance to free the larks!" A soldier pushed the old woman out of his way, and she called him a filthy name on her way out of the station, as the train gathered up its monstrous energy, like a dragon breathing fire, reveling in its own mechanical glory, defying inertia, and prepared to hurtle them all through time and space.

The station quickly emptied of civilians, though not of soldiers, and Cosette and the Starling left hurriedly. She felt something damp, placed her hand under her cloak high upon her shoulder, and found the wound had ruptured and the pain she felt there near her heart was not altogether metaphorical. The blood had seeped through the bandages and stained the plain brown dress. She leaned lightly on the Starling's arm, and he, silent, led her outside, where, once on the street, they heard the shriek of the train, which cut through the lightly falling snow and trailed away from Paris. Cosette squinted into the near distance, where she could see, splayed across a bench, the old woman, her sack of churning larks on the ground.

"Ten francs," said Cosette, to the Starling's dismay, "for the lot of them."

"The larks? Oh no, my dear, they're much more than that. Anyway, from the look of you, you haven't got ten francs to be sparing for a bunch of larks."

"Ten francs." Cosette dug into her pocket and found her last, her only ten-franc piece. "Untie the sack and let them go and it's yours. It's far better than a week's wages I'm offering you. I know the price of bread." Perhaps she knew the price of blood as well; her fingers were pink.

The old woman scratched the wen on her nose and then she snatched the money, unknotted the rope, and the bag fell away. The larks spun upward into the December sky, spiraling overhead in a great noisy conflagration of wings, flying up, high and free, roused from captivity, reveling in the snowflakes, reviving in the cold, dipping, swooping over the tracks and toward the river, flying high above the bridges and the boulevards, the churches and chimney pots, the towers and the twisted streets, the snowy slates and frosted rooftops of old Paris, over the Champ-de-Mars, where new snow fell, shrouding blood from prisoners' executions and sifting over the stones of the rue Jérusalem, where the sewer grating had stained red, over the theatres and the cafés, over the domes and sightless statues overlooking squares and markets, over the new graves in the Montmartre Cemetery, the marked and the unmarked alike.

BOOK III

SECOND EMPIRE

Part I

The Blue Rose

Through demolition and reconstruction, the Paris of his youth,
that Paris he religiously treasures in his memory, has become a
Paris of former times. Let him be permitted to speak of that
Paris as if it still existed. . . . As to himself, the author knows not
the new Paris and writes with the old Paris before his eyes in an
illusion which is precious to him. . . . All those places which we
see no more . . . the image of which we have preserved, assume a
mournful charm, return to us with the sadness of a spectre.

—VICTOR HUGO
Les Misérables

Chapter 1

*T*he dust of demolition settled over the city, a fine-grained, dun-colored snow, and it seemed to Cosette that the destruction of the old Paris paralleled the destruction of her old life and identity. The Baroness Pontmercy dissolved into the gutters and grim impasses of the south side of the Seine, resurrected as the Lark. Like the child she had been, the adult Lark felt the pinch of hunger, the prodding cold, and merely living taxed her every physical resource. Her flesh dwindled, and the knobs of her collarbones and wrists stood out; she developed a dry, relentless cough. Hunted in the present, haunted by the past, yet the adult Lark was not a friendless waif as the child had once been, but connected to a tribe of indigents, shy savages with dirty clothes and open hands. As the old Paris vanished under the pickaxe and a new Paris emerged from the scaffolding, as the people were evicted from dwellings that had stood and leaned and sagged together since the Middle Ages, as those dwellings were reduced to rubble and people found themselves exiled from their old lives, so Cosette became an exile from her own identity. Cosette had lost her family, but she had kept her freedom. She had lost her money, but she had kept her integrity. She came to understand why Jean Valjean had so cherished freedom and integrity. They did not keep you warm at night, but they kept you upright. The education she had received from Jean Valjean was not lost on her, indeed, in these years, she relearned those lessons daily: identity is fluid, integrity is not.

To elude capture, Jean Valjean had rented three different addresses, but Cosette had no such ample means. Ironically, what little she had was the gift of Marius's old royalist grandfather, the rope of pearls he'd given her on her wedding day. Cosette wore it, her wedding ring too, under her clothes, however tattered or grimy they might be. The pearls could be sold one at a time, but to earn her daily bread Cosette joined that vast troop, the rabble, the mob, the people of the streets of Paris, where everything was for sale.

Bodies were more valued than minds. Men sold the strength of their backs and their arms and their hands. Women sold the strength in their arms, joining that brigade of muscled laundresses, or they sewed fancy goods and sold the nimbleness of their fingers, while the rest of their bodies wizened and paled. Their breasts and haunches, the momentary peace or release they could offer between their thighs was as much a commodity as combs or bootlaces or buttons. Any and all goods could be sold, second- and third-hand clothes, clothes that had gone to rag, rags that had gone to tatters, bone, offal, cabbage stumps. In Paris, nothing was without its monetary value, usually paltry. The very beggars made it a point to trade in something—lead pencils, friction matches—or if not a commodity then an enter-taining story of woe, a skill. Music often masked the grimmest lives. Every one-armed man could play the horn. Concertinas were some-times passed down through generations of beggars. In good weather under the trees in the Champs-Elysées, a one-man band, bells on his head, a drum on his back, a guitar in his arms, could play almost any-thing, from the most bawdy and obscene ditty to the old revolu-tionary "Carmagnole" to Napoléon III's anthem, "Partant pour la Syrie," which no one ever requested. (He was forbidden by law to play "La Marseillaise.") There was another beggar in the place Madeleine who played the flute balancing himself on one arm. But Cosette had none of these talents, no strength in her arms or her back since she'd been wounded. But she could write. And that too was a trade, a skill that could be bartered for a few sous.

"The Baroness Pontmercy cannot be a scrivener," declared the Countess Crasseux as she regarded Cosette in the mirror of her small parlor.

"I'll be the Lark again," replied Cosette, picking up the scissors and cutting her hair even shorter. During her long illness, when her wounds had contracted infection and she'd suffered terrible fever, the Countess had cut Cosette's hair short. "The baroness needed all that lovely hair. The Lark needs only to wear caps and hats and wigs."

"Try this," said the Countess with some pride. "I made it myself, just for you."

It was an ancient rusty bonnet, with long gray hairs sweeping around the face and streaming out the back. Cosette wore it with a wool skirt, worn to long tatters at the hem over the usual red wool petticoat, also tattered. Her bodice was frayed, the collar missing, buttons mismatched, elbows worn thin unto invisible, but her new prize possession as the Lark was a warm shawl. On her bare feet she wore wooden shoes, which chafed and scraped her skin raw.

"The thing to do with these shoes is to bind your feet in rags before you put them on," the Countess advised. "Now let me see you walk." Cosette rose and walked about the little parlor while the Countess clucked and muttered. "You remember the story of the Costly Omelette?" she cautioned, for naturally, in the months the Countess had tirelessly nursed Cosette, she'd found occasion to tell her that story. Many occasions.

Cosette smiled weakly. She was pale and frail-looking after the long bout with blood poisoning and fever; her cheeks had hollowed out, and painted across her face, in her eyes, was suffering: the heartbreak of her husband's death, her son's betrayal, separation from her beloved daughter. "You don't understand, Countess, I don't need to invent the Lark. I have been the Lark in the past and I can be the Lark again."

"Perhaps your feet don't remember, though. Perhaps your chin has forgotten. Perhaps the shoulders—" She took Cosette's thin shoulders in her hands and rolled them inward, brought the chin down in the habitual droop of those without hope. She ran her fingertips over a shelf and rubbed the dirt along Cosette's face. From a small pot of a gummy, blackish substance, she took a fingerful and blacked two of Cosette's top teeth and one of the bottom. With a small, smudgy pencil, she darkened incipient creases along her forehead and between her brows. When she was finished, she announced, "Now you're the Lark."

She came to be known as the Plumed Lark; that was her scrivener's signature, a little drawing of a lark holding a quill pen at the bottom of each letter. A wedding pearl, sold through the Countess's connections, bought her a little booth, more like an umbrella with canvas sides, pens, paper, a blotter, a bit of ink, a seal, and a wooden box on which to work, and she became a scrivener, one of those peripatetic Parisians who would write letters for the illiterate. She plied her trade near Saint-Julien-le-Pauvre, the place Maubert, near Saint-Sulpice, up and down the rue Mouffetard. The woman who had once ignited readers in *La Lumière* now wrote letters for people who spoke with thick provincial accents, who sometimes spoke a patois, scarcely French. For these workers and beggars and servants, prostitutes and thieves, she wrote letters asking for money, sending money, sending sympathy, asking for sympathy. She wrote abject, begging letters and cringing apologies. Sometimes, when a death, an illness, a catastrophic injury had to be put into words, words failed these people and they wept, while Cosette framed the letter as well as wrote it. More than one pale, pregnant girl asked Cosette to write her relatives in the provinces that she was well and happy, that her master did not mistreat her.

Most of Cosette's customers, the men especially, had come to Paris for the work, which was plentiful, assured, if not well paid. Napoleon III, determined to emulate the emperors of Rome, set out to create a truly imperial city. And to that end the old city came down, especially those areas where the barricades had so quickly gone up, where workingmen had halted whole armies, streets where people were volatile, habitually hungry, disaffected, but not dispirited. The new boulevards were so broad they could support a cavalry charge. The new buildings regarded one another with uniform opulence. Baron Haussmann, prefect of the Seine, the regime's primary civil servant, became the head of yet another empire inside the Second Empire, an empire of contractors and subcontractors, of landlords and bankers and builders, suppliers and sharpers, knaves and cheats and inside traders, who flocked to the court of Napoléon III, and, at the base of all this money, corruption, and vision there was an army of laboring men who came in from the provinces and up from the gutters.

The Starling was part of this army, anonymous, unskilled, faceless. Every day that he had work, he took up his tools, a hod, a shovel, a pickaxe, and, dressed in coarse, loose clothes, the blue-blouse insignia of the workingman, he was one of the men no one saw, whose sweat and blood transformed Paris. He wore as well a skullcap stuffed with rags so he could carry the heavy trough of mortar balanced on his head, up and down scaffolding, sometimes six or seven floors, twenty and thirty times a day. He grew lean and hard and enormously strong. He worked eleven hours a day and made between two and four francs. He worked all over Paris along-side men from all over France. With them, he picked up his axe and struck at buildings that had been there since the gargoyles of Notre-Dame; he pulled out whole neighborhoods that had wound themselves around twisting alleys since the time of Saint-Louis. The Starling and men like him wrecked their way through the haunts of *les misérables*, and the dust and crust and rime of the lives lived here over centuries billowed out from the Starling's pickaxe, into his face and eyes; he breathed it, he spat it, it covered his clothes. Streets the cholera had ravaged vanished; streets so narrow and overgrown that light never touched the paving stones, those vanished; streets where people had lived grim lives and died quick deaths, all that vanished. The rue Jérusalem vanished. The rue du Haut-Moulin vanished. The rue Judas vanished. Even the rue de Combray vanished. The rue de la Chanverrerie had vanished. Streets where the very rats had pedigrees for centuries, all those vanished, and at the same time Paris, like a gaudy Second Empire courtesan, put her enormous skirts over the suburbs and pulled them unto her.

The vermin could be easily displaced, but the people, once evicted, could not so readily accommodate. For people like Pajol and Germaine Fleury, their wash was hanging out the window one day, and the order to evict came the next. Rents skyrocketed and housing became abysmal and scarce, and those who could not afford to crouch in the shadows of the new splendor were forced out to encampments at the old *barrières*.

Where once working people like Pajol, Germaine, the Starling, and the ragpickers had gone out to the *barrières* to drink cheap, untaxed alcohol, to enjoy a good time, high spirits, political intrigues under the guise of singing societies, where once open fields met the eye, there now sprang up rickety warrens of the dis-placed as well as the impoverished. The same people who had fash-ioned barricades of barrels and omnibuses now put that experience from the streets into building shelters for themselves, barricades against the wind and cold, built from scrap and tin and wire. Forced from the city, these people clustered in *barrière* enclaves, called the *cité,* where their dwellings rambled and shambled alongside one another without streets or sewers, without lights or a source of water, some lacking heat, some with chimney pipes protruding from the roofs of shacks whose walls were canvas. The best-sheltered lived in decayed buildings long abandoned or small, snug wagons with roofs, which kept them off the ground and protected from the rain and snow. The least fortunate huddled on straw-covered dirt floors, their roofs cobbled of boards too soggy to burn, their walls of uneven scraps or canvas, sometimes no more than rags stretched and tacked to sticks and wire. One family covered with canvas a steel hoop support for a lady's great crinoline, and they hunkered there, as in an igloo; somehow they had stolen the steel hoop and gotten it through the city undetected. They were much admired.

In these huddled *barrière* villages the human impulse toward beauty was sometimes visible in a ragged geranium by the door, a bit of paint, sweet peas climbing wires, curtains in a window that had no glass. But for the most part the ragpickers lived here amidst the garbage and the litter, the human refuse; the moneyless scum floated out here on a tide of demolition, flotsam and jetsam bobbing from the wreck of their old lives, beached finally here at the *barrières,* people like the ragpicker Toutes-Nations and her granddaughter Marie-Josephine and her man and their children. In 1856, when the layette for the Emperor's newborn son cost one hundred thousand francs, Marie-Josephine's second child died with scabies infesting his body and rickets infesting his bones. And yet it was amidst these hovels, misery underfoot, ignorance overhead, among the people with the least that the Lark found the most kindness and connection.

As the wife of Baron Pontmercy, Cosette had waltzed under candlelit chandeliers. Now she used a wick soaked in ten centimes' worth of oil. Cosette's library had been heated by two fireplaces; the Lark paid five centimes in winter for the coal man to fill a foot warmer with coal and ashes. Cosette had presided over one of the great tables of Paris; now she bought her bread "by the notch" like everyone else, the baker keeping a wooden stick for the Plumed Lark, cutting it each time she bought, tallying at the end of the month what she owed. And the price of bread doubled in three years. Cosette had drunk vintage Bordeaux; the Lark drank cheap *vin bleu.* Madame Pontmercy wrote for *La Lumière,* but the Plumed Lark plied her scrivening trade, selling lines by the sou. Madame Pontmercy had lived at the rue des Filles-du-Calvaire for nineteen years, but the Plumed Lark paid by the week in winter for an airless garret, where she shivered alone. Spring, summer, the early autumn she much preferred the *barrière* encampments, and she moved out there where the pinch, the poverty, the cold were more tolerable amidst the camaraderie, the candor and affection.

One night in the autumn of 1854, Cosette sat around the communal fire, a good fire, fed this night by the Starling and a few other young men, who had garnished wood they'd torn down during the day, carried it in a ragpicker's cart all the way out here to the *barrière* d'Italie. Cosette too lifted her cup with its bit of bread, held it out for a ladle of hot broth and the splendor of a bit of onion grated over, while the flames snapped before them and overhead the uncaring stars looked down. At least they were safe from the police here. These *barrière* enclaves were insular as villages, with their own codes and signals, and no police agent would venture here at night, so Toutes-Nations could say with impunity, "That Louis-Napoléon, I'd like to rub his face in shit."

"And Haussmann, that pig," Marie-Josephine pulled her toddler away from the fire and opened her blouse for the baby, "his liver should go in a jar and his knees to the boneyards of Montfaucon."

"His cock to Montfaucon," added the Ark, picking through some scraps of cloth.

"Yes, well, his great new boulevard is going to go right through my street," grumbled Toutes-Nations. "Everything will be gone, torn down and no one to throw anything out anymore. Everyone evicted. Me, I've worked that street for twenty years. I had a good—" she made a vague obscene gesture—"with all the concierges. I could have had the wings off flies. True, mine were not rich streets, not fat, but there was marrow in the bones." Toutes-Nations blew her nose on newspaper, regarded with some interest a drawing advertising Russian leather boots, beaded with crystals and tasseled with silk, for eight hundred francs. "Now at my age I have to start all over." She threw the paper in the fire and sulked. "And even if I find another street, how do I know they won't pull it down next, eh?"

"They're carving their way through the city like a hot knife through shit," grumbled the Captain, using his fingers to lift his bread from the soup before it fell apart.

The Starling blew on his soup, letting the bread dissolve. "There'll be no more barricades built in ten minutes, defended for a few hours, and then on the run, off you go to the next to fight, leaving the army there to blast its way through the one you built. Now they will be able to run battalions, artillery, whole squads of cannon across the city easily. They're destroying the battlegrounds of the armies of the poor."

"There's nothing to protect us," said the Captain, sighing.

"Once we had the Code Napoléon," mused the Lark, both hands wrapped round her cup. "Now we have the Toad Napoléon."

To her surprise this remark brought gales of laughter as it rippled to the farthest reaches of the group, the drunks and children at the edges, the children taking up a chant and making a game of Emperor of the Toads.

"Shut up, you little lice!" yelled Toutes-Nations. "That makes the people into toads. It's the Emperor who is the toad."

"He's not even a French toad. They say he speaks like a Swiss chicken," remarked a ragpicker whose clothes, cooking in the warmth of the fire, made others move away from him. But he got a round of applause when he imitated a Swiss chicken.

"Bonaparte reminds me of the La Fontaine fable that—" the Starling bit back *Mademoiselle Pontmercy* because they never used Cosette's real name or alluded to her old life, and he only said Fantine's name when he was alone; sometimes he could not bear to say it at all, and sometimes he whispered it incessantly like a chant. The Starling too had been marooned from his old life and his young love. "Someone lent me the book. You remember?"

Cosette nodded and smiled.

"There is a story about the frog who envied the ox. The frog tried to puff himself up, to be huge and handsome like the ox—"

"Like Louis-Napoléon thinks he is his uncle, Napoléon the Great!" The Ark snorted.

"Yes, but finally, puff and try as he might, the frog exploded with wind and vanity."

Toutes-Nations let a well-timed fart, eloquent comment on wind, vanity, and the Toad Napoléon.

The Starling went on, "And then there's the one about the ass carrying holy relics. How does it go?"

Cosette could not recite it, though she remembered it. She pulled Marie-Josephine's toddler into her arms and rested her cheek on the little boy's head. Cosette's face and arms were tanned, coarsened by the sun, though her short hair was still bright because she always wore the bonnet with the gray hair when she went out. Her eyes were creased at the edges, and though her face had thinned, her mouth was still full and generous, her expression astute and watchful, poignant.

"The ass is so vain, so stupid, so certain as he walks in the holy procession," Le Sansonnet laughed and looked across the fire at the dirty faces, "that when people bow before the saint's relics he believes they're honoring him."

"'The brute clothed in the law's regalia,'" quoted Cosette.

"The stupid brute," griped Toutes-Nations. "Bonaparte thinks his fireworks and pageants and great spectacles will buy our loyalty."

"They will buy our silence," Marie-Josephine burped her baby, "for the time."

The Starling obliged them all with more of La Fontaine's fables, those witty cautioning tales, poking fun at greed, vanity, pomp, and certainty. As the Lark listened, she prodded the fire with a long stick. The flames etched up, red against the black sky, and Cosette marveled at the heat they gave, the light, *la lumière*.

Chapter 2

Le Sansonnet to Fantine, February 1852

Chère mademoiselle—Unfortunately I must write with some bad news. Your mother has got blood poisoning and is seriously ill. My grandmother looks after her with a dedication only you could match. I do not wish to worry you, or cause you pain, but I thought you would worry the more if many more weeks passed without word. She is with us, safe from harm. Her heart is broken but I think her spirit is not, and it is my belief, my hope, she will recover. You must not write back. When it is safe, perhaps you can send letters to the old place near Saint-Sulpice, but the police are closing down hundreds of cafés in Paris alone, even when it is the customers who get drunk and sing "La Marseillaise." The trials of those arrested during the coup d'état go swiftly, but we hear almost nothing because there are no newspapers except for the two belonging to Bonaparte. The word going around is that most prisoners will be transported to Cayenne and New Caledonia. Probably they will not execute many men. They don't want martyrs. They have one in your father. The story of his eloquence at the barricade, of the candles blown out to protect him, of the soldiers' refusal to fire, that story goes all over Paris.

Most of the men who were arrested that night, they have all been exiled. Thiers, we hear, has gone to Switzerland, but many have gone to England. As you have gone to England, mademoiselle. I hope, though, you are well and that Madame Carême too is well. I hope to have good news of your mother's health soon. I think of you in England. Paris is bleak without [scratched out] *sun this winter and they say there will be no carnival.*

Fantine to Jean-Luc, March 1852

My dear Jean-Luc—I regret to inform you that Mama remains unreconciled to your desertion and refuses to write to you. I alone will write to you. Added to Mama's uncertain health and the sorrow of Papa's death, we suffer too the confusions of exile in a country hostile to us and to our religion. Madame Carême and I look after Mama. Madame Fitzpatrick, her childhood friend Helen Talbot, is very kind and good to us, but she is a widow and lives on a small stipend, and so we are four women managing on very slender means. London is expensive.

Jean-Luc to Fantine, May 1852

. . . I have some news that will distress you both. In these months as I have been going through Papa's affairs, I find La Lumière was bankrupt. Papa would have had to close down this year in any event. This was a shock to me as I had counted on something from his estate, as no doubt you did. The sale of La Lumière's presses will bring something, but printing presses are not in much use these days. There are no more radical papers at all. All editors favor Bonaparte and all criticism of the regime is forbidden, so we read nothing but fashion, theatrical gossip, art gossip, café gossip, musical gossip, and the like. Papa's politics have cost us everything but the house. I dare not move as long as Aunt Adelaide lives. She sends her best to you and Mama in England and wishes you would return to France. Madame Touchard has suggested that I allow her to put the matter before Louis-Napoléon himself. He is a very humane man.

The Starling to Fantine, August 1852

Chère mademoiselle—Your mother's progress continues slow but certain. My grandmother says only the beasts or the blessed can live through a siege of fever like this one. They have become fast friends, Madame Pontmercy and my grandmother. They laugh over unlikely things. It pleases me to hear your mother laugh at last. The loss of your father left her devastated. We speak of you daily, mademoiselle, and you are always on our minds.

There was a huge fête last week in the Champ-de-Mars. Sixty thousand soldiers. Six hundred priests. The archbishop of Paris officiated. He blesses everything Louis-Napoléon does. The church and the military, they worship this tyrant. I am happy to say, though, that God and nature do not. A terrible wind and rainstorm came up and destroyed all decorations all over the city and the fireworks. The banner of Bonaparte on horseback and fireworks of laurel wreaths, all that was rained out and blown away. Madame Fagennes says café owners will get the blame. I say, let the police hunt down the wind and arrest the rain.

Cosette to Fantine, October 1852

My darling daughter—I think of you daily, pray for you daily, but I am writing now to tell you how at every turn you are with me. I am living for the winter in a tiny room at the top of the cour du Dragon. However grim and cold, I smile still to remember your affection for Sainte-Marguerite. Above the archway to the cour du Dragon there is carved in stone a dragon, head upraised, wings outspread, talons poised, his scales perfectly sculpted. But I now know Sainte-Marguerite could not have emerged unscathed from the belly of the dragon. Once there, once she came through the experience, she would have been transformed. I have lived through such despair, black as the belly of the dragon. I have emerged at last from that despair, but not unscathed. I see my own reflection in windows and I wonder— who is that woman? She looks so thin and meager and haunted. She has a strange cough I do not remember. But she and I have survived and that mere fact makes me both proud and humble. Perhaps Sainte-Marguerite too felt humility and pride, but as a saint she could admit only to humility. I am not a saint. I understand the anguish of Sainte-Marguerite, not her beatitude, but her transformation.

I embrace you, my darling daughter, but you must stay in England till it's safe. Do not write. Gabriel saw Clerons in the Café Rigolo recently. Gabriel put his head down on the table, pretending to be dead drunk, but clearly Clerons has chased him that far. We are fortunate that Clerons did not inquire for him

*by name, or Madame Fagennes would never let him come there
again.*

Jean-Luc to Fantine, February 1853

*Dear Fantine—As even the English must know, Louis-
Napoléon has declared himself Napoléon III, Emperor of the
French, and we have a new empire, a Second Empire, and a
new imperial family, as last month His Imperial Highness married Eugénie, a Spanish woman of undisputed beauty and
dubious origins. Here in Paris we are embarked on a round of
gaiety unequaled, unparalleled, unprecedented. We are beside
ourselves with joy as the empire means peace and it also means
prosperity. Huvet has suggested I invest, along with his father,
in sugar beets in Clermont-Ferrand. When my financial affairs
are in order, I intend to marry Mademoiselle Nicolette Lauriot.
I have taken the money from the presses, there was not much,
and invested in sugar beets. In the near future I will send you
more than I could have otherwise.*

Fantine to Jean-Luc, March 1853

*As you have sent us nothing at all, we would have been pleased
to receive the pittance rather than the promise. Please do not
abandon us to the charity of Madame Fitzpatrick, however
generous her nature. Mama's health is poor and this is a grim,
gray country. In London the air is so black that during the day
in winter one pays an urchin to carry a lantern before crossing
the street. Tribes of wretched children make their living this
way. The fogs are so black here that every week someone is killed
by an omnibus or a cab. Knocked down in the dark afternoon,
the person rolls under the wheels and dies. I saw such an accident myself yesterday. It is terrible here and not at all like Paris.*

Gabriel to Fantine, August 1853

*Chère mademoiselle—Your mother says I should write to you on
my own behalf and not on hers. I have tried, but can find so
little to say of any interest to you that the ink has dried on my
pen before the words have touched the paper. It was a desolate
spring here, a desolate summer, mademoiselle. I hope you are*

well and happy in London. I am happy knowing you are safe, but I wish I were your student again. I think back to those old days not as the past, to be remembered, but as a dream gone forever. Once this summer I went to your house, around the back, and climbed on the carriage house roof and lay there looking at the garden and the windows and imagining you in the library choosing a book for me and scolding me for being a stupid lout. I stayed till someone, Mademoiselle Lauriot, came out. Walking to the strawberry patch, she looked up and saw me, recognized me, I think, and looked away. I will not go back.

Fantine to Jean-Luc, September 1853

You ask why I have not commented on your intended marriage to Mademoiselle Lauriot. To drape your name on a palm-frond waver is to squander that name, to throw bonbons in the barnyard for common fowl to peck at. Mama refuses to hear her name spoken, and if Papa were alive you would be studying law, not escorting actresses and listening to Monsieur Huvet's advice on sugar beets.

Cosette to Fantine, October 1853

I found a newspaper in the Café Rigolo and read an obituary for Mademoiselle Adelaide Gillenormand. Surely Jean-Luc has told you of her passing. One must pity a life spent so secluded and in such fear. But she loved Jean-Luc wholly and completely and without ambivalence, and to have loved at all is our reward for the pangs of life and death. He is her only heir. I fear he will now sell the house at Number 6 rue des Filles-du-Calvaire. Please ask him to save the silver candlesticks on the library mantel. They are my only legacy from my father, and I pray one day to hold them again. Clerons has been to the Changer's twice in two months, looking for the Starling. Why should he want Gabriel? He's done nothing. Perhaps you are truly safest in England if Clerons continues to pursue the innocent.

Fantine to Jean-Luc, November 1853

I understand our aunt is dead. How appalling that I should have heard this news from a source other than you. Poor Aunt

Adelaide must have long felt a relic in this world, and it is a pity that you were the only bright star in what was otherwise a dark firmament. She left you everything. Now will you be good enough to offer your mother and sister some slight assistance here in England?

Jean-Luc to Fantine, January 1854

Perhaps I was remiss in not telling you and Mama of Aunt Adelaide's death, but the money from her estate is sadly depleted and was before she died. I borrowed on my inheritance and sugar beets had a hard year of it. Huvet's father assures me there is a fortune in salt pork, especially with war raging in the Crimea.

However, Paris itself is the gold field. There are wooden towers set up all over the city with high platforms so it may be accurately mapped before it is destroyed and rebuilt into a city befitting the Second Empire, with broad boulevards, parks, and gardens in what once was waste ground, and the old dens of vice and crime and cholera wiped out, light and air brought in. Haussmann will put all this into effect, and Madame Touchard knows him well. She knows everyone at court well. She is on intimate terms with the Emperor, though not as intimate as she once was in New York. However, as might be expected, the Empress is not fond of her. The Empress loathes all things American and Madame Touchard seems so very American, although she is French.

Madame Touchard has been good enough to introduce me to Baron Haussmann, who knew our father as a student at the Lycée Henri IV. I quickly told him I too had gone there. Haussmann was good enough not to refer to my father's unfortunate death and praised only his unimpeachable honor. I feel my father's death and mother's exile a great burden. I am excluded from the court and from the great circles of wealth and influence, even the possibilities of wealth. Huvet is invited to the Emperor's winter ball. Of course his father has grown even more wealthy with the war, and I am indebted to him for his advice, but it's not enough. Still, Huvet has been very good to me. In fact you should write to me c/o of him in the rue de la Paix. I am

*selling Number 6 rue des Filles-du-Calvaire. You and Mama
need not worry about your things. I shall be storing them until I
have my own apartment, which I would happily share with you
if you would return to France. Madame Touchard says the
Emperor may be approached. I'm sure Mama's exile could end.
Already His Imperial Highness has allowed Monsieur Thiers to
return to Paris, though he had to sign a document promising not
to engage in politics. Monsieur Thiers might just as well have
promised not to breathe. A most unpleasant man. I saw him
recently and he cut me cold. Can you imagine? Beaujard has cut
me. Coligny. Even Cousin Théo does not speak to me. Am I
responsible for my father's death and my mother's exile? Of our
parents' old friends, Madame Touchard alone is kind.*

Cosette to Fantine, January 1854

*My darling daughter—The winter bears down brutally on us
here, the cold and frost, the rain and biting wind keep the chari-
table at home, and so very bad for beggars and the rest of us who
tread these streets in search of our livelihood. Madame Fagennes
will sometimes let me have a corner at the Café Rigolo if I have
someone who needs a letter, but that means the expense of a glass
of her dreadful wine. This winter I had a bed in a boardinghouse, twelve of us to a room, the beds with scarcely any room
between. They're hard-working women and girls here, laundresses mostly from the rue Mouffetard. The landlady makes a
broth from sheep's head, but we must supply our own bread. In
the morning and at night when we return, we get a bowl of
broth and it only costs one sou. You must keep your bread with
you at all times or it is stolen, or if the landlady finds it, she
gathers the pieces up and throws them in the pot. Nearly all these
women and girls are good-natured, coarse, energetic, but the
competition for men is terrible, and there have been more than
six fights this week. I had another boardinghouse earlier in the
winter, fewer people, and cheaper, but the beds were over a
weaver's workshop and it was terrible to watch the girls there,
some younger than you, working from five in the morning until
eleven at night, doing all the housework too for the master's wife.
On Sunday they were allowed six o'clock mass in the morning*

and then back at it. The girls were all yellow and joyless, the dust from the looms lay thick on everything, suffocating even the vermin. I had to leave. I could not bear it and my cough was much worse. Then I moved in with the laundresses. Better to be chained to a washpot than a loom. I had to leave there too. I could never take my bonnet off. With my hair cut so short, I am conspicuous. I could not rest. So at great cost, which I can scarcely afford, I have rented a tiny garret room on the rue des Marmousets where I'm close by Pajol and Germaine and their family. Pajol has got work, not worthy of his abilities, but at least he's printing, and Germaine says he's not happy without ink under his fingernails.

You must not think from my letter (I read what I have written and am appalled!) that I am suffering. My health continues to withstand the rigors of this life and I have many friends whose kindness and affection brighten my days. I suffer only when I think of you in England. I bless you. I miss you. I embrace you. I trust my dear friend Helen Talbot to have made you and Madame Carême welcome, but I hope Jean-Luc is sending you money so you're not cast on her charity, or your own resources in a foreign country. Sometimes I cry thinking how sad it is that your adoring papa wanted to keep you in dancing shoes and now he is dead and you are exiled and I huddle here alone. Did I do wrong to send you to England without me? Perhaps you should ask Jean-Luc for money for a ticket to return to Paris. Surely there can be no retribution visited on you.

Ah well, you can see from my hand I shiver, but the spring will come and one day we will be together again, you and I. That hope, that conviction alone gives me strength. My little scrivening trade gives me bread and shelter. My love for you and for your dear papa keeps my faith bright. So perhaps the life of my body is poor, but the life of my heart and mind is rich. Dear, dear girl. I hear your sweet voice in my head and I pray you are safe and happy, and God willing we will be reunited in this life.

Gabriel to Fantine, April 1854

Chère mademoiselle—At last winter ends and there is work in Paris for those of us with no trade but the strength of our backs.

*The pay is not good and the work is dangerous, but I am happy
to have work with a mason. I carry a trough of mortar up six
floors about twenty-five times a day, and I have to be fast at it.
If the mortar sets before I get it to the mason, he can't apply it
and it's lost. Two of those lost batches and they hire someone else,
and I am on the street without a sou. The work is difficult and
exhausting, coarse work, common. You would find me common
and coarse, even more than when I was a runner. But I am not
a thief. I wanted you to know that I could not, I did not return
to that old life. I hope you will sometimes think of your student.
I think of you [scratched out] and hope you are well and happy
in England. I know Madame Carême does not like me, but I ask
to be remembered to her as well.*

Fantine to Jean-Luc, May 1854

*I have waited to write this letter in hopes that you would see fit
to send me some portion of the money realized from the sale of
our childhood home. However, you have put me in a humiliating position with regard to Madame Fitzpatrick and her
ongoing kindness, which now that I have no money constitutes
charity. At least Madame Carême has a skill, something she can
do well. The English think she actually was married to Carême,
and it has stood her in good stead here. I have taken in a few
pupils, teaching French, but the work is demeaning, dispiriting,
and ill paid. London is full of impecunious young women with
genteel educations and empty pockets.*

Jean-Luc to Fantine, September 1854

*Naturally I intend to share with you and Mama the proceeds of
the sale of our old home. However, I have invested the money in
some land near the Parc Monceau, which, if my sources serve
me well, will become very valuable in the near future. Perhaps
that investment will further others, as I am at last to appear at
the court of Napoléon III, thanks to Madame Touchard. Her
eldest daughter, Eponine-Hortense, is to be presented at court
and I shall be her escort. Madame Touchard has recently been
made the Countess Troussebois in recognition of her daughter's*

parentage and her late father's services at the battle of Waterloo. I am deeply grateful for her patronage and friendship. Without court favor one can only gape and gawk at the passing fête. You may imagine, if you will, your brother in court dress— required—shoes, silk stockings, tights, a waistcoat with lappets, a velvet coat with standing collar, a cocked hat, and a sword! Once my finances are in order, I shall marry Mademoiselle Lauriot.

Fantine to Jean-Luc, November 1854

News of your sniveling up to Louis-Napoléon in the shadow of Madame Touchard does not amuse us here in London. Mama asks that you spare us in the future.

Does memory serve, or did you ask Mademoiselle Lauriot to marry you some time ago?

Jean-Luc to Fantine, February 1855

Mademoiselle Lauriot and I have been engaged for some time.

Huvet and I plan to come to London with our friend comte LaSalle, and at that time I shall bring you more money than I could hope to send. However, it must wait till after the Universal Exposition, which opens here this spring. The festivities, the decorations, the buildings are breathtaking, unparalleled in all history. The war in the Crimea casts some small shadow, naturally (but none on me as my salt pork contracts flourish). They say that every hotel room in Paris will be filled all summer, that all the world is flocking here to see what the French Emperor hath wrought. Even the English queen will come to see how well we live here in Paris—the new parks, the new boulevards, the color and dazzle. Monsieur Offenbach is refurbishing an abandoned theatre in the Champs-Elysées, and he will open a musical farce there in July, in which Mademoiselle Lauriot will have the lead role. So you see I cannot leave Paris now. I wish you would prevail upon Mama to allow Madame Touchard to say a few words to the Emperor on her behalf. Madame Touchard (Countess Troussebois) assures me she wishes to be of service to her dear old friend.

Fantine to Jean-Luc, April 1855

I feel I can no longer withhold from you the truth of my situation. No doubt the path I have taken in life would have given Papa pain, but then the path you have taken would have broken his heart. In any event, I find my new life preferable to genteel beggary or the teaching of nervous English girls.

Madame Carême and I have hired out as cooks. French cooks. We have been doing this for some time informally and have found ourselves much in demand. We shall soon be accepting a position to cook in a rich London establishment, St. James Square, where they have ample means and even some taste. I am Madame Carême's assistant. I speak English. She does not. She refuses to learn. She says the language of people who eat boiled mutton must itself be flavorless, stringy, and wanting in savor. You may continue to write me at Madame Fitzpatrick's. She is very fond of us and Mama will stay on with her.

Do let us know when you marry Mademoiselle Lauriot.

Jean-Luc to Fantine, May 1855

How can Mama allow you to take up such low work? You say nothing of her shock or outrage. If you truly believe that a baron's daughter should be up to her elbows in flour like a common kitchen slavey, I can only imagine what London has done for your morals.

Jean-Luc to Fantine, August 1855

I enclose with this letter (at great peril to myself; you'll note I have wrapped it several times in newspaper) a seditious pamphlet, a traitorous document, a scurrilous reworking of the fables of La Fontaine. I write now to describe to you in some detail several incidents that have occurred of late which lead me to believe I have been the victim of a cruel hoax.

As all Paris and much of Europe has gathered here for the Universal Exposition, I have been afforded unwanted opportunities to see people connected to my parents' past. As I was escorting Mademoiselle Lauriot through the Palais d'Industrie, in the exhibit of the uses of iron in building I happened to see

Beaujard. His work was not accepted for the exhibition of French painters, and he no doubt came to belittle the work of better men than he. In the past, Monsieur Beaujard has been extremely cold to me, but on this occasion his manner may only be described as garish. He was full of courtly observations to Nicolette, Mademoiselle Lauriot, who once modeled for him, and then he asked if I had heard from my mother. When I replied I had not had the honor, he laughed uproariously and went on his way.

When we had moved on to the English exhibit of the uses of rubber in industry, I happened upon Monsieur Thiers. There are those who say he is a man of wit, but no one would accuse Monsieur Thiers of humor. And yet, when he saw me, he began laughing in a most familiar, vulgar, inappropriate fashion. He too asked if I had seen Mama. When I replied that patriotism to the Emperor had long divided us, his mirth seemed altogether out of proportion to the circumstances.

Standing there before the exhibit of electrical apparatus, I was subject to the same sort of humiliating exchanges from Gallet, who was either drugged or drunk or both, as well as Coligny, whom I had heretofore merely thought a peasant in a boulevard disguise, but an honest man.

Then, recently, dining at the Café Riche with Huvet and the comte LaSalle, someone sent to my table, anonymously, the pamphlet I enclose. There are spies everywhere, even at the Café Riche, and clearly this was done to embarrass me, perhaps to get me arrested. Anyone seen with The Toad Napoléon *is arrested immediately. Anyone selling it is transported. The person who wrote it will be shot.*

You will note that no publisher or printing office claims to have printed The Toad Napoléon. *But there is an illustration, a torch, very like the torch that used to adorn the pages of* La Lumière. *Indeed exactly like it, and the author is noted only as* La Lumière. *Since my father is dead, I can only surmise that someone is using* La Lumière *to connect our family with treason.*

Or possibly you and Mama have abused my trust for years. I believed her to be sick, angry, wounded, and impoverished in London. I demand a letter from her in her own hand.

Fantine to Jean-Luc, September 1855

I laughed, I wept, I shouted to read The Toad Napoléon *to think that though Papa is dead* La Lumière *burns on. The London papers tell of* The Toad Napoléon, *of the stir and trouble it has made for the Emperor, how children salute his troops with croaking noises in the streets, but until I read it I had no idea of its wit, its satire, and indelible effect. Louis-Napoléon has a true enemy in* La Lumière. *I smile, Jean-Luc, with my arms in flour to the elbow, I sing "La Marseillaise" as loud as I like in this kitchen. I bless Sainte-Marguerite to have led Mama from the belly of the dragon of despair. She has indeed been sick, angry, wounded, and impoverished. But she has never been in London.*

And you, my dear brother, I bid you adieu as you have joined the imperial carnival, haven't you? Go on, go with the gaudy, giddy pleasures, false as carnival. Be part of their parade. Roll on, Baron Pontmercy, with your Bonapartist title and your sugar beets and your land around the Parc Monceau, your salt pork contracts fattening on the carcasses of dead soldiers. Wear your court dress, Jean-Luc, wear your silly sword and party cocked hat and ride about with your friends who trade high-stepping horses and women with equal indifference, strut with La Lauriot, whose fame or ill-fame is such she makes the London papers. I shall watch this procession, and envy only the ragpickers, who will sweep up behind you, even over you, who will linger upright in the dust long after you are gone.

Chapter 3

*I*t began in blood and it would end in blood, but in between that beginning and its assured closure, the Second Empire was all brilliant, amoral, shallow, splendid, and repressive. It granted few liberties, but many fêtes and fireworks. The passions of 1848 were reduced to ridicule, and prestige, vanity, pomp, even whimsy took the place of real power. The empire itself turned on the axis of the military, the church (to keep the peasants quiescent), and the splash, the rustle of money. Paris was the center of the world and *la vie Parisienne,* as the Offenbach musical suggested, the most envied in the world. While Cosette and the ragpickers huddled at their *barrière,* rich men of the Second Empire adjusted their cravats in mirrors with gilt frames and danced on marble floors and ate from tables dazzling with silver; their women wore acres of lace and crinoline, ropes of jewels, and hothouse flowers. Their women were mostly gilded beauties of the demimondaine and their money just as false, speculative, and abundant. The city was full of foreigners— Americans, Mexicans, English, Russians, Italian princes, Spanish, Turks, Middle Eastern potentates, and lesser Hapsburgs, all of them swept into Paris by railways, which extended in every direction, and new broad boulevards that connected the stations (themselves marvels of iron and engineering) with the riches, the pleasures of Paris, the center of the world. Telegraph lines, gas lines, sewers that would have dazzled Jean Valjean came into the city. Haussmann moved out the dead to make room for the railways, and when they were destroying the old Convent of the Perpetual Adoration (the nuns long since dead, buried in the garden) to lay iron tracks, some enterprising person saw Jean Valjean's blue rose. It still bloomed in the wrecked convent garden, where clouds of white butterflies would soon be replaced by clouds of black cinders. Rescued, taken to the Jardin des Plantes, Jean Valjean's blue rose came, via Jacques Offenbach, to be forever associated with Nicolette Lauriot. The blue rose was at least as immortal as the Second Empire; most of them perished in the Prussian siege of Paris, the winter of 1870.

For her part, Nicolette felt no misplaced nostalgia for the old Paris, though even Jean-Luc suffered a twinge of sadness when the rue du Haut-Moulin fell to the axe. Nicolette brought the only part of her old life that she valued, Jean-Luc, into her new life. No more cold dressing rooms with a single gas jet and a single chamberpot. When the Universal Exposition of 1855 closed, Offenbach moved his Bouffes-Parisiens to the rich district of rue Monsigny, and from this stage Nicolette reigned, as much the Empress as Eugénie. Now the voice of La Lauriot was the voice of Paris and the aisle leading to her dressing room known as the Passage of Princes.

No more third-floor latrines and acrobat concierges; as the star of the Second Empire stage Nicolette now lived with a bevy of dogs and a flotilla of servants in the rue de Chaillot near the Champs-Elysées. Watteau had painted the ceilings and the wallpaper was purple and gold and the gilded bed reputed to have belonged to Marie-Antoinette, or one of those well-born, long-dead harlots. Nicolette's house had a glass-and-iron conservatory, steam-heated with pumped hot water, which housed a jungle with indoor waterfall and impossible tropical plants. She also kept here a tribe of monkeys, gorgeous parrots, and flamingos, who sickened and died one after the other, and were the devil to replace. The girl who once posed for artists as obscure and controversial as Manet and Beaujard now had her portrait done by Winterhalter, painter to the court of Napoléon III.

Paris lays down more than the law, Victor Hugo once said, Paris lays down fashion. In that regard, La Lauriot laid down the law. When the Englishman Worth wished to establish his house, he went to the Empress at the Tuileries and to La Lauriot at the Bouffes-Parisiens. To have Nicolette Lauriot wear and display his clothes, Worth would make her anything she wished for two thousand francs, gowns of cashmere and chantilly lace that cost everyone else twelve thousand francs. In the winter Nicolette wore Lyon brocade, sable, and ermines, and in the summer hand-embroidered muslins, sewn by girls who were paid perhaps two francs a day for their skills, indeed, their art. Nicolette was the first woman in Paris to throw away her prim, face-concealing bonnet and replace it with a smart hat. This shocked the bourgeois matrons, but started a rage and endeared Nicolette to young women all over Paris. Even those who made less than two francs a day cut her picture out of *L'Illustration* and *Le Figaro* and hung it by the shard of mirror serving dozens crouched in squalid rooms behind Haussmann's new and splendid façades.

At the fashionable afternoon hour, Nicolette rode in the Bois de Boulogne in one of her carriages (she had three), drawn by fine, matched chestnut horses (gift of an English duke's son), or sometimes she rode with one of her many admirers, men who would pay five thousand francs for a single night of her company. She rode and dined and danced with men who were willing to pay even for the reputation of having slept with her.

Sometimes she rode and dined and danced—but did not sleep—with the man whose name was endlessly entwined with her own. Jacques Offenbach was tall, blade-thin, pince-nezed and stoop-shouldered. Often he was caricatured as one of the birds in Nicolette's menagerie, but he was not truly comic. In the course of about fifteen years he wrote thousands upon thousands of zesty pieces for hundreds of venues, from operettas to concerts to songs for café singers to private theatricals, where he could be really risqué. He was, they said, the Mozart of the Champs-Elysées, and his tunes were sung everywhere, some, like "The Nicolette Waltz," were immortal—at least as immortal as the Second Empire. When La Lauriot sang it, Offenbach made it heartbreakingly wistful, putting a cello behind the melody line. But that same song, engorged with a full orchestra and speeded up, drove audiences mad, and in the café-cabarets, at the dance halls, the gardens of the Bal Mabille, women danced the cancan to it, their heels kicking high enough to meet the chin whiskers of their partners. "The Nicolette Waltz" was played by every beggar with a wheezy concertina and whistled by workingmen like the Starling on their way to demolition or construction sites all over Paris.

Jean-Luc loathed Offenbach. Often (out of Nicolette's hearing) he would parody the composer's German accent. Perhaps Jean-Luc saw him as a rival, not for Nicolette's favors, but for her affections. On the fifth of every month, Offenbach, a generous, convivial, and courtly man, sent to Nicolette's dressing room a dozen roses, as he had on Thursday, 5 July 1855, when they had first opened together. For a while he sent red roses. Then he sent white. Then he found the blue rose: absolutely extravagant, artificial-looking, and exotic, though not for long. To send a blue rose to a lady became, in that era, to advertise oneself as a man of fabled wealth, like Auguste de Morny (whose half-brother, the Emperor, had elevated him from comte to duc). Morny had delivered to Nicolette's home a single blue rosebud with the inscription FOR YOUR BEDSIDE TABLE. When the rose opened, a sapphire ring fell out. Unfortunately, Jean-Luc was on that side of the bed.

"What should it matter?" Nicolette asked, slipping the ring on her finger and examining it, as well as her own pink and polished nails and smooth hands. "If Morny wants to shower a few sapphires on me, let him. I'm certainly not the only woman in Paris he's been known to flatter, admire."

"And pay."

"Really, chéri, what would you have me do? Leave the theatre and go to a nunnery?"

"I would have you marry me, Nicolette, as you well know. As you have known for years."

"Oh, marriage." She rolled over, pressing up next to him. "This conversation is so tedious, so predictable."

"It doesn't have to be. You could say yes, you'll marry me."

"I've explained it a thousand times."

"I haven't asked a thousand times."

Nicolette wriggled provocatively, but he remained unmoved, his hands beneath his head. She sighed; clearly the quarrel lay between her and the rest of her day. It was after eleven now. Monsieur Worth and his entourage would arrive for a fitting, then her hairdresser, then there would be the usual dozen or so for lunch in the jungle conservatory, a ride in the Bois de Boulogne, then off to the theatre, and afterward, supper at the Café Anglais or any number of famous restaurants. They each lay before her, days as full of pleasure and indulgence as perfect pearls on a string. But for Nicolette the greatest of these pleasures was the work. The theatre.

It never ceased to exhilarate her, all of it, from the orchestra tuning up to the scent of the oranges the audience brought back after the entr'acte; the peculiar smell of the gaslight and the lush bouquets in her dressing room, the thick rush of the curtain when it came down on all that applause, the great promise of the curtain when it went up on all that pleasure. The music, the breathless mad music, and above all, the adoration. When Nicolette stood, center stage, her gloved arms outstretched to the audience, she was making love to every man, from the duc de Morny to the clerk whose inkstained hands tingled with clapping. She looked out upon tier upon tier of women in diamonds, dripping with camellias and blue roses gathered at their opulent, white bosoms. She loved the pleasure she saw even on the face of the dullest bourgeois, the face of the foreigner who understood not a line of her lyrics. But of course everyone understood everything La Lauriot did. That was part of her success: she could radiate high spirits with her body, with her walk, the old walk, at once insouciant and provocative, the lift of her chin, the wink of an eye, the pursing of her lips. She had a sumptuous body, succulent even, and she could communicate promise and innuendo with the wave of a hand. Now she held up the hand with the sapphire ring and watched it catch the light spilling through the gauzy drapes. She rolled over and nibbled on Jean-Luc's shoulder, determined, if she couldn't avoid the quarrel, at least to make fun of it. "Now, tell me, would you love me more if I married you?"

"This is your old trick. I won't fall for it."

Perhaps not, she thought, but he was certainly starting to thaw. Or heat. As the case may be. "Tell me the truth."

"If I say yes, you accuse me of not loving you. If I say no, you have proved your point."

Nicolette nibbled her way across his chest. "Very well, if you won't love me more if I marry you, will you love me less?"

"Emphatically no." Jean-Luc kicked one of the dogs off the bed and swore at another one. One Pekinese barked nastily and mounted the other.

"If I married you, you would do what every man in Paris does, you would immediately take a mistress. And where would I be left? I would have to take a lover."

"You already take lovers."

"Would you leave me with the matrons and the brats?" She plucked one of his chest hairs from her lips. "Abandoned, while you trot around with some high-priced tart?"

"Whereas if you don't marry me, you can be the high-priced tart."

"Marry someone rich, *chéri,* someone dripping with money, and then you can keep me in the manner I've come to relish, and we'll all be happy. I don't need to marry you to love you, Jean-Luc," she continued more seriously. "Marriage is a silly bourgeois affectation, it's a banking arrangement, nothing more."

"But I love you, Nicolette, I need you, I need you the way the bee needs and loves the flower. I don't like sharing my flower with the butterflies."

She rolled onto her belly and rested her chin on his shoulder. "I am not some small savage country to be conquered by one man or another. I don't want to be colonized, all my boundaries staked out, my capital occupied, and my customs changed."

"What nonsense."

"It's not nonsense," she insisted, "you want to colonize me. To deprive me of the theatre while you cavort with actresses. You already cavort. Why should I be deprived?"

"If you married me, I would cavort only with you. My father never took a mistress. Neither will I."

"Truly?" Nicolette was appalled. "He and your mother . . ."

Jean-Luc went glum. "They were their own country. I don't want to talk about them."

"Well, you're absolutely right. I allow no serious conversation in my bed, Monsieur Pontmercy, if you hadn't noticed all these years. Frivolous only." Her hand moved frivolously down and she watched the sapphire ring catch the morning light. "In fact, you should be pleased Morny is interested in me. He and Haussmann are the most powerful men in Paris. Perhaps, since he's taken a fancy to me, I can get you into the Jockey Club."

"I don't have enough money for the Jockey Club."

"Perhaps I can help you get enough money. Perhaps I can do better than Madame Touchard in picking up those little bonbons of information she passes on to you."

"Madame Touchard does not sleep with Haussmann or Morny."

"She'd sleep with them if they'd have her. Has she slept with you?"

"Don't be ridiculous. She's old enough to be my mother."

"They say they're grateful, older women," Nicolette murmured. "And anyway, if you're not sleeping with her, then it's comical the way she obliges you to escort her here and there, her and her silly daughters. Where's the so-called count?"

"At the gaming table. Besides, you underestimate her."

"No, *mon amour,* you overestimate her. She is an aged tart with a bastard brat she passes off as the Emperor's love child."

There was a swift, strangled silence, and then Jean-Luc reminded Nicolette she had very nearly had a bastard brat.

"Please don't do this."

"I love you."

"And I tell you I can't marry you. I won't. I don't want to. I'm sorry about the child. I know you wanted it, but it wasn't to be. Oh, Jean-Luc, isn't it enough that I love you? Can't you accept my love without invading my own small country, my life? It wasn't my fault about the baby. You heard the doctor. The doctor said mine was not the body for having babies."

"I want you. I want to marry you."

She slid over the blue satin sheets, eased over him eloquently. "You have me. You know that. No words can mar or touch or change that."

Swiftly he rolled her underneath him and braced himself on one arm as morning light streaked across the blue sheets in long yellow wisps. "But you won't marry me?"

"I loathe virtue."

Chapter 4

Zelma Thénardier cultivated Jean-Luc Pontmercy as a farmer might a prize cabbage. Mercenary as she was, the rat in satin, Zelma cherished above all, savored, and saw in Jean-Luc the opportunity to revenge herself on Cosette and Marius. Perhaps in her entire life Zelma had only truly loved two people, one the ill-fated major in Helena, Arkansas, and the other her sister, Eponine. Her mother had died in prison, and as for her father, Zelma too had felt his belt and boot, and it wasn't till she outweighed him that he'd given up beating her. While Zelma had been forced into American exile and years of grim struggle, Cosette had been loved, adored, had lived in comfort on the strength of a convict's legacy. Ironically, though, Zelma owed her current success to that American exile, to the twenty thousand francs (courtesy of Jean Valjean) Marius had put in a New York bank, awaiting Zelma and her father. This money lifted Zelma from the Parisian gutters and endowed her with sufficient social standing to meet that other French exile, Louis-Napoléon, and share his woes. In fact, old man Thénardier had ordered Zelma to demand payment for sleeping with Bonaparte, but Zelma was shrewder, more the gambler, less the light-fingered thief. The gamble had paid off. The girl who had played on a gun carriage abandoned in the defeat of Waterloo now brought to the court of Napoléon III a certain American élan, the brighter because she offended the Americans at every turn, shocking everyone with tales of how they ate corn off the cob. Just like the pigs. These truly terrible tales she told out of the hearing of her former lover, for Napoléon III liked Americans and had enjoyed his brief stay there (no doubt the more for Zelma's presence). Zelma had no affection whatever for America, but any reference to her time in New York made her positively misty. To her disappointment, Louis-Napoléon did not resume their old carnal relationship, but he rewarded her for their American idyll, flattered to have fathered such a beauty as little Eponine-Hortense.

Zelma's presence at his court was ubiquitous, and she had access to the highest circles of power, as well as a good deal of practice in sharing an exile's woes. Jean-Luc felt himself unfairly exiled from the court, from opportunities the court offered, from society and money. His father's death alone was enough to exclude him. (The Starling was quite right: the story of Marius's tragic death had circulated all over Paris, and indeed, through market people, carters and hostlers and construction workers, who went back to their districts and spoke low in cafés, the story had gone all over France.) With the appearance of *The Toad Napoléon*, Jean-Luc could scarcely show his face in Paris; not only did all the world know, or at least guess, who La Lumière was, but worse, everyone knew that he had been duped by a mere girl, Fantine, assuring him for years that Cosette was in London.

"Your mother always was sly and treacherous, even as a child," Zelma assured him as they drove through the Bois de Boulogne one afternoon, Eponine and Corinne sitting across from them. The carriage was Zelma's. Gone were the days when the girls played cards by the light of a single candle and splurged with a bit of coal. "But that bit of seditious filth, *The Toad Napoléon*, that was truly low and vile. Tell me, what does La Lauriot think of *The Toad Napoléon*?"

"Nicolette cares nothing for politics. She's probably the only person in Paris who hasn't read it. I'm grateful she doesn't care. At least I don't have to absorb her laughter and ill will, the smirks of all Paris—it's humiliating."

"And deprives you of many useful friends." Zelma sighed, twirling her parasol. It was green-and-purple-striped silk, much in fashion at the moment, and tasseled with gold braid. "Only an unnatural mother would do such a thing."

"What's an unnatural mother, Ma?" asked Corinne.

"One who indulges herself at the expense of her son."

"Or her daughter?" asked Eponine-Hortense, who had grown up saucy, sharp-tongued, and beautiful, with black hair, dark eyes, but the only thing Napoleonic about her was her temper. Fully aware that she was the root of the family's happy financial situation, she lorded it over them unmercifully whenever possible. Since French standards of behavior relegated unmarried girls to a role reminiscent of little dogs who neither bark nor bite, Eponine had one ambition: to get married quick and rich. Once married, she could be free of her mother, ride in the Bois by herself, or with a husband. Better yet, with a lover. Married women and actresses had all the fun. Eponine assessed Jean-Luc, across from her now in the open landau. He was certainly beautiful; she'd been half in love with him for years, and her mother had constantly thrown her in his path. Eponine found this odd; everyone knew he wasn't rich and that he came, moreover, from a family with disgraceful political beliefs. Arsène Huvet seemed more her mother's type—charmless, ugly, and dripping with money.

As if in answer to Eponine's thoughts, Arsène's landau approached them. He was in the company of a ravishing dancer from one of the minor theatres. Everyone saluted, but just then the wind caught under the dancer's crinoline and it billowed up over her face. Eponine and Corinne laughed uproariously as Arsène's hands ran all over the girl's lap, trying to bring the skirt down. Fashionable women were now marooned in their skirts, and the custom of a man offering his arm to a lady had died out: men could not reach the ladies. Women were moated about with yards and yards of tulle and lace and flounces, skirts tiered and beribboned and fringed and draped over cages, hoops that freed one's legs from the heavy petticoats but left women looking rather like the new construction of Les Halles, where lacy iron supported roofs with nothing much underneath. As a result, the skirts of fashionable women prohibited them from taking omnibuses or theatre seats. Or like Arsène's dancer, they could become instantly, hopelessly comic in a high wind. Eponine made a crass remark on the low quality of the dancer's underwear and laughed at her own joke. No one else did. Jean-Luc thought her forward and overly indulged for a girl.

The appearance of *The Toad Napoléon* dampened and depressed Jean-Luc's life in many ways. Clerons came back, naturally, sardonically inquiring if he had heard from his mother yet in London. The minister of the interior himself had given Clerons responsibility for finding La Lumière and putting out that torch once and for all.

"I am for the Emperor," Jean-Luc vowed. "These people who are calling themselves La Lumière, they are traitors and I would be the first to—"

"Your mother is calling herself La Lumière," Clerons corrected him acidly. "The whole gang of them are in on it. Pajol is doing the printing. The Starling is linked to it too. I would settle for any one of the three," he added, stroking the half circle of scar that showed above his beard. "*Toad Napoléon* has gone everywhere, all over Paris. All over France. We can't seem to stop it, but we can stop it from happening again. I've been through all the Starling's old haunts and he's flown. I've been through Pajol's too. He and the Fleury woman have fled their old street. I've offered rewards and put a dozen *mouchards* in the rue Mouffetard, Saint-Julien-le-Pauvre, Saint-Sulpice, all that area where the Starling and Germaine are best known. Someone will turn them in sooner or later. I'd prefer sooner."

"Someone will do it for the reward. My mother shouldn't be too difficult to find."

"You think not? I've put the reward for La Lumière, Baron, because the Baroness Pontmercy has so completely vanished that if it weren't for *The Toad Napoléon* I would think she died with your father. I would think she was in London—as you thought all this time," he added, taking his leave, and abandoning Jean-Luc to writhe with the humiliation of it.

As the notoriety of *The Toad Napoléon* spread, Jean-Luc saw and heard insult in every quarter: the waiter who brought him his coffee, the flower seller at the Bouffes-Parisiens, even his own valet, he was certain they all made croaking noises when he passed, or just behind his back. Amongst his own crowd only Arsène had the loyalty not to refer to *The Toad Napoléon,* but Arsène's father sent word that there would be no more sugar beet and salt pork suggestions to the son of a traitor.

This announcement came at a particularly vulnerable moment financially for Jean-Luc, and he took his troubles to Madame Touchard, now Countess Troussebois, where he was certain of sympathy. He stalked the Turkey carpet in her drawing room down to its woof, while Zelma smoked cigarettes and clucked appreciatively. "Your mother is heartless as a possum," she said, throwing in one of the Americanisms that had given her a reputation as a wit. "A crow in lark's clothing. A nasty, filthy city starling."

"If I could, I'd turn the Starling in to Clerons instantly, I'd cheer to watch him transported, to see him hanged or guillotined. I despise him, I always have."

"The Starling?"

Jean-Luc told her the story of his mother's having saved the Starling from arrest in the rue Mouffetard all those years ago and bringing him to *La Lumière*. "He is the original filthy city starling, a thief, a liar, and a beggar. The bastard son of a five-franc whore. And to think my mother trusts him!"

Zelma rose, put her cigarette out, and walked to the mantel, handed Jean-Luc her invitation to the next court ball. There were four each winter, with perhaps six thousand guests each. They were the required invitation for anyone with any pretensions at all. Zelma watched the expression on Jean-Luc's face. "You didn't receive one? It appears His Imperial Highness has declined to favor you." She always lingered over Louis-Napoléon's titles, as though they had chocolate centers. "How narrow of him. He didn't even think *The Toad Napoléon* was funny."

"He read it?"

"Everyone read it. Don't delude yourself."

"I'm ruined." Jean-Luc sank down into one of her satin-striped chairs.

"You can hardly blame His Imperial Highness. After all, your mother writes sedition and your father died fighting the coup d'état. Have you read the newspapers today? They've found the plates for *The Toad Napoléon* down in the sewer. A sewer sweeper came upon them, but he couldn't read and thought they might be melted down and sold for profit. But *voilà*, when the *merde* came off, someone who could read took them to the police for the reward."

"What do the plates matter if they didn't find Pajol, the printer?"

"They'll find him. The plates were near where the sewer comes into the river at the quai de la Rapée. They're searching the whole Saint-Antoine quarter, from the place de la Bastille out to the place du Trône. Troublemakers, all through there—"

"He's not there," Jean-Luc said glumly. "Pajol may have dumped the plates there, but that's not his ground."

"Well, you had better hope they find him. You had better hope he doesn't reset and print more of these lovely pamphlets, which will put you in for a nasty turn of poverty, I'm afraid. The duc de Morny has suggested I drop you altogether, or run the risk of hurting His Imperial Majesty's feelings. And after all, on behalf of our daughter, how can I not comply? How can anyone fail to respond to the imperial pleasure?"

Jean-Luc had not told her that the elder Huvet had withdrawn his patronage. Was that what she was doing too? Without her, without the real-estate information she had access to via her friendship with Haussmann and Morny, the future lay bleak before Jean-Luc, a future without Nicolette, without anything at all.

"La Lauriot won't like you very much poor, will she?" Zelma commented, as if reading his mind.

"Nicolette is an expensive taste."

"Surely she doesn't make you pay, does she?" demanded Zelma, indignant as an English parson. "She has a heart of iron, that slut."

"But she has skin of satin and eyes of gray and hair of gold, and I have loved her since the day I saw her."

"Why haven't you married her?"

"Don't be ridiculous. Why should I marry her?"

"Permit me to observe, my dear baron, on the strength of my long acquaintance with your parents and the fact that they are not here to advise you, that in all likelihood Mademoiselle Lauriot will never marry you. You're impoverished, if I'm not mistaken, and now that you've lost the support of that root-grubbing peasant in Clermont-Ferrand—"

"Huvet—"

"Huvet's father," Zelma clarified coldly.

Jean-Luc was not a great judge of character, regarding others always in the light of his own needs and seeing them only insofar as he saw himself reflected in their eyes. What he saw in Zelma's eyes perplexed him, perhaps for the first time. He'd always assumed he was using—and entitled to—her goodwill, her court connections, her bits of useful information. Might she have been using him as well? All along? The thought was preposterous. Jean-Luc had a tin ear, a tin heart (where everyone but Nicolette Lauriot was concerned), but not a tin head; he had as well a good deal of unalloyed charm, which he now exerted. "Perhaps I have not fully expressed my deep appreciation to you, Countess Troussebois, for those pieces of luck you have thrown my way."

"You come from a thankless family, Baron Pontmercy. Your mother was ever ungrateful, and so I am not surprised she had a thankless son."

Such bluntness stunned him and he felt himself slipping into unknown waters. "I don't believe you've ever told me quite how you knew my parents—or when."

"I met them in their, in our, youth. Before I had the opportunity to go to America, before I met, enjoyed the friendship—" Zelma sucked on the word as if it dripped nectar—"of His Imperial Highness. And now my little Eponine-Hortense has captured the Emperor's goodwill. Better yet, she has captured his fancy. To have caught his fancy, even his whimsy, is everything. Read the newspaper." She thrust it at him. "In the one column we see the plates for *Toad Napoléon* found, the search for a seditious printer, and beside it, look, the Emperor has sent the Légion d'honneur to a ragpicker he passed on the way to Compiègne. The ragpicker now has the honor to be His Majesty's personal ragpicker. You see how it works? That ragpicker owes the Emperor everything. As do we. The Emperor dotes on his daughter Eponine-Hortense."

"As well he should, Countess. She is a beautiful girl."

"She is a sharp-tongued little shrew, who thinks by marrying she can escape her family."

Jean-Luc took up a cigarette, and seeing the way before him grow clearer, he replied, "That depends on the man she marries."

Zelma gave him the cabbage farmer's grin, the cabbage farmer who has just seen pigs eat the competition. "Eponine has many suitors. Some titled."

"I have a title."

"I am speaking of men whose titles come directly from the Emperor himself."

"Mine is an ancient title," Jean-Luc said proudly, adding as an afterthought, "Well, perhaps not ancient, but won on a field of honor, Waterloo."

"And mine was plucked off the guillotine. Snatched from some gibbering aristocrat dragged there kicking and screaming in 1793 to have his head cut off. Why shouldn't I wear it? It looks good on me, this title. Eponine must get her own title. She fancies Huvet. Did you know that?"

"No." Jean-Luc cleared his throat. "I can't imagine anyone fancying Huvet."

"Not even for his money?"

"Aside from his money."

"Aside from money, what is there?"

The answer was too obvious to make, so Jean-Luc smoked, considered the possibilities of Eponine-Hortense. Shrew that she might be, she was a beautiful shrew, whose mother did not wish her to marry into independence. If Eponine were to marry him, they would both be dependent on Zelma. Jean-Luc already was. At the moment Zelma was Jean-Luc's one hope. He glanced around the Touchards' comfortable drawing room, with its hand-painted wallpaper, its gas chandeliers, parquet floor, marble figurines and ormolu ornaments, gilded picture frames around cherubic Fragonards. A creamy shawl, perhaps one thousand francs of hand-worked silk, was tossed over the piano like a rag on a beggar's shoulder. "Naturally you'd want the best husband for your daughter, a man who would love her but who would always have the family's best interests in mind. As well as hers." He flipped his cigarette into the dancing flames.

"I would be only too happy to help my daughter's husband make his way in the world, and I've often thought," Zelma's big teeth gleamed, "how lovely is the name Eponine Pontmercy."

"If you are being so kind as to offer me your beautiful daughter's hand in marriage, madame, I would accept with pleasure. I am honored beyond all measure. Indeed, beyond all words."

"One word will do," Zelma snapped.

"*Merci.*"

Zelma rang for the servant and told him to bring a bottle of champagne, two glasses, and Mademoiselle Eponine-Hortense, and when she arrived, Zelma merely said that Baron Pontmercy had something to say to her. With cigarette smoke coiling behind her like a serpent on the air, Zelma left the two alone, the better to allow for the spontaneous combustion of opportunity and lust.

Chapter 5

*T*he wedding of Hortense-Eponine Touchard and Jean-Luc Pontmercy was the first Monday in March, a great social event, so of course it collected more than the usual crowd of gawkers and indigents, begging musicians who gathered at the doors of the church of Saint-Roch in the fashionable rue Saint-Honoré. The crowd was swollen by fishwives and vegetable vendors, market porters from the nearby Saint-Honoré market, and various inebriated communicants of the church of Saint-Monday reeling home.

In this crowd, leaning on a cane, was the Plumed Lark, a black-toothed crone, whose face was streaked with dirt and grime; she wore a tattered bodice; a mudlark's skirt hung slack from her hips, and her bare calloused feet were thrust into wooden shoes. On her head there was a rusty bonnet with unkempt gray hair streaming out. Her lips were swollen because they had been bitten and her eyes were red-rimmed from weeping. Cosette stood at the back and watched with the others as the carriages began arriving. Emerging from them was a panoply of beautiful women in sumptuous gowns accompanied by men in dashing uniforms, who tried their courtly best to spare the ladies embarrassment, but the laws of physics would not allow a steel-cage crinoline to pass easily through a carriage door. The rabble watching were treated to the sight of some of the most celebrated legs in Paris and moments unfairly comic as the beauties balanced there like great beribboned mushrooms tottering on their stalks. The guests had the bristling self-conscious air of revelers at carnival, preening, prancing, posing.

From one coach stepped a tall man spangled with medals and honors, and someone shouted, "Haussmann!" An egg, a couple of apple cores, and cabbage stumps just missed the prefect of the Seine, but the incident had the advantage of identifying police spies in the crowd, who descended on the malcontents and escorted them briskly away. Cosette was especially wary. She felt Clerons's presence everywhere. Everyone in the rue Mouffetard talked about the reward, laughed, and went on at great length about what they'd do with the money. The military beggar had even asked the Plumed Lark what she'd do, and Cosette vowed to have his medals polished.

On seeing the imperial carriage come down the street, the rough musicians, playing a couple of broken-back violins and a braying flute, flailed out "Partant pour la Syrie," now France's de facto national anthem. For Cosette it was a dirge of defeat, the squealing echo of the old swing at The Sergeant of Waterloo. When she had read her son was going to marry the daughter of Zelma Thénardier, only the efforts of the Countess Crasseux had kept Cosette from some exorbitant gesture to save him. "You can't save him," declared the Countess. "He was lost to you a long time ago."

"He's my son," said Cosette, weeping.

"Not anymore."

But the Countess could not talk Cosette out of coming to the church of Saint-Roch, to stand deep in this crowd of the eager and impoverished, who cheered to watch the imperial guards line up at the church door and Louis-Napoléon's lackeys throwing coins to the crowd as he and Eugénie (the Spanish slut, as she was called at the *barrières*) moved toward the church. How ugly Bonaparte was, with his short legs, waxed mustache, thin hair, and eyes that looked somehow opaque, expressionless as empty fishbowls.

At that very minute a market porter, reeking of sweat and wine, croaked "Toad Napoléon! Scum! Bonapoléon," he slurred drunkenly. The imperial guards moved hastily to subdue him, but he seemed to be under the impression they were comrades there to haul him off to another café. "Stinking Bonapoléon!" he shouted to the delight of the rabble, who only moments before had been cheering the Emperor. Seeing that he'd created a sensation, the porter cried out "Bonapoléon!" several more times before they managed to wrestle him to the ground, but by then the ridiculous and offensive name had caught fire, echoed through the crowd, the epithet compounded, as the porter was hauled away. He would serve six months in jail for his indiscretion. Such is the penance of Saint-Monday.

Bonapoléon—Cosette considered—it had a certain flip and comic ring to it. She noticed across from her a couple of journalists making notes of the arrest for their pages. The sight revolted her. Louis-Napoléon had so strangled the press that they filled their columns with gossip, ribbons of gray print dedicated to flummery, fudge, and frenzy. Marius would have been appalled.

What would Marius have thought to see the groom's carriage arrive and their son emerge with Arsène Huvet? Cosette could not keep back her tears. To see Jean-Luc on his wedding day was to see Marius all over again, save that the son had his mother's blue eyes. And he did not have his father's expression. Jean-Luc did not look like a man in love. He looked, however, enormously pleased.

"Don't cry for him, old girl," another old beggarwoman said, patting Cosette's back as she wept. "He's a handsome handful all right, but these rich ones, they're bald where it counts." She patted her skirt in the place where she, presumably, was not bald. "Their hearts are dry and their hands are wet. It's the only time they sweat, when they get into bed or go to the bank. This, this wedding, it's both. The bed and the bank. No real marriages for them. No real love."

Cosette accepted the stranger's consolation and wept the more. Cosette had had a real wedding, a true love; she had borne a son, this beautiful young man, adored him as a baby, doted on him as a child, loved him still.

Following the groom came a parade of frivolous women and men spangled with ribbons and medals. The American ambassador himself accompanied Corinne Touchard. They could tell he was the American ambassador because of his plain black clothes. Next came the bridal carriage, and the first to emerge was Monsieur Touchard, the Count Troussebois. Cosette had seen him only once before, and still he looked malleable as new butter and just as slick. With difficulty the bride's mother dealt with her voluminous skirt, golden wheat sheaves worked into green brocade billowing from her waist and a froth of tulle around her bony, broad shoulders. Zelma paused at the step of the carriage and looked out over the throng of musicians, beggars, journalists, market women, gawkers with filthy clothes and pale faces.

She knows I'm here, Cosette thought. Clerons is here too. Somewhere. We're all here, survivors of 1832, bound together by the past, though, God willing, not the future. Cosette regarded the rat in satin critically. Zelma had gone oddly gaunt in the years her fortunes had waxed fat. Of course Cosette was gaunt too these days, hardened by her circumstances, her beauty eroded. Zelma's looks had been artificially heightened, her hair crimped and curled, a dry, blazing, bottled red that actually rather suited her coloring, cheeks rouged, lips carmined, eyebrows unnatural black. They all looked that way, Second Empire women, but Zelma had at least learned to smile with her lips closed to conceal her big teeth. Nothing, however, could conceal the look of triumph in her eyes.

When the bride got out she drew everyone's attention, even Cosette's. A black-eyed beauty, young Eponine did not look like any of the Thénardiers, and Cosette assumed her to be the image of her father. Whoever he was. She did not begrudge Eponine the joy of her wedding day. After all, it should be the one day unsullied for any girl. Remembering her own wedding day, Cosette was inclined to charity, and no doubt Eponine was as much a pawn in Zelma's plans as Jean-Luc. I hope you love him, Eponine, Cosette thought. I hope he loves you.

She was about to drift toward the church to find herself a back pew when word ricocheted through the crowd that the carriage of La Lauriot was coming. Cosette stayed for that. Even in the rue Mouffetard, the place Maubert, and Saint-Julien-le-Pauvre, even in the belly of the cour du Dragon, they knew of La Lauriot. Immediately the mountebank musicians struck up a ramshackle "Nicolette Waltz." The carriage stopped and Jacques Offenbach stepped out. Preternaturally thin, his huge nose supported a pince-nez, and his gray hair had retreated from his forehead, fanning out in enormous mutton chops, converging in a thick mustache. Monsieur Offenbach, acknowledging the music, the applause, deigned to conduct briefly, and then, as though the curtain were about to rise, he offered his hand to Nicolette Lauriot as she stepped out.

Cosette stared, trying to place the face, the eyes, which were unforgettable. It was the girl from the Luxembourg Gardens. The girl who'd been with Jean-Luc that last day before the coup. The palm-frond waver. Had Jean-Luc said her name? Cosette could not remember, but she could not forget this face. Had this girl's union with Jean-Luc lasted all these years? Why was he marrying Zelma's daughter if he loved Nicolette? Did he love Nicolette? In the name of love, Cosette might have been prepared to forgive her son almost anything. If he were capable of love, she would know there was hope for him.

To the crowing delight of the rabble, La Lauriot also had difficulty with her enormous crinoline and the steel cage supporting her skirt of gossamer green silk, with a wash of Valenciennes lace, and a brocaded shawl that looked as though it could cover the whole rue Saint-Honoré. The steel hoops tipped forward so her legs showed. High-heeled white satin shoes. Blue stockings held up with jeweled garters. Men and women alike exhaled in unison, and the journalists scribbled away, and the beggarwoman who had had such contempt for the rich remarked, "In a month's time every *fille publique* will wear blue stockings, even if she starves."

Clearly aware of the impression she created, Nicolette paused a moment on the step to savor it, and the question crossed Cosette's mind: Was Mademoiselle Lauriot a heartless mercenary or a consummate actress?

Nicolette beamed as she moved through the aisle of admirers, positively beamed as she entered the church of Saint-Roch, radiantly beamed accepting applause for what was without doubt the finest performance of her life.

Chapter 6

*I*n Jean-Luc's spacious new apartment near the Parc Monceau every window was a balcony, all of them fancifully grilled with iron, and on every balcony two white hydrangeas in Chinese lacquered pots. The flowers were for Eponine-Hortense Pontmercy; the hydrangea, also known as *hortensia*, had always been associated with Hortense Bonaparte. The flowers were the wedding present of the Emperor. One of his wedding presents. The marriage had clearly already altered Jean-Luc's fortunes for the better; Nicolette could tell as much from the manner of the concierge. The concierge of this building was not a snuff-snorting slattern, no fish and cabbage smells, no leering, ham-handed old man. This woman, decently widowed, looked severe as a sister of charity, and she icily informed Mademoiselle Lauriot that the Baron Pontmercy was not at home to receive her.

"I don't need to be received. I have a key."

"He's gone on his wedding trip."

"I know where he's gone, you pump-sucker." Nicolette was famous for her beauty, not her charm. "I'm going up to remove some of my things."

"Nothing leaves the baron's apartment without his express, written permission."

"There is a portrait of me up there. Naked. Do you think his bride will enjoy it? No doubt the baron will reward you for failing to let me pass."

But once inside Jean-Luc's apartment, Nicolette knew she was not alone. From the drawing room there came raucous sounds of a single voice singing a crude rendition of "Camptown Races." To Nicolette's complete surprise, she opened the door to find the Countess Troussebois in her underwear, her steel-cage hoop across the room with the skirt lying in a frothy puddle nearby. Zelma's high-heeled shoes were swinging in the air as she lay on a sofa before the fireplace. All around it on the marble floor there was broken glass and on one table nearby an armada of champagne glasses and bottles of iced champagne, some empty. Zelma peered over the sofa, stood, in her awkward way pirouetted over to the table and asked if Nicolette would like to drink to the bride.

"I don't believe we've met," said Nicolette coldly.

"Forgive me for not waiting for a formal introduction, but everyone in Paris knows you, the men in the biblical sense."

"Drunkenness ill becomes you, madame."

"*Au contraire*—it's very becoming. A few more bottles and I intend to invite in street musicians to play for me so I can dance the cancan!" She emptied one bottle, most of it, into a glass, the rest splashing on the inlaid table and the floor. She thrust this glass into Nicolette's hand and struggled, cursing the cork of another bottle, till it shot off and the champagne frothed down the bottle. Then she poured some for herself. "To the happy couple."

Nicolette stood stony and inert.

"Very well. To Eponine Pontmercy!" Zelma downed her champagne in one gulp and flung the glass into the fireplace, where it shattered with the rest of them. "She got him!" Zelma crowed. "My daughter got your man."

"Don't flatter yourself."

"I ask you, Who is the Baroness Pontmercy?"

"He married her for her money."

"My money. Eponine needs me. Your lover needs me. They have nothing unless I am good to them. Which I intend to be, you'll be happy to know. Sponge off him if you like, you'll never marry him."

"I never wanted to marry him. What do I care who he marries? He loves me."

"No, he loves money." Zelma drawled the phrase out, bludgeoning it in the American fashion. She put down her glass, picked up a cigarette, and crunching through the broken glass, she walked to the mantel, brought down one of the heavy silver candlesticks to light it. "That's what he really loves. Money. That's why he and I get on so splendidly. I'm going to make him a rich man. I'm going to make him into everything his mother despises."

"What has she to do with this?"

"Seditious traitor, that's what she is. *The Toad Napoléon*. Surely you've read *The Toad Napoléon*."

"I never meddle in politics. I care nothing for politics."

"Ah, as stupid as you are beautiful then. You must be the only person in Paris who hasn't read it. It's funny. Truly. It's treason, but it's amusing treason. She wrote it."

"Jean-Luc's mother? She's in exile in England."

"She's in exile, yes, but she's right here in Paris somewhere. She was there today. I know she was. Clerons knew it, but she scooted past his spies. I know she saw me." Zelma smiled un-self-consciously her big-toothed grin and poured some more champagne. "I wanted to shout, *I've strangled you at last, Lark! You're not singing now, are you, Lark? Come, let's hear you! Sing!*" Zelma finished the glass and flung it. "These were her glasses, these gold-rimmed beauties from her home in the rue des Filles-du-Calvaire. Cosette was drinking from these crystal glasses all those years—the fine house, fine carriage, fine clothes, the adoring husband." Zelma spat on the floor like the Americans she so abhorred. "She had all that while I was teaching French to girls who scalded their own hogs. Well, wherever Cosette is now, she isn't drinking out of these. They're my glasses now and I can do with them what I want. Her son is my son, and I can do with him what I want."

Nicolette put her glass down, but she could not tear her eyes away from the half-clad woman before her, gazing mawkishly at an old sign she'd stood there against the mantel mirror. Hand-painted, crude, with two hooks at the top, it was much faded, a thick slab of wood depicting a soldier, a cannon, and corpses in the background.

"Well, old man," Zelma said to the Sergeant of Waterloo, "I've done it for you, you thieving bastard. And for you too, old lady, you broken-up wheezing old beggars. Monsieur Marius pays our rent, does he, for charity? Oh, *merci*, monsieur, we kiss your ring, Monsieur Marius. And Jean Valjean, the convict so very fond of charity, oh please, sir, help the less fortunate, the truly deserving poor. They both thought we were horse knackers, slaughterhouse pickers. Well, we are the Thénardiers, the great Thénardiers! And Cosette, little Cosette so frightened in the garden that day . . ." Zelma took a deep swill of champagne. "Cosette couldn't be told today from anyone in that crowd of beggars and drunks and thieves. You've got what you deserve, Cosette. The man you loved is rotting in a common grave in Montmartre Cemetery." Zelma finished her cigarette, flung it, wobbled over to get more champagne, and said to Nicolette, "And I've got what I deserve. Champagne. I lift my glass to my father. He beat Cosette silly. And my mother—now, there was a woman with an arm and a temper. Many's the time I watched my mother beat Cosette with a broom that was bigger than she was."

"Who is Cosette?"

"A bastard. Spawn of a slut and convict. A slave. Slaves in Arkansas eat better, live better than Cosette lived when she was little. We'd feed her what the dog wouldn't eat."

"Cosette, Jean-Luc's mother?"

"Yes! Now she's on the run, like we used to—outrunning the police, the cold, the hunger, the filth." Zelma wrestled with another bottle, and once her glass was filled, she again lifted it to the Sergeant of Waterloo.

Nicolette picked up her glass and sipped cautiously. "Did you know Madame Pontmercy as a child?"

"There is only one Madame Pontmercy," Zelma snarled, her lips drawing back grimly. "My beautiful Eponine." She turned again to the Sergeant of Waterloo. "I have done for you at last what you wanted, what you deserved all along, Eponine, you wanted him, you died to get him, and I've got back at them for you, oh, Eponine—" Zelma wept unabashedly, but when she heard Nicolette leaving, she stopped, ran her hand under her nose, and called out, "My daughter sleeps with your lover. He's on his way to Rome now, to bed down with my daughter. Months and months in Italy! She'll keep him. I know my own daughter. You've lost him. Whatever you think, you've lost him."

The retort died on Nicolette's lips as some terrible premonition crawled up the marrow of her bones, that deep, visceral, and certain. She left the drawing room and went into the bedroom, the bed she had shared with Jean-Luc that wasn't her bed, and now, suddenly, the man was not her man, the lover not her lover. "Ridiculous," she chided herself, going to the window nonetheless. "He's never loved anyone but me." But the question came to her, unbidden, Had he ever loved anyone at all? And Zelma's reply, *He loves money*. Nicolette opened the French doors and stepped out to the balcony with its twin pots of white hydrangeas. She gripped the ornate iron grille, breathing in the early spring evening, the smell of earth turned and the city demolished, the dust of stones destroyed, wood and ancient mortar axed, lumber shorn and sawdust scattered, the streets dug up, the sewers laid down; the cries and ringing hammers of workingmen no longer sounded in the last of the twilight, but the dust they'd raised, the grit lay everywhere, even on the white hydrangeas, and it seemed to catch in Nicolette's throat. She looked down at her hands; her gloves were dirty. Dusting them off, she stared through the surrounding trees, which were bare and crooked, knobby, reaching like the arms of children with rickets, and she raised her eyes to the sky, where a spectral spring moon rocked like a cradle in the dusk. Then she turned, went back in, took a painting from the wall, and carried it, with some difficulty, downstairs. She was a woman in blue stockings carrying *Woman with a Blue Hat*.

Chapter 7

*T*here had been a brothel there, where the rue du Coeur-Volant met the rue des Mauvais-Garçons, for a hundred years, but both streets (and their ironic congruity) were now joined under the name of a sixth-century bishop, Gregory of Tours, who would have been very uncomfortable here. The brothel remained, keeping the former name, and a café evolved that adopted the latter. It was a low café, not so low as to have cups chained to the walls, but it took on the brothel's coloration and, when possible, its customers. Registered prostitutes were all across the street, so the women in the café Mauvais-Garçons were unregistered and subject to arrest by the Morals Brigade if they could be found in bed with men who did not know their names. But here at these crude tables, the men sniffed at the possibilities, and the women, sitting on their fortunes, waited to name their price, four francs. Less for soldiers.

The landlord drank and scarcely paid any attention to his customers, unless, like the man who had just entered, they seemed unlikely patrons of so unsavory a place. This man, dressed in shabby, frayed clothes, had auburn hair and beard slightly salted with gray, and an air of curiosity; he carried a thick pad of paper, and perhaps a dozen pencils stuck out of his pocket. He took a corner table and ordered a glass of wine. The windows of the Mauvais-Garçons were all open, and the noise of the street—mostly men leaving the Coeur-Volant, domestic quarrels, and a few hawkers selling guarantees against impotence—wafted in with the breeze. The café was dim, damp, and smelled of stale tobacco and spilled wine.

Beaujard went to work sketching the men and the women. Months had passed since the Pontmercy wedding, and several of the women here did indeed sport blue stockings, showed them off provocatively. Well might they rely on their legs, for little else was provocative about them, Beaujard thought. One woman sat persistently alone, declining all offers of company; through the smoky light he tried, several times, to capture her expression, but his rendition never satisfied him. He turned his attention to a couple in the shadows conducting truly strange negotiations. He could hear the man's voice, wheedling and threatening in its pitch and inflection, if not the words. The woman sat, shoulders rolled forward, eyes downcast into the cloud of absinthe floating in the glass before her. When she finished the drink, they both rose and came toward the open door, and it was there in the light Beaujard recognized Clerons.

In a brusque fashion, Clerons thanked the woman, put five francs into her outstretched hand. Her glove had holes in the fingers and her skirt had tiny burns from cigarette ashes. Without another word, she left, but Clerons's gaze rested on Beaujard, and the two men assessed one another warily. Finally Clerons said, "You've developed low tastes since we last met, Monsieur Beaujard."

"They're not my tastes. They're my work. I'm an artist."

"You're a painter. Only men whose work is accepted for the Salon may call themselves artists." He leaned over and glanced at the sketches. "As long as you paint five-franc whores, I doubt you'll have that pleasure."

Beaujard's gaze followed the woman who had just left. "I might remark on your own low tastes."

"I'm here to put out a torch, Monsieur Beaujard. The Emperor was not amused."

"Loyalty to anyone, even an Emperor, was never your strong suit, Clerons. Betrayal is your natural element."

"People who break the law must expect to be betrayed." He bid Beaujard goodbye and left.

Undrinkable as the wine was, Beaujard sipped from sheer relief. He ordered another and went back to sketching, though his hand was less sure, and in time he checked his pocket watch.

"You are fortunate your watch is not picked from your pocket in a place like this, monsieur," said a woman approaching him. She didn't have blue stockings, nor a crinoline. Her skirt hung on lean hips, and knobby collarbones peeked out from under her shawl. It was the woman he'd been trying to sketch, the one whose gaunt, haunted expression eluded him, although the rest was easy, the garish red lips, rouged cheeks, and high-piled dry hair under a bonnet frayed at the edges and tied with soiled ribbons. Except for her eyes, she looked like any other four-franc prostitute, wary of the police, crudely assessing a potential customer. To his consternation and despite his protests, she sat down next to him and asked him to buy her a drink. "I'm not interested in your wares, madame."

"Of course not. You are an artist."

"My God—is it? Cosette?" His shock deprived him of the required formality, and he looked into her eyes, as much interested in his failure to bring her likeness to paper as in her identity. "You are so changed."

"I am transformed, my friend."

"Why are we meeting here? You saw Clerons?"

"Bad timing or bad judgment? I thought this place would be safe. I'm shocked Clerons was here. He must have moved in closer than I'd thought." She was pale beneath the garish makeup, and her blue eyes dark with fear.

"You truly are transformed. He could not have known you. I did not know you and I looked for you here, knew you would be here."

She took his arm as if in prelude to some other, more intimate association, the sort most often practiced at the Mauvais-Garçons, and she kept her voice low and confidential. "I'm very grateful to you for coming. I know it's dangerous and probably not wise."

"My dear Cosette," he patted her hand, "a man can die from a surfeit of wisdom, as much as from danger."

"But not in prison."

"They didn't arrest—" he stumbled over his inability to say Pajol's name, as though Clerons had left a *mouchard* ghost in this low café.

"No, but you heard about the plates."

"Yes, and I know why they were found on the quai de la Rapée, so far from, well, from home."

"They closed in on him. They were very near and that was the only thing possible. I carried the goods to the quai de la Rapée so there should be nothing to incriminate him. I could never forgive myself if anything happened to him and those children, and Germaine. It would be terrible. They would starve and I would be powerless. He must be protected. They moved to Montmartre, where they can pass for foreigners."

"To move a few streets in Paris is to give up your own brother. To cross the river is to die."

"In this case, to avoid dying. The Starling's trying to find him some work now, but you know he's never done any work but printing, and his hands, the ink is ingrained in his hands."

"Like Verdier."

"Yes. His hands give him away."

"Your hands give you away, too," he said, almost tenderly. "A painter notices hands. Perhaps a policeman does not. Yours are brown and inkstained. Prostitutes' hands don't look like that."

The landlord lurched by with the bottle, and for his benefit Beaujard seemed to be quarreling with the lady over the price of her services. He paid for another glass for each of them, though the wine was unendurable and Cosette rubbed reflexively between her brows.

"It's impossible now, for the moment," she lowered her voice to a husky whisper, "that Pajol should be anywhere near a press. And yet there is—there could be—the need for a press. For a printer. For an ally. There is an ally in Brussels. Pajol gave me the address. I thought perhaps you would, you might, you could go to Brussels now and then, yes?"

Beaujard considered the proposition. "If I did, if I went to this address in Brussels—"

"All I would ask, do ask, is that you leave something there, not that you should bring it back. Into France there are many avenues. Out of France, very few. I'm only asking, Monsieur Beaujard, and if you decline, I understand completely."

Pascal Beaujard sipped and considered. "You know that as a veteran of *La Lumière* I am unemployable in the Second Empire, so I must rely on my painting. It goes well, usually." He shrugged. "There are even days when the painting is intoxicating. But there are days when I can't paint, when I sometimes just mourn— Verdier, Monsieur Pontmercy, so many who lost so much. When I think of the life you have been forced to, my heart breaks. Your husband's heart would have broken if he knew."

"Marius's heart would have broken in any event. I'm not certain truly that he ever recovered from the June Days, when he watched the revolution become civil war, when he watched the Republic he had dreamed of devour the revolution he had worked for. He was an idealist and they are not supple creatures, able to bend with the breeze and bow with the hurricane. They must always stay upright," Cosette paused and looked down the long void of the past to the rue Mauconseil, where the future had irrevocably altered, "until they fall."

Beaujard sipped his terrible wine. "I worked for Marius Pontmercy for almost ten years, and I never met a man of such courage and intensity and conviction. Now, it's so unfair, so terrible, that our passions of 1848 should seem comic. All that commitment to change and social justice now appears silly and fatuous. And yet—for those of us who lived it, how can we ever describe what it was like, that one moment, that spring—that glorious spring of 1848—when we had changed the whole world?"

"It's as vanished as the rue de Combray, isn't it? The Republic is gone, and Marius is gone, and there's not so much as a slab of marble to note the passing of either one. Sometimes I am so sad I can barely breathe, Monsieur Beaujard, but it does please me to be a thorn in Bonaparte's side. My father once told me I was a rose, not a lily, and I should keep my thorns." She smiled. "All I really want is to remind people. That is my sole ambition, really. To be certain that the ass in the law's regalia is still recognizably the ass, that people will know that the toad who puffs himself up to be an ox is still just a—"

Suddenly Cosette found herself pulled into Beaujard's embrace, drawn down in a single movement, so swift the glasses spilled and the wine ran over the ends of the table; she was held tightly, firmly in Beaujard's arms and stretched across Beaujard's lap, his face covering her face in a passionate kiss, and she realized there had been a dark shape at the café door. She wrapped her arms around his back. Beaujard and the woman in his arms looked like two people who have settled on their price.

Beaujard finally looked up, but he did not raise his face from hers, murmuring against her cheek, "Clerons returned. He's gone now, but you must leave immediately. Be very careful."

"Monsieur Beaujard, you take my breath away."

"Madame Pontmercy," he whispered, "for the pleasure of that kiss, I would deliver your manuscript to the toad himself. Where do I find it?"

A very unlikely place. Pascal Beaujard found himself across the street from the Mauvais-Garçons, in the Coeur-Volant, dealing with Mother, while the half-wit son regarded him suspiciously. They did not often get men in coats and vests, even frayed. And this one must have Mimi? Mother assured him there were many finer girls, certainly younger girls, more, well, athletic, vivacious—

"It must be Mimi. I've heard she's fantastic."

"Really?" inquired Mother, impressed. "That'll be six francs. You'll have to wait."

He paid. "Do you mind if I sketch?"

Mother didn't and he had several sketches of her and of the other women waiting in varying states of undress. They smoked, drank warm beer and wine, played cards, hummed Offenbach tunes, and gossiped about the latest of the Emperor's many amours, the Bonapartists among them proud of his appetites, to say nothing of his reputed prowess. Also, they argued about what Nicolette Lauriot had last worn to the Maison d'Orée; *Le Figaro* said one thing, *L'Illustration* another. In the meantime Mother sent a message up to Mimi via the undermistress, an inflated title given to a slattern who sold oranges and tobacco and cleaned up vomit.

Mimi's client came down and Mother sent Beaujard right up, no need to waste time. He found Mimi barefoot but clothed, just finishing buttoning her bodice, a look of wooden immobility on her face.

This was the woman who had just left Clerons in the Mauvais-Garçons. Cosette had told Beaujard nothing save that the manuscript was with Mimi for safekeeping. Safekeeping? He went to the window to open the Venetian blinds, but Mimi stopped him.

"I'm sorry it's so hot in here. But the police, you know, they don't allow us to open our shutters."

"The police?" His hands went cold.

"Well, the Morals Brigade, you know, they register the prostitutes, haul us in for sanitary checks, arrest the unregistered. I guess they're not really police, but they are to prostitutes. They are their own police, their own courts, their own jails." She spoke without inflection, without indignation or humor or anything. She asked if he'd like the light left on and if he had anything special in mind.

"Actually—" Beaujard looked around the room—"I do."

It later became famous, the painting of this anonymous woman and the little room with wallpaper bloated from the damp and no carpet save for a bit of rag in front of the bed, which had an iron frame and was pushed against the wall to save space. A soiled cloth covered a small table, where things were spread and spilled, coffee grounds, sugar, a cup on its side, a lamp, a syringe, and a needle. Mimi's underclothes hung over the chairs, and the dresser gaped open, the drawers full of flimsy tissue-pink pawn tickets. A small stove glowered in the corner, the flue clearly faulty, and black smoke crawled up the walls. Despite the stifling heat, the stove was lit and an iron and curling irons cooked there. Combs with broken teeth, paint pots, and a burnt cork lay on the shelf beneath a large mirror, the most striking thing in the room.

"Could I draw while you—do whatever you want?"

"Draw me? How?"

"However you'd like."

"You don't want—" she made a little gesture, and for the first time her face lost some of its passivity.

"No, I just want to draw."

She took off her clothes in deference to the heat, threw them on the bed, and picked up the curling tong, applied it to her hair in front of the mirror. Her hair sizzled under the iron, and the smell filled the little room.

"I saw you with Clerons in the café."

"He gave me five francs. That was nice."

"For what?"

"For nothing. He wanted—" She turned to him. "You're the one."

"Am I?" Beaujard demanded. "Am I also going to walk out of here and be arrested?"

"I did not expect Clerons. He surprised me."

"And for five francs you'll send me out of here with a manuscript that will get me sent to New Caledonia, blackwater fever, and certain death?"

Mimi did not turn around, but regarded him in the mirror as she fried her hair, one lock at a time. "Monsieur—whatever your name, I don't want to know—for five francs I will get into bed with you. I will let you get whatever it is you need, or want, out of my body, or into it. It makes no difference to me. I will let you grunt and thump and hump. I will let you cry if you want. Some of them do. Some of them aren't happy unless the woman cries. Some don't want to see anything at all, so it's very dark. Some just don't want to see my face while they're at it, so my nose is pressed into the bed or I look at the wall. So yes, for five francs I will go over there and lie down and spread my legs and take you in my arms and sell you my body, which I don't care about anymore. But if you think for one moment that for five francs I would betray my own son, that I would betray the woman who saved his life in the June Days when the Republic—" Mimi spat on the stove and it sizzled—"wanted to kill him, to imprison him, to transport him to his death, to take my only son away from me forever, then it is you who are the degraded one, monsieur. Not I."

Beaujard's pencil had stopped moving, and he regarded her reflection in the mirror. "Are you the Starling's mother?" he asked incredulously.

"What did you think? He came out of a cocoon?"

Beaujard mumbled something inadequate and asked her name.

"Mimi. Mimi Lascaux. Just like Gabriel's name. Lascaux."

"Madame, I—"

"Mimi is fine. What you want is in the bureau there. One of those drawers."

He found a package wrapped in used paper and tied with a stringy red ribbon.

"I put the ribbon," she said. "I thought the color suited the contents, but really, I don't care about all that, you know. What does it matter who's on top of us? Emperor? King? It's always someone, isn't it? Someone's always on top of you, and then it's the grave and probably someone's on top of you there. But it matters to Gabriel. Gabriel's very passionate about it."

"And Clerons?"

Mimi quit frying her hair and turned to him. "He shows up now and then. Five francs. He thinks one day he will catch me when I'm not myself. I'm always not myself. Sometimes I watch from a long, long ways away, I see myself from a distance, and I am interested, but not fascinated. Do you understand?"

"Madame—" Beaujard stammered, moved, humbled, distressed.

"Bonsoir, monsieur, if you're done. You should be done. Mother doesn't like things to take too long."

He picked up the package with its red ribbon and wrapped it in the sketches he'd made, and he left her waiting on the bed like a child to be called down to Sunday lunch with relatives, absolutely certain of the boredom ahead and knowing she was doomed to it, as though her incorrigible innocence lay both barricaded and protected in a fortress of absinthe and morphine.

Part II

The Garden of Louis-Napoléon

*Revolutions have a terrible arm and a fortunate
hand; they strike hard and choose well. Even when incomplete,
even degenerate and abused . . . they almost always retain
enough of the light of providence to prevent a fatal fall.
Their eclipse is never an abdication.*

—VICTOR HUGO
Les Misérables

Chapter 8

*H*e stood outside staring at the sign over the door, shuddering miserably, unprotected from the September rain, so wet Madame Fagennes hoped he would not come in at all, but he did. He muddied her floor, which annoyed her, and when he opened his mouth, his accent betrayed him as a gross provincial, and when he spoke, she was instantly on guard.

"I want to speak to someone named the Starling. Is he alive? I was told I could find him here, if he was alive."

Madame Fagennes busied herself with a glance around her café. Perhaps a dozen people, men, women, one of them the Plumed Lark, driven off the street by the rain, sitting near the stove with a single glass of wine. Madame Fagennes did not know most of these customers by name and feared them for that reason. In honor of the Emperor's spies, Madame Fagennes kept not one but three cheap plaster busts of Napoléon III on her zinc counter and the shelf below the mirror, which was new. She had a framed medallion of him on the wall and, rather than answer this boy, she whistled "Partant pour la Syrie."

The boy looked perplexed and exhausted. He was about fifteen, wearing masons' clothing, including the skullcap, but he carried no hod or pickaxe. "I need to leave a message for the Starling," he insisted in his harsh provincial voice.

"I take no messages for the Starling. I'm for the Emperor," she announced.

"I have work starting tomorrow. I can't keep coming here, looking for this Starling."

"Why look here?"

"This is the Café Rigolo, isn't it?"

"I'm for the Emperor."

"I have to leave a message for this Starling. If I don't, my father will disown me."

"From the look of you, you won't inherit much anyway. If you want to leave a message for someone, you'll have to put it in writing. Maybe I'll see this person. And maybe I won't."

"I can't write," complained the boy.

"There is the scrivener over there, chased inside by the rain." She nodded toward the Plumed Lark by the stove, her face concealed by the rusty bonnet with its graying locks. "She does a fine letter, so they say."

Cosette studied the boy, who seemed distraught as well as damp, confused, and at the same time ridiculous: no one in Paris would come into a strange café and ask outright for a strange man, a man they weren't even certain still lived. She too glanced around at the other people in the café, for spies. One need fear only the men. She even feared this boy.

Slowly, La Lumière's *Bonapoléon,* printed in Brussels, had made its way back into France. On the little pamphlet—La Fontaine again reworked to the Emperor's detriment—the printer was not noted and the author a mere picture, the torch. *Bonapoléon* eased and eked and squeezed and bobbed and rolled its way into France, not in any great numbers, but steadily. And as with all things in France, it made its way to Paris. Every wagon can't be stopped at the border, emptied of its straw. Every traveler can't be stopped and searched. Though all of those who looked like radical rogues could, people with coarse hands, coarse clothes, coarse tongues and manners. Every troupe of circus acts can't be inspected for hollow stilts; the acrobats of course are blameless and near-naked anyway. Every itinerant cobbler and *compagnon* can't be checked. *Bonapoléon* could be packed in watertight containers, and an expert sailor could maneuver his little craft into a quiet bay, an inlet, and unload on the tide. *Bonapoléon* became the most prized and hated pamphlet in all of France. And through all this rising tide of sedition and oppression, Cosette plied her scrivening trade obscurely, taking no chances. She looked to be no more than an old woman, gray hair streaming from her bonnet, bent, missing teeth, who yet wrote people's letters with a sure hand. But she studied her every customer, especially this one, whose youth might only camouflage his true intent.

He bought a glass of *vin bleu,* and sat down across from the Plumed Lark. "I need two letters. They are short."

"Short letters cost less. Still, you understand, there is the paper and the ink, the time."

"How much? I have no money."

She put the price above what she thought he would pay, and the haggling process was not nearly as lengthy and full of bluff and gesture as it would have been with a Parisian, but it gave Cosette a chance to assess not merely the boy but the Café Rigolo and her chances of escape if need be. There was only one door and no chance of escape. She debated leaving immediately. "Are both these letters to this person Starling?"

"No. One to my father. Alphonse Grincourt, Saint-Simon."

"Is there an address?" She reached down into her wooden box on the floor, pulling out paper, ink, a pen, and blotter.

"In Saint-Simon?" He chuckled. "Everyone knows my house. It's the only one that isn't crumbling. Why should I pay extra for the address? Father—" He stopped and used his fingers to count, presumably words. The boy spoke French haltingly and with a tough provincial crust to the words. "I have done—no, say this—I have left the message. I could not wait. Tomorrow I have work and I must take it. Paris is fine. I will bring money home when I return. Truly Papa—well, just say I did my best. Denis. Your son, Denis, if it will cost no extra."

"Do you want to make your mark so your father will know it's from you? Can he read?"

"Yes. He's tried to teach me, but I am a stupid lout." He was proud of it, and he took the pen and made a laborious D. "Now for the message to this Starling. Short too."

Her fingers trembling slightly, Cosette took up her pen.

"I don't need to pay for an address. I'm just leaving it here."

Cosette shrugged.

"Go to the old Corinth, rue Mondétour. On the wall, *Vive le peuple!* In the wall, a note."

Cosette's blue eyes widened and the blood seemed to leave her head as she gripped the table, and her breath beat against her ribs. She dropped her pen; ink splattered everywhere. "Who sent you with this message?" Cosette managed to whisper, though whatever the boy might have said she could not hear over the shot, the single shot, the one she had heard over and over since that December night. She could not see because everyone had put out their candles so as not to illuminate the target for the enemy, as if the whole street, perhaps the whole world, had wanted to protect Marius as he walked down the rue du Petit-Carreau toward the rue Mauconseil and the army awaiting him there, his arms outstretched, his words falling into the night and into the wind, the revolutionary wind blowing across Europe. She heard the wind, the words, the snow as it settled on her shoulders just before the shot, and after that? What? Jumbled and shattered, jagged with despair, a memory she could never quite summon, a pain she could never quite dismiss. The air, the breath, the very life had been knocked out of her with that single shot. But others followed and one had pierced her shoulder when she'd tried to climb over the barricade to reach Marius, to stop him, to save him. Then the volley as the army attacked. And then, the only other words she remembered, perhaps because she had heard them once before, so long ago, as though the events set in motion in 1832 before found their long-denied fulfillment: Verdier's voice: *It's finished. It's over. There's nothing you can do.* It was Verdier's farewell.

The boy across from her picked up his wine, and Cosette ran her rough hands over her dry lips, sipped her wine, held the glass. Later, after the fighting, Thérèse had found Verdier's body, claimed and buried him. But not Marius. Thérèse had looked. Jean-Luc had looked. But Marius had gone into the common grave. And over the years Cosette thought it was not so very terrible after all. Marius would probably have preferred that. All his life Marius had fought for the anonymous men and women of France. He should lie with them in death. She collected her composure with difficulty and spoke very softly. "Who did you say sent you with this message?"

"My father."

"Ah," she read the first letter, "Alphonse Grincourt? Saint-Simon?"

"Yes. He's a mason. Here in Paris you need armies of masons, that's why I've come here, for the message and the work. In Saint-Simon, what is there in Saint-Simon?" he shrugged. "The church and the prison."

With an effort, Cosette asked, "What prison?"

The boy seemed bored. "The old fortress, Ham, nearby. The fortress where the Emperor was once a prisoner. It was all before my time," he added, sensing undue interest. "What do I care?"

"Your letters are free. Say as much as you like. Quietly."

"To my father?"

"No. This one. To the Starling."

"That's all. That's all there is, all I was told to say."

Go to the old Corinth, rue Mondétour. On the wall, *Vive le peuple!* In the wall, a note.

They milled with market crowds, but Les Halles were not at all the old twisted streets Marius had once fought in. The bold, broad rue Rambuteau had erased the old rue de la Chanverrerie, and Cosette and the Starling walked, sheltered from the rain, by high glass roofs supported by lacy ironwork protecting Haussmann's temple to the bounty of France, the testament spread here to the honor of France's cuisine, the glory of her seas, her fields, her meadows. Fish lay displayed, dappling, their scales like shining silver coins, fat pears like golden teardrops, cabbages stacked like cannonballs, and eggs lined up, tier after tier, like white choirs, aromatic wands of fennel waved before the fine-herbs markets, and plucked white geese and yellow chickens hung unprotestingly upside down in the poultry halls, and across the street in the rue Pirouette, in the window of a shop, there were sausages thick as the arm, tied up like gifts. Cosette and the Starling, accustomed only to their bit of bread and broth and onion, were dazzled by the markets, the endless provisions, though they felt no true hunger. Their guts were coiled, tense, listening for the shriek of a police whistle over the cries and calls of Les Halles.

"It's a trap," the Starling cautioned grimly. "You wait for me in the church of Saint-Eustache."

"But, Gabriel, I know where it is. I told you. During the February Revolution, I found him there. He told me, showed me where it was, but I said—" Cosette bit her lips against the tears. "I said I didn't want the note. I had the man."

"Only two men from that 1832 barricade yet remain alive, madame."

"Please don't call me madame."

"Sorry, Lark. Pajol and Clerons. We know Pajol knew nothing of this note. I asked him. So the only other possibility—is Clerons. If Clerons has sent this message, then—well, perhaps this boy looks to you like a bit of provincial veal—" he waited till a market porter had passed them, his cart laden with pink hams—"But if I go in there, I will be arrested and you will have to vanish."

"They don't want you."

"They will settle for me, but they want you very much. They want to see the torch out. They want La Lumière to be as dead as La Fontaine."

"I couldn't bear it if you came to harm because of me. I can't bear what's happened to Pajol."

"Pajol is not dead or imprisoned, is he? Now you go to the church and wait. If I don't come, go to the *barrière* d'Italie. You'll be safe there. They will protect you with their lives out there."

"They don't know who I am."

"They know enough to know what they don't want to know."

"It shouldn't be so much to protect me."

"There you're wrong, Lark."

"Au revoir, Starling."

"If I don't come back, you'll tell Mimi and the Countess."

"I'll tell Fantine too."

Whatever he might have said, he didn't, but sadness settled across his features like an autumn twilight. His face was now a man's face, rough-shaved and dirty, the nose still crooked, the smile lopsided, if not ugly, unique. He turned and walked away.

Cosette walked to the church of Saint-Eustache, pushed open the heavy door into the chill vaulted dimness, determined to wait there all night if need be. She could hear the very candles drip and the mumbled prayers of old market women, who somehow brought with them into the church smells of turned earth and warm animals and silvery fish. Cosette, in her rusty bonnet with its escaping gray hairs, her roughed hands, her coarse clothes, and hardened feet thrust in wooden shoes, looked like any of them; she bent at the rail as they did, knelt, hands clasped. But underneath her shawl she drew out a different sort of rosary, wedding pearls, her gold wedding ring. She knelt there, prayed, wept, believing for all these years she'd had only Marius's memory and now, here before her was the prospect of time. *He's alive, he's alive, my love is alive, by some miracle he lives. O thou just and merciful God to have kept him from the grave, and if the prison has claimed him, at least it's not the grave, he's alive, alive, alive.* And she stayed thus for what felt like days, though only hours passed, and she did not see or hear the Starling as he came down the aisle and put in her folded hands a piece of paper, crimped tight as a bullet, written a quarter century before: the words outside of time, the lover still within time's purview, that old blessed edifice of mortality, flesh.

Chapter 9

Napoléon III carried on the court festivities at his palace at Compiègne, some hundred and fifty miles north of Paris, and the train bearing him there shrieked through the countryside, steam and smoke swirling on the autumn air as the engine harnessed time and velocity, wish and efficiency, and hurtled forward, leaving only cinder and the scent of dry ash in its wake. The Lark and the Starling, however, were helping a farmer with his cart. The wheel had come off, and together they had helped him repair it and put it back on, while the horse waited patiently and leaves swirled around them. The cart, happily, was empty, the farmer returning to his home near Saint-Quentin from Paris, where he had sold his duck pâté, the best in the world, he claimed; he waxed on at length once they'd got the cart up and moving. Cosette and Gabriel were grateful for the ride. Quite the poet of duck pâté, he pontificated on the care and engorging of duck livers and how he hoped one day to send his goods to Paris by railway, but in the meantime the cart would do. Properly prepared, duck pâté kept well, he said, and his wife made the pastry casings.

"Are you very near the fortress of Ham?" inquired Cosette, when he had run the thread of conversation down to the needle of his wit.

"The most illustrious prison in France! Everyone knows our Emperor himself was once a prisoner there. And after the coup, he sent his most dangerous opponents to Ham, Cavaignac and Thiers, but they never tasted my duck pâté. The Emperor did, though. I personally brought it to the fortress for him. I have always been a Bonapartist and my wife as well. We came to Ham to see His Imperial Majesty and the Empress when they visited in 1853. They say when the Empress saw the three little rooms he'd lived in for six years, she threw herself into his arms and wept. He showed her his garden and some flowers he grew."

"Perennials, I assume," Cosette remarked acerbically.

The duck enthusiast regarded her oddly, and the Starling explained that his mother was tired. "We're going to see my aunt in Saint-Simon. It's been a long journey from Paris."

The duck farmer had had many experiences in Paris, and they were obliged to listen to all of them, liberally spiced with tales of the Parisians' cruelty, pomposity, and mistaken notion that France ended at the city's *barrières.*

When at last they reached the cutoff for Saint-Simon a few miles west he let them out, and went on north. The Lark and the Starling trudged in the last of the afternoon light toward Saint-Simon. To these Parisians, the village looked crouched, a cross between animal and vegetable, the houses shaggy, thatched, ill plastered, with steep-sloping roofs; some of them had so grown into the ground they were perhaps upheld by the virtual beams of braided ivy. Save for the church, the plaster and stonework everywhere was crumbling and ill tended, and then, in the last of the long rusty twilight, they came on a house where the stonework was well maintained and the plaster not crumbling, the door hung properly without chinks of light showing around it and the bricked chimney upright and drawing properly. Clearly, this was the house of a stonemason.

Cosette's knock was answered by a woman strong, stout, her hair pulled back severely from a face dominated by close-set eyes. The Lark and the Starling were oddly speechless, knowing their speech would condemn them as Parisians, till finally Cosette inquired, "Madame Grincourt?" The woman assented wordlessly. "We have a message from your son, Denis. From Paris. The boy is fine," she added when the woman's face suddenly darkened. "Well and fine. The message he sends is for his father."

Madame Grincourt drew them into a large room with a fire-place and, mark of modernity, a stove on which a huge pot bubbled, filling the room with delicious smells of leeks, sage, and rosemary. There was a dresser where dishes lined up smartly. Strings of onions, garlic, and apples and bunches of leeks hung from separate gibbets in the rafters. A large featherbed absorbed one whole corner, and the wooden floors shone as though the very dust had got wrestled to the ground. A single lamp pooled light over a table, where a man sat smoking a clay pipe.

"You have a message from Denis?" he inquired coldly. "Odd, since I have had a letter from him."

"You asked your son to take a message to the Starling?"

"I told you so," the wife lamented. "I told you your meddling would bring us to this. I told you it would bring us to grief, to death." She flung her apron over her eyes and wept.

"Stop it, woman! You'll have me in Algeria before they do." He eyed the newcomers with hooded eyes. "Why would they send a woman anyway? Who are you?"

"You sent a message for the Starling, and I am here."

"I sent no message to anyone in Paris."

"This is my mother, the Plumed Lark, who wrote your son's letter. What do you want for proof?"

"I want not to go to Algeria," declared Monsieur Grincourt. He was nearing forty, rough-shaved, wiry, but not gaunt. The skin on his enormous hands was dry and hard as mortar, and a drooping mustache concealed his mouth, but his eyes were shrewd and secretive. To the Starling, who had worked with many such men over the last several years, he seemed a typical mason; they were, in general, a taciturn lot, unless drunk, and it was a hard life.

"We know who the message was from," said the Starling. "That's why we're here."

Cosette stepped forward, picked up a pencil from the table, and drew the Plumed Lark. "Monsieur Grincourt, I would not send you to Algeria. I will testify for you at heaven's gate, Monsieur Grincourt. You and your son have brought me the possibility, the hope, that God might yet return to me what I thought Louis-Napoléon had taken, that from the grapes of despair I can still press the wine of hope, that God is good after all, and that miracles can happen. Once before, Monsieur Grincourt, I've had a miracle in my life. I was rescued on a Christmas Eve, but it was so long ago I had forgotten—forgotten to believe in miracles and believed only in memory. When your son sent that message to the Starling, the grave opened up, Monsieur Grincourt, and however terrible the prison is, it is not the grave. My husband was wrong, the scaffold is not better than the gutter. The gutter is better than the grave. I bless you, Monsieur Grincourt. I would have come this far just to say that."

Under his heavy mustache Monsieur Grincourt's lips remained firm. He reached to the mantel, took a candle and a taper, lit it, and inquired of her earnestly, "La Lumière?"

Chapter 10

*T*he gatekeeper at the fortress of Ham was a fanatic Bonapartist, whose daughter had been Louis-Napoléon's laundress and mistress and had borne his two sons, both of whom now lived in Paris. Never minding that his daughter had married someone else and moved away, the gatekeeper was insufferable on the subject of Bonaparte. When the mason Grincourt came to work at the fortress, the old man drove him to jaw-clenching fury with his remarks about His Imperial Highness. But the work was steady, the pay decent, and the radical mason kept his mouth shut.

Now the mason's new assistant had to keep his mouth shut. Grincourt explained to the gatekeeper that his son had got another job, and this man, Jondrette, was a distant cousin, a mute from Amiens. The illiterate Jondrette signed in with a mark, while the gatekeeper made deprecating remarks about men from Amiens, mute or not. He also said Grincourt would have to apply to the commandant for the mute's pay; wages for one assistant did not mean necessarily wages for another.

Cosette remained at the Grincourt home, Madame Grincourt still hostile and putting forth the story in the village that Cosette and her mute son were cousins from Amiens. She started this rumor the day after their arrival, when she took her eggs to the small village market. The Grincourts' garden supplied them with surplus produce and they kept besides some chickens, a pig, and a horse to draw the cart. Madame Grincourt's fondest wish was to own a cow.

"And you had better be mute yourself," she cautioned Cosette in her kitchen as she surgically removed the top of a pumpkin, "or they will know you for a Parisian instantly. In a village like this, they know everything, and if they don't, they make it up, the maggots. I'll tell them what I want them to think, and you live up to it, and you keep that bonnet with the gray hair on too. If they find you here, a woman with hair cut short as yours, they'll think you've brought the fever with you, or escaped from a nunnery after debauching the priest."

Dutifully Cosette put the rusty bonnet back on. "Please give me some work, Madame Grincourt. Any work, however hateful. I want to be of use."

"You could have been of use staying in Paris." Madame Grincourt brought up whole handfuls of pumpkin innards with such vengeance they might have been Louis-Napoléon's entrails. "After the coup, by Christmas, you Parisians, you were back at it, the old cancan in the streets, that's how soon you gave in to Bonaparte. Well, madame, it took them months to crush us out here in the provinces. In some places, it took years. My husband almost went to prison, prison or Algeria or Cayenne, and he would have, but I kept a tight hold on him. These villagers, they denounced us to the priest, they said we were reds, socialists, that in the village of Saint-Simon we were Saint-Simonists after that radical freethinker. I had to go to the priest and soothe him. Yes, and it cost me my pig that year, given to the church. I've kept my husband straight since then, but these peasants, they are Bonapartists to a man. Do you know what they told the peasants when Bonaparte took power? Go into the fields, life will be so good, put your heads back, open your mouths, and cooked larks will drop from the sky."

"I have heard that," Cosette replied dryly. "Please give me some work, so I can help earn our bread while we stay here."

After she finished heaping deprecations on her neighbors, Madame Grincourt added she hoped Cosette and her son would not be here long. "You know, madame, you are the most wanted woman in France. That bit of sedition, *The Toad Napoléon*, everyone in France has read it. In Saint-Quentin, when soldiers pass, the boys make toad noises, grunting at them, and then cut and run down the alleys. Here in our village the priest burnt your book in the square. He said anyone caught reading *The Toad Napoléon* would be denied communion."

"If France is so happy with Louis-Napoléon, if five million men legitimized the coup d'état, then why are there so many willing to read an attack?"

Madame Grincourt raised her eyes to heaven, her bare arms deep inside the pumpkin, scraping out its flesh. "How funny is it, madame, when a poor man falls off his donkey? He falls, you say, ah, there is an oaf in the mud. But to watch a bishop fall! To see him clad in all his finery and tumble in the mud! To see the Emperor tumbled into a toad, even the Bonapartists of this village, they laugh at that. Who in France will not laugh to watch the king walk in shit? Your tales, madame, the toad who envied the imperial eagle, mistook the eagle for the vulture—we all remember Boulogne, madame. Especially here. And then the toad who puffs himself up so with vanity and air he deflates like a bladder." Madame Grincourt smiled in spite of herself. "The ass who stands upright admiring himself in the mirror as he puts on the robes of the law. That was all very funny, madame. Those who could read it did, and those who could not, they all heard the stories. They are all very funny. They are dangerous. You are dangerous, and I don't like you in my house."

"If you won't let me work, at least let me pay you."

"Your son is sleeping in the shed with the horse. Anyone can sleep on straw. You are sleeping in the bed of my Denis, who is gone, more's the pity. The bed is empty. What do I care?"

Cosette drew out her much-depleted pearl necklace and began to untie it, but Madame Grincourt stopped her.

"Put away your pearls, madame," she took a huge platter of rind and offal, "and go throw this before the swine out back. There are water buckets to fill in the corner. The well is down the road. Speak to no one. My husband would never allow me to take money from La Lumière, not just you, madame, but your husband. My husband admires Monsieur Pontmercy above all men. He read *La Lumière* faithfully for years and years. He read it on our wedding night. I should have known what I was getting into," she added bleakly. "Now, go."

Chapter 11

*T*he fortress of Ham was a great brooding hulk of medieval stone rising from the plains of Picardy. Once there had been a moat around it, but it had dried over hundreds of years to a marshy bit of waste ground, where reeds and cattails grew, and the inner walls had been allowed to fall entirely to ruin after the invention of gunpowder. The outer walls were new, as fortresses go, seventeenth century, but time had not improved either the chill of the stones or the bite of the drafts that ripped around them. Water came from a well in the outer courtyard. The inner courtyard, originally of stone and the site of a gibbet, had been enlarged in the nineteenth century, with a wall knocked down to allow for an anemic garden, though nothing could disguise the squeal of the heavy gate on iron hinges, the snap of the locks, the tread of the sentry who kept watch. The medieval battlements and towers had not altogether crumbled, and so it was perhaps not altogether ironic that the men imprisoned here in the nineteenth century were again guilty of the old medieval crime: disloyalty to the reigning lord. Other than Marius Pontmercy, the other prisoners were radical leaders of provincials who had rebelled against the coup here in the north of France, socialists for the most part, imprisoned—rather than transported to Algeria or Cayenne—because they could and would lead others. Louis-Napoléon did not trust them to conventional prisons, but kept them isolated here at Ham, where he himself had spent six years at what he called the University of Ham, reading, writing, playing endless games of after-dinner whist, till his escape, disguised as a workman, in 1846. It was, in short, a prison he knew, and he knew, moreover, that it was the only prison that could stifle Marius Pontmercy, extinguish the torch. Perhaps Louis-Napoléon relished the irony of it, his most ardent and eloquent opponent locked away where he himself had been locked away, the irony heightened because Marius and *La Lumière* had originally been his most ardent supporters. No doubt both men felt themselves betrayed.

Marius had been doomed by his integrity and saved by his eloquence. The soldiers in the rue Mauconseil would not shoot him, the officer had to do that. And when the soldiers found him wounded, even then they would not shoot him, as they were doing with all the other insurgents. They took him instead to a military hospital, where the doctors had not very much to do. Military casualties from the coup numbered about twenty-six and the wounded not much more. The military doctor, however, was one of those whose medical repertoire was as shallow as his arrogance was deep, and he sewed Marius's guts up so badly that ever after he could not stand altogether straight. But he lived. He almost died of infection, but he lived. He strained his body's every resource, but he lived. He was transported to Ham in secret, and the world believed he'd died. There were never official lists of the dead that December, and to this day no one knows how many died.

At Ham after a long and painful convalescence, Marius had time and memory. Indeed, that was all he had. He used the time for the memory—the painful present, the empty future—to write his recollections of the past, his sense of the struggles in which he'd taken part. He wore no convict's chain or cap, but he felt the degradation: to be Louis-Napoléon's prisoner was to be his serf, dependent upon him for bread, clothes, light, heat, to be without rights, in Marius's case, without a life worth living. His thoughts returned endlessly to Jean Valjean, and his youthful cruelty and certainty came back to haunt him. He learned, though, as Jean Valjean had learned, that to part with hope was to part with one's humanity.

In the interests of his dearest hopes, he besieged the fortress commander with requests for news of his family, and finally, after some six or eight months had passed, the commandant sent written word that his wife and daughter were in exile in England, and that no retribution would be visited against his son in Paris. Marius held the note, pressed it to him, as if it had come from Cosette herself. Cosette had lived. Cosette was safe in England with Fantine. He blamed himself ruthlessly for taking Cosette into danger, and he blessed God for leading her to safety. In the small room allotted him in the fortress, the windows were high but offered a view beyond the outer wall and across the plains of Picardy. The windows looked to the west, and sometimes he tried to imagine his way to the sea, to Boulogne, to the Gérards' inn, where he had last made love with Cosette, to the sea beyond Boulogne, to England, where she was safe.

From the imperial budget six francs a day were allotted for the prisoner Marius Pontmercy, more than the provincial rebels got but less than Louis-Napoléon had once had. From this came his food, his wine, his clothes, light, coal, and wood (the room had a stove and was not altogether lacking in comforts), pens, paper, and ink, though of course he was allowed to send nothing out and nothing came in. His solitude was almost complete, save for a few words exchanged now and then with sentries. For a man who was accustomed to a family, to friends, to life in a great city, and writing he would see quickly into print, Marius might well have died of the loneliness, save for the writing of *Recollections of 1848,* which, even that, seemed futile. But if print did not vindicate his efforts, at least the effort validated his time. And his memories.

Too, his solitude was somewhat eased when, eventually, he struck up conversations with the mason who came to repair the inner walls, to take old stones from the ruins where Louis-Napoléon had planted his straggling flowers, which were indeed perennials, daisies. They were ugly as only prison flowers can be, but each year as Marius watched them scrape themselves back to life, he regarded them as a token that he had survived one more year, though not as a harbinger that he would see them again the following spring. He would never have thought that ruined stone could be of interest till the mason pointed out that you could see where the medieval defenders of this fortress had tried in vain to fight off cannonade. He showed Marius how these walls, built only to withstand bows and arrows, had been burrowed out and stuffed with refuse and metal, fortified in the age of gunpowder—to no avail, of course, but occasionally interesting things could still be found where they had been allowed to fall to ruin.

"They knew they'd never be able to make them strong enough." The mason pulled out a bit of old metal, a shield perhaps, and gave it to Marius. "So they gave up on these and built the outer wall."

"I suppose the outer wall could stop the cannon."

"But not the ideas that make men fight," observed the mason, flinging debris.

Marius turned the shard of ancient metal over in his fingers. "Ideas can only be imprisoned by ignorance."

The mason stood upright. "I have heard, and I believe, Better the sword than the scaffold, better the scaffold than the gutter."

"Yes, but it leaves out the prison, doesn't it, that equation?"

The commandant at Ham, a man of no very great imagination, believed that all his prisoners, having taken up arms against the Emperor, should be shot. But since no order to that effect came through, he merely ignored them. To him, Marius was the model prisoner: no attempts to escape, no overtures, no plots, not a word of protest about his treatment, once he'd been assured his wife and daughter were out of the country and his son safe. By the time Marius struck up his conversation with Grincourt, the commandant had long since ceased to notice him, and the other soldiers took their cue from him. Life in the fortress (save for the brief imperial visit in 1853) proceeded with the banal regularity of a well-oiled clock, the oil in this case provided by alcohol, in which the commandant managed to pickle such intelligence as he had. He nursed his wounds, those inflicted on his pride, believing that command of a medieval heap like Ham, sheltering a few provincial reds, was beneath him, especially when French armies were marching all over the world—the Crimea, Italy, as far away as Indochina and Madagascar, seventy thousand troops in North Africa alone, thirty thousand in Rome, and the word was that soon forty thousand French soldiers would invade at Vera Cruz, Mexico, to support Archduke Maximilian as Emperor of the Mexicans. Oh, it was all glorious to consider, what he could be doing—the battles, the blood spilled, the wine spilled when he could no longer hold the bottle to pour, the ink spilled when he could no longer hold the pen to sign documents the subaltern put before him. He might have forgotten about Marius Pontmercy altogether had it not been for *The Toad Napoléon*.

Inquiries came from Paris immediately. The commandant bristled, bestirred himself, stayed comparatively sober for weeks, dictating letters to Paris demanding to know how they could so much as suggest that anyone under his charge might have the opportunity to commit treason. Marius himself knew nothing of this. His isolation was complete, but he guessed that something had happened because at night two sentries paced before his door. Not until the fall of 1856, digging in the old ruins, the garden of Louis-Napoléon, did Marius find a well-wrapped copy of *The Toad Napoléon* the mason had buried there for him.

It was an act of audacity and courage. Merely to have the pamphlet, much less to share it or sell it, was a serious offense, resulting in arrest, instantaneous prosecution. To be passing *The Toad Napoléon* to a prisoner put Grincourt's whole family at risk, but Grincourt was certain that the thin, graying, pensive prisoner who walked in the old yard was a man of some importance, a Parisian certainly, and over time he came to believe him affiliated with *La Lumière*—not the publisher, Pontmercy, who was dead, but someone, someone important. When *The Toad Napoléon* found its circuitous way into his hands, Grincourt suspected that *The Toad Napoléon*'s La Lumière was connected to the prisoner, somehow, perhaps no more than a signal, some promise, some portent that the ashes of dissent might yet blow and the cinders ignite in the wind.

To Marius it meant Cosette was alive. Alive. Speaking to him and for him, writing to him and for him, whispering to him and for him. Moreover, though she might well be in exile, he felt certain she was not in England. The pamphlet somehow yet reeked of Paris. Now when he stood on the chair and reached his arms through the bars, westward to the sea, his imagination embraced only as far as the shores, the cliffs and inlets, the beaches of France. His love was in France. But it wasn't until he was using the bit of metal Grincourt had given him to scrape a hiding place in the wall for *The Toad Napoléon* that he was reminded of the scraping of Feuilly's knife, digging in the wall of the Corinth to hide a note that would tell Cosette he loved her beyond death, as much outside of time as ever a man could within its confines. Confined now, but not by death, Marius thought, might it be possible that a note he'd written twenty-five years before, when he expected to be dead, could be used to convey the opposite message?

He dismissed the idea, tried to bury it in the stone with *The Toad Napoléon,* but it kept coming back to life, like the scrawny prison daisies. Even so, who to carry such a message? How to deliver it? He had not asked the commandant for news of Verdier, Pajol, or the Starling, fearing if they'd survived he might bring them under unwanted scrutiny. If they had lived. Had they all died? Verdier? Pajol? The Starling? And, even if one or all had lived, escaped prison or transportation, how to send a message to Cosette without putting them and her in danger? Once he had been deluded enough to take Cosette to a barricade, to risk her life with his. He would not do that again. Marius paced his solitary room, stood on the chair and watched from his window as the fields of Picardy puckered and dried with the autumn winds, as the months passed and the birds circled high overhead, flying, sweeping across the sky. If he had lived, the Starling was the one. If he had died . . .

If he had died, who was that? Marius stood on his chair, looking out the window, down at Grincourt and someone else, but not his usual assistant, his son, working on the prison well, which was near the shed they used for shelter for their tools. The two men worked, looked up, went back to work, and then took their midday meal there by the well. They ate their bread and sausages, and then the Starling removed his cap. He stood, pulled the bucket from the well, and drank from it. There, in full view of Marius's window, the Starling raised his arms in a gesture that might have been that of a workingman uncrimping his muscles, and Marius's heart soared.

One day in early October, a nondescript woman, unkempt, her graying hair straggling from her bonnet, stopped at the gatekeeper's lodge to bring the midday meal for the mason and his mute assistant. The gatekeeper checked her basket and let her pass. She went to the shed and put the basket inside. Then she went to the well and stood where the Starling had told her to stand, and when the autumn wind came up, she pulled her shawl close, folded her arms over her thin chest, lifted her face to the windows where the Starling had told her to look. She did not weep or cry out: she knew she could bring him to that window on the sheer power of her love, that love alone could perform its old cannonade, blast unto rubble these stones, these prison walls, melt the iron bars in the crucible of adversity, and still emerge, love could, unalloyed and gleaming, sterling and strong. Two hands thrust through the bars, hands outstretched, a man's hands, strong hands, seeking, beseeching, reaching for the Lark.

Chapter 12

*W*hy shouldn't irony have its day and that toad Napoléon be left to snap at gnats? If escape had worked for Bonaparte, why not Marius Pontmercy? Cosette ruffled her hands through her short, soft hair and drew them thoughtfully down her face as she sat around the table with Grincourt and the Starling, listened to the hiss of Madame Grincourt's irons as they moved effortlessly across the linen. Cosette always marveled at Madame Grincourt. She was as efficient and energetic as Haussmann himself. The autumn wind counterpointed the iron's percussive thump, and the four pondered the possibilities. Cosette had come to Saint-Simon only with the mad hope that Marius might be alive, believing that simply to know he was alive would sustain her for the rest of her life. For Marius to know that she lived and loved him, that would be enough. Her cup would splash over with happiness. But perhaps the cup had grown because, when his hands reached out to hers through the bars, her ambitions rose on the tide of her dreams. Perhaps he could be freed.

Monsieur Grincourt disagreed. "His health is very bad. He's not the man you remember. I wouldn't send a horse to a military doctor. That's where they sewed him all wrong. He can't move quickly. He can't stand altogether upright. In winter he sometimes needs a cane."

"Is his health so fragile we would risk his life?" asked Cosette.

"Would he risk his life to have his freedom?" added the Starling. "If we try, then we have to believe the answer is yes."

"Would you risk your life?" Madame Grincourt inquired of her husband. "Our lives?"

Grincourt sighed and smoked his clay pipe. "Bonaparte walked out with a wig on his head and the plank over his shoulder obscuring his face, impersonating a worker named Badinguet.

Monsieur Pontmercy's walk is no longer a workingman's walk. Not anymore. And besides, the only workingman there is me."

"And me," the Starling volunteered.

Madame Grincourt sniffed, "It's impossible."

"Louis-Napoléon had money. He had a valet and a doctor and a mistress in on the plot," Grincourt argued. "He had a horse and carriage to take him to Saint-Quentin and then another to take to the train at Valenciennes and money for the ticket to Belgium. What do we have? My horse and cart, that's all."

"No!" Madame Grincourt wagged her finger at him. "Not our horse. Not our cart. They will arrest you! You will be the one in prison! You will leave me a widow and your son an orphan and share the rest of your life with Algerian rats."

"Perhaps it is too much," Cosette conceded. "Perhaps we should just return to Paris."

But they did not return to Paris. Each day Cosette walked to Ham from Saint-Simon. Each day she brought the workingmen their midday meal. Each day she passed the gatekeeper, who had lost interest in the contents of her basket, and who had never had any interest in this witless crone in the first place. Each day she put the basket in the shed. Each day she stood before the well. And each day, as Marius's arms reached through the bars and out to her, they seemed not merely to reach, but to wring her heart, as though they were not only the hands of her lover, but the hands of her father reaching through the bars that had incarcerated nineteen years of his life; they were the hands of Pajol, of the dead Verdier, of the bereft Thérèse; they became the outstretched hands of the beggars in the rue Mouffetard, the hands of the ragpickers who reached out and swept spangles off streets, where women spent twenty thousand francs on a single gown, the hands of hovel dwellers, men, women, and the children of the *barrières* reaching toward the communal fire for warmth.

One day as she walked back to Saint-Simon, she thought, perhaps they did not need money to go to Valenciennes, nor money for the train to Belgium. Perhaps they could cross into a foreign country, a no man's land, without papers or passports or tickets. The ragpickers were the only free men in Paris, the *barrière* enclave, their filthy *cité*, a no-man's-land, so ragged and so without laws or addresses or amenities that people thought the ragpickers were savages. Perhaps they were. But they were savages with their own codes and their own contempt for the society that had spurned them. They had nothing but contempt, nothing at all. They were their own foreign country. Perhaps there, amid the garbage and the litter . . .

"Perhaps," Cosette ventured one night, "Marius does not need to walk upright like a workingman. Perhaps he could be a woman." Madame Grincourt quit rocking and her knitting needles hushed their incessant gossip. "A woman's bonnet. A woman's skirt. My thick shawl."

"He has a beard," said Grincourt.

"He could cut it, shave it. Surely he doesn't look like an Old Testament patriarch."

"He looks old, Lark. But, well, perhaps yes. The beard is trimmed, but his hair is gray."

On the table, Cosette placed her ragged bonnet with the gray hair sewn into it; it looked macabre and unnatural, like the hair that continues to grow on a corpse.

"The sentry—"

Cosette put the remains of her wedding pearls and her wedding ring on the table.

"The gatekeeper," said the Starling.

Cosette sighed. "He is the great problem. The commandant is a drunk. The sentry, let us hope, could be bought off with these pearls and the gold ring, the gatekeeper does not usually notice me, but if he does—"

"I am a widow!" screamed Madame Grincourt, while her husband smoked. "Your son is an orphan, Alphonse! They'll know your part in it at the fortress. They'll arrest you, you'll have to go to Belgium with them!"

"Not to Belgium," said Cosette. "They'll expect that. It's what Louis-Napoléon did. It's so close. They might even expect us to make for La Manche and England." She rested her blue eyes on the Starling, who at the word England seemed to start, his crooked features brightening. "As much as I want to see my daughter again, no, we can't try for England. It's Paris. Only Paris can absorb us. What do you think, Starling? The *barrières?*"

He shrugged in the Parisian fashion. "There are no natives to the *barrières,* there are only exiles. But Paris is a long distance, a difficult journey in a horse and cart and keeping off the main roads with a man who isn't well."

"No! In exchange for your husband, you want my husband!" jeered Madame Grincourt. "You want my horse and cart? I care nothing for your husband! I care nothing for La Lumière. I care nothing for the Emperor, for any of it—"

"Suzanne, I'll send the boy home from Paris. He'll work. You'll manage. You already manage. What good is it for me to talk revolution, to argue for a social justice, to believe that workers—"

"It's no good! I thought you'd learned that! Didn't 1848 teach you that? Didn't 1851 teach you that? There is no justice! There is no mercy! There is no liberty! There is only work and sleep and shit and suffer, and to believe anything else is to be a saint or a fool, and you, Alphonse, are no saint! And you, the rest of you—" she cast a withering look at Cosette, at the Starling—"hasn't that vile revolution cost us all enough?"

In her words, her certainty, the Starling heard the voice of the Countess that day they were looting the Tuileries, so long ago now it seemed as though it must have happened in ancient Rome and not within his young life at all. He heard Fantine's weeping for the death of her father. He heard Mimi's passive acquiescence to the indignities life had dealt her. He heard the Pincher's voice at his ear, giving him back the life he thought he'd lost, and yes, he would agree that the vile revolution had cost enough, but it had not been achieved. He laced his fingers together and studied his calluses.

Cosette raised her eyes to Madame Grincourt, whose lip twitched in disgust before she slammed out into the night without so much as a shawl against the autumn chill. The three sat silently and listened to her chop wood, one log after another, chop and curse and cry.

It was perhaps a vile revolution. Cosette would not have argued the point. Rebellion, resistance, revolution had separated her from her daughter, estranged her from her son, and, she'd thought, killed her husband. But she had learned, too—she was now convinced—that the lives of workingmen and women and their children could be, should be, more than work and sleep and shit and suffer. She knew as well, unfortunately, that a saint is every bit as dangerous as a fool.

Chapter 13

*T*wo miles from the fortress of Ham there was a small, lonely
graveyard, gated and set about with ancient elms and poplars,
and here, since the seventeenth century, insignificant lives had been
insignificantly buried, their graves so indifferently upkept that the
names on the stones—the last whisper these lives might have made
in this world—had been effaced by time and the winds of Picardy,
which swept down brutally. By early December—2 December, in
fact, was the date they had chosen; they were not immune to irony—
the wind had stripped the trees and the leaves had all been driven
against the stones, the low fence where, trapped, they sometimes billowed upward, spooking a horse harnessed to a cart in which a small
man sat, cap pulled down, collar pulled up, holding the reins in inex-
perienced hands. Overcast skies glowered and rooks cried out from
treetop choirs, and it seemed to the man—who was really a
woman—that nature had conspired in all this noisy grandeur when
all Cosette wanted to hear was the soft percussion of feet through the
underbrush, as they had planned and prayed for, rehearsed twice, the
feet to come from the meadow to the wood, through the wood to
this graveyard where she waited with the Grincourts' horse and cart.

On this day Grincourt had taken his tools and gone to work
alone at the fortress, even carrying the hod and, in the hod, the
basket that Cosette habitually brought, the whole covered with
canvas loosely secured to the trough. His mute assistant was not
with him, and when the gatekeeper commented on this, Grincourt
shrugged eloquently, suggesting in that single gesture that the mute
from Amiens was worthless. Grincourt walked to the well and in
the shed nearby he left the basket, making no sign but knowing he
was watched from the high window looking west.

He went about his work, and near midmorning he pushed a
barrow toward the old inner courtyard, where he was to collect

some stone from the old demolished wall of Louis-Napoléon's garden. The daisies had long since withered and died by December, their stems in sodden heaps. At the usual hour the sentry brought Marius Pontmercy to the yard and unlocked the gate. The mason's broad back, clad in a blue smock, was bent over as he freed the stones, lifting them one by one into the barrow. When he turned around he was gratified to see the prisoner clean-shaven, but so pale and gaunt he had not before realized what the beard had masked. Perhaps his health was so fragile that escape would be the death of him in any event, but one look at his eyes and Grincourt knew that the prisoner would gladly risk his life for his freedom.

The sentry who had let him in left, and they heard him swearing as he tried to light a cigarette in the wind. He went inside to do it and the gate, though closed, was not bolted, the gaping lock hung open. Marius nodded to Grincourt, then turned, pushed the prison gate open.

Keeping close to the old inner wall, he passed the low windows of other prisoners, windows affording them only a view of the outer walls. One by one these men came to the windows, pressed their faces against the bars, and watched his furtive passage around the old wall toward the well. Between Marius and the well there lay an open space, between the well and the shed, an open, unsheltered space.

The Starling for his part lay at the edge of the wood, with a view of the fortress, the gatekeeper's lodge, and the old moat. Between these woods and the moat there was a meadow where sheep placidly fed as best they could off winter's thin offerings. The Starling lay in some leaves at the lip of a ravine, perhaps the very ravine where archers once stood and aimed at the old fortress. The Starling prayed he wouldn't have to use his weapon, a mere kitchen knife. He peered over the edge of the ravine, past the sheep, waiting to see a stooped woman emerge from the fortress, but instead he saw a convoy of three supply wagons come along the road from Saint-Quentin, accompanied by an officer and a small troop of infantry. They lumbered up over the moat and the gatekeeper, officious as ever, insisted on checking everything before he allowed them into his fortress. The officer argued volubly and their quarrel was lengthy and noisy, but when he could not convince the gatekeeper otherwise, the officer dismounted from his horse, walked to the gatekeeper's lodge, and urinated on his door and step. The urine steamed when it hit the cold air. The gatekeeper's rage was towering and the officer's sangfroid equal to it; the wagons went in, the large gate closing behind them. There was a smaller gate for foot traffic, and this remained open.

Once in the shed, Marius's eyes adjusted quickly to the dimness, and he found the basket and pulled out clothing Cosette had worn daily, coming at a prescribed time, leaving at a prescribed time, only today she would be leaving without ever having come. He pulled the skirt on, fastening it low at the hips so it would cover his boots. (They were the same boots infantrymen wore.) The bonnet he tied under his chin, and taking care that gray locks streamed out, he pulled the brim as far over his face as possible. Flinging the shawl over his shoulders, he checked the security of the papers he'd strapped to his body the night before. He'd tied them around his abdomen, where the scars from the wounds of that other December day still lay purple and twisted and painful. It had seemed to him that, in risking all, if he were caught, the papers would make no difference, and if he went free, they would make a great deal of difference. He took the basket up on his right arm, took a deep breath, and stepped outside, pausing only briefly at the well to look up to the west-looking window, where in his room the bed was stuffed with blankets and clothing molded to a humanish lump, and the guard (the one not blessed with Cosette's wedding pearls) had been told he was sick and unable to eat.

The commandant was certainly able to eat, awaiting only the arrival of the officer with the wagons. From his window, the commandant looked out to see the supply wagons stirring the dust as they rattled toward the inner yards, the raucous cries of soldiers echoing off the walls. In the distance he watched the old woman coming out of the shelter, passing the well, and he commented to the subaltern who was laying the table that he did believe the mason Grincourt was getting his wick wet with that hag who brought in their meals. He laughed to think of it and might have paid more attention to the hag, noticed she was more stooped than usual, that she walked rather more swiftly and with unusual unease, had the subaltern not popped the cork on the wine bottle. The commandant's favorite sound.

In the inner courtyard Grincourt loaded the stones on the barrow and pushed it toward the gate, closed it behind him, and snapped the lock shut with audible finality. Sweating with anxiety, he pushed the barrow in the same path Marius had followed and stopped where he had a view of the shed and the well. He felt under his own loose clothing for his money belt and his knife. The presence of the money and the knife both comforted and depressed Grincourt when he saw the woman emerge from the shed, walk toward the well, pause, and go on toward the gate. They had rehearsed the journey, agreeing that Grincourt would meet them on the outskirts of the hamlet of Guiscard some six miles away, but suddenly Grincourt knew it had all been a blind and foolish mistake, a gross miscalculation that would end in Algeria, because however smug the gatekeeper, however seldom he deigned to notice the woman who brought the workmen's meals, he would have to be struck suddenly blind not to see the error here: clean-shaven or not, even stooped, the figure was tall, and bonneted or not, no one could have mistaken Marius Pontmercy for the Lark. He walked, struggling with the skirts, as no woman struggles. Grincourt stepped out from the wall and wobbled his barrow in the woman's wake, keeping the ungainly figure in full view.

As Marius approached the gatekeeper's lodge, he looked through the foot-traffic door to the long tongue of a moat that led to open fields. He hesitated then, and plunged on when he heard from inside the lodge the sounds of a violent domestic quarrel. The gatekeeper's wife insisted she would not clean up the officer's piss, and the gatekeeper demanded that she do so immediately. She wept and wailed she never thought she'd see the day when officers pissed on her door and her husband did nothing about it. For this the grandfather of the Emperor's sons slapped her, and as the stooped and awkward figure hurried beyond their door, their quarrel took on a screeching nostalgia as she wept and bellowed that when Louis-Napoléon was sleeping with their daughter no one had dared to piss on their door.

From the ravine the Starling saw Marius pass through the gate, and he watched, appalled that an officer's chance fit of pique had stood between them and certain detection, certain failure, Cayenne, New Caledonia, and blackwater fever, between them, the sword and the scaffold, because however stooped, there was no way that a man of Marius's awkward gait and great height could have fooled anyone accustomed to seeing the diminutive Lark. "Run," he whispered to the figure leaving the moat, stepping into the fields where the sheep bleated, as though they were calling to the gatekeeper.

The gatekeeper, flinging a bucket of water on the step, closed his door and flung another bucket on the door, but then he turned and regarded the figure moving, not toward the Saint-Simon road but toward the woods. He might have called out, called the guard, but his wife burst through the door with a broom and attacked him, beating him about the head and shoulders till he snatched it from her and their oaths and cries resounded against the prison walls. The Starling, having scampered out of the ravine, awaited Marius in the trees, which were bare, gaunt, and remorseless, offering neither curtain nor shadow, so overcast was the day. The figure did not run, kept its steady pace, but as he approached the Starling it was clear that the stoop was not affected and the face framed by the bonnet so pale, so gaunt and altered, it seemed he gestured to a stranger, who nonetheless embraced him and gripped his hand. The Starling pulled Marius through the woods, the route marked out, timed, and rehearsed twice. They splashed through the leaves, the fallen branches, while overhead naked boughs moaned and gasped in the Picardy wind. They ran, as best they could, as best Marius could, sweat dripping off his brow as he flushed and paled and stabs of pain shot through his lungs, his abdomen, his joints, but he didn't stop. He followed the Starling all the way to the little cemetery, where the restless horse stamped, breath fogging in the cold, and a small figure sat alone, waiting to hear the footsteps of the living crash through the silence of the dead.

Part III

La Vie Parisienne

*Yes, that's Parisian life, full of breathless pleasures /
. . . Oaths and promises swept away by the wind! /
Babbling songs, kisses taken and returned /
Sparkling bottles, bring forth the best wines!
Et pif et pif et pif et pouf!
Unfaithful husbands brought back to the fold! /
. . . Dramas and comedies unfold /
And after these follies, a general amnesty!
Et pif et pif et pif et pouf! Yes, that's Parisian life!*

—LUDOVIC HALEVY AND HENRI MEILHAC
Libretto for Offenbach's operetta *La Vie Parisienne*

Chapter 14

*O*n the doors of two of her three carriages, Nicolette Lauriot had a large *N* in blue, surrounded by a laurel wreath in gold, an insignia very like the *N*'s and laurel wreaths on the pont de Solférino to this day. It was very Napoleonic, so much so she received a letter from the minister of the interior communicating His Imperial Highness's ire, concluding, "When people see a carriage with the Emperor's characteristic symbol on it, even if yours is blue and his is green, they believe it to be the imperial carriage and are consequently disappointed." Nicolette wrote back blithely that they would only be disappointed to find they had erred on the imperial side.

Through the newspapers, the story spread all over Paris, and though Jean-Luc did not think it funny, Nicolette entertained dozens of people with her version at the Café Anglais, the Maison d'Orée, in the Passage of Princes at the Bouffes-Parisiens, and at her famous lunches, which, to her guests' delight, she had started serving in the jungle conservatory so they could all tease the monkeys and feed the stoic flamingos.

However, it suited Nicolette to keep one carriage undistinguished. She used this carriage when she sometimes followed Jean-Luc to the haunts of dancers and courtesans (both the aspiring and the infamous), and it gave her scant pleasure to know she had been right: once married, Jean-Luc took many mistresses, none for long, none seriously, certainly none to compete with Nicolette. All these women were not merely an acquired taste but a necessity for a man of his new station in life and the money that marriage had brought him. Perhaps that money enriched Jean-Luc, but to Nicolette's perception it had impoverished him. He remained an ardent lover, an accomplished lover, but the streak of passion in him, the fiery certainty that had amused and inflamed her, that dwindled.

The man who had been brokenhearted when Nicolette had miscarried was unmoved when his daughter was born within a year of his marriage, interested only insofar as to object to naming her Louise after the Emperor. However, once Louis-Napoléon agreed to be godfather, of course there was no question what the child's name would be. After all, through his intimate court connections, his friends in government, Jean-Luc had access to Haussmann's plans; the transformation of Paris brought about a transformation in Jean-Luc's fortunes. He belonged to the Jockey Club now, consorted with men like the duc de Morny and, if not quite as rich as Arsène Huvet or the comte LaSalle, at least with them, he frequented Longchamps racecourse, gambled at the Jockey Club, maintained five horses and carriages, and rode in the Bois de Boulogne at the fashionable hour. Usually he rode with Nicolette Lauriot, but he seemed to her less immersed in the pleasures of her company than he was in the possibility of whom they might see and who might see them.

Nicolette could not and did not complain. She had got her wish after all. He had married, if not a rich woman, a woman who had made him rich. He could keep Nicolette in the style she'd become accustomed to. He showered her with expensive, outrageous presents: an hourglass with diamonds instead of sand, a sapphire as blue as the Nile and the size of a fat fig. But somehow the heavy sapphire hurt her neck, and the diamond-hourglass depressed her.

When she had time to be depressed, which wasn't very often. Offenbach's *Orphée aux Enfers* ran for over two hundred performances, and night after night, as Eurydice, she stood on the stage to be pelted by blue roses. Her pleasure in her work never dimmed, the adulation never failed to gratify, even surprise her, the sweetness of her triumph absolutely unalloyed save for those moments when a glance at Jean-Luc's box revealed that his eyes were on the shepherdess in the chorus. Occasionally she was also daunted to see him there with his wife and mother-in-law. Whenever Nicolette saw Zelma, she knew that the prize was Jean-Luc and she feared Zelma had got him.

So it was in this unmarked carriage that Nicolette Lauriot went to the studio of Pascal Beaujard, the same studio where she had first met Jean-Luc. It was a snowy day in late February, and she kept her hands warm in an ermine muff and pulled a veil over her face, a useless precaution, as no one would have expected to see La Lauriot in this quarter. Although fashionable neighborhoods were pushing west, Beaujard's haunts retained their bohemian spirit, and even the ragpickers here seemed to be posing to have their portraits painted.

Nicolette was gratified that her unexpected appearance astounded her old friend, who was painting a pale, anemic-looking woman, sitting naked before him, not coyly posed with rosy haunches, but the plain, unadorned flesh God gave everyone. Introduced to Nicolette Lauriot, the model seemed never to have heard of her. Beaujard asked Mimi to get dressed and said they would work again soon. She dressed with no particular haste or interest and took her five francs.

"She seems an uninspiring model," Nicolette commented when Mimi had left.

"She inspires unconventional emotions."

Nicolette walked around the studio; the high walls were covered with paintings, and many more leaned, stacked two and three deep against the walls like bored extras awaiting their cues. "Did they accept any of your paintings at the Salon this year?"

Beaujard, cleaning his brushes, shook his head and said he and some of his friends would probably exhibit a few canvases each at a gallery, but the Salon refusal had clearly depressed him. He looked up at last to see her leaf through the stack of paintings he'd done in Boulogne in 1848. "That was a miraculous summer, an island of peace and well-being in between two deluges, the June Days and the coup d'état. There was a kind of magic there I don't expect ever to feel again.

Pondering the paintings one at a time, Nicolette said, "You have put the magic here, on the canvas."

"Perhaps, but they are not mythological subjects, nor historical paintings, nor allegorical. They are not classical, hairless nudes, nor maidens *in extremis*. They stand for nothing but themselves."

"Is this Jean-Luc's father?" She came to the painting *Garden Study*.

"His death was a terrible loss to the world."

"Even I heard how he died—and you know how little I care for any of that," Nicolette added with a laugh. "He must have been a powerful sort of person, but Jean-Luc never speaks of him. Is this his mother?" She paused at the picture with the direct gaze, the narrow black ribbon, and light flooding her face. "She is beautiful."

"She is the most remarkable woman I have ever known."

To this Nicolette could make no amused rejoinder. She continued to look at the paintings, asking finally, "Could I buy these from you? All of them."

"I doubt seriously that your lover wants to see pictures of people he betrayed on the wall."

"Jean-Luc did not betray his family. He just didn't go to England with them. His mother didn't go either."

Beaujard stopped cleaning his brushes. "What makes you say that?"

"She was at his wedding."

"That's impossible. She's in England," he insisted.

"Everyone knows the author of *The Toad Napoléon* is in France. That's why I'm here. I want you to arrange a meeting for me. I want to meet with Jean-Luc's mother, Cosette Pontmercy. La Lumière. Everyone knows she is La Lumière, why do you look so surprised? This is an honest request. It has nothing to do with the police."

Beaujard, whose role in the publication of *Bonapoléon* was, as far as he knew, a secret, rinsed his brushes and stood them upright in a vase. "The current Baron Pontmercy would betray her in an instant," he said, "Cosette, and everyone connected with her."

"Perhaps. Perhaps you do him an injustice. In any event, I would not. I care nothing for politics. This is a personal matter." Nicolette rose, walked with her old insouciant grace around the room, looking at him now and then over her shoulder.

"I have no idea where she is. London?"

"Oh, Monsieur Beaujard, let us spare one another all this coquetry and posing. I had so hoped on the strength of our old association—"

"I have no contact with Madame Pontmercy."

"But you know who does." She stopped again in front of the canvases from 1848. "You could not spurn or forget the people in these paintings."

"I have not spurned them. Marius Pontmercy is dead. Fantine

is alone in England. Jean-Luc has moved on to another world and Cosette, Madame Pontmercy—"

"Is somewhere still in Paris. Please, Monsieur Beaujard. Just convey my message. I will meet with her any time, any place she likes. She need have no fear. I shall be absolutely alone. When you've arranged it, come to my house with the information—and the price of the paintings."

"I'm not selling my friends for my paintings, Nicolette."

"Of course not. You are selling your paintings to a friend."

"This is impossible. She will never—she won't—"

"Tell her I want to talk about her son. She'll come."

Chapter 15

*T*he *barrière* absorbed Marius and Cosette as if they had been dropped into the ocean. Indeed, as if they had been buried at sea and their silent bones rocked, as La Fontaine put it, in the vasty deep. For Marius the analogy was not altogether metaphorical: the rigors of the escape and the long and difficult journey back to Paris, his wounds and the years of imprisonment all took their terrible toll, and when they finally arrived at the *cité* it appeared he had exchanged the certainty of the prison for the certainty of the grave.

The ragpickers' encampment at the *barrière* d'Italie lay at the ragged end of the rue Mouffetard, just beyond the old city wall, where it lost shape and the road went slack and lumpy, unpaved, rutted and bedraggled with garbage. When Cosette came home from plying her scrivening trade, in that last bit of light, the hour, as they say, between the dog and the wolf, only the most desperate could be found out here where the ghosts of those murdered wandered unimpeded. Now, in winter, tiny clumps of brown grass clung to the soil with the tenacity of children who know they are about to be abandoned, and near-dead elms straggled along the roadside, their bare limbs hanging pendulous as empty gibbets. Miscreant odors of sulfur and the astringent smells from the tanners along the Bièvre River blew past, miasma from the dyers' works. A turn to the left would have led Cosette to the insane asylum for women and the horse markets, and she sometimes passed animal skinners and butchers going home, their clothes horribly stained, their hands as well. She kept her eyes down and hurried by, fearing that they were not men but ghouls, and the stench that followed in their wake must surely have come from hell. Sometimes horses died before they got to market, and mules pulled the corpses and men cursed. Many buildings out here were abandoned altogether, taken over by ragpickers and beggars or inhabited by people who did not stir during the day. Packs of dogs roamed. It was the geography of *les misérables*, the place and the phrase where the unfortunate and the infamous are confused, compounded, ground together under the pestle of want and mortared with dirt, dust, mud, and sweat. It was near this very *barrière* that Marius, as a student, had lived in the same rundown tenement as the Thénardiers, and where Cosette had first entered the city, her little hand in that of Jean Valjean.

Marius and Cosette, once Fortunatus and Fortunata, now lived in a one-room shack just high enough for Marius to have stood upright, in the days when he stood upright. The walls and roofs were cobbled of boards scavenged from the demolition of Paris, likewise the worm-eaten shutters and thin glass in the window. But at least it had glass and shutters, which could be closed against the storm, and the previous occupant (who had died) had stuffed the chinks with rags and paper, so that only small bits of light pierced in the daytime and darts of drafts at night. The door opened with a leather thong, and though it was hung on iron hinges, the pins were wooden and protested when, at the end of a hard day, a short winter's day, the Plumed Lark returned to find Marius where she had left him, indeed how she had left him: lying on the straw bed, dressed and under blankets (the heavy clothes and blankets donated by the Countess Crasseux) and shivering, sometimes blue with cold. His joints were swollen and he could not move without pain. The scar down his belly was still livid, and the old scar, the one that had given his beautiful face such ineffable sadness, now trailed down a face gone gaunt with suffering, his beard and hair gray.

Cosette took off her bonnet with the gray hair and dipped a rag in a bit of brown water floating in the tin bowl (if it had not frozen) and washed the grime off her face and rubbed the blacking off her teeth. Then she chafed his hands and feet and he tolerated her ministrations, even enjoyed them, but he seemed to know he was dying, and with such strength as he had he stroked her hair and murmured, "Don't worry, Cosette, and don't cry. I was dying anyway in prison. I was dying without you, and now that I have you I am alive again."

Yes, she thought, gulping back tears, alive again only to die. Having rescued him, must she once again suffer his death? One death swiftly dealt by a bullet, one death grindingly slow. How could anyone endure that awful loss twice in one lifetime?

"I have you," he whispered, eyes closed, "I have my freedom. I don't need anything else."

This was not true. There were many things he needed, but Cosette's earnings as a scrivener could not support two people, and with the wedding pearls gone, they had no resources save for the letters the Plumed Lark sold by the line. They had limped through the one winter and straggled into spring. In summer they were no less hungry, but at least they weren't wretched with cold. As the fall dwindled down, the days short, the chill waxing and the light waning, Marius's strength ebbed. If his spirits likewise failed, he took care not to let Cosette see. He saved his every morsel of energy for when she returned home. With the approach of another winter, Cosette braced. Winter was hard on the scrivening trade; people stayed off the streets and holding a pen with frozen fingers sometimes proved impossible. For herself she could have borne it; she was thin and sometimes weak, the dry cough never quite left her, but in the years since she had dipped below the social horizon she had achieved a sturdiness and toughness of spirit and hide; everything inessential had burned away from her life in the refiner's fire of experience, and what was left was hard and bright and brilliant. But they were starving just the same.

Cosette could only buy their bread by the notch (and the notches mounting up). For broth they were dependent on cups of soup from Marie-Josephine's communal soup pot, which bubbled when there was anything to put in it and wood to keep it cooking. In their tiny hovel Marius and Cosette had a little makeshift stove the Captain had made for them, found parts and rigged the rest; it smoked terribly, but it remained cold in any event. They had no coal and little wood, and often the ink in the scrivener's well kept its thin shell of ice all day. But some mornings, too, Cosette would open their door and find a small pile of wood scraps left anonymously by some generous soul. And sometimes the ragpickers shared candle stubs they found, lighting them for Marius so that when the Lark came home she could see, even from a distance, a bit of light wavering and know he was not lying in the dark. Otherwise, she used little bits of string soaked in resin, affectionately (and appropriately) known as cellar rats. When he could, the Starling brought meat scraps, which Cosette was loath to take because she knew it meant he went without, but take them she did.

She sat on the stool by the bed, Marius's hand in hers, as Marius dozed and the Starling by the light of a cellar rat studied him. "It looks bad for him, Lark. I hope we did the right thing. Maybe it was all too much for him."

"We have to believe we did the right thing, don't we? We have to believe, as you said, that he would risk his life for freedom, but I'm afraid, Gabriel, because Clerons must surely know we didn't go north, that we didn't go to Belgium, he'll know, guess we're here in Paris somewhere. If he comes down on us too close, if I can't sell letters, Gabriel," she glanced at Marius to be certain he was asleep, "if I can't work—what will happen to him?"

"You can get another disguise from the Countess."

"But not another trade. What can I do?"

"I don't know," he conceded. "I wish I did."

"I feel as I did in Boulogne those years ago, when we were caught in a storm and our boat was wrecked and we would have died, but the *Saint-Joseph* came to our rescue, and a man whose face I never really saw pulled us to safety, took us to port, and then vanished. I saw the boat again. Once more. The second of December 1851. I think the *Saint-Joseph* was there to take us to England. We were supposed to go to England then, and didn't." Cosette sighed. "So now there's no *Saint-Joseph*, and we're sinking in waves of want, poverty, and desperation."

The Starling stretched his legs out and seemed to contemplate his feet. Finally he said, "I have to tell you something. Mimi gave me a message from Beaujard. Nicolette Lauriot wants to meet with you. She wants to talk about Jean-Luc. They're not to be trusted, Lark, any of them."

Cosette replied disdainfully, "What is there to say about Jean-Luc? He is the son I have lost. You are the son I have gained." She sighed and brushed the gray hair from Marius's sleeping brow.

"Monsieur Grincourt sends you his regards."

"You've seen him?"

"I see him often at a masons' café. He's always working, but he calls himself Auguste now. I think he quite likes Paris," he added with a wry grin. "I told him to be careful, though. They're sniffing around everyone ever connected with us, with any of us. We may all have to vanish again."

"Sometimes I feel as if every time I vanish there is less of me to come back."

"Perhaps we should pity Clerons, Lark. After all, it's difficult to search for a man everyone believes to be dead." As soon as he spoke, the Starling wished he had not. In the wavering and uncertain light of the cellar rat, they both regarded the pale, sleeping Marius, neither of them willing to say what both were thinking.

Chapter 16

On summer nights the pleasure gardens of the Bal Mabille on the rue Montaigne near the Champs-Elysées were the scene of uproarious gaiety, all-night gaslight, and cancan, and underneath its long lighted archway came visiting sheiks, unleashed Englishmen, a potpourri of monocled foreigners, boulevard dandies, would-be rakes, out-of-work actresses, shopgirls, and professional dancers to show off their high-kicking skills, surrounded by a forest of palm trees made of zinc, in short, all the wine, women, and song that money could buy. In winter, though, the Bal Mabille stood ghostly and empty, snow settled on the lamps and trees and zinc palms, the cherubs frozen, their smiles turned to grimaces, the orchestra's lacy pavilion silent as it was on this afternoon in February when an unmarked carriage waited before the gates. Nicolette had been given a time, a place, a date, nothing else. She'd already waited half an hour, and the coachman was so cold he pulled out his flask, but put it away when a grim-looking nun approached. When the nun got in, he was so surprised he took an extra swill.

The nun and the Empress of Offenbach regarded one another as the carriage lurched forward. Nicolette wore a Worth day dress of Lyon brocade scalloped with lace of Crimean green, a smart fur hat, a cape trimmed with sable, and a muff of the same. Courtesy of the Changer, Cosette wore a nun's habit, a wimple, wooden shoes, and not so much as a shawl.

Nicolette thanked her for coming, but Cosette had long dispensed with empty civilities; she had agreed to come with terrible misgivings, prompted by some still-lingering maternal hope of reconciliation. "My son, mademoiselle, Jean-Luc wants to see me? That's why I'm here, yes?"

Uncomfortably Nicolette replied, "I'm afraid not, madame, oh please, don't leave. I do want to talk about Jean-Luc, but he has no idea I'm seeing you. I promise. He knows nothing of this." She pushed the footwarmer toward Cosette, and they rolled along in silence. "Did you know you are a grandmother?"

The surprise that lit Cosette's face answered the question. "When?"

"Not long after they returned from their honeymoon in Italy. As far as I can tell, Jean-Luc cares nothing for the child. He was with me when she was born. The Emperor is the girl's godfather."

"My granddaughter has Louis-Napoléon for a godfather?" Cosette ran her roughened fingers over her forehead, in what had become an automatic gesture of pain.

"Zelma Touchard's granddaughter too. They have named her Louise."

Cosette groaned. "Is the child Jean-Luc's?"

"I'm afraid it is. They say young Madame Pontmercy was, still is, besotted with her husband, that the months in Italy were glorious. But Jean-Luc is a Parisian, and once returned to Paris," Nicolette shrugged, "perhaps even in Italy . . . For a man of the Second Empire, well, no one believes in fidelity. It's ludicrous. Jean-Luc is not like his father."

"What do you know of his father?" snapped Cosette.

"I know he never took a mistress. I know you never took a lover. Jean-Luc says the two of you were your own country."

"Ah." They were circling the Madeleine, passing Durand's Restaurant, where the Second Republic had been born that glorious February in 1848, driving past the small flower market, where the flower sellers still held up tiny bunches of forced yellow freesias, and Cosette could close her eyes, return to that other February, the wedding day, smell the freesias cooking in the candlelight, tied to the chandeliers by cream-colored ribbons. Today is my wedding anniversary, she thought. She had not remembered before; now she could all but see Marius's old grandfather saluting the bridal couple, his spry dance steps to the Haydn trios, and the wedding pearls he'd given her and the wedding ring gleaming new on the bride's left hand, as she gazed at the beautiful ebullient groom. She turned back to the elegant woman opposite her. "Love is its own country," she said at last, "but it is not its own world. Many things can alter or invade the country of love. Death, for one."

"But Jean-Luc has never lived in such a country, madame. Not even with me, though I think we came close, and I don't regret my decision. I did not want to marry him and I would not trade my independence for his name. Besides, why should I be his wife when I can be his mistress? They say that Eponine is trying everything to keep his affections. Perhaps he sleeps with her, but he does not love her."

"Does he love you?"

"He has always loved me. On my Saint-Francis-of-Assisi days, I pity Eponine Touchard."

"Because she is a small animal?"

Nicolette laughed, her old rippling, musical laughter. "No, because her mother, Countess Troussebois, is the most vulgar and demented witch I've ever met. Surely you know that. You grew up with her."

Cosette's breath seemed to freeze in her lungs, and her blue eyes darkened as she looked out the carriage window over new boulevards so broad they looked like snowy fields, the city transformed, everything that once was ground under and gone. "We were all children once."

"At The Sergeant of Waterloo Inn?"

Cosette turned her gaze sharply. "You brought me here to talk about my son. What has my son to do with any of that?"

"He's married her daughter, hasn't he? I should think he has a great deal to do with it. He doesn't know she's using him to triumph over you, over her own past."

"If Zelma wants to believe she has triumphed over me, it is by her own standard and not a standard I would recognize," Cosette declared proudly.

"I don't think Jean-Luc subscribes to your standards, madame. I could have told you that much that day we first met, do you remember? The Luxembourg Gardens?"

"How could I forget? It was the day my old life ended."

"What I fear is that Jean-Luc subscribes to Madame Touchard's standards, oh, not that he would marry for money, that is commonplace."

"Common, I think is the better description. Vulgar."

"Perhaps, but worse, I know that Madame Touchard uses the money as a tool, a forge, and from that forge she expects to bring forth a whole new man, in her image. He's enormously wealthy now, did you know that?"

"I despise it."

"That's what she said. She said she was turning him into everything his mother despised."

Cosette reflected on her own brash challenge when she had declined to be blackmailed, advising Zelma to find some other form of revenge. She's used my own son against me, Cosette thought, and against Marius; she'll tire of it one day and then she'll destroy Jean-Luc. They rode in silence for a bit until finally Cosette asked, "Have you brought me here to break my heart?"

"Forgive me. Forgive him. But I wanted you to meet with me because you are the only person in the world who also truly loves Jean-Luc, but we have more in common than that. More than you might think."

"I'm not certain I do love Jean-Luc. He moves me to tears. And you and I—" Cosette reached out, and with her bare, coarse, inkstained hands, she touched the rich dress worked with golden sunflowers. "What could possibly unite us?"

"My mother died coughing out tiny bits of thread like this brocade," said Nicolette plainly. "It's true. She worked from five in the morning to nine at night, and she earned, on good days, one franc eighty centimes a day, and she breathed in these bits of thread and they caught in her lungs and choked the breath out of her. My sister Valentina went into the same weaver's workshop, and in two years she coughed herself to death too. My father was a navvy, a well digger, wielding a shovel and lifting a glass. He dug all day standing in water, and his feet literally turned green, but at least it slowed him when he was drunk and he would come after us, my brothers and me. We lived in a single room, with a stove and no money for fuel. We burned the pawn tickets finally. We ate bread cooked in water with garlic. We sold the beds. When people would cover the streets nearby with straw because someone was sick or dying, we stole the straw and brought it home to keep warm with. Finally, my youngest brother, he ate the straw he was so hungry, and he died the most harrowing death you can imagine." Nicolette took out her lace handkerchief; she had taken the precaution of bringing more than one. "Now I stand on Monsieur Offenbach's stage, and the Emperor himself comes to my performances. But I tell you the truth of it, my older brother, he bought, or stole, a little tin flute and he learned to play, and out we went on the street corners. Sometimes, when Jean-Luc is very angry with me, he says that without Monsieur Offenbach's music I would be frostbitten and singing on a street corner."

"Does Jean-Luc know any of this? Have you—"

"No. He thinks I come from a family of solid, stuffy bourgeois and that is what I want him to think. How could I ever tell Jean-Luc that my father took everything we made, my brother and I, and beat us anyway, and brought a woman in to drink with him, to sleep with him. One night when we'd finished singing on the street, my brother took half our money and he put the flute in my hand and said he wasn't going back, he was going to Paris. He couldn't take me with him because a girl was a liability, but he said I should come later and find him. Well, I couldn't play the flute and sing too, could I? My father and his woman tried to put me into the same weaver's workshop that had killed my mother and Valentina, and so I ran away. I hired out as a servant so I could eat off the plates of others and sleep near the stove. It wasn't too bad." Nicolette shrugged in the Parisian way.

"Except that the master was all over you?" volunteered Cosette.

"Great garlicky pig. One night, so drunk he could hardly find where to put it, he banged away, and every time he thumped it into me, I could hear money jingling in his pockets. He passed out afterward and I lay there, knowing that another girl in this house had stolen some jam and got a year in prison for it."

"If you had been caught, it could have been death."

"It was death anyway. I knew God had given me this chance, and if I did not take it, it would not come again. So I stole everything he had and left. And I came to Paris and found my brother."

"How old were you?"

"Oh, fifteen or sixteen, it was the year before the revolution. He was living in a boardinghouse near the place Maubert, where men slept twenty to a room and ate soup boiled from sheeps' heads. He had work though. At Montfaucon he held the horses' heads while they slashed their throats. For this he got one franc fifty a day and some horsemeat, diseased, no doubt. I was horrified to see him. He was dying. He knew it." Nicolette twisted the handkerchief in both hands and gazed out the carriage window. "He gave me a little money, what he could spare, and he said to me, Nicolette, you have the voice and the face, take it on the street. Now. Trade now for what you can get while you still have your looks and your strength. Don't come back, Nicolette. Don't come back to this."

"You took his advice?"

"What else was there but outright whoring? I sang in front of the Palais-Royal and in front of the Thèâtre Saint-Martin and the Thèâtre Ambigu and the Variétés, and by the time of the February Revolution, I was an extra at the Théâtre Olympic on the boulevard du Temple, not singing, but—I was happy there. I had the feeling that anything could happen. In fact we were about to rehearse a play during the February Revolution when a mob surged by and another extra dressed like a general was out front smoking a cigarette and they grabbed him and took him to the Hôtel de Ville to lead the new Republic."

"I saw that. I remember watching the mob put him on horseback and a great crowd following. He looked like Lafayette."

"He still does," Nicolette scoffed. "Only he's not a general anymore, now he's comte Châteaurenaud and he's got some post or another at the court. He's actually got the Légion d'honneur! Amusing, yes? What a performer. Sometimes when I am riding in the Bois, his carriage passes mine and he tips his hat. Sometimes he takes a box at the Bouffes-Parisiens. Sometimes I see him at the Café Anglais, the Maison d'Orée, places like that, but we have never exchanged a word since the February Revolution."

"What happened to your brother?"

Nicolette's mirth evaporated. "In the June Days, there was a barricade at the Petit-Pont. He died in a draper's warehouse, the Deux Pierrots," she added bitterly. "I found his body at the Panthéon, stacked like so much human wood, so I knew he died, but I could not claim him. Me, I had no money to bury him. They killed him," Nicolette shrugged, "let them bury him. But when I left the Panthéon, when I walked out of there, I knew my life had changed irrevocably. I know what it is to have someone you love thrown in a nameless grave."

"The pain is unendurable."

"The question is—what do you do with the pain? You, madame, you took that pain and turned it into a weapon. *The Toad Napoléon, Bonapoléon,* everyone in France knows these fables, whether they can read or not. La Fontaine himself is not so well known as La Lumière."

"I am not La Lumiére."

"I took my pain and turned it into an ornament. I turned my back on everything that killed my brother. I waved palm fronds, and Monsieur Needlemaker paid my rent, and I didn't, I don't, give a damn who is in power, who puts the saddle on the working people riding them to death, who puts the bit in their mouths and takes the food out. I don't give a damn for the fact that the price of bread has doubled, the rent in Paris quadrupled, that there are people living out at the *barrières* in inhuman squalor. I don't care. I vowed I would never care. I care nothing for the Republic, or for the Emperor, or any of it. I want only to stand on the stage, to sing and have people adore me. I want only for Jean-Luc to adore me."

"And does he?"

"Probably, but—" Nicolette slumped—"now I wonder if I could have saved him from Madame Touchard."

"No," said Cosette dryly, "you could not have saved him from that."

"Nothing will stop me loving him."

"I believe you, Mademoiselle Lauriot." Cosette gave a wan smile and said, "And I hope he loves you. I hope he loves something truly."

"Madame Touchard says he loves money."

"I could not say what he loves. I don't know him anymore. He was not brought up to love money."

"I also wanted you to come for another reason," Nicolette said after a time. "I thought if I could not save Jean-Luc from Madame Touchard—"

"From himself."

"Then at least I could erode the rest of her triumph, and even if she didn't know it, I would know it, we would know it, you and I." From under her sable cape Nicolette took a small silk bag (embroidered as well with a blue *N* and gold laurel leaves) and she put it in Cosette's hands. "This is so Madame Touchard will not triumph in every way. She may have got your son, but there is no reason for her to be right about what's happened to you. Since the day of Jean-Luc's wedding, when she told me about The Sergeant of Waterloo, drunkenly, of course, I wake in the night hearing her horrible laughter, and it seems to me I see you as a child and I see her beating you with a broom, brutalizing you as a child, I see myself and Valentina and my brother being beaten. I see all the rest of them, the people I've loved, the deaths of people I've loved, I feel the cold, the brutality, the drunken beatings, the rapes, the men and women who live like that, not because they're not human but because they are. The soul dies before the body, madame. The soul is reduced to pulp before the body. The soul is more fragile than the body, but the body has to be protected for the sake of the soul. There's fifty francs there. There's more where that came from."

Cosette's hands closed over the silken bag. There was a time when she might have spent twice this on a bonnet and thought nothing of it, but this money, given now, was a fortune, and she knew she would take it though she would protest. Struggling for composure, Cosette finally drew on some well of poise she had thought long since dry. "How can I take this when I can't earn it?"

"You can earn it. I'd like to give you work, madame, not glorious work and perhaps dangerous for both of us, but Madame Touchard believes you starving, living with beggars and drunks and thieves, that her triumph is complete. It would please me to have some part in proving her wrong. I have work for you, if you'll take it."

"I'll take it," said Cosette, not knowing or caring what that work was, bidding inward goodbye to the Plumed Lark and greeting the prospects of food and fuel and medicine she could buy for Marius; she would take on any work at all to see Marius well, upright, walking, and strong.

Chapter 17

*T*he priest at Saint-Julien-le-Pauvre told the story for years, and of course no one believed him, how a lone nun entered his church, genuflected, reached under a pew to pick up a bundle of something he was certain squirmed and cried, carried it to a side chapel to Saint-Joseph, and when he went to look for her, the nun had vanished. The priest was certain it was a miracle. His listeners were certain he'd been at the communion wine. No, he declared flatly, someone had left an unwanted baby there under a pew, a nun appeared from nowhere, rescued the child, and vanished. Perhaps it was not a miracle, but certainly it was a visitation. He had a witness. The Plumed Lark, the scrivener from the rue Mouffetard. She was there. She was there in the side chapel. She saw the nun and said she vanished.

From Saint-Julien-le-Pauvre the Plumed Lark hurried directly to the Changer's to return her nun's habit. (The Countess had very strict rules against people's returning clothes while they were still on their bodies.) The Countess remained suspicious of Nicolette, even of the money, but she gave Cosette a string to tie the bag around her neck and cautioned her against thieves and getting out to the *barrière* after dark. "There are men out there who would kill their own mothers for two francs."

The Lark, in her usual sorry plumage—the gray-haired bonnet, old shawl, and bedraggled skirt—hurried toward the rue Mouffetard as a melting rain turned the afternoon snow to slush. Shops and stalls displayed their wares under rickety awnings and umbrellas; cabbages cooking in the comfortable apartments above steamed the windows, while horse dung steamed in the street and the voices of children mixed with the laughter of men in the cafés and vendors crying out. Her first stop was the wineshop, where the smell was all cold bottles, straw, and bright gaslight. "Two, please, and nothing that's been opened up and doctored," she cautioned the merchant in a voice reminiscent of the Baroness Pontmercy. She hurried on in the fading light and bought two loaves of bread at the baker's who had very nearly had the Starling arrested all those years ago. She went there rather than to her usual baker, where she bought by the notch, because he would have demanded full payment. The coalman, his apron, his hands, his face and lips black with coal dust, asked to see her money before he gave her two francs' worth of coal. At the butcher's, Cosette chose a bone with meat still on it and an extra small chunk, cut fine. The butcher asked what she was celebrating. The Lark did not reply for fear of betraying her happiness, but when the street musicians and lamplighters, most of them blue-lipped and grim with cold, greeted the Plumed Lark with boisterous reflections on her good humor, she called out, "It's going to be a beautiful spring!" and left them shaking their heads.

In the Market of the Patriarchs she bought three candles, and at a creamery stall a fine cheese, soft and ripe, and butter. Amongst the vegetable vendors, all about to close down, she found onions, cabbage, carrots, all especially dear, especially sweet in this bitter cold. In winter the ragpickers counted themselves fortunate to find stumps of cabbage and carrots, the rinds of cheese, and moldy onions. "Is this a party, Lark?" asked the vegetable woman with a grin.

"I'm celebrating, because life is two parts courage and one part chance and, truly, the unexpected can unfold."

"Ah," said the woman, wrapping up the vegetables in news-paper, "those words! That's why you're the scrivener, Lark."

Mud, churned up by horses and wagons, sucked at Cosette's wooden shoes, and under her heavy load her strength almost deserted her, but her spirits remained buoyant as she approached the ragpickers' enclave, where, over a few hummocks, she could see fires burning low, the smell not sweet like woodsmoke, but acrid, leaving a question mark in the air as to what was burning at all. The glare from these fires made a red smudge across the darkness, and she could hear the crying of hungry children, the scraping of a two-string violin somewhere, a woman's good-natured laughter, and from another direction, a man's brawling anger as he staggered out of a decrepit shed and the Captain told the Ark to bite off her own red rag of a tongue as he tried to piss at the moon. Cosette stepped over the broken bits of tin and porcelain, rag and blowing paper, the refuse of other people's lives, that lay everywhere about here. Everything at the *barrière* had been cast out of the city—including the people who lived here.

She approached her own small hovel and caught the red-eyed glare of a scurrying rat. She cursed it and the cats here, who were sated and fat, so sleek they would watch a rat pass with the disdain of a gourmand declining stale bread. By her door she picked up the lid to the tin pot that collected water. Fresh water was precious, rain and snow the only source, short of a long walk back to Saint-Médard's public fountain. She lifted the latch and walked in to find Toutes-Nations sitting on a stool by Marius's bedside, both of them asleep, one snoring.

Toutes-Nations roused quickly and grumbled about having slept while the candle stub burned. "He is the same, Lark, he hasn't moved all afternoon. Starling came by to see him, and he roused for him, talked even, but it cost him and the Starling said he should sleep."

Cosette put her parcels on the small table, where the ink had already frozen in the well and Marius's book, the fugitive papers he'd salvaged from imprisonment, were neatly stacked with a brick atop them. He did not have the strength to read or write, but it seemed to please him to see, from the bed, *Recollections of 1848*. She pulled off her old bonnet and went directly to the bed, sat there, stroked his hair, pushed it from his forehead, kissed the scar that ran down his face, called his name.

"His gizzard needs something to grind, Lark," said Toutes-Nations sadly.

Cosette put her arms around his shoulders. His eyes opened slowly and a smile lit his face as she whispered endearments. With an effort Marius lifted his hand, ruffled her short hair, and said he had missed her. "Do you know what today is?" she whispered. Cosette smiled and turned to Toutes-Nations. "It's a holiday today, our wedding anniversary, Christmas—something really special. Watch!" Quickly, she cracked the shell of ice in the basin and washed her face clean, dried it on her sleeves, took two wine bottles out from her pack and held them aloft, like trophies, as the onions, cabbage, and carrots tumbled out.

"The Lark's taken to thievery," observed Toutes-Nations. "It's not a bad life. A short life, but not bad. There are worse."

Cosette took three candles and lit them from the stub, and the place seemed to dance with light. Aside from the bed, which had coarse straw ticking, a splintery table, there was a wooden stool, and on a bit of shelving, mended tin plates, a pan, and a basin leaned against one another. She showed off her two loaves of bread and took the coal over to the little stove, which was ill ventilated; smoke streaked the wooden walls, but as the stove was cold and unlit (and had been for days) the pleasure of seeing flames brighten up, fed by newspaper, completely made up for the inconvenience of the smoke.

"And what do you think this is!" Cosette held the parcel aloft. "Meat! Yes, truly! And this parcel, this is a bone *with meat on it!* Now, Toutes-Nations, you take all this," she bundled back up all the vegetables but two of the onions, "and put it in Marie-Josephine's soup pot. And you take this second bread. And the second wine. I insist."

"This'll sluice our gobs good, Lark."

"And thank you for staying with him, but you'll see, tomorrow Marius is going to start getting well. He's going to be well, so well, so soon," Cosette gave a wink, "we'll get a lock for our door."

Toutes-Nations gave a coarse, affectionate chuckle, made an obscene gesture, and left singing a little ditty about a man with a remarkable appendage and all the women who would love him for it.

Cosette returned to the bed where Marius lay, his arms under his head, a quizzical smile on his face. "Now don't ask me where it is from. Don't waste your strength. I didn't steal it. I'll tell you everything. But what's important now is that you're going to get well, my love. You are. You're going to be so strong soon you'll make love to me as you always did, you remember?"

"All those nights," he moistened his cracked lips, "all our nights together. We never thought it would end. Never knew . . ."

"It's not going to end, oh, my love, sit up. Please. Can you? You must try."

The pain in his swollen joints twisted all across his face, but he pulled himself up in the bed, and she wrapped blankets around him. "Cosette, I'm such a failure as a man and a husband. I can't provide. I can't protect—"

"You're not a failure. Our vows were mutual, we were to love and cherish and protect each other. To see you free from prison, oh, I don't think saints have known such happiness as I felt that day I saw you and Starling come through the trees. My love, we are together. Never leave me again. Look, the room's getting warm now. See what a difference that makes?"

"It does, doesn't it? Warmth," he smiled. "Warmth."

With effort she pulled the cork on the wine bottle and splashed some into two tin cups, put one in his hand. "Here, Marius, you can hold it. You can. You're going to be well, my love. There's going to be lots of warmth and food and light." She touched her cup to his. "To us, Marius, as we were all those years ago, as we shall ever be, Fortunatus and Fortunata." Cosette drank her wine and crawled into bed beside him, wrapping her arms around him as he shivered still. He stroked her hair slowly as the warmth from the stove filled the small room, and the warmth of the wine expanded in his veins. Cosette closed her eyes and held him, her head pressed against his chest, listening gratefully to his heart beat.

Chapter 18

"Remember the story of the Costly Omelette," advised the Countess as she outfitted Cosette in the small parlor tucked high in the upper reaches of her warehouse. Piles of discarded clothes lay about, and the ones chosen for Cosette's new life had been set upon the empire divan; they had more in common with the nun's habit than the Plumed Lark of the rue Mouffetard. The bodice was of a mustardy sateen with iron buttons reminiscent of prison locks, and the hoopless skirt was a thick gray, with a horse-hair petticoat to give it girth. The Countess was working now on the finishing touches, which made all the difference, she said, between the two kinds of conviction: the first convicts the victim of the intended scam, the second convicts the perpetrator and sends him to prison. Cosette sat in her underclothes before a mirror while the Countess fitted a wig on her short hair, a wig mouse-gray and moth-brown in color, parted in the middle, pulled, braided, and knotted at the back. "The aristocrat fleeing the guillotine in 1793 dresses as a peasant, licks and scrapes, and bows all the way to the sea only to order an omelette."

"Not likely I'd ask for twelve eggs," said Cosette.

"The point is, Lark, if you don't want your tongue waving goodbye to your guts, then never forget who you are. You must change the inside as well as the outside. Now, who are you?"

"Mademoiselle Nicolette Lauriot's dresser. A toad eater. The poorest, most humble of female relations, willing to accept all insults. Pious, and from the provinces."

"People from the provinces don't say that."

"A spinster from Amiens. Too poor to wed, too ugly to bed."

The Countess smiled and handed her a pair of tiny green spectacles to put over her eyes. "Weak-eyed too. Can't bear the light. Don't forget that. Your eyes will give you away."

"She says Jean-Luc never comes backstage anymore. That he can't bear to see all the men crowded there."

"Keep the spectacles on. Now, here." She handed Cosette a huge, heavy crucifix and a brooch, a wreath woven of a dead woman's hair. "You tell them this is for your dear, dead mother."

Cosette could hardly bear to touch it. "Who cuts the hair of the dead and makes jewelry of it?"

"The English and the Americans. Savage, yes?" The Countess shivered or shrugged, it wasn't clear which. "Actually your mother's hair was more blond. More blond than yours."

"You knew my mother?" Cosette snatched the wig off and turned around. "Why have you never said?"

The lift of the Countess's shoulders expressed volumes of equivocation. "How many Fantines can there be? She left Paris when you were about three. She was just a girl herself. Not yet twenty. When I met you, I saw her all over again, though thirty years had passed. When I met your daughter, the day of the coup d'état, I knew for certain."

"And my father?"

"A student from somewhere. A law student, I think. There were four of us, *grisettes,* four girls and four student lovers, and they left us all on the same day—a holiday in the country, dinner paid for, then they took the mail coach back to their old lives, we walked to Paris. You had to laugh at it. It was a good *rigolo,* but Fantine did not laugh."

"What was she like, my mother?"

"She adored you, doted on you. She would rather sew little clothes for you than sew to put bread in her mouth, so she starved. But she was certain she could make a better life for you if she left Paris. I told her, Don't go, but she was a romantic and they are always doomed. In the *quartier* Latin, it was always the students who go back to where they came from, and the *grisettes* find new lovers till it's time to get a husband. But Fantine was small and serious."

"Like my daughter."

"Yes, I'm afraid so."

"He's in love with her, you know, Gabriel is."

The Countess harrumphed. "I have known it longer than you. I warned him, I told him, Better to court disaster than Fantine Pontmercy. But now, well, it seems futile to oppose something . . ."

"That will never happen? That Fantine is in England and can't come home? I should never have let her go, Countess. I should have kept her here in France no matter what. But at the time—"

"At the time you didn't know what Clerons would do. And she would be dependent on your son here, Lark. Don't forget. You could not protect her from that . . ." The Countess left the rest unsaid.

"My son breaks my heart for the choices he's made. My daughter breaks my heart for the choices I've made."

"It's impossible, Gabriel and Fantine. Impossible. He should set himself up with a woman and live with her. But, no, he pines after your impossible daughter and reads impossible books and runs from the police and stirs up rebellion when all the people want is to be fat and satisfied."

"I run from the police and stir up rebellions," Cosette chided her. "It's a worthwhile enterprise."

"But you have been loved, you've had that, Lark. Everyone should have that, shouldn't they? Not forever, not for good, but something, even false love, everyone should taste that much from life. Gabriel will never have that as long as he is in love with your daughter. Impossible love," she scoffed, "with your impossible daughter."

"If Fantine loved him—I would welcome their wedding, I would never stand in their way."

"Me, I do not stand in the way of the Starling," the Countess toyed with the wig. "No one does. He just flies over you. He always has. He—" She put a finger to her lips when a little bell rang, and she went to a cupboard, opened it to reveal a series of ropes and pulleys, each one toned and tied to a different tiny bell. "Police. You know what to do."

Still clad in her underclothes, Cosette grabbed a shawl and exited by a door that appeared to be a shelf. Indeed, it was a shelf, complete with broken bits of porcelain, but they were glued on and it opened inward, giving onto a passage, a narrow walkway, lit only by a small high window at the opposite end, where a rope ladder hung. Cosette scrambled barefoot along the walkway to the rope ladder, climbed it, and pulled it up after her. This was the high overhead catwalk, where clothing hung in fetal-looking cauls from the rafters. There was enough room for Cosette to stand, but she went on all fours, softly, toward the front, so she could hear the Countess at her great desk, and from this perilous perch, she chilled all the way through to hear Clerons's voice and the tramp of military feet clattering about the Changer's vast warehouse, along many passages and in stairwells. She heard the name *Grincourt* drift up and *Saint-Simon.* The name *Pontmercy*, however, did not resound; Clerons could not admit he was looking for Marius. You'll spend your life looking for him, Clerons, Cosette vowed to herself, you'll spend your whole life and never find him and he will hang over your head like these bags of clothing above you, always out of reach. With my last breath, I will keep him safe. At the same time, however, she winced to hear Clerons ask after the Plumed Lark. So he knew that much, did he? Without the work and safety Nicolette offered her, Marius would have surely died, because the Plumed Lark would have to die.

Everything in the Countess's tone of voice suggested she was resoundingly ignorant. Gabriel, it seems, was in China. Bits of their exchange floated up softly, like smoke along the rafters.

"He's in Paris," Clerons insisted. "He's been seen, out where they're building the new boulevard by the Parc Monceau."

"What business would my grandson have in the Parc Monceau?"

"He's not strolling there, you old fool! He's shoveling earth into a cart and pushing it like a beast. Fitting, that a man who tore up streets for barricades should now be tearing them up to make boulevards. He was seen by a man who would recognize him, Baron Pontmercy."

"Baron Pontmercy is dead," the Countess remarked without irony.

Clerons let it pass. "I think I can take the word of a man of Baron Pontmercy's stature over that of a ragpicker and a prostitute."

"I'm no prostitute."

"But your daughter is. Her card can be revoked, you know. She'd starve without it."

"At her age, she'll starve with it."

Clerons walked around the warehouse, his voice directly beneath Cosette, who held her breath for fear of disturbing a single dust mote that might drift and catch his attention. "The Starling can return from China with impunity, you know. The Emperor has forgiven all. He's proclaimed an amnesty, and everyone who was exiled after the coup d'état may return to France, even those whose exile has kept them in France, like La Lumière," he added sarcastically, returning to the Changer's desk.

"It is not up to the Emperor to forgive La Lumière," retorted the Countess. "It is up to La Lumière to forgive the Emperor."

"How do you get those bags of clothes down?"

"A long staff and a basket."

"It must be a very long staff. What's above them?"

"Heaven, Monsieur Clerons."

Clerons's boots echoed as he walked around the warehouse, looking up, Cosette was certain. She could not keep herself from shivering, however much she wanted the dust undisturbed. He seemed to have paused right beneath her when the Countess made mention of the scar on his cheek, pronounced it "nasty." He marched over to her desk and Cosette could hear the Countess's ancient ledgers thudding on the floor as he swept them from her desk.

"He goes from one menial job to another, your grandson, he changes his name every time, and everywhere he turns it seems there are people willing to protect him, but he can't fly anymore. He's not a boy. Up until now, the Emperor would not have bothered with him, but all that's changed, you old ragpicker, all that's changed, and the game he's playing now is treason. That comes with a very high price. I'll catch him. I'll catch them all. You tell him I said so."

"Tell him yourself."

"Tell him yourself," said Madame Fagennes. "I take no messages for the Starling. I am for the Emperor. You see?" She leaned over and resoundingly kissed the plaster bust of Napoléon III sitting beside the wire fruit stand and the gaily colored bottles. "I haven't even seen the Starling in months. Years. Ever," she added, giving the zinc counter a bit of polish.

Clerons sipped his wine, frowned, and put it down. He had come to the Café Rigolo alone, leaving the two police to go through the Changer's vast warehouse. "We know that you get messages for him here. We know you get letters from England."

"I get nothing for the Starling. I have always thought he was a little piece of vermin, from the time he could walk. I am for the Emperor."

"There is a girl in England who writes to him here."

From the corner of her eye, Madame Fagennes watched one of her customers swing his body and look away, though this conversation at the counter had arrested the attention of everyone else. This man, small, petulant, and greasy, could as easily whine as strut after a few drinks. He was known to Madame Fagennes only as Griffon, not a name but a description of his left hand, which was horribly deformed, the fingers irrevocably curled inward, the fingernails grown long like claws. A man good only for spying, she thought, angry that she hadn't detected this swine *mouchard* earlier. "If there is a girl in England who writes to the Starling, I know nothing of it. Nothing of her. Nothing of him."

"And Grincourt? Do you know Grincourt? A mason from the north?"

"Never. I don't like provincials. They're shifty."

"And the Plumed Lark? A scrivener who calls herself the Plumed Lark, that's her mark, a lark and quill pen."

"What about her?"

"Does she write letters for people in here?"

"Sometimes when it's raining. She—" Madame Fagennes shuffled through her customers rapidly as a deck of cards: the boy with the thick provincial accent, the message he wanted to leave for the Starling; the Plumed Lark had written it for him. Madame Fagennes remembered watching the poor old Plumed Lark at the table. But no letter had been left at the counter. Madame Fagennes ground her teeth and she vowed to gag the Griffon on his next glass of wine. "She's flown. I haven't seen the Plumed Lark in weeks. Months. Years."

"Has she flown with the Starling?"

"The Plumed Lark is a pitiful toothless hag."

"The Starling is in a lot of trouble. He flies with a radical flock these days, people who tax the Emperor's patience and his good-will." Clerons waited till Madame Fagennes finished waxing herself silly lauding the Emperor's goodwill. "Thievery is nothing compared to what the Starling's doing these days. Thievery will get him transported. Treason will get him shot. Do you know La Lumière?"

"A rag. Years ago. I forbid it in the Café Rigolo."

"Not that *La Lumière*. The author, La Lumière."

"The Starling?" Madame Fagennes laughed coarsely. "Never. Sassy and snotty, but not clever."

"But he's in league with people who are clever. Like the Plumed Lark."

"That ugly crone? That poor slut who keeps her carcass together writing letters?" Madame Fagennes patted the round, fragrant oranges in her wire basket; the pat turned to a pinch. Could it be that the Plumed Lark could write more than letters? Could she write, for instance, *The Toad Napoléon? Bonapoléon?* Had the Plumed Lark and the Starling, that little bastard, could they have put her whole life in jeopardy? "Perhaps she's dead. Go check the gutters. Drag the river. Don't come to the Café Rigolo."

That night after she had closed the café and before she mounted the stairs to her flat above, Madame Fagennes took a candle, put it on the floor before the wine casks, and with much grunting and straining reached behind and pulled out perhaps a half dozen letters that had arrived and remained uncollected. Now she knew why. It was true she had not seen the Starling or the Plumed Lark in a very long time. She took the letters over to the stove, cursing herself for ever agreeing to let the letters come here at all. But the years pass, after all, the old fears and passions, like anything else, they get spindle-shanked and impotent. The coup d'état, the bloodshed, the barricades, the fighting, the arrests and exile, who thought of them anymore? Besides, there was the amnesty, after all, the Emperor forgiving all who had opposed him, allowing exiles to return. Nowadays, people were satisfied. Of course there would always be the scrounging poor like the Plumed Lark. But those who could earn a living, they were satisfied. Madame Fagennes was satisfied. The rerouting, the expansion of the rue de Rennes, the building on this side of the river, had brought many new customers to the Café Rigolo. Look at the wire fruit stand. The oranges. The gaily colored bottles. What the truly rich did or thought, Madame Fagennes knew only what she read in the papers, but who cared if the old *liberté* had become libertine? One heard Offenbach tunes in the street. Who wanted to sing "La Marseillaise" anyway?

She took a long fork, lifted open the door of the stove, stirred the coals with tongs, threw the first letter in. The second, hmmm . . .

Dear Starling—

It's quite late as I write and I am tired, but I could not sleep without replying to your letter, which was so welcome. Of our news here, there's little. Madame Carême and I are the best cooks in London, we know that. Last week a duke tried to hire us away. Madame Carême, I think, will not leave this place. Though she objects to the English in general, she has no objections to a particular butler here in this grand house. As lovers they are quite funny, Starling. Old as they are, they must keep themselves as plaster saints before the rest of the household. The English insist upon it. Madame Carême says they never laugh in bed. I would not know. I have been the object of the valet's unwanted attentions, which I recently cut short, quite literally, Starling, snipping before his very eyes the fat from a loin of beef while I told him I had no ambitions beyond returning to France one day, to see Paris, my beloved mother, to see you . . .

"Bah!" Madame Fagennes cast it into the fire and opened the next. More of the same, the foibles of the English, the aching for France, the loneliness of exile. She tossed that into the flames.

My dear Gabriel,

So many months have passed with no word from you and no word from Mama that fear overwhelms me. I have written to Monsieur Beaujard, who has heard nothing either, though he assures me Mama has not been arrested, that certainly he would have known had Mama been arrested. Though perhaps not. Perhaps they would—

"She should have been arrested, Gabriel," snorted Madame Fagennes, feeding this letter to the fire and grumbling audibly, swearing at La Lumière, passing as the Plumed Lark. "Just let that hag come back to the Café Rigolo," she growled, "the police will be informed immediately." Opening the last one, which had arrived just last month, Madame Fagennes read by the firelight, flames provided by its predecessors.

Dear Gabriel—

I fear you are not receiving my letters and that perhaps my writing is adding to your jeopardy, your woes, or those of my dear Mama, so I shall not write again unless I hear from one of you, and I shall only trust God to care for you and to bless you both, to let you know [scratched out] *even now I feel as if I am dropping these words into a bottle, which I should fling into the Thames and let it drift to sea, to cross La Manche and bob along to the mouth of the Seine, to wash up under the bridges of Paris. Perhaps my letters have done you harm. Perhaps you have never read them. Will you never read this one? What then can it hurt or harm, Gabriel, if I tell you now I think of you daily, never does a day pass when I don't see your crooked smile before my eyes. I thank you for your loyalty and affection to my poor dead father, my fugitive mother, to me. I have not deserved your affection, Gabriel. I cringe to remember the cruelty I visited on you when we were children, hating you because you were poor and ugly, while I was loved and comfortable. No doubt you are still poor, Gabriel, but you are not ugly. I think you beautiful. I do not know if you are comfortable, but you are loved.*

Fantine

Madame Fagennes snorted, flung the letter into the fire, but at the first lick of blue flame, she picked up the tongs and snatched it out, stomped it on the floor, pressed it flat, making certain the charred edges no longer burned. She put it in the pocket of her ample apron and made her way upstairs to her flat, cursing Mimi Lascaux and the claw-handed Griffon *mouchard*, cursing La

Lumière and Napoléon III, cursing the Plumed Lark, cursing the Starling and this girl in England who loved him. She cursed as well her own good nature and big heart, her soft streak, which might better have been described as a soft seam, so narrowly did it thread through the fabric of her character.

Chapter 19

So the Plumed Lark vanished or died, though without leaving so much as a pile of feathers. As for the Starling, who would notice one more or less of that flock of pests? Who would notice one more or less lean, muscled man swinging his axe to bring down an old building, climbing scaffolding to bring forth a new one, filling carts with earth, pulling a grader harnessed to him as to a beast? Paris was full of such men, differentiated only by their accents and the forms of fighting they indulged in when they drank on Saint-Monday. Clerons continued his search for the missing Lark, the vanished Starling, though his true object was a man he could not even admit lived. In fact, Marius almost didn't live. The money from Nicolette saved his life. Strength and some mobility returned, though he would never have his old robust health. The wages Cosette earned as Nicolette's theatrical dresser also allowed her to repay the ragpickers' kindnesses, acknowledge their unspoken loyalty. She contributed so regularly to Marie-Josephine's soup pot that around the *barrière* her name evolved from the Lark to La Mauviette, the cooked lark. The regular wages not only bought food and fuel enough to save Marius but to save others. When there was a sick child, a breadwinner injured, a difficult birth, Toutes-Nations inevitably delivered a parcel, remarking with her customary shrug that it was just as Louis-Napoléon had said, Go into the fields, open your mouths, and cooked larks will fall from the sky. In her new life Cosette could help Pajol and Germaine; it was too dangerous to see them, but the Starling acted as a courier between the two families, between the erstwhile printer and the erstwhile Plumed Lark.

Cosette now fathomed her father's insistence on charity, on repaying the goodness one has been shown. Jean Valjean seemed to be wonderfully present in Cosette's life now, as he had seemed only a ghost when she was Baroness Pontmercy. Indeed, Jean Valjean virtually appeared to her when she entered Nicolette's dressing room that first time and saw everywhere vases of blue roses. Cosette slowly removed her green spectacles, ran her hard brown fingers over the petals, watching them fall, one by one, moved to tears to think of her father's work blooming after his death, surviving even the destruction of the convent. Now, over those nuns' bones, gleaming steel rails rumbled and sang, and the only perpetual adoration was the railway timetable. Truly this blue rose was her father's epitaph.

But then, she put the spectacles back over her ears (careful not to dislodge the wig) and became once again the Toad-Eater, the Vegetable (so they called her, Nicolette's bright crowd, as well as the snickering stagehands). A few even dubbed her the Oyster for her complete lack of volition or character, but the name that stuck to Nicolette's new dresser was Mea Culpa. It suited her demeanor as she scurried away along backstage passages, begging pardon, regretting inconvenience, keeping humbly close to the walls, her mouth pinched, fusty skirts pulled close, the crucifix clanging on the metal buttons at her breast.

Nicolette declared she had hired this grim, prim, pious relic because at least she could be certain Mea Culpa wouldn't steal as the last dresser had. (The disappearance of the duc de Morny's sapphire ring confirmed these suspicions.) But gossip had it otherwise. Gossips whispered that Nicolette kept Mea Culpa because she could not bear the presence—or the competition—of another pretty woman.

This rumor gained credence when, at one of the Opéra masked balls, Nicolette found Jean-Luc in the company, indeed in an amorous embrace, with a singer from the Bouffes-Parisiens chorus, and the scene that ensued was worthy of grand opera, not merely operetta. The theatrical fights, the operatic reconciliations of Baron Pontmercy and La Lauriot were legendary in Paris, as were the outrageous parties at the rue de Chaillot, all of it horrifying bourgeois readers of the daily papers and the illustrated weeklies, and delighting everyone else. Nicolette cared nothing for chamberpot notions of propriety, acted always with imperial aplomb. Did not her talent and beauty give her extraordinary rights over the rest of the world, or at least all Paris, which was the same thing? Certainly she had regal disdain for the feelings, the reputations, the regard of those poor mortals pulled into the drama of her life, the men who fawned and fluttered round her, flattered her, snapped jeweled garters on her by now famous blue stockings, paid her rent, her bills at Worth.

As for the women whose path crossed that of Jean-Luc, she regarded them as little better than flies to be swatted with her wit, like the café-cabaret singer whom Nicolette dubbed The Screamer. At a luncheon in her jungle conservatory, while the monkeys scampered and the parrots shrieked, Nicolette would uproariously imitate The Screamer, who reached for a high B-flat in the throes of passion. Nicolette's guests laughed so hard they cried, and Offenbach mused that if The Screamer married the man who could make her reach her high B-flat, the idea could be, well, amusing, could it not? Private theatricals, naturally. He wrote uproarious music, and as a private theatrical it was performed at Nicolette's country house, herself in the starring role. Jean-Luc applauded, but that night in her bed he remarked laconically that he had indeed been able to make The Screamer reach her high B-flat.

He did the same evidently for many women, dancers, singers, courtesans who attracted his fancy. He made wagers with the men at the Jockey Club, where gossip about women and horses was itself a kind of currency. One of the girls whose affection Jean-Luc had shared had recently captured the heart of a count, and thoughtless words exchanged in the Jockey Club led to a duel. This count was newly vested, created by the Emperor for his services supplying swords to the imperial army then about to march into Mexico. Jean-Luc quipped to Arsène (who acted as second) that perhaps he'd chosen the wrong man to offend when the parties met at the appointed hour, just before dawn, in the corner of the Bois de Boulogne gentlemen favored for this sort of thing.

As the challenged party, Jean-Luc had chosen pistols. Perhaps he'd also chosen the wrong weapon, he reflected in the light of a tired, waxy moon hovering on the horizon. His opponent was singularly humorless, and when he lifted his weapon, it was not to the trees. Jean-Luc fired to miss and then stood there, while the count took aim, admittedly to miss, but not to miss altogether. The shot grazed Jean-Luc's left arm, and the count declared himself avenged, waited while his own doctor quickly bound up the wound, and produced cognac from a traveling case for everyone.

Arsène's carriage left Jean-Luc off at the rue de Chaillot, and he found Nicolette pacing in the garden and, he thought, talking to someone. Barefoot, clad in a lacy negligee, the hem grass-stained from the new English lawn she had had put in, Nicolette cried to see him. Her hands flew up to her face when she saw the sling, and she kissed him, wept, admonished him, all rapid-fire. It seemed to Jean-Luc that a breath, a figure, passed behind the boxwood hedge, the shed at the back of the garden, but he gave his attention to Nicolette, who wept against his unwounded shoulder while he held her, assured her he was unharmed, promised never to fight another duel, stroked her beautiful loose hair, kissed the tears from her cheeks and the corners of her eyes, and wondered why he ever made love to anyone else, wondered what possessed him to believe there could be anything worth having outside the circle of Nicolette's embrace.

About the time of the duel Nicolette and Jean-Luc provided Paris with another spectacle, a sort of grand *rigolo,* this one involving a millionaire Manchester mill owner, Mr. Benedict, who escaped the mills and England altogether whenever possible, coming to Paris, where he developed a passion for La Lauriot, which she allowed him to indulge. He ransomed her time, though not her affections. One summer afternoon he drove her and her fusty dresser, Mea Culpa, out to Argenteuil, a river town not far from Paris, where the wine was bad and plentiful and the figs were good and plentiful. It was an unlovely town along the Seine, where already that strange mixture of industry and amusement coagulated. Iron works and plaster works, a factory that made boxes, and a tannery all left their smudges along the sky, and at the same time, sails of little boats sauntered out along the river. It was the haunt of Parisian shopgirls and clerks on Sundays, complete with makeshift cafés, picnics along the riverbank. It was not the sort of place amenable to the Empress of Offenbach. Her heart sank when Mr. Benedict asked his driver to stop before a monstrosity of a villa, handed her the key, and declared the country house a surprise.

"I wish you'd asked," Nicolette remarked.

If he'd asked, she could have had a country house in Fontainebleau, but as a foreigner, Mr. Benedict had been duped into believing Argenteuil a place of great fashion.

As Mea Culpa followed humbly behind, Mr. Benedict conducted Nicolette through the place. The ceilings were so high they dwarfed all human enterprise, no doubt a reflection on the man who had built it, a recently failed factory owner who had unloaded this elephant on the unsuspecting foreigner. Whatever might once have been of value or interest had been stripped, much to Mr. Benedict's dismay. He swore to Nicolette (even to Mea Culpa) that it did not look like this when he bought it.

He promised to furnish it and would have, had the American civil war not broken out, depriving his mills of cotton and depriving Mr. Benedict of trips to Paris. No one missed him. No one remembered him, save that Nicolette's country house came to be known as the Benedictine Folly, and perhaps that's what finally endeared it to her. It was a ridiculous place, an impossible place, its own *rigolo*—and the huge garden full of color and surprise. It was close by the river, where Nicolette and her friends could rent yachts for day excursions, and even the shriek of the train whistle nearby came to have a kind of charm and whimsy. It had novelty too, gas and running water. Its empty walls and tall windows rather reminded Nicolette of Beaujard's studio in those long ago days and she invited him to paint here. He stayed for a whole summer; his enthusiasm brought other artists to Argenteuil, and they delighted in painting the boating and the factories and each other in the act of painting, and it seemed to Nicolette that, even more impressive than being the Empress of Offenbach, she was the queen of this unlikely country, where a democracy of talent reigned, where clever, artistic, and exciting people could meet away from Paris and all its restrictions.

Mea Culpa seldom came, not only because she was neither clever nor exciting nor artistic, but because of Marius, whose health was slowly improving, though his joints were still swollen and painful. He was stooped, but his strength returned and even his ambition: he cleaned up around their little hovel, and Starling helped him plant some sunflower and nasturtium seeds and took a real pleasure in watching them come up. In good weather Marius and Cosette would sit on overturned crates in the sunshine. Cosette would not have thought she could be so happy. At first she blessed every day that Marius did not die. And gradually she blessed his every bit of laughter, the very sun that fell on his upturned face. Cosette laughed to see the fiery radical, Marius Pontmercy, worrying over his sunflowers, chatting with the Captain or Toutes-Nations. He and the Starling, who visited whenever he could, listened endlessly to Cosette tell stories from the theatre, of Nicolette and the monkeys and the parrots and flamingos, of the actors and extras, the drunken porter. Sometimes she brought home blue roses hidden in a coarse sack, and the efforts of Jean Valjean lit up the *barrière* hovel, the promise of continuity, fruition, and love bloomed even here, amongst *les misérables*.

Chapter 20

*A*rgenteuil was a mere twenty minutes from Paris by train, and when Nicolette Lauriot descended on the town, the cabdrivers ferried them to the Benedictine Folly and took the rest of the day off to drink. She came always with troops and tribes of people—lovers, friends, followers, hangers-on, servants; the drivers charged an astronomical two francs per journey, and not one of Nicolette's friends ever complained. She brought her dogs as well, four or five of them, and it suited her, more often than not, to bring the monkeys, who delighted children in the first-class railway carriages and horrified their mothers.

One afternoon the monkeys scampered over the last of the lunch, laid out on a long table in the Folly's large, sun-and-shade-mottled garden, and while the Pekinese dogs humped each other unmercifully, one of Nicolette's guests brought up Mea Culpa. She brushed it off, since Jean-Luc was present, but the question persisted, so she fed the last of her fig to a monkey, lit up a cigarette, and explained Mea Culpa's sad story, how she had been destined for the convent, but when her insufferable family lost their money, the convent wouldn't take her without a dowry. "Poor Mea Culpa," sighed Nicolette. "I thought, why not the theatre? We're our own sort of convent, aren't we? We have our regular services, our prayers."

"No novices," observed Jean-Luc.

"Yes, but we have our priests." She winked at Offenbach.

"Our bell ringers," suggested a young British dandy running his hand up the leg of Arsène Huvet, who jumped up so quickly he spilled his wine.

"Oh, confess," comte LaSalle said, teasing a monkey with a bit of orange, "you keep Mea Culpa for the reason you keep the monkeys and flamingos. It amuses you to outrage people."

"Yes," replied Nicolette with exaggerated sweetness, "but the monkeys are more grateful."

"I must meet this terrible Toad-Eater one day," said Jean-Luc.

"Oh, she would frighten you," Nicolette declared.

"Where did you find her?"

"On the convent steps, of course, like all foundlings."

So Foundling was added to the many disparaging sobriquets clever and artistic people slathered on poor Mea Culpa, but after she had been named, defamed, slandered, sullied, the object of gossip, jest, and ridicule, there wasn't much fun to be had and the novelty wore off. Mea Culpa became just another backstage lackey as she made her way to Nicolette's lavish dressing room, walking underneath smelly, uncovered gas jets and the squeal of pulleys, the hiss of the new hydraulics as the beautiful illusions painted on huge muslin screens were lowered and raised high into the theatre vaults. Pious Mea Culpa (whose character owed a good deal to old Toussaint, complete with righteous snort) moved through knots of flirtatious and quarrelsome chorus girls and dancers, amid smells of irons heating, paste and paint, rope and oil, fumes of faulty plumbing, tobacco, sweat, old wine, old beer, unwashed tights, costumes too long worn and hair cooked with curling tongs, enough flowers for a state funeral, orange peels, apple cores, scorched corks and chamberpots. Cosette loved to hear the groan and squeal of the ropes, to hear men scurrying overhead on catwalks, to watch the prompters leaning out from ladders like lovers offering poetry, to watch the ennui of dancers awaiting their cues. She was thrilled to see the concentration on the face of the gas man as lights dimmed or flared and as he applied gel for color to create high noons or twilit shadows; pink for love or innocence, green for envy, red for hot anger, blue for cold pique, yellow-gold for fulfillment. She enjoyed hearing the musicians tune up before the performance and grumble afterward as they moved from the stifling pit through the huge, unheated room beneath the stage on their way to have a smoke outside. From this room prop men brought up impossible creations by a variety of trapdoors—a whole locomotive and a railway station for the opening scene of *La Vie Parisienne*. In the play, the Trouville train (complete with steam) was created onstage. Many in this audience, Jean-Luc included, were floating railway bonds to connect Paris and Trouville, energetically developing Trouville as the *ne plus ultra* of fashionable seaside resorts, and naturally enhancing their investments. No doubt their profits inflated with every puff of steam from the stage locomotive at the Bouffes-Parisiens, as with the Trouville trains leaving Paris. On stage, the Trouville train was made possible by half-clad men with dirty brows and hard hands. Offstage, the Trouville train was made possible by men in evening dress, with white hands, calloused only by paper that passed through them, tissuey notes of promise, deeds, contracts, and bonds. Perhaps on the stock exchange these men created as much illusion as the burly backstage scene-shifters. Perhaps the men of *la vie Parisienne* were no more substantial than the actors of *La Vie Parisienne*.

Onstage, Cosette never failed to succumb to the magic, to be moved to wonder, though she saw the play every night and recognized manufactured illusion. Still, the transformational moment enchanted her. On cue, dancers shed their mere-mortal coarseness and floated on stage colorful as sea anemones, light as butterflies; singers in the chorus ceased to be quarreling snits and lifted their hearts and voices in gorgeous unison, to make the hearts of the audience rise as well. The insufferable actor who played Bobinet in *La Vie Parisienne* shed his pompous self, emerged on stage as sparkling and high-humored. And at the center of this magic, Nicolette Lauriot created illusion from her body, her voice, her smile: then she turned this whole world upside down, took her bows, no longer the Empress of Offenbach, but the humble vessel of talent, there merely to be filled with the audience's adoration, in turn to spill that adoration back over the entire theatre, to touch and move every person in it. And all this marvelous magic, these breathless transformations were created and destroyed. Nightly.

Cosette's life reflected this theatrical rhythm. Mea Culpa was created and destroyed nightly. Sometimes when she returned to the little gardener's shed at rue de Chaillot and took off the hideous brooch, the crucifix, the bodice, and fusty skirts, the spectacles and the wig, washed her face and brought it up dripping from the basin to the mirror, Cosette wondered who the blue-eyed woman was who looked back at her. Mea Culpa? La Mauviette? The workingman who walked back and forth between Nicolette's and the *barrière* twice daily? The Plumed Lark? La Lumière? The Amiens cousin? The Baroness Pontmercy? Could these transformations go on indefinitely without somehow eroding the grain of the essential Cosette? Would there come the day when she would lift her face dripping and not know her own eyes? Would her son even recognize her if he did come backstage?

He never came backstage. Cosette saw him from the wings, sitting in his box, his eyes hooded and his mouth twisted in a sardonic smile. He had his father's intensity, but not his integrity. Marius asked after him every time she returned home to the *barrière* encampment, and Cosette replied that their son looked well, rich, pleased with himself, and Marius knew, of course, what that really meant.

But Jean-Luc's presence in his box was clearly essential for Nicolette; without him there her performance was exciting, but not inspired. Cosette worried over her, as a mother as well as a friend. Plagued by terrible headaches, Nicolette nonetheless lived and worked and played to exhaustion like a child who fears if she goes to sleep all her toys will be gone when she wakes. Mea Culpa, protective and alert, was always in the wings, ready for those few moments between scenes to give Nicolette a splash of cologne for her temples, a touch of paint, a refresher of powder, something cooling for her throat.

From the wings Cosette looked out over the theatre, where Offenbach's music defied gravity and rose up through the tiers and balconies and boxes, where men in black-and-white evening dress framed women in crinolines huge as ponds, so their every movement undulated waves of frothy purple, reed green, peony pink, gowns in impossible shades of saffron and mauve, magenta, white as lightning, bright as embers, elusive as sunset, all of them tied with bows and furbelowed, camellias cascading from their shoulders and diamonds sparkling in necklaces, tiaras, and rings, powder glowing on their white shoulders and rounded breasts. They were to a woman (and some of the men) rouged, their lips carmined, their eyelashes blacked. She saw people from her old life, Emile de Girardin and his wife; Thiers, unchanged since 1851 save that more of his hair had fled, making his head look all the bigger and even less proportionate to his scrawny little body; he was, as ever, dwarfed by his mother-in-law and shadowed by his wife. Even cousin Théo escorted women whose expansive vulgarity matched his own. Cosette thought perhaps her old convent schoolmate Sophie might yet exist in the opulent flesh and false curls of a woman flirting with a bespangled military man. She recognized Arsène Huvet, who still fit his headmaster's description in 1848: blameless, charmless, vapid, and all too eager to please. Did the theatre create or only reflect the amnesty declared by Louis-Napoléon? There was the duc de Morny, who had engineered the coup d'état, his box beside those of men like Thiers, who had been arrested. The exiles all now returned to Paris, the former republicans no more protesting the Second Empire than rats protest the squeaking of a parquet floor.

There was Louis-Napoléon himself and Eugénie, their box hastily draped with bunting of green satin and set about with imperial bees, all of it gathered in the center with a shield sporting a green N encircled with a gold laurel wreath, the whole having been concocted in ten minutes' time of nothing more than papier mâché and gilt. For the imperial occasion, the orchestra played "Partant pour la Syrie," Offenbach himself conducting as Louis-Napoléon stood and gave a sort of benediction to resounding applause. Mea Culpa did not applaud. How ugly he was, thought Cosette. The years since 1848 had not been kind to him. His eyes were still utterly opaque and pale, his face gray, and the thinning hair clearly dyed auburn, as were his heavily waxed mustache and goatee. Louis-Napoléon sat down gingerly, the caution of a man who suffered pain in his testicles. And yet, they said, he had the appetite, the sexual hungers of a goat, that he had had battalions of women, from actresses to acrobats, that he plucked ladies from the gatherings at the Tuileries Palace like flowers at midsummer. Many of the women in this audience had slept with him. And what of the beautiful Eugénie? Such *sangfroid* for a Spaniard.

Cosette's attention returned immediately to the stage when she heard Nicolette falter, not a note missed, only wavering in its intensity. The reason lay in Jean-Luc's box, where Zelma had entered, late, bearing in her wake her two daughters and a swarthy, hirsute, mustachioed man, clearly foreign and dripping rich. Zelma trilled *pardons,* excusing herself noisily, waving until she caught the attention of another of her lovers, the comte de Châteaurenaud, the former lineless extra ennobled by a regime that was itself full of actors.

It came to Cosette that the audience and the stage were mirrors, not there to entertain, but to reflect. There was certainly as much false hair, as many false eyelashes, false jewels, false titles, false coloring on stage as there was in the theatre. Perhaps more makeup. The actors, after all, created effects, but had no need to maintain them. The audience must create and maintain effect. But for how long? The train for Trouville was as important in *La Vie Parisienne* as it was in the lives of this Parisian audience. In the play, an actor portrayed a Brazilian millionaire, and after the performance he would peel off his mustache, beard, hair, peel off his accent as well, wash his face clean, light up a cigarette, and be someone quite else. Might not the rich nabob with Zelma do exactly the same? Could the audience-side of this reflection be dismantled as easily as the stage-side? As easily as the set could be struck and a locomotive moved offstage to get ready for the second act? Could the whole Second Empire be as insubstantial as the bunting draped over the imperial box? Could this whole cast be disbanded and the real people yet triumph?

As the first shell pink of dawn infused the sky, Cosette, dressed in workingman's smock, pants, and cap, emerged from a small building behind the boxwood hedge at the back of Nicolette's garden, a garden she had had torn out and redone in the English fashion, which was just then all the rage. The effect was less than natural, but less than manicured too. Cosette paused at the lawn's edge, looking across to the high white balcony where wisteria twisted, the summer's first flowers hanging pendulous as heavy grapes. On the balcony there stood a figure in white, the sleeves dripping lace, Nicolette, looking less than natural, but less than manicured, her face still smeared with makeup, bleared with lack of sleep, her brows knit in pain, a glass in her hand. Cosette recognized the headache powders Nicolette poured in water. In looking for a cure for her headaches, Nicolette had been to every quack and most doctors in Paris. She looked so lonely and beleaguered that

Cosette wanted to go to her, but Nicolette waved a long greeting, then turned, went back into her bedroom, while Cosette left by the back gate, locked it, and walked toward the river.

She made this long journey twice daily on foot because after the performance it was too late and too dangerous to return to the *barrière*. When Nicolette volunteered a carriage to take her back, Cosette only laughed: one did not take a carriage to the *barrière*.

Actually, in good weather, Cosette enjoyed this dawn walk, this nebulous hour, queerly lit, when, so it always seemed to her, two armies emerged and met: the ragpickers and the revelers. The latter, unarmed, wove homeward, their faces haggard or flushed or grayed, depending on the nature of the night's excesses, the women's gowns bedraggled at the hems, their gloves soiled, their camellias all browned around the edges, the men's evening clothes stained with wine, with cigarette burns. These revelers emerged from clubs, bordellos, and boulevard cafés, from palaces and dance halls, oblivious, perhaps altogether ignorant, of the other army. The ragpickers, armed with staffs and baskets, picked through the night's garbage, loaded it on their carts and on their backs. As the mists rose off the river, those who had slept under bridges roused, and the river ravagers set out in their skiffs to ply the Seine up and down, looking for last night's suicides, their mournful cries echoing along the water now lit by long ribbons of dawn. Street sweepers pushed yesterday's horse dung before their brooms. The muddy embankments at the river resounded with the groans of men straining under great sacks of coal, walking up and down planks stretched between the barges and the quayside warehouse. Each morning at this moment, before gaudy dawn gave way to banal day, these two armies met and, as if by mutual consent, postponed the battle.

She crossed the river at the pont des Invalides (thus allowing her to avoid all places where the old Plumed Lark had roosted) on her way to the *barrière* d'Italie, where the ragpickers' encampment fires from the night before still smoked. Cosette hurried toward their shack with its homely sunflowers braving the Parisian weather, and nasturtiums a riot of color along the ground. She pulled the leather latch and stepped into the low-roofed dimness, lit only by chinks of light slatting through those cracks between boards, but enough to see to the bed, to see Marius awake, awaiting her as she shed her coarse workingman's costume, shed Mea Culpa, shed La Mauviette, shed the Lark, shed every identity save that of a woman in love, who went, naked, toward his open arms.

Chapter 21

*W*hen she had worked in the kitchen at Saint James Square, Fantine endlessly embroidered a daydream: Somewhere in Paris her real life was going on, and when she returned home (for that's how she always thought of France) she would meet and merge effortlessly into that Parisian woman, have her memories and prospects, her friends, her brocaded shoes and bonnets. Fantine, however, lived so long in London that the daydream itself metamorphosed; the bonnets, for instance, disappeared and hats took their place. And slowly, over the ten years, the self who remained in Paris, with whom she was to merge on her return, dwindled, a tiny kernel rattling inside the dry husk of the dream.

Now, as she stepped off the train in Paris, Fantine felt as if the dream must surely be real—and herself the dry kernel. The pleasure of hearing French spoken all around her was enough to make her cry, but she didn't. One does not live amongst the English all that time without learning not to cry. She looked up and down the platform for her brother, for someone who might conceivably be her brother. Even wildly she imagined her mother coming toward her, perhaps the Starling; these, the last two faces she had seen as the train left Paris all those years ago, the faces she most longed to see now. But, she chided herself, that was a truly ridiculous daydream. They did not even know she was in Paris. Perhaps no one knew. Certainly no one was here to meet her.

The porter regarded oddly her one small bag, and carried it for her into the waiting room, where she sat with it primly at her feet. For all the years she'd lived in England, she'd brought back very little. The one prize, secreted in the valise, a book of Madame Carême's recipes, had to be hidden always, from everyone, especially Jean-Luc.

Fantine owed her being in Paris at all to her cooking. One of Jean-Luc's friends, comte LaSalle, returned from London and complained to the chef at the Jockey Club that his cooking was less than superb. The count waxed on at length about the lobster *à la parisienne,* the hot quail pâté, the soufflé *à la reine,* the creamed oyster soup, and so on he had eaten at a friend's home in London in Saint James Square. The meal had so delighted the French guests that they had asked their hosts to call up the cook, and behold, who should enter but two Frenchwomen! One stout, middle-aged, brisk, and suspicious, the other slender, young, and serious. The former was introduced to LaSalle as the widow of the great Carême (and the count believed it too) and the latter as Miss Pontmercy, pronounced in the English fashion, as though the word could be broken in half, split open like a melon. Not until LaSalle returned to Paris and sat opposite Arsène Huvet and Jean-Luc did he realize what the name actually was, and of course everyone had a fine laugh. They all thought the name merely a coincidence, but they teased him anyway.

Huvet alone knew the truth of it. Jean-Luc never spoke of his family to anyone. Why should he? Who needs to carry the carcasses of martyrs, traitors, and exiles around Paris? But he immediately sent his sister a ticket, some money, and instructions that she was never to mention her kitchen life to anyone. Ever.

There was no one at the railway station to mention it to in any event. Perhaps Jean-Luc's forgotten me altogether, she considered. Perhaps on purpose. The crowds and cries of reunion and vexation thinned, but Fantine continued, exquisitely sensitive to the beautiful sound of her own language cascading around her, and had she not been so intent on the language she might not have heard a small girl ask her mother why *l'Anglaise* was staring at them so rudely. Fantine averted her gaze quickly and with half a mind to tell the brat she was not English. But as she more closely regarded the people in the station, she realized she did not look French either. Certainly not Parisian anymore. The crinolines for one thing. One never saw such huge hoops in England, large yes, but the women of Paris looked like small countries on legs. All of them, from the demimondaine to pinch-lipped matrons, were splendid, opulent, gilded, upholstered, braided, and bemedaled as generals, trailing pennants of perfume. She brushed a bit of cinder from her gray traveling dress. She wondered if she would even recognize the dream Fantine, the girl whose life had gone on in Paris.

She scarcely recognized Jean-Luc. So changed, so rich, so cold, such puffiness in his face, and a sneer now his native expression. But he smiled to see her, kissed her fingers (inspecting them perhaps for flour under the nails), and bade madame welcome.

"I'm not madame," she corrected him.

"After a certain age, all women in Paris are madame."

"I mean, I'm your sister. I shouldn't be madame."

"Very well, welcome to Paris, Fantine."

She knew, in that moment, her name had not crossed his lips in years; she had not crossed his mind in years. The gulf between them yawned, the more terrible for the blood tie.

Jean-Luc's carriage was drawn by a pair of fine, high-stepping grays, and though Fantine knew the old house in rue des Filles-du-Calvaire had been sold long ago, still that's where the dream Fantine lived, and now it was odd to be riding toward a section of the city she did not know at all. As they entered the great circulating arteries of Haussmann's Paris and she saw everywhere construction and destruction, scaffolding and demolition, streets torn up and houses torn down, Fantine realized it was not this section of the city that was foreign, but Paris itself.

"Paris is completely transformed," her brother remarked as they trotted toward his new home, which was still in the Park Monceau area, but the luxurious apartment given up for a newly built mansion. "The old forty-eight districts have been abolished, and the suburbs attached. You left a city still stinking in the Middle Ages. You returned to the nineteenth century. Just look."

Fantine nodded, tried to smile. Perhaps she had come home to be foreign, exchanged one exile for another.

The household Fantine joined was already filled with women: the daughter, the wife, the sister-in-law Corinne, and Zelma. The latter two had moved in when Count Troussebois died. Zelma believed it would be so much better for Corinne's chances on the marriage market to live in an opulent establishment with a wealthy brother-in-law than with a widowed mother. Opulent it was; the whole house dripped with gilt and ormolu, stuffed with velvet, no corner left unfringed. That first night Jean-Luc merely said they would all meet tomorrow, instructing the servants to take Madame Fantine up to her room, which shared with the rest of the mansion an oppressive ostentation. After the clean floor, iron bedstead, plain rug, and dormer window overlooking leafy Saint James Square, the furniture here seemed smothering, shackling, heavy as leg irons.

The following night, that first terrible meal was clearly a harbinger of things to come. Zelma rattled on at length, with exaggerated courtesy, always bringing the discussion back to Fantine's unfortunate flight, plight, and exile, throwing in observations that always began with "Dear little Cosette," and, to the clenched-fist anger of Jean-Luc, she congratulated Fantine on her cleverness in misleading him all those years to believe that Cosette was in England. "And England, how did you amuse yourself there, dear Fantine? What did you do in England all those years?"

"Nothing." Fantine looked to her brother for protection, for guidance, for support, but he poured one glass of wine after another.

"I understand you left Paris with the family cook," said Eponine archly. Eponine and Corinne were clearly nursing some deep personal enmity, the tensions between the sisters overt and painful. Eponine, still beautiful, had thinned, and the fire in her eyes seemed to have burnt out hollows in her cheeks. Corinne, always in Eponine's shadow in the past, had picked up a haughty air visible as a peacock feather, and now and then, her mother's big-toothed smile. "What happened to the cook?"

"Nothing," said Fantine, twisting her napkin in her lap, strangling it. "In ten years nothing happened to anyone."

"Well, now it's up to Jean-Luc to find you a husband, isn't it? A husband worthy of you," commented Zelma. "Have you anyone in mind?" she inquired of him.

Some fleeting emotion, costumed as a grin, crossed Jean-Luc's face, and he said to the evident consternation of all the Touchard women, "Arsène Huvet."

The horrible meal mercifully past, they all vanished, out for the evening, and Fantine climbed the stairs to her room. In her head she wrote one of many letters to her mother. In her heart she wrote letters to the Starling. How would she find him? Would she even know him? He was a boy then. She was a girl. She turned up the gaslight and went to the beveled, gilded mirror, and studied herself. She was too slender and too strong and too pale for beauty, her hair lifelessly brown. Her full lips pressed against tears. Perhaps the ten years that had passed had stolen irrevocably, not merely her youth, but her life. "He's a man now." Perhaps the Starling had his own woman. Perhaps a wife. "And I am an old maid of twenty-five, queer as a four-legged duck." And maybe his long silence did not mean he was in danger, only that she was something he'd forgotten, put away with childhood.

Chapter 22

*A*s a newcomer to Paris, Fantine could not have known the role Arsène Huvet played in the fantasy life of matrons of the Second Empire, especially those with marriageable daughters. Matronly speculation escalated all over Paris when Arsène's mother died; after all, if the father remarried, the son's estate would be considerably cut. These matrons were reassured by gossip that the old man was feeling the pinch of his own mortality, and believing he had not long in this world, he was pressuring his son to marry. The competition for Arsène was indeed cutthroat, but the former Zelma Thénardier was equal to the task, and to keep Arsène, so to speak, in view, Zelma had moved herself and Corinne into the Pontmercy home after the demise of her late husband, a man of whom it could truly be said: He served well.

"One marriage for love," Zelma was fond of saying to her daughters, "one for money." Presumably Eponine's was the first, Corinne's to be the second. Corinne was neither stupid nor vile, but at twenty (and a few shades over, really) she was sick of the role of unmarried girl, sick of Zelma's holding out for the big prize, Huvet. She envied her sister's freedom, the freedom only marriage could confer. Arsène would certainly do. Whatever his deficiencies in charm and looks, they were amply compensated: the only son of the sugar beet king, the salt pork king, one of the richest industrialists in France. And too, Arsène was frequently at the Pontmercy home, there even more frequently once Eponine took him as a lover.

Eponine took him literally, not figuratively, with a kind of rapacity, a capacity for revenge her old grandfather would have relished and recognized. Arsène was the first of many men Eponine took into her bed when she realized that all her dreams had decayed beneath the splendid edifice of a marriage, a title, a life at the center of Second Empire society, with its elaborate balls, hunts, and festivities at court. She had made the grave error of falling in love with her husband. Those months in Italy following her wedding were the most golden moments of Eponine's life. Two hours back in Paris and her husband was in the arms of Nicolette Lauriot.

She wanted him back. She set about it with a lack of scruple her mother recognized, even found endearing. Eponine wanted Jean-Luc's love, and if she could not have that, at least she wanted his tenderness, affection, and interest, and to that end she used her daughter, Louise, born the following year, used her as casually as old man Thénardier had used Zelma. But beyond briefly contesting the name Louise, Jean-Luc had no interest in his daughter and was absolutely immune to ploys on her behalf. Perhaps it was then that Eponine, too, lost all interest in the girl, leaving Louise to be observed, perhaps even attended, but never truly cared for by nannies, governesses, and servants, adults impatient only for her to grow up.

Toward Jean-Luc, Eponine was alternately capricious, cajoling, adoring, seductive, bitter, cutting, cruel, and violent. One afternoon after a screaming bout that had echoed all over the mansion, Fantine came downstairs to see the floor littered, the servants calmly sweeping up an entire service of Sèvres porcelain. It was replaced the next day, and Fantine assumed her brother must have a standing order. Perhaps many such orders. One morning, walking past closed doors to the drawing room, Fantine stopped, listened as Zelma uttered again her unfortunate phrase, "One marriage for money, one for love," which sent Eponine into a foaming wrath. The crash of porcelain resounded.

"One for love! Love! Well, you failed there, didn't you, Ma?"

"*Mama.* How many times must—"

"How can you even say the word *love?* It should stick in your throat and choke you like an Arkansas mule. You don't know what it is to love! I had a chance at it!" Eponine shrieked and wept, "I had a taste of it! I could have been loved!"

"By Jean-Luc?"

"Why did you want him so, Ma? He's nothing. Beautiful, that's all. Without your connections, he was an impoverished nobody.

His father was a martyr, his mother a traitor, and his sister a cook! Why did you want him?"

"I didn't want him for myself, Eponine."

"You didn't want him for me! I'm the daughter of the Emperor! I'm the Emperor's love child! I could have married anybody! I could have married Arsène Huvet! Why aren't I married to him?"

"Huvet will be in the family. Isn't that enough?"

Eponine seemed to strangle on her own breath. "It's done, then?"

"Negotiations are proceeding," replied Zelma with Bismarckian finesse. "I think this can be accomplished."

"So my sister is going to marry my lover? *My lover!*"

"Such passion," Zelma said, sighing, "so unbecoming in a lady of the Second Empire. What do you care about Huvet? You're married to a rich man. A beautiful man."

"But Huvet's riches do not depend on the favors, on the good will, of others, do they? They are his. Completely his."

"Unless his father should remarry," Zelma mused.

"I've met his father. He's ugly as a louse. Liver spots all over his bald head. A great hairy mole on his cheek."

Zelma speculated on the probable looks of Arsène's mother, while Eponine swore like a coachman, and the door against which Fantine leaned cracked with the impact of Jean Valjean's candlesticks. A passing servant shrugged, as if to say, *Get used to it; we're bored.* Fantine was shocked; servants in the house on Saint James Square would have relished a scene like this for months.

"Well, then, Ma, just out of curiosity, why didn't you marry *me* off to Arsène Huvet? It's not like you to pass up a rich man for a poor one. Why did you want Jean-Luc? To keep Nicolette Lauriot in the family?" she added acidly.

"Nicolette Lauriot is a whore, and when her good looks fail her, she'll be begging at the *barrière*. You are protected. You are the Baroness Pontmercy. Eponine Pontmercy."

"Like your sister Eponine, Ma?"

"Poor Eponine. She died of consumption when we were just girls, coughed herself away, just like the lady of the camellias."

Eponine's pacing back and forth could be heard squealing on the parquet floor. "What was it, Ma? What drove you to marry me off to a man who had nothing except your goodwill? I could have married anyone," she lamented again. "I could have married a man who would have adored me. I deserve to be adored."

"Your lovers adore you, don't they?"

"My husband adores Nicolette Lauriot."

"Don't be tedious and bourgeois."

"I've been cheated."

"Nonsense. Jean-Luc sleeps with all sorts of women. He isn't faithful to Nicolette."

"You know nothing of love, Ma, nothing of its glories and nothing of its pains."

"Oh, Eponine," Zelma snapped, "the only thing worse than passion is sentiment."

Eponine's voice, when at last she replied, was neither passionate nor sentimental, but cool, appraising, and grim. "You made some sort of devil's bargain, didn't you, Ma? Some bargain with the past. Something you're not telling me. Something I don't know. Does he know? Does Jean-Luc know how you used him? You bargained for your own past and used me for currency."

"And very attractive currency you are, my dear."

Chapter 23

*T*he clothes Fantine had brought from England were not merely cast off, but cast out, and eventually graced *barrière* belles at a ragpicker's wedding. But to become a woman of Paris, Fantine was obliged to master the crinoline, an art requiring time and practice. She was cinched in, pushed up, a steel cage draped over her hips, and at first she felt like a ship under full sail, the plaything of the wind, but she gradually got used to it, and within a few months could maneuver as gracefully as anyone clad in a half acre of hoops.

But it was by no means as easy a task to navigate through Jean-Luc's world. He expected her not merely to fit into this world but to marry into it. He put her forth like something in a shop window, introducing her to the galaxy of possible husbands in his wide acquaintance. Fantine found that men of the Second Empire could be occasionally amusing, often charming, but they seemed to her predatory or wallowing, slack and spiritless. In a word, "Insubstantial," Fantine described them. Jean-Luc thought the word, the very notion, silly, priggish, and he asked her if she had got it from the English, as though it might be a disease.

Undaunted, though, he escorted his sister to salons, boulevard cafés, to café-concerts in the Champs-Elysées, to masked balls at the Opéra, to the Opéra itself, and to the racecourse at Longchamps. She refused, however, to attend any balls or festivals at the court of Napoléon III. Refused and refused to be budged.

"I will not dance at the court, nor to the tune of the man who killed my father," Fantine declared. "You may call him Sire if you wish. I call him murderer."

"That's my father you're speaking of," Eponine snapped.

"Oh, Fantine, Fantine," Jean-Luc implored her, "don't you know all that's vanished? The rue de Combray has vanished, the

Paris you knew has vanished, the people have vanished. No one cares about any of that *liberté, égalité,"* he scoffed.

"Don't you care? He was your father. Your mother is out there somewhere living in God knows what kind of gutter—and you live like this?" She flung her arm out and upset a wan porcelain shepherdess.

"Our parents made their choices. *The sword, the scaffold, and the gutter?*" he quipped with an indulgent smile.

"How can you sleep at night knowing Mama must be cold or hungry?"

Jean-Luc stormed out and did not come home for three days, and in that time Eponine tongue-lashed Fantine at every opportunity; Zelma passed out nasty observations on her behavior and her family in general, estimations Fantine returned in kind; and the whole house seemed ready to burst like a great cyst full of female vituperation. She was a prisoner in her brother's house and an anomaly in the Second Empire: a well-bred woman with a skill, an unmarried woman with experience outside the home. Absolutely dependent on Jean-Luc, she could not go out without him; he bought the clothes on her back and dictated the people she could see. She was ignored and despised by the Touchard women and precipitated tremendous fights by criticizing their cook. She rattled about the mansion like the dried-up kernel of her dream. She cried herself to sleep at night.

Of all the social venues where Jean-Luc tried to introduce her to men, the theatres were the least painful. At least she was amused at the theatre. He had boxes at several, including the Bouffes-Parisiens, and he took her there to watch Nicolette Lauriot work her old magic on *la vie Parisienne,* both onstage and off.

"She is very beautiful," Fantine conceded, rippling her fan over what felt like her completely exposed bosom as they watched Nicolette enchant the audience. "And her voice is spectacular."

"She is the most desirable woman in Paris."

"Why didn't you marry her? Why marry Eponine?"

"Don't be impertinent."

"I'm not a child, Jean-Luc, to be put in my place."

"Women like Nicolette don't marry. They don't have to."

"Then why should I? Why do you insist on trotting me out like a prize cabbage?"

"Your language reeks of the kitchen," he replied icily. "Besides, you're nothing like Nicolette. No one is."

At the entr'acte Jean-Luc insisted on taking Fantine backstage, where the porter greeted him rapturously, rattling on at great length about how long it had been since he had seen Baron Pontmercy and how well Baron Pontmercy looked, and so on. At least five francs' worth.

"Why has it been so long?" asked Fantine as her great hooped skirt of burgundy silk caught in the narrow backstage passages.

"I don't need to come backstage, to stand in line with every geriatric duke and penniless prince."

He tried Nicolette's door, but it was locked, and so he knocked abruptly, answered by a prim, scratchy voice. "So very sorry, sir, but Mademoiselle Lauriot—"

"She'll see me," he announced; the door opened and he came face-to-face with a wizened little creature with mouse-brown hair twisted in a matted knot, a crucifix banging against her mustard-colored bodice, and green spectacles. "Mea Culpa, no doubt," he said politely.

"Jean-Luc!" Nicolette cried out as Mea Culpa inched back, shoulders hunched, eyes to the floor. "What—brings—you—"

"Here? Why are you so shocked?"

"You never come backstage."

"I have someone who wants to meet you since you are the most famous woman in Paris, excepting the Empress."

"What do you mean? The Empress is a pious, Catholic cow."

"Mademoiselle Lauriot, my sister, Mademoiselle Pontmercy." He ushered Fantine into the dressing room, which was large but not large enough for two women in crinolines, and so hot that they had opened the great door in the floor that led to the storeroom underneath to catch the drafts which swirled up.

"Your sister?" Nicolette blanched as Mea Culpa fluttered amongst the costumes, grabbed hold of the costumes as if she might fall and pull them all with her. "I thought your sister was living in England."

"She's spent the last ten years at an English finishing school," he said without a rattle of irony.

Fantine burst into gales of laughter. "Is that what you've been telling people about me? Ten years in an English finishing school? Oh, Jean-Luc, that's—" she caught her breath for laughing, more difficult since she was laced into the gown within an inch of her life. "Oh, yes, I am finished. Polished to perfection."

Jean-Luc rebuked her, "Unmarried girls should watch their tongues."

"I am not a girl, Jean-Luc! Look at me."

"But you're certainly unmarried and likely to stay so."

"Please, Mademoiselle Pontmercy." Nicolette tried to draw them both into the stifling room, upsetting a vase of blue roses. She fussed and fluttered over Fantine, asking questions, trying her best not to look at Mea Culpa, who fumbled amongst the costumes while Nicolette stumbled amongst the formalities. "How long will you be staying in Paris?"

"Until Jean-Luc can marry me off to some gouty underdone friend of his," snapped Fantine, "or until I can bear it no longer."

"Mea Culpa, that's enough," Nicolette reprimanded her. "You're clumsy as a drunken louse. Leave us." Mea Culpa scraped and bowed hastily backward toward the door in the floor where steps loomed, leading down into the storeroom. She turned and fled down the steps and into the dim, drafty vaults of the storage area and found herself a throne left over from some ancient play, where she could laugh and cry, where she could thank God and pray for guidance, rock back and forth and say her daughter's name, where she could leave by the back door, out into the rue Monsigny, and brave the long, lonely road out to the *barrière* by night to tell Marius that Fantine was back in France.

Their quarrel at the Bouffes-Parisiens was not the first nor the last, but it served to make Jean-Luc merciless in his efforts to marry Fantine off, perhaps more to the point, to make Fantine so miserable she would marry out of petulance and he'd be rid of her. He made pointed references to her dependence on him, which enraged her and she alternately sulked and fumed. The strife between Fantine and everyone else in the house (saving for the child, Louise) exacerbated during the elaborate preparations for the wedding of Corinne Touchard and Arsène Huvet, a wedding of such staggering ostentation and expense it took the breath away.

As part of the wedding festivities, Zelma rented the whole of a boulevard restaurant for one of many luncheons. At the head table sat the two families to be united, Fantine put at the end of the table beside Arsène's old father, who was soft, smelly as an old cheese. She wondered if Jean-Luc thought this a joke, or worse, perhaps he seriously expected her to charm old Monsieur Huvet with an eye to his millions.

Perhaps it was a form of punishment to be captive here behind the monstrous floral decoration, enduring an endless, overdone meal, listening to this liver-spotted brigand tell fascinating tales of sugar beetery and salt porkery and a new machine he was bringing to France, a patent he'd copied or stolen, from a Cincinnati slaughter yard, where the pigs were first splayed, then strapped to mechanical sleds, and on a conveyor belt powered by steam they were struck with a mechanical knife, slit right along the throat. The elder Huvet demonstrated this with his index finger. Then, still on the sled, the blood running down in gutters on either side of the conveyor belt, the pig was pushed along, brushed down, scraped with steam-driven brushes, two for each side, then mechanically quartered and hung. "Total time," said Monsieur Huvet, "eighteen and a half minutes. Not a minute more."

"Those were my sentiments exactly. You will be so good, I hope, as to excuse me."

Swiftly Fantine made her way through the noise and smoke of the restaurant and the nearly five hundred luncheon guests to the front, where she asked for the coat to her cream-and-pink-and-green-striped silk gown, and for the matching hat, which she tied under her chin, and left as quickly as possible, turning right on the boulevard.

Late-April sun softened the green fists budding on long, parallel lines of trees, giving the effect of a chorus line all stretching and yawning in unison. She walked westward, looking for the rue de Combray, disoriented to find the surrounding streets still there, altered but extant. The rue de Combray was one of those erased, vanished as her father's life and work. But even to Fantine the notion of dying to defend an idea seemed completely at odds with the spring afternoon, with the smart tap of her boot heels on the broad sidewalk as she strolled the new Paris, which, to use the

Haussmannian phrase, circulated: carriages, taxis, omnibuses, promenades, the broad avenues of commerce populated by shoppers, people of wealth if not distinction, of pretension if not wealth, for whom clothing was culture. The beggars had all been swept up and swept off the boulevards, as had the itinerant noisy vendors with their cries and horns, the shops all spiffed up, shined, and manned by shopkeepers respectfully indoors and behind counters. The indoor rustle and shuffle of money counterpointed the outdoor orderly clip-clop of hooves and the hum of steel wheels over newly macadamized streets. Every third man wore a military uniform, and every third woman exuded expensive satisfactions.

Fantine walked to the Tuileries Gardens, where twice a week in the afternoon military bands played, bright brasses, thumping percussion, this time rousing out "The Radetsky March," while well-dressed Parisians randomly grouped themselves on gracefully curved iron chairs, skirts billowing, or moving through the trees like silken apparitions, accompanied by men in black, their top hats bobbing, nodding. Fantine picked up her own striped skirts to join the informal disorder, the throng, as all around her people chattered, fluttered, flirted, gossiped, children with hoops, women walking little dogs, parasols twirling as the music rose and fell and laughter tinkled up through the budding trees. A child ran past her pushing a hoop and another played with a ball, while here and there artists sketched. She watched them with special interest, hoping to see Monsieur Beaujard somewhere amongst these matrons and dandies, the babble of foreign tongues. She recognized only Monsieur Thiers, smiling, eyes closed, sitting on a chair, his tiny feet tapping out of time, his great mother-in-law like a toad protecting the fly.

When the band picked up a particularly catchy waltz, a round of applause sounded, and all heads turned toward a tall, stooped man, a halo of gray hair under his top hat, on his huge nose a pince-nez, and on his arm a blond woman of surpassing beauty. Nicolette Lauriot. The name rippled through the crowd, as though Nicolette had agitated, ravished them just by being there, as though she exuded such glamour as to diminish the very sun. Fantine studied her, wondering if perhaps she'd been hasty in declining Nicolette's invitation. No doubt most of these people would have thought themselves honored to have Mademoiselle Lauriot requesting the honor of their presence. She had sent Fantine a note the very day after that dreadful episode in the dressing room at the Bouffes-Parisiens, a fulsome note, an imploring note, inviting her to the rue de Chaillot. Fantine debated going only because she knew how enraged Eponine would be, and the thought of vexing any of the Touchards gave her pleasure. Still, to act on that low impulse would have been unworthy of a Pontmercy, and she had penned a brisk reply, saying that previous engagements would deprive her of the honor. Another invitation arrived, however, and another after that, and now, watching Nicolette, she rather regretted her stubbornness and she wondered if Mademoiselle Lauriot might provide an avenue of escape from her brother.

Crossing through the gardens, she came to the Seine and watched it roll by, looked at the Panthéon across the river, realized that for the first time since her return she was a free woman in Paris. There was no question what she would do with that freedom.

She crossed the pont de Solférino and wandered south, looking the more odd as she progressed through the working life of Paris, dressed as she was in her silken crinoline, satin coat, embroidered gloves, and smart hat with glossy bow tied underneath her chin. Since this side of the Seine was foreign to her anyway, the streets, rerouted, broadened, and ripped from their old fabrics, did not seem as strange until she came to construction altering the rue de Rennes, where she looked up and beheld the cour du Dragon. Just as Mama had described it, the stone dragon flared above the entry to the courtyard, its head raised, talons poised, wings outspread, the dragon of despair, from which one must emerge transformed or not at all. She walked through the miserable court, where her mother had once lived, staring into hostile faces, thinking too of the story: how they wanted Sainte-Marguerite to marry a man of the Roman Empire, just as they wanted Fantine to marry a man of the Second Empire. Church bells sounded and Fantine left the squalid little court, followed the bells to Saint-Sulpice, and there, in its shadow, the Café Rigolo.

The woman behind the counter had not changed since 1851, but the place had an air of tidy prosperity that was new: new mirror, the oranges in the wire stand, gay bottles. The busts of Napoléon III everywhere diminished Fantine's resolve, though, and she asked only for a lemonade, while Madame Fagennes, washing up, watched her in the mirror. Fantine's opulent dress stood out weirdly amongst the half dozen customers, some looking very bedraggled, some very bewildered.

Fantine put the glass down on the zinc, bit her lip, spoke softly. "I'm looking for someone. Perhaps you can help."

"Perhaps not," snapped Madame Fagennes, casting a quick glance over at the interested Griffon. That crippled spy clung to the Café Rigolo like a wart.

"A man who goes, used to go, by the name Starling."

"Never! Go away! Leave! I am for the Emperor!"

"I'm not," came a voice from the back, a slight voice, a thin and shallow voice, a voice behind a glass of absinthe. Mimi Lascaux fortifying herself. Mimi rose unsteadily and came to the counter, studying Fantine's gorgeous clothes, picking up the pink-and-green-striped satin and running it between her fingers, making appreciative noises.

Madame Fagennes stepped briskly around the zinc counter, took one arm each of Mimi and Fantine, and escorted them out of the café. "You are the girl from England, aren't you? Otherwise you would know better. You must be more careful, mademoiselle, you must be very careful. That Starling—" she shot an evil look to Mimi—"will get you in trouble. He will get everyone you know in a lot of trouble. The police, everyone, is looking for him."

"Dogs," said Mimi casually, "swine."

"Did he get my letters?" Fantine implored Madame Fagennes. "Does he know I'm here? Is he here? Is he married or—"

"I know nothing of Starling. Ask his mother," she nodded curtly toward Mimi. "But don't ask in my café. They say they have liberalized the regime, mademoiselle, well—fine—good—but me, I am going to tell you there are names still dangerous in Paris. The Starling is one of those names, the Lark, La Lumière, Pontmercy, do not say those names in Paris."

"But it is my name, Pontmercy."

"Mother of God!" cried Madame Fagennes.

Mimi's eyes cleared. "Fantine? You are Fantine?"

"Shoo!" cried Madame Fagennes as if to scatter a flock of starlings. "Scat!"

Mimi pulled Fantine after her, threading through narrow streets going toward the river, Fantine looking like a balloon pulled in the wake of a broom. Mimi had pawned her crinoline, so her skirt hung slack on her hips, and her hat was frayed and her gloves soiled. Fantine knew she was being led through the streets by a *fille publique*, humbled to be in the debt of this prostitute who would lead her to Gabriel.

But instead she was led to the Changer's warehouse, where Mimi banged on the door and made a great ruckus, echoed by the ever-present dogs. "I've come for the Countess, you old mute," Mimi announced, pushing past a Jondrette, pulling Fantine after her. Once inside, she released Fantine's hand and wandered out in the gloom where the costumes hung overhead in their wombs of net. "It's me, Countess! It's me!"

After the bright sunshine outside, Fantine's eyes adjusted with difficulty to the dimness. She remembered the place, of course, remembered the day her whole life had changed when she'd come here last. Perhaps that's why they called it the Changer's.

"Mimi?" called the Countess down through the dust. "Mimi?"

Mimi walked over, head back, and cried, "It's me, all right. It's time to make this right."

"Oh, Mimi, have you—"

"I've brought the daughter of the Lark."

"Not here, have you? Oh, Mimi—"

"She wants the Starling, Countess, and she deserves him, and only you can find him."

Chapter 24

*F*or nineteen centuries there had been a bridge with this same name at this same spot. Destroyed eleven times since the Romans first put up a wooden structure, the Petit-Pont had been demolished in 1852 because the old wooden structure reeked of revolution. The men who tore it down wished they'd set fire to it in June of 1848, before the cannon rolled across. Rebuilt of stone, solid, indeed still standing, there squatted near it, this particular evening on the south side of the Seine, a beggar, one eye patched, the other squinting, a tin cup on a long chain shackled to his ankle. His clothes were but layer upon layer of rags, his whole body collapsed beneath a floppy slouch hat; he was a pile of motionless tatters, alive only insofar as the cup rattled piteously. Apparently he could not see that all that clanked within was a button or a bone, some worthless trifle. His arms were open to the spring night, and clearly he was of that lowest class of beggars trading on his bodily afflictions. Both arms and the hand that held his miserable cup were festering, blistered, horribly white and scarred, as though they had been once plunged into boiling oil or scalding water, the poor man left in permanent pain and unfit for labor of any kind.

He sat there, collecting horrified stares as people hurried past him, until a woman approached. She was thin, tough as jerked beef, her feet thrust into wooden shoes, her hair wild, her face dirty, her mouth pressed into a thin seam, disgust, perhaps. She might have been anywhere between thirty and fifty. "The Monkey is ready to fly," she said.

Slowly the beggar got to his feet, unsnapped the chain from his ankle (the chaining a common practice among beggars to save their cups from thieving boys), and carrying it, he followed her abjectly along the quai Saint-Michel, where they slid down toward the river, which glowed in the glare of sunset and winked with the lights on the bridges. They faced the old morgue, where bodies of suicides were taken once pulled from the Seine.

"Your arms are disgusting, Lark."

"It's nothing. A thick coating of soap and then you pour vinegar over it and it blisters like this, mottles and turns its awful color, but it doesn't really hurt very much. Pity the beggars of the past who had to inflict real damage on themselves for their livelihood."

"I've no pity left for anyone but my man and my children."

"I understand that. How could it be otherwise?"

"I have no room for pity, but I have mansions of hate, Lark. I hate those fat ones. I hate the military. I hate the clergy. I hate the men who put their feet on our necks, their well-shod feet on our dirty necks, and then tell us to look up and see the fireworks, the spectacles, the universal expositions, tell us these are better than freedom. They give us war and call it peace. They give us crumbs and call it bread, but at least," Germaine shrugged that articulate Parisian shrug, "we're not starving like we were in '48. From the bones of their luxuries we can at least make soup."

"How can poor people believe that their best interests lie with the rich? The best interests of dogs, perhaps," Cosette added, thinking of Nicolette's vile little Pekineses, pampered, fat, and too lazy to do anything but mount one another. "The dogs of the rich are right to slather after them. The rest of us can't."

"No, Lark. The rest of them do. The few of us won't. Pajol is digging sewers for Haussmann. I weep to see him, not because he's ill or injured, or working in the sewer, but because he is a printer and that's all he knows. Without a press, he feels . . ." Germaine sighed.

"Incomplete?" offered Cosette. "As Marius is incomplete without a pen."

"It was a miracle your man lived, Lark. And a miracle you got him back."

"And then I had to watch him sicken all over again, starve, freeze, I was powerless to care for him, to change or alter anything. I know the pain and terror that you face, Germaine."

"Pajol has decided he must leave us. He says if he stays it's only a question of time before Clerons sniffs his way along a trail of ink to Montmartre. We've taken different names and no one knows us in Montmartre, but he says it's safer for him to live apart from us," she said, sulkily. "I told him, let's move out to the *barrières*—"

"It's not that easy. They are their own country now, those encampments, suspicious of the police, suspicious of thieves and murderers, and there are many of those too, pushed out of the old haunts—" Cosette nodded across the river, where the old Ile-de-la-Cité, once a noted den of thieves and filth, was in the throes of reconstruction. "You need an entrée at the *barrière* as you need an entrée at court. To bring Pajol to the *barrière* d'Italie where we live, it's too dangerous for Marius. I must keep Clerons away from Marius at all costs. But I have a place for Pajol, Germaine. A good place, unlikely and uncomfortable, but if he's careful, it's safe." Cosette grinned and reached into the recesses of her rags, first pulling out fifteen francs. Germaine wept to wrap her hand around it. "Now and then I'll send more, with Pajol, with the Starling. We won't let your family starve, Germaine. We'll do what we can, Marius and I." She dug deeper into the tattered layers she wore and drew out a key on a red ribbon, which Germaine put around her neck and dropped down her dress; it seemed to clatter against her ribs. "At the back of the Bouffes-Parisiens theatre, there are two doors. One is a big door for getting scenery and stage flats into the theatre. One is smaller, for props and the like, for the musicians to go outside and have a smoke during the entr'acte. This is the key to that door. Tonight, after the performance—"

"But the rue Monsigny, Lark! That's near the passage Choiseul, the smartest shops—a man who looks like Pajol would be arrested immediately for breathing in the passage Choiseul."

"What choice have we? He'll have to be very careful. It's a safe hiding place. It's not warm and there are legions of mice, but few rats, I think, and no one will ever think to look for a printer amongst the abandoned props, the gas pipes and pulleys. It's a huge room, it goes the entire length and depth of the stage, and I have rigged a corner there for Pajol. Tell him to come after the performance, and once inside to lock the door again and turn to the right and hide behind some trees. Cardboard trees, fake trees," Cosette offered, replying to the surprise on Germaine's face. "Everything below the stage is false, as is everything on the stage, and," she added reflectively, "in the theatre itself. Everyone, too. Tell him to wait there for me and I'll show him where he can sleep. He'll have to learn to get in and out without being noticed, and I don't say it will go easy, but even Clerons won't look there."

"Clerons has not yet looked for you there, has he?"

"Not yet." Cosette laughed grimly. "I think he's still going through the feathers of the poor Plumed Lark, looking for vermin."

"He is vermin. If I could, I would take my man and my children and leave this city."

"Paris is the best place, Germaine. There is no safe country except perhaps for the country of love, and sometimes your heart can live there, but your body cannot. At least in Paris, you know you have friends."

"Yes, Lark. We have friends. If we have friends like you, we can bear having enemies like Clerons. You know Pajol vows nightly to kill him. Sometimes, when I sleep beside him, his dreams are so violent they wake me."

"Clerons was the one who told us it began in blood and it will end in blood, but not just now, Germaine. Go home to your children."

Cosette ambled down to the river, ducked beneath the bridge, and washed her hideous arms in the waters of the Seine, which clouded with the affliction. She pulled off the layer of rags, the slouch hat, the eyepatch, wadded them in a bundle with the beggar's cup, and left them beneath the bridge. She mopped the beggar's thick grime from her face, and using a burnt cork she had hidden in a pocket, she blacked her jaw, her chin, above her lips with what looked like three days' growth of beard mulched with dirt. From inside her blue workman's shirt, she pulled a broken-down hat and put it on her head. The workingman who passed before the Palais de Justice, whistling, heading to the other side of the river, looked as comfortable and jaunty as a man who has never feared the law.

The long ebullient run of *La Vie Parisienne* was coming to a close. A new operetta would open in the fall, and even the locomotive would be dismantled and packed away, stored in pieces in the large, low-ceilinged room below the stage.

As after every performance, once her stage makeup was off

(and her street makeup on), La Lauriot bade Mea Culpa open the door of her dressing room to the Passage of Princes and they flocked in. Eventually they flocked out to boulevard cafés or restaurants, to cabarets in the Champs-Elysées, and Mea Culpa hunched over and cleaned up alone. Tonight she worked especially slowly, and when they had all left, she gathered up a blanket she had hidden in a trunk, in which she'd tied bread, candles, and matches. She lifted the heavy trapdoor in the dressing room and went down the ladder, carrying a candle because gaslight was turned off. As always, drafts swirled up and her candle sputtered, but it did not go out as she dropped to the floor below.

It was a kind of morgue, this room, a morgue of theatrical pasts and pleasures, everything jumbled uncaringly, as if in a common grave. Through this mausoleum Mea Culpa walked slowly, her path insufficiently lit by the flame, mice scurrying before her. Overhead she could hear the footsteps of the porter and the last of the scene shifters getting things ready for tomorrow's performance. Threading her way to the back, she found Pajol, as she had hoped, hunkered down behind some painted trees. He moved them carefully and rose, stood before her. He was still lanky, almost completely bald, such hair as he had ringed his head like that of a monk or a priest, and his expression reminded Cosette of Verdier, though he was not as Old Testament grim.

They greeted each other warmly in the wavering light and Pajol promised, "We'll light the torch again. I found a clandestine press—you know, one of those little ones they used a hundred years ago. It needs to be fixed—but then, you have to write something for me to print."

"I must be more careful now, Pajol. I have Marius to think of and not just my own safety," she said, leading him back through a maze of discarded props and haphazard scenery. "My daughter's back in Paris. I want her to stay safe. The stakes are suddenly raised." She brought him to a small enclosure, walled off by stacks of scenery and a few stage flats. An elegant divan (left over from Pluto's palace in *Orphée aux Enfers*) was pushed against the wall. She gave him the bundle—the blankets, the bread, and candles— and warned him again about remaining absolutely silent if he were there during performances and being very careful coming in and out of the theatre. "I'm going to get you some clothes that will make you look more like a stagehand and less like," she held the candle up to him, "a navvy digging sewers for Haussmann."

"It's work." Pajol shrugged. "I'm grateful to the Starling for getting me some work. Even if I can't print, I have to work."

"Well, Pajol," she wrinkled her nose and smiled lightly, "it would be better for you to look like a stagehand, and smell like one too."

"*Merci*, Lark."

"Not the Lark. Not here. Mea Culpa here."

"I can't say that. I never admit to guilt."

Chapter 25

*I*t was a grave disappointment to Cosette when Fantine replied with brisk dismissals to invitations to the rue de Chaillot. Nicolette suggested that they try once more, that Cosette should write this invitation in her own hand and hope Fantine recognized it. It was dangerous, true. Jean-Luc could recognize it too. But perhaps this was the only way to get her attention. Having taken the risk, it would have wounded Cosette to see that Fantine did not open, did not even look at the note or the handwriting. There was another letter that arrived that same day.

Following the instructions in this latter note, on a glorious Sunday in May, Fantine announced she was going to mass, then took a carriage to the Luxembourg Gardens and found (as was not too difficult) the Fountain of the Médicis, its long silent waterway lined by stone urns on either side, presided over by a mossy, monstrous figure, Narcissus, about to plunge fatally in love with himself. Here she waited, pacing. Like a lady of the Second Empire, Fantine was swathed, head to foot. She wore a voluminous, unwieldy gown of apricot silk with a matching coat and hat, and carried a silk-fringed shawl as well. With gloved hands she touched up her hair which had been brushed smoothly from her face and curled in the back, the curls cascading from under the hat. She checked her tiny pocket watch more than once, but she remained alone with Narcissus. Poor company.

She saw the reflection in the pool before she saw him: tall, broad-shouldered, dressed in a plain black suit he'd got from his grandmother. Clearly he was also manicured for the occasion, clean-shaven, his dark hair smoothed down, and he wore no hat. His nose was still crooked, his smile too, but his dark eyes were alert, his skin tanned. All that wavered, shimmered in the reflecting pool before she raised her eyes, almost afraid to look, to put the image with the name, the man with the memory, the past with the present. "Starling."

"You are so beautiful."

"You are so—so substantial," she faltered, for lack of anything else to say.

He walked down the length of the reflecting pool, coming toward her while her heartbeat pounded all the way out to her fingertips. As she watched him move, she could see how the boy's body had filled out with manhood and strengthened with labor. For this sight she had returned to Paris. For this man. For this moment.

But to her grave disappointment, when he reached for her hand he called her mademoiselle. "Don't—" she interrupted him. "Please, surely after everything that's happened to us, we're beyond such formalities."

"What has happened to us, mademoiselle? When we last saw each other, we were children."

"I was a beast. I behaved like a little beast and you had every right to hate me."

"I never hated you. Even your cruelties meant you noticed me. How could I have hated you?"

"Please say my name. I've waited so long to hear you say—"

"Fantine."

They walked beneath the gaze of stone-eyed statues, around the pavilion where children rented boats, their cries and bright sails amplified across the little lake. They sat on benches set up before the harp player who delighted small children and old folks, while nearby laughter resounded from those amused by a puppeteer's antics and noisy children played, and newspapers, escaped from readers' hands, blew about in the May breeze. They walked down leafy avenues of trees in that last moment of hesitation before full bloom. The moment suited Fantine and Gabriel, who told her that he had not been able to go to the Café Rigolo to get her letters.

"When I didn't hear from you, I quit writing. I thought perhaps my letters were putting you in danger, in more danger. I thought perhaps you and Mama had been arrested, but Monsieur Beaujard assured me he would tell me if that happened. How is Mama, Starling? Do you see her often?"

"Not as often as I'd like. She sends you her love and she's well and happy, truly, but I can't tell you more than that now. I can't even tell you why I quit writing. It's still too dangerous, not for me, but for others."

"For Mama and who else?"

"Others. For a long time I wasn't even in Paris, and then when I came back, it was all I could do to live, to work, to evade Clerons. And even now, mademoiselle—"

"Don't. Please—"

"Mademoiselle, for me to be here with you is—it's unwise."

"But you came."

"Yes."

The silence between them was the more poignant for the noise everywhere else. The respectful distance remained as ever, save that he was not as humble and she was not as lordly. No doubt they looked very odd together, she the opulent lady and he a plain-looking man, a laborer uncomfortable in Sunday clothes. She wished she had not worn the apricot silk, but something simpler, less likely to point up their differences. She gazed out over the park, over the plain of the last ten years of her life, exile and loneliness tempered only by work and by the dream that the Starling loved her, that their love could be simple and sterling despite the time and distance between them. The belief in this love had buoyed her in those long, grim London years, but perhaps it was just that, a mere dream, easily dissolved on waking, of no more substance than lies sweetened and condensed. If that were so, Fantine felt she could not live another moment without knowing the truth. "When you quit writing I thought perhaps you'd got married or fallen in love."

"No. It was not that."

"But you have a woman," Fantine shrugged, "all men have women."

He walked a while beside her, and when he did not reply, Fantine changed the whole tenor of her conversation, nervously, wretchedly chatted about the weather, music playing in the garden, the old people, the golden carp swimming in the fountain where finally they stopped.

"I have had women," he said at last. He looked to the center of the fountain, where stone horses plunged out of the water, hooves high, wild, and fearful. "But I have only ever loved one woman. I have only ever loved the one woman I can never have."

"Why not, if you love her?"

Le Sansonnet reached out and took her hand, turned it over slowly in his own, then deliberately, he undid the buttons along her inner arm to her wrist. Fantine's mouth went dry as she watched him, and everything else dimmed save for the sound of splashing in the fountain and her own quickening breath as his strong fingers twisted the tiny mother-of-pearl buttons. His palms were hard and calloused, seamed and dry, the nails trimmed, but labor was ground in all around them, and on the backs of his tanned hands, veins and sinews stood out. But for all that, his touch was so light, so assured, so without haste that Fantine's eyes closed and she bit her lip, certain that whatever else happened between men and women, it could not be as intimate as this, as moving, as stirring. He took the glove off, threaded his big fingers through hers, and drew her hand up to his lips, kissed it, his mouth lingering against her flesh.

"Look at my hands, Fantine," he said finally, without releasing her. "Look at yours. It's no more possible now than when we were children. It's no different."

"I have worked, Gabriel. I have worked as you work." She clutched his hands, both of them in hers, stepping as close as the steel hoop permitted. "My hands are strong, Starling, feel them! They're soft but they're strong. These are not the hands of a Second Empire flea hopping from dog to dog. My hands have done work. These are not the hands of a woman afraid of work. I am my father's daughter, my mother's daughter, not my brother's sister."

"I came this day because I could not bear to let it pass, but I know, you know as well as I, Fantine—oh, Fantine, I read once a letter your father wrote and he told your mother truly that love is its own country, but not its own world. The world invades that country, Fantine. It invaded our country long ago and we cannot ignore it. Everything is against us and there's too much at stake." He pulled her up against him and she closed her eyes to be kissed, but only words fell from his lips. "I can't see you again. You mustn't go to the Café Rigolo again. It's too dangerous. I can't tell you— there's too much I can't tell you."

"You can tell me that you love me." She broke away from him and stepped back defiantly. "Because if you do love me, then it doesn't matter. Not any of it—what you can say and what you cannot say, where and if there's a place for us, what your hands are like and what mine are like. If you love me, we have time, and all that will come with time. If you don't love me, then all we have is memory." She regarded him without coquetry or whimsy. "It can be enough, memory, and I don't begrudge it, but I have to know."

The Starling looked into the fountain, where ignorant carp swam peacefully in thick, green water and up to the energetic horses plunging out of the fountain's center, crazy to escape— what? Time? Memory? Responsibility? He regarded the beautiful woman before him, more beautiful than he'd even imagined she'd be, than he'd remembered, than he'd hoped. This was the reunion he'd dreamed of, and yet he carried the resonsibility for others, for Marius, Cosette, Pajol. He thought of the Lark, of the look on her face when he'd given her the note that told her Marius was alive. Love like that could fortify and sustain and strengthen you all your life, no matter how the world invaded. To have a chance at such love was not given to everyone. Perhaps everything was against them, but he had lost Fantine once and loved her anyway. He could not give her up now, not when she'd returned, not merely returned to France but returned his love. That had to be a miracle, a gift, a chance he knew he must take. Gabriel smiled at her, the old crooked smile, and he told her he had loved her forever, always, from the time he was a boy, and in the years that had parted them, no day had passed without her name on his lips, without her face before him, without his heart breaking because she could not be in his arms, as she was now. This moment.

Chapter 26

*I*mpossible! Disgusting! Revolting!" Jean-Luc jumped up and paced the drawing room, his lassitude exploded with anger.

"You are my brother, not my father."

"And you are no longer the cook's assistant!"

"You cannot tell me to turn my back on love, to live as you live. This house stinks of unhappiness. Sometimes I think I will gag on the rampant unhappiness here! Your life is loveless and ugly—"

"Have you forgotten Mama plucked that guttersnipe Starling from the jaws of prison? He was in prison before he'd sprouted hair under his arms. He's been in prison since. He'd be in prison now if Clerons could find him! He comes from ragpickers!"

"Nothing you say changes my mind. I love him, I have always loved him, and I'm going to marry him. I'm not asking for your permission, I'm telling you because I won't sneak around and skulk off like a kitchenmaid with the valet."

"You should certainly know what the kitchenmaid does," he observed with his usual sardonic grin.

"You can't offend me, Jean-Luc. You're not invited to the wedding. One day you'll wake up and I'll be gone."

"You'll marry who I tell you to marry. You'll love who I tell you to love."

The noisy quarrel, escalating, drew the attention of Eponine, who flounced into the drawing room, leaving the doors wide open as she sat down, smoothed her skirts upon the sofa. "Please do go on. I adore quarrels about love."

"Get out, Eponine. This is a family matter."

"Really? Am I not your family? Your daughter will be sad to hear this."

Jean-Luc rubbed his forehead in a gesture which, though he could not have known it, was exactly like Cosette's. "Why must I live with all these difficult women?"

"Is Nicolette difficult?" inquired Eponine earnestly. "What a pity for you. And I thought you went there for solace. And that little gutter-truffle from the—"

Jean-Luc reeled on her, bearing down like a force of nature, and Eponine gave him an arch, closed-lipped smile.

"I forbid it," he said returning to his sister.

"It's not your place to forbid it. I'm not a green girl waiting for Mama and Papa to arrange a suitable match for me. My life might have been like that, but it wasn't. I have earned my living, Jean-Luc, I have worked. You disparage me for it, but you drove me to it. You left me in England with nothing. I bless God I had Madame Carême and a skill she could teach me."

Ignoring her point, he clenched his teeth and stated with ambassadorial finality, "It is out of the question for my sister to marry a common thief, a beggar, the bastard son of a whore and a convict."

Zelma regarded them all coolly from the doorway. "Which whore and which convict are under discussion?"

"My quarrel is with my brother, madame. It goes back to our childhood and has nothing to do with you." Fantine rose and walked to the door, past all three of them. "I am like Sainte-Marguerite, do you remember her? In the belly of the dragon? Mama once wrote me that to come through the belly of the dragon you must be transformed. I am transformed, Jean-Luc. I have emerged from the dragon and my life is my own."

Nearly a week passed and then one night, very late, Jean-Luc knocked on the door of his sister's room. She lit a candle and opened the door. Without a word he came in, moved to the chair before the unlit fire, resting his elbows on his knees.

Drawing on a wrapper, Fantine turned up the gas, surprised to see in the light how haggard and old he looked, not elderly, not with the creases of age, only the erosion of his youth. A great fatigue emanated from him and a peculiar odor of patchouli, tobacco, and hashish floated off his clothes.

"So you think this house stinks of unhappiness, Fantine? The poor must also stink of unhappiness."

"They stink of want. Of desperation and cold and sickness. This house stinks of—"

"Spare me," he snapped, but he leaned back and crossed his well-shod feet. "Still, sometimes I pity the girl Louise."

"She has no childhood. Not like you and I had."

"Don't get soggy about the rue des Filles-du-Calvaire. Papa off to prison all the time, to provoke the king into granting freedom of the press. Freedom of the press—what a stupid notion. License for bores." He laughed ruefully. "It's really quite comic, yes?"

"Papa would not think so."

"So damned serious, wasn't he? You are very like him, you know. You daunt me, just as he did. So, Fantine, I will make you a bargain. You want to marry this common thief, this guttersnipe, this coarse laborer, I will not stand in your way. I'm not altogether immune to love, Fantine. You can even see him here if you like, but not upstairs. He'll have to come downstairs like a servant, to that little room off the kitchen, like the basement room we used to have at the rue des Filles-du-Calvaire. You remember?"

"Very well."

Jean-Luc sighed. "I had this house built, new and up-to-date, everything, and when I saw that room, I felt as if someone had attached my childhood to it without my permission."

"All kitchens must have a storeroom."

"Ah, yes, well, you would know, wouldn't you." He rose, staggered slightly, and added that was a joke. "Not laughing? Well, you may see your childhood sweetheart in my home if you wish. You may marry him. You may have a hundred brats by him. I ask only two things. One, that you will sign this paper." He drew it out and left it on the mantel. "It's nothing, but it frees me from any legal obligation—ever—to you or your children. In effect it dissolves all my responsibilities to you."

"I'll sign it, with pleasure."

"Read it first. My second condition is that you and the Starling leave Paris. I don't care where you go."

"Do you want me to sign something to that effect also?"

"No." He reached out, steadied himself slightly on her shoulder. "I just want you to know that I am not so jaded that I no longer believe in love. I do believe in it, Fantine. I have even tasted it. On occasion."

And so, much as Cosette had done many years before, Fantine readied the basement room for an important visitor. But not for her father. She sent a message to Gabriel via the Changer assuring him it would be safe, they would be alone, the servants off, Eponine and Zelma gone to Trouville, Jean-Luc at the Longchamps racecourse. "Only Louise and her governess will be here," Fantine wrote, "and they stay imprisoned in the schoolroom. You and I will have this time like ordinary lovers. Please come. It means so much to me."

At her bidding, servants swept, mopped, dusted, put a rug before the small grate and curtains on the windows. Even the iron grilles outside the windows were to be brushed and cleaned and the sills swept free of dust and leaves and debris. There was a small, discarded sofa that she covered with a silken shawl. Jars and bottles on the shelves were more neatly arranged, and on the morning of the great day, Fantine picked two great vases of pale peonies, pink and white, two bouquets, each one enlivened by a few scarlet flowers. Very dashing. Besides, they suited the dress she was wearing: a billowing white silk with tiny narrow stripes of blushing pink that gave an iridescent quality; bishops' sleeves dripped with lace and lace gathered over the bosom, tied there with a narrow black ribbon.

In getting ready she struggled into the bustier, slipped the steel cage over her head, and put the dress on over white stockings and satin shoes brocaded with gold and pink. For effect she also tied a narrow black ribbon at her throat. From her old home she could find only the silver candlesticks that had once graced the library, and she requisitioned these, put them on the narrow mantel between the vases of peonies. Fantine regarded herself in the servants' kitchen mirror; she made certain her curls were properly piled and the small curls caught around her face. Perfect. Yes, perfect. She was, she realized with a pang of pleasure, pretty. Perhaps beautiful.

"Oh, Fantine," said the Starling when he came to the back door like a servant, "you take my breath away."

"Good." She drew him in, locked the door, and kissed him.

"I came because you wanted me to, but Fantine, this isn't wise."

"It's very foolish, but we deserve to be foolish! We have had to be wise for so many years." She kissed his chin, his lips, his cheeks. "Come with me." She locked the door and led him to the small room, which—for all its poverty of purpose, the shelving, the grilles on the windows—was festive as springtime. Peony petals seemed to fall audibly, one at a time, or perhaps the rustling was that of the white silk dress, the lace rippling as it cascaded from her wrists. The Starling could not take his eyes from her.

"Do you want to sit down?"

"No, I'm too nervous. I can't believe Jean-Luc agreed to this. He has hated me since we were boys. I have hated him," Gabriel added, going to the window, noting that it did not open. The iron bars behind the curtains made him wince. "It isn't like him, Fantine."

"I had to make two promises to him. I had to promise we would leave Paris."

"And did you?"

"Yes. Why do you look so pained?"

"I don't think—I can't leave. There are people here who need me."

"Like Mama?"

"Please, Fantine, keep your voice down." He moved to the door and shut it firmly.

"We'll take her with us. Wherever we go. We'll change our names."

"Oh, Lord, Fantine, all this feels wrong to me."

"What? Us? Our being alone here?"

"If we are alone." But he wrapped his arms around her, anyway, pulled her close, pressing her up against him, kissed her long and deep. "I love you—more than life itself, I love you—but I can't marry you."

"Why not? You don't mean—"

"I love you and nothing changes that, nothing ever has, but think of it, Fantine. To marry, you must present documents and baptism certificates, all that. Do you think there's a priest or public official in Paris who wouldn't turn me in?"

"I don't need a wedding, Gabriel. I need you. I want to live with you. I want to love you. As I have always loved you. I want to have our lives together, and that's all I want. I have no fear of a *union libre*. Give me a time and place where you and I will vow to love each other, that's all I care about. Put a ring on my finger and a kiss on my lips—"

He did not have the ring, but he had the kiss, and he held her in his arms, kissed her, rubbed his clean-shaven cheek to hers, his hands through her hair, his lips at her throat, and they had tumbled to the sofa, his hand at her breast, Fantine murmuring *Yes, yes,* when the sound of carriage wheels crunched over gravel and horses' hooves clattered in the stone courtyard at the back of the house. They froze, regarded each other as if they had been stabbed and the surprise alone might kill them. Shouts, running feet, boots rattled all around them, passed the grilled windows, dashing for the kitchen steps.

"Oh, Starling! I've been tricked. I've led you to this trap!"

"Not you." He got off her quietly, moved toward the storeroom door, when they heard the key turning in the kitchen door and the lock snap open. "Fantine, this is goodbye."

"No it isn't." She got hurriedly to her feet, stepped to the mantel, grabbed her white silk skirt in each fist, and lifted the steel cage hoop. She nodded to him and he went under it.

When Clerons burst through the door, he seemed momentarily shocked: there before him, framed on either side by vases of pink peonies and silver candlesticks, was a lovely young woman, with dark eyes, light hair falling down, curling round her face, her high coloring set off by the pale dress, in her hand a closed fan. Soldiers' boots clomped overhead as they searched the house. "Mademoiselle Pontmercy, or should I say Madame Lascaux?"

"Say what you like, Monsieur Clerons, if it will make you any more appealing than you were when we last met," Fantine retorted. "You have not improved with age."

"Your brother said you were very like your mother, and so you are." He glanced around the tiny room. "Where is your intended?"

"He heard you coming. He got away."

Clerons rubbed the half-circle scar on his cheek. "I'm going to catch him this time, mademoiselle. I'm going to see he's transported to New Caledonia. They say people all die of blackwater fever out there. No civilized man can live there." Clerons walked from one window to the other. The gray of his hair, his beard and waxed mustache, his fly-away eyebrows contrasted with the unremitting black he wore. "That's what happens to traitors, mademoiselle."

"If there are traitors in this house, then you, you and Jean-Luc, are those men. You both betrayed my father."

"And you betrayed your own lover," he offered caustically.

"Yes," she faltered, "not knowingly. Stupidly, I admit."

Clerons reached out, his index finger coming perilously close to her left breast as he picked up one of the long, narrow streams of black ribbon. "I see from the ribbon on your dress that your heart pounds." He dropped that one, reached up to her throat, where that ribbon too pulsed rhythmically. "It's a sad thing to see the daughter of a baron bedding down with the son of a whore and a convict." He dropped the ribbon and sat irresolutely on the sofa before her.

"Please leave me alone, Monsieur Clerons. Search where you like, but—"

"I'll wait here. The soldiers are effective." He lit a cigarette and asked her to move so he could throw the match in the grate. Fantine took two distinct steps to the left. "Your mother never told you of her father? Jean Valjean. A convict, one of that ragged band that used to be, thirty, fifty years ago, chained in hulks, branded with numbers: 24601, that was your grandfather's number. Your mother's mother was a prostitute. Named Fantine. Your mother named you after a prostitute, so perhaps you and the Starling are well suited to one another after all." He smoked thoughtfully while Fantine fanned herself. "The soldiers are prepared to tear this house apart. I will find the Starling. And when I do, the rest will all crawl out of their holes and they will be arrested and shipped off to die in New Caledonia, and there will be no more talk, rumors of La Lumière being invincible, invisible. There will be no more ridiculing the Emperor. Your heart pounds, Mademoiselle Pontmercy. Have I frightened you?"

"No more than you frightened my father."

"Thirty years is a long time," Clerons mused, snapping the end of his cigarette into the grate. "Thirty years ago at that barricade at the Corinth, your father and Verdier, they escaped me. It was a smirch on my honor to have lost them. Now, of course, Verdier's dead. So is your father," he added quickly.

"Now you hunt for my mother like a hunting dog sent out by his master, Monsieur Clerons."

"Don't be so certain of your own immunity. When I arrest the Starling, I could arrest you too."

"You won't arrest him. Not now. I told you, he escaped. Your soldiers may look where they like," she said as Louise's frightful tantrums echoed from the upper stories, "but you cannot compel me to speak to you further."

And she did not. She stood there, the fan moving faster and faster, while he waited, smoking one cigarette after another. In the tiny, airless room, the very peonies seemed to brown with the smoke. One by one his soldiers reported back to him, and while he waited, he talked, cast aspersions on Fantine's grandparents, her parents, on her lover, on everything that these people had believed in, suffered for, died for, but she stood still, silent, fanning, her emotions betrayed only by the quick and rhythmic pulsing of the two narrow black ribbons, one at her throat, one beneath her breasts.

When the soldiers said they could not find him, Clerons sent them back out, till at last one said he'd found an open window, the dining room, and no doubt this is where the Starling had slipped out.

"No, we would have seen him. We have guards outside."

"He could have scaled the garden wall."

"Impossible. That wall is eight feet high." But Clerons went to see the window himself, and when he returned to the storeroom where she remained, unmoving, he growled, "I will get him, mademoiselle. I will. I'll get Pajol too. He thinks by changing his address he and that Fleury woman are safe from me in Paris, but they are not. Your mother—I would never have believed a woman with a pen in her hand could be so dangerous. I'll get them all. They'll be transported. They'll be shot at sea, and the fish will eat their bones. You will regret this, mademoiselle."

"I already regret it."

He closed the door on her and left.

But Fantine remained exactly where she was, the ribbons still pulsing, as outside the soldiers mounted their horses and the carriage clattered out, and the long fingers of afternoon light stirred smoke, still caught in the basement room. The peonies wept their pink petals. The ribbons at her throat and breast pounded more violently after the soldiers left. Her fan dropped and her hand tensed upon the mantel, as Fantine held herself upright with some difficulty, flushed, her breath coming in quick, short bursts, eyes closed, as the vast white crinoline undulated, and at the wordless suggestion of her lover, she moved her feet apart, no longer silent, making now small involuntary noises, moist cries of freedom and ecstasy and fulfillment.

Chapter 27

S he packed swiftly; there wasn't much to take, and though the house was quiet, she waited till midnight to steal downstairs and take the silver candlesticks from the mantel. She packed them too. Then, clad in traveling clothes and wrapped in a shawl, Fantine stationed herself near the door, pulling her feet up in an opulent, uncomfortable chair, awaiting the return of her brother, knowing he might not come home at all.

She slept only fitfully, incensed with herself that she had been tricked into betraying the Starling. She was more angry with herself than with Jean-Luc, perhaps most bitter that Jean-Luc had invoked the name of love. And she had believed him. Her lack of caution or her ignorance (one was as bad as the other) had very nearly cost the Starling his freedom, his life—and by extension, her life. She understood now why her mother had followed her father to the barricade. She hoped one day she would have the opportunity to tell her so.

Dawn in summertime is unequivocal, and the light was unkind to Jean-Luc's face when finally the key turned in the lock and he arrived home. Fantine stood, pulled the shawl around her. "He failed, you know," she said, squaring her shoulders and facing this great brooding wreck of a man, his youth squandered, his skin gray, and the smell coming off him something Fantine could not name, nor did she wish to. She said it again, that Clerons had failed and Gabriel escaped, but Jean-Luc scarcely seemed to see her. "How could you do something so low, so vile?" she demanded.

"I heard it before, I mean, you can't help but hear these rumors, rumors and people in Paris, really, who think my father's alive. Ridiculous." He blurred and slurred and burbled on drunkenly, alternately heaping abuse on the rumor, or amused by it. "Can you 'magine, 'Ponine?"

"I'm not Eponine! Listen to me!"

"People always do that, you know, think they see saints on the street, bloody apparitions carrying their old heads under their arms. We had a servant at the rue des Filles-du-Calvaire, she swore Louis XVI talked to her at night, his head on his lap." He snorted, "Well, that's what comes of my sniffing out gutter-truffles, listen to her prattle. I told her, the pox has gone to your head, sweetie, no one lives through that, after all this time? My father—"

"Your father would die all over again to see you like this, Jean-Luc, to know you betrayed me."

Jean-Luc threw his top hat on the floor, removed his gloves, his opera cloak, and pulled off his wilted boutonnière, stared down at Fantine, and focused with difficulty. "I did it as a favor to you. You'd have married him and had brats. How can you even think about sleeping with someone like that?" He peered at her more closely, and his face lit with a queer smile. "You've already slept with him, haven't you? How did you manage that?"

Fantine colored. "I despise you, Jean-Luc. I'm leaving here and—"

"I don't care what you do, what any of you do." He trudged slowly up the stairs, clinging to the cold marble banister.

When he had vanished down the long hall, Fantine went up, pulled on her walking boots, the only shoes she'd taken, and tip-toed up to the top floor, where, even this early, the servants had roused little Louise and were giving her breakfast, while the grim governess awaited her in the schoolroom. The sound of the little girl's spoon in her cup, scraping out chocolate, had a sad chink to it, like a prisoner's solitary meal. Fantine knelt by the child's chair. "Louise, I am leaving now, and you might hear your mama and papa say terrible things about me."

"Oh, they say terrible things about everyone, Aunt Fantine. You mustn't worry about it."

"Well, I wanted you to know, before I left, that I want to be your friend, and if ever, one day, you should need a friend, you must think of me."

"I will think of you even if I don't. I'm sorry you're leaving. Is it because of those soldiers yesterday?"

"I'm afraid it is."

"They even looked in the water closet! They were disgusting."

Fantine confessed herself equally shocked, kissed the girl's forehead, both cheeks, and made her farewells.

Carrying her valise, her portmanteau, her veil fashionably tied, Fantine walked at a quick clip toward the Gare Saint-Lazare. In her crinoline she felt like some vast Arab tent on the boulevard, but the smile had not left her lips since the day before, when she had had every reason to bless her hoops. She walked with a kind of buoyancy, perhaps only the morning's lovely collusion with the knowledge that she was loved. He was the Starling and he had flown, where she did not know. When or how they would meet again she did not know. If they could ever marry she did not know. And between the Gare Saint-Lazare—where feet clattered and steam and smoke, cinder and ash blew about, heavy machinery squealed and thunked beneath the high, glassed vaults—and the unknown moment when she would again be in Gabriel's arms, no map presented itself. No plan. No possibility. Still, in leaving Paris, there was, at this moment, only one place for her to go.

"One ticket, one way for Argenteuil," she said to the man behind the grill.

She found a bench to wait for the early train and put the ticket in her pocket alongside the letter received just yesterday, before the Starling's visit, from Mademoiselle Lauriot, another invitation. Fantine did not respect Nicolette Lauriot, and moreover did not trust her, but without that letter in her pocket, what would she have done on leaving her brother's house? Blown about Paris like a cinder? After Argenteuil, something will come to me, she promised herself—but nothing presented itself. She pulled Mademoiselle Lauriot's note out and reread it. The Benedictine Folly? Preposterous name. Argenteuil struck Fantine as an unlikely place for someone of the dash and luster of La Lauriot in any event. Trouville, perhaps. Shopgirls took their Sundays at Argenteuil.

The early train pulled in, and Fantine joined the throng pressing out to the platform, these same shopgirls and their clerk sweethearts, women who carried packs of things to sell to Sunday's pleasure seekers, natty commercial travelers, and red-armed matrons with squalling brats in tow. The men ogled her, the matrons envied her, the shopgirls and their lovers felt superior, and the vendors ignored her, but unaccountably Fantine smiled at them all. She might have embraced them, because despite the nebulous future, the uncertain present, she felt as though on this day—which is to say, the day after yesterday—the train spewed blossoms instead of cinders. It shrieked and pulled out of the station, and with every westward revolution of the wheels, Fantine felt certain her heightened sense of possibilities would gather momentum.

However, twenty minutes later the train shrieked over the bridge at Argenteuil. This was not enough time for possibilities to gather momentum, and Fantine found herself suddenly in a small, squalid country railway station. She had not replied to Nicolette's note, so perhaps no one expected her. As she stepped outside into the square, she realized she had no idea why she was here or what she would do. She looked around the town of Argenteuil: behind her a few tall smokestacks with their black smokescarfs wafting, and in the distance a sloping hillside with rippling red poppies cascading downhill in the sunlight. A woman with a parasol followed a path, a boy behind her.

A man with toxic breath and a corrugated face startled Fantine, pointing drunkenly to his threadbare carriage and nag. Could he drive her to the Benedictine Folly for two francs?

"That's rather a lot, isn't it?"

"Yes, madame, but all those who come to Benedictine Folly have money, and if you don't like the fare, you must blame your friends."

"They're not my friends," she said, whereupon he promptly lost interest in her. Fantine had very little money and no prospects in sight, except for Madame Carême's recipe book (which was packed and not in sight) and the conviction that the Starling loved her (also invisible). She asked for directions and walked.

The path took her along the river, where pleasure boats, spare masts rocking, clustered against the shores, though a few white sails brisked about on the river and there was a small canopied boat in which a painter rocked and dabbed. In the distance, smokestacks from the surrounding factories looked like rooted masts, tall poplars lined the path, and the bridges looped evenly over the thick, green water. Her walking boots crunched on the gravel as the sun rose high. She undid the buttons of her coat and the first few buttons of her dress, took off the impossible gloves, lifted the veil of the hat, wishing she'd paid the two francs, and debating the wisdom of having taken the heavy silver candlesticks. But at length, following the driver's instructions, she came to a house, a great pink stucco monstrosity of a house, with a high-walled garden. Lattices crawled up the side of the house, and the green shutters were all closed despite the brilliant June day. She paused, perspiring, not merely from the heat and her heavy clothes. This was not a good idea. Jean-Luc could arrive. Nicolette was not trustworthy, and there were no other prospects in sight.

The gate squealed under her touch, and Fantine walked slowly toward the house, feeling her resolve grow heavy, leaden bravado gilded up to imitate bravery. She peered through the window next to the door, looked down a carpetless, clean hall with tall windows at long, regular intervals. After the upholstered world of Jean-Luc's mansion, the gilt and filigree of the rest of Paris, this place seemed oddly unfinished, as though the lives here were all on easels rather than in frames. What choice had she? She knocked and in her mind readied a speech for the servant.

"You've come at last!" cried Nicolette Lauriot, to Fantine's extreme surprise. "Oh, I'm so happy to see you!" She brought Fantine inside, took her valises, dropped them, and drew her down the hall.

Fantine halted, pulled herself up like a cadet. "You should know, madame, I have left my brother's house forever. I shall never speak to him again, and if my being here is dependent on his good-will—"

"Oh, don't be silly!" Nicolette gave one of her ravishing smiles; she was wearing a light muslin gown, no makeup, and her hair was merely tied back, not arranged. "You're here! That's all that's important!"

Fantine could not escape Nicolette's embrace, redolent of orange and bergamot, and when finally she was released, she asked, "Why are you so happy to see me?"

Impatiently Nicolette grabbed her hand, led her down the long, uncluttered hall out toward the garden, where noon sunlight lay like a bright pond, surrounded everywhere by banks of shade, aggressively encroaching. Nicolette released her, gave her a little shove toward the inky blue-green shadows beyond the small, round table, told her to go. The shade here was so deep even the geraniums seemed extinguished, and Fantine's eyes, adjusting from the brightness, concocted Gabriel's image, coatless, hatless, his dark hair, his crooked smile, his open arms that came to her, enveloped her, his mouth on hers as soon as she pushed his name past her unbelieving lips. He pulled her with him back into the shadows, where Fantine had the sense of swimming, looking up to see the curve of the water, the curve of the earth from underneath, as a veteran of the vasty deep might see it, might look down, deeper into underwater shadows where bones sink and ghosts float, not ghosts, dreams, the voice of someone lost to you. "Mama? Mama!" She wept to feel her mother's embrace, to see her face and hear her voice, hold her hand and be led further into the thick and turgid shadows toward the dream, the ghost, toward a figure stooped and gray, but not ghostly, with flesh, solidity, and voice to answer a child's whispered cry, "Papa?" And as in a dream, the dead speak, they answer, they live.

Part IV

The Costly Omelette

There are vast numbers of unknown beings
teeming with the strangest types of humanity, from the stevedore
of the Rapée to the horsekiller of Montfaucon . . .
Cannot the light penetrate these masses?
Let us return to that cry: Light! and let us persist in it!
Light! light! Who knows but that these opacities will become
transparent? Are not revolutions transfigurations . . .
Look through the medium of the people and
you shall discern the truth.

—Victor Hugo
Les Misérables

Chapter 28

*T*he Pincher was amongst the first to notice the change in *la vie Parisienne,* in the way it ended. He was a river ravager now, up before dawn daily, in his skiff, plying the Seine for corpses. Military life had eroded his skills as a thief, but the Pincher was certainly inured to death, and this was not a profession for the squeamish or the weak. Moreover, he could use his old instincts without taxing his old talents because any corpse hauled out of the river was instantly inspected, and naturally all suicides were impoverished, which is to say they had no money or jewelry by the time they arrived at the morgue. But there are only so many suicides, and a few weeks' bad luck could ruin a man. River ravaging was intensely competitive because (even without the above-mentioned gratuities) the morgue paid handsomely—twenty-five francs for an adult, five for an infant or fetus—a sum that could, so to speak, float a man. Moreover, this was the only job in Paris where, with a strong back, strong legs, and a strong stomach, one could be finished with work by noon.

They were a fiercely independent lot, the river ravagers, and they had their own traditions, which included the obligation on those who had been successful the night before to buy a round of drinks when they gathered, about noon, at a low riverside café, really no more than a door, a rough plank, and a few small tables set near a stove. The stove was crucial. Sometimes river ravagers never warmed up, and perhaps that's why they drank a gut-busting concoction of bad brandy and cayenne pepper. It was here that the Pincher, being of a philosophical turn of mind, first began to expound his theories, to ask his peers if they had noticed that there were more of them buying drinks more often. This elicited a general happy exchange regarding the upturn of business. Then the Pincher inquired if they had noticed that the bodies were getting heavier, and the others solemnly assented. The river ravagers' stock-in-trade was waifish girls (seduced, abandoned, the old, unlovely story), but even those visibly pregnant were usually so scrawny, their clothes so thin and scrappy, they could be hauled on the skiff with no more effort than it took to land a fish. But lately, the Pincher pointed out, after a stiff swill of his drink, the girls weren't so waifish. Many of them weighed more and they wore more clothing, some of it good-quality, rich, warm clothing that soaked up and held the water and made it a terrible struggle just to pull them in. Men too. Like everyone present, the Pincher had pulled in his share of leather-aproned, lovesick youths, flinging themselves (stupidly, thought the Pincher) into the Seine because they'd got thrown out of bed or thrown out of work. And, too, he'd hauled in his share of old men of forty-eight or fifty, men whose sheer brute strength was failing and without that strength their lives had become intolerable and their bodies a burden, so off they went from a bridge. And, if not admirable, such suicides were understandable. But of late, the Pincher ruminated, had the assembled company noticed many more men in good clothes, warm coats, fine linen shirts, the devil to pull from the river, the devil to explain at the morgue, why all these well-fed men unanimously removed their fine shoes, coats, shirts, and often even their trousers before dropping into the Seine. (Toward female corpses, the river ravagers observed an informal code: turn in too many naked women and you got a bad reputation at the morgue.) The Pincher was illiterate but astute, and he surmised that the rise in the numbers of suicides of worth and bulk and substance reflected, was connected, somehow, with the stock market, the fluctuations and easy fortunes, the paper castles men built of credit, built on war and real estate, on railways and buoyant profiteering. Wrecks from the sea of speculation were dredged from the river Seine and gave the Pincher fodder to muse with his brandy and cayenne pepper.

The Pincher would even wax philosophical about the bridges themselves; he had theories as to who jumped from which, so he was surprised early one September morning, so early the mists yet lay across the bridges like smoke, the fog only just granulating, to be pulling up under the Pont de Solférino and to see a woman standing there. This conflicted with his theory. The Pont de Solférino was a man's bridge.

She stood above the *N* surrounded with laurel leaves, a well-dressed, veiled woman, he could see that even in the half shadow. "Take off your hoop, madame," he called out, "or you'll float like a pip downstream and I won't be able to get you."

There was a long silence, the veiled woman peering over the bridge into the shadows, the water lapping around the Pincher's boat. "To save me?"

"I'm not a saver, madame, I'm a ravager, and by the time you get to me, there's no saving, no mercy, but no blame either. But me, I say *merci* to you, madame, to you and all your kind. A social service you're providing. The man who wizens his guts with poison, who sucks off the muzzle of the gun, who turns over his slop pail, puts a rope round his head, kicks the pail, and dances for a bit, what do they accomplish for their fellow men? A mess, that's all. They make a mess, and no one is the better for it and everyone the poorer, from the family to the landlord—after all, no one will rent suicides' rooms. But the man or woman who jumps into the Seine, why, that's the kindest exit you can make. The concierge is happy, the family happy, the jailer cheated, and a service done the men who ply this river and who are paid to haul the unfortunate out. So the mission of mercy is yours, madame, and a mercy it is. If you're primed to jump now, then I say, step out of that hoop and make it like a winter's day, short and dirty. Do it now and let me bless your name."

"You don't need my name."

" 'Deed I don't, but I need your twenty-five francs. You can see I've had a poor night of it." And in the grainy, autumnal dawn he held up a slack little bundle by its pitiful feet, naked and unprotesting.

"Put that away!" came the cry from the bridge. "Oh, put it away!"

"As you wish. You can tell from his color, least I can, that this little fellow never drew breath. There's some along the river who won't even bother with a baby. Not enough money in it when times are as fat as these. What's five francs for a fetus when there's so many rich men offing themselves? Jumping in sometimes two and three a night. Yes, there's them who would say, Forget the infant, forget the fetus, why scoop with a spoon when you can scoop with a shovel? But not I. A man of honor, I am, and I say this little brute deserves burial."

"Perhaps he deserved a life."

"Perhaps he did, madame, but the choice was taken from him and he died blameless."

On either side of the river the city began to emerge from the rough coat of dawn, and the Pincher could see that the woman on the bridge was tall, dressed in smart clothes, opulent clothes, a black-and-green-striped dress, her gloved hands resting on the bridge, watching him as he worked. She asked why his business prospered now.

"It's September, isn't it? September's a peak month. It takes courage to jump in June, but they all jump in September. Cowards, if you don't mind my saying so."

"Death takes the same courage always."

"You're wrong there, madame. Any gibbering fool—deaf, dumb, blind, lame, their ballocks in a bag between their knees—any fool can live through the summer and jump in September. It takes courage to jump in June. The nights are shorter for one thing, and besides, the summer is there before you, just a lovely prospect. But September, ah, that's the cruel one, September, you can feel the old death, the old yearly death creeping up your marrow, the light failing, the cold moving in."

"You admire the summer suicide?"

"No, me, I admire the ones with real courage, the winter suicides. Sometimes, just pulling them out, my hands get froze off. Not a pretty picture, the river in winter."

A sluggish autumn dawn penetrated the thick rind of clouds across the sky, and behind the woman on the bridge, wheeled traffic picked up, cabs and carriages, carts and wagons full of goods. On foot, ragpickers trooped in from the *barrières*, carrying their baskets, pushing carts, some with dogs trotting along behind. From under a bridge a cat came out and blinked in the morning light, and the Pincher could see the woman well now, could see she was young and beautiful.

"You've missed your chance now, madame," he shouted. "It's light. Too late. It's never done in the day, *la mort Parisienne*."

"I guess I prefer *la vie Parisienne* after all."

"You mean the show, madame? Even along the river we know that show has closed."

"Has it? Well, perhaps I shall have to settle for the real thing."

"I'm out my twenty-five francs then. Pity."

"You have shown great pity." Leaving the bridge, she crossed to the quay and tossed him two twenty-franc pieces. "Such pity should be rewarded somewhere besides in heaven."

"*Merci,* madame, especially since we can't be sure of heaven."

"We can be sure of hell, Monsieur Ravager."

Nicolette turned, walked along the quai de Tuileries, crossing the vast place de la Concorde, the green-and-black-striped dress trailing unconcernedly behind her, making no effort whatever to lift it from the street. Sweeping in the dust, dung, debris, the bottom of the dress was brown and bedraggled as she passed the rue Montaigne and the Bal Mabille, deserted at dawn, looking the more sad and tawdry for all the vanished gaiety. Once arrived at the rue de Chaillot, she stood before her own front door and stripped off the black-and-green dress right there, left it in a satin puddle, and instructed the servants to burn it without bringing it into the house.

Chapter 29

Sitting by the window, rocking back and forth on the bare wooden seat in third class, Mea Culpa rode the train from Argenteuil to Paris that same morning, her shoulders hunched, clutching a shawl across her bosom despite the September sunshine. She smiled to think how she resembled old Toussaint, from whom she copied—if not learned—piety and humility, just as the nuns had taught her needlework, and now, all these years later, the lessons of her youth were essential for the masquerade of maturity. Life was not a trajectory from birth to death, but a series of arcs and spirals, an ongoing education in the unexpected. Born in the shadow of Waterloo, raised a slave at The Sergeant of Waterloo, Cosette had danced at the presidential palace and huddled, freezing, in a ragpicker's hovel, and if there were no constants in life, yet if you were very fortunate—as she counted herself to be—there were givens, gifts. Cosette had had such gifts, Marius's love, for one, which for all their years together seemed somehow to bloom anew this summer, to bloom afresh, to take and give new sustenance. Though his health was permanently affected by his imprisonment, his strength had gained over this wonderful summer at Argenteuil, where he and Cosette both basked in their reunion with their daughter. Marius would stay there with Fantine to care for him, but Cosette had to return to Paris. Rehearsals for the new operetta, *The Little General*, would start tomorrow, and Cosette had her own role to play, Mea Culpa.

At the other end of the carriage Cosette caught the eye of a young workingman, ostensibly snoozing, arms crossed over his broad chest. He winked. My son-in-law, Cosette thought contentedly. Though she had seen Jean-Luc's wedding in a church, Cosette could not think of him as married. For Fantine and the Starling there had been no wedding, but Cosette could not think of them as other than married. They were married in a free union without a formal ceremony, and Marius, in the beginning, had been much against the informal one.

"Can you imagine what your father would have said to such an arrangement?" Marius had asked her as they lay in their bed. "If we had simply declared ourselves married and gone to bed together?"

"We could only marry legally, my love, because you were not arrested, and if we had been denied the ceremony, I would still have gone to bed with you."

"But you knew nothing of what happens between men and women. When we married—"

"I knew what I wanted. I wanted you. I would have slept with you no matter what."

"But your father, Cosette!"

"There are things a girl doesn't tell her father. They love each other, Marius, you can see that, and they deserve to live together with our blessing."

"But they need to marry—"

"To marry legally would endanger all of us. We would have to be present, to trot out baptismal certificates and declare ourselves the Pontmercys. We can't do that. We would endanger Nicolette as well." She kissed the crease of his eyes, the sad scar she had first kissed thirty years before. "To love someone is to fly with the angels, and if you're lucky, as we have been, your hands and heart are connected, your body, your soul, they are all connected. Fantine and Gabriel, they deserve our blessing."

And so, as she had wished, Fantine got her ring, and, with Gabriel, said her vows. After that day in June she began calling herself Madame Picaut, going about the town of Argenteuil as a cook at the Benedictine Folly, her husband, Monsieur Picaut, a servant there, both for the time being. Picaut suited them, seemed to partake of both Pontmercy and Lascaux, and in any event those names were impossible now.

Because they were impossible, the Starling was on the train with Cosette, returning to Paris. He looked an ordinary working-man, Cosette thought, save perhaps for the happiness that radiated off him like steam. One would never guess him to be at the center of a network throughout Paris, a network of rebellion, no, that was too strong. Refusal. People like Grincourt who continued working in Paris under another name, people like Pajol and Germaine, people who refused to give up the old notion of *liberté, égalité, fraternité*. They might not live to see the Third Republic, but they would not succumb willingly to the Second Empire.

The ride to Paris was brief and undramatic, and once in the station and with a single nod to Cosette, the Starling vanished into the crowd and Mea Culpa followed a flock of nuns, trailing out of the station behind them like a small, brown comet.

Once arrived at Nicolette's in the rue de Chaillot, Mea Culpa knocked at the back entrance, and to her surprise, one of the servants, a strapping young woman of about twenty, grabbed her and drew her hurriedly in, chattering all the while, kicking the Pekinese aside as they flew upstairs. "This morning, she comes in at dawn, takes her dress off outside—really, Mea Culpa, in the street—tells us to burn it, goes into the conservatory, and won't come out. She won't eat or drink anything. She just cries. She needs your help." They stopped at the door to the jungle conservatory. "She relies on you. Everyone knows that."

"What's happened to her? Why—"

She made a gesture at once cruel and dismissive. "It's finished with Baron Pontmercy. Yes, this time it's truly over."

"But she just spent July and August with him in Trouville."

"Nonetheless, when she came back to Paris last week, you could see she was truly alone. A blind man could see how alone."

Underneath the high glass ceilings held up with fanciful constructions of ornamental iron, the atmosphere inside the conservatory was humid, torpid, and thick; a sickly-sweet stench wafted slowly, amid the chaos of quarreling monkeys and the irregular squawking of parrots. The indoor waterfall had been stilled, and Cosette found Nicolette before the rocky pool, clad in her chemise and petticoat, sitting on a cushion on the flagstone feeding an apple to a monkey.

"When love dies," Nicolette said ruefully, "it has an awful stink, doesn't it? It's intolerable, the smell of dead love, sorrow, and irony. The irony is really putrid." Her eyes were red and painfully swollen, and her face was pale. Cosette asked how long she'd been back in Paris, and she said a week.

"Rehearsals don't start until tomorrow. Why should you be alone in Paris for a week?"

"I am never alone. I am Nicolette Lauriot. I have tribes, whole tribes, of slavish admirers, fawning friends, unctuous enemies."

"And Jean-Luc, is he still in Trouville?"

Nicolette tossed the apple, and the monkey scampered after it. She wiped her hand across her lap. "No. Jean-Luc is in Paris. I discovered that last night." Her gray eyes filled with tears. "It's over, Cosette. Truly."

Sitting on a cushion beside her, Cosette took her hand. "But your letters to us from Trouville, we all thought—"

"How could I put my misery on paper? To let it stain or touch your happiness?"

"Because we are your family now." Cosette brushed the tumbled-down blond hair from Nicolette's tear-stained face. "You are my daughter even if you are not my child," she said, echoing what Jean Valjean had told her all those years before. She held Nicolette while she cried, the sound magnified in the moist air, ricocheting off the chattering monkeys and the cries of the brilliant parrots. "You loved Jean-Luc better than he loved himself. Longer than he loved himself."

"For years I've watched him slip away from me," she said, sobbing, "like a boat drifting out to sea, and always I thought I could pull him back to my own shore, that the line was long enough and strong enough, but he's gone. I left him in Trouville, but he left me long before that." She mopped her face with her petticoat, which was stained with her makeup. "Zelma and Eponine have got him. I should have married him to save him from them."

"No one could save him from them. He embraced them."

"But they've sucked his soul out, Cosette."

"I don't believe that. I don't believe anyone can have your soul unless you let it go. If that's what happened to my son, then he was as much to blame as they are. Perhaps more. You know that, you've known it for a long while. That's not what makes dead love stink." Cosette wrinkled her nose against the smell.

Walking to where the now-silent waterfall pooled, Nicolette splashed her face and flung some water at the stoic, sickly flamingos. "I have an old story to tell you. The world's oldest story. The oldest one of all."

"Oh, Nicolette!" Cosette's whole face lit when Nicolette nodded. "Are we to be grandparents? Oh, that's wonderful! Marius will be so pleased! So thrilled!"

"Jean-Luc wasn't. Jean-Luc was—" she looked around as though the word might be lying on the floor—"indifferent. At best, indifferent. He seemed to think it nothing more than a monstrous inconvenience to him."

Cosette pulled off Mea Culpa's wig and unfastened the hair brooch, unbuttoned her bodice. She rose and, taking Nicolette's arm, they walked amidst the drooping ferns, giant, lacy ferns, ferns mottled with spoors, and ferns with tentacles, passing thick-leafed, fleshy plants that dripped with their own perspiration and orchids with mauve hearts, and pungent, creamy gardenias. "When will this marvelous baby be born? This wonderful child?"

"Oh, I have a long wait. I think it's only about six weeks now. When I told Jean-Luc, he said, If you know this early, you should Do Something. He said for five francs the porter at the Bouffes-Parisiens will give me a name."

"For five francs the porter there will give you the clap."

"I miscarried once, years ago. Jean-Luc was devastated. When I think back, when I remember how passionately he felt, I can scarcely believe it was the same man in Trouville last week."

"Perhaps it wasn't."

"He blamed me then for the loss of that child. He wanted it and I didn't. I was glad for the miscarriage. I was even glad when the doctor told me I hadn't the body for bearing children, for conceiving. I thought, so much the better, but now I wonder about that lost child. I wonder how different my life would have been."

"Those questions are too difficult, too complicated, Nicolette."

"You have asked them of your life. Why shouldn't I?"

"My life has been less my own construction than yours. You have forged a life, burned off your past, and brought forth something quite different and wonderful and new."

"So have you."

Cosette smiled. "But not by choice. I married before I was eighteen. I was madly in love with a man who wanted to reshape the world, change the way people lived, the way they thought, and so I followed him because I loved him. To change the world would not have occurred to me on my own. You have ambition, Nicolette. I had love, but no ambition."

"I had love. Jean-Luc loved me. He did."

"I know he did. While he was capable of love, Nicolette, he loved you. Now," Cosette shrugged, "I don't know what he's capable of."

"I do," she said grimly. "You must promise me, please, if anything should ever happen to me, whatever happens to me, you'll care for my child, won't you? You'll never let Jean-Luc have my child. He mustn't ever. Promise me."

Cosette only came to Nicolette's shoulder, but she put her arms around and held her. "We are your family, Nicolette. We will always be your family."

"I want this baby so much." She wept and wiped her eyes. "I want to hold it and love it, and I can feel myself filling up with life and at the same time I watch the life draining out of Jean-Luc. I said to him, I'm offering you a life, a family, and he told me to find someone, to farm the baby out somewhere and he would pay. He's abandoned me altogether. It feels like a shipwreck."

"He is the wreck. Not you. You are ours, mine and Marius's and Fantine and Gabriel's, and we are yours. You saved Marius's life. You gave Fantine and Gabriel a place for their love. You gave me shelter under Mea Culpa's wig, and you gave me work at your own peril. These are the gifts of love and of family. You are my daughter, our daughter. And your child will be our child. And I will promise to care for your child."

"And protect it—boy or girl—from Jean-Luc."

"And protect it from Jean-Luc and the rest of the world, to love and protect this child, Nicolette."

September sunlight dappling in through the glass escalated the heat and humidity, the ribbon of stench intensified too, and they sat on an ornamental iron bench where bushy palms brushed near them and tropical flowers rotted in the standing water. Nicolette mopped her face with her hands. "When I told Jean-Luc I was leaving him, he only said, Oh, Nicolette, you'll be back. You can't live without me. You need me. And I said, Yes, yes, I need the man you were, but not the man you've become. But when I came back to Paris, I was so lonely without him, so lonely thinking about being without him, so much of my life connected with him, and now, this child, and I thought, I can't bear it." She rubbed the heels of her hands into her eyes, sniffed ungracefully, and swallowed hard. "I sent a telegram to the hotel in Trouville. I told him I loved him. I would always love him. I said, Please come back to me." Even the monkeys overhead ceased their quarreling, and the parrots squawked and then quieted, resting in the branches of the palms. "The stupid desk clerk gave the telegram to Madame Pontmercy rather than Monsieur Pontmercy and Eponine very kindly answered my telegram."

"Eponine? I thought she and Zelma were in Clermont-Ferrand with old Huvet!"

"She came to Trouville after I'd left, after Jean-Luc had left too, so I found out. She sent me a telegram saying I didn't need to wait for Jean-Luc to come back to me. I could go to him. He was in Paris. She gave me a name and an address." Nicolette pulled a gardenia off its stem and plunged her nose into it to obscure the scent of the old decay, the death of love, which overpowered, overwhelmed them both. "I went to this address. Last night. Late."

"Where was it? What did you find?"

"I can't tell you that," she said flatly, "you're his mother."

Cosette turned her head away and caught sight, deep in the lush foliage, of a splash of pink on the ground. The stench here was not the death of love, nor even sorrow and irony, but a dead flamingo. Another of the flamingos had sickened and died, and its impossible pink color lit up the thick greenery in these forced unnatural tropics. Cosette resolutely took Nicolette's arm and led her out of the conservatory, away from the stench and decay, the death of the poor flamingo, native to some other country where it could fly free and be with its own, but in Paris a useless ornament, a whimsy, a gaudy slave to the Second Empire.

Chapter 30

The following day Mea Culpa and La Lauriot arrived at the theatre to begin rehearsals for the new operetta. The ravages of unhappiness on Nicolette's face eased as she flung herself into the work, the title role of *The Little General.* Despite her personal heartbreak, her fatigue, nausea, headaches, the drain and strain of the new pregnancy, Nicolette continued to rehearse *The Little General* tirelessly, though more than one person commented that La Lauriot was not seen along the boulevards at night, and wags remarked with some relish that Baron Pontmercy was paying assiduous court to the wife of comte La Salle. Could it be, people smiled knowingly, and behind their fans women giggled, that the fabulous La Lauriot was losing her touch with men? Losing her vast popularity? Why were there no more great parties at the Benedictine Folly? No more rides in the Bois de Boulogne? No more crazy luncheons with the chattering monkeys? After rehearsals, La Lauriot was seen no more, and her rivals began carving up her empire of admiration.

The Little General was a typical piece of Offenbach frivolity, with a streak of satire the size of the Seine and the story (everyone hoped) balanced to amuse more than offend the censors. Set in an unnamed country of Germanic affectations (thus, the foibles here could not be ascribed to the French), *The Little General* told the story of a lineless actor getting ready for a performance, dressed in a military costume, who is plucked from the theatre and carried off by the mob to take part in historic deeds. The whole operetta was suggested to Offenbach by Nicolette, who had laughingly told the story of Châteaurenaud à la Lafayette at a dinner party one night. In the operetta, though, the Little General is carted to the front to lead a battle. When asked what the soldiers should do, the Little General shrugs in that very Parisian way and says, *Boom boom boom*. The *boom boom boom* tactics are victorious, the enemy defeated, and, showered with honors, the Little General returns to meet the king (a thuggish-looking Hanoverian sort, not at all like Louis-Napoléon). Fêted by one and all, the Little General, through a series of tortured plot twists, is finally unmasked, and at the end marries the king because the Little General, it turns out, was a woman all along, her mezzo-soprano voice apparently not eliciting undue interest heretofore.

Word went all around Paris that La Lauriot would be on stage in men's military clothes, trim, tight trousers and a flared coat.

"It looks very smart on you," said Cosette, applying the finishing touches opening night.

Nicolette patted her abdomen, pulled it in, her shoulders back. "Now I understand why the Empress Eugénie invented the crinoline to cover up her pregnancy."

"Pity the rest of the world has to live with it now that the prince is nearly seven years old."

"I could carry the performance longer if I wore a hoop skirt instead of skin-tight trousers."

"Maybe the play won't run for long anyway. Louis-Napoléon is in the audience. The minister of the interior as well."

Nicolette had a brilliant patch of rouge on one cheek, but the other one went pale. "On opening night?"

"I overheard the porter telling the scene shifters he'd just got word, and they'd best go down to the storage room and get the Emperor's bunting out." Cosette picked up her green spectacles and put them on, checking her own costume in the mirror.

"You know the minister of the interior was not fond of *Orphée aux Enfers,* neither was the Emperor, and they nearly closed us down then. They can close down any play they think the least bit critical of the regime." Nicolette brushed burnt cork over her eyebrows and shaped them so they looked bushy and masculine as she inquired obliquely, "And Jean-Luc? Is he out there?"

"He wasn't when last I looked."

"He has not missed an opening night of mine since my debut with Offenbach in 1855. I don't think I can sing if he's not there."

"Shall I go look again?"

"Please, and will you take some of these flowers out? I think I'm going to be sick again, and there are so many of them. And can you open the trapdoor? It's so hot in here." The Little General dashed for the chamberpot to retch. Mea Culpa lifted the handle to the door that led to the storage room. It creaked badly and a musty draft swirled into the dressing room. Then she gathered up whole armfuls of flowers, mostly blue roses, and took one batch down to the extras' dressing room, where they were needed because extras still shared a single basin, a cracked mirror, and unventilated space where their sweaty costumes hung too near the stove.

"Hey, Toad Eater," one of them quipped, "tell La Lauriot to send her leftover Russian princes, will you, not these flowers."

"I wouldn't kiss a Russian even if he was a prince," retorted another girl, "would you, Mea Culpa?"

"Mea culpa," she murmured and she could hear them making coarse jokes about her love life. She carried the rest of the flowers to the porter's lodge.

The porter's lodge was up some stairs, and from this outpost he guarded the stage entrance like a basilisk. The grim view out his window was a gaslit alley with a central gutter, but he defended this alley as though it led to the Tuileries Palace. He had the cherry-splotched nose of a confirmed inebriate, and he admitted only actors, musicians, the crews, and of course the critics, the theatrical claques, and any gentlemen who greased his palm with five francs. It was rumored he was rich. In the gaslit alley yet another wagon pulled up, and the delivery boy rang the stage-door bell. Mea Culpa humbly implored him not to send the flowers to Mademoiselle Lauriot. "They make her sick."

"I can see where they would. It's like a state funeral here."

Cosette returned to the wings, where, from a tiny slit in the curtains, she could peer out into the house, brilliantly lit by a huge crystal chandelier. They had indeed got the imperial bunting up, but the giant *N* wreathed in laurel was upside down. She laughed to see it.

"What's so funny out there, eh, Mea Culpa?" teased a scene shifter, a burly man with great ringed epaulets of sweat. "The Toad Napoléon? What else besides a toad could make the Toad Eater laugh?" And he hoisted away half a dozen cardboard boulders for the battle scene.

In Jean-Luc's box Cosette saw Eponine enter, followed by Corinne and Arsène, who were the very picture of marital boredom. Eponine, more than usually animated, held up her opera glasses and scanned the house, waving. Next came Zelma with Arsène's old father in tow. Oh, thought Cosette, Zelma will make salt pork out of that old sugar beet. She smiled to remember Fantine's tales of Zelma's pursuit of the rich widower. She was about to turn away when Jean-Luc entered the box, taking his place beside Eponine, exchanging words with her. His great frame had gone to bulk and he looked bloated, surfeited with cynicism. He wore the required Second Empire waxed mustache, but it did not conceal a mouth that was slack and sullen. He exuded the air of a man of experience without adventure, of satiation without satisfaction, of excess without substance. He was her son and she pitied him.

Offenbach himself conducted for opening night and *The Little General* with his *Boom boom boom* brought peals of laughter from the appreciative audience and sustained applause for the music, especially the soldiers' chorus march and the song of the mob in the first act. In this scene little shards, fragments of "La Marseillaise" and other old revolutionary anthems could be heard. The cannons were a marvel of stagecraft, actually billowing smoke, and the funny cart used to convey the Little General around the stage looked suitably crude beside the weapons of theatrical war. Aside from Nicolette's masterfully sly *Boom boom boom*, the line that brought the house down did not belong to her at all, but to a stumpy actor with a turnipish complexion who played the king's foreign minister and who bellowed in a thick Prussian accent, *Have we defeated the French? Have we beaten the French?* At this the Bouffes-Parisiens rocked with laughter.

After the intermission, when the curtain rose, everyone, on and off stage—actors, prompters, singers, dancers, from the call boy to Offenbach—all eagerly scanned the house, Mea Culpa included. The foreign minister's box was vacated. The Prussian ambassador had gone. Count Châteaurenaud had vanished. But everyone at Bouffes-Parisiens sighed happily, gratified to see the minister of the interior still there. And Louis-Napoléon and Eugénie. Offenbach especially breathed more easily. He had fretted over those bits of "La Marseillaise"; he had kept them in but he did not want to pay too dearly for the imperial tweak.

Throughout the performance the Little General herself kept surreptitiously glancing toward Jean-Luc, seeing on his face, perhaps, the occasional pang of pain or heartburn, but not the old hunger and dazzle and adoration. One never forgets that. One never ceases to recognize it. In the imperial box, Louis-Napoléon regarded Nicolette with the old hunger. For dazzle and adoration you need a shared past and shared anticipation. For hunger you need only a body.

At the end of the operetta, the applause deafened all Paris, and *The Little General* was, without doubt, a smash success, as the backstage was invaded and the Passage of Princes thronged with rakes and dandies, peers and theatrical critics, dissolute journalists, the usual array of English dukes, and, rumor had it, a Persian potentate, all awaiting the moment when Mea Culpa would open La Lauriot's door and admit them. But the noise and laughter, the bustle and thump of backstage life seemed to cease when a knock sounded and Mea Culpa shuffled to answer it, grumbling that La Lauriot was not ready to receive.

But once the door was opened, Cosette found herself face-to-face with Louis-Napoléon, as close as he had been on that occasion when they'd danced in 1851. Cosette's shock registered even behind Mea Culpa's green spectacles. Louis-Napoléon smiled broadly; he was something of an actor himself and he did not rush the timing, but of course he had no eyes for Mea Culpa, only for Nicolette, her makeup half off, her wrapper fetchingly undone.

He was shorter than Cosette remembered, and time had not been kind to him. After working in the theatre, she recognized instantly that he wore rouge to heighten his color and powder to smooth out his pallor, but the powder collected in the many creases around his eyes. Wax on the tips of his elegant mustache had caught a bit of dust, which balanced there perilously, and his auburn hair was thinning, growing out gray at the roots.

"Will Mademoiselle Lauriot receive an admirer, madame?" he asked of Mea Culpa. "I would wait with the others—" he gestured behind him to the Passage of Princes, thronged now with chorus girls hoping to pick up La Lauriot's leftovers—"but there must be some advantages to being Emperor."

Must there? Cosette wanted to reply as Mea Culpa stepped aside to let him pass, closing the door on the gawkers and catching Nicolette's astonished expression.

Nicolette rose, curtsied. Louis-Napoléon took her hand and pronounced himself *enchanté*, adding he had admired her for many years, but her performance tonight as the Little General was superb and the costume most becoming. "Would you do that for me sometime privately, mademoiselle?"

"The Little General?"

"Boom boom boom."

"With pleasure," replied the Empress of Offenbach.

"You will receive a letter from my chamberlain then, shortly, with the particulars, and I shall look forward to that. Now, if you will excuse me—" and with a suitably military style, befitting not only the play but his uniform, his ribbons and medals and insignia, Louis-Napoléon clicked his heels and bowed. He turned to Mea Culpa, bowed to her as well, actually took Cosette's hand in his, and—with the charm that had endeared him to market women all over Paris—the Toad Napoléon declared himself *enchanté* to make the Toad Eater's acquaintance.

Chapter 31

ouis-Napoléon, like all the actors in his masquerade empire, wore rouge. He had worn rouge first in 1846 to cover his prison pallor when he escaped as a workingman from the fortress of Ham. In 1870 he would wear rouge at the last to conceal the ravages of painful bladder stones, so that on horseback he could lead French troops to ignominious defeat by the Prussians in a grisly bit of *boom boom boom*, called the Franco-Prussian War, which would bring down the Second Empire altogether. And Louis-Napoléon wore rouge to bed.

Ordinary Parisians, who might not have had the opportunity— or the wish—to sleep with Louis-Napoléon, came to know this fact by way of a small, scurrilous two-page pamphlet, progeny of *The Toad Napoléon*, called *Tadpoléon*, which, within six weeks of the opening of *The Little General,* caused its own *boom boom boom,* an operetta of sedition, unstoppable as an Offenbach melody.

The author of *Tadpoléon* was identified only by a crudely drawn torch; the paper, crude and cheap, the type itself so crude and old-fashioned police finally concluded it was printed on a small, clandestine press, last used against the *ancien régime*. Clandestine presses, they explained to Monsieur Clerons, were perhaps no more than three feet high, the shape vaguely, unhappily reminiscent of the guillotine, but they had advantages for radicals, discontents, and traitors, in that they could be quickly dismantled and inconspicuously stowed. Police were quite certain this one was stowed in Paris. Perhaps Montmartre.

Somehow the old eighteenth-century typography suited *Tadpoléon,* which was loosely based on the fables of La Fontaine, the one about the stinking old king of a lion who invited the other animals to his lair. *Boom boom boom,* laughter echoed, resounded from the boulevards to the *barrières,* from the Coeur-Volant to the Bal

Mabille, from the Café Rigolo to the Café Anglais, from the puppeteer in the park to the Théâtre-Français, along the new extension of the rue de Rivoli, all the way from the place de la Bastille to the Champs-Elysées, as *Tadpoléon* found its seditious way into the garrets and marketplaces, into garters of the *filles publiques,* into the fingers of glovemakers and the packs of ragpickers, pockets of fried-potato sellers, the aprons of brewers and bakers, the calloused hands of masons and joiners and bill stickers, the black hands of coal merchants, the blue hands of dyers—but not booksellers, who assured police, who swore their hands were clean. Absolutely. They would not risk their licenses to sell a pamphlet that suggested, albeit by innuendo, that the Emperor's presentation was toadlike, while his equipment was, well, tadpoleon, that his performance in bed, like his performance as Emperor, was rouged, artificial, and unsatisfying. Booksellers—from the lowliest street peddler to the gaslit shops along the rue Saint-Honoré and passage Choiseul—would have nothing to do with a libelous pamphlet invoking the classic characters of the sacred La Fontaine to imply that the old lion's appetites were unimpaired, but his abilities drooped, that in the course of amorous exertion the wax melted and his mustache drooped. As in La Fontaine's fable, the monkey, the dog, and the fox (the latter the only one to escape) were invited to the lion's lair, but in *Tadpoléon* they were told they may kiss the lion anywhere except upon the mouth. As if even a dog would kiss the old lion on the mouth! All who entered the stinking lair were told to strip off their clothes in one room and proceed naked to the next, where they heard the door lock behind them, to walk to the bed, get in, and satisfy—quickly—such appetites as might be aroused by the sight of the lion naked.

Cosette had argued against it, advised, insisted Nicolette not sleep with Louis-Napoléon, that it was too dangerous, to say nothing of disgusting. But Nicolette, capriciously and in high spirits (having clearly put to rest rumors of her waning popularity), replied that if they were to be a family of traitors then let it be unanimous, and just think what she could take from the Emperor's bed.

She did: she left that bed with enough flint and tinder to light La Lumière's torch again. Cosette wrote *Tadpoléon,* but with misgivings, and she thought it unwise to publish. But Pajol had fixed the ancient clandestine press and wanted to print, and if *Tadpoléon* could not be distributed outside Paris, no matter. The Starling was for it. Marius too, his journalist's instincts roused, declared the danger was worth it. After all, so many years had elapsed since *Bonapoléon,* and besides, Marius told Cosette, everyone would understand what was truly being said.

Everyone did. Immediately upon *Tadpoléon*'s clandestine appearance, the old draconian press laws from the early days of empire were thrust upon the press and public, and a campaign of repression began. Offenbach hastily removed those bits and bars of "La Marseillaise" from *The Little General.* The censors came down ferociously on anything thought to imperil imperial credibility. The newspapers outdid one another in an orgy of frivolity, flummery, fudge, and fluff: the Empress's clothes became obsessively important. The minister of the interior invited Monsieur Clerons to his office to make explicit the gravity of the situation. If the interview itself weren't sufficient for that purpose, the duc de Morny was also present, and both reminded Clerons that for years the Emperor had relied on him to stop La Lumière, and that he had roundly, soundly failed.

"Not simply over the last several years," the minister of the interior barked, "but the records of the previous regime suggest that Marius Pontmercy has eluded you for thirty years."

"That's not true," Clerons defended himself. "He was in prison frequently during—"

"We don't want him in prison," said the duc de Morny. "We had him in prison, if you recall. We don't want him martyred. We don't want his wife martyred. We don't want them fished out of the Seine. We want them vanished. Silenced. Do I make myself clear?"

"Are those the Emperor's orders?"

"Those are your orders when you leave this office, and if you cannot comply with them, perhaps you would prefer guard duty in Algeria, or better, New Caledonia."

Clerons began with the lowest, the weakest, the meekest. Mimi Lascaux was marched out of the Coeur-Volant at the point of a bayonet and her squalid room searched, turning up no more than morphine. Mother informed Clerons that Mimi had few regular customers, but one of them was a painter, bizarre, perverted in the extreme, whose tastes ran to, well, painting.

Clerons's soldiers next marched across the Seine out toward Clichy, and they took hours tearing apart Beaujard's studio, looking for the clandestine press, while Beaujard sketched them.

At the Café Rigolo the *mouchards* tripled like flies waking on a hot window, and (figuring the spies were obliged to be there) Madame Fagennes doubled her prices, losing many of her old customers, hoping she could ride this out. It was enough to make a red republican of her. Every night before she went upstairs she spat on all three busts of Napoléon III.

The Countess Crasseux was served with eviction papers, told the landlord had sold the old tobacco warehouse and it was to be torn down like all the other old rats' nests near the river. Clerons brought the notice himself, explaining that she might be allowed to stay on, the demolition put off if . . .

She heard Clerons out. If people are intent on speeches, she had learned, it's best to give them that satisfaction. While Clerons spoke, she looked over his shoulder, up to the rafters, where fetal-looking cauls of clothing hung high overhead, and she reflected on the time it had taken her to build not merely the business, but her reputation for shrewdness unimpeded by emotion. She was almost seventy years old, she thought, and perhaps what was happening here, now, was a sort of rehearsal for that big eviction. Evicted from the flesh. That journey one makes carrying nothing, leaving finally, only reputation. Moreover, business had dropped off in the last five years. Dramatically. She'd thought perhaps there'd been a drop in the number of knaves and sharpers, foreigners drawn to the court of Napoléon III, but that was not true. If anything, more arrived each year, until the whole court was gorged with them; they were stately and steeped in protocol, suffocatingly opulent, so opulent and so numerous they no longer needed the Changer for that costume of conviction. They were their own Changers nowadays. And if they lived in squalor behind Haussmann's boulevards, when they stepped out to "circulate," their identities matched the garish façades of the uniform buildings staring at one another across those broad fields of wheels and feet. They were not even people she could caution with her tale of the Costly Omelette—no one cared if the outside and the inside matched. The outside was all that mattered. No, the Countess thought, listening raptly to Clerons, she had greeted Louis-Napoléon enthusiastically without foreseeing that when the knaves and sharpers were absorbed into *la vie Parisienne,* she would be out of work. "An interesting proposition," she granted when Clerons had finished. "You assure my grandson's safety and that he won't be transported out of France?"

"The Starling did not write *Tadpoléon.* He did not print it. I want the people with ink on their hands."

The Countess spat out her invisible seed. "Me, I need to think about it. Three hours, monsieur, no more."

Clerons was about to protest, but she seemed so reasonable he agreed, leaving two sentries there, their feet splashing as they marched in the puddles in the impasse.

Three hours later, returning to the old tobacco warehouse, Clerons found the Changer's emporium silent. Only the leather backs of the Changer's record books remained, charred but unburned in the grates and stoves. The cash gone. The Countess gone. The Jondrettes too. The long-snout dogs were gone. The sentries had seen nothing. Floating forlornly overhead, suspended from their high gallows, the clothing bags were mute, testifying only to the passing of all fashion, indeed, of all things.

Not until the duc de Morny provided Clerons with a list of the women who had shared the imperial bed over the last six months did he realize that in pursuing the Starling he would find only feathers. On this list—one name among many—was that of Nicolette Lauriot, identified here only with the words *Bouffes-Parisiens,* as though she were still an anonymous palm-frond waver and not the Empress of Offenbach—to say nothing of the fact that she was the mistress of Baron Pontmercy.

The trees in the Parc Monceau were giving up their greenery as gracelessly as aging belles on the autumn day Clerons called at the Pontmercy home. Zelma had long since gone to live with Corinne and Huvet (for obvious reasons) and to the dismay of Arsène, and the disgust of Corinne, shortly after the appearance of *Tadpoléon,* Eponine moved in too. Even if she was the Emperor's love child, her last name doomed Eponine to imperial disfavor, and though a husband could not be easily shed, he could be quickly abandoned. Eponine did this without a second thought, putting the stunned Louise in a convent school, telling her it would be good for her.

Perhaps the only person who did not abandon Jean-Luc was Arsène, who even defended him when the Jockey Club wanted to expel him after La Lumière's *Tadpoléon* made its way there, through the scullery no doubt, the bootblacks and the grooms. Under pressure from Arsène (or his money), the Jockey Club grudgingly kept Jean-Luc, but no one wanted to be seen with a man even remotely connected to the infamous, treasonous, scurrilous *Tadpoléon*, and so perhaps that's why Jean-Luc was home at all on the afternoon Clerons came to call, shown to the drawing room, made to cool his heels till Jean-Luc saw fit to come down, clad in a dressing gown.

"Coffee?"

"This is not a social call."

Jean-Luc rang for coffee, lit a cigarette, saying immediately he had no idea where his mother was, he loathed, despised, and hated sedition as much as Clerons, more in fact, and in general made a great show and protestation of loyalty to the Emperor.

Clerons interrupted him, "Are you aware that your father is alive?"

Jean-Luc's volubility ceased. He stumbled, faltered, murmured something about rumors, and lit another cigarette though one yet burned.

"Surely the possibility must have occurred to you in 1851. You told me you could not find his body."

"I . . . it was, the bodies were . . . I thought . . ." Jean-Luc cleared his throat. "They said my father walked, open-armed, toward the soldiers, who refused to obey their officer's command to fire, that the officer himself had to fire, did fire, point-blank range. How could he have lived through that? Impossible."

"Nonetheless he did. He was badly wounded and they thought he wouldn't live, but he did. He was imprisoned at Ham."

"Where the Emperor was a prisoner?"

"A bit of irony. The Emperor is not without a sense of humor."

"Why didn't they try him with the rest of the rebels?"

"Your father was already a martyr. At least when he was at Ham he was a silenced martyr."

"He's not there now?" Jean-Luc threw both cigarettes in the dry grate.

"He escaped." Clerons watched as Jean-Luc swore under his breath, lit up again, his fingers trembling slightly. "A mason named Grincourt helped your mother and Starling, and he escaped. We thought at first they escaped into Belgium, but if they did, they returned, and they're here in Paris." Clerons trod heavily about the room; he seemed to be inspecting the academic art on the walls, paintings in heavy gilt frames that complemented the gold braid lacing the drapes, the gold fringe on satin cushions, ornate carvings on dark, heavy wood. He picked up a music box, which played "The Nicolette Waltz," and shut it. "Where is your sister? I haven't seen her since the day you assured me I could catch the Starling here with her." He rubbed the scar on his cheek, just visible above his gray beard.

"Yes, well, if you didn't, it's your own fault. Your men are incompetent fools. She ran off the next day, if you must know. Disgusting, isn't it? She's bedding down somewhere with the son of a whore and a convict."

Clerons stopped before a painting of a pink and fleshy nude looking heavenward, while romping cherubs floated around the heads of sleeping warriors. With a low rumble that in someone else might have passed for a laugh, he said, "She would not be the first. The children of whores and convicts are everywhere. Even in your family."

Jean-Luc jumped up, brandishing his cigarette like a weapon. "What do you mean by that, Monsieur Clerons?"

"Spare me the Jockey Club dueling code. It's ridiculous altogether and it's especially ridiculous for a man like you. To pretend you have any notion of honor is to flatter yourself unduly. Does the name Jean Valjean mean anything to you?"

"Should it?"

"Jean Valjean, number 24601, was a convict who later amassed a fortune—or killed and robbed a man who had, it's not clear how he came by the money. He was thought to have died, drowned. But he didn't. He took upon himself the care of an orphan, a little girl, the bastard daughter of a prostitute. He brought this little girl up to be a lady, educated her at a convent. She married, of course, a rich girl, she married well."

"Married whom?" Jean-Luc's fingers shook as he smoked.

"May I?" Clerons took a cigarette and continued to pace and smoke, his gray-bearded jaw outthrust. "I met Jean Valjean once. I was one of five men in 1832 to leave a barricade where everyone else was going to die. They all knew it. They were willing to die, believing that their deaths would make a difference to the way people thought, to the way people live, that their sacrifice was for the greater good of France. Stupid, yes? Even the word *sacrifice* smells of the moth and the worm. Like the word *honor.* Like *love,* for that matter."

"You sound like an old red republican yourself, Clerons. Most unbecoming," said Jean-Luc, gathering up some of his old poise as the servant brought in a tray of coffee and left.

"I never claimed to practice these things, but I recognize love and honor and sacrifice. I see them as weaknesses, but you don't see them at all."

"Go on with your dreary story." Jean-Luc poured himself some coffee. "Who did this girl marry?"

"The girl who was the daughter of a prostitute, raised by a convict, that girl? That girl is your mother, Monsieur Pontmercy. Your father too owes Jean Valjean his life. Marius Pontmercy would have been killed or at least arrested and imprisoned in 1832, but he was saved by the convict." Clerons finished his cigarette. "So you see, you and the Starling have more in common than you suppose. Perhaps your sister has merely sunk to her origins. Your family came from the gutter, why should she not return?"

The coffee tray, pot, cups, and spoons all went flying, smashed into the unlit fireplace, as with a single swoop of his arm Jean-Luc sent them all flying. "Since the day I met him, the Starling has dripped of mud and *merde.* Gutter sludge."

"Even your wife has more in common with the Starling than you might suppose."

"My wife? My wife, as all the world knows, is a shrewish, grasping, ill-tempered beauty, the daughter of a shrewish, grasping, ill-tempered hag."

"If my records are correct, the Countess Troussebois was born Zelma Thénardier. Her mother died in prison and her father was a vicious thief, a forger, a thug, and a sewer rat, who once owned an inn, The Sergeant of Waterloo."

"You misunderstand. Her father was a sergeant *at* Waterloo. He served the first Napoléon. She knew my mother as a child. She knew . . ." The ugly possibilities dawned on Jean-Luc.

"No doubt the Baroness Pontmercy and the Countess Troussebois played on the same muck heaps and fought for the same scraps as infants," Clerons continued, "but in 1833 Zelma Thénardier went to America with her father. They went to New York to avoid a death sentence for him in France. Perhaps, there in New York, His Imperial Majesty begat a child on Mademoiselle Thénardier, and perhaps he merely bedded down with a French whore in an American bed." Clerons shrugged. "The difference is moot since the Emperor has more or less acknowledged your wife as his offspring, but it makes for a rather grimmer picture than the Countess Troussebois has no doubt painted for you."

Jean-Luc's big frame collapsed on a velvet sofa, and his eyes seemed to empty of all animation.

Clerons regarded Jean-Luc without any more scruple than he would have donated a moth he was about to smash. "Your bad luck—or bad taste—in women extends to your mistress, Nicolette Lauriot."

"Mademoiselle Lauriot and I are finished."

"Was that before or after she slept with the Emperor?"

"Impossible. She hasn't slept with the Emperor."

"But she did. I have her name on a list."

"When?"

"Early October."

"Impossible."

"Why? The Emperor has slept with many women, probably thousands of women."

"She's pregnant. It's my child."

"And you think that would stop her from sleeping with the Emperor?" When Jean-Luc did not reply, Clerons scoffed. "Have you read *Tadpoléon*?"

"Everyone's read it. The illiterate have read it."

"The story was that the smelly old lion called many animals to his lair, many dogs and monkeys but only one fox. I think Nicolette Lauriot is the fox."

"Nicolette, the one who betrayed the Emperor to La Lumière? Impossible! Ridiculous. Nicolette loathes politics. She always has. She never pays any attention to anything she can't wear. All she cares about is collecting applause and jewelry and money from rich men. She never even reads the papers."

"No one reads the papers except for gossip or fashion news."

"What does it matter to me if she slept with the Emperor? I am sick of her. I've been finished with her for months, but if you think Nicolette Lauriot has anything to do with La Lumière, then you truly would pull the teeth from hens' lips." Listlessly he kicked a shard of coffee pot in his path. "I've told you, I would bring them all to you in chains if I could."

"Even your father? Never mind, it's an improper question. Betrayal has an old-fashioned ring to it, quite like those other words, love and honor, pity, sacrifice. Even cuckoldry is almost impossible now. Still, a woman may betray a man in other ways."

"Women are good for one thing only and bad for it too."

At that moment the drawing-room door opened and a girl entered. Her dark hair was unbound and she was barefoot, draped, rather than clad, in a satin bedsheet the same creamy color as her skin. She was young, perhaps fourteen, but her voice had a mature, coarse edge when she asked Jean-Luc what was keeping him, why he didn't come back to bed.

"Get out of here," he barked and the girl gave Clerons a bored, discriminating look and turned, leaving the door ajar.

Neither man spoke. Clerons took out a pencil and a bit of paper casually as if filling out a pawn ticket. "You know Mademoiselle Lauriot's domestic arrangements? You know her servants? How many has she?"

"Three, four, five perhaps if you count the coachman and the gardener at the rue de Chaillot. Of course I know them."

"And at the country house, the Benedictine Folly?"

"No one. She takes the Paris servants with her."

"Are any of her servants new?"

"No, they've been with her for years and years. They're like the damned dogs and the monkeys—"

"In *Tadpoléon* the lion sleeps with dogs and monkeys," remarked Clerons.

"Mea Culpa." Jean-Luc's tongue ballooned as if he had been snake-bitten and the poison racing through his veins. "Mea culpa," he got the phrase out harshly, like coughing out a human hairball. "Mea Culpa."

"Forgive you for what, Monsieur Pontmercy? What are you guilty of?"

"Mea Culpa." Jean-Luc looked suddenly bereft, betrayed, and he repeated over and over, *mea culpa mea culpa mea culpa.*

Chapter 32

*W*hen the Pincher pulled the body of the comte Châteaure-naud out of the Seine, he got only the usual twenty-five francs at the morgue, but the papers got hold of the story and the erstwhile extra's sorry death captivated Paris. Some of the newspapers (though not the government's official papers; it was not imperial policy to allude—ever—to the lost Second Republic) sent men to the river ravagers' low bistro to ferret out the Pincher, who extolled, embellished with relish and solemnity, obligingly informed them that the uniform the comte Châteaurenaud had been wearing when he jumped from the pont de Solférino was the very one he'd worn that day in 1848, complete with false medals made of tin, and moreover, the ex-actor was absolutely penniless, not a sou in his pockets.

The count enjoyed a posthumous celebrity, which had eluded him—save for one brief moment—in life, because the newspapers, unable to criticize the empire in their columns, waxed eloquent over his story, his role in the February Revolution, making those events sound naturally, fashionably ridiculous, innocuous, and passionate, but at the same time, the story somehow raised ghosts, the old ghosts of *liberté, égalité, fraternité,* comic ghosts now, to be sure, silly as the *boom boom boom* at the Bouffes-Parisiens. But someone at *Le Figaro* even remembered (with a good deal of surprise) that Lamartine was still alive, and both they and the weekly *L'Illustration* asked the old poet to write an account of his meeting with Châteaurenaud that day in February 1848, when the king abdicated and the mob looted the Tuileries. Alongside Lamartine's article (written in turgid, fervid, still-incendiary 1848 prose), *L'Illustration* ran a hilarious caricature of Châteaurenaud's career, depicting how, picked up by the February Revolution, he had eventually soared to the top of the Second Empire, only to sink finally into the Seine.

The trouble was, in the caricature Châteaurenaud was sketched so as to resemble Offenbach (rail-thin, big nose, bushy mustache, and muttonchops, but no pince-nez). Everyone knew the dead man's story had provided the basis for *The Little General,* currently collecting raves and revenues. Nonsense, declared Offenbach to the press. Did Châteaurenaud ever fight a battle? Ever say that sainted phrase *boom boom boom?* Was Châteaurenaud a woman? Was he? wondered the giddy press, as they ran off to rifle the dead man's clothes, his past, his unlikely rise to the peerage, his sordid death.

Nicolette was devastated by his suicide. Everyone knew *The Little General* had profoundly depressed Châteaurenaud, who had left no note, no word of farewell before his fatal leap. Everyone knew Nicolette Lauriot had given Offenbach the idea, that she had told the count's story in such an uproarious way that Offenbach had laughed till tears ran down his face: the story of that February day, and how the false and silly general lived up to what the revolutionary moment obliged of him, how he later became a silly count, false as everyone else in the court of the Second Empire. Shattered by Châteaurenaud's death, by the pain and shame of it, Nicolette very nearly took the name Mea Culpa herself. She went to confession, but the priest was more interested in her sexual transgressions (it had been a very long time between confessions) than in a bit of dinner-party conversation. Besides, the priest advised her after he handed out the penance, suicide was a sin and Châteaurenaud did not deserve her pity.

But she did pity him. She pitied herself and she pitied the man she had loved and the child she was carrying, the dreadful wreck of her dreams, before she realized that beyond what she had already achieved onstage, she didn't have any dreams. She had had ambitions and assumptions. She had fulfilled the ambitions, and as for assumptions, well, she'd assumed she and Jean-Luc would be, that they would always be. And now they weren't. And never would be. She envied Fantine and the Starling the clarity of their love, and she envied Cosette and Marius the longevity of their love, but she left the church without performing the penance and went home, cried into Cosette's lap that she'd never meant to bring sorrow or trouble or death to anyone.

Cosette tried to comfort her, but certainly sorrow and trouble pressed all around them. Cosette faulted herself for their troubles; she should have outright opposed Marius's, Pajol's, Gabriel's, and Nicolette's unanimous blithe insistence. Even Marius admitted he'd been wrong; *Tadpoléon* had not served any purpose, save to make Louis-Napoléon look ridiculous and to diminish La Lumière, to make it less a torch than a mere candle, teasing the imperial rump. *Tadpoléon* had amused people without arousing them. No, the specters of the spring of 1848—that betrayed promise, those dead prospects, moribund hopes—all that seemed to rise out of the river with the dripping corpse of Châteaurenaud. His suicide, not *Tadpoléon*, had started whispered dialogue, even nostalgia for the old honor and sacrifice, a need to see *liberté, égalité, fraternité* flourishing again in France. These words had been effaced, erased from all public buildings, but they had not been erased from people's hearts or minds. Obscured, perhaps, but not erased.

Cosette stroked Nicolette's hair and soothed her guilt, but she could not soothe her fears. She shared those fears. Everyone did. Clerons and the police went so far as to comb through the rag-pickers' enclaves at the *barrières*—by day—including the *barrière* d'Italie, where they ruthlessly plunged into hovels and marched the poor out. The Countess vanished; her whereabouts and the whereabouts of the Jondrettes remained a mystery. The Old Changer's warehouse came under the axe. With Mimi's *fille publique* license revoked, Mother immediately evicted her from the Coeur-Volant. Mimi fled to Beaujard's studio, and he hid her there, both of them afraid of every footfall on the stairwell. The Starling vanished without a trace or word to anyone. At Argenteuil Fantine prayed for her husband and looked after her father and put into effect the code they had all agreed upon: each day she wrote a note to Mademoiselle Lauriot informing her that the figs were fine. Each day all Paris read in the press of old radicals being raided, their apartments and premises torn apart, a level of repression last seen in December 1851, as Clerons looked for the clandestine press and the plates of *Tadpoléon*.

Tadpoléon had actually been printed late at night in Pajol's tiny alcove in the room beneath the stage at the Bouffes-Parisiens. Painstakingly he had operated the clandestine press by hand through the night, going out at dawn, giving those he'd printed to the Starling, who distributed them amongst his wide acquaintance on both sides of the Seine, people he'd known since he was a thief as a boy, to the men he'd worked alongside building boulevards, digging sewers, swinging axes, and climbing scaffolding, to men along the river and ragpickers at the *barrières*. Pajol and Gabriel changed their meeting place every day. But one day the Starling wasn't there, and that afternoon Pajol waited beneath La Lauriot's trapdoor till he heard feet overhead. He climbed the ladder and knocked softly on the floor.

Mea Culpa, alone there, awaiting that knock, knew who it was and why. She bolted the door to the Passage of Princes, then leaned over and swung open the heavy trapdoor and looked into Pajol's blue eyes. She climbed down the ladder and faced him in the dim patch of light. "They have arrested Germaine," she said with a heavy heart. "The Starling was not there to meet you this morning because he's trying to find out where they've taken her. They arrested her yesterday in Montmartre." She handed him a newspaper. He held it in a fist and brought that fist down savagely against a Doric column with velvet ivy, which clattered down, hitting a papier-mâché battlement. "Oh, Pajol," Cosette whispered softly, "what can I say? What can any of us say? We never should have done it. *Tadpoléon*, it was the Costly Omelette, Pajol, that last wrong-headed gesture."

Pajol reeled and clung to the ladder as a drowning man might cling to a line that would pull him from the sea. "If I had been there, they would have taken me. They would have left her. I've done this to her. To my children." He wrapped his arms around the ladder and covered his face with his hands.

Cosette wept. "The papers say Germaine is the common-law wife of the man thought to be the printer of seditious material. They won't even use the name *Tadpoléon*. They say they found ink and composition boxes and rolling brushes at your Montmartre apartment."

"I'll kill him, you know. I'll kill Clerons for this. I have my pistol from the June Days. I haven't used it since. I should never have left her. I thought I was protecting her," he said over and over, "I thought I was protecting her. I'll kill the man who hurts her, Lark, I will."

"The Starling says Verdier's daughter's come for your children and she'll look after them."

Pajol nodded grimly. "Germaine gave me back my life when I returned to Paris. Verdier and Monsieur Pontmercy, they gave me back my work, but Germaine gave me life, and me, I have delivered her to the prison I left. You cannot know what the prison will do to you till you've been there."

"Marius knows."

"Perhaps," Pajol conceded, "but to a man of his stature, they don't do this." He rolled back his sleeve to reveal the numbers 23974 branded on his inner arm. "Do they?"

Cosette could not reply. Had her father borne such numbers on his inner arm? Would they brand Germaine Fleury with numbers? Pajol was powerless to protect Germaine, and Cosette was equally powerless. If they found Fantine, they would find Marius. If they arrested Nicolette, they would find Fantine. Cosette considered turning herself in to protect the rest of them, discussed it late one night with Nicolette, who refused to hear of it. "No," said Nicolette, "we take our chances together."

Chapter 33

*T*hat night, as she did before every performance of *The Little General*, Mea Culpa looked out through her slit in the curtains to see if Jean-Luc was in the Pontmercy box. He was never there anymore, and malicious rumors wafted along the Passage of Princes, odoriferous as the smell of gas and faulty plumbing. But tonight, perhaps ten days after the suicide of Châteaurenaud, Jean-Luc was there. He and Eponine and Zelma. Mea Culpa was about to return with this information when she realized they had not brought any of their usual camp followers. They were quite alone. Through the slit in the curtains she studied her son's face: Jean-Luc no longer looked like Marius, but a rather bleak and bloated parody of Marius. The intensity in Marius's dark eyes reflected some commitment, an almost palpable integrity, even when he was broken in health and living in a ragpicker's hovel. In Jean-Luc's, the intensity seemed false and burnished, like the eyes of the Second Empire belles, who rubbed belladonna in their eyes to make them shine. Cosette puzzled over the three of them: Zelma, Jean-Luc, and Eponine neither bickered nor bantered, nor chattered and ogled everyone else as the entire rest of the audience was doing before the curtain rose. Their mouths were set in identical seams, and they were sober as judges. Cosette risked lifting her green spectacles to have a better look.

"They look like judges," she told Nicolette as she put the finishing touches on the Little General's costume. The first set of tucks had already come out, but at four months the pregnancy was not yet evident or visible.

"Even Jean-Luc?"

"Especially Jean-Luc."

The call boy's knock sounded on the dressing-room door, and they could hear the rousing overture start, galvanizing the audience. As a last touch, Cosette took a paintbrush and applied a layer of lacquer to the huge plume on the hat, to keep it erect and shining. She pinned the mock-Napoléonic hat to Nicolette's high-piled hair, and the Little General marched out, Mea Culpa humbly behind her, carrying her basket with the jar of water, cologne, combs, powder, and rouges for the offstage touch-ups.

After the brilliant overture, the packed house hushed and the curtain rose on a scene depicting an extra's ugly dressing room, where the Little General sang her opening number, a whimsical musical complaint about how she never had any lines; she was a great actress trapped in a silly general's costume and musically bemoaning her talents going undiscovered. On cue from the wings there poured onto the stage a mob, looking drunk and disorderly and not at all revolutionary. (And, Cosette reflected, that's probably why we escaped the censor's wrath.) These louts, men and women, carrying rakes and shovels and brooms, ragpickers' staffs, sang a tune ("La Marseillaise" shards removed) compounded of Offenbach's reworking of the old *Carmagnole* and other 1789 ditties. The Little General looked out her window and the mob cheered her. Her face a caricature of rouge and blackened eyebrows, the Little General quickly slapped on a fake mustache and turned to the audience, including them in the ruse, and strutted outside. The dressing room, on a turnstile (turned offstage by four sweating men), rolled into the wings, and the great production number ensued, the louts extolling their new leader's virtues, the Little General sopping up their applause.

Cosette looked out upon the audience. Everyone amongst the acres of silk, the cashmere shawls, the froth of tulle, the flash of diamonds and fluttering fans—the entire audience—was clearly enthralled. Except in Jean-Luc's box. Their expressions had not altered. The gas man brought up the proscenium footlights on the Little General and her loutish supporters, and a great round of applause brought down the house and the curtain.

In the wings Cosette heightened Nicolette's rouge and added more because she was so pale. "I've never known Jean-Luc to look like that," Nicolette whispered urgently. "He's a complete stranger."

The grind and squeal of pulleys sounded as the stage flats, vast muslin sheets of landscape, were lowered into what was to be the distance, to give the illusion of fields that stretched into forever. Grunting and panting, scene shifters pushed the fake cannons into place on stage. The curtain went up and the chorus, who had so recently been a drunk and disorderly mob, hurriedly changed into uniforms, readied themselves to take orders as soldiers. Their uniforms were decidedly not French, but garish green and yellow and Prussian blue. The king and colonel and the foreign minister went on and sang their numbers, hand-wringing, gibbering melodies, about how they were losing their battles and needed a savior.

Cosette moistened Nicolette's lips and throat with the water just before she stepped into the cart that soldiers pushed on stage, and the Little General sang her bright, braggadocio song to the king, the colonel, and the foreign minister, declaring, as the cart was being pushed about, how many battles he had won, the glory he could drape upon this army. She was coming to her famous *boom boom boom* line, and Cosette could somehow feel the whole audience lean forward toward that moment. The king and foreign minister, still gibbering, earnestly inquired of the Little General, what would be his strategy, but at the very minute Nicolette was to have uttered the operetta's most famous line, one of the cartwheels broke off, the cart tipped, crashed, the wheel rolled away, and Cosette gasped to see Nicolette tumble, fall, lie for a moment, dazed, on stage. Nicolette looked wildly from Cosette to the Pontmercy box. Jean-Luc had vanished. Eponine and Zelma sat alone. Smiling.

Mea Culpa had to be held back from rushing out to Nicolette, because somehow the sight of the disabled cart shot through her, a long, jagged knife of memory, some shard of time that yet reeked of memory she could not quite collect or connect. The gun carriage at The Sergeant of Waterloo? The carts overturned and fashioned into street barricades? The broken cart on the road to Saint-Simon? Or something else, less tangible, more terrible? She was seized with heart-stopping fear, as if that three-wheeled cart on stage had suddenly spilled her whole life.

Certainly it had spoiled the whole performance. The poor conductor limped along, slowing the musicians, who, down in the pit, could not see that Nicolette had remained splayed, disoriented, unable to sing, unable to speak, her mouth open, her gaze on

Cosette. The cannons, however, were timed to explode at a certain moment, and though the Little General had not given her *boom boom boom* cue, the cannons boomed-boomed all the same, the smoke belched, and the orchestra hurried to catch up with them, to provide the thundering, thumping, musical *BOOM BOOM BOOM* required to time perfectly with the smoke now billowing, all of it like ghosts, wafting high into the vaults, as Nicolette, her cues missed, her poise vanished, got to her feet, but instead of *Boom boom boom*, she beseeched Mea Culpa, *"Run run run!"*

Mea Culpa turned, pushed past the actors in the wings, past the prompters on their ladders, past the scene shifters, the gas and prop and rope and pulley stagehands, past the call boy with his cigarette, past the sandbags and stage flats, she ran back toward the stage door, the porter's lodge. Behind her, onstage, the soldiers' chorus sounded as they marched around the Little General. From the porter's window, and with the astonished old man, Mea Culpa looked down into the gaslit alley, where there was another soldiers' chorus. Marching feet. Not on stage. Muskets not made of cardboard. Bayonets not made of tin, but gleaming in the gaslight, tramping, approaching the stage door of the Bouffes-Parisiens, while the porter swore, By God, they wouldn't close down the performance like this!

Cosette saw before her the sword, the scaffold, and the gutter: Marius in prison, Fantine suffering Germaine's fate, Gabriel with numbers burned into his arm, Nicolette's baby born in a prison infirmary, and herself torn once again from the ones she loved, the family she had so labored to bring together; the lovers, Fantine and Gabriel, the promise of children, of Nicolette, of Marius, Marius, Marius. They had taken their chances together and their luck had run out. Cosette had but one chance: to get Nicolette offstage and out of the theatre before the soldiers invaded. To get her to safety—a place Cosette could not even imagine.

Darting through the usual backstage melée, Mea Culpa ran into the dressing room, bent double, and with a great effort, hoisted the trapdoor open. She was about to run back to get Nicolette, when she looked in the mirror and saw, beside her own reflection, her son. Jean-Luc stood unevenly. Desperately drunk, and with a deep, cynical bow, he introduced himself to Mea Culpa. "The traitor Mea Culpa," he added grimly.

Cosette took off her green glasses. "If there's a traitor here, it's you. When I think what you have done to your sister, to Nicolette, to your father—"

"He's alive? Was Clerons telling the truth?"

"What kind of son betrays his own father?" she lashed out, though tears spilled down her face. "Think of your father—"

"Think of your father," he replied coldly, "the convict."

Cosette smeared the tears across her face, and drew herself up with dignity. "Jean Valjean the convict would have despised you. I despise you."

"How clever the two of you must have thought yourselves, you and Nicolette, playing me for one of her monkeys, keeping you here, under my nose, all this time. She must have really hated me to do this. She must have—"

"You hated yourself!" Nicolette said, marching in between scenes. "You betrayed everything I loved in you!"

"You've wrecked everything I've worked for, you slut!"

"What have you worked for?" Nicolette pushed past him but he grabbed her wrist. "You never worked. That man with grease on his hands who lowers the stage flats, who raises the curtain, he works! The gas man works! Ragpickers work! Whores work! You have sniveled and snaked and wormed and married your way into money! You have cheated and traded on information, but you have not worked!" She sobbed as he tightened his grip on her. "I loved you, I loved you, and when I see what you've become—"

In a harsh whisper he pulled her up against him, "You told me, 'Marry for money. Marry a rich woman and we'll all be happy.'"

"I was wrong." Nicolette wept, eyelash blacking, rouge, and powder running down her face and dripping off her chin, her mustache heaving off her lip. "We're not happy. We're not any of us happy. Let me go, you coward, you—"

"Let her go!" cried Mea Culpa, flailing at him, as on stage the foreign minister brought down the house with *Have we defeated the French?* and the trumpets rose in clarion unison for the military march that brought the curtain down on the second act, and Cosette could feel looming into the dressing room a bulk, a presence, a past. Nicolette screamed at her to run, but Cosette turned slowly to confront the rattle of the old chain at The Sergeant of

Waterloo Inn, the gates of the fortress at Ham, the clank of the door at Sainte-Pélagie, the stench of the prison.

Clerons, in a single, fluid movement, reached out, grabbed Mea Culpa by the arm, yanked the wig off her head to the gasping shock of everyone backstage, extras, actors, crew, who crowded in the Passage of Princes, drawn there by the uproar, staring gape-mouthed, watching Mea Culpa, snatched bald and fighting like a cat.

Were they more surprised by that or by the imperial guard who invaded? Uniformed men pouring in from the stage door, their red-white-and-blue-clad figures sweeping like an army over the backstage barricades. The soldiers' chorus, clad in their bizarre uni-forms, reflexively resisted, fought the French; the stage army beat the soldiers back, beat them down, engaged in hand-to-hand combat, beat them with rubber muskets, thrust their tin bayonets, grabbed any weapon nearby, weights, sandbags, props, the fight spread swiftly, the whole place wrecking and falling down in chaos as they tried to maneuver the stage cannon to fire into the wings.

His great hand still gripping Cosette's arm, Clerons reached out to grab Nicolette too as Cosette cried out, shrieked for her to run.

Nicolette, with a glance to the yawning trapdoor in the floor, actually smiled, took off her great hat, held it aloft in what seemed a gesture of salute, of departure, of defiance, perhaps even victory, lifted the hat so high the lacquered plume flared in the naked gas jet overhead, and she held it till the whole hat burst into flames, burning brilliantly, and as Clerons lunged for her once more, she thrust this into his face, at his cinder-gray whiskers. With a single piercing scream, he knocked the fiery hat away, and it flew across the room into a pile of tulle, fine as spiders' webs, which blazed up instantly, the flames bursting, gnawing at the frail silk costumes; those hanging fell to the floor, and the flames licked along the skirted dressing table, while Jean-Luc watched, with a drunk's fas-cination, till at last he tore off his coat and flailed at the fire, suc-ceeding only in whipping it further, as flames clung to the floorboards and crawled up the thin wooden walls. Clutching at his singed beard, Clerons released Mea Culpa, who yelled and fol-lowed the Little General down the ladder to the storeroom below, where already long plumes of smoke wafted through the floor-boards, and Nicolette screamed to come face-to-face with the burning blue eyes, the thin, horrible face of Victor Pajol.

"It's Pajol," Cosette cried, grabbing her hand, "he's all right. Pajol, come with us, Pajol! They're here! Clerons—"

"Is that so?" Pajol took his place at the foot of the ladder and the next body to come down was Achille Clerons. Pajol waited for him to turn, to look, waited even for his expression to go slack as he clung to the ladder. "I told you thirty years ago, I told you I'd return to Paris to kill you. You've sent Germaine to a hell I can't save her from. Me, I swore I'd kill you and now I will. I'll kill you." And he did, firing his pistol point-blank at Clerons's face, and both women screamed, cried out as blood sprayed, freckling their bodies and hands and faces, smeared over Pajol's face as he looked up the ladder and saw staring down at him through the smoke-filled trapdoor, Jean-Luc. "You are a pig, monsieur," said Pajol evenly, "but you are also the son of the Pontmercys. Don't make me kill you. I will. As your mother and your woman watch, I swear I will shoot you where you stand, you hear me? Close the door and back away."

"No!" Cosette yelled. "Pajol, no! I beg of you! The fire! Jean-Luc!"

"Step down here, follow these women," Pajol shouted, "and you're a dead man."

Jean-Luc closed the trapdoor while Nicolette cried his name over and over and Cosette flung her arm around the Little General and bent low through the hovering smoke, followed Pajol, who pulled them, holding Cosette's hand, pulled them through the labyrinth of old scenes and sets and props toward the doors that led to the alley. Overhead, the flames ate between the floorboards.

Pajol took his key, the key Cosette had stolen for him, still on its red ribbon, and unlocked the small door. Then he stepped toward the large door, the one big enough for huge painted flats, and he shot off the inside lock, with a grunt he pushed that door open, and ran outside into the alley, shouting to the guards stationed there that he'd found the press, he'd found the printer too, "Arrest him! We need soldiers! Come arrest him! Follow me!" And Pajol ran back into the smoke.

The soldiers ran after him, poured into the theatre, while Cosette and the Little General ducked out the smaller door and into the alley, where already, on steps leading from the porter's door, soldiers (soldiers of the chorus and soldiers of the empire) piled out, tumbled together in their eagerness to escape the smoke billowing after them; they fell and flailed together, and soon those soldiers who had followed Pajol in, they too ran back out coughing, choking, gasping because the fire had burst through the thin walls of Nicolette's dressing room and burnt along the Passage of Princes, exploding in stands of paint and muslin stage flats, those backgrounds meant to simulate the *boom boom boom* of battle. Now little explosions boomed and popped as fire ran up the flats, devoured the wooden frames and the paint pots lying everywhere about, the cans of varnish and lacquer made fiery love to the painted canvas, burned through one and the next and the next and the one after that, crawled up, gnawed the ropes, turned the ladders red hot, snaked along the floor, smoke roiling forth, enveloping the whole backstage, rolling out so that when the curtain went up (and it did) great streams of smoke billowed like the Beautiful Blue Danube, out over the audience, who applauded. Wildly. The orchestra played on—the musicians in the pit ignorant, the conductor believing the stage cannons had misfired, afraid to put down the baton, especially as the audience clapped, cheered, believed it was all part of the effect, part of the false battle, the masquerade enacted on stage, *boom boom boom. Have we defeated the French?* Even when smoke rolled into the house, up toward the enormous chandelier, made the boxes and front rows cough and choke, the audience applauded, till the conductor, seeing flames bringing up the rear, advancing toward the proscenium, seeing a chorus of hard, bright, yellow flames marching toward him, dropped his baton and ran, crying *Fire Fire Fire,* up the center aisle toward the doors, followed by musicians and more soldiers, imperial soldiers and soldiers of the chorus, who had been trapped backstage, ran out alongside men clutching violins and trumpets, along with the stage king and the turnip-complected foreign minister, and perhaps only then did the tiers and boxes of spectators, besotted with effect, only then did they seem to understand this was not effect, but cause.

Many, though not all, fled. Some stayed to watch. Was this not another of the Emperor's great spectacles? Fireworks! Parades! Marching military men, though these soldiers weren't marching, but running, shoving, pushing, using their gun butts, these soldiers, as they had on the boulevards in 1851 when they fired and bayoneted anyone in their path; here, too, they slashed anyone between them and the doors, hacking with their gun butts men and women who fought for the doors, the ladies' great steel-cage hoops supporting acres of tulle tearing, catching in the doorways, blinding, tripping, trampling people as they lost their diamond tiaras and their camellias and their blue roses, their silken shawls and false hair, screaming as the waves of smoke roiled forth. Flames burnt along the stage itself, dazzled their way toward the proscenium, leapt up, as though preening, bowing before the audience, wrapped their fiery arms around the footlights, and the gas in each one exploded like cannon *boom boom boom,* an operetta of illusion, illumination, the noise of battle, and surely enough heat, enough flame, enough *la lumière* to satisfy everyone.

Epilogue

Boulogne
March 1867

When Marius and Cosette first began escaping to Boulogne in 1833, very little there would have suggested the tide of prosperity that had inundated this seaside town in the years following. Not merely the fishing, shipping, and boat building that had traditionally sustained Boulogne, but an influx of holiday makers came to the beaches, and many English not only disembarked but stayed. There came to be quite an English community, mostly of women, as very often well-to-do Londoners established their mistresses here on the more tolerant shores of France, including, it was rumored, the mistress of the great Charles Dickens. The Gérards' inn, alas, did not share in the enormous prosperity washing over Boulogne. Monsieur Gérard was genial but not able, expansive but not discriminating, and when his wife died in 1853, the place rapidly tumbled downhill, scraping by on the leftovers of other, more prosperous establishments, which would send the guests they had to turn away to Gérard's, with its unreliable beds, gritty floors, unpleasant odors, indifferent food, and the wine a suspicious blue.

By 1867, however, a man might inquire after Gérard's Inn and receive, instead of the sigh of condescension, the sniff of professional pique, which is what happened to a tall man clad in black, with a top hat and umbrella, who, inquiring at the hotel where he was staying, was given directions to Gérard's. He made his way uphill against a stiff wind and rain so insistent it seemed to hover rather than fall. Gérard's was in an old section of the town and not especially at any pains to draw attention to itself, and it could be easily missed. He missed it. He was certain he had missed it. Rain dripping from his umbrella, he stood in the street looking around for someone to ask.

"Valentina! Valentina!" came a woman's cry. "Come back home now and out of this rain!"

From under his black umbrella the man watched as a small child, bundled against the damp, turned in a doorway and seriously lectured a cat, who watched her with grave interest. The little girl apparently regarded the cat as a hopeless student, and threatened no herrings whatever if the lessons weren't learned properly tomorrow. Then she splashed across the street and through a door. Above the door there hung a faded sign, GÉRARD.

The taproom, not by any means full at this hour of the afternoon, was nonetheless noisy with English voices. The little girl flung off her coat, aimed for a chair, missed, and left it on the floor as she waltzed in through the smoke to find the taproom cat curled near the fire. She proceeded to lecture this cat as well, adding that it was very much smarter than Monsieur Choufleur across the street. She was fair, this child, with a great tangle of blond, unruly hair. He had no idea how old she was. Three? Four? Five? He was no judge of children.

He took a seat in the shadows, away from the English and the warm fire, quite alone. The woman at the bar sent the little girl over to ask him what he wanted.

She stood before him with saucy poise, her great brown eyes meeting his with equanimity. "What will you have, monsieur?

"Are you Valentina?"

"Yes, monsieur."

"And who is that, over there?" he nodded at the woman behind the bar.

"*Grandmère.*"

"Where is your mother?"

"I am to answer no questions, monsieur, and to tell you it's very rude to ask such questions."

"In England? On the English stage? Is your mother singing on the English stage?" Receiving no reply, he frowned. "And your father?"

She rolled her eyes in an excess of beatitude. "With the angels in heaven. Now, what will you have? Cider? We have the best cider in all Artois here. Beer? We keep a lot of beer for these English. They love beer. Me, I have no use for it. It makes people burp. Very undistinguished, you know. They burp continually." She nodded toward the fire, with no regard for the feelings of her guests, who seemed absolutely oblivious of her French. "They like us here because we speak English," she confided, "but they understand not a word of French. Now, for wine, monsieur, we have very good wine. Red or white. No blue in this establishment. No absinthe either. My aunt says it kills the brain and clouds the palate. The one is as bad as the other. Make up your mind, monsieur, or on your way."

"Do you send all your guests off like that?"

"Those who can't pay, yes."

"Ah. Well. I can pay. A glass of wine. Red."

"And to eat? If you are French, you have surely come here to eat. All true French do. They come too," she nodded toward the English, "because we can keep them happy, cook the things they like, but all the French who come to Gérards' are rewarded."

"*Merci.* Nothing to eat. But I would like to talk with your grandmother, Valentina," he lingered over her name. "Can you ask her to come over here?"

She nodded and tripped back to the bar, where she held a quick conference with her grandmother, who, bringing the glass of wine with her, approached the table, blanched, spilled the wine down her apron and to the floor, clutched the glass with white knuckles, and looked quickly to the door, expecting to see a squad of police.

Cosette's once-short hair had grown out and grayed, and she wore it in a simple knot loosely coiled at the base of her neck. She was still small and slender, but not with that brittle and bony finality of the ill-fed. Her cough was gone. Her hands were capable and strong and the backs tanned. She had creases between her brows and laugh lines at her eyes, but no tissue of fine wrinkles, and her mouth remained unpinched and supple, and her eyes a still-bright blue.

"I'm alone. I promise. I'm alone—" Jean-Luc paused as though the word *Mama* were a great boulder in his mouth, a word he could neither say nor swallow. He opted finally for the latter. "I am truly alone. I thought I might find you here in Boulogne, and when

I heard the reputation of Gérard's cook, I guessed as much. You have made a living here."

"We have made a life," Cosette replied, breathless as if she had run a long distance, or only feared she might be obliged to run a long distance. She kept looking at the door.

"You have nothing to fear from me. I promise. I give you my word."

"You gave your word to your father in 1848," she reminded him tartly. "As I recall, you promised to behave honorably."

"Mama, I promise. I will never again do anything to endanger any of you. Never. Could I see—" but *Papa* was even more difficult—"my father. I have not seen him since that day in the Luxembourg Gardens when I introduced you to Mademoiselle Lauriot."

"We remember that day. We remember it very well." She turned to Valentina, who had pulled the unwilling cat to the zinc counter, where she was trying to teach it to dance. "Valentina, will you be good enough to mind things here for me? I'll be back. If someone needs something, go fetch Monsieur Gérard."

"If someone needs something, I shall see to it." Valentina spoke with childish majesty and regarded the English gathered in the taproom as Queen Victoria might have regarded them.

Flinging a shawl over her head, Cosette led her son out a backdoor to the inn's stone courtyard, set about with empty flowerpots, where the rain sluiced down in perfectly placed gutters into rain barrels; the plasterwork was smooth, the wood painted, the stones even. The kitchen ran along the back of the inn and the courtyard, and Jean-Luc paused near an open window, to look in where he saw his sister, elbow-deep in flour, making a well in the center with her fist, pouring in the eggs and working the puff pastry expertly with her hands, while a man he recognized as the Starling ground the blades of the kitchen knives along a whetstone. Between them a small, dark-haired boy put his fingers in a bowl of sugared apple slices and snagged two of them while his mother and father pretended not to notice. Jean-Luc heard the Starling remark that the boy would have to improve his technique. Fantine laughed, and her laughter wafted out the window, along with delicious smells from the copper pots on the stove. Rain dripping off his top hat, Jean-Luc stayed there momentarily, and then he followed Cosette up a

short flight of stone steps to the chicken coops and other outbuildings, all neat and well-maintained, and there, in a small, sturdy
structure at the end of the garden, candles burned in a window,
though it was afternoon.

Cosette opened the door and walked to Marius, put her arm
around his shoulders, and whispered something in his ear. He sat
at a desk, as he had sat at a desk most of his life, pen in hand,
blotter before him, inkstains on his fingers. He was nearly sixty
years old, and he looked every bit of it; his hair gray unto white, he
still bent over the old 1851 wounds, and his knuckles were so
swollen he clearly held the pen with difficulty, but hold it he did.
He turned, took off his spectacles the better to see his son. Cosette
stayed right behind him, her hand on his shoulder; he reached up
and put his hand over hers, but he could not speak. None of them
could speak.

The rain gusted in, rattling his papers, and when Jean-Luc
closed the door, his candles went out. "I promise you I have come
alone," Jean-Luc said again. "No one knows you're here. Any of you.
All of you. I have been a fool. Worse than a fool. A traitor." He
removed his hat slowly and glanced around the small room: the desk,
a high bed, a washstand, a shelf of books, a stove, all of it modest,
sufficient without being superfluous, completely at odds with Jean-
Luc's whole way of living; in contrast to his parents, his sister and the
Starling, Jean-Luc had made a living without making a life. "I'm on
my way to England. Taking the boat this afternoon. To see Nicolette. To ask, well, maybe just to see. Maybe that's enough. Can't you
even speak to me? Even the prodigal son got spoken to."

"The prodigal son only abandoned his father," said Cosette.
"He did not betray him to the police."

Marius patted her hand, held it tightly. "I never expected to see
you again, Jean-Luc," he said at last.

"I never expected to see you at all. The rumors that you'd lived,
I didn't believe them. Now everyone believes them. People say the
torch, *La Lumière*, will never go out."

"We haven't written anything else. We haven't—"

"It isn't what you've written, it's what you are. Both of you." He
struck a match, moved to the desk, and relit the candles in the
silver candlesticks. Stepping back to the door, he crossed his hands

over his tall hat. "The little girl, Valentina, she's my daughter, isn't she?"

"You will have to discuss that with Nicolette," Cosette said sharply. "She's Nicolette's daughter."

"If Nicolette will talk to me. Perhaps she won't. But I'm going to try. Paris has not been the same all these years. Paris has been, well, Paris has gone on, I have not. I have not been the same without Nicolette. Her flamingos all died, you know, and the monkeys escaped. They say they live in the sewers where it's humid. I don't know. That's just what they say. And the parrots, well . . . I ask your forgiveness." He took a steep breath. "I don't expect you to give it now, or easily, perhaps at all. I don't even say I deserve it. But I ask it. As I am going to ask it of Nicolette. And I ask it humbly, knowing how little I deserve it. I am, as you see me, sobered these days and lonely. I am not the man you are, Papa, but I am not the man I was either."

Cosette stared at her son across the tiny room and the great gulf of the past. He ought to have been in the prime of his life, but he looked gray, exhausted as a man who has been shipwrecked crawls to the shore, clings to the very rocks and barnacles that cut his hands. Could he be forgiven for what he'd done? Could she forgive him? Before she could forgive him, she would have to trust him.

Marius rose slowly, reached for his cane, and walked to Jean-Luc. "I forgive you. For myself, I forgive you. Not for Cosette. Not for Nicolette. Not even for Valentina or Fantine or Gabriel. Perhaps I forgive for the wrong reasons, nostalgic reasons. A man I wronged once forgave me when I did not deserve it. He opened his heart to me. He once told me that I had no idea of the charity, tolerance, and forbearance that life would require of me. Because he forgave me, it is perhaps easier for me than for your mother. I owed him a debt of honor I have spent my whole life trying to fulfill. Do you know of whom I speak?"

"The convict, Jean Valjean. Clerons told me."

Marius nodded sagely. "That's good, then. It's good that you know. He was a great man." Marius went back to his chair, and Cosette put her hand again on his shoulder. "I will not withhold my forgiveness, Jean-Luc, because perhaps I don't have a whole life yet before me to fulfill my debts of honor. It's best not to carry those debts to the grave."

"Please, Marius—" Cosette implored him. "Don't."

"I'm not going there yet, my love. I speak theoretically." He smiled and the old scar down his temple creased with the effort. "I forgive you, Jean-Luc. I will not cling to the wrongs of the past, but as I say, I speak for myself."

Jean-Luc glanced at his mother, who made no move to echo Marius; she stood stony and silent. "I had better get down to the harbor. The packet to England leaves at four, and my bags are already on board."

"*Au revoir* then," said Marius, patting Cosette's hand in a kind of code they had long ago established.

In answer to that code, Cosette took from the hook behind the door a nondescript coat, a hat, and an umbrella, and she followed her son into her rainy stone courtyard, where voices from the kitchen rippled around them. "Do you want to see Fantine and Gabriel?"

"No. Not now. It's too much. Too much to ask of anyone. My heart's already broken to see Valentina. She is the image of Nicolette."

"She is the Empress of Boulogne," said Cosette as they walked around the front of the inn and down the street toward the harbor, where wind-whipped sails snapped and halyards clanged, steam engines puffed and chugged, and fishermen hauled in their nets and the day's catch. The packet for England was loading.

Cosette turned to him. "I won't say goodbye. I have had too many farewells. Too many goodbyes without the formality of farewell. I will just say I wish you well, Jean-Luc. You are my son and I wish you well. I can say that much now."

"Maybe over time you can say more, Mama."

"Over time and memory."

She turned and left him, but she did not go back up through the town. The rain eased as she wandered along the harbor and toward the beach. The beach was rocky, and low tide had stripped it to its unvarnished worst: boats, wrecked long ago, jutted up through the sand; abandoned pilings stood like jagged rows of decayed teeth. Down the beach voices caught her attention as oyster gatherers scraped and shoveled, loading the shells noisily into a cart drawn by an aged horse. The cart's wheels made vanishing grooves in the sand, and Cosette meandered beside them. The waves rolled in, gray, turbulent, oblivious of the rain, and the wind brought with it the smell of spring, salt, fish, and pungent low tide. In the west the clouds lifted, and a long ribbon of blue sky unfurled, and Cosette knew the storm would pass before she got home.

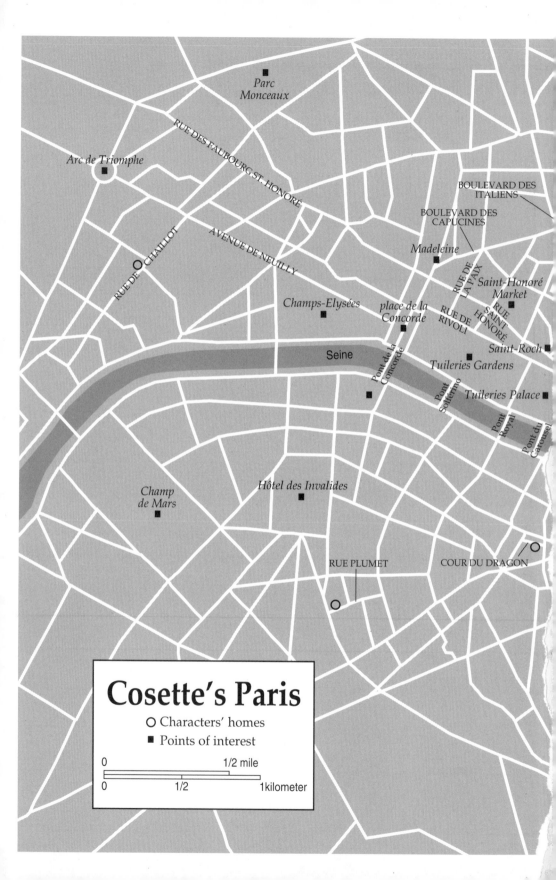

Cosette's Paris

○ Characters' homes
■ Points of interest

| 0 | | 1/2 mile |
| 0 | 1/2 | 1kilometer |

Parc Monceaux

Arc de Triomphe

RUE DES FAUBOURG ST. HONORÉ

AVENUE DE NEUILLY

RUE DE CHAILLOT

BOULEVARD DES ITALIENS

BOULEVARD DES CAPUCINES

Madeleine

RUE DE LA PAIX

Saint-Honoré Market

RUE SAINT HONORÉ

Champs-Elysées

place de la Concorde

RUE DE RIVOLI

Saint-Roch

Seine

Pont de la Concorde

Tuileries Gardens

Pont Solferino

Tuileries Palace

Pont Royal

Pont du Carousel

Champ de Mars

Hôtel des Invalides

RUE PLUMET

COUR DU DRAGON